SHADOW OF THE LARIAT

SHADOW OF THE LARIAT

edited with an Introduction
and Prefaces by

JON TUSKA

PROMONTORY
PRESS

First Promontory Press edition published in 1997.

Published by Galahad Books
A division of BBS Publishing Corporation
450 Raritan Center Parkway
Edison, NJ 08837

Promontory Press is a registered trademark of BBS Publishing Corporation.

Published by arrangement with Golden West Literary Agency.

Distributed by Sterling Publishing Co., Inc.
387 Park Avenue South
New York, NY 10016

Distributed in Canada by Sterling Publishing
c/o Canadian Manda Group
165 Dufferin Street
Toronto, Ontario, Canada M6K 3H6

Distributed in Great Britain by Chrysalis Books Group PLC
The Chrysalis Building Bromley Road, London W106SP England

Distributed in Australia by Capricorn Link (Australia) Pty. Ltd.
PO Box 704, Windsor NSW 2756 Australia

For information about special sales, premium and corporate purchases, please contact Sterling
Special Sales Department at 800-805-5489 or specialsales@sterlingpub.com

Library of Congress Catalog Card Number: 97-73068

ISBN 10: 0-88394-099-X
ISBN 13: 978-0-88394-099-0

Printed in the United States of America.

ACKNOWLEDGMENTS

GREY, ZANE: "The Great Slave" first appeared in *Ladies Home Journal.* Copyright © 1920 by Curtis Publishing Company. Copyright © renewed 1948 by Lina Elise Grey. Reprinted by arrangement with Golden West Literary Agency, Zane Grey, Inc., and HarperCollins, Publishers. All rights reserved.

COBURN, WALTER J.: "Riders of the Purple" first appeared in *Lariat Story Magazine.* Copyright © 1925 by Real Adventures Publishing Company, Inc. Reprinted by arrangement with the Golden West Literary Agency. All rights reserved.

CUNNINGHAM, EUGENE: "The House of Whispering Shadows" first appeared in *Frontier Stories.* Copyright © 1928 by Doubleday, Doran & Company, Inc. Copyright © renewed 1956 by Eugene Cunningham. Reprinted by arrangement with Golden West Literary Agency. All rights reserved.

BRAND™, MAX (pseud. Frederick Faust): "Lawman's Heart" first appeared in *Star Western.* Copyright © 1934 by Popular Publications, Inc. Copyright © renewed 1962 by Jane Faust Easton, John Faust, and Judith Faust. Reprinted by arrangement with Golden West Literary Agency. All rights reserved.

FLYNN, T. T.: "The Pie River" first appeared under the title "The Pistol Prodigal" in *Western Trails.* Copyright © 1937 by Magazine Publishers, Inc. Copyright © renewed 1965 by Theodore Thomas Flynn, Jr. Copyright © 1995 by Thomas B. Flynn, M.D., for restored material. Reprinted by arrangement with Golden West Literary Agency. All rights reserved.

LeMAY, ALAN: "Lawman's Debt" first appeared in *Dime Western* under the byline Alan M. Emley. Copyright © 1934 by Popular Publications, Inc. Copyright © renewed 1962 by Alan LeMay. Reprinted by arrangement with Golden West Literary Agency. All rights reserved.

HAYCOX, ERNEST: "Stage Station" first appeared in *Collier's.* Copyright © 1939 by Crowell Collier Corporation. Copyright © renewed 1966 by Jill Marie Haycox. Reprinted by arrangement with Golden West Literary Agency. All rights reserved.

SHORT, LUKE (pseud. Frederick Dilley Glidden): "Brand of Justice" first appeared in *The Country Home Magazine.* Copyright © 1939 by Crowell Collier Corporation. Reprinted by arrangement with the Golden West Literary Agency.

BLACKBURN, TOM W.: "Where Trails Divide" first appeared under the title "Epitaph for an Unmarked Grave" in *Star Western.* Copyright © 1939 by Popular Publications, Inc. Copyright © renewed 1967 by Thomas Wakefield Blackburn. Reprinted by arrangement with Golden West Literary Agency. All rights reserved.

CORD, BARRY (pseud. Peter Baptisto Germano): "The Ghost of Miguel" first appeared in *Lariat Story Magazine.* Copyright © 1945 by Real Adventures Publishing Company, Inc. Copyright © renewed 1973 by Peter B. Germano. Reprinted by arrangement with Golden West Literary Agency. All rights reserved.

SAVAGE, LES, JR.: "The Beast in Cañada Diablo" first appeared in a slightly different form under the title "The Ghost of Gun-Runners Rancho" in *Lariat Story Magazine.* Copyright © 1946 by Real Adventures Publishing Company, Inc. Copyright © renewed 1974 by Marian R. Savage. Copyright © 1995 by Marian R. Savage for restored material. Reprinted by arrangement with Golden West Literary Agency. All rights reserved.

CUSHMAN, DAN: "The Conestoga Pirate" first appeared in *Frontier Stories.* Copyright © 1944 by Fiction House, Inc. Copyright © renewed 1972 by Dan Cushman. Reprinted by arrangement with Golden West Literary Agency. All rights reserved.

NEWTON, DWIGHT BENNETT: "Reach High, Tophand!" first appeared under the byline D. B. Newton in *Lariat Story Magazine.* Copyright © 1947 by Real Adventures Publishing Company, Inc. Copyright © renewed 1975 by Dwight Bennett Newton. Reprinted by arrangement with Golden West Literary Agency. All rights reserved.

BONHAM, FRANK: "Furnace Flat" first appeared under the title "Gun-Dog of Furnace Flat" in *New Western.* Copyright © 1948 by Popular Publications, Inc. Copyright © renewed 1976 by Frank Bonham. Reprinted by arrangement with Golden West Literary Agency. All rights reserved.

DAWSON, PETER (pseud. Jonathan Hurff Glidden): "Colt-Cure for Woolly Fever" first appeared in *Big-Book Western.* Copyright © 1949 by Popular Publications, Inc. Copyright © renewed 1977 by Dorothy S. Ewing. Reprinted by arrangement with Golden West Literary Agency. All rights reserved.

OVERHOLSER, WAYNE D.: "Stage to Death" first appeared in *Lariat Story Magazine.* Copyright © 1944 by Real Adventures Publishing Company, Inc. Copyright © renewed 1972 by Wayne D. Overholser. Reprinted by arrangement with Golden West Literary Agency. All rights reserved.

CHESHIRE, GIFF: "Stagecoach Pass" first appeared in *Blue Book.* Copyright © 1950 by McCall Corporation. Copyright © renewed 1978 by Mildred E. Cheshire. Reprinted by arrangement with Golden West Literary Agency. All rights reserved.

FRAZEE, STEVE: "Payroll of the Dead" first appeared under the title "Knife in the Back" in *Complete Western Book Magazine.* Copyright © 1957 by Stadium Publishing Corporation. Copyright © renewed 1985 by Steve Frazee. Reprinted by arrangement with Golden West Literary Agency. All rights reserved.

ATHANAS, VERNE: "The Clown" first appeared under the title "Boy with a Gun" in *The Saturday Evening Post.* Copyright © 1961 by Curtis Publishing Company. Copyright © renewed 1989 by Alice S. Athanas. Reprinted by arrangement with Golden West Literary Agency. All rights reserved.

PAINE, LAURAN: "The Silent Outcast" first appeared in *Double Action Western.* Copyright © 1953 by Columbia Publications, Inc. Copyright © renewed 1981 by Lauran Paine. Reprinted by arrangement with Golden West Literary Agency. All rights reserved.

PATTEN, LEWIS B.: "Gun This Man Down" first appeared in *Dime Western.* Copyright © 1954 by Popular Publications. Copyright © renewed 1982 by Catherine C. Patten. Reprinted by arrangement with Golden West Literary Agency. All rights reserved.

HENRY, WILL (pseud. Henry Wilson Allen): "The Streets of Laredo" first appeared in WESTERN ROUNDUP (Macmillan, 1961) edited by Nelson Nye. Copyright © 1961 by the Western Writers of America. Copyright © renewed 1989 by Henry Wilson Allen. Reprinted by arrangement with Golden West Literary Agency. All rights reserved.

CONTENTS

INTRODUCTION

What a year this has been! The first Western novel I read as a youth was THE LONE STAR RANGER (Harper, 1915) by Zane Grey. It was not until 1994 that I learned that this book was not a novel at all in the conventional sense. Zane Grey had written a long serial titled "The Last of the Duanes" and sent it to editor Bob Davis at *The Argosy*, one of the pulp magazines published by The Frank A. Munsey Company. Davis was shocked to find upon reading it that eighteen persons were killed in the course of the story. He considered this much too violent to publish. What he agreed to run was a drastically abbreviated version which appeared as "The Last of the Duanes" in a single installment in *The Argosy* (9/14).

When it came time to offer the book to Harper & Bros., Grey had lost faith in the story as he had written it. The book that emerged as THE LONE STAR RANGER is, for about the first 200 pages, the manuscript of "The Last of the Duanes" and is called Book I The Outlaw. The remainder of the novel, called Book II The Ranger, is the serial which appeared in three parts as "The Lone Star Rangers" in *All-Story Cavalier Weekly* (5/9/14-5/23/14). The consequence of all this was that THE LAST OF THE DUANES as Zane Grey wrote it would first be published in book form eighty years later.

The first issue of a Western pulp magazine I purchased and read was *New Western* (12/48). The most memorable story in that issue was showcased in top position on the front cover and came first in the magazine. It was titled "Gun-Dog of Furnace Flat" and was written by Frank Bonham. I suspected even then what I confirmed eventually to be true. The story the editors considered the best in a particular issue came first in the table of contents. What I didn't know until much later is that an author's title for a story rarely survived after acceptance. The oftentimes garish covers pulp magazines had were no less reflected in the penchant these magazines had for attaching similarly garish titles to stories. Frank Bonham had titled this story simply "Furnace Flat." Really, that said it all, for it is a story set in Death Valley and the terrific heat of that place is as much a part of the story as any of the human characters in it. "Furnace Flat" now has had its title restored for this encore appearance.

SHADOW OF THE LARIAT is something to celebrate because it permits me to bring together stories by many fine writers some of whose wonderful stories filled the pages of *Lariat Story Magazine* which, as all of the subsequent magazines which specialized in Western fiction, could trace its origin to that fateful day in 1919 when, just before leaving on a trip to France, Ormond G. Smith, president of Street & Smith, told Henry Ralston to sell the *New Buffalo Bill Weekly* for whatever he could get. The real Buffalo Bill Cody had died in Denver, Colorado, on January 10, 1917 and, with his passing, interest in his ongoing adventures had waned. When Ralston found no takers, he came up with another idea which he presented to George Smith, vice-president of Street & Smith. Why not revamp the magazine into one devoted to general Western fiction and call it *Western Story Magazine?* George Smith liked the idea and gave Ralston a free hand to do just that. On July 12, 1919, the first issue of *Western Story Magazine*, dated September 5, 1919, and priced at 10¢, went on sale at newsstands.

Beneath the title was a notice that ran for the next eight weeks: "Formerly *New Buffalo Bill Weekly*," and also a reminder that its contents were "Big Clean Stories of Western Life." Already in the first issue there was established an editor's page titled "The Roundup" and, among other things, readers were promised that "the best writers of Western adventure stories will entertain you." In large part, throughout its thirty-year history, this proved to be a truthful statement. Henry Ralston's name was still on the declaration of ownership when it was published for the last time in August, 1949.

Lariat Story Magazine—the similarity in names was scarcely coincidental—came about precisely because of the extraordinary success of *Western Story Magazine* which by 1923 had an average weekly circulation of 2,500,000 copies with a cover price of 15¢. Fiction House which was owned by J. W. Glenister, who was president, and J. B. Kelly, who was secretary of the corporation and also the principal editor, had launched a similarly successful fiction magazine titled *Action Stories* with the first issue dated September, 1921, going on sale August 11, 1921. While there was every kind of action story conceivable in *Action Stories*, Western stories were definitely in the minority. Walt Coburn had become something of a fixture at *Western Story Magazine* by early 1924 when Jack Kelly came to California to see him in an effort to rectify this situation. Kelly offered Coburn 3¢ a word and would feature a 25,000-word novelette every month by Coburn in *Action Stories* as well as provide Coburn with top billing on the covers. "I'll build you up, cowboy," he told Coburn, "until you'll be the highest paid Western writer in the game. Max Brand will never catch up with you. While he's a good writer, he knows nothing about the West." To a degree this was pure salesmanship on Kelly's part. During the decade of the 1920s Frederick Faust, one of whose pseudonyms was Max Brand, was paid 5¢ a word by *Western Story Magazine* and he was contributing between a million and a million and a half words a year to it. Coburn never attained that level. However, during the 1930s and early 1940s, he would average 600,000 words a year for the pulp markets. In another way, Kelly's offer was fortuitous because it brought Coburn financial stability. He was paid $100 a week by Fiction House and at the first of every month he was sent a check for the difference between the $750 owing for the month's 25,000-word story and what had already been paid to him. Fiction House billed him as "The Cowboy Author," running biographical sketches of him and his authentic background, and showcasing his name on covers.

Glenister and Kelly felt the time was ripe in 1925 to give Street & Smith further competition. They launched *North-West Stories* with the first issue dated May, 1925, subtitled "Outdoor Stories of the West and North," published by a subsidiary they formed called Glen-Kel Publishing Company. They had earlier organized the Real Adventures Publishing Company to introduce a new magazine called *True Adventures* which was to feature only true and factual stories of adventure. Why a different company for each magazine? Magazine publishing was a speculative, high-risk business and, if one company failed, the other, more successful magazines could not be attached. *True Adventures* lasted for all of seven issues when, just as the *New Buffalo Bill Weekly* before it, the magazine underwent a transformation. Carrying over the issuing sequence from the former magazine, the first issue of what was called *The Lariat Story Magazine* appeared, a monthly dated August, 1925, indexed as Vol. I, No. 8 (when it was *really* No. 1), and priced at 20¢.

Zane Grey's early novels such as RIDERS OF THE PURPLE SAGE (Harper, 1912) were serialized in pulp magazines. By 1915, however, he had graduated to the better paying smooth paper mass-circulation magazines such as *Ladies Home Journal* and *The Country Gentleman*, both then owned by Curtis Publishing Company which had also acquired *The Saturday Evening Post*. "The Great Slave," the story I have chosen to include by this author, first appeared in *Ladies Home Journal* (12/20). While few would have suggested while he was alive that Zane Grey ought to be regarded as one of our classic American authors, he has indeed become exactly that. More Americans were reading RIDERS OF THE PURPLE SAGE in 1994 than were reading it in 1912 when it first appeared! It is available in paperback editions from HarperCollins, Pocket Books, Bantam Books, Penguin Books, has been reprinted in a bargain hardcover edition by Seafarer Books and as a three-in-one from Avenel, and "The Authorized Edition" with a Foreword by Loren

Grey, the author's youngest son, has appeared in a trade paperback edition from the University of Nebraska Press that even at three times the price of the mass merchandise paperback editions had well over a thousand pre-publication orders! Max Brand's THE UN-TAMED (Putnam's, 1920) in 1994 appeared in a hardcover reprint edition as well as in a trade paperback edition from the University of Nebraska Press, in a full-length audio version from Books on Tape, and for the first time in a Czech language edition. How many other novels published in 1912 and 1920 respectively are able so many decades later to generate this kind of interest among the reading public?

Our "shadow of the *Lariat*," so to speak, begins with the second story, "Riders of the Purple" by Walt Coburn. Although Jack Kelly would persuade Walt to simplify his name in 1926, he was still using the early byline Walter J. Coburn when this story appeared in first position in the first issue of *The Lariat Story Magazine*. Coburn had grown up on the Circle C ranch in Montana and knew whereof he wrote first-hand. To illustrate this story, the cowboy artist and later author, Will James, was chosen for the opening sketch above the title and other of his sketches are to be found in that first issue, just as he had been commissioned three years before to paint the first Western cover for *Action Stories*. In "The Corral," the section of the magazine where readers and editors could communicate, Coburn was chosen as spokesman to solicit new stories by working range men. "One hundred dollars, in addition to the regular rates, will be paid for the best story written by a working cowpuncher, says the big boss," Coburn wrote. Later on in "The Corral," the reigning movie cowboys of the day, each with his likeness reproduced in a photograph, welcomed the new magazine: Tom Mix, William S. Hart, Jack Hoxie, and Hoot Gibson. "I have been a constant reader of *Action Stories* and *North-West Stories*," Hoot Gibson wrote in his testimonial, "and I am particularly interested in this kind of literature, as you know, and shall watch it closely for available material for my Jewel productions." Jewel was a brand name at the time of Universal Pictures Corporation where Gibson was under contract.

That first issue of *Lariat* also contained the first installment of a four-part serial by William Colt MacDonald titled "The Red Raider." Harold Hersey, an editor for the Clayton magazines and later a pulp magazine publisher himself, claimed in PULPWOOD EDITOR (Stokes, 1937) that he "bought Allan W. C. MacDonald's first Western novel" for *Ace-High Magazine*, a Clayton publication. Surely, here, he was mistaken, since the first Western novel by MacDonald serialized in *Ace-High* was "Don Gringo of the Rio Grande," which began with the First June Number in 1927, a full two years after MacDonald's Western serial in *Lariat*.

With the second issue of *The Lariat Story Magazine*, S. Omar Barker, one of the finest and most beloved of Western storytellers in magazines, known as much for his poetry and his fact features over the next four decades as for his stories, made his first appearance with "Jack Emmett, Bulldogger," a rodeo story. In the third issue Barker had a poem, "The Cowboy's Religion," which Jack Kelly annotated with the comment, "A good one to recite at the next stag." Here is the concluding stanza:

> Though out on the ranges of square-shootin' men
> Us boys never hears much preachin'
> I reckon God hears us a-worshipin' when
> We follow His Nature's teachin'.

In the first issue, Kelly had announced that Colonel E. Hofer of Salem, Oregon, would pass on each story published in the magazine for authenticity and accuracy as well as literary merit. The colonel had been publishing for some time a magazine devoted to poetry and literary criticism called *The Lariat*. A reader wrote in a letter reprinted in "The Corral" in the third issue that "you are to be commended on your choice of Col. E. Hofer as the man to pass on your Western stories. I know Col. Hofer well and wish to say that he is one of the finest men I ever met. He reminds one of the old Spanish Dons that were so typical of Old California years ago. In the Garden City of Salem, Oregon, he reigns supreme as the guiding genius of the literary circles. . . . [He] lives in a moderate home on one of Salem's shaded boulevards, surrounded by his immediate family." Now, of course, you cannot copyright a title, but I have often wondered if Jack Kelly invited Colonel Hofer to be field editor for this new magazine precisely because he wanted to placate any objection the colonel might have had to the similarity in names. In the event, the colonel, whatever his following in Oregon, soon was out as field editor and Fiction House quietly dropped *The* from before the magazine's name and it became forevermore simply *Lariat Story Magazine*.

The first issues had carried the subtitle, "Stories of Cowboy Life." In 1926 this was changed to "Cowboy—Life Stories" and thus it remained until 1938 when it was slightly altered to "Cowboy—Life Romances" and this was henceforth the subtitle until the final issue. For many who may recall Fiction House magazines, most memorable of all was the symbol of the bull's eye which appeared on the cover of *Lariat* after January, 1929. In the beginning the logo around the bull's eye read "A Fiction House Magazine." This logo was altered after April, 1930, to read "Fiction House Magazines." In early 1934 it was replaced by the emblem of an eagle within a circle indicating that the magazine was a member of the

National Recovery Act. In early 1936 the cover had no symbol or emblem, but the bull's eye returned for the January, 1937, issue. It was also announced in this issue that *Lariat*, which had become a bimonthly, would now again be issued monthly. It still was in February, but then a hiatus of two months without any issue ensued before advent of the May issue. In May it was again a bimonthly, but with its sequence of issuance reversed from the even-numbered months to the odd, and thus it would remain for the rest of its days.

Walt Coburn wrote his finest book-length novels in the late 1920s and all three of them were serialized in *Lariat*. Coburn's second novel and my favorite among them, MAVERICKS (Century, 1929), is set in the Chinook district of Montana and in it Coburn creates a complex and captivating community of diverse families and social forces. There is a hot-head who in an argument shoots his father so that his father loses an arm, but they are later reconciled. Lance Mansfield inherits his British father's ranch. He intends to make the Circle 7 a success, only to be framed as a slow-elker. Tonnie Kirby is the heroine, in love with Lance but estranged from him by siding with her brother Dick after he shoots their father. The novel falls into three discrete episodes: in Montana before and after the Great War and during the war in No Man's Land. Coburn eloquently described the impact of the war on these Montana cowboys, some of whom "would return, even as these utterly weary, soul-sick men were coming back—with the eager light forever gone out of their eyes and, in its stead, the glaze of horror that is war; young men who had lost something that is an essential part of youth. They would never forget, those men who returned. For God has somehow neglected to bless men with that forgetfulness of war pain. He saves that gift for mothers in childbirth."

By the end of 1926 Eugene Cunningham began appearing on the roster of *Lariat* almost as frequently as Walt Coburn. Harrison Leussler was field editor for Houghton Mifflin in the western states. W. H. Hutchinson, Eugene Manlove Rhodes's biographer, remarked about Leussler that "he loved everything about the Old West—person, place, and incident—and worshipped at his shrines with an eloquence, fervor, and zeal only possible to a converted New Englander. His devotions resulted in some distinguished contributions to his firm's list of Western Americana." It was Leussler who brought Cunningham to Houghton Mifflin as a Southwestern writer. In Cunningham's case, as much later in Will Henry's, those novels which Houghton Mifflin accepted were published under the Eugene Cunningham byline, while those which it did not were issued under another byline, Leigh Carder, and published by Covici, Friede. A case in point is "Buck from the Border" which ran serially in five installments in *Lariat Story Magazine* (12/27-4/28) under the Eugene Cunningham byline and appeared in book form as BORDER GUNS (Covici, Friede, 1935) by Leigh Carder. It is also worth noting that when more than one story by an author appeared in a single issue of a pulp magazine, one of them would almost invariably be run under a pseudonym or a house name. This was not the case with Cunningham at Fiction House. In the same issues in which this serial was running, Cunningham's series of short stories about Bar-Nuthin' Red Ames also appeared on the table of contents under Cunningham's own name.

As is true with Eugene Manlove Rhodes (who wrote primarily for *The Saturday Evening Post*) and Clarence E. Mulford (who created Hopalong Cassidy and the Bar-20), some of Cunningham's most engaging characters are Mexicans. At the top of the list, certainly, is Carlos José de Guerra y Morales, better known simply as Chihuahua Joe. He ably assists Lit Taylor in bringing an end to Frenchy Leonard's violent career in DIAMOND RIVER MAN (Houghton Mifflin, 1934), serialized in *Lariat* in five parts (11/26-3/27). Chihuahua Joe speaks a charming border English as when he tells Lit how he identified the murderer they have been hunting: " '¿*Por supuesto?* W'en I'm hear him laugh, w'en we're outside, then I'm know! ¡*I'm know!* In all these world, Lit, she's only one fella w'at's laugh like that. . . .' " Joe was too fine a character to be confined, as Rhodes would confine his finest Mexican character, Monte, in "*Pasó por Aquí*" serialized in the *Post* (2/20/27-2/27/27), to a single appearance. He returned in "The Trackless Bunch," a five-part serial in *Lariat* (8/27-12/27) and which appeared in book form as TEXAS SHERIFF (Houghton Mifflin, 1934). Lit Taylor in this sequel is now in New Mexico Territory managing King Connell's ranch when Curt Thompson arrives on the trail of a gang known as the "trackless bunch" and it isn't long before Joe helps Curt the way he had Lit before him.

Chihuahua Joe also puts in an appearance in what was destined to be Cunningham's most influential novel in the next decade, RIDERS OF THE NIGHT (Houghton Mifflin, 1932). It originally ran as a five-part serial in *Lariat* (9/28-1/29) under the title "The Mesquite Raiders" and would be reprinted in one installment as "The Gun Tamer" in *Western Novel and Short Stories* (3/36). Since Jack Kelly had been so instrumental in encouraging Cunningham's career as a magazine writer, it was *con razón* that Cunningham dedicated RIDERS OF THE NIGHT "To J. B. Kelly Editor, Publisher, Friend." In writing this novel Cunningham seems to have synchronistically arrived at a plot similar to that of Dashiell Hammett's novel, RED HARVEST (Knopf, 1929), which had appeared serially in four separate, but related, short novels in *Black Mask* (11/27-2/28). The last of these was appropriately titled "The 19th Murder" and there is so much killing in this story that the characters are said to have become "blood simple." In the course of RIDERS OF THE NIGHT some thirty-five men are killed and another thirty-five are known to be killed off stage. The reason there is so much necessary killing is that there are two kinds of law, as summed up by Carewe, a lawyer, in conversation with hero Burk Yates: " 'There's the law of the books, Burk—too damned much of it. Cluttered with ambiguous terms and Latin phrases; even to lawyers very frequently anything but clear-cut. But there's a fundamental law, too; the simple, primitive code . . . that law which gives a man, for instance, the right to protect with his own hand the property that is his.' " Chihuahua Joe has only a minor role in this story because a new concept of support for the hero was introduced in the trio of Sandrock Tom, Three Rivers, and Happy Jack, known as the "Three Mesquiteers." This notion obviously struck William Colt MacDonald since, presently, he introduced his own Three Mesquiteers in LAW OF THE FORTY-FIVES (Covici, Friede, 1933)—adding Lullaby Joslin to Tucson Smith and Stony Brooke whom he had first introduced as a duo in "Restless Guns," a serial in *Ace-High* in 1928 published in book form the next year. This was the first of a series of Three Mesquiteer novels over the next twenty years along with fifty-six motion pictures based on these characters, eight of which starred John Wayne as Stony Brooke. In the same issue of *Lariat* in which "The Mesquite Raiders" concluded a new Cunningham serial began titled "Buckaroo" (1/29-5/29), published subsequently as BUCKAROO (Houghton Mifflin, 1933). In this story Cunningham expanded the number of villains in need of killing to three hundred, taken on and defeated by three Texas Rangers, Vern Dederick, Dud Blaze, and Ody Gardineer who form another trio of heroes. The Establishment is utterly corrupt, as it is in Hammett's detective fiction, and in league with the principal villain, Snake Stett. It is interesting that Hammett who was sufficiently left-wing to be thought a Communist by the House UnAmerican Activities Committee and Cunningham who was such an outspoken state's righter that the War Department thought him pro-Fascist should have agreed that the most expedient solution to crime was killing criminals. Of course, Cunningham had been developing this plot in other stories as well, perhaps most notably in "Rider of the Red Trails" in *Action Stories* (1/29) where soldier-of-fortune Surry Newcum in Nicamala, a fictitious country in Central America, holes up in an armory and shoots down eighty men in the army of the Nicamalan dictator, Gonzatto, before Gonzatto sues for peace, dismissing the carnage as " 'a few of these peon-dogs killed!' " In "Rider of the Red Trails," sympathy is with Newcum who is forced to fight, but not with Gonzatto's attitude. In RIDERS OF THE NIGHT and BUCKAROO there are no such moral ambiguities. The killing is unequivocally justified.

There had been frequent bloodshed in the action Western ever since Clarence E. Mulford introduced this and other dime-novel elements into the mainstream of the Western story in his Bar-20 saga, but Cunningham elevated killing on a scale and in numbers as no one before him. In the same year that saw RIDERS OF THE NIGHT appear in book form Dane Coolidge in FIGHTING MEN OF THE WEST (Dutton, 1932) lamented that "now times have changed and a new school of writers have given us a bloodier West. If this crime wave of fiction continues, someone is liable to believe these boys—they may even believe themselves. The net result, up to date, is a division among our readers. Some are game to swallow anything, even the myth that, in those days, to kill a man was considered a huge joke. The other and wiser class is developing a wearied cynicism concerning everything they read about the West." Yet, notwithstanding the irony of such an observation, the Western story subsequently passed into an even more brutally realistic period. The savagery of the Great War which so disillusioned those authors who had lived through it was compounded a hundred-fold by the Second World War with its massive slaughter of millions, endless bombings of civilians, and its death camps. Such highly mechanized arts of murder could not but have an impact on the Western story, something that becomes increasingly a part of the fiction in this collection beginning with Dan Cushman's "The Conestoga Pirate" from 1944 and that, if anything, became further intensified as a result of the Korean conflict and the devastation of the Vietnam War. Indeed, the Vietnam War created national wounds so profound they will take generations to heal . . . if they ever do.

In the early 1930s Foster-Harris began appearing regularly in *Lariat*. Many of his finest stories have their setting in the oilfields of his home state of Oklahoma. Foster-Harris went on to found the first academic program to teach commercial writing in the nation at the School of Journalism of the University of Oklahoma and included among his students Bill Gulick, Jack M. Bickham, and Jeanne Williams. Michael Tilden, later the editor of *New Western* who would retitle Frank Bonham's stories (and everyone else's for that matter), also began appearing in *Lariat* in 1931.

Jack Kelly died in 1932 and Fiction House went into a period of re-organization. Arthur Anderson (yes, *the* Arthur Anderson) was made Treasurer, T. T. Scott became Secretary, and Jack F. Byrne, who had written for Fiction House magazines before becoming Kelly's assistant, was now made general editor. In 1929 Fiction House had purchased *Frontier Stories* from Doubleday, Doran & Company, so in 1932 with *Action*, *Frontier*, and *Lariat* it had three magazines featuring Western stories in whole or in part being issued monthly. For a time in 1933 all publication ceased. T. T. Scott was quoted in *The Business Week* (1/26/33) that "the influx of lower-priced magazines and the incidental cheapening of product has created a market situation which is unsound." Fiction House magazines cost 20¢ and were having a problem competing with new magazines such as *Dime Western*. Publication resumed only slowly. *Action Stories* became bi-monthly, then quarterly. *Lariat* became bi-monthly and remained, except for the two consecutive months in 1937, a bi-monthly. *Frontier Stories* had the longest hiatus, first from January, 1933, until it resumed in January, 1934, continuing bi-monthly until September, 1934, when it ceased again and was not resumed until spring, 1937, this time as a quarterly. Notwithstanding, Fiction House magazines kept their prices fixed at 20¢ until 1950.

The response among regular contributors was immediate. Eugene Cunningham concentrated on turning his previously published serials into hardcover novels. Walt Coburn expanded his markets. He wrote even more for *Adventure*, wrote again for *Western Story Magazine*, and became a regular contributor to Popular Publications pulps such as *Dime Western* and *Star Western*. In 1935 he and his wife, Pat, moved to Tucson, Arizona, because she suffered from respiratory problems and there built a ranch-style house with a small adobe out back for Walt. Coburn's drinking, always a problem for him, intensified as the years passed. He did not read what others were writing and so, increasingly, what he wrote was but a replay of the same themes and characters and situations. His remaining novels prior to 1951, LAW RIDES THE RANGE serialized in *Lariat Story Magazine* (7/29-12/29) as "Marked Men" and first published in book form in 1935 and SKY-PILOT COWBOY (Appleton Century, 1937), have none of the power and ambiance of earlier efforts. Mike Tilden confided to Frank Bonham when Bonham visited him at the Popular Publications editorial office in New York that most of what Coburn wrote after the Second World War had been written while drunk. It had to be edited severely, the rambling verbosity cut back to the bone while still paying Walt according to his original word count. He was living mostly on his reputation. After Fiction House re-organized, Coburn began contributing on a story-by-story basis. Jack Byrne was joined by Malcolm Reiss in editing the magazines (Reiss had begun his career by writing Western stories for *Star Western*). They were not willing, as Jack Kelly had been, to publish anything Coburn submitted. After 1942 Coburn rarely appeared in a Fiction House magazine and, when he did, it was a reprint from many years before. Before the hiatus at Fiction House, a special one-time issue titled *Walt Coburn's Action Novels* appeared, consisting of four reprints, but it was not until November, 1949, that Popular Publications inaugurated *Walt Coburn's Western Magazine*. The Coburn stories in it were all reprints, although he contributed a regular column titled "Walt's Tally Book." It ceased publication in May, 1951, after sixteen issues.

If *Lariat Story Magazine* had a Golden Age, it was in the 1940s when Malcolm Reiss and Jack Byrne were editing it. It was in this decade that Frank Bonham, Tom W. Blackburn, L. P. Holmes, Dean Owen, Barry Cord, Wayne C. Lee, Wayne D. Overholser, Giff Cheshire, Will C. Brown, D. B. Newton, and, above all, Dan Cushman and Les Savage, Jr., filled its pages with so many fabulous stories. If the original *Lariat* had been a celebration of the cowboy and the Western story, in the 1940s Reiss and Byrne encouraged writers for *Lariat* to explore other periods in American frontier history. Many of Savage's stories are set in a period prior to the Civil War. Tom W. Blackburn specialized in unusual professions much of the time, from insurance investigators to civil engineers. Barry Cord's "The Ghost of Miguel," which as I note in the headnote to that story he later expanded into a novel, is set in the Spanish southwest.

I discovered *Lariat* late in its career. T. T. Scott owned it by then, Malcolm Reiss was General Manager, Jack Byrne and Jack O Sullivan the principal editors. However, when you come to read the story, "The Beast in Cañada Diablo" by Les Savage, Jr., you will realize, as I did, that this magazine carried a most unusual, exotic, dramatic, and gripping kind of Western story. "Blood-Guns of the Crazy Moon" by Les Savage, Jr.—he had titled it "Table Rock" and his agent, feeling this was too bland, retitled it "Triggermistress of Table Rock" upon submission to Fiction House—appeared in the January, 1950, issue. For Savage it was a story which intrigued him so that in 1956 he requested an assignment back to him of the story from the magazine and set about expanding it into a book-length novel. When he died suddenly, there was no book publisher in New York in 1958 who wanted to issue it. That had to wait for nearly forty years when, finally titled as he had wanted, TABLE ROCK (Walker, 1993), it appeared as he had written it in an American hardcover edition, followed by a British hardcover edition, and a full-length audio version from Books on Tape.

Savage's agent, August Lenniger, had warned him already in 1956 that stories he was encouraged to develop and write for *Lariat Story Magazine* would be considered far too off-trail among book publishers. Editors, of course, were setting up these parameters as to what was acceptable in a Western story, not readers. Those who loved the marvelous freedom from conventions and the true frontier spirit of adventurous publishing found in pulp magazines as late as the early 1950s had to say good-bye to those kind of stories as they bid the pulp magazines adieu and welcomed their successors, the original paperback novel.

It was a matter of cost of production, methods of distribution, and—on the part of the public—perceived value. A Dell map-back reprint of a Western novel, a Pocket Book reprint with a stitched binding, an Ace double-novel, a Fawcett Gold Medal original novel by Les Savage, Jr., Dan Cushman, or Dudley Dean were more compact and seemed more durable and portable than a seven-inch-by-ten-inch pulp magazine and, often, the authors were quite the same. The financial rewards were also greater for authors. Fiction House had paid Savage $520 for the story he titled "The Beast in Cañada Diablo." At nearly the same time that Doubleday paid Savage an advance of $500 for a hardcover Western novel like LAND OF THE LAWLESS (Doubleday, 1951), Fawcett Gold Medal paid him an advance of $3,000 for RAILS WEST (Fawcett, 1954). Dell Publishing, the editorial division of Western Printing and Lithographing Company in Racine, Wisconsin, had got its start in the pulp magazine business with such titles as *Five Novels* and *All Western*. Fawcett began in the magazine business with *Triple-X Magazine* and others before branching out into comic books before it entered paperback publishing. Ace Publishing had made its mark earlier with *Western Trails* and *Western Aces*. Even Pocket Books before it issued the first inexpensive paperback reprints in 1939 was publishing *American Cavalcade*.

Today we have gone through another revolution in publishing and the mass merchandise paperback novel is rapidly becoming as much a relic of the past as the pulp magazine. One of the new formats that is replacing it is a book such as this one which brings together a wide and stimulating assortment of outstanding fiction for what remains a bargain price.

Lariat Story Magazine appeared on newsstands for the last time with the fall, 1950, issue, but the power and vibrancy of much of the fiction to be found in it during its twenty-five years of life are reflected in the pages which follow. Lauran Paine, Lewis B. Patten and Will Henry, whose stories I have also included in this collection, came on the scene too late to entertain any hope of appearing in *Lariat*. Yet I believe the stories I have chosen for them represent the kind of story *Lariat* would surely have accepted. After you have read over a hundred issues of a magazine you do have some idea of the kind of fiction which proved appealing to its editors. I mention in the headnotes for the stories short fiction by particular authors that I feel is especially worth reading, as well as recommending Western novels by them. This saves me from having to introduce each one of these stories separately in this introduction and instead I am able to conclude now with a brief comment on the criteria I have used in selecting these stories and the tremendous significance of the Western story and the Frontier story for Americans of all ages, and for people throughout the world. There are naturally some considerations which remain the same for all kinds of fiction: that a story have a beginning, a middle, and an end; that it focus on a single, circumscribed series of events that have such an impact on the characters whom we come to know and care about that it changes them and their lives; and that the best stories are ones

we enjoy so much, or which move us to such a degree, that we wish
to share them with others and to read them over again ourselves.
Personal taste being what it is, I also know beforehand that each
reader is going to find certain stories in this collection that he or she
particularly enjoys, and some that will seem not of the same quality.
I have tried to select stories that will appeal to as broad a spectrum
of readers as possible, which is the ideal toward which any anthologist
must strive.

Beyond these general considerations, however, the Western story
constitutes the single most important literary movement in the history of the United States and the only unique body of literature
which this country has contributed to the wealth of world culture
because of where it is set: in the American West. There was no
place in all history quite like it before and there is no place quite
like it now. But this does not mean that the origins of the Western
story are easy to trace. They are not. It is so because in its way the
Western story grew up with our nation and passed through all
those painful periods of internal or external conflict which have
shocked, torn, and divided, as well as united and made bold and
visionary, the people of our land. How else could it have been for
a nation of so *many* nations?

The West of the Western story is an imaginary West. It draws its
life blood from the belief—even now—that there can be a better way
and that, if we have the grit of character and the fortitude needed
to endure the ordeal, we shall find it. Conventions in the Western
story have changed, what marketing departments say is wanted,
what editors claim is allowable have changed in the past as they
will in the future, but not this. This can never change because if
once a people lose faith in themselves the result is no different than
when an individual does. Having spent the better part of my life
concerned in one way or another with the Western story, that is
the conclusion to which I have come. It is why the Vietnam War
years so hurt the Western story—we could see only the tragedy of
our nation's past, the toll in human lives, the suffering, and not
the other side, the fact that what the American frontier experience
offered from its beginning, and still offers today, is a second
chance—indeed, a third, and a fourth, and a fifth chance. Nor has
the frontier really closed. The Western story has kept it open and
real and available to us and the hope that it holds out.

The Western story at base is a story of renewal and that is what
has made it so very different from any other form of literary enter-
prise. It is refreshing, even revitalizing, in these days of a medically
over-educated culture obsessed with health and terrified of old age
and dying to behold once again generations of Americans to which
such obsessions and terrors meant nothing. It is spiritually encouraging in these days of political correctness, timidity, and herd-

notions such as one-settlement culture which wants everyone to believe in a lock-step approach to life to contemplate those generations where individual, cultural, and ethnic differences were abundant, where not one culture but many co-existed even if warfare between them was unceasing. We have benefited from that time. There is no one idea and no one cause that can possibly ever win endorsement from everybody. We still live now with that reality of the frontier as part of our social existence.

Above all, the greatest lesson the pioneers learned from the Indians is with us still: that it is each man's and each woman's *inalienable* right to find his own path in life, to follow his own vision, to achieve his own destiny—even should one fail in the process. There is no principle so singularly revolutionary as this one in the entire intellectual history of the Occident and the Orient before the American frontier experience, and it grew from the very soil of this land and the peoples who came to live on it. It is this principle which has always been the very cornerstone of the Western story. Perhaps for this reason critics have been wont to dismiss it as subversive or inconsequential because this principle reduces their voices to only one among many. Surely it is why the Western story has been consistently banned by totalitarian governments. Such a principle undermines the very foundations of totalitarianism and collectivism because it cannot be accommodated by the political correctness of those who would seek to exert power over others and replace all options with a single, all-encompassing, monolithic pattern for living.

There are authors of the Western story—some of whom I have been able to include in this anthology—who have recognized in the depths of their being that the past does have something to teach us, if we are willing to learn from it. They have believed that the Western story is the ideal literary form through which our American past can be evoked vividly and painfully—painfully, because often it was painful. The story of the American West is not so much romance, nor is it necessarily tragedy, although it can be both. It is most often, even when the circumstances are tragic, as Æschylus understood so well, a paean to human nobility. Most of all the Western story is about human beings in nature, not the denatured, mechanical, sterile world that increasingly has come to serve as a backdrop for human activity in other kinds of fiction. In this sense, the American West is just what the Indians always believed it to be, the land *just before* the land beyond the sun, the Spiritland, and it can still enthrall us when an author is able to conjure its magic.

SHADOW OF THE LARIAT

THE GREAT SLAVE

ZANE GREY was born Pearl Zane Gray in Zanesville, Ohio. He was graduated from the University of Pennsylvania in 1896 with a degree in dentistry. He practiced in New York City while striving to make a living by writing. He married Lina Elise Roth in 1905 and with her financial assistance he published his first novel himself, BETTY ZANE (1903). Closing his dental office, the Greys moved into a cottage on the Delaware River, near Lackawaxen, Pennsylvania. Grey took his first trip to Arizona in 1907 and, following his return, wrote THE HERITAGE OF THE DESERT (Harper, 1910). The profound effect that the desert had had on him was so vibrantly captured that it still comes alive for a reader. Grey couldn't have been more fortunate in his choice of a mate. Trained in English at Hunter College, Lina Grey proofread every manuscript Grey wrote, polished his prose, and. she effectively managed their financial affairs. Motion picture rights brought in a fortune and, with 108 films based on his work, Grey set a record yet to be equaled by anyone since.

His Golden Age as an author of Frontier and Western fiction spans the years from 1910 to 1932. His masterpieces include, surely, RIDERS OF THE PURPLE SAGE (Harper, 1912) and its sequel, which is even finer in my opinion, THE RAINBOW TRAIL (Harper, 1915), THE LIGHT OF WESTERN STARS (Harper, 1914), WILDFIRE (Harper, 1917), THE MAN OF THE FOREST (Harper, 1920), and, unquestionably his most spiritually searching novel set principally in Death Valley, WANDERER OF THE WASTELAND (Harper, 1923).

Zane Grey was not a realistic writer, but rather one who charted the interiors of the soul through encounters with the wilderness. He provided characters no more realistic than one finds in Balzac, Dickens, or Thomas Mann, but nonetheless they have a vital story to tell. "There was so much unexpressed feeling that could not be entirely portrayed," Loren Grey, Grey's younger son and a noted psychologist, once recalled, "that, in later years, he would weep when re-reading one of his own books." More than stories, Grey fashioned psycho-dramas about the odyssey of the human soul. They may not be the stuff of the real world, but without them the real world has no meaning—which may go a long way to explain the hold he has had on an enraptured reading public ever since his first Western romance in 1910. "The Great Slave" was first published in *Ladies Home Journal* (12/20) and first anthologized in TAPPAN'S BURRO AND OTHER STORIES (Harper, 1923).

A voice on the wind whispered to Siena the prophecy of his birth. "A chief is born to save the vanishing tribe of Crows! A hunter to his starving people!" While he listened, at his feet swept swift waters, the rushing, green-white, thundering Athabasca, spirit-forsaken river; and it rumbled his name and murmured his fate. "Siena! Siena! His bride will rise from a wind kiss on the flowers in the moonlight! A new land calls to the last of the Crows! Northward where the wild goose ends its flight Siena will father a great people!"

So Siena, a hunter of the leafy trails, dreamed his dreams; and at sixteen he was the hope of the remnant of a once powerful tribe, a stripling chief, beautiful as a bronzed autumn god, silent, proud, forever listening to voices on the wind.

To Siena the lore of the woodland came as flight comes to the strong-winged wild fowl. The secrets of the forests were his, and of the rocks and rivers.

He knew how to find the nests of the plover, to call the loon, to net the heron, and spear the fish. He understood the language of the whispering pines. Where the deer came down to drink and the caribou browsed on moss and the white rabbit nibbled in the grass and the bear dug in the logs for grubs—all these he learned; and also when the black flies drove the moose into the water and when the honk of the geese meant the approach of the north wind.

He lived in the woods, with his bow, his net, and his spear. The trees were his brothers. The loon laughed for his happiness; the wolf mourned for his sadness. The bold crag above the river, Old Stoneface, heard his step when he climbed there in the twilight. He communed with the stern god of his ancestors and watched the flashing Northern Lights and listened.

From all corners came his spirit guides with steps of destiny on his trail. On all the four winds breathed voices whispering of his future; loudest of all called the Athabasca, god-forsaken river, murmuring of the bride born of a wind kiss on the flowers in the moonlight.

It was autumn, with the flame of leaf fading, the haze rolling out of the hollows, the lull yielding to moan of coming wind. All the signs of a severe winter were in the hulls of the nuts, in the fur of the foxes, in the flight of water fowl. Siena was spearing fish for winter store. None so keen of sight as Siena, so swift of arm; and as he was the hope, so he alone was the provider for the starving tribe. Siena stood to his knees in a brook where it flowed over its gravelly bed into the Athabasca. Poised high was his wooden spear. It glinted downward swift as a shaft of sunlight through the leaves. Then Siena lifted a quivering whitefish and tossed it upon the bank where his mother, Ema, with other women of the tribe, sun-dried the fish upon a rock.

Again and again, many times, flashed the spear. The young chief seldom missed his aim. Early frosts on the uplands had driven the fish down to deeper water, and as they came darting over the bright pebbles Siena called them by name.

The oldest squaw could not remember such a run of fish. Ema sang the praises of her son; the other women ceased the hunger chant of the tribe.

Suddenly a hoarse shout pealed out over the waters.

Ema fell in a fright; her companions ran away; Siena leaped upon the bank, clutching his spear. A boat in which were men with white faces drifted down toward him.

"Hal-loa!" again sounded the hoarse cry.

Ema cowered in the grass. Siena saw a waving of white hands; his knees knocked together and he felt himself about to flee. But Siena of the Crows, the savior of a vanishing tribe, must not fly from visible foes.

"Palefaces," he whispered, trembling, yet stood his ground ready to fight for his mother. He remembered stories of an old Indian who had journeyed far to the south and had crossed the trails of the dreaded white men. There stirred in him vague memories of a strange Indian runners telling camp-fire tales of white hunters with weapons of lightning and thunder.

"Naza! Naza!" Siena cast one fleeting glance to the north and a prayer to his god of gods. He believed his spirit would soon be wandering in the shades of the other Indian world.

As the boat beached on the sand Siena saw men lying with pale faces upward to the sky, and voices in an unknown tongue greeted him. The tone was friendly, and he lowered his threatening spear. Then a man came up the bank, his hungry eyes on the pile of fish, and he began to speak haltingly in mingled Cree and Chippewayan language:

"Boy—we're white friends—starving—let us buy fish—trade for fish—we're starving and we have many moons to travel."

"Siena's tribe is poor," replied the lad; "sometimes they starve too. But Siena will divide his fish and wants no trade."

His mother, seeing the white men intended no evil, came out of her fright and complained bitterly to Siena of his liberality. She spoke of the menacing winter, of the frozen streams, the snow-bound forest, the long night of hunger. Siena silenced her and waved the frightened braves and squaws back to their wigwams.

"Siena is young," he said simply; "but he is chief here. If we starve—we starve."

Whereupon he portioned out a half of the fish. The white men built a fire and sat around it feasting like famished wolves around a fallen stag. When they had appeased their hunger, they packed the remaining fish in the boat, whistling and singing the while. Then the leader made offer to pay, which Siena refused, though the covetous light in his mother's eyes hurt him sorely.

"Chief," said the leader, "the white man understands; now he offers presents as one chief to another."

Thereupon he proffered bright beads and tinseled trinkets, yards of calico and strips of cloth. Siena accepted with a dignity in marked contrast to the way in which the greedy Ema pounced upon the glittering heap. Next the paleface presented a knife which, drawn from its scabbard, showed a blade that mirrored its brightness in Siena's eyes.

"Chief, your woman complains of a starving tribe," went on the white man. "Are there not many moose and reindeer?"

"Yes. But seldom can Siena creep within range of his arrow."

"A-ha! Siena will starve no more," replied the man, and from the boat he took a long iron tube with a wooden stock.

"What is that?" asked Siena.

"The wonderful shooting stick. Here, boy, watch! See the bark on the camp fire. Watch!"

He raised the stick to his shoulder. Then followed a streak of flame, a puff of smoke, a booming report; and the bark of the camp fire flew into bits.

The children dodged into the wigwams with loud cries; the women ran screaming; Ema dropped in the grass wailing that the end of the world had come, while Siena, unable to move hand or foot, breathed another prayer to Naza of the northland.

The white man laughed and, patting Siena's arm, he said: "No fear." Then he drew Siena away from the bank, and began to explain the meaning and use of the wonderful shooting stick. He reloaded it and fired again and yet again, until Siena understood and was all aflame at the possibilities of such a weapon.

Patiently the white man taught the Indian how to load it, sight, and shoot, and how to clean it with ramrod and buckskin. Next he placed at Siena's feet a keg of powder, a bag of lead bullets, and boxes full of caps. Then he bade Siena farewell, entered the boat with his men and drifted round a bend of the swift Athabasca.

Siena stood alone upon the bank, the wonderful shooting stick in his hands, and the wail of his frightened mother in his ears. He comforted her, telling her the white men were gone, that he was safe, and that the prophecy of his birth had at last begun its fulfillment. He carried the precious ammunition to a safe hiding place in a hollow log near his wigwam and then he plunged into the forest.

Siena bent his course toward the runways of the moose. He walked in a kind of dream, for he both feared and believed. Soon the glimmer of watersplashes and widening ripples caused him to crawl stealthily through the ferns and grasses to the border of a pond. The familiar hum of flies told him of the location of his quarry. The moose had taken to the water, driven by the swarms of black flies, and were standing neck deep, lifting their muzzles to feed on the drooping poplar branches. Their wide-spreading antlers, tipped back into the water, made the ripples.

Trembling as never before, Siena sank behind a log. He was within fifty paces of the moose. How often in that very spot had he strung a feathered arrow and shot it vainly! But now he had the white man's weapon, charged with lightning and thunder. Just then the poplars parted above the shore, disclosing a bull in the act of stepping down. He tossed his antlered head at the cloud of humming flies, then stopped, lifting his nose to scent the wind.

"Naza!" whispered Siena in his swelling throat.

He rested the shooting stick on the log and tried to see over the brown barrel. But his eyes were dim. Again he whispered a prayer to Naza. His sight cleared, his shaking arms stilled, and with his soul waiting, hoping, doubting, he aimed and pulled the trigger.

Boom!

High the moose flung his ponderous head, to crash down upon his knees, to roll in the water and churn a bloody foam, and then lie still.

"Siena! Siena!"

Shrill the young chief's exultant yell pealed over the listening waters, piercing the still forest, to ring back in echo from Old Stoneface. It was Siena's triumphant call to his forefathers, watching him from the silence.

The herd of moose plowed out of the pond and crashed into the woods, where, long after they had disappeared, their antlers could be heard cracking the saplings.

When Siena stood over the dead moose his doubts fled; he was indeed god-chosen. No longer chief of a starving tribe! Reverently and with immutable promise he raised the shooting stick to the north, toward Naza who had remembered him; and on the south, where dwelt the enemies of his tribe, his dark glance brooded wild and proud and savage.

Eight times the shooting stick boomed out in the stillness and eight moose lay dead in the wet grasses. In the twilight Siena wended his way home and placed eight moose tongues before the whimpering squaws.

"Siena is no longer a boy," he said. "Siena is a hunter. Let his women go bring in the meat."

Then to the rejoicing and feasting and dancing of his tribe he turned a deaf ear, and in the night passed alone under the shadow of Old Stoneface, where he walked with the spirits of his ancestors and believed the voices on the wind.

Before the ice locked the ponds Siena killed a hundred moose and reindeer. Meat and fat and oil and robes changed the world for the Crow tribe.

Fires burned brightly all the long winter; the braves awoke from their stupor and chanted no more; the women sang of the Siena who had come, and prayed for summer wind and moonlight to bring his bride.

Spring went by, summer grew into blazing autumn, and Siena's fame and the wonder of the shooting stick spread through the length and breadth of the land.

Another year passed, then another, and Siena was the great chief of the rejuvenated Crows. He had grown into a warrior's stature; his face had the beauty of the god-chosen, his eye the falcon flash of the Sienas of old. Long communion in the shadow of Old Stoneface had added wisdom to his other gifts; and now to his worshipping tribe all that was needed to complete the prophecy of his birth was the coming of the alien bride.

It was another autumn, with the wind whipping the tamaracks and moaning in the pines, and Siena stole along a brown, fern-lined trail. The dry smell of fallen leaves filled his nostrils; he tasted snow in the keen breezes. The flowers were dead, and still no dark-eyed bride sat in his wigwam. Siena sorrowed and strengthened his heart to wait. He saw her flitting in the shadows around him, a wraith with dusky eyes veiled by dusky wind-blown hair, and ever she hovered near him, whispering from every dark pine, from every waving tuft of grass.

To her whispers he replied: "Siena waits."

He wondered of what alien tribe she would come. He hoped not of the unfriendly Chippewayans or the far-distant Blackfeet; surely not of the hostile Crees, life enemies of his tribe, destroyers of its once puissant strength, jealous now of its resurging power.

Other shadows flitted through the forest, spirits that rose silently from the graves over which he trod, and warned him of double steps on his trail, of unseen foes watching him from the dark coverts. His braves had repeated gossip, filterings from stray Indian wanderers, hinting of plots against the risen Siena. To all these he gave no heed, for was not he Siena, god-chosen, and had he not the wonderful shooting stick.

It was the season that he loved, when dim forest and hazy fernland spoke most impellingly. The tamaracks talked to him; the poplars bowed as he passed; and the pines sang for him alone. The dying vines twined about his feet and clung to him, and the brown ferns, curling sadly, waved him a welcome that was a farewell. A bird twittered a plaintive note and a loon whistled a lonely call. Across the wide gray hollows and meadows of white moss moaned the north wind, bending all before it, blowing full into Siena's face with its bitter promise. The lichen-covered rocks and the rugged-barked trees and the creatures that moved among them—the whole world of earth and air heard Siena's step on the rustling leaves and a thousand voices hummed in the autumn stillness.

So he passed through the shadowy forest and over the gray muskeg flats to his hunting place. With his birch-bark horn he blew the call of the moose. He alone of hunting Indians had the perfect moose call. There, hidden within a thicket, he waited, calling and listening till an angry reply bellowed from the depths of a hollow, and a bull moose, snorting fight, came cracking the saplings in his rush. When he sprang fierce and bristling into the glade, Siena killed him. Then, laying his shooting stick over a log, he drew his knife and approached the beast.

A snapping of twigs alarmed Siena and he whirled upon the defensive, but too late to save himself. A band of Indians pounced upon him and bore him to the ground. One wrestling heave Siena made, then he was overpowered and bound. Looking upward, he knew his captors, though he had never seen them before; they were the lifelong foes of his people, the fighting Crees.

A sturdy chief, bronze of face and sinister of eye, looked grimly down upon his captive. "Baroma makes Siena a slave."

Siena and his tribe were dragged far southward to the land of the Crees. The young chief was bound upon a block in the center of the village where hundreds of Crees spat upon him, beat him, and outraged him in every way their cunning could devise. Siena's gaze was on the north and his face showed no sign that he felt the torments. At last Baroma's old advisors stopped the spectacle, saying: "This is a man!"

Siena and his people became slaves of the Crees. In Baroma's lodge, hung upon caribou antlers, was the wonderful shooting stick with Siena's powder horn and bullet pouch, objects of intense curiosity and fear.

None knew the mystery of this lightning-flashing, thunder-dealing thing; none dared touch it.

The heart of Siena was broken; not for his shattered dreams or the end of his freedom, but for his people. His fame had been their undoing. Slaves to the murderers of his forefathers! His spirit darkened; his soul sickened; no more did sweet voices sing to him on the wind, and his mind dwelt apart from his body among the shadows and dim shapes.

Because of his strength he was worked like a dog at hauling packs and carrying wood; because of his fame he was set to cleaning fish and washing vessels with the squaws. Seldom did he get to speak a word to his mother or any of his people. Always he was driven.

One day, when he lagged almost fainting, a maiden brought him water to drink. Siena looked up, and all about him suddenly brightened, as when sunlight bursts from clouds.

"Who is kind to Siena?" he asked, drinking.

"Baroma's daughter," replied the maiden.

"What is her name?"

Quickly the maiden bent her head, veiling dusky eyes with dusky hair. "Emihiyah."

"Siena has wandered on lonely trails and listened to voices not meant for other ears. He has heard the music of Emihiyah on the winds. Let the daughter of Siena's great foe not fear to tell of her name."

"Emihiyah means a wind kiss on the flowers in the moonlight," she whispered shyly and fled.

Love came to the last of the Sienas and it was like a glory. Death shuddered no more in Siena's soul. He saw into the future, and out of his gloom he rose again, god-chosen in his lofty frame that the Crees quailed before him and marveled. Once more sweet voices came to him, and ever on the soft winds were songs of the dewy moorlands to the northward, songs of the pines and the laugh of the loon and of the rushing, green-white, thundering Athabasca, god-forsaken river.

Siena's people saw him strong and patient, and they toiled on, unbroken, faithful. While he lived, the pride of Baroma was vaunting. "Siena waits" were the simple words he said to his mother, and she repeated them as wisdom. But the flame of his eye was like the leaping Northern Lights, and it kept alive the fire deep down in their breasts.

In the winter when the Crees lolled in their wigwams, when less labor fell to Siena, he set traps in the snow trails for silver fox and marten. No Cree had ever been such a trapper as Siena. In the long months he captured many furs, with which he wrought a robe the like of which had not before been the delight of a maiden's eye. He kept it by him for seven nights, and always during this time his ear was turned to the wind. The seventh night was the night of the midwinter feast, and when the torches burned bright in front of Baroma's lodge Siena took the robe and, passing slowly and stately till he stood before Emihiyah, he laid it at her feet.

Emihiyah's dusky face paled, her eyes that shone like stars drooped behind her flying hair, and all her slender body trembled.

"Slave!" cried Baroma's gaze, but spoke no word. His gift spoke for him. The hated slave had dared to ask in marriage the hand of the proud Baroma's daughter. Siena towered in the firelight with something in his presence that for a moment awed beholders. Then the passionate and untried braves broke the silence with a clamor of the wolf pack.

Tillimanqua, wild son of Baroma, strung an arrow to his bow and shot it into Siena's hip, where it stuck, with feathered shaft quivering.

The spring of the panther was not swifter than Siena; he tossed Tillimanqua into the air and, flinging him down, trod on his neck and wrenched the bow away. Siena pealed out the long-drawn war whoop of his tribe that had not been heard for a hundred years, and the terrible cry stiffened the Crees in their tracks.

Then he plucked the arrow from his hip and, fitting it to the string, pointed the gory flint head at Tillimanqua's eyes and began to bend the bow. He bent the tough wood till the ends almost met, a feat of exceeding great strength, and thus he stood with brawny arms knotted and stretched.

A scream rent the suspense. Emihiyah fell upon her knees. "Spare Emihiyah's brother!"

Siena cast one glance at the kneeling maiden, then, twanging the bow string, he shot the arrow toward the sky.

"Baroma's slave is Siena," he said, with scorn like the lash of a whip. "Let the Cree learn wisdom."

Then Siena strode away, with a stream of dark blood down his thigh, and went to his brush teepee, where he closed his wound.

In the still watches of the night, when the stars blinked through the leaves and the dew fell, when Siena burned and throbbed in pain, a shadow passed between his weary eyes and the pale light. And a voice that was not one of the spirit voices on the wind called softly over him, "Siena! Emihiyah comes."

Tne maiden bound the hot thigh with a soothing balm and bathed his fevered brow.

Then her hands found his in tender touch, her dark face bent low to his, her hair lay upon his cheek. "Emihiyah keeps the robe," she said.

"Siena loves Emihiyah," he replied.

"Emihiyah loves Siena," she whispered.

She kissed him and stole away.

On the morrow Siena's wound was as if it had never been; no eye saw his pain. Siena returned to his work and his trapping. The winter melted into spring; spring flowered into summer; summer withered into autumn.

Once in the melancholy days Siena visited Baroma in his wigwam. "Baroma's hunters are slow. Siena sees a famine in the land."

"Let Baroma's slave keep his place among the squaws," was the reply.

That autumn the north wind came a moon before the Crees expected it; the reindeer took their annual march farther south; the moose herded warily in open groves; the whitefish did not run, and the seven-year pest depleted the rabbits.

When the first snow fell, Baroma called a council and then sent his hunting braves far and wide.

One by one they straggled back to camp, footsore and hungry, each with the same story. It was too late.

A few moose were in the forest, but they were wild and kept far out of range of the hunter's arrows, and there was no other game.

A blizzard clapped down upon the camp, and sleet and snow whitened the forest and filled the trails. Then winter froze everything in icy clutch. The old year drew to a close.

The Crees were on the brink of famine. All day and all night they kept up their chanting and incantations and beating of tom-toms to conjure the return of the reindeer. But no reindeer appeared.

It was then that the stubborn Baroma yielded to his advisors and consented to let Siena save them from starvation by means of his wonderful shooting stick. Accordingly Baroma sent word to Siena to appear at his wigwam.

Siena did not go, and said to the medicine men: "Tell Baroma soon it will be for Siena to demand."

Then the Cree chieftain stormed and stamped in his wigwam and swore away the life of his slave. Yet again the wise medicine men prevailed. Siena and the wonderful shooting stick would be the salvation of the Crees. Baroma, muttering deep in his throat like distant thunder, gave sentence to starve Siena until he volunteered to go forth to hunt, or let him be the first to die.

The last scraps of meat, except a little hoarded in Baroma's lodge, were devoured, and then began the boiling of bones and skins to make a soup to sustain life. The cold days passed and a silent gloom pervaded the camp. Sometimes a cry of a bereaved mother, mourning for a starved child, wailed through the darkness. Siena's people, long used to starvation, did not suffer or grow weak so soon as the Crees. They were of hardier frame, and they were upheld by faith in their chief. When he would sicken, it would be time for them to despair. But Siena walked erect as in the days of his freedom, nor did he stagger under the loads of firewood, and there was a light on his face. The Crees, knowing of Baroma's order that Siena should be the first to perish of starvation, gazed at the slave first in awe, then in fear. The last of the Sienas was succored by the spirits.

But god-chosen though Siena deemed himself, he knew it was not by the spirits that he was fed in this time of famine. At night in the dead stillness, when even no mourning of wolf came over the frozen wilderness, Siena lay in his brush teepee close and warm under his blanket. The wind was faint and low, yet still it brought the old familiar voices. And it bore another sound—the soft fall of a moccasin on the snow. A shadow passed between Siena's eyes and the pale light.

"Emihiyah comes," whispered the shadow and knelt over him.

She tendered a slice of meat which she had stolen from Baroma's scant hoard as he muttered and growled in uneasy slumber. Every night since her father's order to starve Siena, Emihiyah had made this perilous errand.

And now her hand sought his and her dusky hair swept his brow. "Emihiyah is faithful," she breathed low.

"Siena only waits," he replied.

She kissed him and stole away.

Cruel days fell upon the Crees before Baroma's pride was broken. Many children died and some of the mothers were beyond help. Siena's people kept their strength, and he himself showed no effect of hunger. Long ago the Cree women had deemed him superhuman, that the Great Spirit fed him from the happy hunting grounds.

At last Baroma went to Siena. "Siena may save his people and the Crees."

Siena regarded him long, then replied: "Siena waits."

"Let Baroma know. What does Siena wait for? While he waits, we die."

Siena smiled his slow, inscrutable smile and turned away. Baroma sent for his daughter and ordered her to plead for her life. Emihiyah came, fragile as a swaying reed, more beautiful than a rose choked in a tangled thicket, and she stood before Siena with doe eyes veiled.

"Emihiyah begs Siena to save her and the tribe of Crees."

"Siena waits," replied the slave.

Baroma roared in his fury and bade his braves lash the slave. But the blows fell from feeble arms and Siena laughed at his captors.

Then, like a wild lion unleashed from long thrall, he turned upon them: "Starve! Cree dogs! Starve! When the Crees all fall like leaves in autumn, then Siena and his people will go back to the north."

Baroma's arrogance left him then, and on another day, when Emihiyah lay weak and pallid in his wigwam and the pangs of hunger gnawed at his own vitals, he again sought Siena. "Let Siena tell for what he waits."

Siena rose to his lofty height and the leaping flame of the Northern Lights gathered in his eyes. "Freedom!" One word he spoke and it rolled away on the wind.

"Baroma yields," replied the Cree, and hung his head.

"Send the squaws who can walk and the braves who can crawl out upon Siena's trail."

Then Siena went to Baroma's lodge and took up the wonderful shooting stick and, loading it, he set out upon snowshoes into the white forest. He knew where to find the moose yards in the sheltered corners. He heard the bulls pounding the hard-packed snow and cracking their antlers on the trees. The wary beasts would not have allowed him to steal close, as a warrior armed with a bow must have done; but Siena fired into the herd at long range. And when they dashed off, sending the snow up like a spray, a huge black bull lay dead. Siena followed them as they floundered through the drifts and, whenever he came within range, he shot again. When five moose were killed, he turned upon his trail to find almost the whole Cree tribe had followed him and were tearing the meat and crying out in a kind of crazy joy. That night the fires burned before the wigwams; the earthen pots steamed; and there was great rejoicing. Siena hunted the next day, and the next, and for ten days he went into the white forest with his wonderful shooting stick, and eighty moose fell to his unerring aim.

The famine was broken and the Crees were saved.

When the mad dances ended and the feasts were over, Siena appeared before Baroma's lodge. "Siena will lead his people northward."

Baroma, starving, was a different chief from Baroma well fed and in no pain. All his cunning had returned. "Siena goes free. Baroma gave his word. But Siena's people remain slaves."

"Siena demanded freedom for himself and people," said the younger chief.

"Baroma heard no word of Siena's tribe. He would not have granted freedom to them. Siena's freedom was enough."

"The Cree twists the truth. He knows Siena would not go without his people. Siena might have remembered Baroma's cunning. The Crees were ever liars."

Baroma stalked before his fire with haughty presence. About him in the circle of light sat his medicine men, his braves and squaws. "Siena is free. Let him take his wonderful shooting stick and go back to the north."

Siena laid the shooting stick at Baroma's feet and likewise the powder horn and bullet pouch. Then he folded his arms, and his falcon eyes looked far beyond Baroma to the land of changing lights and the old home on the green-white, rushing Athabasca, god-forsaken river. "Siena stays."

Baroma started in amaze and anger. "Siena makes Baroma's word idle. Begone!"

"Siena stays."

The look of Siena, the pealing reply, for a moment held the chief mute. Slowly Baroma stretched wide his arms and lifted them, while from his face flashed a sullen wonder. "Great slave!" he thundered.

So was respect forced from the soul of the Cree, and the name thus wrung from his jealous heart was one to live forever in the lives and legends of Siena's people. Baroma sought the silence of his lodge, and his medicine men and braves dispersed, leaving

Siena standing in the circle, a magnificent statue facing the steely north.

From that day insult was never offered to Siena, nor word spoken to him by the Crees, nor work given. He was free to come and go where he willed, and he spent his time in lessening the tasks of his people.

The trails of the forest were always open to him, as were the streets of the Cree village. If a brave met him, it was to step aside; if a squaw met him, it was to bow her head; if a chief met him, it was to face him as warriors faced warriors.

One twilight Emihiyah crossed his path, and suddenly she stood as once before, like a frail reed about to break in the wind. But Siena passed on. The days went by and each one brought less labor to Siena's people, until that one came wherein there was no task save what they set themselves. Siena's tribe were slaves, yet not slaves.

The winter wore by and the spring and the autumn, and again Siena's fame went abroad on the four winds. The Chippewayans journeyed from afar to see the great slave, and likewise the Blackfeet and the Yellow Knives. Honor would have been added to fame; councils called; overtures made to the somber Baroma on behalf of the great slave, but Siena passed to and fro among his people, silent and cold to all others, true to the place which his great foe had given him. Captive to a lesser chief, they said; the Great Slave who would yet free his tribe and gather to him a new and powerful nation.

Once in the late autumn Siena sat brooding in the twilight by Ema's teepee. That night all who came near him were silent. Again Siena was listening to voices on the wind, voices that had been still for long, which he had tried to forget. It was the north wind, and it whipped the spruces and moaned through the pines. In its cold breath it bore a message to Siena, a hint of coming winter and a call from Naza, far north of the green white, thundering Athabasca, river without a spirit.

In the darkness when the camp slumbered Siena faced the steely north. As he looked a golden shaft, arrow-shaped and arrow swift, shot to the zenith.

"Naza!" he whispered to the wind. "Siena watches."

Then the gleaming, changing Northern Lights painted a picture of gold and silver bars, of flushes pink as shell, of opal fire and sunset red; and it was a picture of Siena's life from the moment the rushing Athabasca rumbled his name, to the far distant time when he would say farewell to his great nation and pass forever to the retreat of the winds. God-chosen he was, and had power to read the story in the sky.

Seven nights Siena watched in the darkness; and on the seventh night, when the golden flare and silver shafts faded in the north, he passed from teepee to teepee, awakening his people. "When Siena's people hear the sound of the shooting stick let them cry greatly: 'Siena kills Baroma! Siena kills Baroma!'"

With noiseless stride Siena went among the wigwams and along the lanes until he reached Baroma's lodge. Entering in the dark he groped with his hands upward to a moose's antlers and found the shooting stick. Outside he fired it into the air.

Like a lightning bolt the report ripped asunder the silence, and the echoes clapped and reclapped from the cliffs. Sharp on the dying echoes Siena bellowed his war whoop, and it was the second time in a hundred years for foes to hear that terrible, long-drawn cry.

Then followed the shrill yells of Siena's people: "Siena kills Baroma . . . Siena kills Baroma . . . Siena kills Baroma!"

The slumber of the Crees awoke to a babel of many voices; it rose hoarsely on the night air, swelled hideously into a deafening roar that shook the earth.

In this din of confusion and terror when the Crees were lamenting the supposed death of Baroma and screaming in each other's ears, "The Great Slave takes his freedom!," Siena ran to his people and, pointing to the north, drove them before him.

Single file, like a long line of flitting specters, they passed out of the fields into the forest. Siena kept close on their trail, ever looking backward, and ready with the shooting stick.

The roar of the stricken Crees softened in his ears and at last died away.

Under the black canopy of whispering leaves, over the gray, mist-shrouded muskeg flats, around the glimmering reed-bordered ponds, Siena drove his people.

All night Siena hurried them northward and with every stride his heart beat higher. Only he was troubled by a sound like the voice that came to him on the wind.

But the wind was now blowing in his face, and the sound appeared to be at his back. It followed on his trail as had the step of destiny. When he strained his ears, he could not hear it; yet, when he had gone on swiftly, persuaded it was only fancy, then the voice that was not a voice came haunting him.

In the gray dawn Siena halted on the far side of a gray flat and peered through the mists on his back trail. Something moved out among the shadows, a gray shape that crept slowly, uttering a mournful cry.

"Siena is trailed by a wolf," muttered the chief.

Yet he waited, and saw that the wolf was an Indian. He raised the fatal shooting stick.

As the Indian staggered forward, Siena recognized the robe of silver fox and marten, his gift to Emihiyah. He laughed in mockery. It was a Cree trick. Tillimanqua had led the pursuit disguised in his sister's robe. Baroma would find his son dead on the Great Slave's trail.

"Siena!" came the strange, low cry.

It was the cry that had haunted him like the voice on the wind. He leaped as a bounding deer.

Out of the gray fog burned dusky eyes half-veiled by dusky hair, and little hands that he knew wavered as fluttering leaves. "Emihiyah comes," she said.

"Siena waits," he replied.

Far to the northward he led his bride and his people, far beyond the old home on the green-white, thundering Athabasca, god-forsaken river; and there, on the lonely shores of an inland sea, he fathered the Great Slave Tribe.

RIDERS OF THE PURPLE

WALT(ER JOHN) COBURN was born in White Sulphur Springs, Montana Territory. He was once called "King of the Pulps" by Fred Gipson and promoted by Fiction House as "The Cowboy Author." He was the son of cattleman Robert Coburn, then owner of the Circle C ranch on Beaver Creek within sight of the Little Rockies, whose life story Coburn would later detail in his remarkable contribution to cow country history, PIONEER CATTLEMAN IN MONTANA: THE STORY OF THE CIRCLE C RANCH (University of Oklahoma Press, 1968).

His father believed a college education vital if Coburn was to be a successful cattleman. Coburn planned to attend Stanford, but his application was rejected. The reason, as Coburn would later recall, was that he "had lost the battle to John Barleycorn." It was not to be the last time he lost that battle. Coburn persuaded his father that a college education was unnecessary for what he planned to do. The Coburns now lived in San Diego while still operating the Circle C. Robert Coburn used to commute between Montana and California by train and he would take his youngest son with him. When Coburn got drunk one night, he had an argument with his father that led to his leaving the family. In the course of his wanderings he entered Mexico and for a brief period actually became an enlisted man in the so-called "Gringo Battalion" of Pancho Villa's army.

Following his enlistment in the U. S. Army during the Great War, Coburn read a Western story in *Adventure*. It had been written by Robert J. Horton, a man he had known when Horton had been a newspaper sports reporter in Great Falls. Recognizing in Horton's story the nucleus of a tale Coburn had once told him, Coburn wrote to Horton and asked him how one went about becoming a writer. Horton was very responsive, setting down principles that would remain Coburn's working philosophy all of his years: to read Roget's THESAURUS; to read O. Henry, Jack London, and Joseph Conrad, but not other Western fiction writers; to live a story as it was being written, never plotting it out beforehand; and *never* to rewrite.

Coburn put Horton's suggestions into practice and for a year and a half he wrote and wrote, earning endless rejection slips and becoming so depressed at times that, once, he even considered submitting to a glandular transplant offered by a quack doctor to cure his mental state. By this time Coburn was living and working in Del Mar, California, and one day instead of a returned manuscript he found an envelope from Munsey Publications. Bob Davis, editor of *Argosy-All Story*, had accepted his short story, "The Peace Treaty of the Seven Up." Payment was $25 and the story appeared in the July 8, 1922, issue. It was another six months before a second Coburn story appeared in print, this time in *Western Story Magazine*.

16

F. E. Blackwell, then editor of the magazine, wrote Coburn asking to see more (as if, Coburn thought, he had not rejected a dozen or more stories before accepting this one). *Western Story Magazine* became an important market for Coburn in 1923. He was writing and selling enough to quit his job in Del Mar and move to Santa Barbara where he rented a small cottage near the old mission. In Santa Barbara Coburn initiated what would remain his routine. He would try to write at least 2,000 words a day, never rewriting, six days a week, with Sundays off, never working more than four or five hours a day but also never taking a vacation of longer than two or three days once a story was completed.

It would be daunting to list Walt Coburn's contributions to *Lariat Story Magazine* since he had a story in almost every issue for nearly a decade. "Riders of the Purple" was the first of them, in the first issue. Other notable short novels or short stories include, surely, "The Glory Hunter" (4/26), "Ghost Riders" (12/26), "The Wild Bunch" (2/27), "The White Lily" (1/28), "Cow Country Creed" (1/29), "Dude Wranglers" [a four-part serial] (12/29-3/30), "Lead Poisonin'" (4/30) and reprinted (11/41), "Three Mules to Skin" (2/35), and "He Rides Alone" in *Action Stories* (10/27) reprinted in *Lariat* as "He Heard the Owl Hoot" (2/36). Coburn's early fiction from his Golden Age, 1924-1934, is his best. In these stories, as Charles M. Russell and Eugene Manlove Rhodes, two men Coburn had known and admired in life, he captured the cow country and re-created it when it had already passed from sight.

I

"RIDERS OF THE PURPLE"

Time was when a man could ride from the Rafter T ranch on the Missouri River to the Bar L ranch on Milk River and never open a gate or pass through a lane. The distance, as the crow flies, was one hundred miles. Just where the Rafter T ended and the Bar L range commenced, no man could say. No sign post or drift fence marked the division. Many a Bar L cow wintered on Rafter T hay, fed to her by a Rafter T cow hand. Every second maverick on the Bar L range was put in the Rafter T iron by the Bar L man who ran across the critter. The owners of these two big cow outfits swapped hay, men or horses with the same unconcern that two brothers trade hats. The friendship of Pete Carver of the Rafter T and Ike Rutherford of the Bar L was a by word throughout Montana.

Pete Carver was a short, square-built man, quick talking and active as a panther. No better rider ever forked a spoiled horse and his skill with a rope was uncanny. His temper was as quick as his tongue. The indomitable will of the grizzled cow man showed in the jutting squareness of his jaw and the steely coldness of his eyes that glittered from under abnormally bushy iron-gray brows.

Ike Rutherford reminded one of weather-toughened rawhide held together by barb wire. Lean, sinewy, his tanned face interwoven by myriad lines, he stood over six feet with his boots off. Easy and sure of movement, he could, with miraculous ease, go down a taut rope and, in the space of a minute, twist down the bawling, struggling yearling bull at the end of that rope. With equal ease, he was known to "ear down" a striking, fighting bronc. He knew every brand, earmark, and wattle mark between the Canadian line and the Pecos. A beef man *par excellence*, and as quick as a rattler with six-shooter or fist. Hard winters and endless hours in the saddle had whitened his hair. His eyes were of the same sunny blue as Montana's summer skies. A staunch friend and a hard hater was Rutherford. Men either blessed him or cursed him.

These two had come from Texas with the early trail herds, put their money in cows, and helped make cow country history in one of the finest, yet harshest cow countries that men ever rode. With the passing of years, their herds grew until the hundred square miles of their combined ranges were stocked to overflowing with white-face cattle. Then came the fateful day when these two men faced one another in cold, deadly anger and men held their breath as they waited for the crashing roar of lead-spitting guns.

The break came on a raw November morning when the two cattle-men worked the mammoth beef herd on the sagebrush flat beyond the Chinook stockyards. The bitter wind that swept the bleak flat had chilled the men until they seemed frozen in their saddles. The herd had been hard to hold and the nerves of every man who fought the restless steers had been rubbed raw since dawn. At the yards, impatient trainmen beat their mittened hands and swung stiff arms to restore circulation while they waited for the penning of the herd that was to be shipped to Chicago.

Pete and Ike, cutting strays into the discard herd, had been in the saddle since the first streak of lead-gray sky had heralded the dawn. They were the only men who had not slipped back to the mess wagon for a cup of steaming coffee to thaw the chill in their blood.

Pete worked a four-year-old roan steer to the edge of the herd and his horse, with a quick practiced dash, shooed the animal into the open. Ike, who had just cut a stray bull out, was turning his horse back into the herd when he saw the roan steer.

"Made a mistake there, Pete," he called, and cut the roan steer back.

"Mistake, hell," grunted Pete. "Earmarks show it's a Two Bar critter. Split the right, crop the left. Brand's dim but I mind the day that critter was branded, at the Little Warm corral. It's one uh Jim

Bartlet's steers. That steer's mammy was a brockle-faced two-year-old heifer at the time that roan calf was branded, four years ago. A brockle-faced heifer that I got damn good reason to know was stole from me by that Bartlet skunk. I'll see him in hell afore I ship ary Two Bar stuff on my train."

"I made a dicker with Bartlet to ship his stuff," argued Ike. "He's payin' five dollars a head fer all we ship. I give him my word to ship his steers. I keeps my word regardless."

"You're fergittin' that this ain't the Bar L wagon that's gathered this herd. This is the Rafter T outfit and I'm runnin' it. And I'll tell a man that as long as I am runnin' my own outfit, I ship what I damn please an' cuts back ary steer that don't belong. I'm cuttin' that Two Bar steer into the discard herd. I don't aim that you nor ary other human is goin' to keep me from it."

"Cut back that steer into the culls, Pete Carver, and I cuts every damn Bar L steer I own into that same discard. Ship that roan critter, I tell you, or me'n you splits the blankets here and now."

Both men were white with anger. Each held the other's gaze with a steadiness that caused the listening cowpunchers to squirm uneasily in their saddles.

Then Pete Carver whirled his horse and called in a loud, rasping voice to his foreman, "Ride over to the yards and tell that train crew that I'm cancelin' them cars. We ain't shippin' this herd till it's *clean*."

Then he jabbed his horse with the spurs and cut the roan steer into the discard herd.

When Pete Carver shipped, two days later, the herd was straight Rafter T. That night the grizzled little cow man got drunk for the first time in twenty years.

Over at the Chinook House bar, Ike Rutherford was pouring raw whiskey into his stomach. He had been drinking for twenty-four hours.

Each man stayed in the saloon where he was drinking, avoiding the other. Each was surrounded by his own cowpunchers; they drank their drinks and, when the liquor thawed them, made fight talk.

Big Bob McClean, who had been sheriff for two terms, chewed the soggy butt of a cold cigar and cursed methodically. Then he loaded a sawed-off shotgun and crossed the blizzard-swept street to the Chinook House. He held the gun in the crook of his arm when he stepped into the barroom.

"Ike," he said in a voice that was so deadly calm that it threw an ominous hush over the half-drunk crowd, "I want yore gun."

"Meanin'?"

"Meanin' that I'm placin' you under arrest. There's a good fire a-goin' over at the jail. Bring a bottle along if yo're a mind to."

"Supposin'," asked Rutherford, his eyes narrowing to slits of blue flame, "supposin' I won't be arrested, Bob?"

"I ain't never gone after nobody that I didn't git, Ike. I'm plumb old and sot in my ways. I'm takin' you, Ike."

Ike Rutherford, drunk as he was, knew that the sheriff spoke the truth. The sheriff's shotgun was cocked. With a shrug, he handed over his .45, butt first. His eyes, normal once more, held the sun of summer skies in their blue depths.

"You daged old timber wolf, Bob McClean. Damned if I don't believe you'd turn that there scatter gun loose on me. Now, what in hell is it all about?"

"I heered you was aimin' to kill old Pete Carver on sight, Ike. I don't aim that you'll do it."

The sheriff locked Ike up in a tiny cell, then hunted out Pete Carver.

"Pete, you're pullin' out fer home," he announced as he stepped alongside the cow man who was buying out the Bloody Heart saloon, drink by drink.

"Huh?"

"Yore hoss is out in front, Pete, saddled. You'll make it home by mornin' if you keep goin'."

"What's the joke, Bob?"

"Whatever it is, she's on you, pardner. I'm runnin' you and yore men outa town, plain speakin'."

"Because I 'lowed I was goin' after Ike Rutherford's scalp?"

"Suthin' like that, Pete. You put me in office to uphold the law and order uh this Chinook town. I'm aimin' not to disappoint them as voted fer me."

"If I give the word, Bob, my boys'll jest nacherally pick you to pieces and sling the hunks out in the snow. You're makin' fight talk."

"And I backs up ary talk I makes, Pete. Mebbyso them drunk cow hands will down me but you won't be standin' to watch it. This here gun's loaded and unless you're drunker'n I figger, you kin see which way she's pointed."

"Where's Rutherford?" snapped Carver.

"In jail."

"Jail?"

"You heard me. He's stayin' there till he's sober enough to ride home. Next week, when you two damn old fools has come to yore senses, you'll kiss and make up. Now git and take yore men along."

"Ike Rutherford's in jail, boys," chuckled Pete. "It'll hurt him worse'n shootin' could. Do we quit town or do I make this gun-totin', bad-talkin' sheriff swaller that gun?"

Bob McClean's lips tightened as he read the light of drunken recklessness in the cattleman's eyes.

"Fergit it, Pete," grinned his foreman, who was fairly sober and had done his utmost to span the break between the two cow men. "Let's drag it fer the ranch."

So Pete Carver and his men left town and calamity was averted. But a splendid friendship between the two cattlemen had been ripped apart and there seemed no way of mending the ragged edges.

In the weeks that followed, Bob McClean tried more than once to make peace between them. Cowpunchers on both sides, with the sanction of their wagon bosses, did all in their power to prevent a split in the working of the two ranges that had always been one. Pete Carver, learning of these peaceful overtures, called his foreman into a quiet corner of the big bunkhouse.

"Beginnin' now," said Pete, biting his words till they popped like cracking ice, "I'm firin ary Rafter T man that speaks to a Bar L waddie on the range or in town. It's up to you to carry out these orders uh mine, or damn you, you're fired here and now. Hear me?"

"Yes, sir."

It was the first and last time that any Rafter T man ever called their employer anything but Pete. The foreman had been startled into addressing him as "sir." Pete took it as flippancy.

A short arm swing that traveled but a scant six inches caught the foreman on the point of the jaw and lifted him off the floor. He was unconscious when he slumped to the pine boards.

"Tell him," said Pete shortly, "when he comes to, that his check's waitin' fer him on his bunk. I'll 'sir' him! He's fired! So'r any more uh you that's got any funny sayin's that wants voicin'."

When the Rafter T foreman regained consciousness, he rubbed his swollen jaw and grinned. Pete was at the stable, nursing a heavy grouch.

"Fired, eh?" he grinned. "Fired because I said 'sir.' Fired, hell! I done worked fer Pete Carver too danged long to let him fire me thataway. Him nor no other man kin fire a gent that won't quit."

Whereupon he tore up the check and walked to the barn. Pete, forking hay to his horse, whirled at the sound of spur rowels, anticipating trouble. Hay fork in hand, he confronted his foreman.

"Keep yore shirt on, Pete," laughed the foreman. "I jest moseyed over from the bunkhouse to strike you fer a ten-dollar raise. Do I git it or do I work all winter at the wages I bin gittin'." He rubbed his jaw meaningly.

"Raise you twenty," growled the hot-tempered little cattleman. "You might go to work for that Rutherford polecat, otherwise."

The foreman shook his head. The incident was closed.

"Looks to me like we was due fer a hard winter, Pete. What you aim to do about feedin' the hell-slue uh Bar L stuff that'll need hay to pull through."

"We'll feed 'em, uh course," growled Pete. "Come spring, we'll work our range clean and git shet uh their danged stuff. Every hoof. I'll throw a drift fence across the range and put on line riders to keep Rutherford's stuff back. My quarrel is with Rutherford, son. Not with his pore cows and steers that need hay shoved into 'em. No man kin say that Pete Carver let a Bar L critter starve because they was so plumb unfortunate as to be owned by a danged old bull-headed rannyhan that throws down an old-time friend fer a cow-stealin' skunk like Jim Bartlet."

"Durned if I thought Ike Rutherford could be so low down, Pete," said the foreman gravely. "I've known sheep folks with more principle."

"What the devil d' *you* know about it?" snapped Pete. "I'm payin' you top wages to run this cow spread, not to blackguard Ike Rutherford."

"Shore thing, Pete." He moved away to the further end of the stable before Pete could read the mirth in his eyes.

One week later, the Rafter T foreman met the Bar L foreman in a coulee that afforded some shelter from the snowstorm that was whitening the hills.

"Goshamighty," chuckled the Rafter T boss, thawing the numbness from his fingers preparatory to rolling a cigarette. "He like to run that danged hayfork through me when I 'lowed that Ike was kinda low down. Mebbyso there's hopes yet uh patchin' the thing up. Sore as Pete is around the horns, I plumb believe he'd kill ary stranger that spoke bad uh Ike Rutherford."

The Bar L boss nodded. "Hear the latest news about Ike?"

"Let's have it feller. Ain't got much time. Pete's a ridin' thisaway mebby, and if he ketches me augerin' a Bar L man, he'll like as not shoot my ears off. Gimme the news."

"Ike done bought out Jim Bartlet, lock, stock, and barrel. Then he taken his coonskin off and whipped this Bartlet skunk and two-three Two Bar men fer good measure. He come home with two busted knuckles and a black eye, happier'n a Blackfoot squaw with a red blanket."

"Is he weakenin' any?"

"Not him. He's workin' us like he owned us and he's drinkin' some. We done got orders to whup all Rafter T men on sight. He's gonna build a drift fence, come spring."

"Then we'll be poundin' staples and strechin' wire, side by side, pardner. The Rafter T's throwin' up a drift fence from Squaw Butte to the lone cottonwood on Bull Crick."

The two bosses grinned, finished their cigarettes, and parted.

"See you at the drift fence in May, you Rafter T polecat."

"So long till spring, you Bar L coyote."

II
"WHITE BLANKETS OF DEATH"

Montana stockmen who survived it still shake their heads and look grave when one mentions the winter of '86-'87. Bitter disaster swept the cow country like a white-boned hand of death. Blizzard after blizzard whined and howled across the bleak greasewood flats and left them dotted with the bony carcasses of steers. A hundred thousand wild-eyed steers, drifting with the storm, death glazing their frost-seared eyeballs even before they dropped in their dogged, hopeless trot. Milling, drifting, piling up against the cutbanks until the coulees were filled with their frozen bodies.

Cowpunchers, bundled in wool chaps, coonskins, and mufflers, faced tired mounts into the teeth of that terrible storm and, with heavy hearts, put up a sullen, desperate fight with a heroism that is never to be forgotten so long as men gather and trade tales of the range. No trace of weakening showed on their frost-blackened faces. No word of complaint from lips too stiff to hold a cigarette. If there were some who quit, their pitiful minority is lost in the army of game men who fought their hopeless battle with a grin frozen on their lips. They asked no reward save their forty dollars a month. And when, as the winter wore on and cattlemen whose herds had numbered thousands, were left without a critter to carry their brand, these cowboys worked on, without pay, gathering what stock drifted their way, regardless of what brand marked their tight-stretched hide. God, in His greatness, never made truer, braver men than these laughter-loving, carefree cowboys who without re-straint, without question, gave the best that was in them. Those who lost their battle with the terrible white death that swept the prairies lay buried in the drifts until the warm Chinook wind should lay the hills bare and brown in the late spring. Their comrades, when they found them, would mark their graves with a pile of boul-ders, then ride on.

"Oh, bury me not on the lone prairieeeee!"

The old range song, doleful as a dirge, took on a new significance. Cattle owners were wiped out; cowboys gave their lives; native four-year-old steers died by the thousands. Epic in its devastation was that winter of '86.

Old Ike Rutherford, gaunt, frost-blackened, unshaven, fought his losing fight and doled out scant forksful of priceless hay to the handful of cattle that had not drifted beyond reach with the first driving blizzard.

Each morning he led his men north, into the teeth of the bitter wind, to gather poor cattle and drift home with them at dusk. Hay was scarce. The banks would loan not a penny to buy more. The gaunt old cow man, fighting on when hope was long since lost, grinned gamely and made a pitiful attempt at being jocular with his men. He fooled no one, not even himself.

A hundred miles south of the Bar L ranch, Pete Carver scowled at the long-staggering stream of gaunt Bar L steers that poured into the brakes from the open country.

"Looks like we done ketched everything uh Rutherford's except his milk pen stuff," he growled. "How's the hay holdin' out, boys?"

"Not worth a damn. If this storm don't break in a week, we'll have to quit feedin' to save enough hay fer the saddle hosses. There's a million dead cattle at the head of the brakes. A million, Pete, or I'm a sheep herder. The boys cut open a cow that had jest died. Skinnier than a barbed wire fence. Willow branches thicker'n a man's fist in the pore critter's paunch. I was as fer as the forks of Cottonwood huntin' fer a sign uh that Wyoming boy that didn't git back the night uh the bad wind."

"Find him?" asked Pete in a listless tone.

"Found his hoss at the foot of a shale cliff. Dug fer two hours in the drifts but nary trace uh the boy. Either he'd quit his hoss and was afoot when the hoss went over the bank in the dark, else he's too deep buried. I marked the place so's we could find it, once the snow goes. It's . . . it's hell, Pete."

"Hell'n then some. How's the stuff in the brakes along Rock Crick?"

"Still pawin' to feed. Good shelter in these badlands, Pete. Brush thick too, and there's wuss cow feed than buck brush and willows."

Pete nodded, grinning twistedly. "Yeah. Barbed wire or sawdust is wuss. Still, we'll save enough to make a showin' in the spring. That's better'n some cow men'll do."

"Ike Rutherford," put in the foreman, "will be wiped out, plumb."

"Except fer what's drifted in on us. Which, by the looks uh the string the boys is hazin' into the sheds yonder, is about ten million head. Ain't there no end to them damn Bar L scarecrows? Me shorthanded and no hay, a-wastin' time and feed and men on a outfit that turned down a real friend fer a damn skunk of a cow thief! I'd orter uh lined my sights on his skinny brisket and pulled the trigger!"

"Easy enough to let them Bar L steers drift across the river to yon side, cuttin' back the Rafter T's as the herd passes the pole gate," suggested the foreman.

"Son, don't read no brands when you pass out the hay. It'll shore make old Ike Rutherford happy to see them cattle, come spring."

"Hmmm. Thought you was all but ready to swap shots with him, Pete?"

"Was. Still am, dang his ornery old hide. But that ain't no cause fer me wantin' to see him broke and huntin' work next spring."

So it came about that many a Bar L steer, thanks to Pete Carver, was kept alive through these bitter days, on Rafter T feed.

Hay ran low until Pete gave orders to feed only the horses. Snow plows broke the crusted drifts for the trailing skeletons that followed bawling in its wake. Men worked like fiends from daybreak till long past dark to save the lives of the cattle that huddled in pitiful misery in the low-roofed sheds, gnawing at the bark on the logs, pulling the brush thatch from the roof.

Every Rafter T rider carried a carbine and a belt full of shells, for the wolves and coyotes were growing bolder every day. Each man had orders to shoot any cow or steer that was too far gone to save, and sprinkle the meat with strychnine. Thus the animals were humanely disposed of and the poison would perhaps kill a wolf that, alive, would pull down a cow that otherwise might live through the winter. In this matter of cow shooting, the punchers were ordered to disregard brands. If the animal needed killing, it was killed regardless of what brand it wore. These were days of drastic measures.

III

"LOOKING FOR TROUBLE"

Fifteen miles down the river from Carver's ranch, a cluster of log cabins squatted on the high bank of the river. Above the door of one of these cabins was a rudely lettered sign. SALOON it read.

Here a smoky lamp burned far into the night. In the smoke-laden, whiskey-fumed saloon, unshaved, roughly garbed men played cards or traded stories to the tune of a squeaky fiddle. Trappers, for the most part, with a sprinkling of cowpunchers, half-breed wood cutters, and an occasional tin-horn gambler who had been run out of town for crooked dealing. Sometimes a nameless, hard-eyed man drifted in from the lonely cabin where he was wintering. Silent, bearded, his right hand never straying more than a few inches from his gun, he would buy his quart or gallon of moonshine whiskey, pay for it, and depart.

A half-breed would trade a load of pitch wood for a gallon of vile liquor and stay perhaps, until the jug was empty, then linger on until his credit was no longer good. A wolf pelt or beaver hide bought a quart for the trapper. The tin-horn played solitaire in a far corner and, like a spider in its web waiting for the fly, would bide his time until some man with a craving for poker drifted in.

The squeaky fiddle in the grimy hands of its 'breed owner droned out such tunes as the "Red River Jig" and "Hell Among the Yearlin's."

To this saloon at the Rocky Point crossing came Jim Bartlet and two of his men. In Bartlet's pocket was a roll of bank notes. In his heart a black hatred for the big cow outfits, the Rafter T and Bar L in particular. His face was not yet healed from the beating he had suffered at the hands of Ike Rutherford.

Tall, heavy framed, with the flat features of a bull dog, he saw the world through closely set pig-like eyes of pale gray color. Burly of build, swaggering of manner, he was a braggart who usually was able to prove his boasts. Most men feared his strength and brutality and let him alone. Other men, such as Rutherford, Carver, and Bob McClean, held the swashbuckling bully in contempt.

While it had never been actually proven that Jim Bartlet was a cattle rustler, it remained a mystery how he had built a sizable herd from a few head of cows in so short a time. There were a score of others like him, fringing on the big ranges and fattening their herds with cattle stolen from the larger outfits. Hard riders, heavy drinkers, quick with a gun or lariat. They knew brands and every possible way of changing a brand by blanket, plucking, or working it with pitch. "Sleeper" marking some, "hair branding" others, they gathered other men's calves and moved the animals to their home ranches. Sometimes they drove a long nail into the cow's foot so to lame her that she could not follow. Other cows, whose calves they stole, they roped, threw, and sewed up the poor animal's eyelids or filled the eyes full of sand. An adept at these inhuman practices, was Jim Bartlet.

Drinking, gambling, fighting, he spent his days at the Rocky Point saloon. Always he made his boast of what he had done and what he intended doing to Ike Rutherford and Pete Carver.

"They done run me outa my place," he bawled to his drunken audience. "Damn 'em! Might as well try to run a timber wolf off by throwin' rocks at 'im, eh, boys? I'll git 'em both, hear me? This winter is gonna bust that Rutherford skunk. Me, Jim Bartlet, is gonna finish the job. And when that Pete Carver heaves in sight he'd better come a shootin'. I'm mean, I am. A fightin', snappin wolf, hear me? Drink up, gents."

Night after night, Bartlet and his two men drank until they could no longer stand up to the pine bar. Daytimes they rode into the rough hills and left the saloon keeper to wonder what manner of devilment they were up to. They bought many cartridges at the little trading post across the river. They carried butcher knives. Each night when they returned to the saloon, they would wash frozen blood from their lariats.

"The wolves," Bartlet would chuckle when drink had warmed

him, "is shore a-killin' off a heap uh Bar L and Rafter T stuff. And lemme tell you suthin', gents. That Pete Carver is shore a tricky jasper. He's a-killin' off Rutherford's cattle. Me'n the boys seen him and his men a-killin' 'em and poisonin' the carcasses. I kin show you no less'n a hundred head uh big native steers either shot or with their throats cut. I'm ridin' to Chinook to get the sheriff tomorrow. Drinks is on me fer the evenin', boys. Licker up. And lemme tell you suthin' more. It ain't only Rutherford cattle that's bein' killed off to leave more feed fer Rafter T stuff. No sir. I kin show you ten other brands on dead critters that Carver and his men has killed. Brands that belongs to the little fellers like I was afore Rutherford forced me out and 'lowed he'd run me outa the country. Wait till the sheriff gits here, that's all."

The following day Jim Bartlet left for Chinook. It was a long ride and, during the three days it took him to cover the trail, the man suffered terribly. Only the determination to revenge himself on the men whom he hated kept him from turning back to the Crossing.

After a ravenous meal and several drinks, Bartlet sought out Bob McClean in his office. There he spent an hour in telling his story.

"And you figger I'll make that ride," smiled Bob mirthlessly, "in weather like this, on the say-so of a man uh yore reputation? You're either drunk, Bartlet, or you done gone loco. Yonder's the door you come in. It works both ways. Will you walk out or git carried out?"

"Meanin' you won't go down there to see about this cattle killin' that's goin' on?"

"You guessed it fust time, Bartlet."

"If I go to the district attorney and swear out a warrant fer Pete Carver, you *gotta* serve it!" blustered Bartlet.

"Jest what right, mister, have *you* got to swear out ary warrant? You don't own a single head of cattle. Ike Rutherford, accordin' to yore story, is the man that's loser. I jest can't somehow see no picture uh Ike swearin' out a warrant for Pete Carver. Not if the hull damned Bar L herd was layin' dead in front uh Pete's house! Git outa here, you damned loud-mouthed polecat!"

Jim Bartlet stiffened, his hand poised above his gun butt.

"Pull it, Bartlet," invited McClean. "You'll be drilled afore you git it clear uh the scabbard. If I was so yaller as to let coyotes like you to run a whizzer on me, I'd uh bin dead years ago. Git!"

"All right, McClean," sneered Bartlet, "I'm goin'. But I'm comin' back with uh fist full of warrants and I'm seein' that you serve 'em."

Half an hour later, Jim Bartlet left town. He was gone a week. When he returned, he was accompanied by five men. Each one of these owned upwards of fifty head of cattle on the edge of the Bar L and Rafter T ranges. A grim-lipped, hard-eyed lot, they swarmed into the office of the district attorney.

The district attorney was a young man, fresh from law school, who had been back-slapped and hand-shaken into accepting this office that older, wiser lawyers were wont to decline firmly and with sarcastic thanks. It was an honor that carried too much grief for the pay involved. This young man who held the office was fired with zeal and still cherished many of his university ideals. Secretly he cherished the great hope of reforming Chinook and making of the cow town a city that he could write East about and modestly tell of its reformation under his rule. A worthy ambition, truly. He did not know that this great hope of his was one of Chinook's standing jokes.

Now, as he leaned back in his chair, twirling a pencil and jotting down occasional notations, he nodded gravely as the loquacious Bartlet poured forth a tale of justice blinded by prejudice, of the iron rule of the cattle barons, the gross injustice done the struggling ranchers of lesser means and smaller herds.

"Sheriff McClean refuses to serve the warrants, Mister Bartlet?"

"He shore does. Carver and Rutherford has got him buffaloed. He's scared of their money. Them and outfits like 'em put McClean in office. They kin push him out and he knows it. What we wants is a square deal, mister. We ain't gittin' it. I sold out to Rutherford at the point of a six-gun and I got witnesses to prove it!"

He did not add that Ike had given him an over-generous price for cattle he had stolen.

"You are ready to swear to the truth of your accusations, Mister Bartlet?"

The title of "mister" gave Jim Bartlet an air of importance.

"I kin take you to the spot where the dead animals lays," he boasted. "I got two witnesses to prove what I says. We seen Pete Carver kill the critters."

"What was his object in killing the cows?"

"They was eatin' his grass, mister. No use foolin' with McClean. Wire up to Helena fer a stock inspector that'll do his duty that he's swore to carry out. Let McClean sit alongside his stove and toast his rheumatism. He's too much of a old woman. Slower'n molasses."

"He is an odd old chap," admitted the young attorney, recalling past incidents when Bob McClean had not been overly enthusiastic about carrying out his wishes. "Don't know but what you've made a wise suggestion. I'll wire Helena and get a man here who will look at the matter from an unbiased viewpoint. Drop in tomorrow morning and I think I'll have news for you."

In response to the district attorney's wire, a stock inspector arrived on the midnight train. There was a session behind closed doors in the office of the district attorney. For once, Jim Bartlet had not boasted of his plans and Chinook was unaware of what went on. Bob McClean was at the Rutherford ranch on business pertaining to a loan which he had hoped in vain to make in Ike's behalf.

Sunup found the stock inspector with Bartlet and the five cattlemen, on the trail to the Rafter T ranch. The day was clear but the mercury stood at thirty below zero. In the inspector's pocket was a warrant for the arrest of Pete Carver.

A Rutherford rider happened to meet them as they swung southward along the trail. Jim Bartlet slouched sideways in his saddle to leer crookedly into the cowpuncher's unfriendly eyes.

"You kin tell Ike Rutherford and that settin' hen of a Bob McClean," he instructed the Bar L man, "if you see 'em, that I don't need 'em nor their help to git a square deal in this man's country. Afore this time next week, I'm tackin' Pete Carver's hide on the fence. He'll be lookin' out from between the bars uh the jail. Tell yore boss and that six-bit sheriff uh his'n that they kin go to hell."

Jim Bartlet, with a harsh laugh, spurred his horse into the cowpuncher's mount. Grinning, the other members of the posse followed in the wake of their self-appointed leader. A frown of annoyance clouded the brow of the stock inspector. He was beginning to wonder if he was making a mistake in not conferring with Bob McClean before acting. His instructions from headquarters had been somewhat vague regarding that. The young district attorney had advised against it. Still, he did not like the manner in which Jim Bartlet was pushing matters.

Back on the trail, the scowling Bar L man watched them out of sight, then spurred his horse to a long trot and headed for the home ranch to carry Bartlet's message to Ike Rutherford.

It was dark when he arrived at the Bar L ranch. The old cattleman and the sheriff were playing seven-up. They looked grave when they learned of the threat to arrest Pete Carver.

"There was a law officer with them jaspers, son?" asked the old sheriff.

"Stock inspector, near as I could figger, Sheriff, a kinda young gent with a good-looking rig. Packed a white-handled gun plain' and protrudin' like."

"Some damn glory hunter, Ike," rumbled Bob. "That young D.A. has like as not ribbed him up to thinkin' I'm layin' down on the job. Hell's gonna pop, Ike, if them tin-horns tries to drag Pete Carver out of his hole. They'd a heap better tackle a lion bare-handed."

"A heap," agreed Ike. "Dang his pesky old pitcher. Ornery as snake p'izen, is Pete, but them calf-stealin' buzzards is wuss. Only fer that Bartlet houn', me'n Pete'd be friends this minute. I swear that if them short horns hurts Pete Carver, I'll kill 'em all like they was so many rattlers! Tromp 'em out. That hoss uh yourn good fer a long ride, Bob?"

"Plenty good Ike. Figger we better git goin'?"

"Reckon so, Bob. I ain't doin' myself no good by stayin' here and watchin' my stock die off like flies. I need a hard ride and mebbyso a fast scrap to take the sickish feelin' outa my heart."

"I'm plumb glad to see you bury the hatchet, Ike," nodded Bob.

"Uh?" Ike, shrugging into his enormous coonskin, glanced with mild inquiry at the sheriff.

"Right tickled, Ike, to learn you done quit bein' a fool and are ready to shake hands with Pete and call it square."

"Who in tarnation said I was gonna shake hands, Bob McClean?" roared the cow man. "I'd as lief shake hands with a polecat. I'm not throwin' in with danged old fools that turns down a friend that has gone through hell'n high water with 'em. Let that sawed-off, bench-legged li'l ol' varmint so much as speak to me and I'll claw his hair off."

"Uh-huh. Shore thing, Ike," agreed Bob in a soothing tone that held an undercurrent of laughter. "I'll hold yore coat whilst you does it, too. Never knew a more ornery, bull-headed old fool than Pete Carver. Dunno but what Jim Bartlet was right about him a-killin' yore cattle, Ike. He shore hates you bad."

Ike bit off an end from a ten-inch length of plug and, with a bulging cheek, eyed the sheriff who was scowling as if in deep thought.

"Dang yore old speckled hide, Bob McClean," rumbled Ike, the light of mirth dancing in his blue eyes. "Let's git goin'."

Suddenly both men tensed. Motionless, their faces a study in expression, they stood there in the cabin, listening.

A rush of wind from without whined and howled as it swooped through the giant, bare-limbed cottonwoods.

"*The Chinook!*" croaked Ike hoarsely. "She's done come! The storm's busted!"

With a single stride of his long legs, he was at the door and had flung it open. Bare-headed, he stepped out into the darkness that was filled with the warm wind that meant salvation to the cattlemen.

Silently, his eyes fixed on the blanket of stars overhead, he stood there. Darkness hid the dry sobs that shook him. His lips moved soundlessly. Perhaps he prayed.

Bob McClean, standing in the doorway, watched Ike's shadowy form in the illumination from the open doorway that silhouetted the big man who stood beyond its glare. The old sheriff felt a tight sensation in his throat, for he sensed what was in Ike Rutherford's mind. He knew that for the Bar L cow man, the hot Chinook had come too late. The winter had wiped him out.

After a time, Bob went out and laid an arm across the shoulders of his old friend.

"Some of yore stuff's bound to have drifted into the brakes where Carver's boys'd feed 'em. You'll have some left, Ike."

"I wasn't thinkin' uh the cattle, Bob," said Ike quietly. "Four uh my boys died this winter a-fightin' to save my cattle. I was thinkin' about them, jest then."

MILES FARTHER SOUTH, the warm rush of wind caught the posse under the leadership of Jim Bartlet.

"We gotta keep movin' now, gents," he growled. "That damn hot wind'll cut these drifts like fire. Coulees'll be swimmin' by mornin'. Travelin'll be nigh impossible in some uh the places where we want to ride. The cañons where some uh them dead cattle is will be hell-roarin' rivers. Our evidence will be washed plumb away, like as not."

The inspector smiled to himself in the dark. It was a smile of hopeful relief. He was rapidly growing nauseated at the task that lay ahead. Bartlet's bragging, the whiskey bottles that passed to and from the men whom he had sworn in as deputies to take his orders but who were plainly bent on taking matters in their own hands. There had even been veiled threats of lynchings, shooting, and wiping out of the Rafter T outfit. All were in various stages of intoxication, all ugly. He was wishing he could slip away in the dark but they kept close watch on him, as if he were a prisoner.

"Inspector," said Bartlet, riding alongside the officer, "this damn wind may hide them cattle that Carver and his men shot. These brakes is clean impossible to travel when the snow's meltin'. Gotta keep on the ridges or sink outa sight in the soft drifts with water underneath. Now jest supposin' we can't find them dead critters? Have we still got a case again' the Rafter T spread?"

"No case at all, Bartlet, without the evidence."

"The sworn oath uh me and my men?"

"Won't be wuth six-bits, Mex."

"Hmmm. But if *you* was to see the evidence, yore word as a law officer would go big afore a jury, eh?"

"I'd have to see the evidence, Bartlet." The inspector's tone was firm.

"So? Listen, feller. Stick to me and my friends and we'll see you git paid a-plenty. Swear on the stand to what I tell you and we makes you a purty present uh more money than you ever'll git in a lifetime. Savvy what I'm drivin' at?"

"I think I do, Bartlet." The inspector halted his horse, his hand on his gun. In the darkness, the others surrounded him.

"You're takin' cards in our game?" asked Bartlet.

"Not by a damn sight!" The officer's gun came from its scabbard, hammer clicking to a full cock.

A dull roar. A crimson flash from Bartlet's gun, pressed close against the inspector's side. The officer's white-handled gun spat flame and one of the riders yelped as the slug ripped open his shoulder. Then the inspector slumped in his saddle and fell, dead before he hit the ground.

"Light a match," commanded Bartlet, "while I frisk him fer his badge and the warrants. From now on, I'm inspector. We'll tie this gent's carcass to his saddle and take him along. It's a case uh Judge Lynch fer the Rafter T's now, boys. We gotta go through. This jasper, remember, was killed while tryin' to arrest Carver. That's our story. God have mercy on the man that weakens and don't stick to it."

"We're kinda short-handed to tackle that outfit," complained one of the band.

Bartlet grinned. "Short-handed? I reckon not, pardner. My two boys is to meet us at the Crossin' with ten-twelve men that kin shoot and keep their mouths shut afterwards. When we swarms down on Carver and his gang, we're out-numberin' 'em three to one. Got that inspector tied on? Good. Let's go. Here's where we clean out the big spreads that's done us dirt."

IV

"THE CHINOOK"

Only yesterday, the badlands had been quiet as a tomb. White, cold, silent in the grip of the winter. Now, a hundred noises filled the hills. The warm wind, rushing with a swishing roar through the scrub pines. Swift flowing water, cascading from the ridges into the deep cañons, churning, gurgling, swirling through brush and cutting gorges in the drifts. Cattle, by instinct seeking the high points, clattered up the ridges that were already bare of snow. Startled deer crashed through the buck brush and red willow thickets, escaping the treacherous drifts that were rapidly undermined by melting ice and snow. Slush, mud, and the coulees were filled with torrents of muddy water.

Night came again and the wind still roared in the pine trees. At the Rafter T ranch, the cowpunchers "joshed" one another as they stropped their razors preparatory to ridding their frost-seared faces of the winter's beards. One of the men had fished a service-worn harmonica from his war-sack and was blowing wheezy tunes on the instrument. The lines of worry were fading from the faces of these men who had fought their fight against the blizzards. Pete Carver was the gayest of the lot. Joking, slapping men on the back, jigging when the harmonica whined "Turkey in the Straw" and "Forty-Seven Bottles." The Chinook had come! Cares and grief of the past months slipped from these riders of the big ranges. Joy, unrestrained and carefree, took its place.

At the saloon at Rocky Point Crossing, twenty men, riding in single file along the riverbank, were lost in the shadows of the giant cottonwoods. They spoke in low tones. Cigarettes glowed like fireflies in the dark. An occasional laugh, short and grating, cut through the low-toned banter. A moon rose above the ragged ridge and its white light fell on the butts of carbines and six-shooters.

In the lead of these men, breaking trail through melting snow, rode Jim Bartlet. Half drunk, he slouched in his saddle, bulking big in the moonlight. Fast-emptying whiskey bottles passed from hand to hand. Always the toast was the same.

"To hell with the Rafter T!"

To the north, other riders traveled the treacherous trails. Ike Rutherford and Sheriff Bob McClean, armed and riding in grim silence, pushed their leg-weary mounts southward along the trail. The slush splattered them, hunger and fatigue lined their faces, but neither spoke of the grueling torture of the ride. Floundering through drifts, sliding down ridges into uncharted blackness, their only thought was to keep their guns dry.

Midnight came and the two men halted on the long, bare ridge that led down to the river bottoms where the Rafter T cabins were hidden in the darkness. Loosening their saddle girths, they rolled cigarettes and let their horses rest for half an hour.

Suddenly, from that opaque blackness of the river bottom far below, came the flat, menacing crack of a rifle.

"God!" breathed McClean, and jerked tight his saddle cinch.

"Jackpot's done opened!" grunted Ike, swinging into his saddle.

Indifferent now to the slippery footing, they spurred their horses down the long adobe ridge.

Like popcorn held over a hot blaze, the gun shots cut the night. Streaks of crimson flame. The booming crash of .45s. The flat, echoing crack of .30-30s. Shouts, curses, the thudding of stampeding hoofs as horses ran in the dark. A mêlée of sounds and movement, half cloaked in the blotched moonlight beneath the tall cottonwoods.

In the open, men on foot took shelter behind trees and corrals. In the cabin, Pete Carver and his men, half clothed and bewildered by the unexpected suddenness of the night attack, worked the levers of their Winchesters and took snap shots at the shadowy forms that crossed the moonlit spaces. Hot lead spattered against the log walls and shattered the window panes. Inside the cabin, men groaned from the pain of wounds. Pete Carver swore indifferently at a ragged gash in his thigh and dragged himself to a window.

"Take 'er easy, boys," he cautioned. "We got 'em whupped!"

He spoke with conviction that gave courage to his men. Spoke without reckoning the odds against them. Odds, to Pete Carver, counted less than nothing. He had fought Indians years before when numbers mattered not at all.

"When one uh them varmints looms black again' your gun sights, pull the trigger," he called. "Save yore lead. We ain't got more'n we need. Watch clost there by the door. They're tryin' fer to close in and rush the cabin."

Stealthily, as Indians attack, Bartlet's men dodged from tree to tree, edging closer to the cabin. Now and then a rifle cracked in the cabin and a dodging form spun about, then sank limply, a huddled, shapeless blot on the moonlit ground.

In the shelter of the low-roofed cow shed where frightened steers milled and bawled, Jim Bartlet turned to several men who crouched in the shadows, reloading their guns.

"Only fer some fool shootin' his gun accidental, we'd a snuck up plumb easy on that cabin," he growled, shoving cartridges into the magazine of his carbine.

"What's the odds, Bartlet?" chuckled one of the group, one of the two who had spent the past weeks with Jim Bartlet at Rocky Point. "We got them gents anyhow, ain't we? Makes 'er more interestin' thisaway. If you're rearin' to know who let his shootin' iron go off as we was sneakin' up, I kin tell you. It was my gun. I had 'er cocked and kinda pulled 'er off sudden, when I trips in the dark. What's the odds, anyhow, if. . . . "

Jim Bartlet's gun roared. The man, without a sound, dropped in his tracks, shot through the head.

"Damn him fer a drunken, keerless idiot," snarled the murderer, shoving a fresh shell into his gun. "That'll learn 'im."

Bartlet's ugly face twitched with rage and his voice was coarse and harsh as a rasp. The other men, aghast at the cold-bloodedness of their leader, drew back into the shadow.

"He's got money on 'im," leered Bartlet. "Frisk 'im and split it between you. Who's got a bottle? I need a drink. And don't go gettin' squeamish, boys. That dead un was no good nohow. Cow thief and ex-con from Texas. Knew him down south. Ain't none uh you gents got a bottle?"

One of them produced a pint of whiskey and they all drank. The dead man was searched and his money divided.

"Time we charged that cabin," growled Bartlet, moving away. "Foller me, fellers."

They obeyed half-heartedly, fearful of this killer's wrath, yet nauseated at the cold-blooded cruelty. Cattle stealing, to them, was but a way of making a living. Wanton killing of men was distasteful and dangerous.

"We got the law behind us," called Bartlet. "C'mon. You hired fer tough hands. Play yore string out."

Shifting, blurred shadows, they slipped toward the cabin.

The firing seemed to have increased in volume now. Orange streaks from the rifle barrels cut the dark. Ricocheting bullets droned like hornets.

Into this hail of hot lead rode Ike Rutherford and Bob McClean. Not until the sheriff's horse was shot from under him did the two check their pace. Ike's long arm swung downward, gathered in the stunned sheriff, and the horse sped back to the brush with its double burden.

"Told you we was fools to rush the cabin, Ike," panted Bob. "Like as not it was one uh Pete's men shot that hoss, thinkin' he was bringin' down a Bartlet man."

"Well," growled Ike, wiping blood from his cheek where a bullet had cut the flesh like a knife, "what'll we do? Set here like two long-tailed birds?"

"None whatsomever, you bonehead. Gimme time to think a minute. We ain't doin' nobody no good by chargin' across that clearin', gittin' shot by our friends. Situated as we are, we're as harmful as two prairie dogs. Lemme think, Ike."

"Think! Goshamighty, you danged old horny owl, how kin a man think while seventeen million bad shots is a throwin' lead into our midst? Rid yore manly bosom uh one half-growed, half-reasonable idee fer pullin' us outa this mess and I votes fer you next term. Otherwise I does my best to elect a sheriff that sabes Injun warfare."

"You struck it, Ike," hissed the old sheriff. "We play Sioux with these jaspers."

"Huh?" Ike shifted a long-barreled Colt to his left hand and brought forth a plug of tobacco. Filling his cheek with a generous bite, he returned the plug to his pocket, spun the cylinder of his gun, and spat into the dark.

"We split here, savvy? One by one, we puts these here bush-wackin' snakes outa commission. Spot 'em by their gun flashes, slip up behind 'em and bend yore cannon between their horns. If you got ary hoggin' strings, tie 'em, then step on to the next party. In due time, we has the enemy worked down to our size and under complete and entire control, as the war general says. Kin you find ary blemish on that idee?"

"Nary, Bob. We starts from here?"

"We does. You might kinda keep tally on them that you put to sleep."

"Bet a new hat I downs more'n you does."

"Takes the bet. *Adios.*"

"So long."

With the stealth of Indians, they slipped through the brush. Ike, jaw bulging with tobacco, gun swinging loosely in his big hand, crouched low and made his way toward a tree from whence he had seen a streak of rifle flame. A moment later, he shared the tree with one of Bartlet's followers. The man, thinking him one of the posse, gave him a cursory glance in the half light and lined his sights on the cabin.

Ike grinned, spat, and his gun barrel swung in a short arc.

"Good night, cowboy," he murmured. "May yore dreams be sweet as sorghum."

The gun barrel thudded against the man's skull and he went limp in Ike's arms. The big cow man tied him with his neckscarf and moved on to the next tree.

Suddenly Jim Bartlet's voice roared above the din of firing.

"All ready, boys! Charge!"

With a wild cheer, the attacking party crossed the clearing at a run. Ike, interrupted in the business of tying his second victim, grabbed up his gun.

Squatting, he fired methodically at the swift-moving forms that swarmed across the clearing. His gun empty, he grabbed up the carbine that had fallen from his victim's hands. The tobacco-bulged cheek lay along the gun stock and his long fingers pressed the trigger. Spat! Crash! His gun belched flame until the steel barrel felt warm to his touch.

"Wisht I was among 'em yonder, dang it!" he muttered. "But I better stay put. Pete's a-holdin' 'em, looks like. Yeah. They're comin' back now, what of 'em kin make it. Look at 'em come. Wisht I'd known which was Bartlet, I'd split his brisket with a . . . comin' my way, feller?"

A man was running toward the tree where Ike squatted. The big cattleman got to his feet and leaned against the tree trunk. As the runner slipped behind the shelter of the cottonwood trunk, Ike felled him with a blow on the head.

"That," he grinned, "is what a man might call real accommodationment. Come a-lopin' up, purty as hell, fer his nightcap. Tally three."

He paused to tie three knots in his handkerchief, then moved on.

In the cabin, Pete Carver took toll of his men. One lay dead by the window. Four more were suffering from wounds. Half sick from the wound in his thigh, the cow man called in a cheering tone to the men who crouched in the dark.

"How's the cartridges holdin' out, boys?"

"Not so good," replied a Rafter T man.

"My gun's done gone dry," announced the foreman.

Others made similar replies. Quick calculation disclosed that but a dozen cartridges remained among them.

"Hold 'em fer the next charge, boys," said Pete grimly. "When they hits the cabin, swing open the door and let 'em in. We'll whup 'em at clost quarters. I done recognized Bartlet's voice, fellers. Dunno what kind of game he's playin', but I'm thinkin' we'd be in a bad way if we was to git captured."

Bartlet's men were keeping up an intermittent fire. He moved from one man to the next, giving orders.

"They done quit shootin', yonder in the cabin," he chuckled. "Done run low on shells, I bet. We got a tail holt on the Rafter T now, gents."

He dodged a clear space, slipped into a brush patch, then leaped behind a wide-trunked cottonwood where a man's shadowy outline showed.

"We got the damned T's on the run, feller," he panted. "All we gotta do is . . . McClean!"

The sheriff, grinning wickedly, had stepped into the light that Bartlet might recognize him.

"Stick 'em up, Bartlet!" he said quietly. "I want you!"

The sheriff's .45 was covering the big murderer. Bartlet's hands lifted skyward. McClean took a step forward, gun held in careless readiness.

With a swiftness that was surprising in so big a man, Bartlet leaped sideways. McClean's bullet clipped his ribs. Then the cow thief was on top of the old sheriff, a clubbed gun swinging viciously. A sickening thud as the weapon crashed across McClean's eyes. Again and again it crashed into the old officer's face, across his head, and Bartlet, holding the unconscious man in a vise-like grip, mouthed curses as he swung the blood-spattered weapon. Then, when his frenzy had worn itself out, he flung the limp form from him and kicked it savagely where it lay on the ground.

Standing over the huddled form that lay still as death, he cocked his gun and pointed the muzzle downward.

"I'll pump so damn much lead in you that it'll take a work hoss to pack yore carcass. . . ."

A terrific crash from the cow sheds behind him. Like a thunderclap it made puny the sound of gunfire. Then the earth trembled as if shaken by an earthquake. The next instant the clearing was choked by a sea of fear-maddened, stampeding cattle. Wild-eyed with fright, packed so densely that some of the weaker animals were tossed above the seething mass of hair and horns, they crashed across the shattered corrals, mowing down all that lay in their path.

Tossing, clashing horns, thundering, sharp cleft hoofs, a swift-moving, stampeding death to anything that lay in its path.

A man, caught in its sweep, screamed as the herd caught him. Then the echo of his cry was drowned in the clash of horns.

Bartlet, frightened from his murderous intent, gave an inarticulate cry and ran. Beyond stood a cluster of three giant trees that afforded better shelter than the one behind which he stood. Drop-ping his gun in momentary panic, he ran toward the largest of the trees. Fifty feet behind him raced the herd. He glanced over his shoulder. A quick fearful glance. His spur caught in a bush and with an agonized cry, he fell headlong. With a scream of terror, he struggled to free himself, only to fall again as the spur still held him. Then, shrieking, he threw his arms around his face, half standing, half kneeling. White moonlight fell about him, making of him a grotesque mockery of a man kneeling in prayer. Scarcely fifteen feet away stood the giant cottonwood that meant escape from a terrible death.

Something moved in the shadow of the big tree. A rope shot out, its noose settling about Bartlet's shoulders. A terrific jerk and Bart-let was jerked free and yanked behind the tree. The next instant the stampede crashed past.

Pasty-faced, shaking as if stricken by a chill, Bartlet lay sobbing at the feet of the man who had saved his life. He started to rise. A boot heel clipped him under the jaw.

"Lay down, you damn skunk," growled Ike Rutherford, flattening himself against the tree that shook with the impact of the stamped-ing herd. "Dang me fer a chicken-hearted sheep herder. I'd orter uh let you git ketched. I take after my mammy thataway. How come this here jasper layin' alongside you there was packin' this rope? Speak up, you white-livered, yaller-hided varmint afore I rassels down this here weakenin' heart uh mine and pitches you into them runnin' steers. What's the idee uh this here rope I took offen that gent I knocked between the horns? Is this here a lynchin' party?"

"Yes," came the croaking reply.

"Aimed to hang Pete Carver?"

"Yes." Bartlet's voice was hoarse with fright. His narrow escape had completely unnerved him.

"Thought so. Well, take good keer of that rope, mister skunk. We'll be needin' it, quick as these cows quit a-runnin' past. I'm aimin' to hang you, personal. Brings my tally up to five."

Ike shifted his tobacco to the other cheek and flipped several hitches about the body of his prisoner, binding him securely.

"I'll have to hang you by myself, Bartlet. Don't dast wait fer Bob. He'd like as not raise a kick again' stringin' you up. Kick number four in the belly, will you, and see if he's dead—er playin' possum. Them danged cattle give me a bad scare, jest as I swung, and I'm afeered I hit 'im a mite harder'n I figgered."

There was a hysterical, unnatural pitch to Rutherford's voice that escaped Bartlet. In gaining the tree where he had felled the man with the rope and later rescued his enemy, two bullets had torn through Ike's body, leaving wounds that, while not serious, were bleeding profusely. Blood soaked the leg of his overalls and filled his left boot. The other shot had caught the doughty old cattleman in the muscle of his shoulder leaving a neat hole, thanks to the steel jacket bullet. Now he stood above Bartlet, grinning twistedly and swaying slightly, like a man who sleeps on his feet.

The main force of the stampede had passed, leaving the drag end of weak cows who straggled along, wild-eyed and bawling with fright. Ike saw them but dimly, for the pain and loss of blood was telling on his vitality. He wrapped and tied the rope about Bartlet, then sat down weakly. He felt weak and sick and dizzy like a man stupefied by too much bad liquor. A buzzing, humming sensation came in his ears and he lost consciousness.

V
"BLAZING GUNS"

It was sunrise. Pete Carver and his men, heavy-eyed from loss of sleep and pain of bandaged wounds, talked in low tones. The odor of frying bacon and strong coffee filled the cabin.

In a corner of the cabin Jim Bartlet and ten of his men sat on the floor, arms bound behind them. Sullen-eyed, they maintained a stoic silence. Warrants for the arrest of Pete Carver and Rafter T men lay on the table where Pete had tossed them after reading them.

Ike Rutherford, lying on a cowpuncher's bed, groaned and opened his eyes. He blinked curiously as he looked into Pete Carver's face.

"Howdy, you old sheep thief," he grinned. "Glad to. . . . "

He broke off in his greeting, scowling. Pete had deliberately turned his back, ignoring the peaceful overture of his old friend. Ike made as if to rise, then lay back, puzzled and angry. His hands and feet were tied.

Pete, his broad back turned on his friend, hobbled across the room on a crude crutch, and spoke to his foreman who was bending over a man who lay on Pete's bunk.

"Bob McClean still alive?" he asked listlessly.

"Plumb, Pete. He's bad beat up, but breathin' strong. Whoever beat him up, done a good job. Seems like he's movin' a mite, Pete. He'll come alive directly."

"Call me when he wakes up," said Pete. "I'll be outside. Air's bad spoiled in here by so many skunks."

When Pete had gone outside, the Rafter T foreman walked to Ike's bunk, staring down into the big cattleman's bloodshot eyes. There was no light of friendliness in the foreman's eyes. Ike's lips parted to frame a question, then snapped shut.

"Pete's sent fer a doctor, Rutherford, to patch you and yore outfit up. It's a damn sight more'n you and McClean has got comin'. We're short-handed, bein' you and yore men has crippled and killed half our boys. Them as kin sit a hoss is gatherin' the cattle you stampeded on us last night."

"You mean you think me'n Bob was . . . ?"

Ike broke off with a harsh laugh that held the tone of a sob. Realization that Pete thought them party to such a dastardly attack flushed Ike's lean cheeks with hot anger and humiliation.

"Lucky fer you and yore mule-brained boss that I'm tied, young feller," he growled. "Otherwise I'd whup you both till you couldn't stand. Git away from me, damn you! Clean away!"

"Directly, Rutherford, when I've said my say. Pete's too dang flabbergasted to talk, but I ain't. We did kill some Bar L stuff, Rutherford, along with our own and a few head belongin' to them dirty calf-stealin' snakes settin' yonder. But fer every head uh yore stuff that was shot, fifty was saved by feedin' 'em Rafter T hay. If we done broke the law, we'll stand trial, mister. Pete Carver ain't the kind that runs. Neither is he the kind that sneaks up on folks in the dark. When yore able to serve 'em, Rutherford, you and McClean'll find yore bloody warrants layin' right there on the table."

There was no mistaking the contempt in the foreman's voice. It made Ike sick at heart to be so suspected. The full portent of the Rafter T man's words left the old cattleman speechless with dumb misery. With dulled eyes, he watched the man cut his fetters, then contemptuously turn his back and stalk out of the cabin.

For some time Ike lay staring at the log ceiling, sick with pain and misery. Finally he sat up, swung his legs over the edge of the bunk, and stared across at the bunk where Bob McClean stirred feebly. Then he rose and limped to the stove to pour himself a cup of coffee. Bacon and biscuits stood in their pans on a table but Ike was too sick at heart to eat.

"Well, Rutherford," sneered Jim Bartlet, "how d'you like it out West as far as you bin? How does it feel to be classed with us boys, eh? You're in dang good company, fer onct."

Ike turned on him, scowling from under bristling brows.

"You was nigh the Big Divide last night when I saved yore hide, Bartlet, but not half so clost to sudden death as you are right now. Another word outa you and I'll choke you to death."

"My boys is witness, Rutherford. You'd hang fer it. Best bet you kin make is to throw in with us. You should uh tied us tighter last night. We was all loose when the Carver outfit grabbed us, afore we could bunch up to fight 'em off. Our stories make you and McClean as deep in this as we are. Evidence backs us. We kinda let Carver think you was sorter leader, savvy. Our stock inspector deputized us all. Afore he dies, yonder by the cow shed, I hears him tell you to carry out the raid. He gives you his badge which you pins on yore vest. You're still wearin' it, Rutherford!"

A leering grin on his lips, Bartlet nodded his head towards the star pinned to Ike's vest. In a moment of quick-witted desperation, just as Carver's men swooped down on him in the gray light of dawn, Bartlet had fastened the metal badge to Ike, and shoved the warrants in Ike's pockets as he lay unconscious by the tree.

Ike fingered the bit of shining metal, then ripped it loose and tossed it on the table beside the warrants. Then he gulped down his coffee and made his way to the sheriff's bunk.

Bob stirred feebly and his eyes blinked open.

"Take 'er easy, Bob," said Ike. "Don't make no talk yet till you feel better."

"Where's Bartlet, Ike? How come we're here? Where's old Pete?"

Briefly, in sentences tinged with bitterness, Ike told Bob of their predicament. Bob's lips pursed in a soundless whistle of blank astonishment.

"My God, Ike! You must be loco! Pete'd never believe. . . ."

"But the old fool does, Bob. These low-down calf-thievin' coyotes a-settin' yonder has lied us into the deal, bad, too. Jest the same, a man orter whup that Pete Carver till he can't stand up, for classin' us with them yaller-hided varmints. How you feelin', Bob?"

"Like a yearlin'," lied the sheriff, sitting up and feeling gingerly of the crude bandages about his head, put there by Pete. "Let's have a jolt uh coffee and some grub. Then we'll plan out a scheme. Dunno as we orter be too hard on Pete. He got treated rough last night. Circumstantial evidence says me'n you had throwed with the Bartlet spread. We'll figger a way to win out, Ike."

At a nearby cabin that Pete had converted into a hospital for his men, the Rafter T foreman and his employer conversed in earnest tones, eyes fixed on the river a scant hundred yards away.

"Water's riz three feet in the past half hour, Pete. She's nigh over the banks. A six-foot rise'll wipe us out. Glad I had the boys shove the cattle up on the ridges this mornin'. They'd orter have 'em purty well gathered by now."

"Git four hosses hitched to the mess wagon," said Pete. "We gotta start movin' these wounded boys out to high ground. The cook's out there now, loadin' in what grub we'll need."

The hot Chinook wind, melting the snow on the ridges, had made raging torrents of the cañons. Foot by foot the water rose in the river. The boom of cracking ice crashed like distant cannon. Trees, dead stock, debris of every description, were borne along with the swirling muddy current. A few hours more and the Missouri River would be out of its banks, roaring, churning, carrying with its icy rush all that lay in its path.

"Yonder comes a haystack, floatin' along," said the foreman.

"Looks like a hen house behind it. That'll be the Long X ranch on its way to St. Louis," added Pete. "The X boss was braggin' about them sorrel hens uh his. Wisht we had time to foller that there hen house and ketch 'er when she floats on a bar. Ain't seen a aig since August. Well, son. Better get the team hooked up. Spring movin' come sudden this year. The alfalfa is shore gonna git irrigation."

Half an hour later, four stout horses dragged the mess wagon, loaded with wounded men, up the long adobe ridge. Rutherford and the sheriff watched it leave. The Rafter T foreman led around horses, saddled and bridled.

"All you law enforcers step out," he growled through the open door. "You kin untie yore men's legs, McClean, but leave their hands hobbled. Me'n Pete ain't got time to fool around a-fightin' 'em. Onct we gits the outfit moved to the ridges, we'll go along to town. Not afore then. We got every damn gun on the ranch so you ain't in no shape to argy. I'm escortin' you personal. Rutherford, you and McClean stays here till the wagon makes the next trip. We're short uh saddle horses. Bartlet'll stay, too. We aims to keep you three where Pete kin ride herd on you. Move fast, there. Rattle yore dew-claws, polecats." He backed the command with a .45.

The foreman rode away with his prisoners. Pete Carver, squatted on a stump just outside the door, smoked in silence, a sawed-off shotgun across his knees. He seemed ill at ease as were Ike and Bob.

Jim Bartlet took advantage of the situation to indulge in sarcastic pleasantry.

"We didn't figger on this when we left town, eh, McClean?" he said in a loud enough tone to carry outside to Pete.

The sheriff fixed him with a cold stare and said nothing. The pain in his head and across his blackened eyes was almost blinding.

"Too bad that Helena stock inspector got killed," Bartlet went on. "It'll go hard with Carver."

"You ain't got no witnesses now, Bartlet," said Ike quietly. "I'm still rearin' to carry out that chokin' idee uh mine. Better quit jawin'."

This silenced Bartlet who now devoted his attention to stealthy attempts to slip his hands free of the ropes that bound him. Bit by bit, he was loosening the hastily tied knots. Ike and Bob had turned their backs on him as if the sight of such a human sickened them. Bartlet grinned mirthlessly and slipped a hand free. A few moments and his feet was free of the rope.

Above Bartlet was a window, its glass smashed by the night's bombardment. Ten feet beyond, grazing with dropped bridle reins, was Pete Carver's horse.

Inch by inch, Bartlet edged closer to the window. A sudden leap and he was on the ground outside, running toward the horse. The house shut the fugitive from Pete Carver who rose to his feet at McClean's startled cry.

"Bartlet!" bawled Ike. "Jumped the window. Ketch him, Pete!"

The thud of running hoofs as Bartlet vaulted into the saddle and, bending low on the horse's neck, jabbed the spurs in the sides of the startled animal.

Pete's gun flipped up. His finger pressed the trigger, then eased off.

"I can't," he muttered, lowering the gun, "without shootin' my pet hoss!"

Bartlet swung the horse toward the ridge road, the only passable trail out of the Rafter T ranch. The three men at the cabin watched him go.

"He's turned!" grunted Bob. "He's comin' back!"

Then they saw the reason for the abrupt change of course. The Rafter T foreman and two cow punchers were coming down the trail from the ridge. They were armed. Bartlet had no gun.

"God!" gasped Pete. "He's headin' fer the river! He'll drown hisself and the hoss. Hold on there, Ike Rutherford! Where the hell you goin'?" he shouted as Ike, forgetting the stiffness of his wounded leg, leaped through the open doorway and ran towards the corral where a team of work horses stood, harnessed and haltered to the feed rack.

"I'm goin' after Bartlet!" called Ike without looking back. "Shoot and be damned, you danged old settin' hen!"

With a wild leap, Ike was on the back of the horse that he had untied with a jerk of the rope end. Trace chains clanking, he headed for Bartlet who was racing for the sea of muddy water in front of him.

Back in Bartlet's scheming brain was the conviction that his fabricated tale of law enforcing was too weak to stand the acid test of a jury trial. His own men might weaken; McClean and Rutherford would tell too straight a story. The district attorney was a weakling, too inexperienced to put up a crafty fight in court. Bartlet's safest course lay in flight and, as he headed his horse for the river, he set his heavy jaws and trusted his life to the gameness of his horse. A cold-blooded, calculating killer was Jim Bartlet, but he was no cringing coward. Death lay in that muddy current, but he faced it unhesitatingly.

Below, Ike Rutherford watched for a moment, then urged his horse into the water, heading the animal at an upstream angle towards Bartlet and his mount who were being swept toward him by the current.

"Drop that fool gun, Pete Carver, and git ropes," snapped Bob. "It's time you come outa yore loco drunk. Move, dammit! Ike needs us!"

Pete, an agonizing groan bursting from his lips as he saw the treacherous undercurrent pull Ike and his horse under, leaped to his feet and ran towards the river. Then his leg gave way and he fell.

The sheriff, grabbing up a lariat that lay by the door, followed at his heels, not giving the fallen cow man so much as a passing glance. With Pete hobbling and crawling behind him, Bob reached the riverbank.

Ike's workhorse, tangled in the harness, fought wildly. Ike slipped from his back and struck out against the current. An indifferent swimmer, burdened by soggy clothes, he was hard put to keep afloat. Yet he made no effort to regain the shore. Eyes glued on Bartlet and his horse, he fought the current and waited for his enemy to float downstream to him.

Twenty feet, ten feet, separated them. Then Bartlet and the horse were on him.

Bartlet, twisting sideways, aimed a vicious blow at Ike's white face. It grazed the cow man's cheek. With a grunt, Ike threw an arm up and, with his knees braced against the side of the swimming horse, jerked quickly. Bartlet was pulled from the saddle. Locked in tight embrace the two men went under. The frightened horse, now completely bewildered, pawed at the two struggling men. Shod hoofs lashed the water about the heads of the fighting men, as they came to the surface.

A sickening thud as a steel-shod hoof struck Bartlet on the head. Ike, panting and half blinded by water, felt Bartlet go limp in his arms. Dizzily, one hand gripping Bartlet's collar, he struck out.

A swift side current swung the struggling horse free. Ike, breath coming in sobbing, choking gasps, fought to keep his face above the muddy surface. A whirlpool sucked him under.

Dazed, exhausted, he rose again to the surface. He did not hear the shouts of the sheriff on the bank nor see the flung rope that came within easy reach, then was carried down by the current. His one conscious thought was to hold onto Bartlet, regardless of all else.

Something solid struck him in the face. Something swept harshly across his face, tearing the skin. A tree, half submerged, had caught him. Ike, with a gasp, grabbed a branch and clung to it. In his other hand, clutched in a steel grip, floated Bartlet, blood sluggishly flowing from his gashed head.

Like a man awakened from a bad dream, Ike heard McClean's shouts now. The flying rope struck him full in the face where he lay in the tangle of branches.

"Slip 'er over yore head, Ike," bawled Bob.

Ike obeyed. A jerk and he was pulled free from the floating tree. As the rope pulled him under the surface, Ike shut his eyes and fastened both hands on Bartlet's hair.

To Ike it seemed the passing of hours. In reality it was but a few seconds before he was jerked ashore.

"Ike! Ike! Ike!"

Insistent, like the beating of a drum, the name dinned into Rutherford's pounding, aching ears. With a sigh, he opened his eyes wearily to look into the face of Pete Carver.

Tears dimmed Pete's eyes and his voice was choked with dry sobs.

"Thank God, Bob," he called brokenly. "He's alive!"

"Bartlet?" Ike asked.

"Dyin', Ike" came the sheriff's voice from nearby. "He's conscious and talkin'. Onburdenin' his black soul afore he goes to meet the devil. He's tellin' it all, Ike."

"Ike," groaned Pete, holding the other's head in his lap. "I done wrong. I bin a damn fool!"

"Two of us, Pete," grinned Ike weakly. "Old fools, the both of us."

He sat up, Pete's arm about him. The mess wagon drove up and the Rafter T foreman and his two men gazed with astonishment at the men on the ground.

"There's about enough cattle left in the two brands to make one fair to middlin' herd, Ike," said Pete. "I bin waitin' all winter to proposition you regardin' a pardnership."

The look in Ike Rutherford's eyes spoke louder than any words that could have come from his sob-choked throat.

"When you gents gits through settin' there in the water which has riz till it's got you dang nigh swimmin'," suggested the foreman, "we'll load you all in the mess wagon and pull out fer high ground. You act fer all the world like schoolmarms at a sewin' bee, augerin' to and fro regardless of hell, high water, er the elements. Will you ride yore water-logged hoss which is grazin' yonder, Pete, er does you set in the wagon with these two gents, which you admitted an hour ago, was worse'n skunks?"

The foreman was grinning widely, anticipating the fun he would have telling the Bar L foreman of the reconciliation. Just how it had come about, he could only guess.

"I rides with these two old rannyhans, son," chuckled Pete.

Ike fished a soggy, sodden mass of brown substance from his hip pocket, wiped it on his wet overalls, and held it towards Pete.

"Chaw, *pardner*?" he invited.

THE HOUSE OF WHISPERING SHADOWS

EUGENE CUNNINGHAM grew up a Texan in Dallas and Forth Worth. He enlisted in the U.S. Navy in 1914, serving in the Mexican campaign and then the Great War until his discharge in 1919. He found work as a newspaper and magazine correspondent and toured Central America. Although Cunningham's early fiction was preoccupied with the U.S. Navy and Central America, by the mid 1920s he came to be widely loved and recognized for his authentic Western stories which were showcased in *The Frontier* (later *Frontier Stories*) and *Lariat Story Magazine*. His history of gunfighters—which he titled TRIGGERNOMETRY (Press of the Pioneers, 1934)—has never been out of print and remains a staple book on the subject. Often his novels involve Texas Rangers as protagonists and among his most successful series of fictional adventures, yet to be collected into book form, are his tales of Ware's Kid, and Bar-Nuthin' Red Ames, and ex-Ranger Shoutin' Shelley Raines.

Among his finest short stories and short novels appearing in *Lariat Story Magazine* are: "Bar-Nuthin'—Feud Breaker" (5/28), "Bar-Nuthin' Holds the Aces" (6/28), "Bar-Nuthin' Hunts a Tiger" (7/28), "Six Shot Salvage" [a three-part serial] (5/29-7/29), ".44 Kid" (2/30), "Rough Ridin' Ranny" (9/30), "Gunman" [a three-part serial] (7/31-9/31), "The Quick Six" (10/31), "Gun Sight Chance" (3/32), "Short-Grass Man" (7/32), "Belle of the Border" (10/35), "Gun-Play Gamble (9/38), "Fan Lead, Texas!" (7/39), "The Moonlight Maverick" (3/40), "Short-Gun Pilgrim from the Panhandle" (5/41), " 'Slap Leather, Texas!' " (1/42), and "The Devil's Posse" (7/42). Among his most notable novels are TEXAS SHERIFF (Houghton Mifflin, 1934) recently reprinted in a hardcover edition by Chivers Press, WHISTLING LEAD (Houghton Mifflin, 1936) dedicated to John F. Byrne, RED RANGE (Houghton Mifflin, 1939) dedicated to Harrison Leussler, GUN BULLDOGGER (Houghton Mifflin, 1939) dedicated to Malcolm Reiss, and RIDING GUN (Houghton Mifflin, 1957).

At his best Cunningham wrote of a terrain in which he had grown up and in which he had lived much of his life and it provides his fiction with a vital center that has often proven elusive to authors who tried to write Western fiction without that life experience behind them. Perhaps the best story Cunningham ever wrote about Ware's Kid is "The House of Whispering Shadows" which first appeared in *Frontier Stories* (2/28) and, while never anthologized, was later reprinted in *Zane Grey's Western Magazine* (9/50). In this story Cunningham made use of an incident in the history of New Mexico Territory, when Colonel Albert J. Fountain (who had once been a defense attorney for Billy the Kid) and his young son with their mules and buckboard just vanished from sight. The *Jornado del Muerto* is renamed Satan Land and is moved to a Texas location in this story, contributing to an eerie atmosphere surcharged with menace. Later, giving Ware's Kid the first name of Stephen, Cunningham expanded "The House of Whispering Shadows" to form SPIDERWEB TRAIL: A TEXAS RANGER NOVEL (Houghton Mifflin, 1940).

The country north of Las Tunas is flat, yellow desert, dappled with the varying shades of green found in yucca, greasewood, tornillo, ocotilla and prickly pear; it is hemmed in on either hand by savage red-black mountains as grim as the faces of Apaches who once made the rugged cañons their fortresses; through the flat the river runs in a narrow belt of green and thorny *bosque*.

Ware, who upon a time had served as temporary city marshal of Las Tunas, knew the country vaguely. So he frowned forbodingly when he had finished the letter from Captain Knowles, brought to his hand by the Mexican youth who was often the captain's messenger. Theo' Ribaut was vanished, the captain wrote, gone as if the earth—or yellow sand—had swallowed him, taking at the same gulp the buckboard and span of little Mexican mules, with little Theo'—Ribaut's ten-year-old son—and seven thousand six hundred dollars. The Ribaut family had searched vainly for trace of them, old Theo' and little Theo', when they failed to return from La Piedra. Now, they asked Ranger assistance of Captain Knowles, an old acquaintance of Theo' Ribaut.

"And I got to go wandering through that desert looking for a sand dune that might have Ribaut's body . . . and the kid's . . . underneath it!" Ware said helplessly in English. "All right! *Muy bien!*" he grunted to Antonio, the messenger. "Go you back to *mi capitán*. Say that I ride now for Los Alamos to do all that a man may to make this mystery clear. But if Ribaut had with him so much money . . . why, certainly he is dead, now. Remains but to try to find the manner of his dying and the names of those who killed him."

He saddled up—Antonio had found him in camp—and turned Rocket's head south and east toward a pass he had heard of in the Soldados range. It was a lonely land, savage and sinister, that he rode through for days, lucky to find water-holes every day, making many a dry camp, living off the pronghorn antelopes and rabbits killed with the little Winchester carbine. But if the country were

empty of man, it held much to interest, fascinate, Ware, who had
been bred in much the same sort of land.

He crossed the river and went on east guided now by the directions
given him by a Mexican rider who had seemed none too anxious to
answer questions. The ranch of Carlos Smith—the D-Bar-D—lay at
the head of Wood Creek, said this tawny-skinned, ever watchful
rider. No more than a short two-days ride. Here, he added, a man
might go on eastward to the settlement of La Piedra.

"La Piedra!" said Ware to himself, with narrowing of gray-green
eyes that sent the Mexican's hand creeping toward a bulge beneath
his *serape.* "La Piedra! Hell, I'm getting onto Old Man Theo' Ribaut's
trail! He was supposed to be coming home from La Piedra."

He grinned at the Mexican.

"You may take your hand off that pistol, *amigo mio*! I have no
quarrel with you. Indeed, I thank you most kindly for your directions. A sad business, that of the *Señor* Ribaut, no?"

It seemed to him that the tawny face almost altered; that there
was a flashing change instantly checked, to tell—what? That was
the trouble, Ware thought. A Mexican who had reasons for not de-
siring his every activity to be bared would act as this one did at
mention of Ribaut's name, for fear of having to account for himself
and in proving innocence of complicity in Ribaut's disappearance
prove guilt of something else. Ribaut's murderer would act the
same, because of fear.

"*El Señor* Ribaut?" shrugged the Mexican, lighting a corn husk
cigarette with an airy gesture. "*Sí*, a bad business . . . if the *Señor*
says so."

With that he bowed courteously and rammed his big spurs into
the bony sides of his pony. Ware watched him go, grinning a little—
but not good-humoredly. For he knew Mexicans and this was
doubtless an indicator of what he would encounter on every hand
when he began investigating Ribaut's fate.

Going on toward the D-Bar-D he mulled over what he knew of
Theo' Ribaut. It was not much. He wished Captain Knowles had
thought to include more information about the politician in his
letter.

Ribaut was a man of mysterious antecedents. He had been known
to hint, when in liquor, that his name was an old and famous one,
somewhere back East. He was a lawyer, but more politician than
attorney. In this frontier country his shrewdness, his education,
had made of him a man standing head and shoulders above most.
His manners, Ware had heard, were those of a courtier; he was a
welcome guest at the finest homes of Las Tunas—and he had married a slatternly Mexican woman almost as black as a *negro.*

Partly through drink and partly because of more competition as
the land grew tamer and attracted more men of education, Ribaut

had for three or four years now been losing his grip. Where he had been second, if not first, in political circles, of late he had been barely able to control his own town of Los Alamos; investments, too, had seemed to fail him. He was no longer rich.

All this, Ware had gotten here and there from chance-dropped remarks of men over a great sweep of country. He wished, now, as he jogged up to Carlos Smith's adobe ranch house on Wood Creek that he had taken pains to learn more. He reined in Rocket and looked with interest at the bare dooryard of the D-Bar-D with its squat, fort-like house and rows of adobe cabins behind it, all shaded by giant cottonwoods.

"Howdy!" said an apparent Mexican almost at his side, appearing soundlessly from the shelter of a log corral. "You look like as if you'd ridden a piece, so light and rest yourself."

Ware eyed the man curiously as he swung down. In every detail of feature and dress he was a *pelado*, a laboring Mexican, but his language was that of the cowpuncher, even to the lazy Texan drawl.

"I'm Smith . . . Carlos Smith," said the man with flash of teeth. "You thought I was a Mex, of course. Well, I'm half. The old man drifted down to this-yere country and squatted on Wood Creek. That was thirty year ago. He couldn't find a white woman nowheres handy in them days, so he hiked over to Rancheria, the settlement southwest of yere, and got ma."

"Glad to meet you!" grinned Ware. "I'm heading for Los Alamos and one of your boys I ran into this side the river, he said I might as well come over here and get some grub before I struck south."

"No boy of mine," shrugged Carlos Smith. "I work two-three hands . . . all Mex *vaqueros* . . . and they're all on my east range. Don't know who it could've been you met."

Ware knew instinctively that he was lying, but inwardly he grinned. There was more than a little smuggling in this region and, if Carlos Smith were mixing in it, as well he might with his mixed blood, that was nothing to him.

"Don't know, either," he said indifferently. "Bad business about old Theo' Ribaut, wasn't it?"

"Sho' was!" nodded Smith. "They tell me . . . couple fellas from Los Alamos that come lookin' fer him . . . that I must've been the last one to see Theo' . . . except them that downed him. If," he added with a knowing grin, "he was downed."

"You don't think there's any doubt of that?" Ware said artfully. "Way I heard it, the other side the Soldados, somebody killed him and the boy as they was coming back from La Piedra. He had a lot of money in his buckboard, they say."

"Seventy-six hundred and fawty dollars," nodded Smith. "I ought to know. I paid it to him right yere in this house and took back my mortgage. Sho' glad I done it, too. The money was due the next day and if I'd had to monkey around tryin' to find out who to pay it to, now, some law-shark might've found a way to say my place was forfeit. It's worth twict the money, too."

He gestured toward the house and they went into the cool dusk of the front room, where Smith called to someone in the rear to make a meal ready. Ware was going back to take care of Rocket, but Smith checked him and sent a boy to put the animal in the corral.

"Sit down!" he cried genially. "It's sho' fine to have somebody driftin' in to augur with. I don't see many folks. Old Theo', he came through yere and collected the money from me, then went on to La Piedra. Then he came back and stopped overnight . . . him and the boy and a Mex I never see before. A week or so after, up come Jud Bingham and Whiskers Logan from Los Alamos a-lookin' fer him. And you're the next one to drift in."

Coming to the job that faced him, Ware felt innate suspicion of everyone who might have had the slightest connection with the Ribaut affair. Now, he wondered if this account of Smith's, with its detail, were artless or artful; the indirect alibi of one who knew a good deal, or merely the garrulous talk of a man much alone. But nothing showed in his blank face, his greenish eyes, which he studied.

"Funny the old man would collect the money from you and then go to La Piedra and then bring it back with him," he said absently. "Looks like he'd have dodged all that packing and left it with you till he was ready to hit for home."

"He wanted to!" grinned Carlos Smith and closed an eye knowingly. "But me, I knew that old fox too damn well, I did! Time he got back yere, you see, the due-date'd be passed by and he'd likely have grinned at me and refused to take the money. So I made him gimme back my mortgage and take the money. Then, I told him he could hide the sack somewheres around till he come back. Nah! I knew the old devil too well, Ware! I ain't sayin' he was too crooked to sleep in ary hoss-corral in the country, fer I ain't seen all the hoss corrals. But he was too foxy fer me to take a chanct with."

So, thought Ware, Carlos Smith knew him, had known him ever since he rode up. Thoughtfully he glanced at the wide, bullion-trimmed sombrero hanging on a peg beside the door they had come through. It was not surprising to find himself recognized, after all; the Mexican sombrero, the short jacket of soft-tanned goat-skin with its bunch of flowers embroidered on the back, the wide-bottomed trousers with scarlet insert at the outer seam—these were uniform such as no other Ranger wore at present.

But why had not Smith voiced his recognition directly, voiced it in the beginning, instead of letting it show now by inadvertent use of his name? It might mean nothing, of course, but Ware was trained to hunt for trifles as well as large indicators, in his business.

"I've heard old Theo's pretty sudden in his dealings," he nodded. "I never fancied these political pups a lot. Ribaut was always hunting some government job that'd give him good pay with no work and lots of influence. I've heard about a thing or two he's done by having some sort of loop over somebody. That kind of business don't set level on my stomach."

"My idee, too!" cried Carlos Smith. "He was packin' more secrets, I reckon, than anybody had a right to know. Me, I'm a good Democrat; same's pa was. Ribaut, he was a blamed Republican and so I never had much dealin' with him. But I reckon he knew somethin' about a lot of Democrats . . . the politicians."

"What made you say you didn't really believe he was dead?" Ware asked suddenly. But Smith only lifted a shoulder in the Mexican fashion, by his face quite unperturbed.

"Shucks! Old Theo' wasn't so easy handled as you might figure to look at him. He packed two sixes under his arms and he never needed no day's notice to git 'em out, neither! And he could do fancy-work with 'em too, onct he got 'em out. He went to Las Tunas one time after a Mex and the city marshal delivered the fella to Theo'. Goin' back on the stage the Mex grabbed a gun off'n a fella and brought her down *slo-ow*, grinnin' like a tawmcat, you know. And Theo' he pulled a gun and punctured that-yere Mex three times and done her before the Mex could shoot!"

"I know all about that deal," said Ware sardonically. "The gun the Mex grabbed was empty and the fella he grabbed it from was a hired hand of Theo's. The Mex was allowed to grab the gun."

"Well, mebbe so. Anyway, Theo' was cat-eyed. Looks funny to me that anybody could've got the drop on him. And if he was took by surprise, he'd still have got him a lunch out of the fellas that bushwhacked him. And looky yere, Ware! The old devil was about at the end of his twine, around yere. He was sittin' in the buckboard with seventy-six hundred and fawty dollars and the wide world before him. He knew there was men around yere that'd like a chanct to kill him, because of what he'd done to 'em, or knew about 'em. S'pose he just drove on."

"Can happen! Seems to me you were lucky to have the money to pay him, Smith."

"Lucky, hell!" cried Carlos Smith. "I damn nigh went down onto my marrer bones to old Clem Tooley, at La Piedra, to borrow it off'n him. He's got a mortgage on the D-Bar-D today that sticks tighter'n ary mustard plaster you ever see! And it ain't fer but one year, too; interest a-runnin' fifteen per cent. Man, I just jumped out of one jackpot into a tighter one."

"¡*Comida!*" announced a Mexican woman, appearing in a dusky, rear doorway.

"Le's go git it!" said Smith, getting up.

LYING ON HIS COT that night, Ware lay long awake. It seemed to him that the theory advanced by Carlos Smith was plausible enough: Theo' Ribaut might well have decided to leave this country where—beyond doubt—he had about played out his hand. Men had been known to disappear forever in this wide land, with even less cause than had Ribaut.

But a plausible theory was by no means a probable explanation. Ribaut might have analyzed his situation and decided that it was hopeless—and downright dangerous. But, on the other hand, he might just as logically have clung to the hope so typical of a politician, of putting over a coup that would seat him again in power. If this last supposition were the truth, then there remained the other possibilities Ware had seen from the beginning.

Ribaut might have been waylaid and murdered for the money Smith said he carried away from the D-Bar-D; he might have been murdered by political enemies and robbed as a matter of incident.

Smith's story, plausible enough in all its detail, was still worth nothing in the investigation unless its truth could be indubitably established. So, instead of heading for Los Alamos in the morning, he must ride to La Piedra and have a talk with this Clem Tooley, who had loaned Carlos Smith the money to meet Ribaut's claim against the D-Bar-D.

Suddenly he thought of something Smith had said—the unknown Mexican who had come back in the buckboard with the Ribauts. This was the first mention he had heard of such a one. It might well prove to be explanation of the whole mystery. A third person—also vanished—could answer everything!

He was up at the first sound of shuffling feet about the house. Carlos Smith ate breakfast with him and came outside to watch him saddle Rocket. A Mexican woman brought cooked food to put in Ware's saddlebags.

"Goin' to Los Alamos, huh?" said Smith conversationally. "Well, you can stop tonight at the House of Whisperin' Shadows."

"Stop where?" grunted Ware, staring down at Smith.

"The House of Whisperin' Shadows . . . Capen's place. The house he built on the old Open A ranch."

"How come they call it that?" inquired Ware. Nicknames in this country were apt to have meaning.

"Oh, Capen's a queer *hombre* in lots of ways," shrugged Smith. "Foreigner of some kind, but he talks good as anybody. Drifted into this country twenty year or so back; won the Open A off'n young

Al Twombley and built this big house on it. The Mex are skeered to hang 'round it much; they say the spirits dance underneath it."

"Capen . . . Capen," mused Ware. "New to me. What's his first name?"

"Got none! Which is just another one of the queer things about him. He just signs Capen to everything; always has. Right hefty among the politicos, Capen is. Goin' to be our next sheriff and he'll pack the whole ticket in with him. Him an Ribaut was about the biggest politicians in the country, I reckon. Friendly enough, though, they was," he added quickly.

"I see," drawled Ware without change of expression. "Well, if I'm going to make La Piedra by noon, I'd better hightail it!"

"La Piedra! Why . . . why, I thought you was headin 'fer Los Alamos about . . . ?"

"About the Ribaut business, I bet!" grinned Ware. "Well, I reckon it was a sort of natural guess for you; Ribaut's not showing up and a Ranger riding in would make it look like the Ranger was on the trail. But I got a little private job Piedra-way to do. You haven't had a dark-skinned, bat-eared hairpin ride by, have you? Fella with a white scar on his neck that might call himself Barry or maybe . . . well, most any name?"

"Nary bit!" grinned Smith and Ware wondered if his manner had not suddenly lightened, with mention of the imaginary Barry.

"Of course, a fella not envious to be known might pass up a ranchhouse."

"Yes, that's so. Well, if I come back by here, I'll stop off. S' long."

Ware moved vaguely eastward along the faint trail and as he went, even as mechanically he studied the trail and found, here and there, the marks of buckboard wheels to prove Ribaut's passage a good while before, he mulled the puzzle of Carlos Smith. For, correctly of the reverse, Ware was suspicious of the Mexican-looking, cowboy-talking rancher.

But when he came into La Piedra and found Clem Tooley sitting like a huge Buddha on the gallery of his trading store, Tooley verified the part, at least, of the story Smith had told. Ware, sizing Tooley swiftly, had squatted upon the floor near the storekeeper and introduced himself curtly. Tooley, his big face moveless as an image's, had nodded and continued to smoke lazily, the black Mexican cigarette pushing forth, inch by inch, from his strangely thin lips as it was consumed. When Ware had told frankly of his work and the necessity of testing each step, Tooley had nodded blankly once more, the blue eyes, half-hidden in rolls of fat, twinkling a little.

"Yeh, I loaned Carlos seventy-six hundred and forty dollars. Took a mortgage on the D-Bar-D to cover the loan. It's worth two-three times the money, the outfit is, if I have to foreclose."

"But suppose Carlos Smith hadn't paid the money over to Ribaut?" suggested Ware. "Suppose he'd just rammed it into his pants and Ribaut had foreclosed?"

"Meanin' I'd have had no security? *Tchk!*" said Clem Tooley and his vast sides quivered gently. "These boys around here, they know me right well. They wouldn't none of 'em pull a dirty trick like that on old Clem Tooley . . . unless they was real sure, mightily sure, he was good and dead.

"No-o, I loaned Carlos the money . . . chargin' him fifteen per cent, because I don't like him and never did and couldn't abide his pa before him. I said to Carlos: 'Young fella, you pay Ribaut and git back that mortgage. Then you bring it to me right here and we'll tear it up. Be you sure,' I said to him, 'that you do just that.' "

"What do you think about Ribaut's being missing, you being an old-timer here?"

"Could have happened some several ways," Clem Tooley replied calmly. "Ribaut had lots of enemies, and some men he done dirt to when he was county attorney and holdin' other jobs, they're real salty folks. I'd have been actin' four-eyed on the road if I'd made as many enemies as Ribaut had. And then, too, there's Mex smugglers and cow thieves runnin' hither and yon around the country. They might have cracked down on him, just in case he had somethin' on 'em, or just in case."

"Who was the Mex he took out of La Piedra with him, going back?"

"That was the ghost of Cortez . . . invisible to the naked eye," said Clem Tooley. "He rode sittin' on the boy's lap. "

"Meaning?" inquired Ware. Clem Tooley was a man after his own heart.

"Meanin' that I was sittin right here when Theo' Ribaut finished up a cow trade with Willard Steeves and come by. He stopped the buckboard here and asked me . . . Theo' and me, we've been on the outs for twenty-odd year . . . if he could buy a plug of Star Navy. 'I advertise to serve the needs and wants of man and beast,' I told him. 'So if I couldn't rightfully sell to you on one count, I'll let you slip on the other and only charge you double what folks pay.'

"So he took his chawin' and paid his money with his yaller teeth showin' like a wolf's. Then he licked the mules and went straight down the trail and I could see him for some two mile. So he never got a passenger in La Piedra."

"Of course," frowned Ware, "he could have picked a Mex up on the road."

"Yeh, he could've, but . . . son, you've got a purty good name in the old outfit. Thirty years ago when I was Rangerin', I knew your pa. So I'm goin' to tell you a few things I wouldn't tell most folks and all I want is your word you won't blab out all this or say who told you: All right! Now, she don't make a bit of never mind to me what happened to Theo' Ribaut. Like I said, we been on the outs a long while. If we'd got just a mite more on the outs, Ribaut'd have cashed in his checks. He knew that, too. But if I was a Ranger, now, with the job of clearin' up the way he went out, I'd figure some on Carlos Smith . . . not that Carlos has the guts needful to down anybody, even from behind. Carlos, he'd be afraid that the fella'd turn around!

"But Carlos and Capen are just like dog and master. And Capen's a curly wolf. He'll be sheriff of Piedra County come election day . . . now that Ribaut's out of the way with all he knew about Capen. Capen's been mixed up into most everything a man could figure . . . stealin' cows out of Mexico; rustlin' his neighbors' stock; jumpin' minin' claims when the real owners went up into thin air same as Ribaut has just done; plain and fancy murder. He's had a crew hangin' around the Open A that enough warrants could have been hung on to make 'em look like a Monday clothesline. Whenever somebody come lookin' for one of these hairpins, word always went ahead and Capen, he never knew a thing about the fella or about him being wanted.

"So, if I was a young fella about your size and complexion, I'd figure that if Capen never saw Ribaut last, then he likely knows who did. And figure, too, that Carlos Smith knows a heap more'n he's a-tellin'."

"Thanks!" nodded Ware, though this was more general than he had hoped for. "You figure this election business was reason enough for Capen's wanting Ribaut out of sight?"

"Plenty reason, son! But even if the election wasn't comin' off, Ribaut's knowin' so much about Capen's doin's was all the same as a death warrant without a date, with Ribaut's name on it. Now, if I was you, I'd straddle that black there and cut across country to miss the D-Bar-D and come in along the edge of Satan Land . . . that bare patch of sand that nothin' lives on . . . to the Open A. Ride right up to the house and light and stay the night. But . . . be damned careful of everything you do or say. Capen's some sort of educated furriner and he could turn the average man plumb inside out in a half an hour! Oh, he's slick! Slick as Ribaut ever was!"

Ware nodded, absently eyeing an oncoming rider a half-mile away, a Mexican, who had apparently turned into the trail at that moment and was riding toward the store. Clem Tooley picked up an old brass spyglass from the floor and trained it upon the rider, then set it down with a grunt.

"Florentino Valdez, a *vaquero* of Carlos Smith's," he said. "Reckon Carlos has paid his hands . . . though where he'd lay onto the dinero I don't know. Wonder where Monte Murillo is that's usually Valdez's shadder? Ah!"

Again he picked up the spyglass and leveled it down the road, then nodded to himself contentedly. "Monte's just turned into the road. They're passable fair *hombres*, Florentino and Monte."

The two *vaqueros* came jogging on their shaggy little ponies until they drew rein before the gallery of the store. They nodded gravely to Clem Tooley.

"*Buenas tardes, Señor* Clem!"

"You two have come to buy me out?" the storekeeper asked solemnly, in Spanish as smooth as their own. "One moment, I will have that lazy Manuel move the shelves out here where you may the more easily take my stock away."

"No, no!" grinned the taller of the two. "Not today, *señor*. When Monte and I ave made our fortunes, we will do that. Today, we wish only the tins of peaches and Monte desires that neckerchief of red which he has admired so long. For me, I like the color green and so I will have the neckerchief of that color."

They swung down and dropped their ponies' reins and came at rolling horsemen's gait into the store. Clem Tooley waddled in before them and Ware continued to squat upon the gallery and puzzle the complications which seemed to grow more tangled as he considered this disappearance of the cunning Theo' Ribaut.

Twenty minutes or so went by, then the two *vaqueros* came back outside, both carrying large, opened cans of peaches in each hand. They moved down the store wall and sat comfortably in a shady place. Clem Tooley waddled out and resumed his huge chair. He exhaled a cloud of bluish smoke and regarded Ware calmly.

"Look at this!" he grunted softly, extending his hand.

Ware stared; in the big palm lay a tattered five-dollar bill and a gold piece of the same value. There was absolutely nothing about the note to attract attention but, after a second, he noted that around the edge of the coin the gold was brighter than in the center; it had a sort of rim of clean, untarnished gold.

"Somebody's spending his watch charm," he said, then lifted narrow eyes to Clem Tooley. Something was behind this he knew.

"Somebody's spendin' *somebody's* watch charm," corrected Clem Tooley and into his half-hidden blue eyes leaped a sudden light that illuminated for Ware in a flash the true caliber of this lazy-seeming fat man. "Last time I saw that gold piece, son, she was hangin' on to Theo' Ribaut's watch chain. The bill is one of the fives I give Carlos Smith on that loan I made him. I'm a downright funny jigger, son; born thataway. I just naturally see things and remember 'em."

Ware's slim, brown hand went up in characteristic gesture to his chin; the fingers tap-tapped his lips and he whistled softly to himself. Slowly, levelly, then, his eyes showing a greenish war-flame went to the two Mexicans who sat in the shadow of the wall, cramming the halves of peaches into their mouths, talking lazily, laughing now and then.

"Florentino Valdez, he says Smith gave 'em this money," Clem Tooley drawled. "That is, he says Carlos paid it to 'em couple of days ago."

"Which leaves the gate open for a couple chances," frowned Ware. "Either Carlos Smith stuck up Ribaut and robbed and did away with him, or those two hairpins yonder turned the trick."

"*Umhmm*," nodded Clem Tooley. "If you wanted a lot of glory with no trouble all you'd have to do would be arrest Valdez and Murillo and charge 'em with Ribaut's murder and robbery. Carlos Smith'd deny givin' 'em this money and they got no witnesses to prove he did. Seems they was out on the range when Carlos rode up and paid 'em each ten dollars . . . their month's pay. And they was ridin' range together on the day Ribaut left the D-Bar-D. Looks right black for 'em."

"Does, kind of," Ware agreed. "And too, reputations have been built up in this country on just that kind of deal. But I draw pay for finding out the truth about things so far's I can, not for building up a big rep. I'd be a damn sight better off if nobody knew I was alive . . . or a Ranger. What do you figure?"

"Why, either way it might have happened. I don't figure Carlos has got nerve enough to 've done the job. And I've known these two Mexes a long time. I've always believed 'em average honest and good-hearted. Either guess is like to be wrong, of course. Still, I kind of stick to my reckonin' in spite of it all!"

"All right," said Ware quietly, getting up. "Hang on to those exhibits and I'll yell for them when they're wanted. Reckon we can lay onto these fellas if we need them. Me, I'm hightailing it across country. Reckon I'll go listen to those shadows whispering."

"S'long," grunted Clem Tooley. "And, son," he drawled cryptically, "if you ride back up this way, you'll see me and, even if you don't, maybe you'll see me anyhow."

Ware nodded, if somewhat blankly, then reined Rocket around when he had mounted. But suddenly he pulled up again and once more faced the storekeeper.

"Thcsc two fellas that the Ribaut family sent hunting Theo' . . . they go back to Los Alamos?"

"Yeh. Went back to say they never found nothin'. But Teresa Ribaut . . . the gal, you know . . . she sent 'em out again and they're roamin' around the landscape somewheres right now. Jud Bingham and Whiskers Logan. Two downright serious boys, too. That Whiskers, he's half-Comanche and if he can't smell out a track, nobody can. Tell you, son, if I'd buried anybody in the southwest end of the state of Texas and never wanted that there corpse found, I'd shore-ly hope Whiskers Logan'd die before he come nigh the place!"

"I see," nodded Ware and again spurred away into the south.

*   *   *

SATAN LAND WARE thought well-named. Forty to fifty miles the yellow sand stretched away to southward, a sinister, utterly silent waste that was like a lake the turgid waters of which had been solidified. The wind-carved dunes curled up around cactus and stunted greasewood, threatening to overwhelm even these poor manifestations of life, as if resentful that anything could live in their midst. The rattlesnakes, even, seemed to come out of Satan Land to find their food; their looping or dragging trailings were many.

The faint trail of horsemen led along the edge of the sands. Ware rode with mind busy. Of the many mysteries he had faced, this puzzle of Theo' Ribaut's vanishing seemed the knottiest problem. It would be easy to take those two simple-seeming *vaqueros* who spent money of Ribaut's. But that would not settle the mystery unless Carlos Smith's connection, or lack of connection, with the crime could be established beyond a doubt. And if he had Ribaut's money; if he had paid the two *vaqueros* the money Clem Tooley had recognized; but denied that, nothing could be proved.

He drew up suddenly, in late afternoon. At the edge of the faint track he followed was a rut in the soft earth beside a reef of rock. He stared hard; if that were not the trail of a wheel—he studied the track; it had no fellow, as a wheeled vehicle should have, no faintest sign of a second rut anywhere.

He was well south of the D-Bar-D now. Very soon, he should be reaching the Open A of the mysterious, powerful, sinister Capen, master of the House of Whispering Shadows. It occurred to him, remembering all his talk with Carlos Smith, that the half-breed rancher had somehow given him the impression that Theo' Ribaut, leaving the D-Bar-D on the return trip to Los Alamos, had gone south over the main trail well to westward of Satan Land that moved toward the river by way of The Notch, the pass in the Blancos.

Perhaps Carlos Smith had not said definitely that Ribaut's buckboard had gone that way, instead of this lonelier but shorter trail, yet certainly Ware had come away with that idea. And—here was the track of a buckboard. The absence of the other rut was perhaps proof of nothing, yet suppose someone had wished to remove all evidence of the buckboard's passing this way; suppose this interested person had wiped out the buckboard wheel-ruts, but had missed this one wheel track . . . ?

He shrugged and spurred on and inside the hour, without having seen any other trace of the vehicle, any vehicle, he came to a ridge and saw, lying in a little green valley that was threaded by a creek, the mass of buildings that must be the Open A. There were adobe barracks for the cowboys and laborers, but all were over-shadowed by the great, rambling bulk of the central building, the House of Whispering Shadows.

A cowboy came out of a tornillo-brake, a tanned and efficient-looking young man more than usually well-mounted. A long-barreled Colt hung low on his left side with butt to front; a well-kept carbine was in a sheath beneath his leg. He looked long and hard at Ware, then nodded.

"Howdy!" he said evenly, without warmth. "Goin' up to the house?"

"Reckon," replied Ware. "Crackers and cheese at La Piedra was a sparrow's dinner and a long way back."

They rode down the slope in silence and crossed the creek by a heavy plank bridge. Everything about the Open A was orderly, well-built and well-tended. It was the finest place Ware had ever seen. All the 'dobes, including the House of Whispering Shadows, were smoothly white-washed. There was no litter about the yard; indeed, before the big house itself a green lawn stretched smooth and short.

"Grass!" grunted Ware amazedly. "On a cow-ranch! And a piano player!"

The cowboy grinned slightly, but still without much humor.

"The old man," he said, "he plays a heap. All right, if you fancy his kind of music, but me, I like somethin livelier. Go on up to the house; he'll want to see you."

Ware rode on up and picketed his mount at the hitch-rack beside a corral in the side yard, then went at awkward, horseman's gait along a graveled walk and so into the great veranda. And as he stood before the door, with the sound of approaching footsteps in the dusky interior to tell that his coming had been noted, suddenly something seemed to pour from these thick mud-brick walls, coming like a cloud-shadow across a bright prairie. It was almost as palpable as a faint, cold wind. He shivered slightly and instinctively half-turned to see if outside the late afternoon sunlight were gone.

Then the footsteps in the doorway before him brought his eyes back around. He looked up impassively into the long, thin, wax-like face of the man who could be none other than Capen. Great, shining black eyes regarded him steadily; upon Capen's wide, almost lipless mouth hovered the very shadow of a smile which affected Ware much as had that sinister breath or the house itself.

"Good afternoon," said Capen in a low, soft voice. "You are Ware, the Ranger, of course. You'll stay the night with me?"

"Thought I'd bunk and eat here and go on to Los Alamos come morning," nodded Ware, in no way taken aback at Capen's knowledge of him. For he thought of Carlos Smith and what Clem Tooley had said of Capen and Smith—master and dog.

"You are very welcome. Come in and I'll show you a room. I'll have your horse taken care of."

He stood aside to let Ware pass through the hall into an enormous living room, where furniture and furnishings were an odd mixture of East and West; magnificent tapestries hanging from the green-tinted plaster walls with, over them, Indian baskets, warbows, tomahawks. A grand piano stood in a corner.

"Sit down," Capen invited Ware courteously and waved a long, white hand toward a great chair draped with a jaguar skin.

He took another chair, even larger, so deep that in the dusk of the room, looking across ten feet of intervening space, Ware saw nothing plainly save the white face—so pale that it made his mop of graying hair seem almost dark, by contrast. It seemed to hang in the air and again to Ware came that feeling as of a mist of evil floating out of this house and surrounding him. He was sensitive as a wild animal, almost, to these atmospheres; now, a sixth sense warned him of deadly danger. He sat like a crouching cat, ready to move like a spring uncoiled, yet without seeming tense or nervous.

"Well, what do you think of the disappearance of the esteemed Ribaut?" inquired Capen.

"Why, I've just about got it figured out," Ware answered in thoughtful drawl. "He was killed by folks that didn't like him politically . . . if he wasn't stuck up by somebody that wanted the money he was packing . . . or captured and held to keep him out of the next election. That is, if he didn't just walk off to start all over again somewhere else with the money."

Capen laughed, but as with that watchful cowboy Ware had met above the creek, there was no honest humor in the sound. And Ware felt that he was being probed, now. He moved slightly, merely to feel the touch of the Colts in the Hardin holsters beneath his arms. It was comforting to feel them there.

"But," drawled Ware, "all you folks are just the same. Something happens in your neck of the woods . . . like Theo' Ribaut's dropping out of sight. It looks real big and important to you. A Ranger shows up on a trail and right off you figure he can't be looking for anything but your lost man . . . or rustled cow! This fella Smith up the trail, he jumped thataway when I rode up."

"Then you're not on the Ribaut mystery?" Capen asked abruptly.

"Didn't Smith tell you I was hunting a fella wanted for murder over at San Andres?" countered Ware, putting all the tolerant amusement possible into his tone.

"He said that you said you were," Capen nodded calmly. "But Carlos is not . . . overly bright. It seemed to me that you might well have been suspicious of him and so evaded admission of your real business. Personally, I have an interest in solving this mystery. At the next election I am a candidate for sheriff. I believe that in spite of anything anyone can do, I'll be elected. But in politics one does not safely take anything for granted. If Ribaut is dead, I want to know that. If smugglers . . . or anyone . . . have taken him prisoner, I want to know that, also. If he has merely decided that his race is run in this locality, again I want to know it. For he is supporting my opponent, Bridges. With his assistance, Bridges is dangerous; without . . . not particularly. You can see why I wish to know whether Ribaut is apt to reappear."

"Did you see Ribaut on his trip toward Los Alamos? I mean, did he get this far?"

"No. Carlos Smith told me that Ribaut, with his son and a strange Mexican, left the D-Bar-D early one morning, coming this way. Who saw him after that nobody has yet come to tell us."

"Reckon he could have wandered into Satan Land and ended up there?"

"How? He knew this country well. He had no reason to leave the main trail. He was my political opponent but still he was sure of a personal welcome here. Why should he have taken that back trail? Anyway, *vaqueros* of Smith's were working along that edge of Satan Land. He didn't go that far east."

"Oh, but he did!" said Ware very softly, watching Capen's white face with hawk-like intensity. "He didn't come by the main trail. He came along the edge of Satan Land."

For an instant there was utter silence in the big, shadowy room. Then Capen laughed, a thin, high sound that set Ware's tense nerves on edge.

"The young detective!" he sneered. "My boy, when you are as old and as . . . experienced as I . . . you won't jump to conclusions so quickly. I tell you that Ribaut did not go by that trail or in that direction!"

"Well, maybe I've been misled," Ware conceded with indecision in his tone. "But there's buckboard tracks along there and I figured they must be Ribaut's. Thought maybe he'd strayed out into that sand and never got out."

"Cartwheel ruts, you doubtless saw," said Capen tolerantly. "The Mexicans from Rancheria come across and go around the end of Satan Land to the salt beds. Have from time immemorial. No, you're jumping at conclusions. But you *are* trying to solve the mystery."

"Well, sir, it's this way," Ware told him. "When I hit Los Alamos tomorrow, there may be orders for me to look into this business. They tell me the two fellas from Los Alamos went back without finding track of Ribaut. So I might as well find out all I can and be that much ahead if I do have to hunt Ribaut."

Booted heels sounded suddenly in the hall, a big dark-faced man came rushing into the room.

"Listen, Capen!" he cried. "Them devils, Bingham and Whiskers Logan, are snoopin' around Monument Rock and we better git the. . . ."

Capen rose flashingly and, though Ware saw no gesture, the flood of nervous speech was stopped short.

"If they bother those cattle, after our warnin'," Capen said slowly, "I'll run them out of the country. So long as they were working for Miss Ribaut . . . or pretending to . . . I let them go and come as they pleased on my range. But this present trip of theirs begins to seem very queer to me. I've lost too much stock over the line to be charitable. Yes! Get the boys and warn those killers to leave the Open A at once. But, Jim! No shooting! Don't let them provoke you into it!"

"Yes, sir," stammered the big man.

He looked hard at Ware, half-concealed in the big chair, whirled and went clumping out.

Capen stood motionless for a minute, then went quickly after.

"And Jim!" he called. "Wait a moment. Three men should be. . . ."

He left the sentence unfinished and went through the door. Ware heard the murmur of his voice, but he was far too cautious to try overhearing the conversation. Instead, he sat with racing thoughts.

"Funny," he said inwardly. "Friend Jim wasn't mad when he came in to tell about the trackers snooping around somewhere. He was scared! And if it was rustling that was in his mind, he wouldn't have been scared. He'd have been pining to bend a .45 bullet around somebody. The House of Whispering Shadows. Hmmm! It isn't whispering anything to me yet, except that maybe this isn't going to be too damned healthy."

"Dinner is ready!" said Capen, who had reached the door soundlessly. "I do hope nothing comes of this business! It has been quite a while since we've had to fight off rustlers, though when first I came to the Open A such wars were of weekly occurrence."

Ware followed without reply to the low-ceilinged dining room where a long table gleamed white with snowiest of linen and was set with cut glass and fine china and silver. Two young Chinese in white jackets were standing behind chairs. Capen bowed Ware to one and then sat down at the table's head. He spoke in a strange tongue to the boy behind him and the Chinese bowed and pattered off, to return a moment later and make some report in the same tongue; Chinese, Ware thought. Capen's face seemed to wear a trace of relief.

"You're missing your cocktail," he said genially to Ware. "It is of my own concoction, an improvement upon one I learned to make in Paris, years ago."

"Don't drink!" grunted Ware.

The sixth sense was strong in him now; he obeyed it blindly. Never in his life had he known, so strongly, the feel of deadly danger all around him. Nor was it the plain sort, against which a man might jerk his gun and make a flaming stand. This was like a snake's stroke from the dark.

A shadow of displeasure—of defeat—showed for a flash in Capen's face. But he smiled courteously in almost the same moment. They ate silently, save for an occasional polite remark of Capen's. Once or twice, looking up quickly, Ware found his host's eyes upon him. And in one sort of reading Ware was skilled—the reading of men's faces. Capen was contemptuous of him; he felt that beyond the shadow of a doubt. It was plain in the sardonic lifting of the man's lip-corners; in the drooping of full lids over great black eyes. And in Ware it waked a dull resentment; waked, also, determination to throw a bomb into Capen's supercilious calm.

Capen spoke to the Chinese again in the same harsh-sounding language. The boy nodded blankly, went over to a sideboard and took up the great silver platter upon which a silver-and-porcelain coffee service sat. As he carried this out the door, Ware thought that he saw a fine steam rising from the nozzle of the coffee pot. Why, he wondered swiftly, should the coffee be taken out, when, ready for serving, it had been in the room?

Presently the boy came back with it and brought it to the table. He poured a cup and Ware lifted his hand with a small smile.

"None for me, thanks!"

Capen stared. There was no doubting his barely suppressed anger, now.

"You are quite a temperate young man," he said with the suggestion of a sneer.

"Coffee's no good for a Ranger!" Ware told him solemnly. "Coffee and liquor and cigarettes . . . they're all bad. Lots of Rangers don't use any one of the three. I do smoke." He fitted action to the words and blew rings while Capen toyed with his eggshell cup. A faint drowsiness rose in Ware. Not overpowering, but apparent. And an idea came; he let himself relax a little more with passing minutes, let his eyelids drop. Suddenly straightened and grinned ruefully at Capen.

"Man, but I'm tired!" he cried. "Never knew it till just now. But I've been riding right steady for a week and sleeping hard. If you don't mind, I reckon I would like to hit the blankets."

"Surely," smiled Capen, courteous again. "Your bedroll won't be necessary tonight. Juan, here, will show you to a bedroom."

Having turned back the covers of an immaculate bed, the Chinese boy looked furtively at Ware, who was already pulling off his boots. A sly cat-grin crept over his yellow face.

"I believe that you will sleep soundly here, *señor*," he said in Spanish.

Ware grunted wordlessly and went on undressing. The boy went out and closed the door; his footsteps padded away down the hall. But Ware had ears like a wolf; he knew when the boy returned quietly to listen, perhaps to look through the keyhole of the heavy door. So he blew out the lamp and drooped audibly upon the bed; began to breathe deeply, slowly. And as he lay there, he grinned.

Like every other room Ware had seen in the house, the bedroom was decorated with odds and ends, some Indian, some Spanish, others he could not identify. But the pair of moccasins hanging with a shield on one wall he had seen and planned to use as he came into the room in the wake of the Chinese boy.

He lay listening to such sounds of the establishment as came to him through the half-open window in the house-front wall. An hour passed and still he was silent, patient as an Apache, lying with arms crossed on his breast and hands upon the butts of the twin white-handled Colts.

The room was pitch dark; it was moonless outside. He was alert particularly against sound or movement from door to window. He was sure that nothing came from either and yet he realized suddenly that something approached his bed. His hands closed on the Colt butts. He dug in his heels and was ready for a snake-swift move. Closer and closer; louder and louder; so came the breathing. He grunted and moved a little. The sound of breathing was instantly hushed. He began to breathe audibly himself. Again he detected the sounds of movement, coming closer.

At last he barely make out a dim shape beside the bed. He watched it until he could see the head. And that head was bowing; coming down toward him. The House of Whispering Shadows! Anything was possible here.

When he had first moved, he had drawn the right hand gun and now—without rising, moving only his hand and arm, he flicked up the long-barreled weapon and there sounded a dull crunch. Upon him sagged with the merest suggestion of a groan a soft, limp something. He wriggled out from under it and his free hand leaped to find its throat. But whoever it was, his visitor was senseless.

One of the Chinese boys, his exploring fingers told him. And upon the bed the Chinese had dropped an odd, wavy-bladed knife. Ware left him lying on the bed and with hardly more noise than a snake he went on all fours across the room, got down those Apache moccasins and slipped into them. Jacket and trousers next; then he was ready. How had that Chinese got in? Around the room he crawled until he found a place where a door yawned, a door that had not been detectable in the light.

He hesitated. Then shook his head. He might encounter someone out there, if he took this passage. Someone who would talk Chinese to him. So he crossed to the window and looked out. Nothing he could see in the darkness. He was about to straddle the sill when something shifted positions with little creakings, as of chaps, directly below him.

The hall-door, then, was his only chance. He crossed to it and with infinite slowness and silence turned the knob and let it sag a little open. No trace of danger here, but he slid through it with extended Colt and thumb holding back the big hammer. Down the hall he went like a shadow among shadows. Around the turn and so to the living-room door. Silence in there. He flattened himself against the wall and someone went by him with soft *pad-pad* of feet. Then to the front door of the house. It was open and he edged around the facing and stood against the wall.

If there was anyone on the veranda, he could not detect their presence. So he went on out into the yard. And now sounded the slow *clop-clop* of horses' hoofs, down by the corral at which he had left Rocket. He went that way and found himself following a man who moved with not too much care against noise. Where this one had come from, Ware had no idea, but he trailed him and slid against the log wall of the corral.

Several horsemen drew to a halt within a few feet of him. That man he had followed stepped forward.

"Jim?" called Capen. "Got them?"

"Yeh," a voice answered. "On the mules. Had a hell of a time, too. Them damn mules didn't like that job of packin'."

"Unload them, then! There's no use wasting time. Though our Ranger visitor is soundly asleep and had best not waken!"

" 'Unload them?' " Ware repeated to himself. "Unload Bingham and Logan? Had they been killed or captured by Capen's gunmen? What had he stumbled upon? What had been so carefully guarded from him?"

"I reckon . . . "—this, to Ware's surprise, was Carlos Smith's voice—"that when Whiskers Logan gits to sniffin' around tomorrow he's goin' to be right disappointed. But he shore had me skeered today, when I see him gittin' so close. I sent you word right off, I'm tellin' you."

"Never mind the discussion," Capen said coldly. "Are they unloaded? Jim! Send the boys back to the bunkhouse. You and I and Carlos can manage the rest."

Ware scowled uncertainly. Then these prisoners, or whatever they were, could not be the two trackers hired by the Ribauts. He moved a little nearer. And from the trail came faint, but clear, the sound of someone singing:

> "Oh, onct in the saddle I used to go gailee;
> Oh, onct in the saddle I used to go free. . . ."

"What the devil!" cried Capen. "Who is that coming? Carlos! It's from your way. Who would be coming . . . now?"

"¿Quien sabe? I left Squintin' Mig' a mile up the trail, to ride like hell thisaway if anybody was comin'. What happened to Mig' I wonder?"

"You boys hike for the bunkhouse," snapped Capen. "Jim, you go meet whoever is coming. Carlos, you and I will have to manage this end. Remember! All of you are turned in; you're being waked!"

Men and horses moved swiftly away as Ware stood with drawn guns, undecided as to what move he had best make. Capen and Carlos Smith now came toward him, grunting as under a burden, their steps in duet so that he knew they carried some load between them. Past him they went and on around the corral; he followed and so heard the soft thud of a something being dropped within five feet of him, near a big wooden feed trough on the far side of the corral.

When they went back, he stole out and felt for the thing they had dropped; almost made a startled sound as his hand found a man's cold face. Quicker they came on the return trip; he had barely enough time to slide softly back against the wall of the corral. Clearer and clearer came the sound of singing from the main trail north and west of the House of Whispering Shadows. And to Ware it seemed that actually the darkness about him was a live, breathing, whispering thing. There were small noises, creakings, tiny groans, detectable all around, direction and distance indeterminable.

Again the soft thud, fainter this time, of a burden striking soft earth. One man moved—Capen, Ware thought—but only for a few steps. There was a whirring noise.

"Yes, sir!" Carlos Smith chuckled. "Ol' Whiskers's mug is goin' to be a sideshow, and when they tell him in Los Alamos how them Ribaut mules come home wearin' busted harness, he. . . . "

"I have told you before about talkin' too much!" came Capen's chill, angered voice. "I act always as if the walls had ears. You had best do the same!"

"Hell! Ain't nobody goin' to hear nothin'! If you doped Ware's grub and put that Chinese killer of yours watchin' him with a knife, there's nobody goin' to be snoopin' tonight. And them fellas a-comin' . . . likely it's just them crazy Diamond A boys of Steve's hittin' fer Los Alamos and a big drunk. Ready to pack 'em down below?"

"In a moment. I'll get into the tunnel and you slide them to me. Then we can carry them into the main cellar and I'll slip back into the house so that if I have to make an appearance I can do it instantly. You'll have to stay below."

Suddenly Capen laughed, a thin, metallic sound that sent shivers crinkling up and down Ware's spine so insane did it seem.

" 'The House of Whispering Shadows,' " he chuckled. "Well, if ghosts can wander about, then there is reason for whispers coming from the shadows here! Ribaut and the brat will find old acquaintances among the shadows."

"Like hell I'll stay below!" snarled Carlos Smith shakily. "Nah, I'm comin' right at your coattails or a li'l ahead! Not for me stayin' down there with that gang of yours, Capen, and I don't give a damn what you say about it!"

"All right! All right!" Capen's voice was muffled now. "Push the bodies down. The boy's first."

"Glad I never done the job!" Carlos Smith mumbled, as if to himself.

"Ah, but you profited by it, my friend," Capen laughed from the tunnel mouth. "You received your mortgage and so made seven thousand-odd dollars for disposing of the buckboard and mules and keeping guilty silence. Don't try to act the innocent here, Carlos. They would hang you by the neck, if ever your part were known. Hurry with them! Listen to those hoofbeats. They have stopped!"

"Hello, the house!" came a distant voice and Ware thrilled to it. It was Clem Tooley!

"Hurry!" snarled Capen. "¡*Cuerpo del diablo*! Have you lead in your boots?"

Ware stole forward, following Carlos Smith's grunting passage. Suddenly he had the sense of someone behind him and sprang sideways. He heard a panting exhalation; then something vague lunged by. A hand struck him lightly; he stumbled. The next instant, he was in a squirming pile of men in a narrow space, as end to a dive downward of four or five feet.

His Colts were still in his hands; instinctively he had clung to them. Now, as Capen snarled something, Ware fired. Fists were striking him. He wriggled out of the mass and to his knees, then began flailing around him with the long barrels. Someone cried out; there was the clucking, harsh sound of Chinese—ending in a groan as he struck at the source of that talk. Then stillness—of sound and of movement.

"Ware! Where are you? Ware! Ware!" a faint call came to him.

"Here!" he answered, when he could get his breath. "By the corral feed trough. Look out you don't fall! Tunnel's open!"

"Hurt, son?" Clem Tooley inquired anxiously from the tunnel mouth, showing as a huge, vaguely outlined bulk above Ware. "I heard you shootin' . . . if it was you."

"It was me, all right. I got Capen and Carlos Smith and a Chinese down here spread out all around me. And the two Ribauts."

"Glory be!" cried Clem Tooley. "Let me git a light! The old House of Whisperin' Shadders is livin' up to her name all right!"

Ware moved a little so that he had all his captives before him, then struck a match. Capen lay motionless beneath Carlos Smith, who was beginning to move a little, though his eyes were closed.

Across Smith was that Chinese boy who had taken Capen's orders at the dinner table. He, too, seemed to be breathing, but unconscious. The bodies of the Ribauts were in a corner of the square well.

The match went out. Ware struck another and this time inspected Capen more carefully. He was dead, killed by that one shot Ware had fired. And behind Ware was a dark passageway. An idea came to Ware, who could look with grim calm upon Capen and plan ahead without worry. He caught Carlos Smith by the shoulders, having felt safe in reholstering both his guns. He dragged him backward and a few feet up the tunnel and swiftly lashed his wrists together behind him with Smith's own twisted shirt sleeve.

"All right, son!" called Clem Tooley. "Andy, here, he's comin' down to take this lamp. We'll see what's what down there."

A slender man dropped into the tunnel mouth and in an instant was holding up a kerosene lamp. Then Clem Tooley, moving easily despite his great bulk, joined him and whistled long and shrilly.

"Tie up that Chinese, will you?" requested Ware. "Then come on down here. I got an idea. Where's the rest of Capen's gang?"

"In the bunkhouse!" chuckled Clem Tooley. "I gathered up a bunch of Diamond A boys and drifted this way just in case you got in trouble with Capen, as I figured you likely would. We was just swingin' down at the bunkhouse with Jim Millit makin' us sort of welcome when you unlimbered your hawgleg. So I bent my gun over Jim's head . . . much to his surprise, of course . . . and my boys are ringin' the bunkhouse around. Nobody'll git out of there till Clem Tooley says so."

He straightened above the Chinese boy and came waddling up the tunnel, looking the benevolent, well-pleased Buddha.

"Got Carlos up here, huh? Fine! I been layin' off to smash this Capen outfit quite a spell, now. And when Capen announced he'd run for sheriff and figured he'd likely be elected, I made up my mind right then not to stand for it. You come along right handy. I was goin' to come over here with a bunch and make Capen let me search the place. But this is heaps better. Somebody might've got killed, the other way."

Carlos Smith groaned and Ware bent swiftly to whisper in Clem Tooley's ear.

"Good idee!" cried Tooley. "Come on, Carlos, up the trail with you! We come to look into these here whisperin' foundations we hear tell about. Come along and help us."

"What happened?" groaned Smith. "Somebody hit me."

"That was me," Ware informed him thoughtfully. "I was afraid you'd do something that'd keep you from hanging. Let's go. Now that Capen's confessed that Smith, here, done the Ribaut murder, there's nothing much left to do, Tooley."

"That *I* done it!" cried Carlos Smith. "I never done no such thing. I never knew a thing about it! I. . . ."

"Ah, shut up!" said Ware disgustedly. "You trying to out-talk Capen's sworn statement? You going to get up in court and look him in the eye and try to wiggle out of it? You make me tired!"

"Reckon this-here's the cellar, the big one," grunted Clem Tooley, striking a match.

Black space yawned all around them.

"Yeh, it's the cellar, all right!" cried Carlos Smith. "And that lyin', murderin' rascal, Capen, he's got a half dozen men buried in it, too! He was goin' to put Ribaut alongside Jimmy Thornton that was cashier of the bank in Ancho and that Capen brought here to make him tell the combination of the safe, so's he could rob it without makin' a noise. He shot Thornton. And there's old Snake-Stomper Ledoux that owned Concepcion Mine. And. . . ."

"Well, anyhow, we got the deadwood on *you*, Carlos," grunted Tooley. "You murdered the Ribauts to git back that money. And bein' in Capen's gang you brought the bodies here, of course."

"I never! Ribaut had a half-dozen ropes around Capen's neck and he was goin' to bust him wide open come election. Capen and Jim Millit and Blackie Woll and that Squintin' Mig' that works for me, they done it. I knew about it and Capen give me my mortgage that Ribaut had on him. I hadn't paid him the money a-tall!"

Ware, striking matches, was groping about. Now he found a little stairway and a barred door at its head. It opened into the living room. Tooley and Smith followed him up, the bonds having been taken from Smith's wrists.

"Sit down at the table and write what you told us!" snapped Ware.

He stood over the trembling half-breed until the smeary page was done and signed. Clem Tooley witnessed it and grinned at Smith.

"I'll have the boys rope the ones you mentioned," he said genially. "The others . . . well, I reckon we'll tell them to hightail it out of Los Alamos County. That way'll save heaps of trouble, Capen being dead."

"Capen dead!" gasped Smith. "Why, you said . . . ?"

"You don't ever want to believe all you hear . . . and not much you see," Ware advised him solemnly. "But especially nothing much you hear."

"Nah," nodded Clem Tooley in agreement. "Might just be a shadder whisperin'. Come on, Ware. Le's go collect them other candidates for the cottonwood prance."

LAWMAN'S HEART

FREDERICK SCHILLER FAUST was born in Seattle, Washington. He wrote over 500 average-length books (300 of them Westerns) under nineteen different pseudonyms, but Max Brand™—"the Jewish cowboy," as he once dubbed it—has become the most familiar and is now his trademark. In 1917 Faust met Robert H. Davis, an editor at The Frank A. Munsey Company. Faust wanted to write—poetry. What happened instead was that Davis provided Faust with a brief plot idea, told him to go down the hall to a room where there was a typewriter, only to have Faust return some six hours later with a story suitable for publication. Zane Grey had recently abandoned the Munsey publications, *All-Story Weekly* and *The Argosy*, as a market for his Western serials. Davis was convinced Faust could do as well and encouraged him to write Western stories.

The one element that is the same in Zane Grey's early Western stories and Faust's from beginning to end is that they are psycho-dramas. What impact events have on the soul, the inner spiritual changes wrought by ordeal and adversity, the power of love as an emotion and a bond between a man and a woman, and above all the meaning of life and one's experiences in the world conspire to transfigure these stories and elevate them to a plane that shimmers with nuances both symbolic and mythical. In 1920 Faust expanded the market for his fiction to include Street & Smith's *Western Story Magazine* for which throughout the next decade he would contribute regularly a million and a half words a year at a rate of 5¢ a word. It was not unusual for him to have two serial installments and a short novel in a single issue under three different names nor to earn from just this one source $2,500 a week.

Faust's finest fiction can be enjoyed on the level of adventure, or on the deeper level of psychic conflict. Much more about Faust's life, his work, and critical essays on various aspects of his fiction of all kinds will be found in THE MAX BRAND™ COMPANION (Greenwood Press, 1996). Yet, ultimately, what is most amazing about him is not that he wrote so much, but that he wrote so much so well! It is also worth noting at this point that while Walt Coburn's Montanans speak the way he grew up hearing them speak and Eugene Cunningham's Texans speak the way he heard them speak, Faust in his many Western stories made no effort to imitate regional patterns of speech. The West in a Max Brand™ story is that timeless plain one encounters in Homer's ILIAD and ODYSSEY.

In 1921 Faust made the tragic discovery that he had an incurable heart condition from which he might die at any moment. This condition may have been in part emotional. At any rate, Faust became depressed about his work and consulted H. G. Baynes, a Jungian analyst in England, and finally even met with C. G. Jung himself who was visiting England at the time on his way to Africa. They had good talks although Jung did not take Faust as a patient. Jung did advise Faust that his best hope was to live a simple life. This advice Faust rejected. He went to Italy where he rented a villa in Florence, lived extravagantly, and was perpetually in debt. However, Faust did read Jung's books and Jungian ideas had a revitalizing effect on the kinds of stories he wrote.

In two works published in the same year Faust created protagonists chillingly debilitated by a heart condition, in MARBLEFACE (Dodd, Mead, 1939), serialized as "The Tough Tenderfoot" in *Western Story Magazine* (2/3/34-3-10-34), and in "Lawman's Heart" in *Star Western* (6/34). Both appeared under the Max Brand™ byline. "Lawman's Heart" has never been otherwise collected.

I
"THE HOLDUP"

The place looked safe and it felt safe. The stagecoach had come in sight of its destination at Little Snake. The passengers could wipe the dust from their faces and see the wriggle and flash of the river that crossed the flat and split the town in two. Heat waves dimmed the mountains, and danced over the strata of vari-colored rocks across the flat range. The whole scene was one of peace and somnolence.

Young Larry Traynor, in the driver's seat, knotted his brows a little as he prepared to sweep the stage down the cataracting slopes that led into the flat below. Certainly there was no thought of danger in his mind. He had a good set of brakes and he had a pair of excellent leaders. He hardly needed the long reins to drive them. His voice was enough; and they pulled wide or close according to the curves they encountered.

Besides, when Larry Traynor came in view of Little Snake, something moved like music in his blood, a happy sadness, as he thought of Rose Laymon. Once she had been close to him, but time and another man had put a distance between them; and now there was only the melancholy beauty of his memories. . . .

The stage was rolling over the last of the up-grade and lurched onto the level. Traces and chains loosened. Traynor was about to call to the leaders when a voice barked from a clump of brush inside the curve of the road. The sound of that voice, shrill and piercing, scattered the sleepy unreality of the moment. A long rifle barrel gleamed through the brushes; a masked head rose to view, sleek black cloth with white showing through the eye-slits.

Sam Whitney, the veteran guard who shared the driver's seat with Traynor, muttered: "The damn rat . . . ," and jerked up the double-barreled, sawed-off shotgun which was always under his hand.

He got halfway up from his seat before the rifle spoke. There was no flame, no smoke—just the shiver of the barrel and the clanging noise. Sam Whitney kept on leaning forward. He threw the rifle before him. He fell from the seat as the stage lurched to a stop under the brakes which Traynor had thrown on.

Traynor saw the body of his old friend hit the rump of the off-wheeler. He saw a spray of blood fly. Then Whitney, turning in the air, landed with a solid impact in the road. Sam Whitney lay flat on his back in the dust of the road, and stared up at the glare of the afternoon sky.

Traynor could only see that picture. He hardly heard the shrill voice that commanded the passengers out of the coach. It was a strange voice, too high and sharp to be real. Only something in the subconscious mind of Traynor kept his hands stretched high above his head. Vaguely he was aware that the passengers had their arms high over their heads, also; and that one man was obeying the commands of the robber to throw things out of the boot. There was money back there—more than twenty thousand dollars.

The robber held his rifle under the hollow of his arm while he accepted the canvas sack in his other hand. The passengers faced him in a line. If they tried to follow him, they would catch hell, the masked man told them. The sun glinted for the last time on the rifle as he backed into the brush. The gr en leaves swayed together. The fellow was gone.

And still Traynor sat for a rigid moment with the arms stuck up high above his head. His heart had leaped up into his throat and trembled there, beating too fast for a count. For the last three months, whenever a moment of excitement came, his heart acted like that, paralyzing his body.

Nerves, he told himself. The old woman in him was coming out. Suddenly he could move; he could think. He sprang down into the road and kneeled in the dust.

"Sam! Hey, Sam!" he called.

Out of the babel of voices of men congratulating one another that the robber had not stripped them of watches and wallets, Traynor heard one fellow saying: "He killed the guard, all right."

"Almighty God!" said Traynor.

He could not believe it. Dead men should stare at the world with dead eyes. But there was still the old twinkle of humor in the look of Sam Whitney, just as when he stood at a bar, resting one foot on the rail, hurrying through an anecdote before he swallowed his drink. Now Sam's expression looked as if he were just going to make some humorous retort to the last speaker.

" 'Possums taught me how to play dead," he'd say.

But he said nothing. His eyes would not move from the distance into which they peered. And there was a great red blotch across his breast.

Traynor ran for the buckskin leaders. He had a revolver with him. Fool that he was, he could remember now that he was armed.

He cut the near leader out of its harness, leaped on the bare back, and raced the horse into the brush, up the slope. His passengers howled after him. Their voices were no more to Traynor than sounds of the journeying wind.

Sam Whitney was dead! And there never would be peace in Traynor's soul until the murderer went down. Old Sam Whitney had taught him how to throw a rope. Old Sam Whitney—why, he had always been old, even when Traynor was only a child. He had taught Traynor how to strum a guitar. And how to shoot. And how to stick to the back of a pitching bronco.

"If you're feeling sick, maybe that damned mustang will be feeling a lot sicker," Sam Whitney used to say. He taught Traynor how to fight. "The other fellow looks good when he's hitting; he looks damn bad when he's being hit. Bulldog, bulldog is the trick."

Sam Whitney was dead, but part of his soul would live on in the minds of his friends, and in the mind of Larry Traynor above all. Bulldog—that was the thing!

The buckskin, running like a racer, blackened with sweat already, streaked across the round forehead of the mountain, through trees, into the clear. And yonder galloped a big man on a swift little horse, a quick-footed little sorrel. A mountain man on a mountain horse, no doubt.

The robber turned, the black mask of his face with the white showing through the eye-holes. He snatched up his rifle. And Traynor, as the buckskin ran on, fired twice.

The first bullet hit empty air, and he knew it. The second shot skidded the sombrero off the head of the robber. Then the rifle spoke and the buckskin fell on its nose.

Traynor turned a somersault, got staggeringly to his feet, and fired once more at a dim vision which was disappearing through the thick of the brush. The only answer that came back to him was the clattering of hoofs that disappeared into the distance.

He turned to the buckskin. The bullet had clipped it right between the eyes. Beautiful shooting! Shooting almost too beautiful, because there were not half a dozen men in the mountains who were able to make a snap shot as effective as this. Such accuracy narrowed the field in which he would have to search.

He stripped the bridle and harness from the limp, dead buckskin.

Then Traynor went over to the spot where the sombrero had fallen. It was a common enough hat—a Stetson—and he looked at the sweat-band, where initials of owners are often punctured through the leather, but there was no sign. The hat was new, which made it all the worse as an identifying mark. He tried it on his head. It was a perfect fit, and that made him sigh with a greater despair.

However, he had something to go on. A mountain man riding a sorrel mountain horse, an active little beauty; a fellow who was a dead shot. Or had that bullet been intended for the breast of Traynor when the tossing head of the mustang intercepted its course? As well be hunted for two murders as for one.

Thoughtfully, Traynor walked over the round of the slope and back into the road. The passengers started clattering at him. At least they had had the decency to put the dead body of Sam Whitney back into the coach. Someone had closed his eyes.

"No luck," said Traynor gloomily. "This hat, and that's all." He put the other buckskin leader behind the stage and drove down the sloping road with only four horses, the pointers acting bewildered when they found themselves at the head of the team.

They entered Little Snake. A crowd, half mounted and half running on foot, was already tailing about the stage shouting questions when the fattest and oldest man among the passengers called: "There's Bill Clancy's clothing store. Stop over there and see if he might have sold this hat."

Traynor stopped the coach. The crowd fell on the passengers. Half a dozen attached themselves to each man, babbling questions, getting terse, important answers. When they got into Clancy's store, they first stood at the counter with proprietarial airs, waiting for Clancy to finish examining the hat.

He was a sour-faced little man, this Clancy, and now he took the Stetson on the tip of his finger and caused it to rotate slowly under his eyes. His hands were pale, clean, delicately shaped. He had the air of the artist examining a mystery, and a beautiful mystery, at that. He turned the hat over, regarded the sweat-band, which was only slightly darkened towards the front.

"The gentleman who wore this hat," pronounced Mr. Clancy, "did not sweat a whole lot around the forehead." He turned down the leather sweat-band and looked inside it.

"Gentlemen," he said, "I sold this hat." There was a little grunting sound from the whole crowd, as if they had all been in a conveyance and had gone over a jolting bump. Traynor began to feel cold about the lips.

"I sold this hat," said Clancy, "and the name of the gentleman to whom I sold it was. . . ." He paused, studying something that caught his attention. "I always write in the initials of the purchaser," murmured Clancy, in the midst of his thought. "These initials are rubbed a little dim, but . . . yes . . . this is the hat that I sold to Doctor Parker Channing three weeks ago on Tuesday."

No one spoke. There were good reasons for the silence. Sleek and handsome young Parker Channing had come to Little Snake three months ago on his way to the mountains for a shooting trip. But he found a dozen cases suddenly ready for him and not another physician within fifty miles to rival him.

He lingered on to do his professional duty; then he settled down for an indefinite stay. His reputation was carried on the wings of the wind. When he operated on the skull of Tim Wallace and saved Tim's life or reason, or both, by removing a segment of the bone, his skill as a surgeon was established. And when he saved the wife of Big Joe Mellick from death by typhoid, it was apparent that he was an exceptional medical men, also. If his prices were high, his services were worth it.

He became at one stride the leading professional man of the town. He was an honor to it. He could stick to the back of a bucking mustang as well as the next fellow. He could shoot circles around nearly every man in the district when it came to a hunting party. He was the best of company, had a tight head to hold whisky, and was such an all-around prize that it was little wonder that he took the eye of the prettiest girl in town. He walked her away from Larry Traynor the very first time he met her.

And that was why most heads in the Clancy store now turned suddenly towards Traynor—not because it was his dear friend who had been murdered, but because it seemed apparent that Doctor Channing was the murderer.

Clancy could not fail to rise to a situation of this magnitude. He leaned across the counter and offered the Stetson to Traynor. "I guess you'll be wanting to give this hat back to the gent that owns it, Larry."

Give it back to the handsome doctor? Perhaps receive some lead out of the doctor's gun in exchange? Traynor accepted the dangerous mission with his eyes on the floor. His heart was up there in his throat again. He could not move; he could not speak. A strange, dizzy sense of faintness was sickening him. Then he thought of the dead man and lifted his head suddenly. "I'll look up Doctor Channing," he said.

II

"COWARD'S BRAND"

The stagecoach had to be taken to the station. The passengers left Clancy's store with Traynor, and he drove at a dog trot back to headquarters.

Abe Terry, the general manager of the line, sat on the bench before the station stable whittling a stick and spitting tobacco juice into the deep dust of the street. He did not move to avoid the cloud of white dust that blew over him. He merely lifted his head a little to watch the men who took off their hats before they carried the dead man into the building. He was whittling again and working at his quid when Traynor came up to him.

"Yeah, I've heard," said Abe Terry. "Gunna have a chat with the doctor?"

"I'm going to have a chat with him," agreed Traynor.

"He'll shoot hell right out of you," said Abe, thoughtfully.

"Yeah, and maybe he won't."

"It's your party," said Abe, "but why not wait till the sheriff gets in? He's due some time this afternoon."

"If I can find the doctor, I'm going to have it out with him," said Traynor.

"Well, more power to you. Watch both his hands. The sucker is as good with his left as with his right, they tell me. He's over at the Laymon house on the front porch, chewin' the fat with Rose."

Traynor nodded. "Supposing that anything happens," he said, "put this ten bucks on old Sam, will you?"

Abe Terry took the greenback and fingered it. "What the hell good will ten bucks do Sam now?" he asked.

"Flowers, or something," said Traynor.

"Yeah. Flowers or . . . what the hell?"

"Turn it into coffee and limburger, or whisky for the drunks that are broke," said Traynor. "It comes from Sam. That's all."

"Owe him this?" asked Abe.

"More than that. I owe Sam millions!"

"Oh, that's the way, is it?" said Terry. And he spat into the dust again. "Fond of the old goat, were you? Look here, Larry. Why be a damn fool? Why not wait till the sheriff gets home?"

"If I were the fellow that lay cold," said Traynor, "Sam wouldn't wait for any sheriff."

"Well, go on and play your hand," said Abe Terry. "I'm wishing you luck. Remember, if you start shooting from the hip, you're likely to pull to the right. I always noticed that. I pulled a gun on a Canuck down in Flaherty's saloon, once, and I shot a bottle off the bar right beside his left arm. Then he put a dose of lead inside my hip and turned me into a lame duck for the rest of my life." He waved his hand. "So long, Larry."

"So long, Abe!"

The Stetson was still in the hand of Traynor. As though it were a flag, it called people towards it. There were a half a hundred men and boys walking around the block after him towards the Laymon house.

The men sauntered at ease, each fellow pretending that his way simply happened to coincide with that of Traynor. But they kept advising the boys to get back out of the way of possible trouble. It came over Traynor that he would certainly be left alone to start the trouble with the doctor. The crowd would hold back.

Not that the men were cowards. There in Little Snake lived as many brave fellows as one could wish to see, but Traynor had a special purpose in enforcing this arrest and the crowd would hold back and let him make his try. If he failed—well, even then nothing might be done. The law ought to take care of its own troubles, and the sheriff was the law in Little Snake.

The Laymon house hove in view. It was two tall stories high and had a whole block of trees and garden around it. John Laymon never did things by halves. Thirty miles out from town he had one of the best ranches in the valley, crowded with fat cattle. But he preferred to keep his family closer to the stage line.

Money had come to John Laymon through his patient labor and keen brain. Reputation had come to him some three or four years ago when he had rounded up the entire Wharton gang of rustlers who had been praying on the cattle of the community. He had brought in the sheriff, raised a force of fighting cowpunchers, contributed his own wise head and steady hand, and they had scooped up the gang and sent the Whartons to prison. After that, John Laymon spent less of his time on his distant ranch which lay back among the mountains in a fertile valley. He was more often in town.

But he was not in sight as Traynor advanced towards the house. There was only Rose Laymon in a white dress, and the doctor. Her arms were bare; her throat was bare. She was as brown as a schoolboy, and Traynor could guess at the blue of her eyes long before he actually could see the color.

She was small and slender, but her wrists and her arms and her throat were rounded. Traynor could see the flash of her laughter from the distance, and then he turned in up the path under the big shade trees.

The crowd waited behind him. Some of the men leaned on the fence and some remained clear across the wide, treeless street.

The doctor lounged in a chair near the girl. He wore gray flannels and a white shirt open at the throat, without a necktie. There was no other man in Little Snake who would have dared to wear such clothes—not even Clancy himself. But the doctor had no fear. He wore white shoes, too, and he had his legs crossed and swung one lithe foot up and down.

When he saw Traynor coming with the hat, however, he began to straighten himself in the chair, little by little. He was big and he was lean; he was supple and quick; he had the look of a fellow who might be capable of almost any physical exertion, and as a matter of fact he was as good as his looks.

But what depressed Traynor more than all else was the great sweep of the intellectual brow above that handsome face. The doctor had everything from education to brains. It was not at all strange that he had taken Rose away from Traynor at a gesture. What was Traynor in comparison but a rather stodgy figure, a common cowpuncher not even distinguished for skill with a rope or a branding iron?

He was merely "one of us," and people like the doctor always ride herd on the ordinary men. The immensity of the gulf between him and the murder kept widening in the understanding of Traynor as he drew closer. He could see himself as a mere pawn contrasted with a king among men. It seemed to him miraculous that he, Larry Traynor, could ever have sat on that veranda at the side of Rose Laymon.

He went up the front steps, one at a time, tipping his hat to the girl. He took his hat clear off. Sweat began to run on his hot forehead. He raised his left arm and wiped the sweat off on the flannel sleeve of his shirt.

The girl stood before him, saying coldly: "Do you want something . . . Larry?"

She had started to say "mister," and then shame, perhaps, had stopped her. But he could forgive pride in such a girl. Let the pretty women pick and choose because, once they have chosen, they settle down to trouble enough.

"I want to give this hat back to the doctor," said he. He offered it, with a gesture.

Parker Channing sat forward, rose. He took the hat in a careless hand, examined it. "I never saw it before," he said.

"No?" said Traynor. His heart was beginning to rise in his breast, stifling him.

"No, I never saw it before," said the doctor.

"What's this all about?" asked the girl. "Why do you look at Parker with such a terrible eye, Larry?"

"Because I was wondering," breathed Traynor. "I was wondering whether or not he was a murderer."

The girl made two or three quick steps back. She put out a slim hand against the wall of the house. The heat had crumpled the white paint to roughness.

"Don't pay any attention, Parker," she said. "He's simply drunk again."

That was the way she had been talking to the doctor about him then? A town drunkard—was that what she had been making of him?

"I won't pay too much attention to him," said the doctor. "He's not drunk, though he looks like it!"

His gaze suddenly narrowed, became professionally curious. It fastened like teeth on the throat of Traynor. A malicious interest gleamed in his eyes. What could he see?

"A man wearing this hat," said Traynor, "held up the stage I was driving and shot old Sam to death."

"Not Sam!" cried the girl. "Oh, Larry, not old Sam!"

"Yes. He's dead."

"But he can't be. Only two days ago. . . ." She stopped. Something was passing between the two men that locked up her speech in ice.

"The murderer was wearing this hat. You never saw the hat before, Doctor?"

"Never," said Channing. "Sorry to hear about. . . ."

"You're sorry, are you?" muttered Traynor. There was rage in him to warm his blood, but always there was that horrible fluttering of his heart, and the need to gape wider for air. "You never even saw this Stetson before?"

"I've told you that before, man. What's the matter with you?" asked Parker Channing, coldly.

"Your initials are inside the sweat-band, where Clancy wrote them in when he sold you this hat three weeks ago Tuesday."

The doctor's head jerked back. His right hand darted inside his coat.

"No, Parker!" cried the girl. "No, no!"

Traynor's grip was on the butt of his Colt. He did not draw it. There seemed no strength to draw the gun. He knew, by the cold of his face, that he was deadly white. His eyes ached, they thrust out so hard. And there came over him the frightful surety that he was a coward.

He could not believe it. He had gone through his troubles—not many of them, but he had faced what all Westerners have to face—half-mad horses under the saddle, high dangerous trails, and sometimes an argument with an armed drunkard in a saloon. Yet here he found himself hardly able to breathe, and the tremor from his heart had invaded his entire body.

"You don't mean that he's right," moaned Rose Laymon. "It's not really your hat, Parker?"

The doctor, breathing hard, swayed a little back and shook his head. "No . . . not mine. At least, if it is mine, then someone else stole it. I don't know anything about this murder. . . ."

He was always as cool as steel. But now the coolness was gone. The guilt withered and puckered his face, narrowed his eyes. What was he seeing, briefly, in the distance of time? All the high promise of his life falling in ruins? And in the presence of the girl he had wanted to marry!

"Ah, damn your rotten heart!" said the doctor, and walked straight up to Traynor.

It was the time to stand on guard, but Traynor's arms were lead. The figures before him shifted, were raised from their places, wavered in the thin air. The brightness of the sun was gone. He could no longer feel the beating of his heart. His lungs labored, but the life-giving air would not enter them, it seemed. He could hear a rasping, quick pulse of sound and knew that it came out of his own throat.

The doctor struck him across the face and leaped back half a step, his hand inside his coat, half crouched, on edge to draw.

"You lying dog!" said Doctor Channing.

And Traynor could not move.

"How horrible!" he heard the girl whisper.

And, far away on the street, where the men of the town were watching, Traynor heard a deep, groaning noise. Nothing as shameful as this had ever been seen in Little Snake.

Cowards have been known to faint in a crisis. And Traynor wanted to faint; he wanted to lie down on the flat of his back and close his eyes and concentrate on the frightful problem of getting enough air into his lungs. Instead, he had to stand, like a wretched, crumbling statue.

The girl walked between him and Channing. "Don't touch him again," she said, scornfully. "Whatever you are . . . whatever you've done, Parker, you don't strike a handless coward a second time."

"Certainly not," said the doctor. "I beg your pardon, my dear. It seems, in fact, that I'm in some trouble, here . . . owing to a little misunderstanding that I'll clear up in no time. Will you trust me to do that?"

She did not answer. She looked as white as Traynor felt. She loved this fellow—this murderer.

"In that case," said Channing, as though he had heard a long and bitter denunciation, "there's nothing to do but say good-bye to you forever. And God bless you, Rose. I know you'll mix in a kind thought of me now and again."

He leaned, picked up the Stetson which Traynor had allowed to fall on the porch, and walked down the steps, down the path, out into the open street.

"Gentlemen," he said, slowly, tonelessly, "what is it that you will have of me?"

III

"MURDER TRAIL"

He stood out there in the sun with his hat raised, waiting, and running his eye up and down the men of Little Snake, and not a voice answered, and not a hand was raised.

He turned his back, and walked without hurrying down the

street, and around the corner. He was well out of view before a murmur grew out of the crowd. It increased to a loud humming. Then a yell broke out of one man. It was echoed by another. The whole crowd lurched suddenly into pursuit of Parker Channing, as fast as their feet would carry them.

"You look sick," said the cold voice of the girl to Traynor.

"I'm all right," he said. He was not at all sure that he could walk, but he managed to get down the steps with sagging knees. When he stood on the level of the path, he turned to do his manners and lift his hat to Rose Laymon. But she was oblivious to him. She had her hands folded at the base of her throat. Her face was not contorted by sobbing, but tears ran swiftly down her cheeks and splashed over her hands.

"She loves him!" said Traynor to himself. "She'll never stop loving him. And . . . I wish to God that I were dead!"

He got out from the grounds of the Laymon house, at last, and turned into the emptiness of that wide street. He had to take short steps. His feet would not fall in a straight line but wandered a little crazily. Something akin to nausea worked in his vitals. Something was dead in him.

A pair of boys dashed on ponies around a corner. When they saw him, they reined in their horses. They swept about him in flashing arcs. The hoofs of their ponies lifted a cloud of dust that obscured Traynor.

"Yeller . . . yeller . . . yeller!" they shouted. "Larry Traynor's yeller!" They screamed and they sang the insult. That was all right, and he might have done the same thing, at their age.

The thing was true. He was yellow. And yet he still felt that it was the sick breathlessness rather than actual terror that had kept his hands idle back there on the veranda of the Laymon house. All cowards, of course, would have the same feeling. They were not afraid. No, no! They were just troubled with a touch of ague. They felt a mastering chill up the spine. They could not help growing absent-minded because they were thinking about home and mother.

He could have laughed. Instead, he had to start gasping for air in real earnest. Something was profoundly wrong with him. And the two young devils kept wheeling their horses closer and closer to him, yelling more loudly. Other children were coming from the distance. Better ask mercy from Indians than from these mannerless savages.

He saw the little house of the sheriff, unpainted, with nothing except the long hitching rack, in what might have been a garden patch. He turned in and climbed the veranda with weary legs.

"Look at him! He's afraid! Coward, coward, coward," screamed the boys. "Oh, what a coward! He's yeller! Larry Traynor's yeller!"

Traynor pushed the door open—it was never locked—and walked into the tiny, two-room house. Kitchen-dining room—and then a small bedroom.

The sheriff had left in a hurry, this day, for the neatness of his housekeeping was marred by a soiled tin plate on the table, and a tin cup with coffee grounds still awash in the bottom of it.

Traynor went into the bedroom and lay down. The blankets held a heavy body odor that seemed to put away the supply of air. He got up wearily and opened the front door and both windows and then the rear door to make a draught. He lay down on the floor of the kitchen and spread out his arms.

Lying on his back did no good. Presently he was sinking. A wavering thread attached him to existence, and the thread was running out, spinning thinner and thinner. To breathe deeply took too much effort. He could only gasp in a profound breath every now and again, when he was stifling.

He turned onto his right side, his head pillowed on his arm. By degrees he felt better.

He began to think of old Sam—dead! He began to ride again over the dusty miles the stagecoach had covered. Out of these thoughts he was recalled to himself by the sound of a horse trotting up to the front of the house, the squeak of saddle leather, the thump of feet as a man dismounted.

He sat up. Very strangely, the faintness had left him almost entirely. He rose to his feet, and a moment later the gray-headed sheriff walked into the room.

Compassion entered his eyes when he saw Traynor. Better to be hounded by the insults of the youngsters than to be met by that compassion. But the sheriff shook hands—almost too warmly.

"Sit down, partner," he said. "I'm glad to see you. Mighty glad. I've heard about the stage and everything. A good job you done in skinning away after that crook and getting his hat. We know who the killer is, now, and we'll have a chance to spot him, one of these days. I'll hit the trail after him right this evening."

He ran on cheerfully: "We've found out what made him do it. Faro. He couldn't keep away from the game, and Lem Samuels told us how much he was losing. You can't buy fine horses and trot a girl all around and then hit faro, too. So the poor fool found out about that shipment of cash and decided to help himself. A pretty cool nerve, Larry, when you come to think of it. A stagecoach filled with armed men and only one. . . ."

Here the sheriff's voice died out, as though he realized he was stepping on delicate ground.

"I was mighty sorry about old Sam," he said. "One of the best men in the world . . . and a good friend to you, Larry. I hear the funeral is tomorrow morning."

"I won't be here," said Traynor. The sheriff waited, and he went on: "I'll be pretty far out on a trail. And I want to carry handcuffs with me . . . and a deputy sheriff's badge."

The sheriff whistled softly. He laid his hand on the arm of Traynor. "Ah, that's it, eh? Good boy, Larry. You were down for a minute, but the right sort of fellow always comes back. If you want to go after the doctor, though, hadn't you better go with me?"

"I'll go alone," said Traynor.

"Got an idea?"

"A piece of one."

"I'll swear you in," said the sheriff. "You know what you're doing. You shot his hat off once, and I hope to God that you shoot his head off the next time . . . the damned, murdering, sneaking rat! Wait till I get a badge for you. . . ."

The outfit that Traynor took was exactly what he wanted—some dry provisions, a pot and pan, a couple of blankets, a revolver and a rifle, enough ammunition. But his old horse, Tramper, was much too high to suit the rider. Tramper had not had much work to do since his master began to drive the stage. He had wandered through rich pasture lands, eating his fill, until his body was sleeked over with fat and his heart was rich with pride. He wanted to dance every foot of the way; he insisted on shying at cloud shadows and old stumps; and in the morning he enjoyed working his kinks out with a little fancy bucking.

All of these things would have been nothing to the Traynor of the old days. He would have laughed at the dancing, the shying, the pitching. But the Traynor who survived out of the past was a different fellow. A flurry of hard bucking left him gasping, head down, the landscape whirling before him. And it would be whole minutes before his breath came back to him. Even to sit in the saddle for a few hours was a heavy thing, and he made it a habit to lie down flat beside the trail for a few minutes every couple of hours. Even so, he reached the end of each day almost exhausted.

But a good idea is better than strength to a determined man, and he had the idea. Where would the doctor flee, when he rushed on his fine bay gelding out of Little Snake? Of course he would wish to go far; but what was the greatest distance that he had ever gone from Little Snake through the twisting mountain trails?

A couple of months before, the doctor had been far up on Skunk Creek with a hunting party, and Skunk Creek was a good two days' ride away from the town. It seemed to Traynor a good bet that Channing would head for this distant place among the lonely mountains. From that point of vantage he could plan the rest of his retreat. The sheriff and his men would conscientiously hunt out the sign of the doctor's horse; Traynor preferred to hit far out and take his chance.

The second day was the worst of the two. The altitude made it harder for Traynor. He was continually short of breath. He was continually so very short that he had to gasp like a fish on dry land. About midday, also, he felt discomfort in his feet. By night they were so badly swollen about the ankles that he had to lie with his heels resting on a log higher than his head for a couple of hours before he could reduce the swelling and get the boots off.

On the morning of the third day he simply could not wedge his feet back into the boots. His foot was swelling out of shape. His wrists were heavy, also; and the cursed shortness of breath had increased.

But he was only an hour from the head of Skunk Creek, and he made that distance riding in his socks, his boots strapped on behind the saddle. Something had gotten into his system—some sort of poison, he presumed. And it was settling in the extremities. Some good, hard sweating when he got back into the heat of the valley would probably make all well.

Then he forgot his troubles of the body.

It was the glimmering verge of the day through which he rode; it was only the gray of the early dawn when he came down a gully towards the head of Skunk Creek. He thought, at first, that it was a wisp of morning mist that floated above the head of a cluster of aspens. But the mist kept rising, thin and small, always replenished.

It was fire smoke!

At the edge of the aspens he dismounted and leaned for an instant against the shoulder of the horse. His heart was rocketing in his body. His swollen feet were painful to stand on. His wrists were so thick that the rifle had a strange feeling in his grasp. His eyes felt heavy, too. He could find pouches beneath them by the touch of his fingertips.

He looked for an instant about him. The rose of the morning had entered the gray dawn. The mountains shoved up black elbows against the brilliance of the sky.

It was his country, and he loved it. But the beauty of it gave him no joy now. He could think of nothing except the horrible fluttering, the irregular pulsation of his heart, like a flock of birds beating their wings without a steady rhythm.

Was he to be mastered again—if indeed that smoke rose from the campfire of the doctor—not in battle, but by the maudlin weakness of his own spirit? Not spirit, either. Matters of the spirit do not puff the eyes and make the limbs swell.

Somewhere in the back of his mind he kept a sense of the old mountain tales of Indian witchcraft, and of evil spirits breathed into the bodies of condemned men by the ancient seers. It was like that; that was how he felt, exactly. He went on gingerly through the copse.

Now, beyond the thinning of the trees, he could see the silhouette of a man saddling a horse. He drew closer. The veil of the trees thinned; and he found himself looking out on Doctor Parker Channing in person, in the act of drawing a bridle over the head of that lofty bay gelding. The gray flannels and the white shoes looked a good bit absurd in these mountain surroundings; however smart they had seemed in the town. But the air of the doctor had nothing absurd in it.

That lofty head was carried like a conqueror's. The pair of holstered revolvers at the hips were not there for show, and the Winchester worn in a saddle holster would keep its owner fed fat with the best game the mountains could offer.

No matter what Channing had given up, he was not entirely depressed. It was the blue time of the day, of course, and yet he was singing a little to himself.

Something crackled behind Traynor. That fool horse, Tramper, of course, had followed where he was not wanted! He saw a shadowy impression of the animal behind him; then the doctor was whirling with a drawn revolver.

"Hands up!" yelled Traynor.

"Damn the hands!" said the doctor, and was firing into the trees at what must have been to him a very dim target. Traynor, gun at shoulder, aimed at the breast and fired. He wanted it not this way but another way; but he had to take the game as the doctor chose to play it.

He was certain, as he drew the trigger, that his forefinger was closing over the life of big Parker Channing. Then, as the rifle boomed, he heard the clang of the bullet against metal. The revolver, spinning out of the hands of the doctor, arched through the air and struck heavily against the side of the gelding, which went off like a shot down the side of the creek. And out of the woods, squealing like a happy fool, Tramper bolted after this good example of light heels and feather-brain. But Larry Traynor leaned a shoulder against a slender tree trunk and maintained his bead.

"Don't try for that second gun, Doctor," he said.

"Certainly not," said Channing, politely. "But can it be my old friend Traynor? Well met, my lad! Oh, if I'd only had one candlepower more of sunshine to show where you were among those trees!"

IV

"BULLDOG IT!"

Fear ought not to choke a man when he had an enemy helpless under a leveled gun. Surely there was no fear in Traynor now, and yet his heart was still swelling in his throat and his breath would not come as he walked out of the woods towards the doctor.

"Unbuckle that gunbelt and drop it," he commanded.

The doctor obeyed. His glance was not on the gun, but on the face of the captor. "You're going fast, eh?" he asked.

"Going fast where?" demanded Traynor.

"To hell, old fellow," said the doctor. He kept shifting his glance across the face of Traynor as though he were reading large print. "No, you won't last long," added Channing, as if he were diagnosing a case for a patient.

"Give me your hands," said Traynor.

Channing held them out, and when he saw the handcuffs he laughed: "Ah, a legal arrest, eh? No murder, Larry? Just a legal arrest leading up to a trial, and all that?"

Traynor snapped the steel bracelets over the brown wrists of the other. And the doctor sneered openly: "You poor devil! You can hardly breathe, can you?"

"Better than you'll be breathing before many days," said Traynor. "Step back, now."

The doctor stepped back. But he kept nodding and smiling, as though he were entirely pleased by what he saw. Traynor stooped and picked up the fallen gunbelt. He strapped it around his own hips.

"I'm curious, Traynor," said the doctor, "just how you managed to know that I'd come here?"

"You'd travel as far as you could over ground that you knew. This is the biggest march you ever made from Little Snake."

The doctor stared. "Well," he muttered. "I'll be damned! Am I as simple as all this? Then I deserve anything that comes to me." And he added, almost with a snarl: "I should have gone the entire way, on the Laymon veranda. I should have drifted lead into you before the other people could see that you weren't able to fight. But here we are; what are you going to do?"

"Follow those damned crazy horses, first of all. Face that way and march."

"How far, brother?" asked the doctor, looking down at Traynor's feet, softly muffled in the socks.

"Till I wear the flesh off to the bone!" said Traynor, savagely.

"Is that it?" asked Channing. "I'm to be paraded through the streets of Little Snake with the conqueror behind me? Is that it?"

"Something like that," said Traynor. "You're still going to parade into the Little Snake jail. I don't give a damn who sees you go."

"The fact is," said the doctor, rather with an air of curiosity than of concern, "you never would have bothered about me, except that I seem to have shamed you in front of your townsmen?"

"The man you shot off the stage was my best friend," said Traynor. "You had to go down, Doctor. If I could manage to get a chance at you, I would have followed you the rest of my life."

"That wouldn't have been long, old son," chuckled the doctor. He looked again from the swollen feet to the puffed eyes of his captor. "No, that wouldn't have been long."

"Stop bearing down on me," commanded Traynor. "God knows that I'm holding myself hard. I don't want to do you harm, Channing, but if you keep nagging me. . . ."

They followed the two horses a good ten miles. Five of those miles were backtracking completely away from the direction of Little Snake and, at the end of that distance, Traynor from a hilltop bitterly watched the two animals careening miles and miles away from him down a gulch.

There was little use in following. He could not make the doctor help him catch the horse that was to carry Channing to prison. And Traynor's feet were now in a condition that made walking difficult and running impossible. Gloomily he turned in the direction of far-off Little Snake. "March!" he said, huskily.

The doctor laughed, and turned willingly in the appointed direction.

No man thinks of shoes until there is long marching to be done. But Traynor began to yearn for anything that would effectively clothe his feet. He had to cut off slabs of bark and bind them to his feet with strips of clothes, which he sliced into bandages. Other bandages he used to wind around his ankles, and so constrict the swelling. But the puffiness which did not appear in the ankles began higher up in the legs. To walk began to be like wading through mud. Yet through that entire day he kept heading on toward Little Snake.

In the evening he built a fire and stewed some rabbit, which he had shot along the way. They ate that meat. Then the doctor sat with his back to the trunk of a tree and smoked cigarettes, and smiled derisively at his captor.

There was reason and plenty of it for that mockery, as Traynor knew. He had covered a very short distance toward the town. Each day, it seemed, his feet were likely to grow worse and worse. If that were the case, before many days were out he would hardly be able to make perceptible headway.

Presently he said: "Channing, this is a thing to die of, eh?" He pointed to his feet, to his wrists.

"Die of? Why, you're dying now, man," said the doctor. He laughed again. "You were dying down there in Little Snake, and I saw what was the matter with you when I looked at you on the veranda. Dying? You're as good as dead right now!"

They were in the green bottom of a gulch, and the doctor looked around him with amused eyes. "And yet," he said, "the medicine is here that will heal you. Make you fit and well again. Right here under your eyes, old son. I'll make the bargain with you. I'll take the swelling out of your legs and wrists . . . out of your whole drop-sical body. And in exchange, I'm free to go where I please. What about that? What could be fairer?"

"I'll see you damned first!" answered Traynor, softly.

Where could the healing stuff be? In the bark of a tree? In roots of grass? In some mineral that the doctor had spotted in some small exposed vein?

"Ignorance is the curse of your people," said the doctor. "You ride your horses, raise your cattle, labor all your lives. Your amuse-ments are drunkenness and gambling. Some of you marry and raise a batch of equally damned children to follow your own dark ways. In the end, men of your intelligence come, exploit the opportunities that you have opened to them, and elbow you out of your holdings. And that is fit and right, Traynor. In the eyes of a superior man, like myself, you and your friend of the driver's seat were no more than wild hogs running loose in the forest."

Traynor gripped his rifle with an instinctive gesture. And then he laid the gun back as suddenly. "No," he said. "That would be the easiest way for you, Channing. Dying wouldn't bother you. But to be shamed in front of a lot of people . . . to have Rose pitying you and despising you . . . that would be the real hell. And by God, you're going to taste plenty of it before I'm through!"

He felt very faint, so he tied the doctor to a tree before he lay down for the night. Afterwards, he slept brokenly, and in the earli-est dawn he resumed the march, but not for Little Snake. He knew, too, that he could never make the town.

There was a much nearer goal, however. By swinging to the south he would reach the most outlying ranch, the Laymon place, thirty good miles from Little Snake. Once there, his prisoner would be safely in the hands of the law. Old John Laymon, the fiercest of all the enemies of evil-doers, would see to it that Channing was handed over to the sheriff. And the sheriff would see to it that Parker Chan-ning was hanged by the neck till he was dead!

So to the south they marched. At noon, that day, Traynor told himself that he could go no farther. His ankles and wrists had become elephantine. His eyes were puffed until his vision was dim, and inside his breast there was continually that cursed beating as of wings, great and small, in hurried and irregular flight.

If he lay down on his left side, during one of the many rest peri-ods, it seemed to him that he was slipping down, being moved feet first—for the sound of his heart was like the rubbing of two bodies together—like the vibration of a wet finger against a pane of glass.

There was constant pain. There was constant faintness.

That night, the huge watery puffing of his flesh suggested some-thing that might ease him. He cut shallow gashes with his knife. Not blood but water flowed out, in quantity. That was a relief, and when the morning came neither his wrists nor ankles seemed to have regained their swollen proportions of the evening before.

Every night, thereafter, he made new incisions, or freshened the old ones so that the water would run out of his flesh. In the middle of the next day's march, the cuts would begin to bleed, blood and water commingled.

His eyes were growing bad, very bad. It was difficult for him to shoot game. Images wavered before him. But on the third day chance enabled him to shoot a deer. Afterwards, he could load the prisoner with venison and make him carry the food for the party.

"The worst diet in the world for you, Larry," the doctor said, cheerfully. "You're dying, anyway, but you'll die all the sooner under the effects of this diet. Do you want to know how really bad you are? Cut a reed there on the bank of the creek. Put one end to your ear and the other end to your heart. It will be a sort of stethoscope, old son. You can study your death more clearly, that way."

Traynor cut the reed. He was able to bend without breaking it, and with one end to his ear and the other pressed to his breast he listened to the queer, hurrying, faint vibration of his heart. It passed into flurries so rapid and dim that he could not begin to count the contractions. It seemed to him that legions of ghosts were flickering across his vision. And again there were breathless, frightful pauses in which he was sure the next stroke would never come; and at the end of those pauses would come one bell-like stroke that sent a thin shudder all through his being.

He looked up at the sneering, smiling face of the doctor. "Yeah, Parker," he said slowly. "I'm a dying man, all right."

"But why die, you fool?" asked the doctor, lightly. "Life all around you; plenty to live for . . . and, with what remedies right before your eyes, you might have a long time to go."

Channing began to laugh, blowing out his cigarette smoke in ragged clouds of mirth. "Presently, you're going to fall into a coma. That will be the end, Traynor."

"It's true," said Larry Traynor. "I'm going to pass out. You'll brain me with the handcuffs while I'm helpless. And that's why . . . that's why, after all, I have to do this."

"Do what?" asked the doctor, cheerfully.

To stand entailed too great an effort. That was why Larry Traynor only pushed himself up to one knee. He raised the rifle and leveled it.

"You have to die, Channing," he said. "I won't be far behind you, I suppose . . . but you'll have to go before me!"

"Right!" said the doctor. "Either way . . . it makes little difference to me. But what a fool bulldog you are! Blind, stupid, with fat in your brain!"

Down the barrel of the gun, Traynor sighted. He covered the

breast. He covered the face. He drew his bead between the bright eyes, just where the bullet had knocked the life out of the buckskin leader.

V

"METAL OF A MAN"

There was no doubt that the doctor was a brave man, a very brave man. He sat steady enough; he held up his head high; but to look at death is not an easy thing and, as the seconds ran on, the eyes of Channing began to enlarge and grow too bright.

Suddenly he shouted: "Shoot, damn you!"

Traynor lowered the gun. "I've been trying to. I've been wanting to," he said, slowly. "But I can't. I don't suppose I have the nerve to shoot even . . . a dog!"

He cast the rifle from him and sat with his head between his hands.

"The poorest fool," laughed the doctor, "the weakest and the poorest fool that I've ever met!"

There was a ridge between them and the valley in which the Laymon house stood. They climbed that ridge. It was only a few miles to go, but it took them four days. Sometimes the dying man walked. Sometimes he crawled. He would hear the doctor say: "Keep your drooling mouth shut, will you?" And then he would realize that he had been walking with his mouth open, babbling meaningless words. For the agony had ground out his brain. His wits were spinning; he knew that he carried death inside him, in his very heart.

It was on the second day of moiling up that slope that he reached a little pool of still water and looked at his face in the mirror. The thing he saw turned him sick. It could not be his. But when he opened his mouth, the bloated lips of the image also opened.

The doctor said that day: "To do a thing like this for the sake of fame . . . there's sense in that. But to do it for nothing . . . to do it for the sake of a little hand-clapping in a village filled with muddy-brained yokels . . . by God, Traynor, I've never heard of such insanity! I'm going to take back some of the other things I've said to you. Whatever else you are, as a bulldog, you're magnificent. You're killing yourself for a crazy sense of justice. What good will the legal murder of me do to the soul of your dead friend? And if you'll make the bargain with me, I'll have you practically fit and well inside of three days! Will you listen to me?"

Traynor did not answer. He was saving his breath because he

seemed to need it all. The deadly tremor was entering him more deeply than ever.

They got over the ridge the next day. Below them, Traynor could see the sprawling lines of the ranchhouse and the barns and the shining tangle of the wire fencing of the corrals. That was the goal, under his eyes, in his hand. It was not three miles away.

It took him five days to cover the three miles, though almost every step of the way was downhill. He did not take so many steps. He was on his knees, waddling, most of the time. Although the knees grew bruised, the mere pain was nothing. The burning of the gashes in his legs helped to keep his wits awake.

He had cut away most of his clothes for bandages, by this time. More than half-naked, blood-stained, swollen to a frightful grossness, he could not look down on his body without loathing.

The fourth evening found him still a full mile from the goal. He sat back against a tree, half blind, covering his prisoner constantly with the rifle, though he could only get the tip of a swollen finger inside the trigger guard. And lying there, with an aching throat and a groaning voice, he prayed aloud to God.

He fired shot after shot. He fired them in groups of three, sure signals for help. And yet not a single rider rushed out from the ranch to help him. For four days he had been close enough to catch the attention of some range rider. But when he fired the gun there was no response—there was only the mocking laughter of the doctor.

But for the fifth day he mustered the last of his strength and the whole exhaustless mass of his courage to bridge the final gap. And it was bridged. Just at the sunset time, that poor, rolling monster and his handcuffed man reached the back door of the ranchhouse. The steps up the porch seemed to Traynor almost as insurmountable as Alps.

He shouted; and he had no answer except a feeble echo that flew back to him from the bald, vacant faces of the barns.

Then the doctor said: "I've saved something to tell you. I'll tell it to you now, and be damned to you. I've been crowing over you these five days because, you fool, the ranch is empty! There's nobody in the house. All these five days your bleary eyes couldn't make out the details, but I've seen that not a single soul has left this house or entered it!"

"It can't be empty. It's the Laymon place," mumbled Traynor. "You've got to be wrong . . . you've got to be lying. It's the Laymon place and. . . ."

"If you had something besides death and cotton-batting in your brain," shouted the doctor, "you would have noticed that there are no cattle in the fields. Not a damned one. The place has been cleaned up!"

Traynor waited for a moment. He could see very little. Off towards the west there was a redness in the sky, to be sure. Red—fire—and fire was in his wounds, and the ghastly fog of death was in his brain. So this was the end of the trail, at last!

He said: "Doctor, you ought to die. I wanted to see you hanged."

"Thanks, old son," said the doctor. "I've been appreciating that idea of yours for some days, you know."

"I could chain you here in the house if it's empty, and you'd starve in three days."

The doctor said nothing.

"That wouldn't be pretty, eh? You tied and starving . . . and me spilled out on the floor, my body rotting away before I'm dead. Not pretty, Doctor, eh?"

"My God, no!" breathed the doctor.

"Well," said Traynor, "I can't do it. I'll tell you why. I can't help remembering that Rose loved you. I can't do you in like this, Channing."

He had to pause and fight for breath. The captive stared at him with eyes made enormous by wonder.

"Inside this right-hand trousers pocket," said Traynor through his puffed lips, "there's the key to the handcuffs. You take it . . . I can't get my hand into the pocket anymore. Take it, and set yourself free." He laid down his gun as he spoke.

The doctor, his hands trembling so that the chain between the handcuffs sang a tuneless song, reached into the pocket and found the key.

And when he had it, he stood over his captor for a moment with his hands raised as though he intended to dash the steel manacles into the hideously distorted face.

Pain in Traynor had reached such a point that he could not fear death itself. That was why he waited for the blow with a frightful caricature of a smile. He felt that this was natural. He had given the tiger its freedom, and the first place the tiger struck would be at him.

But Parker Channing stood back after a moment. He scowled at Traynor. He fitted the key into the lock of the handcuffs; in an instant he was free. He hurled the manacles far away from him, and his glance wandered across the mountains. Freedom and safety lay for him there. The discarded hope of existence returned to him with a rush.

From that prospect, he looked back, suddenly, at the helpless man who lay against the steps of the veranda. The sight made him sneer. As for the bloated, visionless eyes, there was little comprehension in them. To crush Traynor now would be like crushing a toad.

But something else was working in the mind of the doctor. It made him take a few paces up and down, muttering to himself. He wanted to be away. He wanted to be putting miles of safety between himself and the society which waited now only the chance to strangle him at the end of a rope. And still the dim life in the eyes of Traynor held him back.

Channing uttered a final exclamation and stepped away. Traynor looked after him without denunciation, without hope. With the sick man, even the effort of thinking had grown to be almost a physical strain. It was better to lie back and feel the damp cold of the night coming over him. It was better to lie still with the dreadful fluttering in his breast, the movement as of dying wings, wings that have flown to weariness over a sea of darkness into which they must fall. Very shortly, as the night closed over him, his eyes would be closed and never open.

A returning footfall amazed him. Through the dimness he saw the tall form of the doctor go past him, up the steps, across the veranda. A little pause at the door, and Channing entered the house. His footfall echoed through the emptiness. There was the rattling of iron, iron sounding like that of a stove. Finally the dying man heard the crackling of fire, more cheerful than the song of a cricket. Pans rattled. A fragrance of cookery moved out on the night air.

The doctor was low; a murdering snake without pity or human compassion, but even in him it was peculiar that he should cook for his own comfort while a man lay hungry and dying within sense-range of the preparation of the food. The footfalls came loudly out of the kitchen, across the veranda, and descended.

"Stand up!" commanded the doctor harshly.

"No use," muttered Traynor. "If I'm in your way here, roll me out of the path. I'm not moving anymore."

"Look," said Channing. "You're rotten. I don't want to touch you. But if you'll try to get up, I'll do something for you."

"Thanks," said Traynor. "And to hell with you, Channing!"

The doctor sighed. He leaned down, fitting his strong hands under the shoulders of Traynor, and raised him into a sitting posture. The brain of Traynor whirled dizzily.

"Let me be," he said, in a thick husky whisper. "I'm almost finished, Channing. Let me pass out, this way . . . no more pain . . . God! Let it finish off like this downhill. . . ."

The fierce hands of the doctor, strong, hard, painful, ground into his flesh and raised him. He was tottering on his feet. Now he went forward, his huge, hippopotamus feet bumping together as he was more than half lifted up the steps.

The kitchen stove, as they entered the room, he heard roaring with fire. A lamp had been lighted. Wisps of smoke were twisting in the air above the stove, and pans over the fire were trembling a little with the force of the flames. Dim hope, now, entered the mind of Traynor.

The doctor got him down the hall and turned him through a doorway into another lighted room. On the incredible softness of a bed he stretched the body of Traynor. He covered him with blankets.

"Stop thinking," said the doctor, standing over him at last. "Don't do any more thinking. It'll wear out your mind. Look at the light. Remember that you're not going to die."

"Not die?" whispered Traynor.

"No."

"Not die?" murmured Traynor again, and his mouth remained gaping open, as though he were drinking in hope with the air. The doctor left. He returned, after a little, with a cup of tea. He raised the bloated, spongy head of Traynor in the crook of his arm. The tea had a foul odor. The taste of it was green, bitter, sick.

"Pretty bad to swallow, eh?" asked the doctor. "But it's life, Traynor. This is the life that was green all around you, as we came through the valleys. Foxglove, Traynor. It's the plant that doctors get digitalis from. Do you know why your body is almost rotting away from you? It's because your heart has gone bad. And digitalis is going to cure that heart. When the heart is well, *you'll* be well. You'll be fit for a normal life again. Here . . . finish this stuff off and have some more!"

And Traynor drank the foul stuff and almost found it good, it was so sweetened by the taste of hope!

In twenty-four hours the change was incredible. The bloating about the face was almost entirely gone. Traynor's whole body and limbs felt lighter. Above all, he could see clearly; he could think clearly; and as he stared up at the ceiling his thoughts led him into a continual maze of wonder.

Channing came back into the room that evening with food, and more of the digitalis tea. Now that his brain and eyes were clearer, he could watch in the face of the doctor the shadow of distaste as he looked down upon the sick man; but mastering that dislike, that horror, there was a keen interest showing through.

He fed Traynor. He held the cup of tea for him, raising his head.

Afterwards he pulled the soggy clothes from the sick man's body and washed him. The exquisite comfort of cleanliness soaked through the flesh, into the soul of Traynor. He had felt too dirty to be worthy of life, or of fighting for it.

And still he wondered, from day to day, as the strength flowed back into his body, into his brain. And the frightful fluttering of wings had left his breast. When he turned on his left side, he could still feel a slight, quick, abnormal vibration; but otherwise the beating of the heart did not trouble him except that now and then there would be a great, single drum-stroke, as though to give him warning of the condition in which he had once lain.

"The digitalis . . . it's done all this?" he asked, marveling.

The doctor nodded, "It's one of the few drugs that are absolutely necessary to modern medicine. It works miracles. You're one of the miracles. You look like a human being again . . . you *are* a human being. You're able to sit up. You could start walking tomorrow . . . and that's the day I leave you, Traynor!"

Traynor stared upwards at the ceiling. "Why did you do this, Parker?" he asked.

"I don't know," answered Channing, scowling. "Partly because you were such a bulldog. Partly because . . . well, because the doctor in me was being tormented by the sight of you. My profession is sworn to relieve suffering, you know."

"And you'll be paid for making me well. Do you know how?"

"How?"

"As soon as I can walk and ride, I'm coming on your trail again."

"Good!" exclaimed Parker Channing. "No damned sentimentality. And we'll fight it out to a finish."

"Yes, we will," said Traynor.

He smiled in a strange way at Channing, and Channing smiled in the same manner back at his patient.

"I understand," said Traynor.

"What do you understand?"

"Why it'll be a pleasure to you to cut my throat. It's because you can't stand the idea of me finding Rose Laymon again, and making her forget that the crooked doctor ever lived."

"You'll never make her forget," said the doctor.

"Women know how to put things out of their minds," insisted Traynor.

A patch of white appeared around the mouth of the doctor. "I'll talk no more about it!" he exclaimed, and straightway left the room.

Their understanding was perfect, Traynor knew. They had made a fair exchange. To the doctor he had restored freedom, and the doctor had given him health and life. Neither needed to be grateful to the other. It was a fair exchange and they could part on an equal footing. Yet—except for the picture of old Sam lying on his back in the dust of the road—Traynor knew that he could be fond of this man.

He was simply an outcrop from the ordinary blood of humanity. His brain worked not as the brains of other men operated. There was a greater logic in him, a detached, impersonal coldness of thought. When he was in need of money, therefore, he was able to conceive a crime. Having conceived the crime, he was able to execute it calmly, efficiently, killing the old hero who attempted to interfere with his scheme.

This picture of cold-minded efficiency was marred by only two facts—the real love of the doctor for Rose Laymon, and the human weakness which forced him to tend his worst enemy, curing a patient who would afterwards go on the trail to end his life.

These thoughts were in the mind of Traynor that evening; in the morning, the doctor would go, sinking himself deep into the mountains, attempting to secure his freedom from pursuit. And Traynor would wait one day, recovering further strength before he started the long walk back to Little Snake.

He could hear the pounding hoofs of a horse up the road; the doctor was stirring about in the kitchen, singing softly. The sound of the horse turned in towards the ranchhouse.

Hinges creaked with a great groaning and vibration, as though a wooden gate were being dragged open. After that, noise of hoofs became louder.

The doctor was no longer moving in the kitchen. His step came down the hall. He looked in at the door of the sick man, and Traynor saw the rifle in his hands.

"Somebody's coming. I guess this is good-bye, Larry," he said.

"Good luck . . . till I meet you again," said Traynor, smiling thinly.

"The same to you," sneered the doctor, "till I sink lead into you."

The noise of the horse had ended. A footfall sounded on the back porch as the doctor turned to slip away through the front of the house. He was checked by a voice that rang clearly through the old building, calling: "Hello! Who's here? Who's here?"

Channing whirled about as though a knife had dug into him. It was the unforgettable voice of Rose Laymon.

VI

"THE FACE IN THE WINDOW"

The doctor leaned the rifle against the wall. He looked white, strained, old. "Call her!" he whispered to Traynor.

"All right." He lifted his voice. "Rose! I'm in here!"

And the girl answered: "Who . . . Larry Traynor?"

She came running. At the door of the room she halted. The ride had blown color into her face. The hat was well back on her head. And there was such an upwelling of light in her eyes, such a gleaming of surprise and caution and excitement, that she looked to Traynor like an Indian girl.

"Larry," she exclaimed, "are you ill? What's the matter? Did you catch up with him? Did that murderer hurt you . . . ?"

She was coming into the room, one small step at a time, when she saw the doctor in the corner, among the shadows. She winced from him with an exclamation, as though she had been struck.

The doctor, whiter than ever, made a small gesture. "Murderer is the word, Rose . . . but not a woman-killer, you know."

She faced the doctor, but she kept backing up until she was close to the bedside of Larry Traynor. There she put out a small hand, and Traynor took it. He could see an agony in the face of Channing, at this gesture which sprang from fear of him. Then the doctor mastered himself. He spoke almost lightly.

"Why not sit down, Rose?" he asked. "I was leaving in the morning, but I'll get out tonight since you've arrived. However, we might all have a chat together."

Her hand wandered behind her, found a chair, drew it towards her while her eyes were still fixed on the doctor. She sat down, close to Larry Traynor.

It seemed as though she had stepped far back in time to the last moment when they had meant so much to one another. With a gesture, in an instant, she had banished the distance that had come between them. And Traynor, turning his own head away from the doctor, watched the breathing of the girl, and his soul extended towards her with an immensity of joy and possession.

"I don't understand it," she said, shaking her head. "Will you tell me what's happened, Parker . . . why you're here with Larry, like a friend?"

"He caught me, and slipped the handcuffs on me," said the doctor. He brought out his words with a cool precision. "We're not friends. His heart went bad on the march in. He turned off to this place to shorten the way. He was close to dying when he got here and, instead of sending me to hell before him, he turned me loose. So I cured his heart trouble for him. We part tomorrow. And we'll meet another day on another trail."

Cold hatred—but respect, too—was in his glance as he stared at Traynor. Yet he went on, forcing himself: "When you and the fools of Little Snake thought that Traynor was showing the white feather the other day . . . that was simply the same heart trouble. I saw the tremble and jump of the pulse, in his throat, and I knew that he was as helpless as a child." He turned to Traynor: "I think this leaves us quits, Larry."

"Absolutely," agreed Traynor.

She almost turned her back on the doctor as she leaned over Traynor. "You know what I thought that day, Larry?" she said. "Yes, because you could see it in my face. Are you going to forgive me?"

"Look," said Traynor. "That didn't happen; that's forgotten. The other things . . . what's to come . . . are all that matter."

A slight shadow like the breath of fear ran across her eyes, then she smiled at him. There was that in her smile that made him glad not to look towards the doctor.

"I'll be getting on," said Channing.

"You can't go," she said. "Not till I've thanked you for the thing you've done for Larry."

The face of Channing stiffened. "That's unnecessary cruelty, isn't it?" he asked.

"Parker, be honest," she said. "It was all a game with you. You never cared a whit about me. I was simply a girl to fill some of the dull hours. Isn't that the truth?"

He stared at her. "All right," he said. "We'd better let it rest that way." Then he added: "No decent girl wants to think that a . . . murderer . . . ever cared for her."

"You're being serious?" she asked.

"My God!" he exclaimed bitterly, "even if there's no heart in you, there ought to be a memory."

"There *is* a memory," she answered. "You meant everything? Did you really mean everything, Parker?"

"There's no good in talking about it," said Channing. "I know what I'm going to do. I've seen what you think of me now. But so far as meaning what I've said before . . . well, I meant more than that, even when my damned supercilious manner denied my words."

After this, there was a pause that alarmed Traynor. He began to look anxiously from one to the other. And when he saw her beauty and the magnificence of the doctor, he could not help feeling that in some way they had been made, destined, for one another.

Then she said: "I'm sorry, Parker."

"You mean that," he answered, very slowly. "And I'm such a poor beggar now that I'm grateful for even pity. Or is your blood still running cold when you look at me?"

"No," she said, shaking her head. "Only . . . it's the horrible waste, Parker. It's the frightful throwing away of all your chances . . . it's the ending of your life that makes me want to cry."

"Maudlin sentimentality!" he answered, half sneering. "I'm ashamed of you, Rose. That's the weak streak appearing. I'll find my way to a new place in the world soon. Our friend Traynor thinks that he'll be able to find me on the outtrail and stop me. For his own sake, I hope that he doesn't reach me . . . ever!" And once more there was murder in the glance he gave Traynor.

A hunger suddenly came up in the heart of Larry Traynor, a burning desire for the future day when he would be able to confront the doctor clad in his full strength, without that deadly betrayal, that horrible fluttering, of his heart and nerves.

"I'll go now," said the doctor.

"You can't go," said the girl. "You can't leave me alone with Larry. And I can't leave him here in danger."

"Danger?" echoed the doctor.

"Of course. The Whartons may swoop on the place at any time. And they. . . ."

"The Whartons are in prison!" exclaimed the doctor.

"They *were* in prison. Haven't you heard . . . but of course not! They broke jail. They, and a dozen other men. They started away through the mountains. They've been sighted here and there, close to this place."

"Ah," said the doctor, "and that's why your father moved off the ranch with the cattle?"

"That's right. The instant he knew that the Whartons were free, he was sure that they'd come straight for the ranch. He knew that they'd run off the cattle and burn the buildings. So he started for town."

"Why couldn't he have brought out a posse from town?"

"Hire thirty men for heaven knows how long? At five dollars a day and keep? Dad would rather die than throw away money like that."

"Rose," said Traynor, "do you mean that the Whartons at any moment may come down on the place?"

"It's true. They were sighted two days ago in Tomlinson's gulch."

"Then what made you come out here . . . at night . . . into danger?"

"I'm ashamed to tell you," said the girl, blushing. "Well, I don't care . . . I'll show you!"

SHE RAN from the room. Her footfall went lightly down the hall, and Traynor smiled, listening after it, until his absent-minded glance crossed the burning eyes of the doctor.

"Some way. . . , " said the doctor. He did not need to complete that tight-lipped sentence. "Some way" he would manage to cross and blast the happiness which she was dawning again for Larry Traynor. The cold white devil in his face glared steadily out at Traynor.

The girl came back. In her hand she held up a rose-colored frock, covered with airy flounces, the square-cut neck bordered with a film of lace.

"My first party dress!" she said. "I looked through the luggage that my father brought in. When I couldn't find it, I made up my mind that I'd take this trip. I couldn't risk the lives of men by asking them to come along. So I told Father that I was going to spend the night with Martha Carey . . . and then I came out here. I could be back long before the morning."

No matter what enmity was between them, the two men looked at one another and smiled. She, lowering the dress, suddenly cried out in a stifled voice of fear. Traynor followed the glance, and at the window, pressed so close to the pane that the nose and chin were whitened, he saw a man's face, rounded out like an owl's with an uncropped growth of beard, a man with eyes narrowed in malice. And the upper lip curled back from the teeth as though the man were a carnivorous creature, a hunting beast of the night.

The face receded, sank out of sight like a stone wavering down into the dark depths of a pool.

"It's Jim Wharton!" gasped the girl. She slid down on her knees. "Oh, God, it's Jim—and all the rest will be with him!"

VII

"CRUCIBLE OF COURAGE"

The doctor got to the window with a leap, catching up the rifle on the way. He pulled up the sash and thrust the rifle out. A bullet smashed through the glass. Thudded into the opposite wall. The doctor stepped back into the corner, while loosed bits of the glass were falling with a tinkle to the floor.

Traynor, half-dressed under the blankets, threw back the covers and began to pull on the rest of his clothes. He had shaped some heavy felt moccasins which he stepped into now.

"We've got to get Larry out!" the girl was crying. "He can't take care of himself, now. Parker, we've got to get Larry out!"

"Do we?" said the doctor, calmly. "We'll be in luck if we get *anyone* out."

He walked from the room and down the hall. Traynor followed. He was weak in the knees, and his head was light, but the gashes in his legs were fairly healed. He would have strength for short efforts, he felt sure.

They stood in the kitchen. The lamp had burned low and crookedly. It was smoking fast, and the sickening sweet smell of the soot hung in the air.

The doctor took control. "I'm going to try the back door, quietly," he said. "It may be that they haven't scattered all around the house, now. If I get out, the rest of you sneak after me. Keep on the left. We'll try to get to the shrubs."

Traynor had neared the door. It was perfectly apparent to him that the doctor was willing to take the risks. But there was a good reason why he should not.

Through the screen on the door, Traynor could see the pale glimmer of thin moonlight, pouring a haze of brilliance over the ground. He could see the gleam of strands of new wire along the corral fence. The barns were bleak and half white, half black shadow. The scene had the very look of death.

The doctor was still speaking when Traynor pushed the door soundlessly open and stepped out onto the porch. He had not taken two steps when he heard the stifled exclamation of the girl, behind him, and the doctor muttering: "Come back, you fool!"

Then, out of the cloudy dark of a bank of shrubs behind the house, a thin tongue of flame darted. The crack of the rifle struck painfully against his ears. A sting greater than that of a giant hornet gashed his neck. He jerked the door shut as a second bullet hissed beside his ear as he sidestepped.

"They're behind the house . . . they're all around the house, it seems," said Traynor.

The girl parted her lips to speak, but no words came. She stood in white suspense while the doctor grabbed Traynor by the shoulders.

"You jackass!" snarled the doctor. "This thing . . . thank God, is only a scratch!" He pulled out a handkerchief and bound up Traynor's neck.

"Why did you do it, Larry?" begged the girl. "Why, why did you go out there, half-helpless?"

"It's glory that the fool wants! Glory!" sneered the doctor.

"Mind you," said Traynor, "I'll be no good to the rest of you. They're going to get me before the show's over, and they might as well get me now. You're the fool, Parker. You're the able-bodied man. It's up to you to get Rose away. You can't show yourself here and there to draw fire."

Channing, finishing the bandaging, stepped suddenly back at the end of this speech. The girl, with moisture welling into her eyes, stared mutely at Traynor.

"You see what he is," sneered the doctor. "A hero, eh? A dead hero before long, I suppose. We're all dead, Rose. And this is no time for damned heroics. Listen!"

Outside, a man shouted. He was answered far and near, from all around the house, by what seemed a score of voices.

"We're walled in," said the doctor.

Traynor sat down and leaned his elbows on the edge of the table. He looked at the floor, forcing his eyes down because he did not want to let the image of Rose fill them. He tried to bend his mind away from the thought of her. As for what happened to him and the doctor, it was no tragedy. Men who live with guns in their hands have to fall by guns in the end, often enough. They were simply playing out their logical parts. But the girl. . . .

She stood beside him, now, resting a hand on his shoulder. The doctor paced the floor like a great cat. No one spoke. The nearness of the danger blinded their eyes and stopped thought.

Then a voice called: "Hello, you inside there!"

The doctor placed himself close to the door. "Hello, outside!" he answered.

"Who are you?"

"I'm Doctor Parker Channing."

"You're Doctor Murderer Channing, are you?" Sneering, drawling laughter commented on his name and presence. "Channing, you'd be better outside than inside. We could use a doctor like you. Open that door and walk out to our side of the fence and you'll be as safe as any of us."

Channing looked down at his hands and dusted them.

"Go on, Parker," urged the girl. "It's the best thing for you. You'll be safer with them than anywhere else. With them you may have a chance to get away."

"What do you suggest, Larry?" asked the hard voice of the doctor.

"You're a fool if you don't go out to them," said Traynor, peering into the pale face of Channing. "But I think you're going to be a fool."

"Do you?" asked the doctor with a slight start. "Thanks!"

"Answer up, Doc!" shouted the man outside.

"Who are you?" called Channing.

"Jim Wharton."

"Wharton, I'm staying in the house with my friends."

A yell of amazement answered him. "Are you crazy, Channing? Are you gonna go home with your friends and let the sheriff hang you?"

"I'm staying here. That's final."

"Of all the damn fools!" cried Wharton. And then he added, a moment later: "There's another offer I'll make to you. Who's the second man in there . . . the one that was flat in bed?"

"He's Larry Traynor."

"Traynor? I got nothing against him. Now, listen: I've got men all around the house."

"I know that."

"Then you know that we can do what we please."

"I know that, too. But it might cost you something."

"Damn the cost. Or else, I can burn you out. And that's what I'll do if I have to!"

The doctor said nothing, but his head bowed a little and he took a great breath. "But there's an easy way out of all of this," went on Jim Wharton. "It ain't everybody in the world that I'm against. It's the skunk that put me in jail. It's John Laymon that I'm going to get even with. Send out the girl to me. She's in there . . . I seen her myself!"

"What sort of hound do you think I am?" asked the doctor.

"I think you got brains. I hope you have, anyway. We won't touch her. But we'll hold her till her old man pays for her, and pays heavy.

Damn him, he's got enough money to pay. And I'm going to have a slice of it . . . a slice right into the red of it!"

The doctor turned his head from the door towards Traynor and the girl. His eyes glazed. Traynor, starting to speak, found the hand of the girl over his mouth. The doctor seemed to see nothing.

"Answer up!" yelled Jim Wharton. "If you think that I'm going to wait an hour, you're loco. I get the girl, or else I burn out the three of you like rats!"

Suddenly the girl cried out, sharply: "I'll come to you, Jim!"

"Good girl!" yelled Wharton. "You'll be safe with us, Rose!"

She had started up. The grip of Traynor fell on her wrist and checked her. "Let me go, Larry!" she panted. "There's no other way for the two of you. . . ."

"They won't harm her," said the doctor. "They won't hurt her. She'll be safe, Larry, and . . . and. . . ." His voice faded.

"What he says is true!" cried Rose Laymon. "Larry, don't you see that?"

"Be still!" said Traynor, sternly. He jerked her down into a chair at his side. Then, his grim eyes never leaving the face of the doctor, he said: "You'd trust her with a gang of dogs like those fellows outside?"

"She'd be all right," panted the doctor. "She'd be . . . I mean . . . *fire*, Larry! My God, if they set fire to this old wooden shack . . . the flames would . . . God! . . . they'd cook us."

"Are you coming, Rose?" shouted Jim Wharton.

"Be still!" said Traynor.

"You damned fool!" shrieked the doctor, his voice shaking to pieces on the high note, "do you want her to be burned to death?"

"Better that than the other thing," said Traynor. "Channing, what a skunk you are, after all!"

"Rose!" called Wharton. "Where are you?"

And her eyes were bright and her voice was strong as she answered: "I'm not coming, Jim. I'm staying here!"

"Rose, if you stay there . . . woman or no woman, I'll fire the house. Do you hear?"

"I hear . . . and I'm staying!"

"It's crazy!" panted the doctor. "It's . . . *fire*, Rose! They'll burn the house upon your heads! They'll. . . ."

"Go out and argue with them," said Traynor, sternly. "Maybe you can make them change their minds."

Parker Channing, leaning against the wall, struck a fist into his own face, and groaned. Then he muttered: "I'll talk to 'em face to face. I'm not afraid!"

"I've given you your last chance!" yelled Jim Wharton. "Of all the damned. . . ."

"Wait a minute!" screamed the doctor. "I'm coming out . . . I'm coming out to talk to you! I'm going to. . . ."

He opened the door. "Can I come safely?" he shouted again.

"Come ahead."

And Doctor Parker Channing slunk out of the house, without a word to those who remained behind. The outer door slammed, rebounded with a jangle, slammed again. And they knew that he would not come back.

"He's gone," whispered Rose Laymon. "Oh, Larry, for him to go . . . murder was nothing, compared to this."

A queer pain wrung the soul of Larry Traynor. "He's a brave man, though. I've seen him laugh at the idea of dying. Yes, with a gun leveled at him. But the fire, Rose . . . that's the thought that killed the heart in him. Never blame him again. The life that's in me, it's Parker that gave it back to me. He wouldn't be here now, except that he stayed to take care of me. . . ."

And a voice rolled in on them, faint from the distance: "Throw the bush up there agin the side of the house. Light that straw and throw it on, too!"

VIII

"INTO HELL"

They could tell the course of the fire by the rising yells of the Wharton gang; then by the noise of the flames, and finally a tremor that went through the whole building. Beyond the window, they saw the smoke driving low in the wind towards the barns, which were wrapped in clouds, with the yellow light of the fire playing on it, until the barns in turn seemed to be on fire.

The two sat still for a long time. The wind carried gusts of heat to them over the floor. They could hear the far end of the building falling, as half-burned rafters crashed, and let down the roofs above them, and with every fall there was a louder roar of the fire.

Rose pressed closer and closer to Traynor. He, with his arm around her, looked steadfastly above her head. There was fear in him, but there was also a dim delight unlike anything he had ever known, a full and quiet ecstasy.

"Back there," she said, "if I could throw the months away . . . then I'd be happy, Larry."

"What months?" he asked.

"Those after I left you, and when I was knowing Parker."

"He is worth knowing."

"Do you mean that?"

"He is the greatest man I ever met," said Traynor, solemnly.

"Larry, have you forgiven him out of the bottom of your heart?"

"I forgive him."

"Then I do, also."

"When the fire comes over the room, Rose, shall we make a break for the open?"

"No. Let's go with the house."

"There's the rifle with plenty of bullets in it."

She looked sharply up at him. "Well . . . that way, then," she murmured. Suddenly she cried out: "But I can save you, Larry! There's still time for me to save you, if I go out and call to them. They'll take me, and they won't harm me. . . ."

"Hush," said Traynor. She was still. He added: "I saw Jim Wharton's face at the window. Do you think I'd let you go out to him? It's better this way."

"It *is* better," she answered.

A strange light began to enter the room. The low-flowing smoke, wind-driven, covered the ground, and the fire reflected from the top of it through the window, brighter than the light of the lamp. This tremulous and rosy glow made the girl as beautiful as an angel to the eye of her lover.

As he looked at her, he said: "Poor Channing! Poor devil! He's out there thinking of this, Rose. He's eating his heart out. He's half wishing to be back in here with us."

"I don't want to think of him," she said.

"He killed poor old Sam. I ought to hate him. If we both lived, I suppose I'd try to go on the trail after him. But this way, I understand him. I'm glad to think of him. If it's God that makes us, He put too much mind and not enough heart in Channing. That's all there is to it! God help him, and God forgive him!"

A voice shouted huskily, as if in fear: "Hey, all of you! Watch through that smoke! Watch through that smoke! They might sneak out that way, through the smoke!"

"And we might!" cried the girl. "Look, Larry!"

There was a great crash that shook the entire house—what was left of it. The walls of the kitchen leaned crookedly. Plaster fell in great chunks from the ceiling and seemed to drop noiselessly, so huge was the uproar of the fire, and the heat was intense. The flame could not be more than a room away. The door of the dining room rattled back and forth as though a hand were shaking the knob.

But out the window, Traynor could see hardly a thing. For the funnels of white smoke, rushing away from the house, filled the air and covered the ground, towards the barns.

"Rose," he said, "there's a ghost of a chance."

He went to the dining room door and pulled it open. Before him a wild furnace was roaring, tossing up a billion-footed dance of flames. The heat seared his face, searched his body through his clothes.

He jammed the door shut again.

"Half a minute!" he called to the girl. "Have you got a handkerchief. Then wet it in that pitcher, and tie it over your mouth and nose. Like this. You see?"

He used the bloody handkerchief of the doctor, unknotting it from around his throat, for the same purpose. When he looked again, the girl was masked in white. She furled up the lower lip of the mask and threw her arms around him. And he, pushing the handkerchief high on his head, took what well might be his last clear view of her.

They only looked, desperately, with great eyes; they did not touch their lips together because each was striving, in divine despair, to see the face before them as it might be transfigured in another life. Then they drew down the wet masks again and went out the door onto the porch.

The full heat of the conflagration struck them at once. And the sweep of the wind hurried them into the boiling columns of the smoke. He had her hand in his.

"Close your eyes . . . I'll guide!" he called at her ear, and jumped with her from the edge of the porch.

He had a deep breath of pure air in his lungs. He ran forward straining his eyes through the smoke that burned them, until the breath was spent in his lungs. They were far from the house, by this time, and the dim outlines of the barn loomed dark before him.

He threw himself flat on the ground and dragged the girl down beside him. She was coughing and gasping. But there, close to the ground, it was possible to breathe and fill the lungs with better air, for the smoke kept rising. Voices were still shouting: "Keep a watch! Keep a watch! What's passing there?" And distantly a rifle cracked. Three shots—at some smoky phantom, no doubt—and the firing ceased. But it was a good measure of the peril into which they were running.

"Now!" he said at the ear of Rose Laymon, and helped her to rise.

His knees were very weak. Yet he could stagger again to a run that carried them on toward the barns. The door of one yawned open right before them. He had carried the rifle slung in his left hand; now he transferred it to the right and, as he did so, he saw forms loom into the shadows of the doorway, peering into the smoke.

"Hey!" yelled one. The voice was a scream. "Here they come . . . here! Here!"

Traynor fired from the ready, straight into the breast of that big, bearded figure. He turned and jammed the muzzle of the rifle into the face of the second man, and the victim staggered backwards, screeching out something about his eyes, firing a revolver repeatedly at nothingness.

The girl and Traynor already were far down the empty aisle of the barn, with flickering lights from the burning house entering the place. Behind them, they heard a great crashing, a loud whistling of the triumphant wind, and a gust of heat and light streamed with a thousand-fold brilliance into the shadows of the barn.

That was what enabled them to see half a dozen horses tethered to the manger near the rear door. The frightened beasts were rearing and stamping and pulling violently back on the tie-ropes to escape.

Rose Laymon threw up her hands in helpless terror at that mill of great, tigerish bodies, as she heard the stamping of the hoofs and saw the frantic eyes of the horses rolling towards the distant fire.

But Traynor, with a knife, cut loose the first two horses. They looked no better than ordinary broncos, but ordinary broncos would have to do. They could not pick and choose. He hung on to the reins of a fiery little pinto as the girl swung into the saddle.

She had the rear door of the barn open the next moment, and Traynor was barely able to hook a leg over the cantle of the saddle before his horse flew like a stone through the doorway and into the open night.

"This way! This way!" a voice was screeching. "This way, everyone! Here they go . . . and on horses! Ride like hell! She's worth a hundred thousand to us. A thousand bucks to the gent that snags her first."

Traynor righted himself with a vast effort in the saddle, then shot his horse in pursuit of the flying pinto; and he heard behind him the swift beginning of the pursuit, the rumble of hoofs growing louder and louder as man after man joined the chase.

IX

"TRAIL'S END"

They went up the easy slope of a hill which was half white with the moon, half trembling with the glow from the fire. The house of John Laymon lay prone, but huge red and yellow ghosts rose above it, dancing, sometimes throwing up great arms that disappeared in the upper air.

There was plenty of light for shooting, and the Whartons used it. "Get that damned Traynor and the gal will give up!" the familiar voice of Jim Wharton was thundering.

The result was an endless shower of bullets. Many of them flew wide. He only knew of their passing by the clicking of them through the branches of the trees or by their solid thudding into the trunks. But others clipped the air close about him, whining small with eagerness, each like a dog that misses its stroke and has to rush on past the quarry.

They rounded the hill. They entered a narrow shoot of a glade that carried them straight out into the road for Little Snake. To have that road under them seemed to insure freedom. He saw the head of the girl go up; he heard her crying: "We're going to make it, Larry! They're not going to catch us!"

But he, glancing back, still smiling, saw that half a dozen riders had forged ahead of the rest and were gaining steadily.

"Ride ahead!" he commanded Rose. "You're lighter than I am. The pinto's a flash. You'll get to help first."

She shook her head, waving her denial. And as he stared at her, the blood trickling again from the open wound in his neck, he realized that she would never leave him—not now—not hereafter.

There are fools, he thought, who doubt the future. Those are the men who have never gone through the fear of death with a friend, in the knowledge that an equal faith is on each side. But for such as have endured the crisis, there must be a promise of life thereafter. An eternity of faith poured over him as he watched her at his side and saw the tight pull she was keeping on the head of the pinto. She could flash away from him in an instant, but all the dangers in the world could never persuade her.

They rushed around a great loop of the road, and behind them the beating of hoofs was louder and louder. Then the voices raised in a sudden triumph that was like a song. He looked wildly behind him, and saw the waving arms in the moonlight and the brandished guns.

He could not understand, until he looked ahead again and saw a solitary rider, straight up in the saddle, rushing his horse down the slope to intercept their way.

Would he come on them in time?

It seemed almost an even race but at the end, as the pinto and Traynor's mustang struggled up a slope in the way, it seemed that the horse of the stranger was losing speed. He did not attempt to shoot. Perhaps he was afraid of striking the girl with a bullet. And Traynor himself held his fire with the rifle.

A roar of angry surprise rose from the crowd of the leading pursuers. Then a twist of the way cut off everything from the view of Traynor. He was amazed to hear an outburst of rifle fire, with yells of high dismay scattered through the explosions.

The beat of hoofs died out. Still the voices clamored furiously, far away. Still the gunfire beat more rapidly.

But the pursuit had died at that spot. What had happened? Well, he could save his breath for the work of riding, for he was very, very tired. His legs shuddered against the side of his horse, and his back was bending.

Hours seemed to flow past him, and more hours. He passed into a sort of trance through which the quiet, cheerful voice of the girl cut into his consciousness, from time to time. She was riding the pinto close to his horse. She was supporting him. And then he saw the lights of Little Snake clustered ahead.

"Do you know what happened back there?" she asked him, as she gave the horses their last halt before making the town.

"Where?" he asked, his mind very dim.

"The rider who came down the slope . . . didn't you know him, Larry?"

"Ah, the fellow who almost cut us off, and then his horse petered out, or his nerve failed him?"

"His horse didn't give out, and he had as much nerve as any man in the world."

"What do you mean, Rose?"

"It was Parker Channing. I knew him by his way in the saddle. I knew him by the wave of his hand when I looked back. And I saw him turning against the rest of them."

"The doctor? You mean that he cut in to help stop them? You mean . . . ? Rose, I ve got to go back to him. . . ."

"Hush, and be still," said the girl. "He died hours and hours ago. They've killed him, and gone on. But not till he let us get safely away."

"Die? For us?" cried Traynor.

"Yes, for us," she answered.

And he knew that it was true. His brain cleared of all weakness. He looked ahead at the twinkling lights of the town and the glimmering stars, and it seemed to Traynor that the glory of the heavens descended without a check and overspread this earth.

Back there at the head of the hill, the doctor had charged in earnest to cut off the retreat of the two, for he felt that he had abandoned all shame and all virtue forever, when he left them in the condemned house. There was nothing for him, now, but to race forward into crime and greater crime and welcome the darkness of the future.

And there was a savage earnestness in his riding as he considered how close the two rode together, Traynor beside the girl. He wanted to kill Traynor—not with guns but with his hands. When the last life bubbled up under the compressed tips of his fingers, then only would he be satisfied!

What was it that changed him? It was when he saw, quite clearly by the moonlight, how Rose Laymon was reining in her pinto until it's neck bowed sharply; it was when he understood perfectly her will to live or die at the side of Traynor.

If his strength was in his mind rather than his heart, perhaps it was in the quiet perfection of his thinking that he saw how the two were blended together for a single destiny that should be far higher than to be trampled down by the ruffians of Jim Wharton. And it was clear thinking, also, that showed him what he must do. No one would know. His reputation would not be cleansed by the act, unless the girl, perhaps, had recognized him by his riding. But he had to face the Whartons and check their pursuit.

So, as he swung into the road at the crest of the shallow hill, he turned straight back towards the pursuers and pulled his rifle out of its holster. He took good aim. The very first shot jerked back the head of the foremost rider, and with upflung arms the man dropped backwards out of the saddle. The second brought a yell of agony.

The party split to this side and to that. With screaming curses the riders fled.

He could ride after the fugitive pair now. But that was not his plan. To his clear brain the future of this act was very plain. His life was cast away. He had thrown it away and made it forfeit with the bullet that killed old Sam. Perhaps he had returned a partial payment by the slaying of the ruffian, who lay yonder, twisted in the road. But there was still more to do—it was a long account.

He got his horse into a nest of rocks and made the animal lie down. By that time, the tail of the pursuit had come up, and warning yells of the Whartons made the other men take cover. They began to spread out to this side and to that. Bullets, now and then, whirred through his imperfect fortifications.

He kept a keen lookout. He saw a shadow crawling between two bushes, took careful aim, and fired. The man leaped with a yell that burned like a torch through the brain of the doctor. One bound, and the fellow was out of sight. But he would remember this night for the rest of his days.

Suddenly, on his right, four men charged right up the hill for him. They came from a distance of fifteen yards. He dropped—one, two—and the remaining pair dodged to the side and pitched out of view behind an outcrop of rock.

One of the remaining two lay still. The other, groaning, got to his hands and knees and started crawling away. The doctor let him crawl. Something in the tone of that groaning told him that the bullet wound was through the body, and if that were the case. . . .

In the meantime, the pair under the rock so close at hand would be a thorn in his flesh. He had to keep his attention at least half for them.

Still he watched until he saw a head and shoulders lift from beside the rock. He had to snatch up his own rifle quickly. He knew that his bullet struck the target. The head bobbed down like a weighted cork, but right through the shoulder and into the body of the doctor drove the answering slug.

That was his end, and he knew it. Calmly—because there was the clear mind in him to the end—he prepared for the last stroke. He could not manage the rifle very well with one arm. But he had a borrowed Wharton revolver. That was in his hand as he roused the horse and slipped into the saddle.

The instant his silhouette loomed, the rapid firing began. He spurred the mustang straight toward the flashes of the guns. And a glory came over the doctor, and enlarged his spirit and widened his throat. The shout that came from him was like a single note from a great song.

So, firing steadily, aiming his shots, he drove his charge home against the enemy until a bullet, mercifully straight, struck the consciousness from him, and loosed the life from his body, and sent the unharmed spirit winging on its way.

They gave Parker Channing a church funeral. And the town of Little Snake followed him to the grave.

There was a very odd picture of Rose Laymon kneeling at the edge of the grave, dropping roses into it. The rest of the people held back. They knew it was her right, her duty, to play the part of chief mourner. And not a soul in Little Snake doubted that her tears were real.

Those who watched kept shifting their looks from the girl to the pale-faced solemn young man who stood not far behind her, with his head bowed. He was waiting for the end of the ceremony. He was waiting for Rose Laymon.

And it is fair to say that in all of Little Snake there was not a man who did not judge that Larry Traynor had come fairly by his happiness.

THE PIE RIVER

T(HOMAS) T(HEODORE) FLYNN (JR.) was born in Indianapolis, Indiana. He was the author of over a hundred Western short novels for such leading pulp magazines as Street & Smith's *Western Story Magazine*, Popular Publications *Dime Western* and *Star Western*, and Dell Publishing's *Zane Grey's Western Magazine*. In fact, his short novel, "The Last of the Black Tantralls," appeared in the inaugural issue of *Dime Western* (12/32) and his short novel, "Hell's Half Acre," appeared in the issue which launched *Star Western* (10/33). He moved to New Mexico with his wife and spent much of his time living in a trailer while on the road exploring the vast terrain of the American West. His descriptions of the land are always detailed, but he used them not only for local color but also to reflect the heightening of emotional distress among the characters within a story. Following the Second World War, Flynn turned his attention to the book-length Western novel and in this form also produced work that has proven imperishable. Five of these novels first appeared as original paperbacks, most notably "The Man from Laramie" which was serialized in eight installments in *The Saturday Evening Post* (1/2/54-2/20/54) and subsequently made into a memorable motion picture directed by Anthony Mann and starring James Stewart. It was recently reprinted in a hardcover edition by Chivers Press and has been recorded in full-length audio by Books on Tape.

TWO FACES WEST (Dell First Edition, 1954) deals with the problems of identity and reality and later served as the basis for a television series. Flynn was highly innovative and inventive and in later novels, such as RIDING HIGH (Dell First Edition, 1961), he concentrated on deep psychological issues as the source for conflict, rather than more elemental motives like greed. His last novel was recently published in hard covers, NIGHT OF THE COMANCHE MOON (Five Star, 1995) and is also available in full-length audio from Brilliance Corporation. Flynn is at his best in stories which combine mystery—not surprisingly, since he also wrote detective fiction—suspense and action in an artful balance. The world in which his characters live is often a comedy of errors in which the first step in any direction frequently can, and does, lead to ever deepening complications. His agent, Marguerite E. Harper, refused to sell any story by one of her clients to Fiction House, which is why Luke Short, Peter Dawson, and T. T. Flynn never appeared in any of their Western magazines, but this story would have been welcome! According to Ted's ledger book, "The Pie River" was sold to *Western Aces* on July 4, 1937, and he was paid $225.00

for it before agent's commission. It was published, however, in *Western Trails* (12/37) under the title "The Pistol Prodigal." For its appearance here both text and title have been fully restored to what the author intended.

I
"A HOT-HEADED POSSE"

"Put a bullet in my belly!" Steve Cochrane taunted. "See what good it will do you!" Between his uplifted arms, Steve Cochrane eyed the men who had crowded into the half-ruined adobe hut.

"It'd give me pleasure!" Reeves, the sheriff, gritted.

A long-waisted cowman growled, "It'd probably save somebody a heap of trouble."

Up in the right-hand corner of the room, where the adobe bricks had fallen in, the late afternoon sun drove a golden lance of color through tangled cobwebs. Buzzing flies made pelting darts of movement up there in the stagnant heat under the sagging ceiling boards.

A pack rat had left trash in one corner; the windows had long been broken; the door hung crazily by one bent hinge. The dusty surface of the dirt floor gritted under restless high-heeled boots. And Steve knew that the thread of his life was no stronger than the strands of cobweb up there under the ceiling.

Caleb Reeves, the sheriff, was in a cold fury, and Reeves had never been noted for his mildness.

For sixteen years, or maybe it was twenty-six years, the Pie River Country had known the name of Caleb Reeves. Steve Cochrane had known it as a boy. Steve had stood on the outskirts of Costerville, the county seat, and watched Caleb Reeves lead posses out after lawbreakers.

In those days Reeves's short, black, upstanding hair had been stiff and wiry as an Indian's. There always had been something of an Indian about Reeves. His high cheekbones, his spare, expressionless face, his steady stare, his mouth that seldom opened unless he had something important to say were like an Indian's.

In less than a year after Caleb Reeves had first pinned the sheriff's badge on his vest, he had swept lawlessness out of the Pie River Country. He had shot men, brought men in to be tried and hung, and followed relentlessly with his hard-riding posses after men who kept going, and stayed away from the Pie River Country if they were lucky enough to escape.

Caleb Reeves hated an outlaw.

Steve had heard as a boy, and never had reason to doubt, that Caleb Reeves found more joy in killing or hanging an outlaw than in anything else life offered him. He was a bitter man, Caleb Reeves, and his bitterness was savage against those who followed the outlaw trails.

A gnarled thumb crooked tautly about the lifted hammer of the old single action gun boring into Steve's middle. A slight shift of the thumb, the space of a breath, and it would be over. Steve felt his stomach muscles tightening, crawling.

Gray streaked the sheriff's temples now; his lean face had grown thinner with the passing years, so that his hooked nose stood out more fiercely than ever. Wrinkles were beginning to trough his leathered cheeks. But his hand was as steady; his eyes were clear and chill; the gun was no less deadly.

And Steve said again evenly: "You can't scare me, Reeves. I haven't got anything to tell you. If you're looking for some excuse to let that hammer drop, fish it out. The deal is yours."

Steve recognized the scowling young man who rolled a cigarette, struck a match, made a comment with a sneer.

"Put a rope over one of those piñon limbs outside, Sheriff, an' stretch his neck a little. Maybe it'll help his memory."

That was Buster Davis, whose father had run the hardware store. Buster still had the scar under his ear where the wall-eyed filly had thrown him when he was eleven. Even then Buster had been a surly, sneering boy, ready to bully when he could.

Steve grinned coldly. "Buster, you must be remembering the time I punched the stuffing out of you and made you cry 'yellow' back of the harness shop."

"You lied as quick then as you do now," Buster Davis snapped.

The sheriff jerked his head impatiently. "Never mind talkin' over old times. Three days ago, mister, you was seen over near Jawbone Mountain with a man who held up the stage a couple of years back. His mask slipped then an' he was seen plain by Henry Simpson here. I trailed him for a couple of days before he shook us off. Now I aim to get him. We trailed you both from Jawbone Mountain to this neck of the woods. Now where's your sidekick?"

"I told you," said Steve, "you're talking Apache. I don't savvy. You can gouge that cannon up under my liver and pull the trigger and I still won't savvy. That plain?"

"Too damn plain!" said Caleb Reeves harshly. "You're coverin' this jasper up! You know where he is!"

"Why don't you look around?" suggested Steve. "Maybe he's hiding under that old windmill, or laying up on the roof, laughing at you."

The gun gouged deeper. "Your ideas," said Caleb Reeves coldly, "don't help you none."

"You men come busting in here," said Steve to them, "waving your guns under my nose and shouting questions. Which is not the way to make me remember anything. Maybe I did meet up with a stranger. I meet plenty of strangers. But I haven't been in these parts for twelve years. I didn't know you were looking for anybody. I'm not one of your deputies. I'm not interested in Pie River law.

"I aimed to camp here for a day or so and mind my own business, while trying to decide what to do now that I'm back home. And you bust in on me demanding answers. You'll get the same answer if you stay till the desert gets blizzards. I'm no outlaw. I'm not interested in outlaws. I haven't any idea where this *hombre* is you're looking for. Now what are you going to do about it?"

Buster Davis snapped, "Buzzards always hang together!"

"If that was always the case," said Steve, "you'd be on your belly with the other snakes."

"Never mind jawin' at each other," said Caleb Reeves impatiently. "What are you doin' back in these parts?"

"Looking around," said Steve.

"What for?"

"I thought I might buy me a piece of land and settle down. I'm tired of sloping."

"It takes money to buy land."

"I've got money."

"Where'd you get it?"

"Gold mining down in Mexico, if you've got to be so damned curious!"

"You made money minin' gold over the border," said Reeves with cold suspicion. "And now you're comin' back to ranch when everybody's losin' money at it. It don't make sense."

"Who said it made sense?" said Steve calmly. "I left a heap of friends in these parts when I went away as a kid. When I figured to settle down, I thought of home. Maybe it doesn't make sense, but it was good enough for me. Now I don't know. If a bull-headed old gun-slinger and this hot-headed posse are a sample of the rest of the Pie River Country nowadays, maybe I was a fool to come back.

"I used to think you was some shucks as a sheriff. You're acting like a boogery steer now. You've been wearing a badge too long. And make up your mind what you aim to do about me. My arms are getting tired."

Caleb Reeves caught an end of his brown-stained mustache in a corner of his mouth and stared. His eyes were frosty blue, gunman's eyes. Looking at the seamed, hard face, Steve knew that here was a man. Bitter, hard, ruthless, Reeves might be, but he'd never run from a gun, never turn his back on danger or a bluff.

"I remember you," Reeves said. "I remember your old man. Pete Cochrane was all right. You had good blood in you."

"Never mind my blood," said Steve. "I'm asking you for a showdown."

"If I thought you was an outlaw," said Reeves, "I'd settle your hash quick. But I ain't sure and I never aim to go off half-cocked."

Two men stepped in from outside.

"Any signs of the other one?" asked Reeves.

"Tracks around the corral," was the answer.

"Reckon he's gone on, then?"

"Looks like it."

Caleb Reeves looked at Steve's blanket roll in the corner, glanced at the rifle leaning beside the door, let his frosty blue eyes wander around the room.

"No sign in here," said Reeves. He shrugged and slowly holstered his gun. "Take down your hands," he told Steve. "Looks like you're tellin' the truth. I hope so, for your sake. If I ketch you with that damned outlaw, or find you mixed up in any crooked business on this range, I'll ride you twice as hard. It don't set kindly with me to have an owl-hoot buzzard make a monkey outa me."

Steve lowered his arms, stretched them, grinned thinly.

"Thanks for nothing. And now, I'll tell you all something. I don't take kindly to being spied on. If I start rambling around looking for a piece of land to buy, I don't want any rannies fogging my trail back where their dust hangs low. Give me my gun and make yourselves at home or drift on. It's all the same."

"Give him his gun," said Caleb Reeves.

The long-waisted cowman at the sheriff's right surrendered Steve's six-gun in silence.

Reeves's cold blue eyes rested on Steve for a moment, while the possemen drifted toward the door.

"I don't know what to make of you," said Reeves. "You talk big." Reeves fingered his mustache, shrugged and decided, "If you stay around, I'll make up my mind."

The sheriff strode out. Buster Davis let Steve see his scowl before leaving.

In the doorway Steve watched them fork leather and gallop down the slope, across the dry wash and up the other slope into the piñons. And when the last man was gone and the noise of their passing had died away, Steve kicked viciously at a rusty sardine tin, and bitterly addressed a buzzard wheeling in slow circles over the piñons behind the cabin.

"Why in hell did something like this have to happen?" he asked bitterly. "Now I've got to stick my head in a noose, or figure myself a skunk. I might have known better than to come back this way."

II

"BROTHER JACK"

Costerville lay in the southeast, where the flood-scoured channel of Hatchet Creek came out of the gullied foothills. Steve rode into the northeast, leading the gray pack mare.

The sun was dropping to the jagged crest of the Jawbone range, some forty miles across the lowlands. Steve rode leisurely through the piñon ridges. Now and then he watched behind. Once he tied the pack mare and circled back to watch the back trail in the fast-fading light. No one seemed to be following.

Miles north of Costerville, where the road began a tortuous climb to the rimrock above, and Paloma Creek came tumbling out of a narrow, rocky cañon, there was a rambling log building backed by corrals and two open-front sheds. A crudely lettered sign over the door said: **Brother Jack, Eats**.

Steve remembered the place. A Mexican had owned it years back, and the Mexican's father before him. Travelers off the rimrock, heading toward Costerville, usually stopped to fill their belts. Going the other way, travelers were glad to stop before making the hard climb to the rimrock and the dry *malpais* country to the north.

Tonight the moon was not yet up over the rimrock when Steve dropped stiffly out of the saddle and tied his horses to the sagging hitchrail.

A buggy, two wagons, half a dozen saddled horses were already at the hitchrail. Loud laughter and talk came through the open door. Tall and stringy, Steve had to stoop when he passed through the door. He squinted against the light and looked around the small, low-ceilinged room.

A man in old sheepskin chaps was tilted back against the wall in a chair held together by wire. He lowered a crumpled newspaper and stared as the stranger entered. On the wall over his head was tacked a yellowed piece of cardboard crudely lettered in red paint.

WELCOME BROTHER, SIN NOT

Other signs were on the log walls.

PEACE TO ALL
REST WITH BROTHER JACK
FRIENDS BE FRIENDS IN HERE
NO CUSSIN PLEASE

Other men were clustered at a plank bar across one end of the room, with whisky glasses and beer bottles before them.

A pretty, black-eyed Mexican girl collecting soiled dishes from a table paused and eyed Steve with approval as he went to the bar.

"Howdy, men," Steve said.

They nodded. One or two greeted him. He spoke to the tall, bearded man behind the bar.

"Got another bottle of beer, mister?"

"Brother, I got a barrel full of bottles," was the sonorous reply. "Here's one that just come up outa the crick. It's good an' cold."

Steve set down the foam-wet bottle half empty and grinned.

"That lays the dust where it's needed."

The man at Steve's right, broad-shouldered, powerful, young looking despite his square-cut, reddish beard, commented:

"You look like you been travelin' through plenty of dust. Come off the *malpais*?"

"Nope, I cut across by Jawbone Mountain."

"Plenty dusty over that way, eh?"

"Plenty."

Brother Jack, behind the bar, rested two big gnarled hands on the age-blackened planks. An old man, Brother Jack was still huge despite the stoop bowing his powerful shoulders. The bushy beard that covered his face and fell down over his chest was dirty white; and the beard grew up past his ears and high up on his cheeks and a drooping mustache hid his mouth. Bushy eyebrows tangled on jutting eye ridges under which large, unwinking eyes stared mildly.

And above the bulging forehead there was no hair, only a polished, leather-colored dome which gleamed in the lamplight. That high, polished skull above the white beard gave Brother Jack a commanding, patriarchal look, and his deep, slow voice seemed to come from a chest that had no bottom.

He said mildly: "Jawbone Mountain's kinda off the trails around here, brother. You musta come up from the border."

"I've been down thataway," Steve admitted.

"Ridin' on north?"

"I'm ridin' ham an' eggs an' fried spuds an' coffee, if you got 'em."

Brother Jack nodded.

"Josita!" he called. "Tell yore old lady to hot up some ham an' fixin's."

"*Sí, señor*," answered Josita meekly. She vanished into a back kitchen with the wet rag she had been using on the table.

Steve ate ravenously, trading smiles with the saucy-eyed Josita who hovered near the table for a time.

Two of the customers went out and a wagon rattled away.

The man with the reddish beard leaned over the end of the bar and talked to Brother Jack in an undertone. From the corner of his eye, Steve caught them both looking at him. Presently the red-bearded man walked out and the pound of his galloping horse vanished in the night.

Brother Jack lifted the hinged end of the counter and came to the table.

"Grub all right, brother?" he inquired.

"Suits me," said Steve, putting down the tin cup of coffee.

"Ridin' on tonight?"

"That depends," said Steve. "I'm looking for a friend of mine who came this way."

Brother Jack stroked his beard. "Lots of folks come this way. Maybe he'll be along tonight. What's his name?"

"Smoky Davis," said Steve, dropping his voice.

For an instant the huge, gnarled hand paused on the dirty white beard. Then the fingers combed gently in, and the leathery dome of Brother Jack's skull caught the lamplight as he shook his head.

"Don't know the fellow," he stated mildly.

"Didn't say you did," said Steve casually as he scraped a piece of bread around the plate. "I reckon he's been here, if somebody ain't put a bullet in him, and that isn't too likely. He's a short fellow, good looking, talks quiet and soft. Riding a roan with a white blaze on its nose."

"Friend, you say, brother?"

Steve nodded.

"How long have you known him?"

"Long enough."

"Long enough for what, brother?"

"Long enough to be looking for him," said Steve calmly.

Brother Jack sat down at the side of the table and smoothed his beard tranquilly.

"You sure this here friend of your'n was by here, brother?"

"Smoky started here an' I reckon he got here," said Steve, reaching for the tobacco bag in his shirt pocket. "Smoky's that kind of a fellow."

"If he shows up," said Brother Jack, "I'll tell him you were here."

Steve flipped a match alight. "It might be better, brother," he suggested, "if you tell me where Smoky is now. I've got business with Smoky, and I don't aim to be put off by any psalm-talking mossy-horn with a mattress on his face. Do you follow me, brother?"

Brother Jack combed his beard with his fingers. His chest lifted in a sigh.

"Son," he muttered, "when I was a young 'un, I didn't like talk like that."

"I reckon you don't like it now," said Steve. "Where's Smoky?"

"I told you. . . . "

"Never mind telling me again." Steve leaned forward, speaking calmly under his breath. "Smoky told me he knew you from away back. Never mind heaving dust in my face. It don't matter a damn to me why you're covering up for Smoky, but I aim to see him."

"Brother, I'm an old man. . . ."

"You'll be a damn sight older when I get through with you, if you don't come through about Smoky," said Steve evenly.

"That ain't no way to talk to me, brother."

Brother Jack's big, gnarled hand smoothed the under side of his beard, and flicked out and rested on the table. And all but concealed under the gnarled fingers was a runty little double-barreled derringer that had come from some hiding spot under the beard.

Brother Jack said apologetically: "There's times I forget myself. I'm only a pore sinner, but I don't take to bein' backed in a corner when I'm tryin' to do my best."

Steve grinned.

"Brother Jack," he said, "you have converted me. The pot is yours, an' now what?"

"Son," said Brother Jack, putting both elbows on the table and dropping his other hand over the derringer, "you talk reasonable. I find myself likin' you and forgivin' yore hasty ways. If yo're a friend of Smoky Davis's, yo're a friend of mine. That's from the heart, brother, from the heart of Brother Jack."

"Brother Jack," said Steve, "you move me deeply. But where in hell is Smoky?"

There was a call from the bar. "More beer, Jack!"

Brother Jack's deep voice bellowed from the depths of his beard, while his eyes stayed on Steve's face.

"Gregorio! Tend bar, I'm busy right now!"

The stolid young man who came from the back of the building was hardly more than a boy, a year or so older than the pretty Josita, and somewhat of a dandy, with his grease-slicked black hair, tight trousers, and a gaily embroidered vest.

Steve wondered about him and the pretty Mexican girl. And the mother who was back there in the kitchen. Were they the Mexican family that had lived here in years past? And if they were, how did Brother Jack happen to be running the place?

But at the moment that didn't matter. Brother Jack was speaking softly in his beard.

"Yore friend Smoky was here. But he's gone. I don't look for him back."

"Where'd he go?"

"Are you sure it's important, brother?"

"Plenty important."

"It's a right smart ride to where Smoky is," said Brother Jack reflectively. "I ain't sure he'll be there when you get there. But I'll tell you, son, an' hope for the best. I'll have to draw you a map. It's

over by Lariat Cañon, on the edge of the *malpais* back of
Costerville."

"I know the place," said Steve.

Brother Jack's heavy eyebrows lifted. "You live around here?"

"I used to, when I was a kid."

"You ain't been around here lately, I take it. I've never seen you
before."

"That's right," said Steve.

"You know how to get there," said Brother Jack. "Go to Lariat
Cañon, where the Twin Rocks is. A couple of miles up, there's a
little side cañon. Smoky oughta be camped there."

"What's he doing there?"

"Smoky didn't tell me his plans, son," said Brother Jack mildly.
"That's all I can do for you. Step up to the bar an' have a bottle of
beer. You got plenty of time to be ridin' yet. The grub is on me, too,
brother. I like yore style."

The Mexican boy vanished into the kitchen. While Steve was
drinking the beer, Brother Jack walked back there, too. He returned
with a paper-wrapped package.

"Here's some grub for you, son. You might get hungry 'long
about midnight."

Steve stacked two silver dollars on the counter.

"No offense meant for refusing the treat. Thanks for the grub. It's
more'n I expected. *Adios.*"

Brother Jack lifted his hand in a gesture that was almost a
benediction.

"Good-bye, brother," he said sonorously. "A pleasant ride to you."

Steve went out, puzzled. There was a queer character. Smoky
Davis had been vague about Brother Jack. One thing was certain,
despite his meekness, the old man could take care of himself.

What was Smoky doing up Lariat Cañon? Why had he pushed
on alone, apologetically, as if no business was more important than
a visit to Brother Jack?

Steve had the lead rope and the reins of the sorrel in one hand
and was reaching for the stirrup with the other when a whisper
came out of the night behind him.

"*¡Señor!*"

She was a slim, vague figure in the moonlight, wary, frightened.
She watched the open door fearfully as she stepped close.

"What is it?" Steve asked under his breath.

"*Señor*, don' go, don' go!"

"Why not?"

"Gregorio hees ride ahead."

"Gregorio gone to the cañon?"

"*Sí.*"

"Why?"

"They keel you, *señor*."

"Who'll kill me?"

"*Señor*, don' go! An' eef you see thees Smoky, tell heem Josita thanks him."

She was gone, a flitting, silent shadow, back behind the building.

Steve swore softly, hesitated, half minded to return to the bar. But that would mean trouble for the girl. He rode off, testing his belt-gun and the rifle in the saddle boot by his leg.

III

"DRY-GULCHER'S PAYOFF"

The Twin Rocks were slender spires where the weather-gutted, eroded *malpais* land dropped down into Lariat Cañon. Under the full moon the rocks were visible long before Steve reached them. They were a landmark. A rough trail dropped down at that point into the cañon.

Before riding down, Steve turned in the saddle and looked off into the southwest. Those faint lights on the lower lands were Costerville, seven or eight miles away. Costerville, on Hatchet Creek. This was a strange place for Smoky Davis to be. Up Lariat Cañon was nothing.

It was also strange that Smoky Davis had gone to see Brother Jack. It was strange that Smoky had ridden on to this bleak, deserted cañon above Costerville. And there was the warning of Josita! Her voice had trembled with earnestness. She had believed she was telling the truth. But she was hardly more than a kid and Smoky Davis had proved himself in the past. There'd be no dry-gulching of Steve Cochrane while Smoky Davis was near.

Brother Jack evidently didn't know that. He had played his cards wrong. Smiling thinly, Steve led the pack mare down the rough trail to the cañon floor, along which a tumbling thread of water burbled snake-like. In the black shadows and quiet, the shod hoofs of the horses rang loudly. But Smoky would be expecting him.

Steve knew the cañon, knew every mile of this country, and it seemed to him that the ghost of another rider kept pace up the cañon, a barefoot boy on a bareback pony, eagerly exploring here on the fringe of the *malpais*.

Then the narrow mouth of the pocket cañon yawned just ahead on the right. When Steve came opposite, he saw the wink of a fire back in a rock-walled pocket hardly more than an acre in size. Back in there were horses, half a dozen at least, picketed near the fire.

Their heads lifted, ears pricked toward Steve. But no men were visible.

"Smoky!" Steve called.

His answer was a crashing gunshot from the rocky slope behind him. A cold flick against his left arm was followed by a loud whinny of pain from the gray pack mare as she staggered and tore the lead rope out of Steve's fingers. The pack mare had walked up abreast when Steve had stopped. She was between Steve and the little side cañon, and Steve was between the mare and gunmen behind him. The bullet had gouged Steve's arm, traveled on downward and struck the mare high in the neck, near the skull.

She staggered, lurched to her knees, rolled on her side, kicking. And Steve barely saw that as the sorrel leaped ahead under slashing spurs.

Josita had been right. This was death, death from behind, grimly without warning. And if Smoky had a hand in it, there was no trust and honor to friendship, no one to whom any man could turn for safety.

The pack mare had fallen inside the belt of shadow near the cañon wall. Steve was out in the white, flooding moonlight. He yanked the sorrel toward that shadow belt as he bolted up the cañon. If Smoky and the other riders off those picketed horses were ambushed up in the rocks, their guns would be reaching for him.

A second bullet struck the sorrel as Steve heard the whiplike crack of the shot. And the sorrel plunged down, too. Steve kicked his feet from the stirrups, snatched for the rifle as he launched himself from the saddle. He landed in a staggering, stumbling run, the rifle muzzle trailing in the sand behind. Instinctively he gripped the smooth wooden stock hard. Without the rifle, and afoot, he had no chance.

The sorrel rolled heavily on the sand and rocks. Here the cañon wall was sheer. There was no cover. Steve spun around in a dodging crouch, shaking the rifle to clear any sand from the muzzle.

Sparks flew as the sorrel kicked against small boulders. And a third rifle shot drove a bullet smashing into the rocky wall behind Steve. A wet gurgling sound came from the sorrel's mouth. It died there, and lay still with blood gushing from its nostrils. Steve threw himself down behind the horse.

The mare was still kicking, trying to get up. But she was dying, too. A fourth shot thudded hollowly into the sorrel's belly. Steve caught a saddle string and pushed it into the rifle muzzle to make sure no clogging sand would split the barrel wide.

The barrel was clear. He pumped a shell into the breech. His eyes were narrowed, calculating. No storm of lead, no fusillade of shots had come from that nest of rocks across the cañon. Four shots only, spaced close together, in the time a fast shooting man might lever shells into his rifle and throw down in quick aim.

One man! If more men were up there, they would have been shooting by now. No matter where the other men were. They might be coming fast, might be closing in from both sides. But at the moment, one man!

Steve peered cautiously past the saddle. The moonlight played on the rocks where the lone gunman hid. He must have counted on dropping his victim with the first shot. Now he was trapped up there himself, couldn't go up or down or show himself.

A fifth shot blasted, and Steve saw the wink of light low down between two big boulders, and he knew where his man was, and it was an easy shot. Steve sighted carefully. The other man would be straining his eyes, getting ready for another shot, would be exposing himself between those two boulders, not sure whether his victim was down for good or not.

Steve squeezed the trigger before the sixth shot came, before the man had time to dodge back to safety. He fired low, where the crouching figure of a peering man would be. There was no cry of pain. Steve fancied he saw a flurry of movement back of the boulders, thought he heard metal strike against rock. Then the silence of death fell over the cañon. Even the gray mare lay quiet now.

He waited, and it seemed that the slow, hard beats of his heart must be audible. The sixth shot did not come. The quiet seemed to press down like a heavy weight. Then a grating cry rang out with uncanny clearness.

"I'm dyin'! Do somethin' for me!"

"You asked for it!" Steve called. "Don't think I'm damned fool enough to walk out there and get potted!"

The man strangled, coughed audibly. "I'm holed, I tell you!"

"Crawl out in the open if you're that bad, you snake!" Steve ordered.

"I cain't move!"

But the stranger did move, with a flopping, twisting motion that brought his body out into view beside a boulder. He slipped, fell, rolled down in plain sight before another rock stopped him.

"Don't move!" Steve called.

He ran across the cañon, rifle cocked, ready, and climbed up the slope. And before he reached the prone figure, he knew this was no trickery. The man was strangling again when Steve bent over him. Dark blood was on his lips in the moonlight. He was half doubled up, clutching his middle.

"I'm all tore up inside!" he gasped. "In my belly an' chest!"

His mustache was black, and he wore rawhide chaps and a leather vest, and a stubble of black beard covered his thin face.

And his eyes seemed to bulge in a frightened stare as the moonlight struck against them.

"Lemme see," said Steve.

The bullet had struck the gunbelt buckle and ranged up through the stomach, probably into the chest. Men did not get well from wounds like this.

"You fixed me, didn't you, fella?"

"I reckon so," agreed Steve heavily. Regret made him gruff. "Why'n hell did you dry-gulch me that way?"

The wounded man did not answer.

"That Mex boy brought word from Brother Jack I was coming, didn't he?"

The man nodded, groaned: "I shoulda told that Mex to go to hell. I mighta known it was bad luck to drop a stranger like that."

"Why'd you want to kill me?"

The answer was surprising. "Damned if I know. You was bringin' trouble, the Mex kid said."

"I was lookin' for Smoky Davis."

"He ain't here."

"Where'd he go?"

Blood was getting in the throat, choking, cutting off air from the chest. The man got his throat clear and lay panting for a moment.

"All I want is to find Smoky Davis," said Steve.

"He's in town."

"Costerville?"

"Yep."

"What's he doin' there?"

"He's with the boys."

"What boys?"

"Hell, stranger," was the weak counter, "doncha know nothin'?"

"I'm Smoky Davis's pardner, that's all I know."

"He's in Costerville." The man began to choke again.

Steve waited.

"Who else is around here?" he questioned, after a moment.

"Nobody."

Steve had to bend close to hear that hoarse, labored whisper. It didn't make sense.

"What's Smoky doing in Costerville? When's he coming back out here?"

The wounded man was gasping, rattling in his throat. He turned half over, leaned back, seemed to relax peacefully. When Steve lifted one of the bloody hands, it came limply, and fell soggily.

Steve's arm was bleeding slowly. The wound wasn't deep. He rolled up the shirt sleeve, tied his bandanna over the furrow, rolled down the sleeve again, and put on his coat. With a little effort he got the saddle off the dead sorrel. The gray mare and the pack would have to stay here. The picketed horses in the little pocket cañon eyed him curiously as he lugged the saddle to them. One already was saddled.

Steve picked out a powerful black horse and cinched on the saddle. The horse might have been rustled, might be recognized by an owner in Costerville, but the risk had to be faced. The black was fresh, full of fire; Steve let him have his head down the cañon, away from that spot of death.

IV

"LARIAT CAÑON"

Costerville had grown larger. But the same main street was there, with the small brick courthouse and jail under the cottonwoods at one end. The church had a new coat of paint and a spire. There were more houses and stores and saloons than Steve recalled. Now, an hour and a half before midnight, hitchracks still were full; stores were open for business.

Steve remembered that this was Saturday night. The town would be awake until well after midnight.

He rode the length of the street, and saw no sign of Smoky. He hitched the horse at one of the courthouse racks and started back afoot to search saloons and stores. And he was wary, tense as he went. That furtive signal that had gone on ahead to ambush and kill him was warning enough that Smoky was flirting with trouble.

Ten minutes later Steve stepped out of Thad Stephens's General Store. Caleb Reeves, the sheriff, was waiting on the walk, thumbs hooked in his gunbelt and a stony, suspicious look on his seamed face.

"So yo're in town now?" said the sheriff.

"Your eyes are right," said Steve.

"One of the boys said he seen you down the street. You seem to be lookin' for something."

The last time I saw this street," said Steve, "I was only a kid. Tonight I'm taking a good look again."

Reeves bent closer. "That a bullet hole in yore coat sleeve?"

The blood had not soaked through; the bandanna underneath was holding it in now.

"That's a bullet hole," Steve admitted. "Some day I'll have it patched."

"Where'd you get it?"

"Ever hear of Torquemado?"

"Nope," denied Reeves suspiciously.

"Then there isn't any use tellin' you," said Steve calmly. "Too bad I wasn't wearin' this coat when your posse jumped me. You could have asked more questions."

Reeves chewed the end of his tobacco-stained mustache, frowning under the broad hat brim.

"I still ain't made up my mind about you, Cochrane. But it don't set too well to see you here in Costerville. Some buzzards are evidently figurin' I'm too old to back up a sheriff's badge an are hornin' in on this range. I'm proddy about it, Cochrane."

Steve grinned thinly. He was as tall as the sheriff, so that their eyes were level. They faced each other across a gulf of years, with a wariness that had all the tension of cocked triggers.

"You always were proddy about outlaws," said Steve.

"I always will be, mister." Reeves clenched a fist. His voice grew harsh. "I'm livin' to get all the outlaws I can while I'm alive. Remember that, Cochrane, while I'm makin' up my mind about you."

"You make it plain, anyway," said Steve. "Have you found your man from Jawbone Mountain?"

"If he stays on the Pie River range, I'll get him," promised Reeves. "An' I'll bring him back in a wagon with his boots on. Watch yore step, Cochrane!"

Caleb Reeves strode away, a tall, wiry, bitter man. Steve searched again, listening for an eruption of gunfire. If Smoky was in town, and was recognized, gunplay would follow.

More than one face was familiar. But Steve was not the boy who had left Costerville. No one recognized him.

A man with a square-cut reddish beard walked diagonally across the dusty street. Steve watched him enter the liveliest saloon on the other side of the street. Years ago the spot had been a vacant lot. Steve crossed the street also. That square-cut reddish beard had leaned over Brother Jack's dirty bar in low-voiced conversation with Brother Jack.

The Stag Bar was still busy, despite the late hour and riders and wagons and buggies leaving town. The bar sign was lettered: **R. B. Davis, Prop**. Steve was in the swinging doors before the name struck him. Robert Davis had been the school name of Buster Davis.

The reddish-bearded stranger was ordering a drink. He saw Steve's reflection in the bar mirror and turned. Their eyes met. The red-bearded man flicked a glance to the rear of the room, and back to Steve. His teeth showed.

"Have a drink, mister?"

"Thank you, no."

At one of the back tables Smoky was sitting, face to the door, unconcernedly finishing a game of solitaire. Two empty beer bottles were at his elbow. Smoky looked up as Steve reached the table. Smoky's lean, cheerful face was blank. He gave no sign of recognition as he scooped up the cards and began to riffle the deck.

"Get the hell outa here," Smoky said when Steve sat down.

"You damned idjut!" said Steve under his breath. "*You* get out of town. There's a pack of trouble pilin' up for you!"

Smoky did not look up. "Don't be seen talking to me. I'm bad medicine tonight, Steve."

"You don't have to tell me," said Steve. "I was looking for you up at Brother Jack's place. He sent me on to Lariat Cañon and sent word ahead to put a bullet in me. I killed the fellow who laid for me."

Smoky cut the cards, stacked them again, and started to deal a new layout.

"You kilt him?"

"He opened up on me from behind. Nicked my arm and got both my horses!"

"Anybody else up there in the cañon now?"

"Hell's fire, no! Didn't you hear me say one of your friends opened up at my back with a gun? What kind of business is this?"

"Keep your voice down," warned Smoky. His own voice was strained, wooden. Smoky looked different. His face might have been cut from a block of stone.

"Are you tied up with that red-bearded gent at the bar?"

"Plenty," said Smoky, hardly moving his lips.

"And with this Brother Jack?"

"You might say so."

"And your sitting there not batting an eye when I tell you what happened?"

"Will you high-tail out of here?" said Smoky through his teeth. "Some day I'll tell you all about it."

Steve felt the blood pounding in his temples as anger grew hot and strong inside.

"Listen, Smoky! We've been pardners. You saved my life down on the border. I owe you plenty for it. We were aiming to drift in here and buy us a ranch and settle down."

"Tell me about it later," said Smoky in the strange, flat voice. Little drops of perspiration were appearing on Smoky's forehead.

"This afternoon," said Steve, "a sheriff's posse jumped me at that adobe shack. They were looking for you. That man we met over by Jawbone Mountain a couple of days ago spotted you as the one who held up the stage here a couple of years ago. I talked 'em off, and rode to this Brother Jack's where you said you were going. The stage didn't matter. I took you as you were since we met up.

"I tried to find you and warn you to get going before a posse gives you noose law. And all I got was a bullet at my back and you trying to run me out now. What are you up to, Smoky? The sheriff has halfway decided I'm an outlaw. If I'm going to have the name, I'm going to know what's behind it."

Smoky looked past Steve, to the bar. A low groan of helplessness burst from him and he dropped the cards, pushed back the chair, stood up, and his hand was on the gun at his side.

"I didn't want this to happen!" husked Smoky. "Stand back, Steve! Hell is due to pop!"

Smoky's eyes were on the bar. Steve turned, taut with apprehension at what he saw on Smoky's face. He hadn't seen Buster Davis come in. But Buster was there behind the bar, at the back, where the gold-scrolled door of a massive iron safe stood ajar. The red-bearded man, and two other men among the customers whom Steve had not noticed, had stepped back into the clear with drawn guns.

The red-bearded man barked a preëmptory order: "Lift 'em, boys, an' you won't get hurt!"

Buster Davis made the mistake of trying to dodge down behind the bar. Smoky's gun roared. Buster staggered against the back bar, his shoulder drooping queerly, while Smoky jumped toward the safe.

"Smoky!" Steve called involuntarily.

The red-bearded man swung on him with quick fury. "Do I have to drop you?"

"Lay off him, Red!" Smoky gritted. "He's with me!"

"Why'n hell didn't you say so? Tell him to get his gun out an' get to work!"

The swinging doors burst open. One of the townsmen looked in to see what the shooting was about. A bullet drove him tumbling back outside. Steve hardly saw it. He was looking at the sneering fury on Buster Davis's face. Buster spoke to him across the bar, while the echo of the shot was still ringing in their ears.

"I knew you was a damned outlaw! Too bad we didn't string you up this afternoon! But we'll get you!"

"Shut up!" Smoky threw over his shoulder.

Smoky had jerked the safe door wide, was clawing open the inner door. From under his shirt he took a stout cloth sack. In it he dropped a money bag that lay on the floor and he swept in gold and bills and silver stacked inside the safe. It took only seconds, and in that time shouts were rising outside. Denver Red and his men were edging toward the back of the room, watching the door.

"Come on, Steve!" rapped Smoky.

Steve drew his gun with a bitter, crooked smile at this twist of fate. Gun killings were not new; holdups he had seen; he had traded shot for shot with men who laughed at death. But this had the harsh mirth of a cruel joke. In sixty seconds, against his will and knowledge, he had been turned into an outlaw. Smoky had tried to stop him. Smoky had tried to explain, and the swift rushing tide of carefully planned action had engulfed them both. Now it was, take it outlaw style or hang.

Two swift shots sounded back of the building.

"Make it fast!" rapped Smoky coolly.

Steve followed him through a narrow hall to the back door. The other three gunmen backed after them.

A sharp voice addressed Smoky as he reached the night: "They're comin'!"

A rider was holding four saddled horses. Smoky turned his head. "Where's yore horse, Steve?"

"In front of the courthouse!"

"Hit it behind me!"

Tumult broke out in the saloon as the three gunmen ran out and dived for their horses.

Around the corner of the building a harsh familiar voice shouted: "They're back here, boys!"

That was Caleb Reeves. And as they thundered off in the moonlight along the alley behind the buildings, Steve glimpsed the old sheriff's tall figure backing the blistering streaks of a blasting gun. Roaring guns from the flying saddles did not stop him. One of the outlaws pitched to the ground.

"Leave him there!" Smoky yelled. "They'll be down on us like hornets in a minute!"

Smoky led the retreat around in front of the courthouse. Here was quiet, peace for a moment as Smoky jerked his horse into a rearing stop. Steve flung himself toward his horse, tore the reins from the hitchrack, and hit the leather as the horse bolted forward. He was thundering up beside Smoky a moment later, and the retreat swept on out of town. Behind them men were shouting; guns were firing; horses were drumming as the first hasty pursuit gathered and roared after them.

They headed toward Lariat Cañon, toward the *malpais* country, the foothills, the mountains on beyond. And the pace was killing. No horse could stand this thundering, breakneck speed for long. The Costerville men seemed to realize it; they saved their horses, dropping farther behind. Their riding had a careful grim tenacity.

But they didn't know about those fresh, strong mounts picketed in Lariat Cañon. They didn't know this killing ride to the cañon would put the outlaws on fresh horses which could draw away with ease. And it happened that way.

The fire in the little side cañon had burned down to a few red coals. The dead pack mare and the dead sorrel were there on the rocks, and only the dead man's silent eyes watched the quick shifting of saddles and a fresh leg of the retreat begun. Smoky curtly explained the dead horses and missing guard.

"Joe tangled with my pardner here. He's dead. Forget about him."

The red-bearded man was the only one who made a comment. "Yore friend seems to be in it every way we turn."

"Which is my business, Red!" retorted Smoky coldly. "I'm givin' orders till the payoff. Shut up!"

Still ahead of the pursuit they rode easily up Lariat Cañon. The cañon floor mounted steadily, and presently the walls grew lower, and after a time they were out in the full moonlight spreading over the gullied, eroded, tortuous *malpais* sweep.

Smoky drew rein on a low ridge from which they could see in all directions.

"There's enough moonlight to see," said Smoky. "We'll split here an scatter."

A coat was spread on the ground. The bag was emptied on it. A hasty count and division were made. There was over six thousand dollars.

"That Davis fellow," explained Smoky to Steve, "owns a big general store down the street, an' another saloon where there's gamblin'. Folks leave money in his safe until the bank opens on Monday morning. He's had a habit of pickin' up the last money an' puttin' it in his safe just about the time he did tonight. He's been askin' for a holdup. They've got too used to dependin' on that prod-headed old sheriff."

"You planned everything out pat," Steve commented colorlessly.

"Yeah," agreed Smoky, counting money swiftly. "Two of the boys are dead. That leaves four piles. Here's yores, Red. Lefty, there you are. We'll scatter out from here. It's every *hombre* for himself."

The red-bearded man stuffed handfuls of coins and bills in his coat pocket.

"I'll string along with you," he decided. "I'm goin' the same place you are."

"Yore mistake," refused Smoky. "We're splittin' up."

"I told Jack I'd come in with you."

"You mean Jack told you to stick close to me," said Smoky, straightening up. "He's so crooked he can't trust himself, but I'm tellin' you what to do!"

"Have it yore own way," was the sulky reply.

V
"OWL-HOOT MAVERICK"

They split up there, fanning out in different directions without farewells. Smoky sat in the saddle till the red-bearded man was beyond gunsight, and then grunted to himself as he lifted the reins and rode off.

"That Denver Red is a mean one," said Smoky.

Steve said nothing.

Smoky looked across in the moonlight. "Sorta feelin' that way about me, ain't you, Steve?"

"No," denied Steve. "I reckon you know what you're doing. When I take a man for a pardner, I take him for bad and good. And you saved my life once."

"We're clean on that. Forget it. I reckon we split up now. If you want to cut off on your own from here, it's all right. I'll understand. I owe you plenty of thanks for tryin' to save me from a tight tonight."

"You're still in a tight," said Steve. "Reeves, the sheriff, ain't a man to take his teeth out of a thing like this."

"He's just a sheriff," said Smoky. "I've handled better sheriffs than he'll ever be. Soon as I turn this money over, I'm ridin' an' I won't be back on this range."

"That goes for both of us."

"I'm sorry, Steve. When I was makin' plans with you, I didn't know all this'd break."

"This Brother Jack is behind it?"

"Yes," admitted Smoky glumly. He cursed. "I'd have killed him if it'd done any good. But this was the only way."

"You didn't have to do this to get money, Smoky. I had enough to get a small ranch. All you needed to do was tell me you were busted."

"I had money."

"I don't savvy this then."

"You never will understand, I guess," said Smoky heavily. "Steve, we never talked about the past. You never asked me questions."

"The past is your own business."

"It's yours now, I guess," said Smoky. "Steve, this ain't nothin' new to me. I was an outlaw before I met you."

"The sheriff's posse made that plain this afternoon."

"There's a hell of a lot of things they didn't make plain," said Smoky. "It goes away back, Steve, back almost as far as I can remember. I wasn't even five years old when I hit the outlaw trail."

"You started pretty young," Steve remarked dryly.

"I can just remember two folks who must have been my parents," said Smoky. "A woman who held me a lot an' musta loved me a lot. And a big man who used to laugh a heap an' play with me. Sometimes I dream about her, Steve, bendin' over my little bed and smilin' down at me. Hell, Steve, do you remember your mother?"

"Yes," said Steve.

"That's all the memory I've got," said Smoky, and there was a strange, wistful hunger in his voice. "The rest of it starts with a man named Dirk Johnson an' the women at Pyote Springs."

"Never heard of the place."

"You wouldn't," said Smoky. "Strangers weren't welcomed there. It was an outlaw hangout. The women were about what you'd expect. They mothered me a little when they felt like it, and slapped me around when I got in the way. Dirk Johnson used to leave me there for long stretches while he was out riding the owl-hoot.

"One woman had been something better than an outlaw's woman, an' she taught me what schoolin' I've had. And as soon as I could ride a horse an' hold a gun an' cover country, Dirk Johnson took me out with him and saw to it I finished my schoolin' on the owl-hoot."

"A hell of a father," Steve commented.

"He wasn't my father. I didn't know it then. But sometimes he'd stand an' grin at me, nasty-like, as if he was rollin' somethin' over in his mind that pleased him a lot. An' he had light hair an' I had dark. We didn't look alike. But I'd been an owl-hoot rider for years before I savvied all that. It was natural to me, Steve. I didn't know anything else. You used your brains an' beat the law an' if you didn't get shot up or caught everything was all right."

Steve said nothing.

Smoky rode in silence for a few minutes.

"Dirk," he said finally, "used to beat me an' act so mean when he was drunk, I finally cut away from him. I didn't think much more about him until I landed back in Pyote Springs and got to talking to one of the women who was still around. She told me Dirk Johnson wasn't my father. Dirk had boasted of it when he was drunk. She said Dirk an' another man had showed up with me one day an' said I was Dirk's kid, an' nobody asked any questions."

"Looks like Dirk Johnson was a man for you to look up," said Steve slowly.

"I looked him up," said Smoky. "It took me four years to find him." Smoky's voice grew bitter. "And then Dirk was dyin' from knife wounds he got in a drunken fight. I asked him who I was an' where he got me, an' he laughed at me. He knew he was dyin'. There wasn't anything I could do to make him yellow.

"He told me he'd taken me from my father an' mother for spite, because my mother had married another man an' not him, an' he'd sworn they'd regret it. So he dropped around when I was only a shaver, an' rode away with me. He said he made an outlaw outa me on purpose. He was laughin' about it when he died.

"Steve, I don't know what I mighta been, instead of an owl-hoot rider. All I know is that maybe that woman who smiles down at me in my sleep sometimes, an' that big man who used to pick me up an' play with me, are maybe waitin' around somewheres wonderin' about me. Like . . . like I wonder about *them.*"

In the far distance coyotes were howling mournfully. The moon hung still and white overhead and Smoky's story suddenly made the night seem empty and lonesome.

Awkwardly, Steve said: "Pardner, I'm sorry. What about this other feller?"

"I've been hunting him," said Smoky. "Three years I've been hunting him. At Pyote Springs, he used to call himself Jack Black. He was a bald-headed man. I reckon I've trailed down a thousand bald-headed men, but none of them was Jack Black. Years ago, he was with the Belcher gang for a time, but he left 'em. About two months ago, when we were down in Nogales, I ran across one of the old Pyote Springs men. He said he heard that Jack Black had settled over here in the Pie River Country, on the road north of Costerville."

"And was calling himself Brother Jack," Steve supplied.

"That's right," agreed Smoky. "That was when I suggested we ride this way. And the more you talked about settling down, the better I liked the idea . . . after I'd got to Jack Black and heard what he had to tell me. That's why I left you today, Steve, to get Jack Black in a corner an' get the truth outa him."

"What'd he say?"

"He didn't say. I found him there, an' recognized him behind his beard. He knew me quick enough, too. He'd taken over that place an' married the Mex woman. She'd been right pretty, it seems, before her husband got killed. If you ask me, Jack Black killed him. But that don't matter. There he was, callin' himself Brother Jack, an' he admitted he knew who I was. Said he was with Dirk Johnson when I was taken. An' he offered me a trade. He'd tell me all about it if I'd help him get this money tonight. He had a hunch this wouldn't go off right unless an old hand like myself was leading the party."

"He must've fooled the sheriff all this time," said Steve.

"I reckon so. Jack Black's been carrying on outlaw business under cover ever since he's been here. The owl-hoot knows his place is the right place to stop. But things have been getting a little warm lately. He's ready to quit an' ride on. He needed this money tonight to get away on. So he wouldn't talk unless I helped him out."

"You had a gun, didn't you?"

"He had me hogtied," said Smoky. "He laughed at me, too. He's the only living man who can tell me what I want to know. I couldn't kill him an' never know."

"I guess so," Steve agreed.

"He offered me a cut," said Smoky. "I turned it down. But I said I'd do the job. One more job wouldn't make much difference, I figured. We could get us a ranch somewhere else. So I've done it, an' I'm takin' Jack Black's money to him an' getting my answer. I reckon it'd been all right if you hadn't showed up."

"After you get your answer," said Steve grimly, "I'll stay behind and see Jack Black myself. He played his cards wrong with me. The Mexicans won't be too sorry at what happens, I guess."

"I reckon not," agreed Smoky. "He don't treat 'em too well. There's a pretty girl there, Josita, who's scared to death of him. He aimed a lick at her while we were talking in the back room, an' I knocked his hand up."

"She didn't forget it," Steve remembered. "And Smoky, I'm wishing you luck in what he tells you. I hope that . . . that woman you remember is there waiting for you."

"I'm afraid to hope," confessed Smoky. "It's been a long time. But at least I'll know. It won't be eating down inside day an' night."

"We'd better ride along," suggested Steve. "This Denver Red'll get there with his story about me."

"I think Jack Black an' Denver Red are figuring on pullin' out together. We'll beat Red there," said Smoky, spurring.

VI

"AN OUTLAW'S BARGAIN"

The moon was a great silvery disk that flooded cold light over the night, and Paloma Creek came tumbling out of the rocky cañon with an unceasing murmur. There was only one wagon and a drooping team before the low log building at the base of the rim-rock. Steve reined up some two hundred yards from Jack Black's place.

"I'll come up easy while you have it out," he said.

"It won't take long."

Smoky galloped on. Walking his horse, Steve saw light shine out of the doorway as Smoky entered.

And moments later, off in the night, Steve heard a loping horse cutting across the range from the general direction of Lariat Cañon. A single rider. That would be Denver Red. Steve walked his horse to cut off the rider. The man was close before he pulled up sharply. A gun leaped into his hand.

"That you, Denver Red?"

"Who is it?"

"I'm with Smoky."

"It's you, is it?" said Denver Red unpleasantly. He holstered the gun and rode up. "Where's Smoky?"

"Talking to Jack Black. We'll wait here till they're done."

"Who says we will?"

"You heard me."

"Why, damn you!" exploded Denver Read, streaking for his gun.

Steve outdrew him. The moonlight glinted on his gun as he rapped: "Hold it!"

Denver Red's arms shot up. He swore under his breath. "What's comin' off here?"

"You're comin' off, mister. Keep 'em up, while I get your guns, and then climb down."

Denver Red uttered another oath as he dismounted and his horse bolted away from Steve's slap.

"I don't like you," said Steve, "so take it easy ahead of me with your hands high. Smoky can handle you when he comes out. I've got business with Jack Black."

"What kinda business?" asked Denver Red sullenly.

"The kind that ought to have been done long ago. I'm bringing the wages of sin. Don't walk so fast. We've got plenty of time."

Denver Red's horse was making for the corrals behind the log building. Steve guessed the horse had been there before. Smoky was still inside. He wondered what Smoky was hearing.

Behind a fringe of mesquite brush across the road a horse nickered. Steve realized then his own horse already had pricked ears in that direction.

He demanded: "Anybody else due to show up here with you?"

"Nobody," retorted Denver Red, staring at the spot. His hands came down slowly. "That ain't a stray horse!"

"Keep walking," ordered Steve.

A yell answered him and it was not Denver Red.

"Cut 'em down, boys! This is good enough!"

A rifle cracked spitefully. And the shot might have been the key that loosed the floodgates of hell. A roaring, rising crescendo of shots followed.

A bullet knocked Steve back in the saddle. He felt a second slug tear through his Stetson crown, just above the scalp. For a second time that night a horse staggered under him in a weaving, helpless lurch that told its own story. It all happened instantaneously. Steve was thinking, acting in split seconds while it was happening.

Denver Red was plunging toward Jack Black's building in a dodging run that made him an uncertain target in the moonlight.

Steve twisted down and out of the saddle while his horse still staggered. And once more he took the rifle, dropping Denver Red's guns. The horse screened him for a breath and, as its legs buckled and bullets thudded into its body, Steve raced after Denver Red.

The chance was slim. They were gunning him like a running rabbit. Unless his ears were mistaken that man who had opened fire with a shout was Buster Davis, venomous for a kill. There'd be no mercy. At least part of Caleb Reeves's posse had known where to come.

The night was full of crashing, screaming death. Dust spurted from the road in front of Steve's feet. He heard slugs screaming close. He lost his hat; it felt as if a bullet had knocked it off. A searing lash slapped across the back of his shoulder, and he knew that only his speed had carried him inches ahead of death.

Light gleamed as the door swung open. Smoky's short, compact figure rushed out, behind him the hulking, bearded Jack Black. Back by the road, mesquite was crackling as riders galloped after the two fleeing men, emptying their guns as they came. Denver Red staggered, kept on with a limp. Jack Black plunged back inside. But Smoky stood there. Red streaks licked from his gun.

The wagon team was backing away from the hitchrack. Smoky's horse screamed as a bullet struck it, plunged back, tore the reins free and bolted away.

Denver Red staggered through the lighted doorway as Steve raced up, calling, "Get inside, Smoky!"

Smoky dodged in and slammed the door. A wooden bar was leaning behind the door. Smoky slammed it down into place as Steve knocked the chimney from one of the lamps, extinguished the flame, and made for the other lamp. As the room plunged into darkness, Jack Black yelled in the kitchen.

"They're out by the corral! We're cornered in here!"

Denver Red was groaning and cursing. "You two brought 'em here, damn you!"

Somewhere in back, a woman began to wail in Spanish. The girl, Josita, faltered in the darkness: "*Señor* Smoky, will they keel us?"

"Get down on the floor behind the bar and stay there!" Steve panted at her.

Glass crashed as a bullet bored into the room. Another bullet tore through the plank door. A rifle barked in the kitchen. Jack Black swore aloud with a savageness new to him.

"Got one, by hell!"

Steve broke out a window pane with his rifle muzzle and peered cautiously out. Smoky did the same at another window. The horsemen stopped, retreated to cover. Out there in the night, men were closing in on foot; hugging the ground, they were hard to see.

"Ain't this one hell of a mess?" asked Smoky.

"They might have dropped us out there in the road!"

"They've got us!"

"Looks like it," agreed Steve. "I'm bleeding. My horse is down and yours is gone. Any more around?"

"Some back in the corrals, I think."

"They ain't doin' us any good now." Steve turned his head. "What'd you find out, Smoky? Did he tell you?"

"He said my old man was a preacher over in East Texas," said Smoky in a tight voice. "Wouldn't it have to work out that way? My old man a sky pilot!"

A gun flashed out there in the night. Steve threw a bullet at the spot, didn't know whether he hit the man. The firing had slacked off. The posse was saving ammunition. In the kitchen, Jack Black was pouring shot after shot from the windows. Steve could hear him shifting about, hear his oaths and orders to Denver Red.

"Damn yore leg, Red! Stand up an' fight! I got enough cartridges to keep us goin' all night. Drive 'em away from the corrals! Damn them sheds! I shoulda torn 'em down a long time ago!"

A shout came out of the night.

"Come out with yore hands in the air! You'll get a fair trial in court!"

Steve answered. "There ain't any doubt what the trial'll be like!"

"That you, Cochrane?"

"That's me."

"Yo're a damned lyin' outlaw!" called Caleb Reeves from a depression nearby, where he was invisible. "But you was raised around here. You know I back up my word. You'll all get a fair trial. There'll be no vigilante mob stringing you up."

Smoky shouted, "Your sheriff's noose fits just as tight! Come in an' get us!"

"We'll burn you out!" roared Caleb Reeves. "An' gun you when you come runnin' out from the fire. This is yore last chance!"

"There's women in here!" Steve called.

"Send 'em out! They'll be safe enough!"

"Josita!" Steve said, turning from the window. "Get your mother an' any other women an' walk out."

Only the two women were inside. They were both weeping as Steve unbarred the front door, let them slip quickly out, and barred the door again. Guns were silent while they ran to safety.

"Brother Jack," called Caleb Reeves, "yo're tarred with the same stick. I've had my ideas about you for some time. That bunch that held up the Stag Bar in town was seen in yore place earlier tonight, talkin' with you! Are you fightin' it out with 'em, or will you take a chance with the law?"

"I'll talk it over with you, Reeves," Jack Black called out. "Walk up to the front of the building. I'll step out with my hands up. If there's any double-crossin', you can gut-shoot me an' even the score."

Advice from the posse was audible.

"Don't do it, Caleb! It's a damned trick!"

"You can't trust snakes like that, Caleb!"

Jack Black called: "Are you afraid of a man with his hands in the air?"

"There ain't an outlaw livin' I'm afraid of!" shouted Reeves. "If yo're workin' a trick, the posse'll get you. I'm a-comin'. Step out in front with yore hands in the air!"

Denver Red protested bitterly as Jack Black left the kitchen. "You won't have any luck talkin', Jack. Are you crazy?"

"Watch them back windows!" Jack ordered. "I know what I'm doin'!"

"What are you doing?" Steve demanded as the big bearded man unbarred the front door.

Jack Black chuckled. It sounded malevolent with sinister humor.

"I'm fixin' to get us outa here, fellow. Hold yore horses. This ain't the night we hang, or I miss my guess. I always keep out an ace or two in a tight game."

Gunpowder fumes bit at the nostrils; the sudden quiet was almost as sinister as Jack Black's chuckle. The moonlight, flooding down on the dusty road, picked out with eerie clarity the two figures who moved into the open. Jack Black, huge, stoop-shouldered, bearded, hands high by his bald head, and the tall, spare, wary figure of the sheriff, who walked grimly, slowly, through the dusk, gun out, ready. They met near the hitchrack. Each word came clearly through the broken windows.

"What are you tryin' to do?" Caleb Reeves demanded.

Jack Black chuckled. "Talk easy, Sheriff; you got a surprise comin'. Maybe the posse better not know."

"Damn you, what kinda bluff are you runnin'?"

"I've heard about you, Reeves. You wasn't always a sheriff. One of them boys inside left East Texas when he was about five years old, an' never knew who his folks were. Are you willin' to burn him out an' shoot him up?"

"Oh!" Smoky gulped.

Steve hardly heard. He forgot for the moment he was holding a rifle. He was looking out into the moonlight, where Caleb Reeves stood stiff, motionless. It was not possible that one man's voice could hold hope and agony, joy and grief, such as burst from Caleb Reeves.

"My boy, my Jimmy, in there!"

And Smoky's agonized husk: "Steve, Steve! I remember now. She used to call me Jimmy!"

Jack Black said: "Dirk Johnson told me the boy's mother married the wrong man, so he evened the score by takin' the kid and makin' an outlaw outa him. Your own flesh and blood, Reeves, yore own son's in there! Are you a sheriff, or a father?"

There was not light enough to see tears, but Caleb Reeves's voice was strangled. "After all these years, I've got to see him! Jimmy, it's yore dad comin' in!"

Caleb Reeves holstered his gun and walked into the dark room.

"Jimmy, my son. . . ."

Voices from the posse were shouting.

"Caleb, what're you doin' in there?"

"You, Jack, stay out there where we can see you!"

And inside Smoky's voice was husky. "I've been lookin' . . . I never figured it'd be like this . . . trouble like this when I found you. My . . . my mother?"

Caleb Reeves cleared his throat. "Three years after you was taken from us, son."

"I was ready to hear it," said Smoky. "And now, there's no use dodging it. I'm the man who held up the stage a couple of years ago, an' made that play tonight. You're the sheriff. I ain't expectin' anything."

Steve spoke. "He's been tryin' for years to find who his folks were. Jack Black, out there, promised to tell him if he'd clean out that safe tonight. He did it, and Black told him his father was a preacher in East Texas. That's all he knew till you walked up."

Caleb Reeves stood silently in the darkness, and woodenly repeated: "I'm the sheriff."

"You heard me," said Smoky. "I'm not askin' for anything. I've got this comin', I guess."

"When it was plain we'd never get you back," said Caleb Reeves, "I put down my Bible an' took up a gun. My hand has been against all outlaws since then." And out of the past, Caleb Reeves, the man of God, spoke the bitter truth he had once preached. " 'Those that live by the sword, shall die by the sword.' Oh, Lord, this is too heavy a burden to lay on me!"

"The Bible," said Smoky, "ain't never been much to me. But I'll play my own game out. You're the sheriff. You can't quit it now when I've put you in a corner."

"I put my hand on the Bible," said Caleb Reeves, "an' took the oath to carry out the duties. I've shown no favors to any man's son. I can't do it now to mine."

"I'm tryin' to tell you," said Smoky gruffly.

Caleb Reeves gulped harshly. "Light a match, son. Lemme look at your face."

Two matches sparked, flared.

Steve saw them in the glaring little circle of yellow light, father and son, two pale, strained faces staring hungrily at each other. The matches flickered out. The faces vanished.

"You're like your mother," said Caleb Reeves in a low voice. "Goodbye, son. . . ."

Caleb Reeves stumbled against the side of the door as he went out, walking like a blind man.

There was a jeering note of assurance in Jack Black's greeting. "Well, sheriff, do we ride away from here?"

Caleb Reeves stared at him. "You knew this, an' never told me anything about it."

"Do you think I'd be fool enough to do that? I didn't know where he was. You'd a' been smokin' after me with a gun. Are you gonna fix it, Reeves?"

Caleb Reeves straightened. He seemed to tower in the moonlight. The threat in his voice had a scornful, warning edge.

"Stand there till I get to cover! You'll get yore answer quick!"

VII
"THE DEATH CIRCLE"

Jack Black was swearing in his beard when the moment came for him to jump back inside. "What'd he say? What's he gonna do?"

"Kill you!" said Steve. "If we weren't in a tight all here together, I'd do it myself."

"You mean he'll gun his own flesh?"

A shout out in the night gave the answer. "Close in on 'em, boys!"

Jack Black rushed to the back windows as guns began to bark and roar.

Smoky said: "Steve, how can I throw down on them now? I might hit *him*."

"You made your choice. He wouldn't want you to go out like a rabbit."

Smoky's reply was cool. "I reckon so. Here goes hell!"

Bullets were smashing through the plank door, screaming through the windows; bottles crashed behind the bar; the raw smell of whisky spread through the low-ceilinged room.

The posse had spread out in a thin circle, was firing from all sides. Now and then a dark flit of movement showed in the moonlight as a posseman ducked forward to a closer bit of cover. They were moving in, tightening the death circle.

The log building had other rooms. Steve and Smoky moved from window to window, in and out of the rooms, watching all sides. Blood soaked Steve's back. Pain was grinding through his shoulder, but there was no time to waste on such matters. Jack Black passed out fresh boxes of ammunition. Their guns grew hot. Steve ducked behind the bar, knocked off the top of a bottle of beer, and slaked a burning thirst. He carried a bottle to Smoky at one of the front windows.

"Thanks," said Smoky. "Steve, the moon'll be up for hours yet. They must have sent back to town for more men."

"They'll have a hundred men out there in an hour or so," Steve agreed. "Every man in Costerville that can pack a gun will come fast."

"I'm thinking about him," muttered Smoky.

"Think about yourself."

"Hell, I'm a goner already. We all are. I'll say it again, Steve. I'm sorry you got drawn into this."

"Now you're talking like a fool! Look out the window there."

Smoky dropped the beer bottle, whipped his rifle to the window. "What is it?"

"I meant look up, see them clouds drifting in. I've been watching them."

"Pretty, ain't they?" said Smoky ironically. "Cloud gazing won't help you."

"Maybe it will," said Steve. "Those clouds are spotty, but they're drifting steady. They'll be over us in a little while. Maybe one of them'll cover the moon for a few minutes."

"You're grabbing at straws, Steve. Our hosses are gone. If Jack Black's got anything back in the corral, we ain't got a chance to catch it an' get goin'."

"The posse," said Steve calmly, "has got horses over there by the mesquite. The men are scattered out pretty thin right now. If we can get some shadow and run for it, we might have a chance of reaching their horses."

"Uh-huh," said Smoky. And after a moment he added, "It might work, if a cloud gets over the moon an' more men from town aren't here yet, an' if we can buck through 'em an' get to the hosses. About one chance in a thousand, Steve."

"More'n we'll have if we stay here."

"Tell Jack Black about it."

"You're crazy!" was Jack Black's decision in the pitch-hued blackness of the kitchen. "Watch where yo're steppin'. Red stood in front of the window too long an' got one in the face."

The posse was edging closer. Around the thin, imprisoning circle guns kept up a ceaseless, intermittent fire. And it seemed that the clouds had stopped in the sky; that time was rushing past with frantic haste, while more possemen from Costerville were coming fast.

But gradually the first scattered clouds drifted overhead, and behind them crawled other patches of heavier clouds.

"It's coming," said Steve. "Fill your gunbelt, Smoky!"

"I'm ready!" said Smoky tersely.

The white, bright moonlight began to dim, fade away. Shadows grew deeper, blacker outside.

"All right, Smoky!" Steve clipped out, and went into the kitchen. "Coming with us?" he asked Jack Black.

"Hell, yes, I reckon so!"

Gun muzzles were flickering red and clear in the new darkness outside. The corrals were almost invisible now as the high, dark cloud overhead blotted out the moon.

"To the left, toward the mesquite," said Steve. "Every man for himself!"

Steve jerked open the door and dived out, rifle in his left hand, cocked six-gun in his right, and they were instantly three racing shadows.

For a moment or two the possemen did not realize what was happening. Then a yell of warning rang out. A gun streaked red. Steve poured a shot at the spot. Another gun a few yards off to the left opened up. Steve fired that way. Over to the right, Jack Black's six-gun was roaring. But between them, Smoky's gun was silent. Smoky was running without shooting—only a man who had heard that meeting between father and son would understand why.

A gun blasted at Smoky's vague, rushing figure. Steve saw the vicious, red muzzle spurt, and turned his gun that way, blasting his last two shots. And the man gave ground, dodging away, and that would not be Caleb Reeves who ran.

Then suddenly they were even with the wide-spaced possemen, then past them, dashing toward the looming mesquite before the nearest possemen realized their purpose. But quickly shots rained after them. Warning shouts bawled raucously through the night.

The cloud began to drift on past the moon. Light swiftly seeped back as they plunged into the fringe of the mesquite. Sharp thorns tore at them. Just ahead, horses were stamping, snorting. A man was swearing angrily. And the gunfire died away as the possemen realized their horses were in danger of being shot.

Smoky was not fast. Steve slowed to keep near him. Jack Black, for all his age, was ahead of them when the man who was watching the horses challenged them.

Jack Black's gun opened up shot after shot and the man dropped. Jack Black was winging up on one of the plunging, rearing horses as Smoky and Steve ran up. He was spurring away when the man he had shot down staggered up to a knee and emptied a handgun at him. Jack Black grabbed the saddlehorn, hung for a second, and fell heavily under the hoofs of stampeding horses.

Steve had grabbed two horses. He shoved reins into Smoky's hand. Smoky dragged himself into the saddle. They rode off with the bolting horses.

From behind them shouts of rage, the crackle of gunfire increased, and then fell swiftly back as the furiously ridden horses thundered across a shallow arroyo, through another belt of mesquite, and on into the open night. Another cloud drew over the moon, and over his shoulder Steve saw more and more clouds drifting up. There would be no clear moonlight the rest of the night.

Riding close, he and Smoky raced into the west, into the Jawbone Mountain country, and there were few horses left for the posse to follow them quickly.

When they stopped the lathered horses miles beyond for a few moments' rest, there was no sound of pursuit. And the clouds were thicker now. Tracks would be almost impossible to follow until daybreak.

"There's a rope on this saddle," said Steve. "Remember those horses over by Jawbone Mountain? We can saddle fresh by daybreak, and outride any trackers before night. South of the border, you can let the old man know you're safe, and where he can meet you if he wants to visit."

"Sounds good," muttered Smoky. "Let's get goin'."

They pushed the horses, hour after hour, across the lowlands, across the piñon ridges and the grass country beyond. The moon went down and, after a short period of blackness, the gray false dawn began to creep in from the east and the foothill slopes of Jawbone Mountain were just ahead.

They were climbing the slopes of Jawbone Mountain when the crimson dawn broke behind them. They topped a ridge and saw in the mountain valley beyond a small bunch of grazing horses.

"There we are," said Steve. "I'll get a couple."

Smoky had not spoken for an hour. He was clutching the saddlehorn now. His face was gray and lined. He turned and looked back over the wide valley into the crimson dawn, and his voice was strained.

"I'm stoppin' here, Steve."

Then Steve saw that Smoky's hand was red with dried blood, and blood had oozed down the saddle and flying drops spotted the white patches of the wary pinto pony.

"Why'n hell didn't you tell me you were wounded?" Steve rapped out as he dismounted hastily and stepped to Smoky.

Smoky tried to dismount and fell into Steve's arms, and Steve lowered him gently. Smoky lay on the ground panting. He tried to lift his head. Steve rolled his coat quickly and put it under Smoky's head.

"I got it while we was runnin' for the hosses," Smoky muttered. "I figured you'd try to stay with me if I didn't keep ridin'."

"I'll get you to a house somewhere, an' have 'em send for a doctor."

"An' have the Costerville men comin' for me?" said Smoky. A faint smile came over his face. He shook his head. "No danger of that, Steve. I can feel it comin'. Roll me a quirley."

With shaking fingers Steve rolled a cigarette, put it between Smoky's lips, and held a match.

"I reckon we're safe enough here for a little," said Smoky. "They won't be tracking us good till daylight. It'll be hours before they get this far."

"I can ride back and cut them off, throw them off the trail."

Smoky ignored that. They both knew it was only talk.

"He'll be leadin' 'em," Smoky muttered. "He'll find me. Write him a letter when you can, Steve, an' tell him the things I didn't get a chance to say. You'll do that?"

"Anything you ask, pardner."

Smoky finished the cigarette. His face was white. He was taking shallow, quick breaths.

Great streamers of color led the glowing rim of the rising sun above the far horizon. Smoky lifted his head and stared at the beauty of the sunrise for a moment, and then dropped back heavily. Once more a faint smile came on his face. His eyes were staring up at the thinning clouds and bright blue sky as he spoke, and it seemed to Steve that Smoky was talking to something up there in the sky, something that only Smoky could see.

" 'Those that live by the sword shall die by the sword.' I reckon if it's good enough for him, it's good enough for me," Smoky muttered. "This oughta help even things up."

Smoky was still smiling faintly up at the sky when Steve suddenly realized that he was alone, and turned blindly away. And when he turned back, Smoky's eyes were closed and Smoky seemed to be peacefully resting.

Steve rode down the slope, roped a fresh horse and shifted his saddle.

Hours later he was waiting beside Smoky when the first dust of riders on their trail showed miles away. Steve swung on his horse then. It would not be long until the possemen reached this spot. And he paused, looking down for the final time at Smoky before he started the long, hard ride toward the border.

"He'll find you, Smoky," Steve said aloud. "And my guess is, he'll be proud of you, like I'm proud of you. Like . . ." Steve looked up at the blue sky where Smoky had last looked, "like I reckon she's proud of you for not comin' out last night with yore gun smokin'. I reckon everything is all right now. So long, pardner."

Steve headed into the south from there, and he was smiling. Smoky would want it that way. Smiling. For Smoky was going home, one prodigal whose folks would understand and be proud.

LAWMAN'S DEBT

ALAN (BROWN) LeMAY was born in Indianapolis, Indiana, and was the author of such classic novels as THE SEARCHERS (Harper, 1954) and THE UNFORGIVEN (Harper, 1957). He attended Stetson University in DeLand, Florida, in 1916 and in 1918 joined the U.S. Army Infantry and was commissioned with the rank of 2nd lieutenant in the American Expeditionary Force during the Great War. Following his military service, he completed his education at the University of Chicago. His short story, "Hullabaloo," appeared the month of his graduation in *Adventure* (6/30/22). He was a prolific contributor to the magazine markets in the mid 1920s. His first novel, PAINTED PONIES (Doran, 1927), was serialized in four installments in *Adventure* (1/1/27-2/15/27) and his second novel, OLD FATHER OF WATERS (Doubleday, Doran, 1928), was serialized in five parts in *Adventure* (9/1/27-10/15/27). The latter, concerned with Mississippi riverboats, anticipates the iconography and setting of his final novel, BY DIM AND FLARING LAMPS (Harper, 1962). PAINTED PONIES in general follows the narrative structure employed years later by Henry Wilson Allen in his Will Henry novels; in this instance the trek of the Cheyenne Indians from their reservation in the Southwest back to their homeland in the Black Hills is interwoven with events in the lives of the fictional characters. Such LeMay themes as the stigma of having Indian blood from THE UNFORGIVEN and the indomitable fanaticism of a quest from THE SEARCHERS are already apparent in embryonic form.

In 1929, two years before Ernest Haycox, LeMay broke into the pages of *Collier's* with the story, "Loan of a Gun" (2/23/29). Feeling that he should preserve the byline Alan LeMay for *Collier's*, Western fiction he published in pulp magazines during the 1930s appeared under the anagrammatic byline, Alan M. Emley. Yet, in virtually all of LeMay's pulp stories, there is always something which raises them out of the ordinary, be it an image, a character, or a circumstance. LeMay Western novels of the 1930s are more conventional than either those from the 1920s or the 1950s. WINTER RANGE (Farrar & Rinehart, 1932), arguably the best of them, opens with an inquest and involves the unraveling of the murder of a wealthy rancher and banker. It was first serialized in *Collier's* (12/19/31-2/20/32) and later reprinted in one installment as "Death on the Rimrock" in *Western Fiction* (5/35). During this decade LeMay wanted nothing more than to be a rancher and his income from writing was intended to supplement the income generated by raising livestock on his ranch outside Santee, California. When he was plunged into debt after disaster wiped out his herd, he turned in the late 1930s to screenwriting, early attaching himself to Cecil

B. DeMille's unit at Paramount Pictures. LeMay continued to write original screenplays through the 1940s, on one occasion even directing the film based on his screenplay.

THE SEARCHERS is regarded by many as LeMay's masterpiece. It possesses a graphic sense of place; it etches deeply the feats of human endurance which LeMay tended to admire in the American spirit; and it has that characteristic suggestiveness of tremendous depths and untold stories developed in his long apprenticeship writing short stories (and quite a few "short, short" stories for *Collier's*). These subtexts often ride on a snatch of dialogue or flash suddenly in a laconic observation, as when he wrote of Amos Edwards in this novel: "Amos was—had always been—in love with his brother's wife." The futility of life hovers here, just as it does in those deep leathery lines carved on the faces of pioneers by the harsh prairies which LeMay had described in PAINTED PONIES.

"Lawman's Debt" first appeared in *Dime Western* (5/34) under the Alan M. Emley byline and has never been previously collected.

Darkness had set in, and the rain was falling in a steady downpour as Dale Jameson, looking like some misshapen monster out of the past, in his yellow slicker and huge hat, entered the tiny cabin of saplings. He had built it in secret in the midst of a dense clump of spruce against this need.

Here he would stay until the hue and cry had ceased. Then, with beard grown and in the garb of a prospector, he would go west over the divide and eventually reach civilization beyond—unknown, unsought, and unafraid.

He pulled off the slicker, and from his back he unstrapped a canvas bag that was stuffed to overflowing with currency and gold.

Quickly he built a fire in the tiny fireplace, put on a coffee pot, and spitted a venison steak on a stick before the leaping flames.

Then, with shaking hand, he opened the canvas bag and poured a fortune out on the pineboard table. It was a huge pile, and he wondered how so much money could come out of so small a bag.

He had no fear of pursuit. His plan had been well made; it had been cleverly executed, and his trail had been well covered. Caching saddle and bridle and turning his pinto loose near Las Vegas cañon was a master stroke. No one ever would think of him leaving his horse and going on foot to a hide-out by a path no mounted posse could follow.

Perhaps, even now, the two men in the bank were still bound and gagged and the alarm not yet given. Or at most the word was being passed that the Pioneer State Bank had been robbed by one man, and that a stranger by the name of Brad Kelly was suspected. Who would know that Dale Jameson, the respected son of a prosperous rancher who lived far away, had staged the daring hold-up?

Slowly and deliberately Dale piled up the gleaming yellow coins.

Carefully he separated the bills into fives, tens, and twenties. There was a thick pack of one-hundred-dollar bills with the figure $10,000 stamped on the band around it.

Fifty-three thousand, seven hundred and forty dollars was the total haul. What a tidy sum to wrest from one institution without bloodshed and without the slightest difficulty!

He had slipped through a back door in the afternoon and hid in a closet till the bank was closed, the doors locked, and the curtains drawn. Then, like an avenging demon, he appeared with handkerchief over face and gun in hand. He tied the two men in the bank hand and foot, looted the safe at his leisure, and walked quietly out the back door and away. In the whole community only a few people knew him, and they knew him as Brad Kelly, a cowboy from the Mancos River country.

Jap Heathcote was right. A man was a fool to work all his life when he could so easily take the proceeds of labor away from those who had less brains or smaller courage. Why should a wolf dig for roots when succulent mutton was nearby, guarded by weak and incompetent dogs?

Weak and incompetent dogs!

Dale grimaced slightly at the thought as he fingered the piles of currency and gold. There was one fly in the ointment! The watchdog of this particular fold was neither weak nor incompetent.

Dale had passed him on the street two weeks before the hold-up, and his eyes had fallen as the keen glance of the sheriff had met his own. He had suddenly found himself facing his boyhood hero— old Bat Masters of border fame—who was his father's best friend. Frequently Masters had come to the Texas ranch in the old days. He had bounced Dale on his knee and let him hold the big .45 that swung at his side. It was a strange coincidence that Bat Masters should be at the scene of Dale's first crime, and that this terror of outlaws should meet his first defeat at the hands of the boy to whom he had been on a par with Robin Hood and Richard of the Lion Heart.

Masters looked a little older now. His shoulders were a trifle stooped; the long sweeping mustache was a trifle grizzled; but there was the same fire in the blue eyes and doubtless there was the same skill in the lightning hand.

Yet Dale had won! He had won against this noted guardian of the law; the man who had brought grief to so many who had stood without the pale.

Dale wished that Jap Heathcote could see him and know what he had done; that he had executed the perfect bank robbery, and had committed the perfect crime. As well for Bat Masters to try and catch the lightning playing above the mountain tops as to try to bring Dale Jameson to justice.

The savory odor of coffee and broiling venison roused him from his reverie and he arose with a sigh.

He turned the steak and shifted the coffee pot, shielding his face from the heat of the flames with his hand. The wind had arisen and the little cabin trembled in spite of its protection from the surrounding trees.

A draught of cold air struck the back of Dale's neck and fanned the flames in the fireplace. The door had blown open. He was not nervous, and he did not turn until the coffee pot was settled where it could simmer instead of boil. Strange that the door should blow open! He must have failed to close it in his haste.

Slowly he turned. Then his eyes grew wide, his jaw dropped, and he stood staring into the round orifice of a six-gun held by a steady hand. Behind it a black and wet slicker gleamed and glistened in the firelight. Above it was a face with a long, grizzled mustache and the keenest of keen, blue eyes.

"Brad Kelly," spoke a calm voice that reminded Dale of the cold steel of edged tools. "I thought so!"

With manacled hands Dale lay on his cot throughout the wild night. He felt a strange comfort in the fact that Bat Masters had not recognized him. It would be easier to endure the long years of prison life if this silent man did not know the one he had taken to justice was the son of his old friend—the boy he had held on his knee.

Thoughts of escape flashed through his mind, but they struggled feebly and died as he looked at this man of iron who was smoking silently as the frail shelter was battered by the wind and rain.

The perfect crime and the clever escape had come to a sudden and inglorious end. This stern, relentless guardian of the law had caught him scarcely before he had counted his stolen loot. It was uncanny how quickly Dale had been gathered in.

Mentally he cursed the memory of Jap Heathcote. Dale was a fool to have been attracted and led astray by the dashing outlaw. His father had warned and pleaded and threatened and cajoled, until there came a final, violent quarrel when Dale left the paternal roof and went his own way.

Jap Heathcote had died with a bullet between the eyes shortly after his young friend had joined him, and Dale had gone on alone.

Only once did Dale speak, and that was to ask how Masters had trailed him.

For some moments the sheriff smoked on without answering. His eyes were on a little colored picture of a doe and fawn that Dale had tacked on the wall. When he spoke, it was with seeming irrelevance.

"There ain't many people in a county like this," he drawled. "A few ranchers, a few miners, a few prospectors and a few business men make up the whole population. But the county has miles and miles of plains, hills, and mountains. A sheriff wouldn't amount to shucks up here unless he knew a good many things that most people wouldn't notice. Sometimes he learns secrets from prospectors and lion hunters and trappers that go to the most hidden places in the wilds. Sometimes he learns something from those that are much sharper than any human.

"Someone tells the sheriff of a strange young man living above Las Vegas cañon. One day the sheriff goes up there. He sees a deer that runs on ahead and disappears. Pretty soon it comes dashing back. Something is up ahead . . . either man or animal. Some jays are screaming in a clump of spruce. They settle down and then rise up again and scold. The sheriff knows there is something in that spruce that shouldn't be there. The jays tell him so. Then comes the sound of a hammer.

"The sheriff slips through the trees and sees a young man building a cabin. That's harmless enough, so the sheriff goes away and the young man is no part the wiser. Later he sees the same young man in town. He looks at him and the young man drops his eyes. He can't look the law in the face. The sheriff asks about him and learns he is Brad Kelly, occupation unknown; supposed to be a cowboy from a Mancos River ranch. A letter from Mancos River says they don't know him. The bank is robbed by a lone man. The description tallies with Brad Kelly who built the little cabin. What's the answer?"

Masters puffed away at his pipe and said no more. Dale lay silent in his misery. What a child he had been when pitted against this machine of the law! How quickly the solution to his perfect crime had been solved! What a fool he was! If he ever got out of this mess. . . . But it was too late now! He had broken the law and must pay the penalty.

Then his thoughts turned to escape. Perhaps even yet there was a chance. Bat Masters had not recognized him. Let him get away and he would be hard to follow. Jap Heathcote had told him: "Never turn yellow if you get caught. Keep your chin up and your mouth shut and ten to one you can crawl out even if they get you behind the bars."

In early dawn the two men left the cabin and started along the path that led down the tortuous decent into Las Vegas cañon.

The rain had ceased and the wind had gone down, but the clouds hung dark and forbidding above them. Every mountain rill and dry creek bed had become a torrent that plunged and snarled its angry way over the rocks.

Coming out on the rimrock above the cañon, they paused and stared without speaking at the stupendous change that had been wrought by the few hours of heavy rain. Normally, Las Vegas River was a clear, small stream that sang and bubbled and tumbled among the boulders. Now it had risen high and was filled with mud and debris. Its dark waters dashed in a wild race for the valley below, churning the brown foam and flinging spray far into the air. The cry of the tortured stream in its travail echoed against the sides of the cañon and reached the men on the rimrock far up against the sky.

Together they slipped and slid down over the wet rocks. It was a dangerous descent for Dale. The handcuffs were still around his wrists, but he would have died rather than ask that they be removed.

An hour later they reached the road at the side of the stream. It continued up the cañon to Las Vegas dam.

Foam and spray dashed over them as they moved down the road. Evidently the dam was full to the brim and the water was dashing over the spillways. Dale shuddered to think what would happen if the dam should break, and the vast store of irrigation water be loosed upon the valley below.

In a little cavern at the side of the road they came to the sheriff's horse, which had waited patiently for him. Masters had removed the saddle and bridle and thrown his blanket over it.

With Dale in the lead, the sheriff walking behind him and the horse following, they emerged from the cañon into the green valley, dotted thickly with hay stacks. For a hundred yards the water was over the road.

Dale looked about him for the slightest chance of escape, but saw none. If he only had his hands free, he might plunge into the stream. It was deep here within a few feet of the road, and he might get away with a long dive and powerful swimming.

On the other side was a thick grove of cottonwood trees standing in the water. The road ran straight ahead a mile or more, then it rose sharply and continued over the hills to the town.

A fine, cold rain had set in, and the two men splashed through the water and mud with hunched shoulders and bowed heads. In spite of his desperate situation, Dale was filled with admiration for Bat Masters. Nearly sixty years old the sheriff must be, yet no storm was too violent, no test was too severe to prevent him from going forth in the performance of his duty, preventing crime, apprehending the criminal and enforcing the law. The institutions of established society must be worthwhile, after all, when such men spent their lives upholding them.

The fortune that Masters carried in the canvas bag was no more to him than so much wheat. No temptation could be great enough for this man to take one penny of it.

A faint trembling of the earth took Dale's mind abruptly from these thoughts. The horse threw up its head and snorted. It snorted again as a roaring came to their ears that grew steadily louder like a terrific wind approaching though the pines.

"The dam!" cried Bat Masters. "It has gone out!"

Dale's face paled at the thought of the danger that faced them. They were directly in the path of the unleashed flood, too far down the road now to reach the safety of the cañon walls! Trapped!

The sheriff acted quickly. He turned to the horse, slapped it with the flat of his hand. "Get out!" he commanded. "Go!" The terrified animal went dashing toward the hills.

"He won't carry double," Masters explained, as he swiftly unlocked the handcuffs and took them from Dale's wrists.

"Climb that tree," he ordered. "It may hold. It's each for himself now."

Dale noted the silent fulfillment of the unwritten code of the West that required the sheriff to stay with his prisoner, as he swung into the branches of a big cottonwood. The sheriff might have escaped alone on his horse, but that was not Bat Masters's way.

The roar grew louder. Suddenly a wall of water burst from the mouth of the cañon a mile away. Spreading like some huge feathered fan, it gushed over the valley.

A white ranchhouse, with its unpainted barn and corral, was swept away like so much straw. A small herd of cattle disappeared in the plunging foam. Then a five-foot roaring wall of water was upon them.

The tree trembled like a reed as the flood struck, and Dale wondered how anything could stand against the battering ram that had been unloosed against them.

On every side was a plunging, seething, pounding sea carrying with it the fruits of destruction. Huge trees uprooted and tossed about, swirled by them, turning end over end or riding low in the flood. There were logs and planks and boards, and once Dale saw the roof of a house that had been torn loose like a toy.

A dead steer came to the surface for a moment and swirled round and round before it disappeared in the brown flood. A huge log struck and lodged against their tree, which shook and trembled under the blow.

The sheriff, clinging to a branch on the other side of the trunk, pointed and shouted. Although Dale could not understand all the words, he knew Masters was saying that their tree must go if enough debris piled against that log, and that nothing could live in that roaring hell.

Again the sheriff shouted, and Dale's eyes followed his pointed finger. From the mouth of the cañon burst a second wall of water. Evidently not all of the dam had given way at one time.

Masters pulled off his heavy slicker and motioned Dale to do likewise.

Dale watched the widening fringe flung out over the valley. Nearer and nearer it came. Trees that had resisted the first onslaught were going down, uprooted or snapped off like toothpicks before the fury of the flood.

The sheriff held out his hand. Dale gripped it hard. No need for spoken words. Their tree, with the log and swiftly accumulated debris of all kinds, could not stand against the impending blow.

Masters smiled, but Dale could not answer that smile. The sheriff could laugh in the face of death for he was going out in the performance of his duty—honest and clean. Bat Masters was a man!

Dale felt that he was about to die, and he had ceased to care. He was neither nervous nor afraid. His one regret was that he could not go like Bat Masters.

With a roar like the loosing of a thousand seas the plunging, surging mass of water was upon them. The cottonwood gave a sickening shudder and leaned slightly out of the perpendicular. The log was torn away and went swinging end over end into the maelstrom. For a moment Dale hoped. The crest of the flood passed. Perhaps, after all. . . .

Again came that sickening shudder. Then, slowly and steadily, the great tree tipped. It touched the angry water with its lower branches, paused a moment and then, as though worn out with the long battle, darted down the stream as the last root gave way.

With both arms and both legs wrapped around the branch, Dale struck the water. Even then his hold was almost broken as the foaming flood tore by.

His head came above the surface of the stream, and he opened his eyes surprised to find himself still alive. The branch was steady for a moment, but this was no assurance for the future. He could see trees as large as this one flung about and turned over and over farther out in the stream.

A whirlpool caught them. Dale took a deep breath as he was plunged beneath the surface. Something seemed to tell him to hang on, and he clung to the limb till it seemed his lungs would burst, clung till there was a ringing in his ears, clung till he thought the end had come and he had descended into the dark and fathomless pit to eternity.

There was a quick heave and he was flung a yard above the surface of the stream, still clinging to his branch. He glanced across the tree. Bat Masters was no longer there.

The cottonwood was floating broadside down the river now, and Dale noticed a foot or more of seemingly still water following along behind the big trunk beneath.

Into this still place came a head. It floated a moment and then sank slowly.

Scarcely realizing what he was doing, Dale reached down and grasped the long hair. Slowly he lifted, and the face of Bat Masters came into view. It was a pitiful face now with its long, dripping mustache. It was white and drawn and the old fire had gone out of the half-closed eyes.

The cottonwood had stopped its mad whirling and was floating steadily. Dale knew that the worst of the flood was over. If he could hang on a few minutes longer, he might yet cheat the death that was reaching for him with dripping hands.

Again the tree turned. Loosing his hold, Dale dropped into the water, seized another branch with his right hand, and passed his left arm around the sheriff.

He could see that they were drifting toward the shore, away from the violent middle of the stream. There was hope if Dale could hang on. A small log dashed against him, knocking the breath from him and nearly causing him to lose his hold.

He looked at the face beside him. The eyes were wide open now, and Dale knew the sheriff was alive and conscious. There was a surge as they sped down a little rapid, and the branch was nearly torn from Dale's grasp. The strain upon hand and arm was terrific.

"Can you help me hang on?" he shouted.

The head moved slightly from side to side and the eyes closed.

The run down the rapid had driven the tree farther toward the shore. Slower and slower it moved. Dale was sure that the flood must be receding rapidly; already it seemed that a thousand lakes as big as Las Vegas had swept past them.

Suddenly the tree halted. It moved again, trembled, and then came to a full stop. Dale's feet touched bottom a moment and then were lifted by the current.

The tree moved again in little jerks, and then the branches caught and the trunk swung downstream. Again Dale touched the bottom and this time he stood firm!

The flood had spent its force. A few minutes later the exhausted Dale carried the limp body of the sheriff to firm ground.

A hasty examination showed a cut on the head, a badly bruised wrist and the right leg hanging limp and twisted. Cutting away the trouser leg, Dale found the limb broken above the knee. The shattered bone showed in a white lump.

"Are you badly hurt?" Dale asked, and realized as he spoke how idiotic his question was.

There was no answer. The blue eyes were open and upon him and Dale was sure that Masters was conscious. He pulled off his scarf and bound the scalp wound, wondering if putting on a wet and muddy bandage was the proper thing to do.

The gleam of handcuffs in the sheriff's pocket brought him to a sudden realization of his opportunity. Dale looked about him, wondering vaguely if the coast was clear for him.

Far away two men on horses topped a hill and disappeared in a little valley as they rode toward the stream. In all the soggy waste-land that the flood had left behind it, no other living being was in sight.

The words of Jap Heathcote came to Dale with double force: "Never turn yellow if you get caught. Keep your chin up and your mouth shut and ten to one you can crawl out even if they get you behind bars."

Jap Heathcote was right! Dale had kept his chin up and his mouth shut, and now he could escape after being in the hands of Bat Masters, the famous hunter of men.

With shaking hands Dale unstrapped the canvas bag which Masters had carried through the jaws of death, and pulled the sheriff's gun from its holster.

The blue eyes were upon him and the old fire was returning, but there was no word and no sign from the injured man.

Dale was very tired, yet the prospect of escape with the stolen fortune gave him new life and new strength. He glanced at the still swollen stream, shuddered, wondered that he had come alive and uninjured from it. Then, with long strides, he ascended the slope that bordered the valley.

Again the horsemen rode into view. They were headed far to the right and there was no danger from them.

Dale paused and looked back at Bat Masters who was lying motionless in a pathetic heap. This relentless, merciless instrument of the law could not follow him now. As for the rest of the community—they would have enough to do in searching for their dead. Dale would get away safely with the wet, sodden loot that was strapped to his back.

The sheriff moved. Slowly and painfully he struggled to one knee and tried to drag himself over the ground. Then he sank down and lay still.

Dale knew he would die there alone unless he was rescued, and who could find him amidst those miles of wreckage piled high in the wake of the flood? The horsemen were still in sight, but they were traveling rapidly and would not come within a mile of the injured sheriff.

Dale reached and touched the canvas bag, now on his back again. Ahead lay comfort and plenty. Behind lay years of prison life.

Then hardly knowing what he did, he shouted loudly! The horsemen rode on. Dale lifted his voice again and again in a call that carried far over the open range.

The horsemen stopped. Still in the grip of an urge he could not name, Dale frantically waved his hand. Presently he saw an answering signal, and the two men rode toward him.

A moment later he was at Bat Masters's side. The sheriff lay in a twisted heap, but his keen blue eyes were upon Dale.

Dale threw the canvas bag down beside him, and shoved the big .45 back in its holster. Then he held out his hands for the handcuffs and smiled into the blue eyes.

"I've come back, Sheriff," he said calmly. "I'll take my medicine and then go straight as long as I live."

"Yeah," answered Masters, and his voice startled Dale coming from one so long silent. "I thought that was what you would do. Sometimes it's hard to go straight, son, a good many people fail when the pinch comes, but after all it's the easy way."

He made no movement to put on the handcuffs. Dale moved him to a more comfortable position and then sat by his side till the men rode up. Dale did not know them.

"Hyah, Sheriff?" greeted one. "Are you hurt?"

"Yes. Busted leg. Put on a couple of splints and I can make it to town on a horse."

The eyes of one of the men fell on the canvas bag as he dismounted.

"What's this?" he asked.

"The money stolen from the bank," the sheriff answered.

"Great Scott, you got him, did you?"

Masters nodded.

"And is this the fellow that . . . that . . . ?"

The keen eyes of the sheriff looked into Dale's young face. It was weary and drawn and showed the strain of the past few hours.

"I caught Brad Kelly and got back the money," Masters said. "Then the flood came and he . . . he's out there drowned. We never will see Brad Kelly again. This young fellow came along and saved my life at the risk of his own. Men, I want you to meet Dale Jameson, the son of the best and truest friend I ever had . . . and Dale's a chip off the old block. I'm proud to be numbered among his friends."

And Bat Masters, relentless scourge of the outlaw, reached out and took Dale's hand in a firm grasp.

STAGE STATION

ERNEST HAYCOX was born in Portland, Oregon, and was long considered the dean among authors of Western fiction. When the Western Writers of America was first organized in 1953, what became the Golden Spur Award for outstanding achievement in writing Western fiction was first going to be called the "Erny" in homage to Haycox. His name became established already in the 1920s as a master of the Western story in all the leading Western pulp magazines of the day, including Street and Smith's *Western Story Magazine* and Doubleday's *The Frontier* and *West*. Haycox's long novelette, "Red Knives," appeared in *The Frontier* (4/25) and in the letters department for that issue Haycox commented that " 'Red Knives' was the result of some research for a historical book. . . . At the time the book was the important thing, but as I read through all the chronicles of what these early pioneers had done the idea of a story came along and wouldn't be denied. For every man struck down by a Shawnee lance or Huron war hatchet there were others to go on, a little grimmer of purpose, a little more determined to see the land beyond the hill and the plain beyond the river. It would be hard, in looking through the history of advancing civilizations, to find another group of men so individualistic in temperament, so buoyant, or stoical." The title was drawn from the color of the handles of the scalping knives supplied by the British to their Indian allies during the Revolutionary War.

In 1931 he broke into the pages of *Collier's* and from that time on was regularly featured in this magazine, either with a short story or a serial that was later published as a novel. In the 1940s his serials began appearing in *The Saturday Evening Post* and it was there that such modern classics as BUGLES IN THE AFTERNOON (Little, Brown, 1944) and CANYON PASSAGE (Little, Brown, 1945) were first published. Both of these novels were also made into major motion pictures although, perhaps, the film most loved and remembered is that based on Haycox's short story, "Stage to Lordsburg," in *Collier's* (4/10/37), retitled STAGECOACH (United Artists, 1939) directed by John Ford. MAN IN THE SADDLE (Little, Brown, 1938) and BUGLES IN THE AFTERNOON are available in full-length audio versions from Books on Tape. SUNDOWN JIM, one of his very best novels, has been reprinted recently in a new hardcover edition by Chivers Press.

Haycox was perhaps at his finest and most accomplished in the short story because, as he himself confessed, it gave him greater freedom to experiment, to explore character and situation, and to concentrate on tension and social psychology. While many of his magazine stories are still in the process of being gathered into book editions, some of the finest of them have already appeared, above all in ROUGH JUSTICE (Little, Brown, 1950), BY ROPE AND LEAD (Little, Brown, 1951), PIONEER LOVES (Little, Brown, 1952), MURDER ON THE FRONTIER (Little, Brown, 1953), and PRAIRIE GUNS (Little, Brown, 1954). "An Evening's Entertainment" in *Collier's* (9/26/31), Clouds on the Circle P" in *Collier's* (7/9/32), "Ride the River" in *Collier's* (5/26/34), and "Born to Conquer" in *Collier's* (3/21/36) are among the Haycox short stories now available in paperback audio from Durkin Hayes.

Haycox almost always has an involving story to tell and one in which there is something not so readily definable that raises it above its time, an image possibly, a turn of phrase, or even a sensation, the smell of dust after rain or the solitude of an Arizona night. "Stage Station" first appeared in *Collier's* (4/22/39) and was first reprinted in the Haycox story collection, OUTLAW (Little, Brown, 1953). It was filmed twice, first as APACHE TRAIL (M-G-M, 1942) and then remade a decade later as APACHE WAR SMOKE (M-G-M, 1952).

Rosalia Dures gave the table one last glance to make sure that the owner, who believed it a sin to be ungenerous, could find no fault with the meal. The arrival of the Tonto stage shattered the hot drowse lying all about Folliard's station. Tobe Urquhart, the driver, called, "Fifteen minutes to eat," and the weary and relieved voices of the passengers ran over the yard. One was a woman's voice.

The light of the desert was a white-hot blast and, when the woman stepped into the thick shadows of this 'dobe-walled room, she put out her hands as though blinded. She laughed gently at the other passengers crowding around her and her shoulders tipped a little and then the owner stepped into the room and the woman caught the front of his shirt with her fingers. She said, laughter still in her voice, "It has made me a little faint."

From the corner of the room, Rosalia Dures observed this with a practical and dissenting interest. The woman was surrounded by men but it was the owner on whom she placed her hands; and the owner looked at her and was pleased. There was, Rosalia thought, nothing wrong with the woman's eyes.

Tobe Urquhart said, "Mrs. King, this is Tom Folliard, who runs this station. It is one of the few stations in Arizona the Apaches ain't had any luck with."

The owner helped Mrs. King to the table and took his own place and everybody, made impatient by time and hunger, fell upon the meal. Rosalia stepped forward, her round and white and firm arms grazing the owner's shoulders as she poured his coffee. It was against his wishes to be served first but Rosalia, obedient in most things, had her own gently stubborn convictions. This was the owner's house and this was his table. Afterward she moved to Mrs. King. There was a perfume in Mrs. King's chestnut hair and a firmness to her skin. The day's heat had deepened her complexion. Small, faint freckles showed around the base of her nose. Rosalia Dures's appearance instantly drew Mrs. King's quick and close regard and there was at the moment no smiling in her eyes. They were cool and made heavy by a dark, old wisdom and they turned from Rosalia to the owner, and back to Rosalia again, until Rosalia knew what the *Señora* was thinking.

Rosalia thought: If it were but true. She circled the table with her own eyes discreetly lowered and went into the kitchen. Her mother moved from the hot stove and said: "I hear a woman. There is danger in the desert for a woman."

Rosalia said, "She would not be afraid," and moved back to the dining room. She stood in a corner, listening. Tobe Urquhart said: "Should be a cavalry guard waitin' at the top of the pass. Any Apache sign around here?"

The owner said: "Not much."

Tobe Urquhart said: "Any sign is too much. All right, folks."

They rose at his word. Tobe Urquhart was a tall man but the owner was taller. The owner had heavy shoulders and heavy legs and he had a voice that made men turn. All the sun in Arizona couldn't darken his skin, and his lips were long and made for smiling, but they were firm at the corners and his eyes were gray.

Rosalia saw how strong was the *Señora's* interest as she watched the owner. The *Señora* was fair and pretty; she was laughing again. She put a palm gracefully toward her head.

"I had not counted on this heat. It will be much worse this afternoon. If you don't mind, I'll stay over until the next stage, Mr. Folliard."

Rosalia thought: Her appetite was not ill.

The owner said, "Certainly," and seemed pleased, and followed the other passengers into the glass-glittering light. There was talk in the yard and the stage's wheels groaned into motion and for a little while the run of the horses was a descending beat in the day. Then the solid, sultry quiet returned to Folliard's station and the owner came in with *Señora* King's flower-patterned portmanteau.

"Rosalia," he said, "which room will Mrs. King use?" Afterward he added: "This is Rosalia Dures."

Rosalia lowered her eyes. *Señora* King said, "How are you, Rosalia?" with a distant civility. Tom Folliard looked at *Señora* King, not understanding the tone.

Rosalia walked down the dusk-gray hall of the 'dobe's rambling wing, into a small room. *Señora* King's stiff dress and *Señora* King's petticoats rustled behind her and the owner's feet softly tramped the rammed earth floor. Rosalia walked to the deep window slit and pulled back the shutter so that some of the day's blinding light might stain the gushed, warm shadows of the room. *Señora* King stood near the owner with her chin lifted and her lips smiling. There was an expression in her eyes. Rosalia thought: It is not modest.

Rosalia, who knew the shape and shadow of the owner's every mood, saw that he was pleased. His words were softened. He said: "If there is anything you need, call Rosalia or me."

Rosalia went back along the hall, still hearing the owner's steps behind her. Luz padded in and out of the room, bearing away the dinner dishes. Luz was a careless Apache boy and needed the eye of authority on him; and so Rosalia stood in the corner and supplied that need. She wore a black skirt and a white linen shirtwaist with short sleeves, and her hair, black as brilliant lacquer, was pulled back from her forehead into a round knot held by a semicircular comb. Her lips were serene and her eyes were dreaming and grave. At her hip was a small chain holding three keys. When she moved, they made a quick and faintly musical sound. She watched the owner cross the room and go into the brilliant flash of day, whereupon she turned to the kitchen.

"Luz," she said in Spanish, "you are lazy. I will speak to the owner."

Señora Dures sat comfortably by a kitchen table, drinking her coffee. At middle age *Señora* Dures had the fine, hard camellia-clear skin and features of a high-bred Spanish woman. Moisture lay on her upper lip but she was very loose and comfortable in the chair and her practical eyes considered her daughter. "I saw the woman," she said. "The best fruit has been picked from that tree. Why is she here?"

Rosalia Dures said: "She has a sickness."

"Ah," said her mother with a broad irony. "The owner is a well-set man and the desires of women have followed him before now." *Señora* Dures sipped coffee, considering her daughter. "But it will do her no good. American men are cold."

Rosalia said: "The owner is not cold."

"Has he looked at you?" pointed out *Señora* Dures. "Has there been in his eyes a thing to make you afraid, or glad? With Tomás Folliard you are as safe as in the tomb. With a Spanish man it would be impossible. It would be a wound to his pride to disregard the possibilities of a woman."

Rosalia said, soft and stubborn: "The owner is not cold. I saw his face when he looked at *Señora* King."

She lowered her eyes from the critical examination of her mother, who said, "You are twenty-three. It is a shame. It is not that you are plain, for you are not. It is not that you are of poor blood. The Dures were great people in Spain two hundred years ago. You do not know your gifts. You are shy. You need younger women to instruct you and Spanish men to try your eyes on. I should take you to Cousin Felipe's in Tucson."

"Spanish men," said Rosalia in expressive scorn. "They do nothing but talk and smoke cigarettes in the sunshine. As you yourself have said. . . ."

"So," murmured *Señora* Dures and sighed. As a young girl she had married Dures, who had been fifty; and on the wedding night he had stayed away, drinking until his friends brought him home and laid him like a log on the bed. Men were difficult at times and though she was doubtful of American ways she had a sympathy for her daughter, and was tolerant. She rolled herself a cigarette and laid her hands across her knees. "If the *Señora* brought a look to the face of Don Tomás, it may be you can learn from her. . . ."

Rosalia said, "It is not the way. A man must see for himself. The owner is lonely and the *Señora* King reminds him of his people. Luz, move faster or I will send you back to the hills."

She went down the shadowed hall, past the door of *Señora* King's room, past the little barroom with its rank smell of tobacco and whisky, and out to the back yard. The hills in the distance were ashen-gray and iron-brown under the beating light; and up there on the bare summits Apaches would be watching.

Always they watched; always, at night, they crept down. This was the heart of Indian country, with no settlement nearer than twenty miles. But the owner's walls were thick and the owner had never deserted his station. Long and low and solid, the 'dobe house faced the wicked emptiness. Behind, lay the ramparts of the hills; in front the white, flat, endless floor of the desert stretched away; and far, far off the heat haze closed down. The stage road's twin ruts came out of the northern desert and vanished in the rocks and stiff-standing cacti southward. A horse laid its nose against the surface of the pool; Guiterrez, the Mexican hostler, slept in a shady angle of the mesquite fence.

Rosalia returned along the dusky corridor to the main room. The owner sat in his big chair by the front door. He had his back to her. His feet were spread forward; his cigar's pale blue smoke spiraled in the room's dusk. The shutters were closed and the door was shut but faint pencil streaks of light searched through the cracks, diamond bright. Rosalia watched the owner's black head roll a little against the chair's rung. His skin was light and his shoulders were very wide. When he raised his cigar to his mouth, she caught the heavy row of knuckles on his fist. She made no sound; she was still, she was dreaming.

He said: "Rosalia."

Rosalia's heart quickened. The owner had sharp ears; he had a sense for things around him. She walked on until she stood before him. His hair was tumbled around his head. He had a sleepy, heavy, troubled look. His lips were big, and tight at the corners, and the gray in his eyes was darker. He was a young man and he was lonely.

Rosalia said: "Was there something for tonight you wanted?"

"No," he said. "I leave all that to you. The keys are yours, Rosalia."

Rosalia thought: The keys are only for rooms; they do not unlock all things. But she said: "You must speak to Luz. He is worth nothing. He is an Apache. He dreams like an Apache, even when he washes dishes. One day he will take a knife and stab you."

He said with a more alert tone: "Bothered you?"

She looked up in some surprise. "Me, Tomás? No." She squared her small shoulders; and then she was willful and calm and afraid of nothing. "I would skin him alive."

The owner's smile took the loneliness from his face. There was a look in his eyes that sent up the beating of her heart again. She held herself steady and knew that he was interested; and kept her lips even and gentle. Something was in his eyes. It came and passed, and was not quite as it had been when the *Señora* King had placed her hands on his chest. Rosalia turned away.

At four o'clock the house awoke. *Señora* Dures's voice was in the kitchen, using hard Spanish on Luz. Rosalia stirred around the long table and the Mexican hands appeared, to water stock and to run in the cattle from the outer range. Tom Folliard went to the barn to see that the relief horses were fed and ready for the Lordsburg stage.

At sundown he returned to the house. The table was set. Mrs. King sat in a chair with her hands in her lap. She watched Rosalia; her head was turned and the side of her neck showed a sharp line and her lips were pressed in from thought. At sight of Folliard this faded and she was smiling and she was softly at ease in the chair. Rosalia stood by the table with her face thoughtfully bowed over its dishes.

Mrs. King's talk was persuasive: "You didn't come from this country originally, Mr. Folliard?"

"No," he said. "I drifted into Arizona Territory as a runaway boy, eight years ago. My people all live in Maine."

She said: "I knew you were a Yankee. So am I. From Rhode Island. I married Lieutenant King the year he graduated from the Academy. He was killed last summer by the Sioux."

It was the way she talked that shook up a man's interest and made him aware of her, and made him aware of himself as well. He said: "For you it's a long way from home."

"I've been visiting at Fort Whipple. Now I'm going on to New Orleans. I have people there." She paused and her hands expressively turned. "I hate to go. This land . . . I hate to leave it."

Her voice was a soft, steady breeze fanning alive a fire in him. Rosalia saw this. The sun dropped over the rim of the desert and there was the distant sound of the Lordsburg stage running up.

Folliard left the room. Mrs. King's breath was a sharp cut in the silence; she stared at Rosalia and her shoulders fell lower in the chair.

The stage came off the desert with a jarring of its wheels and the passengers came into the room, stiff-jointed and weary—and relieved. There were four of them, one an Army major in crumpled blue, with the yellow piping of the cavalry branch running down his trouser leg. The owner came in and for a moment all the men were restrained by the presence of a woman. The owner said: "This is Mrs. King, gentlemen," and the Army major's bow was a faint break at the hips. Afterward they sat down.

Rosalia circled the table, her white round arm poising the coffee-pot, and pouring. She watched the owner's face turn toward *Señora* King; and saw the *Señora*'s quick, frank smile answer him at once, willing and eager. But there was a thing here the owner did not see. The Army major sat opposite *Señora* King, and there were times when his glance touched her and remained on her with a full curiosity. There was a look on the major's face that was not like the look of a stranger; it was bolder and wiser; it was more insistent.

Cull Durrie, who drove this stage, rose promptly at the quarter-hour's end and said: "Time to go." The passengers filed out. The major paused before Mrs. King. He said in his civil voice:

"I have not had the pleasure of meeting you since last year in Tucson."

Rosalia held her shoulders still. The owner was listening. *Señora* King's face, by lamplight, was grave and its color diminished. Her voice hurried out an answer: "I'm on my way to New Orleans, Major."

"I wish you luck, Mrs. King," said the major, and gave his faint bow and left the room. The *Señora* King's smile, small and brief, touched the owner as he followed these men into the compound; and then the *Señora*'s smile died and support seemed to leave her shoulders. She wheeled and sat in a corner chair, darkened by the shadows. She spoke to Rosalia with a tone that hurt: "Bring my coffee here."

Rosalia said, soft and compliant: "Yes *Señora*," and brought the cup. The *Señora*'s eyes lifting to her, were wide open. They were old and desperate.

Luz, the Apache boy, padded in to take away the used dishes. The Mexican hands came in to eat and the owner appeared and took a chair beside the *Señora* King. He put his long legs before him and pulled cigar smoke deeply into his chest. His half-curly hair made a black shine under the lamp. Rosalia, back in the room's corner, saw the owner change. His big fists were loose on the arms of the chair and the corners of his mouth were not tight and he had forgotten—he who so seldom forgot—the Apaches back on the rim of the Mesquites. The owner was dreaming. Rosalia knew what his dreams were. She lowered her head so that her eyes might not see.

Night's startling black swept over the station and heat drifted out of the room and then—because this was the only shelter—men began to creep in from the wild heart of the desert, and in from the treacherous hills. A friendly Mescalero chief came to the room as silently as the cool night came, and ate and sat a while and spoke ten words and was gone. Charles Rice, one of Crook's scouts, came in. He waved a hand at the hills and said, "It is hell back there." A cowpuncher from the Santa Rita rode up. A solitary civilian messenger from Fort Apache appeared. These were all men who knew the country by heart; and it was at night they did their traveling. They ate and talked a while with the drowsy, brief phrases of their kind, and were silent when a rider drummed into the compound. And continued silent as the rider entered. Rosalia said to herself in disfavor: "The bad one again."

The owner, who was a just and impartial man, said: "Hello, Bill. Take a chair."

Peso Bill was old in wickedness but his eyes were bright and careless. He was slim and he could laugh quickly and show these people an insolence, which he did. For he knew how well the owner's hospitality sheltered him as long as he was within these walls. Alkali dust was heavy on his clothes and it caked his face like powder. He sat to the table with his hat on; black, lank hair came down beneath the brim. When Rosalia poured his coffee, Peso Bill stared at her, his smile very sharp. Rosalia moved away at once and the owner's chin lifted a little and he watched Peso Bill with a moment's hardening attention. The silence of the room was a wall surrounding Peso Bill.

Mrs. King said to the owner: "How did you come to pick this place?"

The owner smiled at the question, as though it brought back a fresh memory. "One day . . . this was five years ago . . . I took the stage out of Lordsburg, intending for Tonto. We broke an axle, about here. There was nothing at the time between Lordsburg and Tonto at all. I liked the spot, came back to it later and put up my station. This is pretty fair cattle country. I had five hundred head run off by the Apaches. But someday this range will all be used. It is a matter of waiting."

Charley Rice said, around his pipe-stem: "In the mornin', ma'am, go outside and look at the bullet marks in the walls."

The owner showed a smile which was a sign to Rosalia that he was pleased with the recollection. The owner's jaw was a long solid line and there was no man in this room, Rosalia told herself, who did not have a trust in him. Even Peso Bill trusted him. The owner said: "My people were all sailing men. My father is on the sea now. It is a far cry to the desert. But this is a good land."

The *Señora* King's voice, so graceful, so easy for a man to hear, filled in the silence: "But there is no difference, really. This desert is like the sea. This house is the only thing on it, for miles. You are responsible for these people. You are the captain, Mr. Folliard."

Charley Rice slanted a speculative and taciturn glance at the *Señora*. The fancy attracted him. All these men looked at the *Señora* and were pleased with her presence. Men were men, and made so for a purpose. But they could not see.

Peso Bill reared from his chair. "I'd like a drink, Captain," he drawled, and showed the owner a malice with his eyes. When he stood up this way, his right arm brushed the backcurved butt of his gun. The owner weighed Peso Bill briefly, still holding judgment out of his face. He nodded to Rosalia who walked down the hall with Peso Bill's spurs jingling behind. She turned into the small barroom, unlocked the cupboard, and placed bottle and glass before him.

Peso Bill poured his drink and took it at one impatient tip of his head. He put his elbow on the bar and watched her until Rosalia, who was a discerning girl, saw devils dancing their pinpoint brightness along the pupils of his eyes. There was a greediness in him, and a want. He moved his hand forward until he touched her waist and he waited, cat-like, to see what she would do. Rosalia stood still, composed and scornful. She said: "*Señor* is a fool. You want more out of this bottle?"

"Maybe," he said, and moved around the bar. "A Spanish woman is a hellcat, but I know. . . ."

There was a shadow in the doorway strong enough for Peso Bill to feel. He turned around and Rosalia almost smiled to see this. The owner was a big man but he had come down the hall without sound and stood over Peso Bill with a blackness on his face. The owner's eyes were small streaks of light and the owner had his fury. But he held it back in him and softly spoke.

"Ride out, Bill. And don't come back."

Peso Bill's smile was whiter. He said, "About that . . ." and paused with his head tipped aside. Other men were riding forward through the black, which was a sound that took Peso Bill out of the side door on the run. Rosalia heard his horse rush away, toward the south. Rosalia's lips were smooth and her heart beat faster; she kept her eyes down while she put away the whisky and locked the cupboard again. When she turned to leave the barroom, the owner was still in the door and it was necessary that she look up. The blackness was still on his face. "Rosalia," he said with a roughness, "hereafter I'll wait on this bar. It is a poor place for a woman."

Rosalia said: "Of what am I afraid, Tomás? Certainly of no man."

He kept watching her and this pause was strange, for the owner was no man to hesitate. Men were in the yard; they were coming into the living room. Rosalia said gently: "You have guests, Tómas."

She followed him down the hall, pleased that his back was so high and wide against the lamplight. There were four men in this new party and one was James Breaid, who wore a star. The marshal spoke out to the owner.

"Tom," he said, "Peso Bill has raised hell in Tonto. He killed Lyle McGarrah. His second shot hit Henry Graham's wife. Miz Graham is poorly."

This was as much of a question as the marshal would ask, knowing that he stood under the owner's room. The owner was not a talking man and, if he said anything now, it would be because of the badness of Peso Bill's bullet striking a woman. There was a silence. The owner moved a hand across his jaw. He said then: "I would know nothing about Peso Bill, Jim. Sit up to the table and we'll get something to eat . . . "

"Why . . ." spoke up *Señora* King. "I . . ."

The owner dropped one hand on the chair; it made a brief, arresting sound. He looked at the *Señora* King with a steadiness more important than words. The other men in the room kept still and the marshal's face, as he watched the *Señora*, was faintly amused. Presently he said: "We're a long way from home."

That was all. They went back to the yard. Everybody listened to the fading run of their horses. The *Señora* said: "I'm quite sorry."

The owner said: "No harm done. Jim Breaid knows I can't talk. All kinds of men come to my place. I question no man; and answer none. On the desert it has to be like that."

The *Señora* said: "Is that moonlight I see on the ground?" She rose and Rosalia, watching from the background, saw her wish reach out and lift the owner from his chair. The *Señora* placed her hand on the owner's arm. They left the room.

Rosalia went back to the kitchen and caught Luz idling in a corner. "Luz," she said, "there is still work." She crossed the kitchen and let herself into the rear compound and walked along the baked earth with her arms folded tight and high across her breasts. In the low east lay a new moon's yellow-orange arc, but it shed little light on the soot-black shadows of the desert. The ramparts of the Mesquite Hills showed raggedly along the sky and a cooling wind brought in the dry, aromatic odor of the desert. Folliard's station was a black rectangle solidly resisting the wild loneliness; its light shone out a challenge to the Apaches in the hills.

Rosalia returned to the house and finished her duties. The civilian messenger and the cow hand and Charley Rice had gone to bed; and the *Señora* had turned to her room. In her own room Rosalia listened to the house settle and grow still. She changed to her long white nightgown, and braided her hair in two pigtails and stood a moment, grave and young and caught by some thought that softened her lips and made her eyes glow. She took up a Hopi blanket from the bed and wrapped it around her shoulders, and padded barefooted down the hall, to the edge of the living room. The owner sat in a corner chair with his back to her. He held a cigar poised in one hand. He wasn't smoking it. He would be thinking and he would be lonely. The *Señora* had a way, Rosalia thought, and looked down at her small toes. Her heart quickened and her toes crept forward until they were almost in the room. This was as far as she could go; turning, she returned along the hall to the *Señora's* room.

There was a light shining beneath the door and Rosalia pushed the door before her and entered. The *Señora* sat at a table with her shoulders bowed forward and her glance fixed into a small mirror. The *Señora* jerked about and spoke with a startled sharpness: "What do you want?"

"Did the *Señora* want anything?"

Señora King said, "Come here." Rosalia walked nearer, seeing the coldness of *Señora* King's eyes and the knowledge in them that was not soft. The *Señora* said: "How old are you?"

"I am twenty-three," said Rosalia. "You are older, is that not so, *Señora*?"

The *Señora* King breathed: "Go away. Go away."

Rosalia returned to her room and made her prayers and listened to the broken cry of the coyotes on the bench not far away.

THIS WAS ANOTHER DAY, with the light of the desert growing brighter and hotter and the horizon slowly sinking behind a powder-blue heat haze.

At eleven-thirty Peso Bill rode down from the Mesquites at great haste. Rosalia, moving around the dining-room table, heard the drum of his horse and paused at the slitted window long enough to identify him. Alkali, as before, was thick and fresh on his clothes. He had pushed his hat away from his face; all his features were thin and expressive, and he was smiling at the owner who suddenly appeared. The owner stood before Peso Bill's horse. The owner's voice was slow, but it had closed out Peso Bill. "Keep going, Bill."

Peso Bill said: "A man's a fool to ride alone."

"That's your trouble, not mine. I've got no place here for you."

Peso Bill's grin sharpened. He said: "You wouldn't push a man away without water or grub?"

"Water your horse," said the owner. "And break the dust."

"Maybe," breathed Peso Bill. "Maybe."

"I've told you," said the owner and walked deliberately away, toward the barn.

Rosalia turned back to the table to make sure that the owner, who was a generous man, would find no fault with the food. The stage, coming on from Tonto, would be here in half an hour. The *Señora* King walked from her room and crossed to the door. She wore a plum-colored dress that rustled as she walked. Her chestnut hair lay in smooth folds on her head and her lips were fixed in softness. She went into the compound.

Rosalia hurried through the kitchen to the back door. Peso Bill's horse nosed the water in the dirt pool. Peso Bill stooped over the mouth of the pipe and drank with his hat removed. His lank hair fell down around his ears. He straightened and replaced the hat. Water clung to his face, but he made no move to brush it away. His eyes came over to the kitchen door and saw Rosalia; and he was smiling again.

Rosalia turned through the kitchen. The owner came down the long hall with a quick soft step. His shoulders were wide and heavy against the shadows and his face was very grave as he reached for his gun and belt hanging to the wall. When he strapped it around his waist, he turned to look at Rosalia. Rosalia was straight and still; her eyes were dark, but composure held her lips even. She said, "Tomás . . ." and said no more. The owner walked through the front door, into the compound. Mrs. King was saying something to him. Through the slitted window Rosalia saw Peso Bill round the corner of the 'dobe, without his horse. He walked on with a swing to his hips, faced the owner over a distance of twenty yards, and stopped.

There was talk between them. Rosalia swung to a corner of the room, seized up the rifle canted against the wall, and hurried toward the door. Peso Bill's voice came into the room, high and self-certain: "To hell with you, Folliard."

The owner's voice was deep and steady and complete: "You had my order, Bill. Move back to your horse."

Señora King screamed and that shrillness overrode the two flat bursts of revolver fire. Rosalia ran through the door, into the compound, feeling that sound collapse around her. Her eyes were for the owner. She saw him standing with his feet apart and the revolver half lowered. Peso Bill had fallen. He didn't move.

Señora King ran from the 'dobe wall of the house. She ran with her shoulders pulled together and her arms clenched. She stopped near Peso Bill and her voice was strident and accusing; it had a swift rage in it. She said: "The beast, Thomas! The beast! You shouldn't have given him the chance!"

Rosalia put the butt of the rifle on the ground and laid a hand over her mouth, and drew it away. Astonishment changed the owner's face as he watched the *Señora*. He listened to her and there was a pain in his eyes at hearing that shrillness, that outpour.

Rosalia said nothing. But the owner's eyes came around and he saw the gun she held. Rosalia at the moment looked upon the fallen Peso Bill and her grave features were pitying the man. Even though she would have killed Peso Bill, regret came to her now. She stood straight-shouldered in the full glare of the sun, soft-eyed and sad. This is what the owner saw.

There was a loose ball of dust in the north, which would be the Tonto stage rolling up. The *Señora* King came back to the owner. Her cheeks were brilliantly flushed and she stared at him with willingness on her lips. "You remember what I told you, Tomás? You are the captain."

The owner said, even and courteous: "The stage is coming, Mrs. King. You will have time to pack and eat."

Rosalia turned at once and went into the house. She was there by the table when the *Señora* King entered and walked towards the hall. The *Señora's* eyes were very old; they reached Rosalia and hated Rosalia, and then the *Señora* vanished into her room. The owner appeared through the door and the sound of the stage grew stronger. Rosalia lowered her eyes and her heart beat very fast and strong. The owner was before her and his voice lifted her chin. "Rosalia," he said; and then she saw the look in his eyes, which was the look the *Señora* King had brought there. But it was not for the *Señora* King. It was for her, for Rosalia Dures.

The owner was smiling. "Rosalia," he said. But said no more, for the stage had rolled before the station and the driver's voice, dry and flat, said: "Fifteen minutes for lunch." The owner walked reluctantly out. Rosalia, standing in the shadows, thought: I should thank the *Señora*, for Tomás has seen me and it was she who made him see me.

The passengers came in, speaking with weary relief. It was a hard ride and, these days, a dangerous ride from Tonto to Folliard's. After they had seated themselves at the table, Rosalia moved forward and, when she poured the owner's coffee, her round white arm gently touched his shoulder, and brought out his smile. The owner did not like to be served first, but there was a gentle stubbornness to Rosalia. This was the owner's house, and his table. Next meal she would sit at the table's other end, with Luz serving.

BRAND OF JUSTICE

FREDERICK DILLEY GLIDDEN was born in Kewanee, Illinois, and was graduated in 1930 with a Bachelor's degree from the University of Missouri where he had majored in journalism. Following graduation, Glidden worked for a number of newspapers, but no job lasted very long. He spent some two years trapping in northern Canada before he took a job as an archeologist's assistant in Santa Fé, New Mexico, and met Florence Elder of Grand Junction, Colorado, whom he married and nicknamed Butch. Fred read *Dime Western* and *Star Western* and was convinced he could write a story as well as any he had read. Since he had had first-hand experience living and working in the Arctic, he tried his hand first at North-Westerns. These were met by rejection. Fred and Butch were renting two adjacent adobe houses in Santa Fé which they used as a combined unit from Brian Boru Dunne. Fred asked Dunne if he knew of an agent. Dunne didn't, but he had another tenant who was a writer and who had a good one and he would ask him. That writer was T. T. Flynn. Marguerite E. Harper was the agent. She told Fred to redraft his North-Westerns as Westerns. In October, 1934, Fred sent Harper a story titled "Six-Gun Lawyer" and signed it F. D. Glidden. On April 17, 1935, Harper sold that story to *Cowboy Stories*, a pulp magazine Street & Smith had acquired from the bankrupt Clayton House for the princely sum of $100. It appeared in the issue for August 1935.

Harper told Fred she was concerned about his name. F. Orlin Tremaine, who had come to Street & Smith with *Cowboy Stories*, complained that it didn't sound very "Western." At first Fred thought of Lew Short—he wanted something "short" and memorable like Max Brand—and finally settled on Luke Short without realizing that this was the name of an actual gunman and gambler in the Old West. When Butch started writing Western romances, Harper named her Vic Elder (utilizing her maiden name); and, when Fred's older brother, Jonathan, started writing stories and she sold his first one to Street & Smith's *Complete Stories*, she named him Peter Dawson after an actual brand of Scotch whisky she liked to drink.

The characters in a Western story by Luke Short are hard and aggressive, and the tone in much that Fred wrote has an angry edge to it. However, in life Fred was not at all the person often suggested by his narrative voice. On January 4, 1966, he wrote to Moe, Jonathan's widow, a wholly characteristic letter that reveals how much compassion was a part of him: "I've had no real news from Marguerite in the last two months. She simply shuttles all publishers' correspondence and contracts to me. I don't know

170

what to do about half the business she sends and I feel as if, for the first time in thirty-one years of writing, I haven't an agent. My conscience won't let me dump her while she's in her present state of health, but it's exasperating to have to do her work for her when I haven't the knowledge or experience to handle it. Has she been doing anything for you or hasn't any business come up that requires her to act? In one of her letters she said her trouble was a nervous breakdown. She pleads with me to have patience until she's recovered and I guess that's what I'll do."

The Country Home Magazine was an agricultural journal published in Springfield, Ohio, when the Crowell Collier Corporation which owned *Collier's* and *The American Magazine* purchased it in the hope of using it as a means to compete with Curtis Publishing Company's *The Country Gentleman*. With the issue for December 1939, however, Crowell Collier decided the experiment had not been successful and the magazine ceased publication. Luke Short had three stories published in *The Country Home Magazine*, all in 1939: "Brand of Justice" (2/39), and two non-Western stories, "Ring Struck" (9/39) and "Danger in the Air" (12/39). "Brand of Justice" has never been otherwise reprinted.

The crowd had missed supper to hear the verdict, and now it poured out of the Masonic Hall into Sligo's main street, hungry and disgusted and in a surly temper. The Jake Van Every Mining Company had lost its suit against the huge Union Mining and Milling Company, and Sligo did not like it.

Jim Trimble, in his big fist a piece of raw newsprint filled with notes of the trial, thrust his way out of the door. He was a tall man, young, with overwide shoulders, and his trousers were tucked into half boots that were scuffed and unpolished. There was something about his quick, harried blue eyes and the taut look of his browned face that told an observer he hadn't had much time for the amenities lately and didn't miss them.

Scarcely a dozen steps away from the hall, he was brought to a halt by a tangle of men clotted on the boardwalk in front of Miller's assay office. A girl was backed into the doorway there and was being heckled by a group of rough miners. Trimble heard one of them say, "That's a right pretty red dress, miss. I bet it cost more'n my wages for two months."

"Why, heck," another drawled. "Her old man can earn a dozen of them in a day, just by sittin' still and lettin' big mines steal the little ones."

Jim elbowed his way through the knot of sullen onlookers to the inside of the circle. The girl he recognized as Judge Walcott's daughter, Julia. She had both palms flat against the door, as if she were trying to make herself as small as possible in her fright. Her eyes, brown to violet in the half-light, were full of anger and fear.

One burly miner, just off shift at the Van Every mine, with mud caked on his boots and his hands, said, "Maybe I ought to rub that dress a little and find out if it's silk."

He stepped past Jim Trimble and started for the frightened girl, holding up his muddy hands. Trimble caught him by the elbow and whirled him around.

"Maybe you'd better take my word for it that the dress is silk," Jim said in a low, taut voice.

The miner hesitated, his face ugly. "You're on the Union side, too, eh?"

"The man that says that is a liar," Jim said quietly. "I just don't believe in picking on a man's womenfolks, mister, no matter what I think of him."

He shoved the man into the crowd, which received him in sullen silence. Then Jim turned to the girl. "You should have had better sense than to come out tonight," he said curtly. "Come along, I'll take you home."

Without a word the girl fell in beside him as he made a way through the mob. She came just to his shoulder. He had seen her about town many times with her father, only then she looked a little proud and disdainful, as if she hated this rough world of boom camp. But tonight she was frightened, and somehow it made her seem more human. He was surprised to see that her hair, which he had always remembered as brown, was a deep honey color, piled high beneath her absurd little hat.

At the big Exchange Hotel, the pride of this raw mining camp, they turned into the lobby, which was just filling up with the crowd from the trial. Only this was a different crowd—flashy with easy money, not poor.

Julia Walcott paused at the foot of the wide, red-carpeted stairs and bluntly said to Jim, "Why do they hate me so?"

Jim looked searchingly at her, suspicion in his blue eyes. He decided suddenly that maybe she really didn't know, and his answer was mild. "It's not you; it's your father they hate."

"But why?"

Jim Trimble, recalling the events of this past week, couldn't keep the bitterness out of his voice.

"Why, around here we've got the old-fashioned idea that a judge should be impartial. Your dad used to be and he isn't now, that's all."

A faint flush crept into Julia Walcott's cheeks. She looked at him steadily and said, "That is a lie. Either prove it or apologize."

Jim looked over the lobby. Here were the men who owned the big mines in Sligo, the stock promoters from San Francisco, the men who were the wealth in this town. They were the men he had been fighting in his newspaper these last weeks, fighting with all the power he had. And tonight he knew they had beaten him. He could not keep the contempt from his voice as he spoke:

"Miss Walcott, have you ever heard of a silver ledge?"

"No." Her voice was cold.

"It's where they find silver in ore. These ledges go deep into the ground, thousands of feet. Only they don't go straight down. Lots of times they angle off. The Union Mining and Milling Company is working a ledge now that has angled off until it has got over the boundary line of the Union claim onto the claim of a relatively poor man. That man, Jake Van Every, brought it to court because he believed the Union was looting his ore."

"And Dad ruled the Union wasn't?"

"Not your dad. The jury."

"Then what is your quarrel with Dad? A judge can't decide a case!" She was angry now, and so was Jim.

He said, "But he can order evidence stricken out that is perjury; he can declare a mistrial when he has cause; and he can issue a restraining order closing down the Union until this case is settled." He paused and, when he spoke again, his voice was harsh. "He turned this camp over to the robbers."

"I don't believe it!" she said, her eyes flashing.

"I didn't think you would. Good night."

"One more question," Julia Walcott said. "What right have you to criticize a man whose profession you don't understand?"

"All the right in the world," Jim said softly. "I own the *Sligo Herald*, Miss Walcott. And I'd rather turn up an injustice like that than a gold mine."

He turned on his heel, his wrath unchecked, and left her. Almost to the lobby door, he paused and stepped aside to let a group of men pass him. Judge Walcott, his thin, fine face pale with fury, strode through the wide door, accompanied by an armed bodyguard. Also in that group of men were Miles Overman, the superintendent of the Union, and Big Chig Henry, his assistant. The sight of them brought a wry smile to Jim's face. Overman saw him, saw the smile, and fell away from the group that was marching toward the stairway. A barrel-chested man, big for a country of big men, Miles Overman had a kind of brashness about him that he wore like a banner. He paused now in front of Jim, and regarded him quietly.

"Decided to take your beating, eh, Trimble?"

"What beating?" Jim asked gently.

Overman grinned. "Oh, I thought you'd been trying for two weeks in that rag of yours to start a lynching party against the Union."

"I'm not very lucky," Trimble said, and smiled faintly.

Overman regarded him closely for a long moment. "How long can you hold out, Trimble, now that all your advertising is stopped."

"As long as I can get paper."

"I saw about that," Overman said mildly. "Your credit ain't good any more with the paper people."

"I know. They wrote me. But I've still got enough left to beat you robbers. And, Overman," he added grimly, "don't lose your head and try to wreck my plant, because I'll kill you."

Once outside, he found he hadn't realized how angry he was, but now it came over him in a sick wave of fury. The taste of defeat was bitter in his mouth. He had jumped into the thick of the fight, taking Van Every's side because it was simple justice to him. But in a short time Jake's claim would be worthless, gutted of its ore, since Judge Walcott whose name had always been a byword for honesty would not issue an order to cease operations until the case was appealed. Jim wondered, in his anger, what had come over Judge Walcott.

Ahead of him Jim saw Hugo Fayette turn in at Price's Keno Parlor and, on an impulse, followed him. Fayette, a morose-looking man, a horse-trader by profession, had been the foreman of the jury in this trial. He had an unsavory reputation and Jim reflected that his presence on the jury had been a symbol of the whole shifty business. Fayette was a little drunk and, as Jim casually came up beside him at the bar, he looked up, his eyes furtive and immediately wary.

"Tryin' to wash the taste of the trial out of your mouth, Hugo?" Jim asked. He hadn't meant to be insulting, but now it was out, he was glad.

Fayette came erect, a small wicked light in his eyes. For a brief second Jim thought he was going to fight, and then the light died. He made no response. He reached in his pocket, brought out a bank note, and laid it on the bar. The bartender looked reprovingly at Jim and picked up the bill. He examined it closely, turning it over and over.

"What's this?" he asked.

"It's a bank note," Fayette growled surlily. "Same as money."

Jim said dryly, prodding. "Sure, Barney. Didn't you read in the paper about the banks turning twenty thousand in new bank notes over to the Union?" He looked at Fayette meaningly. "They were going to pay their men in bank notes, but the men wouldn't take them. All except Fayette."

Fayette's face was ugly. "If you think I ever took pay from the Union except for what I sold 'em, you're a liar," he said angrily. He slapped a paper down on the bar. "I sold seventy mules to the Union yesterday. There's the receipt. They paid in bills."

"Sure," Jim murmured. A wave of weariness and disgust flooded over him as he turned and went out. He might suspect that Fayette had been bought by Overman, but he was having trouble trying to prove it.

He made his slow way up the street to the small office of the *Sligo Herald* and slumped down into his rickety chair. This was how it felt to take a licking. There was no sensation at all, not even one of despair. His creditors were slowly closing in on him and by his stand against the Union he had alienated the sources of revenue in the town. He was finished. He thought of Julia Walcott, remembering her face, grave and clean and angry. She wouldn't be a party to shifty business like this, but her father was. Or was he?

A stack of newspapers from the other frontier towns lay on the desk before him. He might as well turn out the exchange news tonight, rewriting the news from the territory that might interest his subscribers in Sligo. It was while he was doggedly reading the *Argus* from Fort Clifton, the Army town on the other side of the Toand peaks, that something started to tick in the back of his head. Here was a story on the front page headed:

ARMY REMUDA RAIDED AGAIN

It went on to tell that twelve more mules had been stolen from the Fort Clifton remuda—a common-enough frontier story.

Jim settled back in his chair, looking at the ceiling. Funny, wasn't it, that Hugo Fayette had sold the Union some mules yesterday just after some mules had been stolen from Fort Clifton. . . .

Jim was still tingling with excitement when he heard the street door open. Judge Walcott and his daughter stepped into the room. Jim rose slowly as Walcott crossed to the desk. He had a long, sallow face, bisected by a black saber mustache, and his eyes were as dark as Julia's. Pausing before the desk, Judge Walcott said bluntly, "My daughter told me of a conversation she had with you tonight. I'd like to hear you repeat it to me."

An unreasoning anger mounted in Jim at the judge's present arrogance. He said ominously, "If she told you that I once thought you were a fair man, and that now I think you're prejudiced, unfair, and not even interested in the justice of the case, she covered the ground pretty well."

"You intend to print that?"

"Naturally."

"It's libel," Walcott snapped. "And I'll close this paper down with a court order so quickly it'll take your breath away!"

"You wouldn't close the Union until the appeal, Judge, but you'll close me," Jim drawled. "I reckon it depends on who you favor, doesn't it?"

"That's not so!" Julia cried.

Jim looked at her with contempt in his eyes, then shuttled his glance to Walcott. The judge was making a visible effort to control his fury. "I won't hide behind a court order. If you libel me, I'll shoot you down like the dog you are."

Jim's voice was thick. "That's a date. Next Thursday."

Walcott drew a deep breath. He said slowly, "I warned you," turned and stalked toward the door.

Julia Walcott hesitated a moment, regarding Jim with puzzlement in her brown eyes. "You think you're right, don't you?"

"I do."

"Then be sure you're willing to die for it," Julia said bitterly, and followed her father out.

Jim settled back slowly into his chair, surprised by this girl's spirit. She was beautiful, even in her rage—but she was wrong, so very very wrong. Then as if something had decided him, he rose again.

"I'm going to bust this town wide open," he said grimly. "Or I'm going to be buried here. It's one or the other now."

The shaft house of the Union Mining and Milling Company was a quarter way up the Toands that towered behind Sligo in giant shoulders of sun-blasted rock. The steady chuff-chuff of the hoist engine filled the desert night with its small noise as Jim rode up the slope to the candle house. He found McGuire, the night super, at the desk in one corner.

He seemed surprised to see Jim. "You're in Indian country, son," he said, smiling.

Jim grinned. "Nobody's shot at me yet. Listen, Mac, I'm writing a piece for the *Herald* on the Union. I want to see how far you've gone. Can I go down?"

McGuire looked troubled. "Well, whatever stinks down there, and some of it does, you know already, I reckon, Jim."

He led the way out to the half-covered shaft where the cable timbers loomed up in a dark tangle. He called to the hoist man, told him to put Jim out at nine hundred. Jim stepped into the cage, heard the clatter of gears, and then the earth seemed to drop out from under him. At last the cage slacked speed and came to a stop at one of the lower galleries.

Jim stepped out, lantern in hand. After a short search, he came to a cross cut that was wider than the others, with a timbered floor—the stable. Inside, the only light a turned-down lantern, were a dozen mules facing a long manger. These animals, for the rest of their lives, would work and eat and sleep in this dank gloom, nearly a thousand feet from sunlight, hardly missing their other life.

Jim worked swiftly. Taking the lantern he moved in among them and began, one by one, to examine their brands. He had a sudden suspicion that he was a fool, and on a fool's errand, but he kept at it. And then, the third from the last mule he came to, he found what he was looking for.

He turned away then, smiling, and quickly made his way toward the shaft. He took an ore skip to the surface, and faded into the night. There was a look of grim and cool satisfaction on his face as he headed back for town—and Malloy's.

Malloy's was a shabby boardinghouse, just off the main street, a slab affair of two dozen airless cribs that flanked a corridor off a greasy-smelling dining room.

"Fayette in yet?" he asked Ed Malloy.

"Yeh. Fifth on your right."

Jim struck a match inside the room, lighted a blackened lamp. Fayette, fully clothed, lay snoring on the bed, his breath filling the room with a stench of liquor. Jim took the bucket of water from the washstand and doused it on Fayette, then yanked him to a sitting position and slapped his face until his head steadied.

"Stand up, Hugo," Jim said softly. "We're taking a trip to the closest U.S. marshal. When I tell him what I know, I think he'll twist your head off."

Fayette's eyes snapped into focus. "What you talkin' about?" he asked.

"Those mules you stole from the Army over at Fort Clifton."

"They were bought!"

"If they were," Jim murmured, "why the hair-branding that changed that U S on the left shoulder to a J 8? You've been playin' this game a long time, Fayette. Selling stolen mules to the Union to put underground where nobody would ever see their brands, and the men who did wouldn't care."

Fayette's glance shuttled to the washstand where his holstered gun lay. Jim smiled. "Don't make a try for it. Just pull your boots on."

Fayette said harshly, "You'll never get away with it! The Union will back me up."

"You fool," Jim said scornfully. "The Union will sell you out. All they have to say is that they didn't know the mules were stolen and you'll stand trial alone."

Fayette struggled to his feet, eyes blazing with anger. "Did Overman say that?"

"He didn't. Do you want me to go to him, so you can prove it yourself?"

The question was intentionally framed that way, and Fayette, even in his fright, saw an alternative. He said, "Then you ain't goin' to the marshal?"

"Not unless you crowd me to it."

They looked at each other briefly, then Jim shoved Fayette down onto the cot.

Jim said softly, "You were paid big money to hang that jury, weren't you?"

The man's lips tightened stubbornly. Jim took Fayette's gun from the washstand and leveled it at him.

"Were you paid?"

Fayette paled. "Five thousand dollars."

"Who paid you?"

"Overman. He was pretty sure of Walcott, but he wanted to be dead sure."

"Was Walcott bribed?"

Fayette shook his head. "No."

Jim could scarcely keep the relief from his voice. "I'm taking you to Judge Walcott. Tell him your story, and then clear out of the country. And clear out fast."

"Overman'll kill me!" Fayette cried.

"Maybe." Jim paused. "Want to take a chance on missing him? Or would you rather go up for ten years for horse stealing?"

Fayette scrubbed his face with his hand and said hoarsely, "I'll take the chance."

Under Jim's gun, he pulled on his boots, and they started for the Exchange.

As they entered the lobby, Jim glanced toward the cluster of chairs behind the big window. Overman was sitting there, his back to them. Jim increased his pace. If Overman saw them, there would be trouble. They had gone ten steps, perhaps, when Jim heard his name called.

He paid no attention. He could see the sweat beading Fayette's brow. They hurried to the judge's room. Jim knocked and, when the door opened, he was facing Julia Walcott. Without a word, he shoved Fayette past her, then stepped in, closed the door and locked it.

They were in the sitting room. Judge Walcott had risen from his chair. Julia Walcott, outraged, stood beside Jim.

"I haven't much time, Judge," Jim said in a low voice. "This is Hugo Fayette, foreman of the jury. Overman gave him five thousand dollars to hang that jury in Van Every's suit against the Union."

A thunderous knock on the door punctuated his speech. The anger in Judge Walcott's face gave way to bewilderment. He looked at Fayette. "Is that true?"

"Every word of it," Fayette said.

The knock came again. It sounded as if somebody was kicking in the door.

"That's Overman," Jim said, his quiet gaze on Judge Walcott.

Slowly the judge's face hardened. He said quietly, "Let him in."

Jim unlocked the door and threw it open. Miles Overman stalked into the room, his glance settling on Fayette, who cringed.

Judge Walcott spoke first, and it was done calmly. "You're under arrest, Overman. Fayette says you bribed him to hang the jury in the Van Every case."

"He lies," Overman said calmly.

"We'll go into that later. You are under arrest."

Overman's eyes were busy. He looked at the judge's face, and then at Fayette, and finally at Jim. Then his gaze shuttled back to the judge. "And if it's true?"

"A mistrial will be declared. And this time," Judge Walcott said stonily, "the bench will issue a writ closing down the Union. Moreover, you'll never get a jury in this country again that won't render a judgment in favor of Van Every, Overman. You tried to buy off justice once; you will never find it again."

Overman was smiling faintly. "And if there's nobody to testify to the bribery?"

It was Jim who first caught the meaning behind those words. His hand streaked toward the gun in his waistband. At the same time, Overman's gun slid out of its holster and swung hip-high in a tight arc. The sight on Jim's gun caught in the lining of his trousers. He tugged frantically at it, swinging it clear just as Fayette screamed and Overman's gun exploded with a roar. Fayette went down with an oath. Jim brought his gun up as Overman's pistol swung around toward him. In a panic of haste, Jim fired, and on the heel of his shot Overman's gun went off. The slug ripped into the carpet at Jim's feet raising a faint geyser of dust. A look of amazement crept into Overman's face, and he raised a hand to his chest. He took one step backward to brace himself, and then pitched forward on his face.

Jim dropped his gun and turned to Julia. He put an arm around her and led her into the next room. Already, there was the sound of running feet in the hall. Jim guided Julia to the bed and she sat down, crying in a kind of wild hysteria that Jim could not stop. Nor did he want to. Her face was buried in his shoulder—the warmth of her close to him intoxicating.

After a long time, Judge Walcott entered, a weary and beaten old man. Standing in front of Jim and Julia, he said, "I owe you my profound apology and thanks, Trimble, as does my daughter. You not only saved our lives, but you saved me from the biggest mistake of my lifetime."

Jim murmured something embarrassedly, and Julia clung to him.

"I thought," Judge Walcott said, fumbling for his words, "that I was a just man. I find I am not. In my eagerness to see this country grow, to bring wealth and prosperity to a desert, I played into the hands of crooks. I mistook power for progress, wealth for right." He looked humbly at Jim. "I forgot to be human, Jim. I won't do that again." He turned blindly and left them.

Julia sat erect, and Jim, embarrassment in his face, took his arm from around her and started to rise.

Julia said quietly, "Sit still, Jim." She did not look at him and she spoke in low tones. "I was beastly, Jim. You see, I sat through the last of the case, and what you said about Dad was true. I knew it, but I couldn't be disloyal to him, could I?" She looked up at him, her eyes questioning.

"No," Jim murmured. "I understood that. And I believed in your dad, too, or I wouldn't have brought Fayette here."

"Believed? Why?"

Jim blushed, but he stammered on. "A man doesn't get that loyalty from a thoroughbred unless he's worth it."

Julia turned her head to look at him. Her brown eyes were beginning to fill with tears. She turned her head away. "I . . . I'm going to cry again, Jim."

"Go ahead and cry," Jim murmured, his arms around her. "I reckon I'll see you plenty of times when you aren't."

"I know you will," she answered softly, and she answered for them both.

WHERE TRAILS DIVIDE

TOM(THOMAS) W(AKEFIELD) BLACKBURN was born on the T. O. Ranch near Raton, New Mexico, where his father was employed as an engineer. The T. O., which controlled such a vast domain it had its own internal railroad system, was later used as the setting for Blackburn's novel, RATON PASS (Doubleday, 1950). Blackburn eventually moved with his family to southern California where he attended Glendale Junior College and then UCLA. In 1937 he married Juanita Alsdorf and, surely, she was the model for many of his notable Spanish and Mexican heroines. Blackburn got his start "ghosting" stories for Ed Earl Repp and Harry F. Olmsted, prolific contributors to Western pulp magazines but mostly of fiction they did not produce themselves. For example, one of the last stories Blackburn submitted to Harry F. Olmsted was sold to Jack Burr at Street & Smith's *Western Story Magazine* for $425.00. It was showcased as the featured novel under the title "Guns of the Buckskin Empire" by Harry F. Olmsted in *Western Story Magazine* (3/2/40). Olmsted paid Tom 3/10 of a cent a word; Tom's "share" came to $75.00.

In the 1940s in addition to writing hundreds of stories under his own name, Blackburn worked as a screenwriter for various Hollywood studios. His longest affiliation was with the Disney studio where, for a time, he was best known for having written the lyrics for "The Ballad of Davy Crockett," a popular television and then theatrical series based on the exploits of this legendary frontiersman.

Among his finest short novels are several which first appeared in *Lariat Story Magazine*: "Mistress of Night Riders' Rancho" (9/43), "Renegade Lady of the Blazing Buckhorn" (1/44), "Bullets Sang in Siesta" (11/44), "Trigger Boss of Wild Horse Creek" (5/45), and "Town of Whispering Guns" (9/49). His first book-length novel, and still one of his best, SHORT GRASS (Simon & Schuster, 1948), was an expansion of a short novel he had submitted to Fiction House titled "Man from the Short-Grass." The title was changed to "The Gun-Prophet of El Dorado" when it appeared in *Action Stories* (2/43). Tom later adapted this novel to a screenplay and it was filmed as SHORT GRASS (Allied Artists, 1951). Other novels by Tom W. Blackburn, no less fine, are NAVAJO CANYON (Doubleday, 1952) which was recently reprinted in a hardcover edition in the Gunsmoke series by Chivers Press, A GOOD DAY TO DIE (McKay, 1967) which concerns the battle at Wounded Knee, and the five-book Stanton saga, beginning with YANQUI (Dell, 1973) and followed by RANCHERO (Dell, 1974), EL SEGUNDO (Dell, 1974), PATRÓN (Dell, 1976), and COMPAÑEROS (Dell, 1978). This saga is really his *magnum opus* and, starting with YANQUI, it is now being reprinted for the first time in hardcover editions by Chivers. Both SHORT GRASS and RATON PASS are available in full-length audio editions from Books on Tape.

"Where Trails Divide" was the twenty-fifth short story Blackburn wrote and just about the first he offered for publication on his own without submitting it to Ed Earl Repp or Harry F. Olmsted. He sent it directly to Rodgers Terrill at Popular Publications on August 22, 1938. Terrill bought it on October 14, 1938, and paid Blackburn $40, or 1¢ a word. Originally Terrill scheduled the story to appear in the February 1939, issue of *10 Story Western*, but he changed his mind and published it instead in the more prestigious *Star Western* (1/39) under the title "Epitaph for an Unmarked Grave." For its reappearance here, its original title has been restored. There is very little that is ever conventional or routine in any Western story by Tom W. Blackburn and that was as true at the beginning as at any point in his professional writing career.

I

The town lay peacefully along the one street that drifted carelessly beneath the cottonwoods. Old Mexico, with her mystery and tolerance of all breeds of silent men, lay a short, swift ride to the south. Cordobal was quiet, a little eddy off the outlaw trail reaching down from the Texas grass ranges to the hidden markets for stolen stock in Old Mexico. Maybe it was the quiet of Cordobal that leathery, stone-faced Kirk Brandon liked. But some folks thought it was something else.

Kirk Brandon knew the answer but, as with all that concerned his own past, he kept a shut mouth. Now he stood idly at the Buckhorn Bar, a weathered man, both in spirit and saddle-toughened body. His guns hung low and his eye was level. He knew good beef, and who raised it. . . .

His head was cocked slightly forward as he listened to the quiet on the street outside. That quiet meant something, now. He shifted position and lounged more easily. For Brandon was a patient man, and a clever one. The faint creak of a buggy's wheels drifted in, but still he stood impassive. The barkeep's low-voiced words brought him nothing he did not already know.

"Them buggies'll be Johnny Carter, takin' his last ride, I reckon."

Brandon said nothing, his gaze riveted to the backbar mirror before him. The barkeep again tried to stir his single customer into conversation.

"Johnny died jest about as thick-headed as he lived. He rid some mighty scary trails after Texas beef for the Mexes, afore his wife drug him back to his place out of town. And he was lucky he come back from the owlhoot with no stronger brand on him than they was. Then plumb-fool like, he lets Cochise and his Last Ten of the Vengeance 'Paches sight him after dark off his own spread. Any gent who'd take them chances rated the arrow in his throat Johnny collected. . . . And him with a wife and kid!"

The barkeep paused expectantly. Talk of Texas beef on border trails was nothing to make in hearing of tall Kirk Brandon. Brandon recognized the bait and passed it up. The sound of buggy wheels was still in his ears. Dregs were in the glass before him and he downed them. Then he spun out the door and stopped near a veranda pillar, his eyes focused on the somber procession before him.

Three black buggies, a shiny hearse, two horsemen and a stray dog. . . . Johnny Carter made his last trip down this familiar street with little enough fanfare. But one figure alone out of the scene caught the watching man's eyes—the tall figure of a proud woman in one of the buggies.

She sat erect and calm in the face of her grief. Her eyes were fastened on the black vehicle ahead. It was only when Kirk became aware of her gaze turning upon him that he suddenly felt detached from all this, a stranger looking at something he did not understand.

Down Buscado way, in the Mexican camp where Kirk Brandon's trail-wolves wound up their wide-looping drives for stock, quarrels came and went. Many more men died than ever rode a black hearse down the one street of Cordobal. But Brandon had never before seen a woman with the courage to match her grief. He was thinking about that woman when he reëntered the saloon.

The barkeep eyed him strangely again. Finally a sympathetic smile crossed his deep-veined face. He shoved a bottle forward quietly. "This one's on the house, Brandon," he offered. "I'm just rememberin' you and Johnny Carter, there, was once saddle-mates."

Brandon's colorless eyes fixed those of the man behind the bar unseeingly.

"Yeah," he muttered. "Yeah. . . ."

And he walked out of the Buckhorn without a glance at the label on the bottle set before him.

When he was in Cordobal, as infrequently he was, there were but two places where Kirk Brandon might be found. One was in front of a bottle of hundred-proof bourbon at the Buckhorn, the other was his corner room on the second floor of the hotel. Having quitted one, he went now directly to the other, his mind still occupied with the woman in the buggy.

It had been a picture to tighten a man's throat, seeing her ride that procession with her lovely face set in calm acceptance of the blow that was hers. Molly had always loved Johnny Carter, and Brandon remembered this bitterly. But she had always been like that, with courage to spare. When her boy was born, Johnny had been in Buscado, delivering a Turkey Track herd to his tall, leather-faced partner. Molly had had her baby all alone in the sod shanty that had been on the Carter place in those days. But her eyes had been bright with welcome when Johnny came home, drunk and ashamed.

Molly loved that kid of hers, too. When folks in Cordobal started talking about raising a kid to be a rustler, to follow in the footsteps of his dad and Kirk Brandon, Molly had acted calmly. She had pulled Johnny home, set him to tending beef with his own iron. Kirk had understood how it was, and he had let Johnny go. For sooner or later on the brush-trail, Johnny would find trouble somewhere and he might bring it back with him to Buscado.

The rest Molly had done was something else again. The kid had been sent north to school in Santa Fé with only letters to keep him near his mother. And Molly had sent him, without showing a tear, though it must have torn her heart out to do it. The kid stayed, learning to be honest, learning out of books a more honorable trade than his dad could teach him. And Molly had turned toward the task of earning a new reputation for Johnny, winning for him in Cordobal the name of an honest rancher. That she had never entirely succeeded was no sign she had not fought grimly for it.

And now. . . . Well, that ride down the street behind a hearse was the beginning of more troubles, and another more drastic test of Molly's courage. That school in Santa Fé cost money and Johnny Carter hadn't been a very good cowman, just as in earlier years midnight hops across the border had brought him but little silver.

A strange deep glow was in Kirk Brandon's eyes. Many a lost-hope deal had come at last to the hands of this man who waited wisely and played his hand as his cards were dealt to him.

He crossed the room to his bureau and took out a small case. From within he took two slips of paper, and a thin, dry grin crossed his face. He looked at the two notes for five thousand each, long overdue.

In Buscado they said that Brandon had been a fool to have let Johnny Carter have the money, but Johnny had been his partner once, and. . . . Now it all didn't seem foolish. A memory of Molly Carter as she had been ten years ago when he and Johnny were both courting her was in Brandon's mind. Molly had not changed much. She still was a likely queen for a borderland empire of renegades down in Buscado.

For a little while Kirk thought of the Carter place beyond the town, of riding out there. Then he shrugged. He was older now, and he had learned patience. Fortune, and a woman, must be won slowly and with consummate cleverness.

With steady hand he scrawled "Paid" across the notes and sealed them in an envelope. In a bold block script he addressed the packet to the man Cordobal was burying today. . . .

When he went out onto the street, a *peonito* squatting in the dust took a quarter from his hand and carried the envelope into the post office.

In half an hour Kirk was riding south. He rode hard and kept to wide country until he breasted the river. Cochise, the dread Apache raider, and the Last Ten still ranged those breaks, seeking their tithe in white blood from lone riders for a wrong none but the 'Paches remembered. And Kirk Brandon never made the mistakes that had hounded Johnny Carter.

After crossing over into Mexico, with the Rio between himself and Cochise's hunting-ground, tall Kirk Brandon's grim face split in a confident smile. For once, Molly's courage would have no play. She had been the business head at the Carter ranch too long not to know that Johnny's biggest creditor, with a generosity she could not believe of him, had freely relieved her of her most pressing financial problem. Molly would think much about this, and about the man who had done it. Brandon rode easily now, for later he would return.

II

But it was three months before messengers from the north brought the news to Buscado, and tall Kirk Brandon rode hard again. And this time he forsook the Buckhorn to visit Sadavan's bank.

Sadavan was old, and folks said he knew the thoughts of every man who faced him. But Kirk Brandon knew this was a lie. None knew what turned within his own mind save himself.

"I'm after cash this trip, Sadavan," he said brusquely. "I'll clean my account out . . . in bills, if you've got it."

The banker looked surprised. His lined old face screwed tighter and he leaned forward. "You quittin' at last, Brandon?" he said slyly. "Made your pile, eh?"

Brandon's eyes were cold and fathomless, but perhaps there was a hint of elation in them, and it colored his words. "I'm closing a deal this trip, Sadavan, that I've been working on for ten long years. I'm making a bid for the thing I've wanted most since I first hit the Big Bend. If my bid is best, I want the green to back it!"

The banker mumbled and turned toward the vault. The dial whispered and later came the crisp rustle of fresh bills counted in practiced hands. Directly he came into the office with a brown, square envelope which he thrust into Brandon's hands.

"No deal west of St. Joe's worth the risk of totin' thirty thousand in cash on your belly! But you'd know that," the banker grunted. "Now I got to write Silver City for more cash to meet the construction payroll on the railroad at Lima Crossing, come the end of the month!"

But Kirk Brandon was gone onto the street, with banker Sadavan's complaint only a vague whine behind him.

In moments he was facing another man, his segundo from Buscado, in his hotel room. The segundo had been well-informed. The brown envelope was opened and a pad of bills removed. Brandon watched his man go out into the hall with the bills in his pocket. Then he sat down to wait.

Time dragged slowly, and his mind drifted back over years now gone into the past which had been his humble beginning.

Two Texas drifters had hit the Big Bend together, riding the high trails with posse-thunder in their ears, for a man lay dead at Silver City and his friends had claimed murder. Kirk remembered that shot, a clean one through the throat of a pasty-faced tinhorn. It had been Johnny Carter who was at the table; it was Johnny's thick wits which had called the tinhorn's double-deal long before Brandon was prepared to capitalize on his own previous knowledge of it.

Kirk had been across the room, his back turned, when he heard Johnny's startled cry of alarm, yet Kirk had still beaten the gambler by a wide margin. The trouble was, there had been too much speed in Brandon's draw. For he was tallied a gunman, maybe masquerading under an unknown name, and the law came baying after them.

They had worked south and finally were forced across the border. Here Kirk saw opportunity for a man with brains. So he had bought, with what money they had, the piece of land outside of Cordobal which became the Carter place. With that as a blind, things had gone well, driving Texas cattle south for Mexican sale.

A dry humor was in Brandon tonight. That Carter place had been good land. Had a man who understood his business ranched that piece, it would have made money—almost as much as the camp at Buscado. But it had been Johnny's lot to get that ranch, as it had been Kirk's choice to rod Buscado and its tough cattle-rustling renegades. It had also been Johnny's lot, with his wide blue eyes and boyish carelessness, to win Molly Haskins—but not for keeps. For Kirk Brandon had learned the way a strong man may win from the world what he wants. And for ten years Kirk Brandon had wanted Molly Carter. Tonight he knew he was close.

Once he got up from his seat and moved nervously to the window. He had planned carefully. It was not in him to believe he might have been wrong somewhere along the line of reasoning that had led up to tonight. She would come; he was certain of that. For Molly Carter was a proud woman and fought her own way.

The sound of steps in the hall roused him again, but they passed on by. He took a long *cigarro* from a battered case and chewed it viciously.

But in the end, Molly did come.

He opened the door with a courteous swing that was something Mexico had given him. Molly was dressed in denim blouse and the divided skirt of a woman who had much riding to do. She carried a folio under her arm, and through the tired wrinkles of strain about her eyes, somehow, a light of happiness showed.

For a moment Brandon believed he had won, hands elbow-high and without need of a showdown. But he soon saw he was wrong. Molly had never laid down a hand in her life and she intended to play out this one.

He gestured awkwardly. "I was hoping to see you, Molly." He stumbled. "These things are hard, I reckon. Johnny . . . well, if I could help . . . ?"

Carefully he framed that speech and carefully he watched its effect. The pleasure faded from Molly's eyes and a puzzled look crept into them. She leaned forward, her hand resting on his.

"Help, Kirk?" she asked. "I got those canceled notes. Johnny never had a thousand dollars at one time, let alone ten, to pay off notes with. Was that your way of helping?"

Tall Kirk Brandon hesitated just a moment. "That was business, Molly," he answered. "Let's say I owed Johnny those cancellations."

Molly shook her head. "A week ago I advertised my stock for sale. Sadavan had a small note on the land out at the place and I had to let him take it. The cattle were all I had left to meet the others Johnny owed. The beef market is in the worst slump in a dozen years. Yet a bidder took my stuff for three times what it's worth! I'm broke now, but every man in town is square with Johnny Carter."

Kirk leaned back in his chair. A smile crossed his face, a bland effort at naturalness. With thirty thousand in cash and Molly at Buscado, an empty life would be full. Ten years might suddenly be forgotten.

His answer was hearty. "That was luck that you deserve, Molly," he said. "The kind of good luck you've won by your own efforts."

Molly shook her head. Her fingers tightened on his. "Not good luck, Kirk, not even luck. Some folks say it is . . . some folks say it's bad luck . . . for me. Word got 'round that the bidder was your man!"

Brandon made no answer.

"More help, Kirk?" Molly asked again. "I know you, Kirk Brandon. Sometimes I think I know you better than I ever did Johnny Carter. You never helped man, woman or beast in your life. Some have

been helped *through* you, but only because through them you made
a deal! You were really working for Kirk Brandon every minute of
your life. And that's what this is, isn't it, Kirk . . . a deal?"

Still Brandon made no answer. Too many words had ruined many
an otherwise sound transaction.

"You knew I couldn't refuse the return of those notes," Molly went
on. "You knew I had to take the best price for those cattle I could
get. You knew that, when it was all done, I still had my boy at
school in Santa Fé, that I still had hopes of sending him East to
college, of making a fine lawyer out of him. And I reckon, Kirk
Brandon, you know me as well as I know you. Your bid tops anything I had dreamed of. What is it you want, Kirk?"

Silence was in the room for a moment, then Brandon's answer
came bluntly. "It's you, Molly!"

The woman rose and crossed to the window. She stood there
staring out while Kirk's *cigarro* burned a half inch of ash. Then she
turned back.

"Yes, I suppose it is me you want. For ten years I've known you've
kept this on your mind. Now you'd take me south to your place at
Buscado. And I'd have those things you promised me the night I
told you I was going to marry Johnny Carter. You've been a strong
man, Kirk, where Johnny was weak. You have money where he had
debts. But it was you who chose Buscado and the renegades to
ranching, and Johnny only followed you. And when you go, you'll
leave nothing behind you. For I loved Johnny Carter. You understand that, Kirk?"

Brandon nodded.

Molly picked up the hat she had tossed on the bureau. "I packed
tonight before I came in, Kirk. I was leaving Cordobal. My bag is at
the stage station. Maybe I hoped your bid was for something else;
maybe I knew it was for me. It doesn't matter. But what about
my boy?"

Tall Kirk Brandon rose to his feet. He took up the brown envelope
with Sadavan's greenbacks wadding its sides. "Your stock cost me
ten thousand," he said. "There's plenty more."

"There'll always be plenty . . . for him?"

Brandon nodded as he opened the door.

III

Ten miles south of Cordobal, pounding along through the breaks
behind a livery team in one of the three black buggies which traveled in Johnny Carter's last ride, Kirk Brandon felt a strange sweat

upon him. The first flush of pride in the presence of Molly beside him was gone.

Some of the bitterness of ten long years came back to sicken him. This was to have been his greatest coup, yet it left him empty. Molly was there, sure, like she always was . . . with courage to spare.

Suddenly he knew who was the stronger, and the answer brought him no pleasure. This woman beside him was sworn to stay at his side as eternally as she had once been to his partner. But there was no solemn ceremony to recall the date in happiness through the years. She was as beautiful as the day the two Texas drifters had first sighted her on the streets of Cordobal, but duty and not desire dictated her presence.

Ten years ago he had whispered of a white-walled *hacienda* below the Rio Grande, of music and moonlight and broad herds bearing his own iron. Now he might build the *hacienda,* but nothing could change Buscado. It would always be the hangout of the border-popping renegades who had called tall Kirk Brandon their *jefe.*

Presently Molly saw the heavy creases ridging his forehead and laid her hand across his arm.

"Don't worry, Kirk," she said gently. "Once you were very fond of me. I know that now. Maybe it will come back to you just like it was, and I will be there. The instincts of a great cowman are in you and after we're married we will live as you once planned, with money and the respect of friends. And my boy will have his chance. I can spare him as I have before to let him make something of himself that the borderland could never produce. We'll all be happy!"

The breaks became less rugged under the flying wheels of the light buggy. The team ahead in the darkness was high in spirits and the broad ribbon of the river drew closer. Brandon hunched lower in the seat. The brown envelope in his pocket gouged his ribs. He took it out and laid it on the seat between them.

The instincts of a great cowman, Molly had said! Grim humor seized him, and suddenly he knew. This was the greatest trial of all for the woman beside him. Grief and the collapse of all she'd ever known meant nothing to the hurt this bargain he had forced upon her brought. Yet chin up and warmth in her eyes for him, she was traveling south to the renegade town she hated.

A rise pitched ahead and he sent the whip out over the team in a sudden viciousness. What did all this mean to him? For ten years bitterness had been his lot because a weakling and a fool had won the single thing he wanted most from the world. Now he had gained what he desired because he was the stronger and had learned to wait. The rest was something beyond the ken of a hard man.

Over the rise ahead the trail split wide. One thin white line laced across the river like an accusing arrow toward Buscado and the other led to Cordobal by a route more direct than the one they traveled.

With lips set grimly in anger against this parade of vagrant thoughts and self-accusations which made his victory an empty thing, Brandon put the flying team against the sharpness of the rise.

And as the buggy rocked up, a sudden hell flared behind them.

Kirk heard the first shrill scream which tore the air about them and his thick-muscled arm sent new speed to the animals ahead. Molly twisted half about in the seat to stare at the mad visions trailing them.

"Near a dozen men," she panted.

Kirk nodded. "Cochise, and the Last Ten!" he snapped.

Molly gasped, perhaps thinking of the gaudy crimson arrow they had found in Johnny Carter's throat. Then her voice was sharp with insistence.

"Take the river road, Kirk," she urged tensely. "Cochise raids this side only. We've got enough lead on them. We can make it. We've got to! It means so much. . . ."

But Kirk Brandon did not hear. He was climbing down from the buggy, a Winchester in his arms. He was shoving a brown paper package more securely into a fold in the cushion of the seat. And then he was staring at the vision in the buggy above him. . . .

Molly Carter was tired. She had almost made a mistake, a more terrible mistake than her life with Johnny Carter could have ever led her into. This realization put a new power in Brandon. For a few moments the crest of the rise they had just topped would shelter them from the view of Cochise and his charging savages.

Kirk Brandon threw the lines of the wall-eyed team up into Molly's lap. His powerful arm swung in a sharp circle and the flat of his palm struck smartly on the rump of the near horse. The buggy leaped forward. They could be kept on the trail, and for miles nothing on earth could stop that team.

Molly's white face was a fast-receding cameo of surprise against the backdrop of the night. Kirk Brandon stared after her for a fraction of a second with the sudden feeling that somehow the emptiness within him had been filled.

His hands arced upward in a salute of farewell and his voice rolled clearly after the woman he was giving back to herself.

"Good-bye, Molly," he said calmly but clearly. "The boy needs you more. Take the north trail. And drive like hell!"

Kirk Brandon took his rifle in his hands, knelt by the side of the trail, and waited. . . .

THE GHOST OF MIGUEL

PETER BAPTISTE GERMANO was the oldest of six children born to Italian immigrant parents in New Bedford, Massachusetts. He only had a year and a half of high school before he had to get a "work permit" as many young people did during the Great Depression. He was a regular, however, at the New Bedford Public Library. In 1948 he took the Massachusetts High School Graduation Equivalency examination at Harvard University and placed first among his group. He would later attend college with the help of the G. I. Bill and eventually would earn a Master's degree from Loyola University in Los Angeles.

His earliest Western fiction appeared in *Western Aces* under the name Peter Germane. The Barry Cord byline came about as the result of having two stories in the same issue of *Sure-Fire Western* (1/39), "A Rustler's Receipt" by Peter Germane and "Mustang Vengeance" by Barry Cord. Germano subsequently came to prefer the Barry Cord name and by 1940, when he began writing Western stories for Mike Tilden at Popular Publications, it was the only byline he used. "Two Trails of Glory" by Barry Cord in *New Western* (5/40) is the most powerful and evocative story he wrote before entering the U.S. Marine Corps during the Second World War. Mike Tilden kept a special place for Germano's stories at Popular Publications and most of his Western fiction following the war continued to appear in *Dime Western*, *Star Western*, and *Fifteen Western Tales* along with an occasional contribution in Fiction House's *Action Stories*. The longest, and in many ways finest, Western story to emerge in the immediate post-war period was "Boss of the Tumbling H" in *West* (5/48). Germano then proceeded to expand this short novel to book-length proportions. It appeared under the title TRAIL BOSS FROM TEXAS (Phoenix Press, 1948), published under the Barry Cord byline. The opening scene is set in the town of Douglas at night during a torrential downpour. Although Germano would later say that he modeled his Western fiction after stories by Ernest Haycox and Luke Short, he never sought to achieve the complexity of character one finds in Haycox's fiction nor the hard-edged aggressiveness of Luke Short's characters. In fact, in TRAIL BOSS FROM TEXAS as in most of Germano's subsequent novels, it is the plot that is quite complicated while the scenes themselves are simply set, with a minimum of description and quick character sketches used to establish what is actually a wide assortment of very different personalities. The pacing is made to seem so swift because of the adept use of parallel plotting, shifting back and forth between different scenes and characters. The atmospheric descriptions of weather and terrain also combine to make the story consistently interesting.

His next two Western novels, THE GUNSMOKE TRAIL (Phoenix Press, 1951) and SHADOW VALLEY (Phoenix Press, 1951), are also expansions of earlier magazine stories. "The Ghost of Miguel" in *Lariat Story Magazine* (1/45) had marked the first post-war appearance of Barry Cord in a Western pulp magazine and SHADOW VALLEY opens with a suspenseful sequence about a mysterious rider known as the "ghost of Miguel" who cuts down his victims with a sword and who wears Spanish armor. The reappearance of the short story below marks the first time it has been reprinted.

Long Jim Evers reined in his bronc, a scowl creasing his long face as he glanced at his pint-sized companion. "Forty miles from nowhere," he grumbled reproachfully. "An' me with my stummick ridin' my backbone! Dang it, Windy . . . what was the idear cuttin' cross-country from Las Cruses?"

Windy Harris shrugged. "Cows," he informed, calmly. He leaned forward, worked his huge quid into a leathery cheek, and spat over his roan's left ear. "From what I heard back in Las Cruses, this section was full of mavericks and sleepers, jest waitin' for an iron. No law in forty miles."

"And not a cow in fifty!" Long Jim snapped. He twisted to survey the gently rolling stretch of sageland that ran into the dirty brown border hills. The sun had set a half hour ago, and the shadows were already thickening in that desolate land.

Evers shifted in his saddle, his tone growing serious. "I'm ready to eat a jack, if I kin spot one, Windy. In fact, right now, I'm willin' to. . . ."

Out on the small flat, under a piñon-butte, a light suddenly winked on. Evers's drawn scrutiny revealed a low, rambling dwelling, the outbuildings of a spread. A hopeful grin creased his humorous features. "Windy . . . we're saved. The horn of Gabriel's a-callin' . . . and I see a light in yonder distance. I kin smell food, already. Good, solid, home-cooked. . . ."

Harris grunted. "Let's go see, Jim."

The main building was of yellow 'dobe, built around a patio. There was a crumbly 'dobe fence fronting the big yard, tall pecans casting shade over pole corrals, a big 'dobe barn, and several lesser outbuildings.

A man came out of the barn as they rode into the yard. A fast-stepping, suspicious gent. Thin starlight seeped through the trees, touched the rifle barrel in his hands.

He faced them, ten feet away, balanced on his toes. He said: "Howdy, gents! What's on yer minds?"

Windy Harris leaned on the horn, stared innocently at him. The man was broad across the shoulders, thick about his Levi-clad waist. He had red hair, snapping blue eyes, and two score years had not dimmed the temper that went with these unfailing attributes.

The bantam spat, apologetically. "Jest now it's that Winchester. A rifle muzzle sets uneasy on my stummick . . . thanks," he chuckled easily as the red-haired man lowered the rifle slightly, but his scowl deepened. "Me and this human beanpole are lookin' for the foreman of this shebang."

The blocky man did not move. His gaze narrowed on Long Jim's six feet three of saddled indolence, shifted to Windy's bare five feet of wiry length. An incongruous pair, these, seamed and slouchy. Saddle bums, evidently. Then his gaze was drawn to thonged-down Frontiers that rode easily on lean thighs, and the cold suspicion spread further across his face. "Yer lookin' right at him!" he snapped. "Spill yer business!"

Windy looked hurt. Evers edged his bronc up close, and shook his head, sadly. "Don't mind him, mister. We're harmless. We ain't et since last night. We was ridin' up yonder, plumb lost and help-less-like, when we seen yer lights. We figgered. . . ."

Over to the right, yellow lamplight suddenly made a long oblong among the dappled shadows. A woman loomed up in the ranch-house doorway. A tall, angular figure in faded gray, black hair tied up in a bun on her neck. "Rolly!" she called with quivering eager-ness. "Who is it?"

The redheaded foreman shrugged, eased the rifle into the crook of his arm. "It ain't him, ma'am," he answered sullenly. "Jest a couple of chuckliners askin' a handout."

The woman came out of the broad, vine-covered porch. The eager-ness faded from her. There was a tired, hollow ring to her tone. "Supper's ready, Rolly. Have them come in."

Rolly scowled. Windy and Long Jim were already out of saddle, heading for the stairs. He followed with soft, springy steps. Twice he stopped, looked out beyond the yard, to the darkening flatland. Little lines etched his mouth corners. His gaze swung back to the two old reprobates, and his scowl deepened as he followed them in.

The meal was solid, the best they had ever stowed away. And plenty of it. The lamp on the table threw light in a small circle that barely outlined the big room.

The angular woman ate little. There was a weary hopelessness in her eyes, in the droop of her mouth. Forty, perhaps, yet she looked fifteen years older.

Rolly sat at one end of the long table, still scowling, eyeing the old wanderers with an intentness that caused Harris to squirm.

At the other end of the table sat a man in a wheelchair. A short, grizzled man with a stubborn, harsh mouth, and furrows in his flat cheeks. He was Lincoln Fervans, owner of the V-Bar ranch. The woman was his wife, Lucy. They had no help, save Rolly, who looked after things—and they weren't thinking of hiring.

This information had been given shortly, almost curtly, by the crippled rancher. They were bidden "draw up chairs and dig in!" Two extra plates were added to the three already on the table. They ate in silence, with none of the usual eager questions asked by people living in out-of-the-way places.

Harris, stuffed long before his voracious companion, felt the strange tension in the room. And he noticed things now, little things that had escaped his first casual glance.

Rolly had deposited his rifle in a corner by the door, as if he figured he might need it. The wooden table had strange grooves, some old, several fresh, as if slugs had scoured its surface. He kept his face noncommittal as his eyes took in the signs. But they narrowed slightly as he noticed ragged tears in the old cupboard across from the near window.

The uneasiness in Windy peaked up. He could see Rolly eyeing the old wall clock, leaning forward intently, his fingers clenched on the table surface. Half-past seven. Even as he looked, it struck the half hour with a solemn, jangling stroke.

The lamp went then, its glass globe disintegrating. The sound of breaking glass mingled with the short, angry crack of a rifle from out in the dark. Harris surged back, hearing Long Jim's surprised curse. He lunged up in the sudden gloom, headed for the door. A dark, squat figure cut across his path. They collided, and he heard Rolly's harsh voice swear in his ear. A hand shoved him roughly aside.

When he reached the porch more glass fell, as if something heavy had been thrown through the window. Harris edged away from the squat foreman, the Frontier in his fist jutting readily. His searching eyes caught a glimpse of a vague figure low-hung in the saddle of a black horse just clearing the low 'dobe fence.

Harris's Colt slapped heavily, its report mingling with the sharper crack of Rolly's rifle. 'Dobe puffed angrily a foot behind the fleeing rider. But the potshooter continued on, crossed a patch of starlight that revealed a small, indistinct figure topped by a huge anthill sombrero—and disappeared. The low drum of hoofs faded.

Harris stood by the door, staring into the shadows. A long figure loomed up behind him. Evers's voice rasped in his ear. "Get the potshootin' galoot, Windy?"

Rolly eased toward them, swearing in a flat monotone. He said: "Reckon that's all, gents . . . for tonight!" He said it as if this had been expected.

They reëntered the house in silence and watched the woman as she lit a candle. She looked up at them with a dull hardness. "You'll have to get some lamps, Rolly, the next time you go to town. That was the last one we had."

Rolly shrugged, his eyes searching the dimly lighted floor. He paced forward, suddenly bent down by the near table leg. Harris's puzzled gaze followed him, lifted to the old rancher, still sitting at the table. There was baffled rage in the cowman's gray eyes. His big-knuckled hands were tight about the chair arms, as if he had tried to lift himself, force his paralyzed limbs to movement.

Behind Windy, Long Jim muttered: "Mebbe I'm loco, but. . . ."

The foreman straightened with something in his hand. It was a piece of sandstone, with a ragged square of brown paper wrapped around it. He unwrapped the paper, looked at it briefly, walked to the old rancher, passed it to him. "Jest like the others!" he growled. "'Cept this time he's givin' you a deadline. You got till Saturday to pull yer stakes!"

The old rancher slowly crumpled the message. His wife walked to his side, placed a hand on his broad shoulder. "We'll go, Lincoln. We've had nothing but misfortune since we bought this place. We can't hold out." She glanced up at Rolly, as if for confirmation.

The foreman said: "He's got us by the throat, Lincoln. And he knows this country better'n we do. We've tried everything. . . ."

Windy and Long Jim shifted uncomfortably, feeling out of things and not knowing quite what to do. The others seemed to have forgotten their presence. The rancher answered, his voice ragged: "Did you see Strauss? Mebbe, if he gave us a hand. . . ."

The other sneered. "I seen Box-Ear Strauss all right. He said he had enough trouble of his own, watchin' out for the Diamond L, without chasin' after ghosts. He said somethin' about missin' cattle, too . . . and I didn't like the way he said it!" At this Rolly scowled. "The Diamond L may not be behind this crazy ghost greaser, but they shore as hell ain't losin' any sleep over our trouble and never will."

Windy shuffled, cleared his throat. "Sorry if we busted in at the wrong time, folks. Me and Jim didn't know. Who is this ghost?"

The old rancher, chewing on his lip, eyed them, and held out the crinkled paper.

Evers looked down over Windy's shoulder. The message was terse:

This is the last warning. You have till Saturday. Miguel.

Long Jim looked down at the crippled rancher: "One man . . . a greaser . . . drivin' you out? Off yer own spread?"

Fervan's lips twisted. He wheeled himself away from the table as his wife started to clean up the mess.

"It ain't as easy as you think, stranger," he snapped. "A man can't lick a thing he can't git close enough to fight!" He leaned forward, his thick hands gripping the chair arms. "I bought this spread over a year ago. There was a story went with it . . . that made me git it cheap. But I didn't hear the story till later.

"This place was once the old de Santoro's *hacienda* . . . had been in de Santoro's hands for generations. But the only right thing they had to the place was the right of possession. The land was granted the first de Santoro by royal Spain. Six years ago, the last of the de Santoros were driven off by a man named Elbow Johnson. Johnson showed a deed from the U.S. government, and backed it with six-guns. He had a craggy bunch of riders with him, and when the de Santoros showed fight, he wiped 'em out. It was a massacre. A young son of Jose de Santoro, a seventeen-year-old kid named Miguel, got free. He went a little crazy, I reckon. He headed into the hills, and for a coupla years nothin' was heard from him. Then he came back."

The old rancher shrugged. "It was hell . . . just plain hell. Johnson was no chicken-livered scoundrel . . . and he had *gunmen* ridin' for him. But this crazy Mex, with a Sharps rifle he got somewhere, just broke 'em. He got Johnson, long range, the second day . . . killed him while he was standin' right outside there on the porch. He wore Johnson's men ragged huntin' him. He ambushed 'em till they were scared to go out alone. At night he drove 'em near crazy slammin' lead into the place. They stuck for about four months. Then, what was left of that craggy outfit quit cold. The *hacienda* went for a year without a buyer. Then a Swede, named Omsen, took over. He lasted six months.

"Finally the sheriff took a hand. There ain't a better man cuttin' sign than Sheriff Breller, and he was born in this section. It took him four months to dig up Miguel. But he ran him down." Fervan's lips tightened. "They shot it out, on Standout Bluff. The sheriff swears he got two slugs into the kid before he fell into the river. But. . . ."

Rolly interrupted, his tone harsh. "The stories have it that Miguel's ghost is still ridin' over the range of his ancestors." He sneered. "Mebbe! But if the gent that's been raisin' hell around here is a ghost he's a god-damned solid one! And he sure knows how to use a rifle!"

The old rancher eased back in his chair. "We been tryin' to hold on. We bought this spread legal . . . and it's a good layout, given half a chance. The day I took over, I drove five hundred head onto its grass. Now Rolly tells me we're lucky if I kin round up a hundred. There was me, *my son*," his lips twisted bitterly, "and Rolly takin' care of things. My son's gone . . . and I'm a cripple. Got the slug in my back while ridin' the west line four months ago!" He ended harshly, "The doc says I'll be in a wheelchair the rest of my life."

Windy shifted uneasily. Rolly straightened. "There's clean hay in the barn, strangers, if you want to hang around till mornin'," he suggested.

Windy and Long Jim grunted their thanks and followed Rolly out. They left the old rancher staring toward the shattered window, sitting unmoving in his chair.

As they crossed the gloomy yard, Long Jim inquired carelessly: "What happened to the old man's kid, Rolly? This rifle-totin' ghost get him, too?"

Rolly did not slow his stride. His shoulders hunched. "It was the old man's fault, I reckon. The kid was one of 'em high-strung colts . . . the kind you gotta handle easy. But the old man is hard, and plumb set in his ways. He tried to break the kid to his way of thinkin'. The kid couldn't see it that way at all. The last argument they had the old man beat hell out of Walt. The kid was nineteen, then. He took his beatin' without a word. But I remember the way he faced his father after . . . his face all bloody, his lips tight, his eyes gray pools of hell. He quit the spread that night . . . headed for the border."

Windy frowned. Long Jim muttered something about the folly of the young being surpassed only by that of the old.

Rolly left them in the barn, went back to the ranchhouse. He had been bunking in Walter's place since the kid had left.

Something troubled the lanky Evers. He walked to the open door, squinted toward the dark rangeland. His gaze swung around to the dim light against the ranchhouse windows. He said: "Hell!" and looked down at Windy, unconcernedly making a hole in clean hay. "I hope to hell this Mex ghost comes back tonight. Seems like we oughta do *somethin'* for that grub we stowed away."

Windy grunted. "If he comes back, we'll take him apart and see what makes a ghost tick. But it ain't our affair, Jim. Come mornin', we'll ride west and see what kind of mavericks the Diamond L have got." He settled himself, made a clucking sound in his leathery throat. "Strauss, huh? Didn't we run across a mean *hombre* with a handle like that up in that Montanny country?"

Long Jim snorted, walked toward the hay. "Shore, you idjut! He was a ghost, too. Don't you remember?"

Windy disdained reply. He squirmed a little, settled back, but a train of thought came through his head, and he worked on it, his eyes puckering. "Ghosts, too, huh? I wonder. . . ."

THE MORNING SUN was hot over the brown land, raising little shimmers of heat. Miles west of the V-Bar, where a jumble of ravines and sandstone cliffs broke the expanse of rolling plain, a thin curl of gray smoke lifted against a tawny ravine wall, and faded before it got above the sheer sides. A score of feet beyond the fire, two broncs stood stiffly, forty feet of rope stretching taut from creased saddle knobs. The sound of profanity faded slowly into the heated air.

"Lie still, drat you!" Windy Harris grunted, dug a bony knee into the steer's flank. Shifting, he attempted to dally a couple of turns around the animal's hind legs. The frightened steer lunged in a frantic effort to regain its feet, the ensuing struggle spilling the pint-sized rustler. For a brief moment there was a flurry of legs, dust and chaps. Then it quieted, and Windy untangled himself slowly. He stood up, glaring at the hog-tied animal, making queer gulping sounds in his throat. Finally, his Adam's apple quit bobbing, and an audible sigh of relief came from him.

The sound of unsuppressed laughter spun him around, a wrathful glare in his eyes. "What in hell *you* laughin' at, you overgrown, pinheaded mule?" he roared. "Can't a man swaller his chaw without you takin' a fit?"

Long Jim rocked weakly by the side of his hog-tied animal. "Hell!" he gasped finally, tears in his eyes. "Damned if I ever saw anythin' like it! Like a sage hen you was. . . ." He went off again.

Windy's glare changed. "Near two bits worth of Ol' Harmony gone to hell!" he snapped. A faintly uneasy expression came to his eyes.

Behind them the small fire crackled. The heat was boxed in between tawny slopes here; it was like a deep, miasmic sea in which no wind stirred. Below them a creek slid through thickets with a soft, cooling murmur.

Long Jim straightened, getting control of himself. He looked down at his animal, his expression changing. "We oughta be in Diamond L country here . . . and these beeves cinch it. The brand on 'em is big enough to be seen from the ranchhouse." His eyes narrowed slightly and he peered closer. "Free iron branded, and the *hombre* who done it was no artist. Huh," he grunted softly, "I'll be eatin' loco weed if the first iron on this critter wasn't a V-Bar!"

Harris swung his attention to his animal. "Looks like we ain't the only runnin' iron experts in this section. Whoever worked on this one did a better job . . . but he was a mite careless in closin' the diamond." He straightened, his leathery face scowling. "Mebbe this Box-Ear Strauss is makin' hay while Miguel's ghost rides, huh?"

Long Jim shrugged, straightened, started to coil his rope. Reaching the range-wise roan, he hung the reata from the horn, swung into the saddle. His gaze dropped to Windy. "I got a hunch . . . and it ain't good," he muttered. "I'm gonna take a look up the ravine."

Windy scowled. What had seemed like the easy prospect of re-branding six or seven head, and herding them through the broken country toward the border, was developing angles. Ghosts and brand-blotting and Box-Ear Strauss.

He grunted, swung away from his trussed steer for the iron in the branding fire. Something sure smelled on this range!

The thud of sand-deadened hoofs jerked him away from the fire, his right hand flicking gunward. He waited, his body alert, till view of the rider cutting around the sharp ravine bend eased him.

"Three Diamond L riders!" Long Jim snapped, pivoting his roan. "Headin' this way." He cut across Windy's remonstrances concerning the trussed steers. "We ain't got time, you fool! Leave 'em! Let 'em guess!"

Windy whipped to saddle, crowded close to Long Jim. They swung back down the ravine the way they had entered it, crossed under a gnarled oak, and suddenly pulled up. Ahead of them a shod hoof clanged sharply against stone!

Long Jim threw a glance back to the fire. His thin face tightened. "Trapped! Looks like here's where two fools come to the end of a rope!"

His shoulders hunched as his eyes swung over the tawny ravine walls. The stream here slid close to the abrupt barrier, and Evers's questing gaze stopped at a slit in the wall beyond, like a wedge cut in the cliff. "Mebbe we kin make it," he suggested.

He glanced at Windy, and was startled by his companion's pale face, a funny flicker in his eyes. He had never seen Windy like this before. "First time I ever saw *you* get white around the gills, Windy. Scared?"

Windy straightened, snapped weakly. "You'd get pale, you bean-pole . . . if you had jist swallered yore chaw! Damn . . . it's shore raisin' hell."

They splashed up the stream, crowded through screening bushes, and made the split. It was a fault in the rock wall, about seventy feet deep, narrowing at every foot. They led their cayuses in till they could go no further, wrapped reins around rock, and left them, sliding back to the opening with ready rifles.

They didn't have long to wait. A rider appeared, jogging a big-chested white horse. A slim, wiry youngster, with a carbine under his right leg, a black hat tipped over his eyes. He looked hard, bitter, and dangerous.

His gaze froze on the telltale fire, the hog-tied steers. The rifle slid into his hands with a smooth, easy motion. He scanned the cañon scene intently, then advanced toward the camp.

As the youngster passed by, Harris muttered: "Here's where we pull our stakes, Jim. This country's gettin' too cussed crowded for two pore rustlers like. . . ."

Evers's fingers closed on his shoulders: "Wait! That kid . . . he looks a lot like that crippled rancher we et with last night. Mebbe. . . ."

The kid was dismounting. He looked warily around, walked to-ward the steers. He paused by the almost dead fire, picked up Windy's running iron. He walked to one of the cows, squatted by it, scanned the carelessly made Diamond L brand.

Three riders appeared around the bend. The youngster dropped the iron, started to run for his ground-reined cayuse. A rifle glinted in the hands of a gnome-like Diamond L rider. A spurt of flame showed, a sharp crack. The kid twisted in midstride, went down heavily. He clawed at the dust, pushed up on one knee. He got unsteadily to his feet, his left arm limp, and faced the oncoming riders.

The two oldsters, who were the cause of it, watched with hard eyes. All thought of flight was gone from them. They were old hands at this game; they knew what would follow.

The Diamond L riders bunched up before the youngster, rifles glinting. They were as craggy looking *hombres* as Harris and Long Jim had ever lined up in their sights. The gent who had plugged the kid was squat, seeming as wide as he was tall, long-armed. He sat saddle of a horse that dwarfed him. The other two were lean, raw-boned, stubby-profiled: they looked like brothers.

One of them took down his coiled rope, with a wide, loose-lipped smile. The gnome-like rider slipped out of the saddle, paced to the trussed steers. He picked up the running iron, examined it, then let it drop. He cut the cows loose, watched them lumber away. Turning, he snapped orders. The man with the reata shoved the kid forward, jerking a thumb toward the gnarled oak.

Harris caressed his rifle. He said, softly: "They ain't losin' any time, Jim. They've got it all figgered oι ι. And the kid's the goat. What you aimin' . . . ?"

Evers scowled. "We got the kid into it. 'Sides, I don't like that midget, nor his friends." He grinned down at the mustached ban-tam as he eased the rifle into the crook of his long arm. "He's yore size, Windy . . . you take him."

They had the youngster astride his big white, arms bound behind him, under the big oak. And they were working fast. The gnome whipped one end of the rope over an overhanging branch, started to widen the slip-noose. He leered at something the kid said.

"We ain't got time for the law, Fervans . . . and it's too far anyhow. We snapped you red-handed usin' a runnin' iron on Diamond L beef. We been losin' plenty, ever since yore pop started that cock-and-bull story 'bout Miguel's ghost. That cinches it. Yore pop's been runnin' a bluff . . . hidin' his rustlin' under cover of that ghost yarn. Even that story 'bout you and him breakin' up was fake. You wanted the Diamond L to think you was out of the section so you could work yore game."

"That's a lie, Card!" the youngster shouted. Pain beaded his forehead, lined his mouth. "And you know it! Why don't you tell the truth? There's no one to hear you. You read the signs around that fire. There was two *hombres* doin' the brand blottin'. Reckon they heard you comin', and hightailed. Or mebbe the whole thing was a Diamond L setup, and like a blunderin' fool I came into it. But I seen enough. Those Diamond L cows were V-Bar."

Card grinned, toyed with the noose. "Mebbe you *have* at that! But you'll do the rest of yore snoopin' in hell."

At the sight of the incongruous pair shuffling toward them, he swiftly closed a hand over his holstered gun. The tall scarecrow had a rifle in the crook of his right arm, a gun holstered on his right hip. The bantam beside him walked as if he creaked. His rifle was loose in his right hand, muzzle pointed toward the sand.

Evers said: "Reckon you gents are plumb hasty with that rope. Me and Windy here was the ones thinkin' of doin' a li'l runnin' iron work when you butted in." A cold grin cracked his long face. "That shore was a sloppy job you boys did on them V-Bar critters. Reckon the brand blotters around here need lessons in their trade. This younger generation . . . tch, tch."

Card sneered, his first grip of surprise passing. This was better than he had hoped for. Like the kid had pointed out, he had read the signs—had known it was not the youngster who had built that fire, roped those steers. Whoever it was must have noticed the careless branding. And he had not liked the thought of someone riding around with that information. But now. . . .

His small red eyes jerked to his two companions, narrowed meaningly. These two old fools would never talk! They had rifles in their hands, and really thought that was enough to hold Card, Cheeky and Sturgeon! Hell!

He minced his cayuse to one side, thick lips twisting. "So you two jaspers want to show the Diamond L how to blot brands?" His sneer faded into a vicious grin. "How you fools lived this long is beyond. . . ."

His long arm whipped up, spinning a Colt. He was still grinning, and he died like that. Harris's .30-30 slug had passed clean through his heart.

Sturgeon, leveling his gun with desperate speed, stiffened as Long Jim's rifle flared. He slid forward, hit the ground a moment after Card.

Cheeky had time to shoot twice, both wild. He was cursing the two oldsters who used rifles like he had never seen them used before, when Harris's slug got him in the left eye—Long Jim's over the heart as he started to sag.

The sharp reports faded slowly down the ravine. Walter Fervans held his frightened cayuse with his knees, and stared with pained, wondering eyes at the three sprawled Diamond L gunmen.

Harris was complaining: "There you go, wastin' lead again! Two slugs fer one polecat."

Long Jim grunted, looked down to the clean-sheared rip where Cheeky's first shot had passed. "My best pair of boots!" he groused, disregarding the fact that they were his only pair. "Dang it, Windy . . . they cost me forty dollars in Cheyenne. And you let that. . . ."

The youngster swayed, his eyes clouding. Long Jim cut him free, eased him down. Walter winced as the shirt was ripped from his shoulder, exposing the ugly hole. Windy knelt beside them, his old eyes pitying.

"Bad!" he acknowledged. "We better get him back to the V-Bar."

The kid jerked his head, his lips white. "No! I can't go back. . . ."

Long Jim shrugged. "You're Walter Fervans?" He nodded slowly at the youngster's reluctant "yes." "Don't be a fool, kid. Yore paw and maw are eatin' their hearts out for you. Shore . . . me and Windy heard the story . . . last night."

Walter's voice was unsteady. "I heard 'bout my pop gettin' hurt, way down in Prietas. I came back. But I didn't know how . . . how to. . . ."

"Jest tell him you're sorry," Long Jim said gruffly. "He needs you, kid . . . needs you bad. An' your maw . . . she's been cryin' inside ever since you went away."

Walter Fervans whispered chokingly: "I reckon I been a fool, strangers. . . ."

"You both have," Windy amended. "But they'll be glad to see you."

THE SHADOWS were long over the *hacienda* when they jogged into the yard. The youngster was slumped in Long Jim's arms, his hair shrouding his white face. Windy followed, leading the kid's big white.

Rolly met them on the porch, surprise in his eyes. The ever-present rifle eased in his hands, he stepped down to meet them. "Wait! What the hell . . . ?" He swung on Long Jim. "What's happened?"

Long Jim told him, leaving out details, of course, of what he and Windy were doing in the ravine. Lucy Fervans's cry smote them as they entered, bearing Walter's limp form. She stood agonized till Long Jim's reassurance calmed the anguish in her. She opened a door, motioned to a bed.

The old rancher wheeled himself close to the unconscious youngster, his furrowed cheeks tight, a lump in his throat. He looked up at the two saddle bums, standing stiff in the uncertain candlelight. "How'd it happen?" he asked hoarsely. "Where . . . ?"

Long Jim repeated the story. Windy said nothing. He kept watching Rolly, watching the glitter in the puncher's eyes.

Lucy Fervans, applying first-aid to the ugly wound, stated anxiously: "We must get that bullet out of him. We've got to have the doctor!"

"I'll go for him, ma'am," Rolly offered. He was fidgety. "I'll take Brownie, the big stud . . . and make it to Las Cruces before dawn." He turned to the pair, his lips grim. "You figgerin' on standin' by, tonight?"

Long Jim hesitated. A heel ground warningly on his toe, brought a pained frown to his eyes. Windy said: "Naw! Reckon me and Jim'll be driftin'. We don't want to git mixed up in something that ain't our mess."

They went out. Long Jim scowled at his partner. Mounting, he followed Windy up the trail; they kept on till they were out of sight of the ranchhouse, then circled.

Under the concealing shadow of trees, Long Jim nudged him, his scowl deep between his eyes. "What in hell you doin'? Playin' a game? We could a' stayed for supper. Dang you, my stummick's. . . ."

Windy cut in: "Yeah . . . I know. Your stummick's allus empty. But I was kinda thinkin' 'bout that crippled rancher and his wife. And that kid. It was our fault he got hurt, Jim." The bantam tugged at his ragged mustache. "Seems like we oughta pay up for what happened."

Long Jim shrugged. "Yeah," he said. "Mebbe we oughta bring 'em Miguel's ghost."

"Shore," Windy agreed. "I got ideas 'bout this Miguel . . . and they ties in with this Box-Ear Strauss we been hearin' about. Box-Ear . . ." he grinned slowly, his homely face lighting up. "Danged if it don't come back to me! It was a li'l homesteader's shack . . . up in Montanny. Remember?"

"You gone loco?" Long Jim asked, peering suspiciously down at his partner. "When did we ever . . . ?"

Windy's quick arm checked his words. He followed Windy's nod.

Pale moonlight washed the flat. A dark figure was riding out of the V-Bar yard—heading west. It cut across the flat, began to fade in the distance.

Long Jim said: "What the hell, Windy! It's Rolly . . . goin' after a sawbones. What you. . . ."

Windy chuckled. "Shore. Which way to Las Cruses?"

The beanpole rustler glared at him. "North, you locoed. . . ." His mouth closed, and he swiveled, his eyes picking up the faint blur of the disappearing rider. "Hell!" he said, understanding.

Windy nodded. "The Diamond L is west . . . and that's where Rolly's headin'. Not for the doc." He shrugged, looked down to the squat, vague ranchhouse where a crippled rancher and a wounded youngster were watched over by a woman with anxious eyes.

Long Jim muttered, "It's a lousy play, Windy. Not fit fer even sheep herders." His gaze turned to the western horizon. "You figgerin' like I am?"

Windy let a gnarled, capable hand drop to his holster gun. "I'm way ahead of you!" he grinned. "Let's get goin'!"

The Diamond L had never been more than an excuse. A two-room flat-roofed 'dobe house, with adjoining 'dobe stalls, a couple of sheds that badly needed repair, a crazy corral, a bunch of willows around a small, gurgling spring. As a ranch it wasn't worth the labor put into it. As a base for rustling, it was invaluable.

Jammed back among the tawny cañons of the Malpais Rim, it was a hop, a skip and a short jump to the border. It lay far from the beaten path, in a section overlooked as inconsequential by the hard-worked sheriff in Las Cruces. All in all, the Diamond L was in an admirable position for its nefarious purpose.

Moonglow lightened the darkness about the spread as Windy and Long Jim dismounted by the willows. Old hands at this game, they talked little. Windy nodded shortly toward the rear of the squat 'dobe, indicating his course of action. Long Jim eased away. His long figure was like a shadow crossing the gloom-blotched yard toward the front of the 'dobe where Rolly's big brown stud stood trailing its reins.

Windy waited till Long Jim had reached a vantage point. Then he cut out in a short arc, a gnarled hand brushing against his gun butt. He reached the back of the house without incident, flattening against the wall, gave wordless thanks to the warmth of the summer night that kept windows open.

A moment later, he was inside the bedroom, skirting a chair. A streak of light cut into the darkness, showing a door ajar. Voices rasped against his ear. He edged to the door, and peered through.

Box-Ear Strauss was swearing vividly as he paced the big living room. Lamplight cast his rangy, hard-muscled frame in long distortion over bare walls. Heavy guns lay thonged against his legs, their pearl handles winking with his long-paced stride. His ears marked him. They were huge, membranous things, squared off as if by shears. They stuck out like billboards on either side of his big square head.

Against the far wall, two men stood nervously watching their boss pacing. One of them, a thin, wiry man with a sharp face, kept fingering his Colt. His mouth kept twitching.

Box-Ears stopped, glared at Rolly. The bogus V-Bar puncher was by the table, his thick body tense. "Damn it to hell!" the Diamond L owner snapped. "Card, Cheeky, and Sturgeon! You know what you're sayin', Rolly? You're tellin' me that. . . ."

"I'm tellin' you, I don't know who they were," Rolly interrupted savagely. "Look like a coupla saddle bums, that' all. One was long, thin, like a scarecrow. A good wind coulda blowed him away. The other was a under-sized runt who walked like he creaked. They were there last night . . . when Card pulled the Miguel play. Card was on the dot. Hell, we had ol' Fervans on the run. Come Saturday, we woulda had the V-Bar for the takin'."

Rolly threw up his hands. "Then, tonight, these meddlin' bums come in, totin' Lincoln's kid, with a slug in his shoulder. That was the first shock. I thought I had fixed things 'tween him and his old man . . . fixed it so's he'd never come back. But he heard 'bout his pop bein' laid up." He shrugged, his lips twisting. "Anyway, the way they spilled it, Card, Cheeky, and Sturgeon are doin' their ridin' in hell!"

Beefy, a thick-waisted, flabby-faced man, siding the nervous-fingered gent, snarled: "Hell . . . you know what that means, Box-Ear! Outside of yoreself, there warn't a better man with a gun than Card! An' Cheeky an' Sturgeon was 'bout as good!" Beefy swore, his eyes dilating. "I'm sayin' we oughta git the hell out, while the gittin's good! We got most of the V-Bar beef up in that cañon under the Tombstone . . . and while it ain't what we started out to git, it'll give us a stake across the Line." His gaze slid from Box-Ear's scowling features to Rolly, to the man beside him. " 'Specially now that there's only four of us in on the divvy!"

Windy waited to get the full picture of the setup. Harsh lines took the humor from his mouth as he started to push open the door. Box-Ear was facing the bedroom, his voice rasping, ". . . gonna give up this play less'n we have to Beefy. We're gonna hit back . . . hit hard. We'll pour enough slugs into that ranchhouse to. . . ."

His voice snapped off, his rangy body shocking stiff. His gaze narrowed on the small, homely-faced gunster who was framed in the bedroom doorway.

He found his voice then, snapped it metallically: "What the . . . ?" His right arm tensed with his intention. But he didn't draw. Didn't move.

A sad voice was saying casually, "Howdy, gents. We're lookin' for Miguel's ghost!"

Indecision held the four of them rigid, eyes shunting from Windy's grinning face to the mock mournfulness of Long Jim's. The bean-pole rustler was in the front doorway, long sinewy fingers hooked casually in his gun belt. His voice was almost sepulchral in that taut stillness. "Windy . . . where *is* Miguel's ghost?"

Windy chuckled. "In hell! In mortal guise he was known as Card." His eyes slanted to Box-Ear and his chuckle took on a harsh note. "Jist like Box-Ear here was known as Rickey Means, up in Montanny. The hardcase jasper who was given a meal and a bed by an old homesteader, and who paid 'em for their kindness by killin' 'em for the hundred dollars they had hid in an old coffee pot. Looks like Rickey is still playin' his old game."

Box-Ear's face was pale, his eyes dark, uncertain. He said: "Windy Harris . . . and Long Jim Evers!" Recognition brought sweat out over his face. His voice choked in his throat. "Damn you, Rolly . . . why didn't you . . . ?"

The nervous-fingered jasper at the side of Beefy sneered: "What the hell, Box-Ear! They're jist two bums, with their cutters pouched! I'll take the runt."

His nervous fingers tightened, pulled on his gun butt. Then he was sliding forward on his face, his eyes bulging. He never heard the slamming reports that followed his move; didn't see the crossing jets of flame, the smoke that had billowed upward. He didn't see anything. He was dead.

Box-Ear staggered with lead in his chest. His eyes tried to focus on the crouched beanpole from whose hip spurted jagged flame. His gun spat aimlessly as he fell, and dimly through the exploding roar in his head, he heard the crash of glass.

Rolly, jumping clear, worked his gun in spurts, his eyes blazing. He caught a blurred glimpse of a harsh-faced runt backed against the inner wall, a long-barreled gun bucking heavily in a gnarled fist. Then a .45 slug caught him in the right eye, sent him spinning backwards. He hit the table with his back, and went down with it.

Beefy, cursing with wild fear, made a running dive for the window. Two slugs hit him at the same instant. His heavy frame crashed through glass—hung limply across the sill—tipped. Clothes made a ripping sound on jagged edges, and then the window was blank. Smoke drifted out of it in slow, wrath-like fashion, and heavy, smashing shots faded out into the night.

Long Jim straightened, wiped a long hand across the gash on his cheek. Windy, unhurt, came to him, eyes grave. "Bad, Jim?"

Long Jim swore. "Naw! But my stummick's near wrapped around my backbone. When do we eat?"

THE BEAST IN CAÑADA DIABLO

LES(LIE) SAVAGE, JR. was an extremely gifted writer, born in Alhambra, California. He grew up in Los Angeles. The first story he wrote was accepted by the publisher to whom it was sent. That was "Bullets and Bullwhips" which Jack Burr was pleased to buy for Street & Smith's *Western Story Magazine* where it appeared in the issue for October 2, 1943. Almost ninety more magazine stories followed, all set on the American frontier, many of them published in Fiction House magazines such as *Frontier Stories* and *Lariat Story Magazine*. The publisher announced on the dust jacket to the first edition of his first novel, TREASURE OF THE BRASADA (Simon and Schuster, 1947), that it was by "a young writer of enormous power and imagination. We are proud to present it as the first novel to appear under the imprint: *Essandess Westerns*." However, due to his preference for historical accuracy, Savage later ran into problems with book editors in the 1950s who were particularly concerned about marriages between his protagonists and women of different races—a commonplace on the real frontier but not in much Western fiction in that decade. As a result of the censorship imposed on many of his works, only now are they being fully restored by returning to the author's original manuscripts.

Savage died young, at thirty-five, from complications arising out of hereditary diabetes and elevated cholesterol. However, his considerable legacy lives after him, there to reach a new generation of readers. Such noteworthy Savage titles as THE TRAIL (Fawcett Gold Medal, 1951) recently reprinted in a hardcover edition by Chivers Press in its Gunsmoke series, THE TIGER'S SPAWN (Chivers, 1994), RETURN TO WARBOW (Dell First Edition, 1955), and BEYOND WIND RIVER (Doubleday, 1958) are examples of the Western story at its finest. THE BEST WESTERN STORIES OF LES SAVAGE, JR. (Ohio University Press, 1991) is now available in a trade paperback edition from Barricade Books.

Savage's first story in *Lariat Story Magazine* was accepted by Malcolm Reiss and retitled "Gunstorm Ghost" (11/43). Reiss became Savage's mentor at the magazine and was responsible for encouraging him to write many of the notable short novels which followed: "Town of Twenty Triggers" (1/44), "Colt-Coward of the Hell Trails" (3/44), "Blood Brand of the Devil's Corral" (5/45), "Gun-Queen of Gambler's Row" (7/45), "Valley of Secret Guns" (9/45), "Where Hell's Coyotes Howl" (11/45), "The Brand Twisters" (3/46), "Drink to a Lobo's Guns" (9/46), "Brand of the Mustang Queen" (1/47), "Six-Gun Bride of the Teton Bunch" (7/47), "Gun-Witch of Wyoming" (11/47), "The Last Ride of Pothook Marrs" (9/48), "Beware of the

Six-Gun Saint" (11/48), "Lure of the Boothill Siren" (5/49), "Hymn of the Hogleg Hellion" (7/49), and "Blood Guns of the Crazy Moon" (1/50). Not one of these titles, of course, was the author's. In making this list I have neglected to include only one story, the one that follows.

When he completed the novelette he titled "The Beast in Cañada Diablo," he sent the manuscript to his agent, August Lenniger, in the summer of 1945. The novelette was accepted by Fiction House on September 10, 1945. The brasada region of Texas where this story is set, named this after the Spanish word *brazada* meaning a region densely covered with thickets and underbrush, was one that particularly intrigued the author. "The Beast in Cañada Diablo" was first published under the title "The Ghost of Gun-Runners' Rancho" in *Lariat Story Magazine* (5/46). It has not been reprinted elsewhere until now. It has been restored following the author's original manuscript.

I

It was the first apprehension Eddie Cardigan had felt since this started. His saddle emitted a mournful squeak as he turned to stare behind him. There was nothing but the gaunt pattern of brush the border Mexicans called *brazada* and the dim shapes of running, bawling cattle, half hidden in a curtain of acrid, yellow dust. Navasato came back wiping his sweating brown face, a burly man in buckskin *chivarras* and vest, bare shoulders and arms patterned by brush scars, fresh and old.

"Why did you stop them here?" Cardigan asked.

"We come to Cañada Diablo."

"All right," said Cardigan, shifting his long body irritably. "All right, so we come to Cañada Diablo. You just gonna sit here and let them catch up to us?"

"We got to go back till we hit the Comanche Trail," said Navasato. "I didn't realize we'd crossed it. We can't go through Cañada Diablo."

Cardigan leaned toward Navasato, his dark eyes narrowing. There was a lean intensity to his face that might have indicated a certain violence in him, and deep grooves from his prominent, aquiline nose to his thin mouth that might have indicated a rigid control of his natural tendencies. The wool vest he wore over his red, checked flannel shirt had not been designed for brush country, and it was ripped in several places, and covered with burrs and dirt.

"You know we'd walk right into them if we turned around now. Why can't we go through here?"

"Nobody ever goes through this part of the *monte*."

"*¿Nagualismo?*" said Cardigan.

"The *nagual*, the *nagual*," said Navasato, waving a square, callused hand half impatiently, half fearfully. "*La onza.*"

Pinto Parker had milled the cattle from the head by now, stopping them, and came trotting his spotted bronc back through the settling dust, sitting his seat with the same broad swagger which marked his walk, white Stetson shoved back on blond hair that took on a tight curl when it got wet with sweat this way.

"What's our tallow-packing pard babbling about now?" he said.

"*Nagualismo*, or something," said Cardigan.

"*Si, si*," muttered Navasato. "*La onza, la onza.*"

Pinto Parker threw back his head to laugh, and Cardigan wiped his hand irritably on his shirt. "What is it?"

"Some crazy Mex story," grinned Pinto, his teeth flashing a white line against his sun-darkened face. "You get it all the time down here. Started with the Indians farther south I think. Has to do with their religion or something. It spread up here and got the *brasaderos* in a big lather."

Cardigan pulled his reins in and felt the jaded dun draw a weary breath and stiffen to go. "Forget your ghost stories, Navasato. We've going through."

"No, Cardigan, no. *En el nombre de Dios. . . .*" With an abrupt decision, Navasato pulled his big Choppo horse around. "I ain't going."

The dun was ready for reaction when Cardigan put his reins against the neck, and it stepped broadside of Navasato's Choppo, putting Cardigan face to face with the man, their animals standing rump to head. "They'll get you if you go back, Navasato," he said through his teeth. "You ever seen a bunch of rustlers hanging from a tree? That's what you'll get, Navasato. No less."

The Mexican turned pale but tried to urge his Choppo on past Cardigan's dun. "I don't care. Let me go, Cardigan. You can find your way to the border from here if you want. Not me. I won't go through Cañada Diablo."

Cardigan realized what a primitive fear must hold the man if he would risk hanging rather than go on, and he understood there was only one thing now, and he did it. "You're coming with us. Go up and help Pinto on the point."

Navasato stared at the big .46 in Cardigan's hand. The little muscles around his mouth twitched. His eyes met Cardigan's for a moment, and Cardigan didn't know whether the fear there was for him, or something else. With a small, strangled sound, Navasato jerked on his reins. The Choppo jumped with the big Spanish bit biting his mouth, turning sharply after the cattle Pinto had started up again. Once the Mexican turned back to look at Cardigan; then he disappeared in the haze of rising dust.

There were maybe a hundred head of the animals, and it would not have been a big job for three men in the open, but through this brush it was hell. Cardigan had ridden brushland before, but nothing like this. The brasada was really a dry jungle, and for hours he had fought it as he fought no other country; the black chaparral clubbing at him constantly with a human malignancy, the *granjeno* clawing his bare hands and face, alkali settling in each fresh cut to sting and burn. Yet, this was the first time they had stopped since running into it that morning, and the utter primal force of the land had not clutched at Cardigan till he had pulled his dun to a stop there a few minutes ago and stared back. Well, they had told him how it would be, hadn't they? Or had tried to tell him. No man could describe in words the sensation that came when he stopped like that, for the first time, with the dust settling back into the stark ground from which it had risen, and the dull, cattle sounds dying out in the emptiness of the brush, and the inimical *mogotes* of chaparral closing in on all sides, black with a hostility that was almost human, suffocating, waiting.

"Hyah," shouted Cardigan, trying to dissipate the oppression in him by yelling at a thirst-crazed *orejano* which had tried to break into the thickets away from the main herd. "Get on back, you bug-eyed cousin to a. . . ."

It was the sound that cut him off. At first he thought it was a woman screaming. It rose to a shrill, haunting crescendo, somewhere out in the brush, and, stiffened in his saddle by the utter terror of it, Cardigan sensed more felinity in the cry than humanity. It ended abruptly, and the silence following beat at Cardigan's eardrums. As if snapping out of a trance, he put spurs into his dun with a jerk, leaping it ahead to meet Pinto Parker as the man appeared in the dust ahead.

"Did you hear it?" shouted Pinto.

"Sounded like a cat," said Cardigan.

"I never heard no bobcat squall like that," said Pinto. "Where's Navasato?"

"I think he was riding point."

"Cardigan!" It was the Mexican, his voice carrying a cracked horror in its tone, coming from the brush somewhere ahead. "Cardigan, I told you, *la onza, la onza.* Come and help me. *Dios,* Cardigan, *madre de Dios,* come and get me. . . ."

The crash of brush around him drowned the cries as Cardigan raced through a prickly pear thicket. His own animal whinnied with the pain of tearing at the thorned plants, and Cardigan's sleeve was ripped off as he threw his arm across his face to shield his eyes.

He pulled the horse up and swung down, hauling the reins over its head and whipping them around a branch. As he whirled to dive through the thicket on foot, he saw Pinto erupt from the prickly pear behind. Then Cardigan was struggling through the beating madness of black chaparral, tearing at the branches with one hand, his gun in the other. He could hear no sound but his own labored breathing as he finally ran into the next clearing, and saw Navasato. He stood there a moment, staring at the spectacle. Pinto crashed through behind Cardigan. Cardigan was the first to move over toward Navasato.

"Dead?" said Pinto, in a hollow voice.

Cardigan nodded, squatting down beside the mutilated body. "No brush clawed him up like that."

Parker was stooped over, looking at something on the ground, beyond Navasato. "What did he say about the *onza*?" he asked.

"Perhaps you had better ask Florida that, *compadres*," said a man's voice from behind them, and Cardigan started to raise his Remington as he turned, and then let it drop again.

The man standing there possessed a strange affinity with the brush. His face was lean and saturnine, and dark secrets stirred smokily in his strange, oblique eyes. He had thick, buckskin gloves on his hands, holding a gun in a casual, indifferent way, as if he wouldn't have needed it anyhow.

Pinto Parker's equanimity had never ceased to amaze Cardigan. Parker spoke to the man now without apparent surprise, a grin crossing his face easily. "You Florida?"

"No, Lieutenant Dixon," said the man. "I am not Florida. I am Comal Garza."

"Lieutenant Dixon?" asked Pinto.

"Yes." Garza's murky eyes passed over the animal lying beyond Navasato's torn, bloody body. "I see you brought the Krags. Where are the rest of them?"

At first, Cardigan had thought it was Navasato's Choppo horse, the dead animal over there, but now he saw it was a mule, with an army pack-saddle on its back. Its throat had been ripped, and steaming tripe was rolling out of a great, gaping hole torn in its belly, and Cardigan did not look long. Pinto had taken his rifle from the saddle scabbard on his horse, and he glanced at it involuntarily.

"Yeah, I got a Krag. What cows does that rope?"

Comal allowed a faint puzzlement to cross his face, studying Pinto. "I refer to the Krags on the mule. Where are the other mules? Stampeded?"

"This is the only mule I seen," said Parker.

Garza's gun had raised enough to cover them again. "What are you trying to do, Lieutenant Dixon? It is unfortunate your guide had to die this way, of course, but you certainly can't blame me. It's rather obvious what caused it. We all knew you were coming today, but we didn't expect you to appear driving a herd of cattle. Did you have to use the beef as a blind?"

"The beef is all we had," said Pinto. "You must have us mixed up with someone else."

"No one else would have come this far south of the Comanche Trail, *señor*," said Garza sibilantly, and he drew himself up perceptibly as if reaching a decision. "I did not expect you to act this way, Lieutenant. But of course, if you would betray others, it's not inconceivable that you wouldn't be honest with us. Did you think we weren't prepared for that contingency?"

"You're riding an awful muddy crick," said Pinto.

"I will make it clearer. I will ask you to relieve yourself of the implements."

Garza inclined his head toward the Krag .30 Parker had. Pinto grinned, dropping the rifle, fishing his Colt out and letting it go. Cardigan did the same.

"Kamaska," called Garza.

Cardigan could not help growing taut with surprise at the man's appearance. He made no sound coming from the thicket behind Garza. He was short and stubby and walked like an ape with his thick shoulders thrusting forward from side to side with each step. Kamaska's broad black belt was pulled in so tight it would have dug deeply into a normal man with a belly as big as that, yet it made no visible impression on his enormous, square paunch. His eyes passed over Pinto and Cardigan with opaque indifference in a wooden face, and Cardigan was expecting him to grunt when he bent over to pick up the guns, and was disappointed. Pinto Parker looked at Navasato in an automatic way, and Garza's voice came with a nebulous, hissing intonation.

"We'll leave him there."

"*Nagualismo?*" said Cardigan.

Garza's head raised, and a thin smile caught at his flat lips. "Perhaps, *señor*. Perhaps. And now?"

His thin black head was inclined toward the prickly pear, and he let them precede him. Pinto swaggered ahead of Cardigan, grinning back at him once, not caring much what this was about or trying to figure it out, because he was that kind. There were two other saddle animals with their horses. There was no room between Kamaska's belly and that belt, cinched up as it was, for the revolvers, so he dropped them in a fiber *morral* hung on the saddle horn of the hairy, black mule he had, and swung aboard with surprising alacrity for such a bulk, still holding the Krag in one hand.

Garza did not mount till Cardigan and Parker were in their saddles. Kamaska led through the brush, moving so steadily and surely that Cardigan finally realized they were following some sort of trail. Mystery was in Garza's vague smile, and his eyes were smoky and secretive.

"We will be there presently."

"I don't suppose it would do to ask you who you are?"

"I am Comal Garza."

Up ahead, Pinto laughed. Kamaska turned for an instant, staring opaquely at Parker as he would stare at an animal he did not understand.

Cardigan had no measure of the distance they rode through that weird brushland before they reached the house. It was hidden by chaparral until they were almost there; then the clearing thrust itself upon them, with several ocotillo corrals on the near side and an adobe structure across the intervening flat that might have been a bunkhouse. Some two hundred yards past that was the main building. It was typical of the dwellings in the southwest, though larger, its rafters formed by *viga* poles thrusting out the top of the wall a foot or so to cast a shadowed pattern across the yellow mud, shutters closed against the heat of the summer sun. A man rose from where he had been hunkered against one of the uprights forming the *portales* which supported the porch roof that ran the length of the front. He wore the usual *chivarras* and a tattered red Chimayo blanket, poncho style, its four corners dangling to his knees. His eyes were small and bucolic and his mouth was thick-lipped and brutal. Garza tossed his reins to the man.

"Did Florida get back, Innocencio?"

"No," said the man. Garza pointed toward the house, and Cardigan took it they were to go in. The living room was dim and musty.

"All right, Lieutenant Dixon," Garza told Pinto.

Parker's mouth opened slightly. "Lieutenant Dixon?"

"You were the one with the Krag," said Garza.

"Krag? It's my rifle."

"I'm glad you admit it," said Garza. "Now, if you'll tell us where you've got the other Krags. . . ?"

"Oh, the Krags," said Parker, as if something had dawned on him abruptly. Grinning, he turned to Cardigan. "Now just where *did* we put those Krags, Cuhnel Cahdigan?"

There were times when Parker's irresponsible sense of humor galled Cardigan. "Shut up, Pinto," he said. "Can't you see they mean business?"

"Yes, Lieutenant Dixon," said Garza. "We mean business."

"Now, Cuhnel Cahdigan, suh," said Parker with mock gravity, "you-all know ahm serious as all hell. I jes can't seem to recall where we put those Krags. By Gad, my name ain't Lieutenant Dixon if I can. . . ."

Garza had taken his forward step before Cardigan realized what he meant to do, moving without perceptible effort, and his hand made a dull, slapping sound across Parker's face. Garza had put no apparent force in the blow, yet it sent Pinto reeling back against the wall so hard, a hand-carved *santo* fell from its niche. Pinto stood there with his hand up to his face. Finally he grinned again, without mirth.

"You shouldn't have done that, Garza."

"I don't appreciate your broad humor, Lieutenant. Or were you being humorous? When Zamora came from contacting you in Brownsville, he said we might have some trouble. If you think of holding out for a higher price, don't. We already made the arrangements, and you are here. Now, tell us where the Krags are and you'll get your money."

"You made a mistake," said Cardigan. "This isn't Lieutenant Dixon. It's Pinto Parker. We were just running some cattle through."

"Your cattle, I take it."

A trace of Pinto's humor had returned. "Now, you don't suppose we'd be herding somebody else's beef, do you?"

"You have a bill of sale for a hundred Big Skillet steers?" said Garza.

"Is that what they were?" Pinto asked.

A thin impatience entered Garza's voice. "Let's quit this sparring. If you chose to use a bunch of rustled Big Skillet cattle as a blind, it is no concern of mine. You know what I'm interested in."

"Oh, is there a woman in the brasada?" said Pinto.

Garza drew a sharp breath; then he inclined his head toward a hand-carved Mendoza chair that sat in high-backed austerity against the wall. "We'll put him in there, Kamaska."

"Wait a minute."

"I would advise you to keep quiet, *señor*," said Garza, turning the gun on Cardigan. "Innocencio will be watching you, and his characteristics are hardly those his name would imply."

Innocencio had taken a singularly evil looking *belduque* from beneath his Chimayo blanket, and he moved toward Cardigan, running a thick, callused finger down the bright blade. Garza was forced to snap the gun bolt before he could persuade Pinto into the chair. Cardigan stood by the wall, bent forward tensely, his breath fluttering white nostrils in a hoarse audibility. Kamaska got a rawhide dally from a wooden stob in the wall. Parker started to jump from the chair as he realized what it meant, then sat back down slowly for the cocked hogleg was aimed at his belly. Kamaska pulled the rope so tight it dug into Pinto through his fancy-stitched shirt. Garza shoved Pinto's white Stetson off and it rolled to the floor.

"Now, Lieutenant Dixon, are you going to tell us where the Krags are? You have one more chance."

Cardigan never ceased to marvel at Pinto's reckless nonchalance; even now the man's grin held nothing forced. "You got us wrong. Parker's my name. We're just a couple of punchers."

"Very well," said Garza softly. Kamaska had gotten an ancient

Spanish nutcracker of beaten silver from the oak table. Pinto's arms were lashed along the arms of the chair with his fingers protruding over the edge. Garza watched Kamaska slip Pinto's right index finger into the jaws of the nutcracker. "It was made to crack Brazil nuts, Lieutenant. It executes a remarkable pressure."

Pinto could not help the gasp, and his grin turned to a grimace of spasmodic pain. His eyes remained closed while Kamaska opened the nutcracker from his finger. The beaded sweat stood out on his face. Finally he opened his eyes and looked at the mashed nail.

"Hell," he said, and grinned.

"*Muy bien*," said Garza. "Very well."

Kamaska slipped the nutcracker on Pinto's middle finger. Cardigan knew his first anger; it had only been irritation before. He had not comprehended fully what it was all about, and it had only been irritation, and a remnant of the revulsion at what had happened to Navasato; but now it was anger. He had seen how Pinto's first gasp drew Innocencio's attention for that moment, and he watched Kamaska begin to squeeze the nutcracker. Innocencio stood facing Cardigan with that *belduque* in his thick fingers. Pinto's face contorted again, and once more he could not stifle a deep moan. This time Innocencio's reaction was less marked. Cardigan barely caught the flicker of his eyes toward the sound, and moved when he did.

Innocencio tried to jump backward and throw the knife at the same time, but Cardigan's foot lashed up and caught his hand before the blade had left it. The knife flew upward to strike the low roof with the impetus of Innocencio's toss.

"I told you to watch him," shouted Garza, whirling with the rifle. Cardigan's jump had carried him to Innocencio, and he caught the man about the waist, whirling him toward Garza before the man could fire. Innocencio struck Garza like a sack of sand, carrying him back across Pinto and knocking chair and all over onto the floor. Cardigan heard Parker shout with the pain of their weight smashing down onto him. Cardigan had tried to set himself, but his legs would not hold the terrible force of Kamaska's charge. He felt himself stumbling backward across the hard, earthen floor, and the wall struck his head and sent a roar of pain through his whole body like a cannon going off.

He tried to roll over and drive an elbow between them as a wedge to keep Kamaska from grabbing him, but the man caught his elbow and jammed it aside, and then one of those thick arms was about Cardigan's neck, and he thought he had never felt such incredible strength in a human being before. He heard the snap of bones and his own scream of pain. Then Kamaska's fist exploded in his face, and the room spun, and then he couldn't even see the room. Somewhere, far away, he felt his own body make a feeble effort at struggling, and one of his arms moved dimly. Then Kamaska's fetid, sweating bulk shifted against him, and he knew that fist was coming again and he knew that would finish it.

"Kamaska!"

At first Cardigan thought he had said it. Then he realized it had come from across the room. Kamaska's arm slipped from around Cardigan's neck, and the man stood up, breathing heavily. Cardigan had trouble focusing his eyes. At first all he could see was the Burgess-Colt repeater held in the small, brown hands of a dim figure across the room, light from the open door glinting on the rifle's silver-plated receiver. Then he heard Pinto's voice.

"I guess I wasn't joking. There *is* a woman in the brasada!"

II

His name was Esperanza, and he shuffled around the bunkshack like a ringy, old mossyhorn, growling through drooping, white *mustachios* so long their tips were dirty from brushing against the chest of his white cotton shirt. After the fight in the house, Innocencio had brought Cardigan and Parker out here to the bunkhouse, a structure even more ancient and odorous than the main building, its roof so low Pinto had to remove his Stetson before entering. Cardigan sat at one end of the long, plank table, still too sick from Kamaska's brutal blows to eat anything of what was before him. Innocencio stood by the door, glowering at Cardigan, nursing his hand.

"*El mano*," he kept repeating.

"You must have broke his hand with that boot of yours," said Pinto, the pain of his mashed fingers having little effect on his appetite. He forked up a huge mouthful from the tin plate grimacing as he spoke around it. "This is the foulest concoction of hogtripe I ever wrapped my lips around."

The deafening crash of guns drowned him out, and he jumped up, knocking over his chair and spewing the food all over the table. Cardigan was bent forward, both hands gripping the planks, staring at Esperanza. The old man held a smoking, stag-butted .45 in each hand, his red jowls quivering.

"You don't like my food," he shouted apoplectically.

"Don't get me wrong, *amigo*," laughed Pinto shakily, staring at the smoking guns with the surprise still on his face. "Your *alimento* is marvelous. I wouldn't eat anywhere else. It's just an old Texas custom. Like throwing salt over your left shoulder. You say it out loud, see. You say this is the foulest concoction of hogtripe I ever ate, and then . . . *Diablo*, he don't come up to get it. An old Texas custom."

"*¿El Diablo?*" said the old man, squinting at Parker, still suspicious. They were literal-minded in many respects, these *brasaderos*, with the superstition of peasantry, to whom the devil was as real as the coma trees in front of their *jacales*.

"All right," growled Esperanza finally, waving one of his .45s. "Sit down and eat it then. I make the best *chiles rellenos* in all *Mejico*. Why do you think they call them the children's dream, ah? I take the greenest of peppers and stuff them with the tenderest of chicken and the yellowest of cheese and dip them in a batter *El Dios* himself would be proud to be dipped in, and I cook them in the purest of hog fat till they come out as golden brown as my very own skin. For twenty years I cook them for General Díaz. Porfirio Díaz Santa Ana Estevan Esperanza. That's me. Why do you think they call me that, ah?"

"Esperanza," said Florida Zamora from the door. "Haven't our guests already been shown enough bad hospitality?"

The grin that spread Pinto's face as he looked toward her held an infinite appreciation. "It's about time you come out," he chuckled. "I wasn't going to wait much longer."

Cardigan had seen women in Brownsville react to Pinto's animal magnetism. Florida took in his great height, and the breadth of his muscular shoulders beneath his fancy-stitched shirt, and his blond hair, and her smile answered his. It drew a resentment from Cardigan he could not understand; and, angered at himself for feeling it, he did not smile when the woman's eyes passed to him. He met her gaze almost sullenly, and her smile faded. Her rich underlip dropped faintly, as if she were about to speak; then she closed it again, and moved to the table. There was nothing masculine about the way her buckskin *chivarras* fitted across the hips, or about what she did to the white silk shirt just beneath its soft collar; and Pinto was taking that all in as she placed the Krag she had brought on the table, and then pulled their revolvers from her waistband and put them down.

"You must forgive us, gentlemen," she said. "Esperanza is an irascible old reprobate. I'm sure you'll overlook his peculiarities. As for Garza, he made a very grave mistake. We were expecting someone else. He mistook you for them."

Cardigan tried to keep his eyes off her, and could not. There was something gypsy in the way she wore a red bandeau drawn tightly about her head, hair with the sheen of a blue roan falling soft and black from beneath that to caress the shoulders of her white shirt. There was undeniable aristocracy to the arch of her thin, black brows, the proud line of her nose.

"I'm glad to see Esperanza fixed up your fingers," she said, and Cardigan sensed her mind was not on the words.

Pinto glanced at his bandaged fingers. "I never knew prickly pear poultice. . . ."

"Will cure anything from *dolor de las tripas* to a .50 caliber hole through your head," smiled Florida, faintly. "Or almost."

Pinto let his eyes cross her features. "You've got some white blood?"

"My father was Mexican," she said. "He married an American woman from Brownsville. This is *Hacienda del Diablo*. It's not really as forbidding as Estate of the Devil would suggest. The country south of the Comanche Trail has always been known as Cañada Diablo. I could never see why."

"*Nagualismo?*" said Cardigan.

Her turn toward him was sharp, as if she had forgotten he was there. "The land was named long ago," she said finally.

"And this *nagualismo* only started lately?" said Cardigan.

"You seem to know," she said.

"Garza seemed to think you were the one to know," said Cardigan. "Just what is *nagualismo?*"

She hesitated, her eyes dropping from his face, then she spoke abruptly. "*Nagualismo* really originates farther south, in the Mexican peninsula. It's a belief among the Indian tribes down there. The Caribs subscribe to it, I think. In Yucatan, a *nagual* is an Indian dedicated at birth to some animal by his parents. The rapport between child and animal finally becomes so strong the *nagual* can change himself at will into the animal."

"A cat, maybe?" asked Pinto.

She nodded. "They have jaguars down there."

Cardigan remembered, then, how Pinto had been bent over beside Navasato, looking at something on the ground, when Garza came. "That's what you found?" he said.

"By Navasato?" asked Pinto, and nodded. "Big ones. Just like cat tracks. Only they couldn't have been cat tracks. Cats don't grow that big in Texas. Or anywhere."

There was something frightened in the silence that fell. Florida stared at Pinto for a moment, then gave a rueful little laugh.

"We're letting our imaginations carry us away. Why even dignify such an absurd superstition by considering it in that light? I've lived in the brasada all my life and admit having seen some strange things. I've never seen any evidence of a man having the capacity to change himself into an animal at will, however. If Garza came on you right after you found your dead friend, you undoubtedly did not get a chance to study the tracks closely. We have large bobcats around here, and a few jaguars come up from Mexico. Even a

mountain lion or two from the Sierras. I'm sure you'd find one big
enough to account for the tracks."

"I've seen the biggest mountain lions they got," said Pinto. "I
never seen one with feet that big. And the way it took Navasato. He
didn't even have his gun out."

She sat tapping the table with a long finger, finally shrugged it
off. "Garza said you were running a cut of Big Skillet steers. Have
you got a bill of sale?"

The abruptness of it took Cardigan off guard, but Parker's grin
was easy. "Garza picked us up so fast we didn't have a chance to
bring our duffel along. The bill was in my sougan."

"I thought so," said Florida.

Parker's look of growing indignation was almost genuine enough
to convince Cardigan. "You don't mean to insinuate. . . ."

Florida Zamora stopped him with an upraised hand. "Never mind.
Whether those cattle were wet or dry doesn't concern me. I just
wanted to know. Men who run wet cattle wouldn't be as particular
about the kind of jobs they do as men who run dry cattle, shall
we say."

"Their discrimination between the legal and illegal aspects of an
occupation might not be as keen as a man who never ran wet cattle,
true," said Pinto.

"Would you like a job here?"

Pinto picked up his Colt, spun the cylinder. "What's going on?"

"Nothing particularly. We just run *mestenos*," said Florida.

"You just run mustangs," mused Pinto, slipping his gun back
into its holster, "yet you'd rather hire a man who might overlook a
legal technicality than one who wouldn't."

"If these weren't your cattle," said Florida, "you couldn't get to
the north without running into a posse. Sheriff Sid Masset's a hard
man to shake if he happens to be riding your trail. On the other
hand, no lawman has come into Cañada Diablo in a long time."

"*Nagualismo*?" said Cardigan.

The woman turned sharply toward him again, a faint flush of
anger rising into her cheeks. With an audible, indrawn breath, she
turned back to Pinto. He had begun to eat again, and spoke around
a mouthful of beans.

"The advantages of your little *estancia* sound pleasing. Tell me
more."

"The financial arrangements might interest you. For a hundred
steers on the wet market you couldn't get more than three pesos a
head. I could see that you draw down more than that in a month
here."

"A man would have to work pretty hard for that kind of chips."

"It all depends on what you do," she said. At Pinto's inquiring look, she smiled, tapping his Krag. "You're not unknown down here. We've heard what you can do with an iron."

Pinto nodded, forking in more *frijoles*. "Then you're not hiring us to run mustangs."

"I'm hiring you to run mustangs," she said. "But if something comes up that necessitates the use of that hardware you pack, I hope I'm right in thinking a man who runs wet cattle would be less reluctant about using it than a man who runs dry cattle, and more skillfully."

Pinto wiped the gravy out of the plate with the last piece of tortilla, leaned back, smacking his lips. "Doesn't sound bad to me."

Florida turned to Cardigan. "How about you?"

"What if we don't take the job?" asked Cardigan.

She hesitated a moment, then spoke with a certain control tightening her voice. "It seems to me you would be better off accepting it."

"You say no lawman has been here for a long time," said Cardigan. "Maybe this *nagualismo* business has scared everybody else out, too. Maybe we're the first outsiders you've entertained in quite a spell. Maybe you'd rather not have us reach the outside again, knowing you were expecting a Lieutenant Dixon."

"You take an unfortunate attitude." Anger was slipping through that control in her voice.

"I just wanted things clear," he said. "Does Garza still think Pinto is Lieutenant Dixon?"

"I don't," she said.

"Does Garza?"

She pulled her lips in impatiently, then shrugged. "All right, so he does. What difference does that make?"

"It might make a big difference."

"What does it matter, Card?" said Pinto. "She's right about us not being able to get out of the brasada by the north now. This is as good a place to camp as any till the Big Skillet ruckus blows over, and we get paid to boot."

"I'm glad you will stay," she said, moving toward the door. She took a last glance at Cardigan, then spoke as she turned away. "We're riding this afternoon. You might like to come along."

Pinto got up and went to the door to watch her walk across the sunlit compound toward the house, making various appreciative noises. He leaned against the door, tucking his good hand into his gunbelt, turning to grin at Cardigan.

"She really must have wanted hands bad."

"Why?"

Pinto laughed softly. "She didn't even ask us if we knew how to run mustangs."

III

The wind whispered through mesquite with a haunted sibilance and the black chaparral was so thickly matted and so low in some places that a man trained in the brush could see a buck's antlers rising above it half a mile away, and so tall in other places a horse-backer could ride for miles without ever seeing more than twenty feet ahead or behind. Riding through it, behind Florida Zamora, Cardigan was filled with a nebulous oppression he could not shake off. They had left *Hacienda del Diablo* earlier that afternoon, riding past the huge cedar-post corrals filled with half-tamed mustangs. They went at a fast trot which kept Cardigan dodging post-oak limbs and ducking outstretched branches of chaparral, his face and hands continually clawed by mesquite. He marveled at the ease with which Florida seemed to drift through the brush, her movements to avoid the growth hardly perceptible. Finally they crossed a clearing, and she allowed her pony to drop back, smiling faintly at Cardigan as he dabbed irritably at a scratch on his face.

"Riding the brush is a little different than open country, isn't it? You don't learn it in a day, Cardigan. I've been running the brasada most of my life, and I still get knocked off now and then."

"Garza seems adept enough," said Cardigan. "I got the impression somehow that he wasn't native to the brush."

"He's only been with me about six months," she said. "He came from Yucatan, I think."

"Funny he would give me the idea you were the authority on this *nagualismo*," Cardigan told her. "If it originated in the Mexican peninsula, I should think a man from Yucatan would know more about it."

"Maybe he does," she said. "How about you, Cardigan? Where are you from?"

"I've been a lot of places," he answered.

"How long have you been with Pinto?" she asked him.

"I met him in Brownsville."

"You're so specific." Then she was looking at his hands. "They don't look like Pinto's."

"They've got ten fingers."

She drew her lips in that way, with irritation. "The rope burns on them are fresh."

"We were working cattle when you found us."

"But all the rope burns on your hands are fresh. Pinto's got some old ones."

"Maybe I got tired being a bank clerk," said Cardigan.

"You don't get legs like horse collars sitting on a stool."

"Maybe I used to tuck my feet in the rungs."

"Then you admit you haven't been in the wet cattle business long?"

"How long have you been in the mustang business?" he asked.

"That's irrelevant," she said hotly. Then she quieted, something pensive entering her eyes. "Who are you, Cardigan?"

"I'm the hand you hired to run mustangs," he said, and saw the impatient anger that drew from her before he had to swoop beneath a hackberry limb. He rose in the saddle again. "I never heard of an outfit this size spending all its time chasing mustangs. What happened to your cattle?"

"Mustanging is a profitable business," she said evasively. "We're coming to the watering hole for a herd we've been after for some time now. We haven't staked out here for a week or so now, and our scent should be gone, and the wind's toward us, so they shouldn't smell us. Tighten the noseband on your animal. When they show, try to keep the *manada* from breaking into thick brush "

"*Manada?*"

She glanced at him. "They run in *manadas*, herds of twenty or thirty mares with a stallion. Get the stallion, and the mares are all disorganized."

"¡*Caballos!*"

It was Kamaska's voice, and it settled an immediate silence over all of them. Garza stood beside his *pelicano*, a stiff, arrogant figure in the gloom. Parker was beside him, taller, his broad shoulders carried back in a sway-backed stance. Parker felt his dun's throat swell with a nicker, and he caught at the noseband. Then he saw them, drifting into the open as silently as a file of thunderheads climbing from behind a peak. The leader was a huge white stallion, prodigiously muscled for a brush horse, his chest and shoulders moving with the striated sinuosity of thick snakes beneath his pale, silken hide. He was wildness incarnate, moving with a delicate ferine prance that barely touched his sharp, clean hoofs to the ground, the proud arch of his neck never still as he moved his head ceaselessly from side to side. Rather than marring his appearance, the brush scars patterning his body only lent it a bizarre beauty. Cardigan watched, fascinated, his breath catching in him as he saw the animal stop and raise its head, and thought it had scented them. Then it went on, switching its long, white tail, and the mares followed. When they were almost by, Cardigan saw Garza turn and lift his foot into the stirrup, and knew it was the sign. Without a word, all of them mounted, the faint stir of movement they made rising above the small night sounds and then breaking into a shocking, thundering noise, as Garza laid the guthooks into his *pelicano* and jumped it through the brush with a pounding crash into the open. Cardigan lost his hat bursting through that first *mogote*, and after that all he could see was the white stallion.

It was reared up at the brink of the water hole, noble head twisted toward them. With a piercing scream it whirled, plunging directly into the mucky water and floundering across. Cardigan drove his horse directly after Garza, hearing someone's wild shouting and not realizing it was his till he was in the water himself.

The spray shooting around him was sticky with mud. He came out on the other bank pawing at his eyes and cursing. He saw Kamaska make a throw at a mare and forefoot her, and the ground shook as she went down. Then Florida passed Cardigan, bent over her pony. She hit the first growth hard on Garza's tail, and passed through its massed brush with a swift ease. Then Cardigan met it. He saw a branch of chaparral dead ahead and dropped off to one side to go under, and put his face right into a growth of prickly pear. Howling with the pain of torn flesh, he tore his head upward to escape that and was caught by the branch he had tried to dodge in the first place. The blow on his head knocked him backward, and he barely caught himself from going over the dun's rump. Blinded, cursing, he was still in that position when some mesquite caught one of his outflung feet, tearing it from the stirrup, and he slid over the other side of his horse.

He managed to catch the fall on his other heel, bouncing it off on his buttocks and rolling over to smash into a low spread of mesquite. He got to his hands and knees, shaking his head, spitting out gramma grass and dirt. Finally he got to his feet and looked after his horse. It had disappeared in the brush, along with Florida and Garza. Then the thud of hoofs from the other direction turned him that way, and he saw Kamaska riding in from the sink on his black mule.

"It takes a lifetime to ride the brasada with such skill as the *señorita* possesses," he said, enigmatically.

"Hell with the brasada," snarled Cardigan, wiping dirt and blood off his cheek. "I thought you were taking care of the mares."

"I have two tied to mesquite trees," said Kamaska. "The *señorita* told me to keep an eye on you."

"I thought, maybe," said Cardigan. "And who keeps an eye on Parker?"

"He knows the brasada," said Kamaska.

"That isn't why she wanted you to watch me," said Cardigan.

Then his head raised slightly. He had never seen Kamaska evince any emotion before. Perhaps it was the man's eyes. The opacity had left them, and they were filled with a luminous, startled light, that changed in a moment to the animal fear Cardigan had seen in a dog's eyes when it sensed something beyond the pale of human perception. Kamaska's dark hands tightened around the reins of his mule till the knuckles shone white, and his voice shook on the word.

"*Nagual,*" he said hoarsely, and gave a jerk on the reins that pulled the mule completely around, sending it crashing into the brush; Kamaska's voice echoing back as he said it again, in what was almost a cry, this time: "¡*Nagual!*"

The wind had ceased and, after the sound of Kamaska's passing had died, the utter silence pressed in on Cardigan with a physical, suffocating weight. The ashen *cenzio* across the clearing was still trembling from the passage of the man who had appeared through it an instant before, only accentuating the complete quiescence of the man himself, as he stood there, and of his two shaggy hounds, moveless, on either side of him. A pair of greasy *chivarros* were his only covering. His black torso was bare, a scabrous covering of fresh scars and scar tissue peeling from old scars giving him a leprous, revolting appearance. His black head was covered with hair like a thick mat of curly gramma grass. The whites of his eyes gleamed in his dark face as he spoke, and his voice held a hollow, bell-like intonation.

"I am Africano," he said.

"Cardigan's mine."

It was almost as startling as watching a statue come to life when the man named Africano moved, coming toward Cardigan with a smooth, flowing, soundless walk. "You came to help *Señorita* Zamora?"

"I didn't know she needed help," said Cardigan, stifling with some effort the desire to put his hand on his gun.

"You must know," said Africano. "You came to help her."

"There are a lot of things I don't know," said Cardigan.

"But would like to."

"I would," said Cardigan. "And a lot of other folks, too."

"But you, especially," murmured the man, his eyes white and shining on Cardigan.

Cardigan studied the negroid features, trying to reconcile the luminous intelligence in those eyes with the primal brutality of the low, heavy brow, the coarse line of lips and nose. "What do you mean, me, especially?"

"Comal Garza thought your *compadre* was Lieutenant Dixon."

"Are we going through that again?" asked Cardigan wearily.

"Comal Garza did not consider you." Cardigan could not help the way the lines deepened about his mouth. It was the only sign, but he realized Africano had noted it. The man took something from inside his *chivarras*. It was a flat leather case about a foot long and five inches wide. The moon had risen, and Cardigan could make out the lettering on the case. *Tío* Bacalar. This time Cardigan tried to keep it from showing, but something must have passed through his face, for there was a satisfaction in Africano's hollow voice. "I thought it might mean something to you."

"He's here, then," said Cardigan, through set teeth.

"What else?" said Africano. "I found it down near *Mogotes Oros.* Camp had been made there."

"Anything else?"

"Rumors," said Africano.

"Why show this to me?"

"There was a man named George Weaver," said Africano.

Cardigan's brows raised as his head raised, wrinkling his forehead when he finally stared into Africano's eyes. "What's happened to him?"

"About a month ago." Africano waved a repulsive hand. "Also down near *Mogotes Oros.*"

"What happened to George?" The grim insistence in Cardigan's voice drew Africano up.

"*La onza.*"

"Don't give me that!" Cardigan dropped the case in a sudden burst of anger, grabbing the man by his thick shoulders, voice rising to a hoarse shout. "Everybody I asked says it that way. I'm damn tired of it. *Nagualismo. La onza. Nagual.* Give it to me straight, damn you. What happened to Weaver? The same thing that happened to Navasato? You know! What the hell made tracks that big around Navasato? And Kamaska. He called you *nagual*? I never thought I'd see him scared like that at anything. Tell me, damn you "

It was the sound that stopped Cardigan, before the actual pain. Africano had stood moveless in his grasp, and Cardigan did not realize why until the guttural eruption from his feet. Then he gasped, releasing his hold on Africano, jumping backward to lash out with his leg. Both dogs were at him now, the one which had bitten his leg leaping away and then darting back in savagely to catch at his swinging arm. Cardigan had been reaching instinctively for his gun, but the slashing pain of teeth ripping his hand caused him to pull it up again with a howl. His backward momentum carried him off-balance, and he went down beneath them, kicking violently with his legs and throwing his arms over his face.

"Tuahantepec," called Africano, without much vehemence, "Bautista," and then it was gone. One instant Cardigan had been the center of a whirling, snarling mass of fangs and fur and claws; the next he was lying there on an empty clearing, the hoarse rasping of his own breath the only sound. He sat up, nursing the slashed hand, blood soaking down his Levi's from the long rip there. Perhaps it was the riders that had frightened Africano away. They came into the open with a crackling of brush, and Pinto Parker was the first to dismount from his steaming horse. Getting to his feet, Cardigan could see Kamaska behind Garza, his eyes still wide and luminous with that fear.

"I told you," Kamaska said. "Look at him, look at him. *Nagual. La onza.*"

Garza swung down, a strange, baffled look in his eyes as he stared at the slashes on Cardigan's hand. "What was it?"

"A *negro* and a couple of big dogs," said Cardigan sullenly.

Cardigan saw relief cross Garza's face, and the man let his breath out, and seemed to force a small laugh. "You must mean Africano. He's not *negro*. He's *mestizo*. Part Aztec, he claims."

Parker had picked up the brown case from the ground, staring at the gilt letters on its flap with a frown that held more than puzzlement. "Who's *Tio* Bacalar?" he said.

IV

They were called *Mogotes Oros*, which meant the Gold Thickets, because of the huisache which grew through them in such profusion and turned yellow in the spring. Almost every Saturday the *vaqueros* held a bull-tailing there, providing almost their only form of entertainment, gathering to eat and drink and gamble. It was two days after the dogs had attacked Cardigan, but he was still feeling mean, his hand swollen and painful as he swung down off the dun and stood there a moment looking at the group of *jacales* to one side of the clearing, the inevitable house of brush and adobe in which the *brasaderos* and their families lived.

A pair of squat, ugly women in shapeless skirts of tattered wool and dirty white *camisas* for blouses had begun building the fire and driving cottonwood stakes into the ground for the spit. Behind a *jacal* was a large corral containing a dozen ringy bulls, the nervous lather about their jaws and their raucous bawls and incessant stamping showing how recently they had been brought in from the brush. And back of the corral, again, was the somber brasada, its depths stirring restlessly when a faint breeze fanned the summer heat momentarily. A saddle creaked beside Cardigan, and Comal Garza's voice was soft in his ear, mocking somehow.

"It is a strange land to a newcomer, no? Perhaps you are beginning to realize how impossible it would be for you to find your way out alone. Many men have been lost here, *señor*. The brasada is more deadly than the desert . . . to those who do not know it intimately."

A mirthless smile crossing his dark face, he moved toward the group of *vaqueros* lounging in the shade of a coma tree. Pinto had dismounted now, hitching the reins of his spotted pony to the mesquite, a narrow speculation in his eyes as he studied Cardigan.

"What's going on, Cardigan?"

"I thought it didn't bother you."

Pinto made an impatient gesture with his hand. "First the girl. Then this Garza *hombre*. What's between you and them? The way Florida watches you."

"Getting jealous?"

"More than that," said Pinto, easing his girth in the saddle. "I wouldn't mind if it was your native charm attracting the girl. But it's something more." He studied Cardigan's intense face. "I really don't know much about you, do I?"

Cardigan shrugged. "I don't know much about you, either. We've got along that way."

"You know what I am, Cardigan."

"You know what I am, Pinto."

"I thought I did," said Parker. "Who is Lieutenant Dixon?"

Cardigan met Parker's eyes. "I don't know any more than you do, Pinto. Evidently this Dixon was bringing a bunch of Krags to Garza, and they expected him the same day we passed through, the same spot."

"Why should Garza want a load of guns?"

"Maybe he has other interests besides mustangs."

"Gun running? Who to?"

"How should I know?" Impatience had leaked into Cardigan's tone. "The revolutionists in Coahilla. The Federales. There's always a market down there."

Pinto shook his head, not satisfied. "More than that, Cardigan. Just a simple little smuggling wouldn't upset the whole brasada like this. I can feel it. See it. This *nagualismo* business is mixed up in it, too, somehow."

He trailed off as the sound of a fiddle rose from across the clearing. A blind *brasadero* was sawing on his ancient instrument and tapping a foot against the hard ground, and one of the younger Mexican girls had already glided into the Varsoviana, the high heels of her red shoes tapping the hard-packed earth like the click of castanets. Cardigan drifted that way, and Pinto cut out in front of him with a laugh.

"Not this time, *compadre*. I'm claiming this first dance with the prettiest gal here."

Florida had been talking to one of the women at the fire, and Pinto caught her with a whoop, swung her out toward the others.

Innocencio had brought his guitar, and as his playing joined in with the fiddle's, the excitement caught at Florida. Cardigan could see the flush climb up her neck into her cheeks, and her eyes widen and flash. She was laughing as Pinto whirled her into the cradle dance they called a *cuna*, and more couples wheeled out until all Cardigan could see was Florida's shining black hair spinning through the brown faces and whirling bodies. He knew a twinge of envy at Pinto Parker's facility with women, and then smiled at himself for that. Garza was drinking pulque from a big Guadalajara jar with Kamaska and three other *vaqueros*, and Cardigan felt them glancing toward him once. Then he saw Parker and the girl had stopped dancing and were coming through the crowd toward him, a puzzled frown on Parker's face. Kamaska left the group of *vaqueros* and moved over toward the horses in his shuffling, anthropoid walk.

"I can't figure what you got on this gal," said Parker as he came up to Cardigan.

"What do you mean?"

Parker wiped his sweating face with a fancy bandanna, and his grin looked forced. "She wants to dance with you."

"I don't dance," said Cardigan.

"Then it's time to learn," Florida told him, and the soft touch of her hand against his back caused him to stiffen. She felt it, and looked into his eyes, and then laughed. It angered him, and he swung her out almost roughly. Why should he let her touch do that to him? Enough other women had touched him. She was still laughing as she tried to teach him the steps. As they swung in the *cuna*, she let herself come up against him with a bold smile, and he thought she was coquetting and his lips spread back from his teeth in a disgusted way. Then he realized it wasn't for that she'd come near. Her breath was hot against the side of his face as she spoke.

"It's the only chance I'll get to tell you. They're up to something. Watch yourself and don't get off alone. I don't know what it is, but they're up to something."

The desperate intensity of her voice caught at him. "Who's up to something?"

"*Señores y señoritas*," called Garza from where the fiddler stood, "if you have had enough dancing, we shall turn out the first *toro* so we can get started with the feasting."

A cheer went up from the *vaqueros* around Cardigan, and they left their partners on the spot, running across the compound toward their horses. With excited squeals, the women scattered toward the *jacales*. Innocencio and another man had driven a bull from the corral; it was a wild-looking bay with brown points, switching its rump from side to side and pawing at the ground.

"*Muy valiente*," shouted Kamaska, leaping on his hairy mule, and the others mounted to follow him at a gallop into the open after the bull.

Garza led his *pelicano* from under the comas. "You have tailed the bull, *señor* Cardigan?"

"I've tailed a few," said Cardigan.

"It is a practice more common near the border," said Garza. "If you watch, you will see how we do it, down here."

Cardigan couldn't help letting it goad him, though he knew that was Garza's intent. He stood by his dun, watching the riders haze down the bull. Kamaska was in the lead and, as the bull broke for the brush, Kamaska ran his mule off to one side of the running animal and came in from there, leaning far out of the saddle to catch at the switching tail. The riders behind were whooping wildly and slapping at their *chivarras* with quirts, and the dust boiled up around the whole group as Kamaska caught the bull's tail and dallied the end around his saddle horn as he would a rope. With his free hand he jerked the reins against the mule's neck and the mule veered sharply away. Cardigan saw the bull's tail stretch taut, swinging the animal's hind feet from beneath it. At that moment, Kamaska released the tail and galloped free, and the bull shook the ground with its falling.

"A good man can break its neck that way," Garza told Cardigan. "Perhaps you would like to ride the next one. Whoever throws him gets the honor of eating his brains."

Kamaska must have broken the bull's neck, for it lay inert as a *vaquero* roped its horns with his rawhide dally and hauled it off toward the fire. Innocencio was goading another bull out of the corral, a big *sabina* beast, hide mottled with red and white speckles, one of its horns growing in a broken, twisted way down across its eye. It's heavy, scarred head was tossing wickedly from side to side as it danced from the corral.

"Ah"—there was a certain satisfaction in Garza's tone—"this one I will ride myself. It is Gotch, *señor*. It will take a real man."

Cardigan swung an angry leg over his dun, knowing the men had little respect for him after the sorry spectacle he had made in the ride after the mustangs. Maybe he didn't know the brasada, he thought, but if he couldn't tail a bull he might as well sack his saddle right here. As he trotted the dun out after Garza, he thought he heard someone call from behind him.

"Cardigan, not that one, not Gotch. . . ."

It was lost in the whoops that rose from the riders as they wheeled their horses out in the rising dust. Innocencio gave the bull a last jab with his prod pole. The *sabina* bellowed in rage, evil little eyes darting from side to side as it shied around the fire; then it spotted the free brush ahead, and the scarred head lowered, and it made its first rush.

"*Viva*, Gotch," yelled Kamaska, his quirt popping against his *chivarras* like a gunshot, and Garza jabbed his *pelicano* with silver-plated spurs the size of cartwheels, and the animal leaped forward with a shrill whinny. A bitter satisfaction swept Cardigan as he jumped his own horse into a run and saw how quickly it closed the space between him and Garza's prized *pelicano*; then the excitement of reckless speed and wild sounds beat at him, and he didn't know whether the drumming beat inside him was the blood pounding through his ears or the thud of hoofs beneath him.

The yells of the *vaqueros* came to Cardigan through a din of galloping horses and the dust rose up yellow and choking and blotted out the brush around him and the screaming women by the *jacales*, and all he could see was a glimpse here and there of a rider through the haze, and the snorting, running bull in front of him. His big dun was long-coupled and set low to the ground the way a good roper should be, and Cardigan could feel the steady, vicious pump of its driving hocks behind his saddle. He passed Kamaska, and the main group dropped behind him, and then Garza was on his flank, beating his *pelicano* desperately with a plaited quirt. Give him a little slack on those ribbons and he might go faster, was Cardigan's momentary thought, and then his long dun had stretched past Garza. In that last instant, his face was turned toward the coma trees where they had hitched their horses, and through the hole in the choking dust, he caught a glimpse of Florida and Pinto Parker. The girl had hold of Parker's shirt, shouting something at him; his broad face turned toward Cardigan, then he whirled toward his pinto. As the dust dropped back between them, Cardigan saw Florida leaping on her own horse.

Then the bull formed its heaving, running silhouette between them and Cardigan, and he was leaning from the saddle to grab that switching tail. He caught the hairy end and yanked upward, snubbing it around his horn. There was just enough room between his running horse and the bull to stretch the long tail tight, and as Cardigan saw it go taut, he laid his reins hard against the inside of the dun's thick neck. The horse responded with all the incredible alacrity of a roper, turning aside the very instant the reins made contact.

Cardigan saw the bull's hind legs slide from beneath the animal, and heard the shriek of his rigging as the weight was thrown against it. He let go his hold on the tail, instinctively stiffening for the sudden release of weight as the tail snapped loose from around the horn, throwing the bull. There was a loud pop, and the saddle jerked beneath him, and in that last instant, he saw that the tail was still dallied onto the horn, and had time to wonder what had happened, and then to know, before the empty air beneath him turned to the hardest ground he had ever hit. His saddle had left the dun completely, and he hit still astride the rig, kicking free of the stirrups as his boots struck the earth. He rolled backward out of the saddle, his head striking the ground with a stunning impact, the bull's tail still snubbed on the horn, dragging the saddle across the ground behind it.

Through a haze of pain, Cardigan felt himself roll to a stop. He lay there a moment with noise droning around him. Then the sounds began separating themselves into something discernible.

"Don't turn him that way," someone was shouting, "you'll drive him right back at Cardigan. That saddle's got him crazy and he'll go right back. Let him go, let him go. . . ."

It was Florida's voice. Sight reeled back to Cardigan. He saw the *vaqueros* had cut the bull off from the open brush; the *sabina* had reversed.

"Let him stop, you fools." That was Pinto's voice, from somewhere behind Cardigan. "Give him a chance to slow down and his tail will slack up and let go that saddle. It's the saddle driving him loco."

It *was* the saddle. Crazed by the bobbing, rattling rig which followed its every movement no matter which way it turned, the gotched bull had reached the point of frenzy where it quit seeking escape, and wanted only to reach its tormentors and vent its wild rage. It whirled toward Florida as she came in from the quarter, tossing her rope at its frothed muzzle. The bull made a wily jump aside and the dally spun on past and dropped on the ground. The *sabina* lunged at Florida's horse and she missed getting gored by inches as she jabbed her can openers into her animal, jumping it past the running bull. With its head down that way, the *sabina* thundered on past the rump of Florida's horse, its momentum carrying the beast straight toward Cardigan. He had been trying to move, in a feeble, stunned way, and it must have been this which caught the bull's attention.

The shaking ground beneath Cardigan told him how close the bull was before he looked. Then his gaze swung up and caught that frothed muzzle and those wicked, little eyes and that great pair of speckled shoulders.

There was no time for fear in that last instant. Only a shocking comprehension of how it stood. He made one last effort to rise, and failed, and knew it would not have helped anyway. Then, from somewhere back of the running bull, he heard a wild shout; dust rose in a great cloud about the animal, hiding movement for an instant, sweeping across Cardigan where he was crouching. The steady shake of the ground to the running hoofs of the bull changed to a great, roaring shudder beneath Cardigan. A dim shape pounded through the dust to his right. He thought it was the bull, and wondered why the beast had swerved. Then the dust began to settle, and he saw it had not been the bull.

The *sabina* lay in a heap not two feet from Cardigan's hand, the hot, fetid odor of its great body sweeping nauseatingly across him, its hind legs twitching in a last, spasmodic way before it lay completely still. The shape which had passed Cardigan was coming back now. Pinto Parker swung off his spotted horse and caught Cardigan's arm, sweat streaking the dust on his face, the inevitable grin revealing his white teeth.

"Guess that will show them how we tail a bull north of the Nueces," he said cheerfully. "You're all right, now, aren't you?"

Cardigan was staring stupidly at the *sabina*, and the full realization of how close death had come to him was bringing its reaction. He got to his feet as quickly as possible, pulling his arm free of Pinto's grasp, not wanting the man to feel him trembling.

"Yeah. Yeah. All right." Then Cardigan turned to meet Pinto's gaze. "Thanks, Pinto," he said simply, and saw the understanding in Pinto's eyes, and knew he needed to say no more.

Florida had brought her horse up, swinging off, with a wide relief in her big, dark eyes, and Garza pranced his *pelicano* in, glancing at the bull first. "I haven't seen a bull tailed like that in years, *Señor* Parker. You should have been born a *Mejicano*."

"Where are you going?" Florida asked.

Cardigan did not bother to answer. He stumbled in a grim deliberateness to where his saddle lay behind the *sabina*; the bull's tail was still snubbed tight about the slick roping horn, and he had to jerk it off and unwind the rigging from around it before he could turn the saddle over. He had to lift the skirt up off the front girth before he could find it, and now he understood why Garza had held his reins in so tight when he was quirting his horse, and why the dun had passed the *pelicano* so easily, and the others.

"That where the cinch broke?" asked Pinto, leading his pinto over.

"No," said Cardigan. "That's where it was cut."

V

Evening fell across the brasada insidiously, darkening the lanes through the outer thickets first, then creeping into the clearing of *Mogotes Oros* till the firelight blazed redly in the velvet gloom. And new sounds came with the night. A coyote began its dismal howl somewhere far out in the brush. A hooty owl mourned closer in. Standing there at the edge of the clearing, Cardigan found it ineffably sinister. It was an hour after Pinto had saved his life; the *vaqueros* and their women were beginning to eat the meat of the dead bulls. Parker came across the clearing from the fire.

"Got your rig fixed?"

"I cut off a piece of my latigo and tied it to the cinch ring," said Cardigan. "It'll last till we get back."

"I still think you're loco, not having it out with them. If they cut your cinch."

"How would that improve our position?" said Cardigan. "It wouldn't bring us any closer to finding out which one of them cut it, or why. It would only antagonize the whole bunch of them. We're hardly in a spot to do that right now. At least we keep them wondering this way. They don't know for sure I found the cut in the cinch."

Parker was studying him. "Why do you want to stay here?"

Cardigan's eyes opened a little. "How do you mean?"

"When a man finds out somebody's after his guts this way, his natural reaction should be wanting to get away."

"Should it?"

Parker studied him a moment longer, then a slow grin crossed his broad face. "No," he said, and chuckled. "No. I guess not. Not a man like you, Card. You'd want to stay and find out. You'd want to stay and nail the buzzard who tried to spill your guts on a gotcho's horn that way."

"Wouldn't you?" said Cardigan.

"Let's go over and get some of that meat," said Parker. "I'm plumb ravenous."

Estaban had come in a *carreta* drawn by a yoke of longhorn oxen, and he was officiating at the spit. "Ah, *señores*," he called, seeing Cardigan and Parker approaching, "you are just in time to see us unearth the head. We have a handful of oregano stuffed in its mouth for flavor, *sí*? All wrapped up in grass and tied with the leaves of the Spanish dagger, lightly roasted in ashes to make the fiber pliable. You have never tasted such a delicacy. And to you, *Señor* Parker, for tailing this *toro* goes the honor of the brains. Would you like the eggs, *Señor* Cardigan?"

"Eggs?" said Cardigan.

"Eyes," Parker muttered, beside him. "Take them. They're ribbing you."

Cardigan let his glance circle the men. He saw the speculation in Kamaska's face, and thought, Yes, you big ape, I know my cinch was sliced, do you? The others were watching him, too. Garza had mockery in his smile.

"Sure," said Cardigan. "Back home I always get the eggs." Then he realized they were not watching him any more. Garza's glance was turned past Cardigan, and the mockery had been replaced by surprise. Kamaska made a sudden abortive shift, across the fire, and then stopped. Parker turned around before Eddie Cardigan did.

There were at least a score of men, and they must have come in on foot that way so as not to make any noise, and Cardigan had seen enough posses before to recognize one. The noise about the fire had dropped so low that Cardigan heard Garza's hissing, indrawn breath before the man spoke.

"Sheriff Masset," said Garza.

Sheriff Sid Masset moved with a graceful ease, surprising in such a prodigiously paunched man.

"Don't anybody do anything foolish," he said, and the lack of vehemence in his tone only lent to its potency. He moved on forward, the .45-90 he held across his hip swinging slightly with the side-to-side motion of his walk. "I'm taking you in this time, Garza. I've caught you outside your damn Cañada Diablo and I'm taking you in and you better not object the slightest because I've got twenty boys here just itching to push that fresh-roasted beef out the back of your belly with some law-abiding lead."

"I don't understand," said Garza. "You have no charge."

"I've got two or three charges. A hundred Big Skillet steers was run off their home range a week back, and we got a pretty good description of the operators, two of which I see among you now. It's the last bunch of cattle you'll take into that Cañada Diablo, Garza."

"They aren't my. . . ."

"Then we got a number of dead men to account for," said Masset, his boots making their last sibilant creak as he stopped in a bunch of short grass. "Deputy Smithers was found dead last month just this side of the Comanche Trail, all clawed up. There was a government marshal named George Weaver found the same way near these *mogotes*. It wasn't no ordinary cat done that, Garza. In fact, there's some think it wasn't no cat at all. The Mexicans say this is some of that *nagualismo* bunk. Whatever it is, your crowd is mixed up in it. Now, I want you to step out in front of me here, one by one, and drop all your hardware."

The irony of it was what struck Cardigan first. To be taken in for those cattle; to have the whole thing spoiled like this for a mangy bunch of Big Skillet stuff, when it wasn't that at all. The fire made its soft crackle behind him, and he had already thought of it. They were standing in a bunch of short grass turned sere by the summer heat; there was a general shift through the crowd of *vaqueros* as Garza moved sullenly forward, and it gave Cardigan a chance to step back without being noticed.

Cardigan toed a coal from the edge of the fire; the heat of it had penetrated the leather of the boot before he had it shoved into the grass. Pinto Parker was unbuckling his Colt when Masset's head raised.

"Stamp it out," he yelled abruptly. "Behind you. Stamp it out!"

Cardigan jumped aside with the heat of the flame searing the back of his leg. The coal had caught in the brown grass, and the fire was leaping forward toward the posse beneath the fan of the wind. Yelling wildly, Cardigan began stamping at the ground on his side of the growing fire. Pinto Parker turned with an immediate understanding, stooping to grab a handful of grass at his feet and pull it up by the roots.

"Throw dirt on it," he yelled.

"Don't be a fool," shouted Masset. "You're just throwing more grass. You'll have the whole brasada afire."

"*Si*," shouted Garza, taking that chance for movement and jumping toward the fire, which brought him nearer the spot where his six-gun lay on the ground. "Stamp it out. You want all of the *Mogotes Oros* to burn up?"

The whole crowd of *vaqueros* were yelling and shifting now, and Cardigan saw Florida kicking more of the coals into the grass. Indecision spread through the milling crowd of possemen, some of them jumping forward toward the blaze, the ones in front of them backing up. The coals Florida had kicked out were catching, and the flames were rapidly forming a blazing wall between the posse and the *vaqueros*. Already Kamaska was turning toward the *vaqueros'* horses, hitched behind the coma trees. Cardigan was still kicking wildly at the fire and shouting, when the full realization struck Masset.

"I'll shoot the first man that moves," he bellowed.

"It's blowing right into us," yelled one of the possemen.

"Do what I say," shouted Masset. "Can't you see they did this on purpose? I'll shoot the first one that moves. Garza. . . ."

Masset's rifle drowned him out, but Garza had already dived through a hole in the blaze, and the roaring flames made his running body a deceptive target. While Masset was still turned that way, pulling down his lever to put in another shell, Cardigan caught Pinto by the back of his shirt, yanking him straight into the blaze. They ran through the flames, choking, gasping. Cardigan heard another gunshot from behind them, and his flat-topped Stetson was jerked off. Then they were on the other side of the fire; Parker's shirt was ablaze, and Cardigan threw himself on the man, beating at the smoking flannel till it was out. He realized someone else was also beating at him and, when Pinto pushed him away, he saw Florida had a saddle blanket half wrapped around him.

"Let's go," shouted Parker, laughing recklessly.

The *vaqueros* were running back and forth all about them now. Garza galloped past on his *pelicano*, followed by Kamaska. The second man wheeled his hairy, black mule toward Florida, jerking his foot from the stirrup. "*Señorita*," he shouted, "climb on with me."

Florida cast a wild glance at Cardigan. "Go on, Kamaska. Everyone for himself now. I'll get my own horse. We'll be safe as soon as we get into Cañada Diablo."

The fire had swept into the possemen, scattering them, and was rapidly filling the grassed-over section of the clearing and breaking into the thickets surrounding it. A great *mogote* of huisache went up in crackling glory and, beyond that, a growth of chaparral began to blaze, lighting the thickets about it weirdly. Three possemen who had run around one end of the blaze burst from the thickets near the *jacales* and began to fire. With a wild yell, Pinto turned on them and threw down with his Colt. Cardigan saw one of the men drop. Then he had reached the horses, tearing loose the reins of his frenzied dun, and the girl's rearing black. The bulls, maddened by the fire, had burst loose of the shaky ocotillo corral and were running wild through the clearing. Cardigan had all he could do to get on his frightened dun.

Parker was the first to break into the brush, the girl after him, a wild, swaying shape, her long hair flying, and again Cardigan knew amazement at her incredible ability at riding the thickets. She drove her animal straight at a growth of black chaparral covered thick with huisache. There must have been a hole, though Cardigan could not see it, for she crashed through the chaparral, trailing the huisache from her head and shoulders, leaving a big aperture for him to follow through. He leaped a low spread of *granjeno* and, while his eyes were fixed on an upflung spear of Spanish dagger and he was dodging aside to miss being impaled, a post-oak branch appeared out of nowhere. Shutting his eyes instinctively, he ducked abruptly.

He felt the mesquite rake across his arm and he knew he had avoided it, and just as he opened his eyes, another outreaching oak branch caught his head.

Pain made a great roar in back of his eyes, and blackness swept him, and that was the way he hit the ground, no comprehension in between the striking branch and the hard blow of the earth. He lay there spinning in a sick wave of nausea, trying to rise, and was dimly aware of a rattling crash somewhere above him. It was Florida, coming back; she drew her horse up onto its hocks and swung down.

"You've got to keep your eyes open," she called to him. "No matter what happens, you've got to keep your eyes open. You'll never be able to ride the brush unless you do that."

"Go on," he tried to wave her away, blood dribbling into his eyes as he shook his head. "If the fire don't catch up with you, Masset will. I'm not worth waiting for. I'll never make a brush rider. I don't want to. The hell with it."

Frenzied by the fire, Florida's horse was plunging and rearing against her hold on the reins. "Don't be a fool, Cardigan. Get on, will you? I can't hold him much longer. "Cardigan . . . Cardigan, get on. . . !"

Cardigan was still too dazed to do more than make a wild, vague grab at the flying reins as the horse plunged forward, taking Florida off-balance, and tearing loose from her grasp. The hoofs made their shuddering pound past him, and the brush crashed, and then the animal was gone. Florida stood there, above Cardigan, her face flushed, her bosom heaving. She looked down at him, and her lips peeled flatly away from her teeth in whatever she was going to say; before, with a disgusted exhalation, she bent to help him up. He was on his feet before they both heard the crackle of brush from the direction of the clearing. For a moment, hope shone in Florida's face.

"No," said Cardigan. "That isn't a horse. I told you if the fire didn't catch up with us, Masset would."

VI

The thickets rose in sinistrous desolation on every side, standing in impenetrable mystery beneath the pale light of the moon that cast the shadow of each twisted bush across the ground in a weird, tortured pattern. This pattern slid constantly across the back of Florida's white silk shirt like some live thing, as she moved beneath the brush ahead of Cardigan. They had traveled on foot southward. The fire and its sounds were lost behind them, and nothing but the haunted silence of the night reached their ears, broken infrequently by the dim howl of a coyote, or the lonely call of an owl.

"We're in now," she whispered. "Masset won't follow us here."

"He doesn't look like the kind of man who'd be scared out by some Indian superstition."

"Masset's brave enough," she said. "So are a lot of other men. You don't see them in here, do you? You don't see any sheriffs or any marshals or any Texas Rangers, do you? The whole brasada's always been a hotbed of border hoppers and rustlers and killers, and a lawman was taking his life in his hands to enter any part of it after a man, and Cañada Diablo is the worst spot of all. Even so, there were always men who'd pack a badge in here. They knew what was waiting for them, and they knew how to fight it. Until this last year, that is. They can't fight this, Cardigan. It's always the same. They send their men in, and a few weeks, or a few months later, some *brasadero* finds him in the brush that way.

"You heard Masset. That marshal, George Weaver. Deputy Smithers. They're only two, and they were the last ones, and that was months ago. And so they've stopped coming. There's no use just sending a man to his death. Especially when there aren't any men left who'll come in. Would you? If you were a ranger, or a deputy, would you come in, knowing what fate all the others had met? Even when they have something definite to follow, like those cattle."

"You didn't talk that way back in the bunkshack," he said. "You weren't going to dignify any Indian ghost story."

She looked up at him in a strained, pale way, then turned her face to the side. "I don't know, Cardigan, I don't know. I've tried to tell myself such a thing couldn't be. All along, I've tried. But it's all around. Just waiting out there."

"And yet you live right in the middle of Cañada Diablo as safe as a kitten up a tree," said Cardigan, and it brought her eyes around to him again. "If someone were doing something in Cañada Diablo, it would be very convenient for them to have this *nagualismo* business keeping the law away, wouldn't it?"

"What do you mean, doing something?"

"It still seems strange to me that a spread the size of yours would devote its whole time to running mustangs . . . or gathering Krags."

She started to answer him, but her mouth remained open without any words coming out, and her eyes were staring blankly into the thicket. It came to him finally, and he let his hand drop to the butt of his gun.

"Masset?" he whispered.

"I told you he wouldn't come in here after. . ."

It was the only way to stop her quickly enough. Cardigan felt her whole body stiffen against him as his arm snaked around her neck, and her lips mashed damply beneath his sweaty palm. The man rustled through the last chaparral and came into the open with his rifle held down at the hip, and Cardigan had met enough men that way to know what the expression on his face meant when he saw them, and to know what had to be done.

He already had his Remington out of leather, and he threw his weight against Florida as he fired. Masset's .45-90 echoed Cardigan's gun, and the slug clattered through brush about the height of Cardigan's chest, if he had remained erect. Masset was already spinning around with the force of Cardigan's slug in him. It turned him in a half circle and by the time he took the stumbling step to keep from falling, it was carrying him in the opposite direction. He was bent almost double when he stopped, still on his feet, trying grimly to retain the rifle and snap its lever down again. From where he had thrown himself, lying half across the girl, Cardigan called to Masset.

"Don't, Masset. I don't want to kill you."

Still bent forward, Masset turned his head. His eyes, squinted with pain, took in the five-shot held at Cardigan's hip. Reluctantly, he dropped the rifle.

Cardigan got to his feet, lips drawn back against his teeth. "Go on back now," he said. "You were a fool to come this far."

Masset had one beefy hand gripped across his shoulder where the bullet had hit. His words came out gustily. "I'm tired of fooling around, Florida. I'm going to clean you out of here if it takes an army. . . ."

"I told you to get out, damn you, before it's too late," snarled Cardigan. "You don't know what this is, Masset. You come in here just for a bunch of steers? You don't know what you're getting into. Now, get out!"

He almost shouted the last, in an anger he could not name himself, and Masset drew himself up, grunting a little with the pain movement caused him, his eyes narrowing even more. "What are you talking about, pard?"

"Just what I said," Cardigan told him.

"*Tío* Balacar?" said Masset.

"What about *Tío* Balacar?" Cardigan's voice held an edge.

"We heard he's been seen in here."

Cardigan was surprised to hear Florida's voice behind him. "Heard from who?"

"That nigger. Africano. How do you think I knew you'd be outside Cañada Diablo tonight?" Masset was looking at Florida now. "What's going on, girl? What's Balacar doing in the brush?"

"Masset, if you don't get out. . . ."

"Sure, I'll get out." Masset swung toward Cardigan. "But I'm coming back, and when I do, it'll be for good!"

He turned heavily and crashed off into the thicket like a ringy, old bull. Cardigan was just starting to get Masset's rifle when the sound came. It seemed far away, at first, and yet close up, somehow, filling Cardigan with a vague awe. He turned toward Florida; her mouth was open, and her eyes, staring at him, were blank with listening. The noise had died before her glance took focus with a perceptible jerk.

"What was it?" he said.

"Cat," she said, in a hollow voice. "Sounded like a cat."

"I never heard no bobcat squall like that," he said.

"Jaguar. Mexican ones. They come down out of the mountains like that." She seemed to twitch then, and something like shame came into her face, and her voice lost its hollow tone abruptly, coming out quick and hard. "Are we going?"

He had not moved yet when the scream rang through the brush, so akin to another scream that his own shout followed it instinctively. "Navasato," he yelled, and then realized the significance of his reaction, and jumped toward the *mogote* into which Masset had disappeared.

"Cardigan," gasped the girl from behind him, "Cardigan, don't go in there. Please!"

But he was already bursting through the thicket of chaparral, Masset's unintelligible cries driving him. He crashed into a small clearing on the other side of the first thicket, face scratched and bleeding, and the screams had stopped. Masset lay beneath a bunch of ripped, trampled mesquite on the other side of the open space, his face mangled beyond recognizability, his shirt torn from his fat, bloody back. There was a rattling out in the brush, and then that ceased. Cardigan stood there, staring at Masset, hardly aware of Florida as she came out of the thicket behind him, and made a low, strangled sound of horror.

"I sent him into that," said Cardigan, a deep bitterness entering his voice. "I sent him into that."

"No, Cardigan." Florida's grasp at his arm pulled it down. "How could you know? It might have caught him anywhere. It wasn't your fault."

He didn't have to go down beside Masset to see if the man were dead, that was patent enough; but there was something else he wanted to see. Pinto Parker had said they were larger than any cat tracks he had seen. Cardigan struck a match for light and bent down. He was right. It gave Cardigan a strange, suffocated sensation to stare at the prints of the huge, padded claws. Florida was staring at them too, and then she was catching at his arm again as he rose, a swift, breathless desperation in her voice, as the flame guttered out.

"You know what this means, Cardigan? Masset was right. I've sensed it all along, but now I know it. This *nagualismo* isn't just a rumor. It's too deliberate. We can't let it go any farther, Cardigan. I can't go any longer trying to feel you out, and waiting for you to make your move. I've got to trust you, and you've got to trust me."

He sensed that what had just happened was bringing it out of her like this. "What do you mean?"

She had him by both elbows, staring into his eyes with a driven intensity. "You think I'm one of them, don't you? You think I'm just rodding a bunch of rustlers and smugglers?"

"It did look like you were top screw in the corral."

"You know that's not true." Her eyes were pleading with him.

"Do I?" he said warily.

"I told you that's got to stop." Florida's voice was rising. "We've got to trust each other, Cardigan. Why do you think I kept them from killing you that first time?"

"I really don't know."

"You *do* know," she almost shouted. "Will you quit evading me like this? There isn't any more time to play that game." She glanced at Masset, revulsion twisting her mouth. "You might be next, I might be next, Pinto might." Suddenly the warmth of her body was against him and her face was pressed into his sweaty, burnt shirt front, and he could see the fight she was making to keep from crying. "Cardigan," she mumbled against him, "please, please, I'm at the end of my dally, and you don't know how long I've been doing this alone, in the brush, all alone, against all of it, and when you came, and I thought . . . I thought. . . ." She twisted her face the other way against him, the hair drawn taut and lustrous across the top of her head. "Oh, Cardigan, please. . . ."

Holding her like this filled him with a strange weakness he had never known before, and all his wary, suspicious control left him, and he spoke in a harsh, guttural acquiescence. "What do you want?"

There was a triumph in the way she lifted her face to him. "Who you are. I've got to know that, Cardigan. I've got to know where I stand now, whether there's anybody at all, or whether I'm still alone. I'm not, am I, Cardigan? Tell me I'm not. Tell me I was right about you."

The movement of her head away from his chest might have been what caused it. Suspicion returned in a swift inundation as he saw the triumph in her eyes. It might have been innocent triumph. He searched her face for guile, and found none. Yet he eased away from her, almost trembling with the realization of how close he had come. She saw what had happened, within him, and jumped backward like a cat in a rage.

"You still won't trust me. You think they put me up to this? I guess I should have let them have you in the first place. You don't care. You know what *Tío* Balacar is up to, but you don't care. You'll just let him go ahead and do this. People think the brasada's a dangerous place now? Wait till Balacar comes. What's gone on before will just be a Sunday school picnic compared with what it will be after he gets through. You told Masset he didn't know how big this thing is? I don't think you know how big it is. I don't think you want to know. . . ."

"Florida . . ."

"Shut up," she spat. "I was a fool to think you were any different than Parker. You're just a couple of tinhorn rustlers looking for a place to hole up till it blows over about those Big Skillet cattle. You were right. You'll never make a brush hand. You'll never make anything. You. . . ."

Perhaps it was the expression on Cardigan's face which stopped her. He had heard the sound before she did, because she was so deep in her rage. Now she heard it, and the angry flush seeped out of her face, leaving it pale in the moonlight. Cardigan's hand tightened around the butt of his Remington, and he raised the gun without being conscious he did it.

"Cardigan," breathed Florida, and took a step toward him, fear turning her eyes dark.

It came again, like the scream of a woman in mortal pain, weird and unearthly and terrifying. Then it ceased, and all Cardigan could hear was his own breathing. His burned, smudged face was greasy with sweat, and he could feel it dripping down his sleeves, from beneath his armpits. The first impulse to move seeped through him vaguely, and he was about to answer it when the brush clattered. Both of them whirled, and the hammer of Cardigan's Remington made a sharp, metallic click under his thumb.

"*Buenas noches*," said Africano, from where he stood beneath the chaparral with his two dogs. Cardigan stared at him blankly, unable to speak for that moment, and the girl stood with her underlip dropped slightly, making no sound. Africano's face bore no expression. "You heard *la onza*?"

"Yeah," said Cardigan finally. "We heard something." His voice took on a patient deliberateness. "What is it, Africano? What is *la onza*?"

Africano's eyes shone white as they dropped to Masset; then they rose again, meeting Cardigan's, and they held something he could not read. "*La onza* is a hybrid, *señor*. A cross between a bull tiger and a she-lion. There is nothing more deadly. There is nothing more terrible."

Cardigan jerked his gun to bear on one of the dogs as Africano started to move forward. "I'll kill those dogs if you bring them any closer, I swear it."

"They will not harm you unless you threaten me, *señor*," said Africano softly.

"How do you fit in with this *onza*?" asked Cardigan harshly. "Maybe Kamaska isn't as dumb as we think."

"If you refer to his belief in *nagualismo*, there is nothing stupid about that," said Africano.

Cardigan couldn't help bending forward sharply. "Then you know. You. . . ."

"I know you had better get back to *Hacienda del Diablo* as soon as possible and never again get separated from your friend Parker as long as you stay in the brush."

"What are you talking about?" It was the first time Florida had spoken.

"*Tío* Balacar has come," said Africano.

VII

The black chaparral surrounded the compound of *Hacienda del Diablo* in endless undulations of skeletal malignancy, and the buildings huddled fearfully beneath a risen moon. One of the horses standing hipshot before the long porch snorted dismally. It was the only sound.

A yellow crack of light seeped from beneath the door, and drew a rectangle around each of the two shuttered windows on the north side. Weary from the long hike through the brush, Cardigan stood by the ghostly pattern of a cedar-post corral, watching the house.

"Any way we can get in without being seen?" he asked.

The quick shift of Florida's head to glance at him caused moonlight to ripple across the glossy toss of her long black hair. "They might not have locked the shutters on my bedroom," she said finally. "There's no reason for any of them to have gone in there."

They skirted the fringe of brush till they were opposite the north side of the house, then cut directly across the moonlit compound. Cardigan was tense with waiting for some reaction from Florida, and it puzzled him, in a way, that she had made no objection to coming in this way, or had not tried to warn them. The heavy, oak shutters on her bedroom window opened with a loud creak, and Cardigan lifted a long leg over the low, battered sill. The bare, earthen floor of her room was as hard as cement, covered meagerly by a pair of hooked rugs he made out dimly in the soft light from outside. He passed her bed, a ponderous, hand-carved fourposter of Spanish origin, and reached the thick, wooden-pegged door. The handle of hammered silver felt cold to his touch, and it moved with less noise than the window. He cast one glance back at Florida before pulling the portal toward him. There was a tense, waiting line to the rigidity of her body. Then he turned his head, looking through the crack and down the short hall that led directly into the living room from this wing of the house.

He saw a broad-framed, thick-thewed man, with the flat hams and skinny, bowed legs of the inveterate horseman, his jack boots black and polished, a fancy gilt-edged sash about his heavy girth. His eyes were small and black and brilliant in the dissipated pouches formed by his puckered, veined, wind-wrinkled lids, and his thick lips moved with sensual mobility. His hands were surprisingly delicate and slender, and he kept moving them expressively while he spoke, as if the words were spawned and shaped and caressed by his supple, ceaseless fingers, rather than coming from his mouth. With his first sight of the man, Cardigan knew who he was.

"I understand your, ah, reluctance to commit yourself, *amigo*," he was saying, and he moved across the living room in a pompous, stiff-legged walk as he talked. "I have myself, at times, endeavored to enhance my financial position by just such means. We will dispense with the moral grounds for our objection to what you are doing, though you will admit there are those who would call your attitude far from honest. We will be merely expedient. Expediency is so much more logical a basis than morality. And you can see the obvious expediency here. You have tried to improve your monetary standing in this way, and have failed. Why don't you just admit your failure and we can all be good *compadres* again and forget about it and take another drink together and you will tell us where the Krags are."

Pinto Parker was seated at one end of the long table with a big jug of mescal before him, and he grinned thickly. "Don' know where any Krags are. I tol' you that."

Comal Garza had been standing a little farther down the table, and his pewter mug made a dull clank as he set it down on the furrowed boards. "I told you we were wasting time, *Tio*. We tried being polite before and it failed. We would have gotten it out of him the other way if Florida hadn't interfered."

"No, no," said *Tio* Balacar, his smile placating and sly at the same time. "We want Lieutenant Dixon to work with us. We want him for our *amigo*. There are things about those Krags we shall have to know before using them. Don't you see what a priceless asset an army officer would be to us, Garza? We will never get any of that by antagonizing him. I'm sure if we could just make it clear to him"—he pulled a chair from beneath the table with a flourish, and put one foot up on it, leaning forward with his elbow on the knee of his white pants—"now Lieutenant Dixon, if you will only tell us what it is you want, perhaps we can come to an agreement. We agreed on a price in Brownsville, of course, but if you want more, say so, and maybe. . . ."

"You got the wrong *hombre*," grinned Pinto foolishly, taking another drink. "Wait'll Card gets here. He'll tell you."

"Perhaps Cardigan will not be getting here," said Garza.

"Sure he will," slurred Pinto confidently. "Nothing can stop Card. Just a couple of cattle operators, see, *Tio*. Just running a bunch of cattle through. Let's have another drink. I haven't wet my whistle like this in weeks. Man needs to get drunk once in a while."

"You are already drunk, Lieutenant," said *Tio* Balacar, and Cardigan could see the brilliant pinpoints of light catch in his small, black eyes. He took his foot from the chair and paced about the table, rubbing his hands together, frowning. Then he turned back, speaking to no one in particular. "It seems we have failed to make the necessary impression on the lieutenant. We offer him logic, and he says he is just a simple *hombre* trying to get along. We fill him with liquor, and his tongue does not become any looser in the direction we wish. There is very little left."

"That's what I say," Garza said.

Parker blinked owlishly at Balacar, patently not understanding the man's implication. Balacar moved around to the chair again, putting his boot up on it and leaning forward on his knee that way once more to peer intently at Parker. Carefully he took the glass away from him; then he put a hand on Parker's shoulder.

"Don't make us do this, *amigo*."

"Do what?" said Parker, reaching for the bottle.

Garza slid in and moved the bottle away. "No, *amigo*, don't make us."

"I don't getcha," said Parker, lurching over the glass.

Balacar moved the glass daintily out of Parker's reach, then picked up the hand which Kamaska had used the nutcrackers on, separating the swollen finger from the rest. "It caused you some pain, eh?"

"Hurt like hell," said Parker.

"We would not want to cause you any more pain," said Balacar.

"I want another drink," said Parker. "Come on, Garza, let's toast to old Texas."

Balacar dropped the hand abruptly, swinging his foot off the chair to walk away from the table in those stiff strides. He stopped, facing the window. He slapped his hands together. "All right," he said, without looking at Garza. "Go ahead."

"No," said Cardigan, stepping into the hall, "don't go ahead. Just stay right where you are."

He had never seen Garza display so much emotion. The man's jaw dropped and his oblique eyes were wide and blank. Cardigan's boots made a hollow tap into the room, and his lips were drawn back from his teeth in that mirthless grin.

"Did you think maybe the *onza* got me, Garza?" he said.

Tío Balacar had swung around and, after the first surprise, his glance crossed Garza's. "Cardigan?" he said.

"Cardigan," said Garza.

Cardigan moved across the floor without lost motion, his .46 swinging to cover what was necessary, and grabbed Parker by the arm. "Come on, Pinto, we're trailing out now."

"Card," laughed Pinto. "I told them you'd be back. They didn't think so, but I told them. Have a drink."

"Get up. I said we're going."

The cold, flat sound of Cardigan's voice sobered Parker momentarily, and he blinked upward in that owlish way. "I thought you wanted to stay."

"Yes." Garza had recovered his composure now. "Yes, Cardigan, you aren't going to leave us now, are you? *Tío* even brought some more men to help us with the *mestenos*. Meet Aragonza. He is the best *jinete* north of Mexico City, and they say a horse doesn't live he can't fork, and he's reported to be just as skillful with his gun."

Cardigan had already taken in Aragonza, standing slim and fancy in a long Durango serape and glazed sombrero by the window, and he knew why Garza had done it. "I can see how many men you got in the room without you pointing them out to me, Garza."

That pawky smile slid across Balacar's thick lips again, and he spread his hands out, palms up. "*Señor*, you misinterpret my *amigo*'s meaning entirely. We would not try to detain you forcibly if your desires lead you elsewhere."

Kamaska's restless shift across the front of the fireplace belied Balacar's words, and Cardigan hauled at Parker with a growing sense of urgency, knowing his one gun wouldn't hold them much longer. "Will you come on, Pinto."

"*Pues*, you are so insistent, *señor*," said Balacar. "Is our hospitality that bad? Is it?"

"I don't think you have Florida to intercede on your behalf this time, Cardigan," said Garza.

"Watch it, Innocencio," snapped Cardigan, twitching his gun toward the man as he saw his hand slide toward his neck. "Parker, will you get up? Damn you, will you come on?"

"Whatsamatter, Card," said Parker, rising halfway, then falling back. "I don't wanna go. Look at all the pulque they got left."

"Don't you see what they're trying to do?" Cardigan almost shouted, and coming out with it openly like that must have been what set it off, because everybody started to move at once, and Cardigan slipped his arm clear around behind Pinto and yanked him upright, giving him a push that sent him toward the door.

"Cardigan," shouted Garza, and Cardigan turned toward him with the gun. Garza stood by the table, unarmed, and even as he realized his mistake, Cardigan had to admire the man's nerve, taking that chance. Cardigan's thumb was tight against the hammer, but he couldn't throw down, somehow, and he saw the triumph in Garza's face as he turned back the other way. It was too late; it had given them their chance, and Cardigan was not around far enough to recognize who it was when the weight was thrown against his arm.

He shouted with the pain of two vise-like hands twisting his wrist back on itself, felt the Remington drop. Then he saw it was *Tío* Balacar's sweating, sensuous face, jammed into his shoulders, and knew time to be surprised that the man's slender hands could hold so much strength. The man's position only allowed leverage on Cardigan's wrist from one direction and, when Cardigan whirled the other way, he felt his arm jerk loose. As he whirled, he let his knee come upward. Balacar's sick grunt was reward for the pain of that wrist.

Garza had been on the opposite side of the table from Cardigan, and he was not yet around it as Balacar reeled back into a chair with both slender hands gripping his groin. Cardigan made a loud, grunting sound, heaving that heavy table over on Garza. Kamaska and Innocencio had jumped Pinto, and he was on his knees beneath their combined weight, head bobbing down due to a blow from Kamaska's fist. It must have taken just about that long for comprehension to get through Pinto's drink-fogged brain, because his reckless shout rang out as Garza went down beneath the long table.

"Well, damn you," shouted Pinto, and the floor might as well have heaved up from beneath Kamaska and Innocencio for all the good their mad struggle did to keep Parker down. He burst from between them like a raging bull, smashing Kamaska in the face with a bony elbow and knocking him back onto the overturned table, butting Innocencio in the belly, swaying up onto spread legs with that wild grin. "It looks like the boys want to fight, Card. That'll finish the evening just right."

"Get out, Pinto, get out," yelled Cardigan, realizing this was their last chance, grabbing at Parker and trying to whirl him toward the door. Then he saw Aragonza over at the end of the room with a gun in each hand, and the first shot drowned all other sound and, before the echoes died, someone else was shouting.

". . . at them, you *necio*, don't shoot at them. We want Dixon alive!"

It was Balacar who had yelled, and he hoisted himself up out of the chair with one hand still at his groin and a sick, greenish hue to his twisted face, and Cardigan tried to shove Pinto out of the way. But Balacar crashed into Pinto, tearing him loose from Cardigan's grip and carrying him on over into the upturned bottom of the table. Before Cardigan could reach them, a heavy body struck him from behind, and he went to his knees beneath Innocencio. Down like that, he saw Pinto bring his knees up between himself and Balacar and lash out with them. It shoved Balacar off Pinto, and the upswing of Pinto's feet brought them past the heavy man's body, and Balacar screamed as both Pinto's sharp-roweled spurs hooked him in the face.

Cardigan knew of that *belduque* and, with Innocencio on top of him, jerked aside as he heard the man grunt. Innocencio's thrust went past Cardigan's shoulder, the long knife sinking deeply into the hard-packed earthen floor. Cardigan caught the man's arm and used it for a lever to pull Innocencio over him onto the floor. Innocencio jerked the *belduque* free to jab again, and Cardigan had to sprawl bodily across the man to block it. From that position he caught another glimpse of Pinto. *Tío* Balacar was holding his bloody face in both hands now and blindly trying to rise from where he had been thrown across the upturned table. Free of the man, Pinto had gained his feet, whirling to jump feet first at Balacar again. This time the spurs crunched into Balacar's hands, and rolled down his forearms, tearing the sleeves of his silk shirt from cuffs to the elbows, dragging deep red furrows through muscle and flesh.

"That's Texas fighting for you, *Tío*," roared Pinto, still filled with liquor, laughing crazily, and launched a final kick at Balacar that struck the man's head and rolled him down the table bottom till he crashed into an end leg hard enough to crack it off.

Cardigan was still sprawled across Innocencio, and had just about realized it was Innocencio holding him down that way rather than him keeping the man on the floor, when a great crushing weight landed on him from behind and his head was driven into Innocencio's chest by a rabbit punch behind his neck. He had seen a man hit that way before and, through the fog of stunning pain, knew instantly who was on top of him.

"Kamaska," he gasped, involuntarily, and then his blind struggle for the *belduque* was rewarded.

He had both hands on Innocencio's knife wrist, and had finally gotten it twisted around beneath his own chest, when Innocencio shouted with the pain of it, and the long blade was free. Sensing above him the stiffening of Kamaska's body for another blow, Cardigan grasped the knife's hammered silver hilt and lunged back over his shoulder, blindly.

"¡*Sacramento!*"

It came from Kamaska, and was so full of animal pain that Cardigan knew he had struck. The blade was held in a solid, fleshy way for a moment, and then jerked a little, and was free in his hand again. Kamaska's weight was slack enough on top of him for Cardigan to thrust himself from beneath it, slashing at Innocencio as the man sought to hold him. Innocencio jerked back to keep from having his face ripped, and Cardigan was free. As he got to his hands and knees, he could see Pinto again.

Garza had finally crawled from beneath the table, and his leap must have taken him into Pinto and carried both of them past Cardigan and Innocencio into the wall, because the two of them were up against the wall now. Whatever Pinto had done to Garza left him lying inert on the floor against the adobe *banco* that ran clear around the room to form a bench against the wall. But Aragonza had jumped in from the other end of the room and had Pinto on his hands and knees above Garza, beating at his head with both those guns. No telling how many times Balacar's man had struck Pinto before this. Parker's blond head was red with blood, and he was dripping it all over Garza's face beneath him, and he was sobbing as he tried to make what was evidently his last attempt at rising. Aragonza grunted as he slugged again with the barrel of his right handgun, and it knocked Pinto flat across Garza.

Aragonza must have seen Cardigan roll from between Innocencio and Kamaska with that knife, for Cardigan was still on his hands and knees, just stiffening to rise, when Aragonza turned from Pinto, and Cardigan saw his intent plain in his face. Maybe they wanted Pinto alive. He was the only one. Aragonza was an old-style gun-slinger, pulling his gun hand up as high as his head so that when he let the weapon drop back, the weight of the gun itself would carry the hammer back beneath his thumb, and it would be cocked as the revolver came down. But as soon as he saw Aragonza's hand begin to rise, Cardigan knew what it meant, and his reaction was without thought. He tossed the knife while still on his hands and knees, throwing all his weight over onto one palm to free the other hand. It caught Aragonza just as his hand reached the level of his head and started to drop down again.

The hammer must have already started to cock from the weight of the dropping gun, because the knife driving into Aragonza's fore-arm hit it so hard the gun exploded at the roof. The weight of the big knife and the force of the throw carried Aragonza back against the wall the way a blow would have, pinning his arm against the mud, the *belduque* sunk hilt deep through his wrist and into the adobe. Even as Aragonza went into the wall, Cardigan was whirling toward sound from behind him. Kamaska was getting to his feet, his hand clutched across one shoulder, blood seeping between the fingers. Innocencio had started to rise, but he seemed suspended there with his knees bent, staring at Aragonza in a stunned surprise, as if he found something hard to believe.

Cardigan flung himself at the man, his weight carrying both of them crashing into the overturned table where Balacar had broken a leg off. Cardigan came up on top of Innocencio, clutching at the smashed leg. There was a good length to it, and the wood came free when he yanked it.

"No," yelled Innocencio, "no," and then gasped wretchedly with the twelve inches of solid oak smashing him across the forehead. Cardigan still had the leg as he jumped to his feet, because he knew what was behind him. Kamaska was already coming at him. He didn't move fast this time, nor slow. He came with both hands outstretched, in a lurching, deliberate walk, each step a little longer than the preceding one, each one a little quicker. Cardigan jumped out to meet him, knocking aside one arm with the table leg. Kamaska cried out with the pain, but did not stop. Cardigan had knocked his arm aside to come in against him, and this time his blow was across the top of Kamaska's head, with all the weight and force he could bring into it. He heard the crack of wood, and Kamaska dropped a full six inches. He stood there a moment against Cardigan, his knees bent, his one arm still outstretched.

Cardigan raised the leg, brought it down again. Once more the cracking sound. Kamaska dropped another six inches, his face buried against Cardigan's belly, that one arm clutched around Cardigan's hips. Cardigan brought it up for the third time. Then he held it that way, staring stupidly up at the short stub of wood in his hand. The leg had broken in two. He stood there a moment longer, dropping his head to look at Kamaska. Then he stepped back. Kamaska went to his hands and knees. Then he slid quietly onto his belly.

Cardigan swayed there, trembling, panting, his shirt ripped from his lean torso and hanging from his belt. *Tio* Balacar was sitting over on the *banco*, bent forward, with his elbows on his knees and his bleeding face in his hands.

"I can't see," he said stupidly, "I can't see. Where are you, Aragonza? I can't see."

Aragonza was crying like a baby as he twisted one way and the other, still pinned against the wall that way, desperately trying to pull the knife free. At his feet, Comal Garza was stirring feebly beneath an inert Pinto Parker. Finally Cardigan's dim perception reached the hallway. Florida stood there holding Garza's gun.

Cardigan spat out a tooth. "Well," he gasped. "What are you going to do?"

VIII

A fog had swept in from the Gulf coast to shroud the brasada in a gray oppression, the morning after the fight. Gaunt mesquite reached out of the viscid mist like helpless skeleton hands supplicating the unseen sky. The *cenzio* sprawling about the bunkhouse door blended its dead ashen growth with the shreds of turgid vapor seeping into the room. Esperanza shuffled in from the kitchen with a bowl of beans, grumbling through his flowing longhorn *mustachios*.

"I don't see why you have to leave now. The whole *estancia* is yours. Everybody's afraid of you. You're the big *toro* of the pasture and nobody comes within ten feet of you."

Cardigan was sitting at the table, wearing one of Esperanza's cotton shirts. "Would've left last night if Pinto was in any shape."

"An' leave the *señorita*?" said Esperanza.

"What does she have to do with it?"

"She don't want you to go."

"What did you do with those?" Cardigan pointed his fork at the beans.

"Those are on foot, *señor*. Boiled. Tomorrow we have them on horseback. Fried. You stay tomorrow and you see why we call them *nacionales*. *Sapodillas*. You should see my *sapodillas*. I make them for Generale Porfirio Díaz himself. Sweet hollow pin cushions of puff paste, *señor*, as frothy as lather from the *amole*. I fry them in deep grease and make syrup to go over them hot. And *bishochitos*. . . ."

"All right, all right, biscuits," said Cardigan impatiently. "Just bring the coffee and forget. . . ."

This time the crash of gunshots did no more than make him jump in the chair. Esperanza stood there quivering with rage, hands filled with his smoking Colts.

"You don't like my *bishochitos*?" he shouted.

"I didn't say that. . . ."

"You don't like my *bishochitos*. I make them for the whole Mexican army, but they aren't good enough for you. What are you, a *hidalgo*? *Sacramento*, no, just a loco *Tejano* who can't even ride through a mesquite tree without getting knocked off. . . ."

"You want me to slit your throat?"

It came from the doorway, and it stopped the cook. He stood there a moment, staring toward Innocencio. Then he let the Colts drop back into their holsters.

"*Madre de Dios*, Innocencio, I was just telling him how I cook my *bishochitos*."

"Get back in the kitchen where you belong," said Innocencio, moving on in. He looked at Cardigan, grinning evilly. "Some *batalla* we had last night, no? I never see anybody throw a knife that way. Just a little flip and it goes in so deep Aragonza can't get off the wall for fifteen minutes."

Cardigan shoved the bench back, rising. "Little Indian toss I learned in San Antone. I didn't want you to think you were the only one could use a pig-sticker around here."

Pinto Parker came from the bunkroom, his head swathed in white cotton bandages Esperanza had put on the night before. He stopped a moment by the table to steady himself, grinning ruefully at Cardigan. Then he nodded toward the door. Cardigan followed him out, serpents of ground fog streaming about his legs. Pinto stopped by a big cottonwood to one side of the shack, turning toward Cardigan.

"You're leaving on account of me, aren't you, Card?" he said.

Cardigan shook his head. "I'm fed up."

"No," said Pinto. "If it was just you, you'd stay. There's something here. I know. But you're leaving because you don't want to let me in for something like last night again."

Cardigan shrugged his acceptance. "Just licking them didn't necessarily convince them you aren't Lieutenant Dixon."

Pinto was studying his face. "They were willing to have you killed at the bull-tailing the other day, but they didn't try anything on me. That's because they still thought I was Dixon. What would happen if they found out I'm not Dixon?"

Cardigan's eyes grew opaque. "They might cut *your* cinch."

"And that's why you're going," said Pinto. "To get me out of it. They've already tried to kill you, but you'd stay if it was just you."

"It's not your roundup," said Cardigan. "It wasn't from the first. I didn't look at it that way when the thing started. I hadn't known you long and you were just a man I trailed with, and I didn't look at it one way or the other. Now, I've known you longer, Pinto. It's not your roundup, and I've got no right to rope you in on it."

"What if I want to be roped in?"

"We're still going," said Cardigan.

"The girl don't want you to go, Card."

"What's she got to do with it?" said Cardigan.

"She didn't interfere last night."

"What cows does that get you?" said Cardigan.

"It shows you she don't stand solid with Garza," said Pinto.

"You're still riding a muddy river."

Pinto's voice was intense. "You know what I mean. She wanted your help somehow all along. That's why she took a shine to you from the first. She sensed what I should have known. You weren't my kind. Just because you came in here trailing a bunch of wet beef didn't make you a tinhorn rustler like me. There was something else. She sensed it; she tried to get your help, but you wouldn't trust her because you thought she rode in Garza's wagon. Hasn't she proved different yet? It was only her arriving when she did the first night that kept Kamaska from killing you. She tried to stop that killer bull at *Mogotes Oros* just as hard as I did. It was her told me something had gone wrong when she saw Garza and the others dropping back and letting you have the bull. And now, last night"—he reached out to grasp Cardigan's arm—"maybe she's in such a position she can't come right out against Garza, Cardigan, until she knows someone else is backing her. You can see how it would be for a gal, all alone like that. You can't run out on her, Cardigan, just because of me."

Cardigan bit his lip, meeting Pinto's eyes. "You'll go, anyway, Pinto?"

"The hell I will! What is it, Card? What is it you're after in here?" He was looking into Cardigan's eyes, and must have seen it there, for his hand dropped from Cardigan's arm, and he took a step backward, his voice sober. "All right, Card. You don't have to tell me if you don't want to. It won't make any difference. Not after what you did last night. Nothing would make any difference between you and me, Card."

The sound of someone's boots made a dull tap across the hard adobe compound. It was *Tío* Balacar, moving toward them in that pompous, stiff-legged walk, the fringed ends of his silk sash ruffling against his polished jack boots. His face was blotched purple with some kind of local herb Esperanza had smeared on the deep gashes made by Pinto's spurs, and one of his eyes was squinted shut and twitching all the time. Aragonza was with him, a pinched, lethal look to his pale cheeks, as he stared at Cardigan. His right arm was bandaged beneath the sleeve of his fancy *charro* coat, and held in a black sling. Garza and Florida were following, and the woman was watching Cardigan with a repressed desperation in her big eyes.

"Well, *compadres*," said Balacar and, though his thick lips held that pawky grin, Cardigan could see the corrosive hatred smoldering in his eyes. "That was quite a rodeo we had last night, eh? I haven't had such a *batalla* since my cadet days in the Colegio Militar. *Pues*, I understand you *Tejanos* do that every Saturday night just for amusement. I'm sure you're already laughing about it, eh? I understand you're leaving this morning, and I'd hate to have us part with a bad taste in our mouths."

"On the contrary," said Cardigan, and he saw hope leap into Florida's eyes, "we aren't leaving this morning," and saw the hope turn to a fervent thanks, "we're staying."

IX

A butcher bird sat preening itself in the leafless *junco*. Mexicans said this was the only bird which would alight on the bush, for the *junco*'s thorns had formed Christ's crown. It was a somber belief, and seeing the bird, somehow, filled Cardigan with an apprehension. He recalled the first time he had felt that, riding the brush this way, just before Navasato had been killed, and turned to look at the rustling mesquite stretching dark and illimitable behind him. They had ridden after mustangs again, and it was the first time since they left *Hacienda del Diablo* that Florida had found a chance to speak with Cardigan. Balacar and Garza had drawn ahead slightly to scout for tracks, and Florida pulled her scarred, little brush horse up to Cardigan's dun.

"I think it was a mistake to come out this way," she said tensely.

"We've got to wait for them to make the first move," he said. "As long as Balacar wants to keep up a pretense like this, we've got to play along."

"It's like sitting on a powder keg," she said. "You can see it under *Tío*'s smile. The way Kamaska watches us. Garza's eyes. Your first slip is your last, Cardigan."

"I think they include you in with Pinto and me now, don't they?" he said, turning toward her. Their eyes met for a moment, and then he reached over and touched her hand. "Florida, if you want to tell me now, I'll tell you."

She grasped his hand and squeezed it with a certain desperate thanks at this evidence of his trust, and her words tumbled out in a swift, tense mutter. "You know who Balacar is?"

"I know he rode with Díaz in the 'Sixties. Turned revolutionist later on. Mixed up with gun-running down in New Orleans. Packs a lot of pull with the peons for what he did in the army. Is that what he's doing here?"

"Gun-running? You know it isn't. You know it's more than that." She glanced ahead quickly. Balacar and Garza were barely visible through the chaparral, talking in low tones. Florida twisted back in her rawhide brush-poppers rig. "You're right about him packing a lot of pull with the peons, though. Almost as much as Díaz. What do you think would happen if Díaz showed up here in the brush with five hundred Krag rifles and as many freshly broken horses?"

"He'd have just about that many men to use them within a week."

"The same with *Tío*," she said. "He was a fiery, popular, dashing cavalry leader, and his exploits in and after the war have become almost legendary among the Mexicans of the border. All he has to do is let it be known he's here and needs men to follow him, and they'll come flocking like so many buzzards to a dead horse. He already has the horses. All he needs is Lieutenant Henry Dixon and those Krags. As soon as he lays his hands on those guns, he'll send out word."

"You're a *revolutionario*?"

"It's no revolution," she flung at him. "Mexican politics don't affect me. And they have nothing to do with this. It'll stay right here in the brasada. Do you remember Cortina?"

"The Red Robber?" said Cardigan. "What Texan doesn't remember him?"

"Then you know what happened when he got going," she said. "He was leading a veritable army before he finished. The whole border had a regular war on its hands. You finally had to call on the United States Army. And it took them ten years to break Cortina's hold down here." She leaned toward him, eyes big and black. "It'll be worse with Balacar if he's allowed to organize, Cardigan. You know what a terrible place this brush is. It's full of men in hiding, and very few law officers who came in after them ever went out alive. Think what it would be with an army in here, under a man like Balacar. Think what a terrible job it would be trying to smoke them out. It would be worse than any of the Indian wars. They could raid any town from here to the Red River. They could rustle cattle till cows stopped growing horns. It could well lead to another war with Mexico. You know how touchy the Cortina trouble left the whole border."

The scope of it staggered Cardigan. "Cortina was a piker beside this bird."

"It's been going on in the brasada, that way, since before Texas broke away from Mexico," she said. "But nobody ever had the nerve to try it on a scale like this."

He glanced around him, realizing what an impregnable fortress this harsh, impenetrable jungle would be for a force like that. "And they want your place for a headquarters?"

"It was the only spot in the brush big enough to corral that many mustangs," she said. "It would have been hard to steal that many horses anywhere, even over a period of time. Besides, rustling such a large number might have given away what Balacar intended in here, and he didn't want that until he was set. They did have to have horses, though. You know half the Mexicans in the brush and along the border don't own an animal. I didn't know exactly what was in the wind when Garza came to me wanting to use my ranch as headquarters for his *mesteneros*. He paid for a six months' lease for the use of my corrals and men. We'd just finished fall roundup and my crew was idle, so I didn't see any harm. By the time I realized something was going on, Garza had won over Kamaska and Innocencio. *Brasaderos* like them would give anything to ride with Balacar. And Aragonza had worked with Balacar before. I couldn't fight them openly, even when I did find out. I tried to reach Masset, but it was impossible. He's always thought I was mixed up with the rustlers in here. The *nagualismo* business starting about that time didn't help much. Two of Masset's deputies were killed that way and he connected me with it."

"You could have gotten out."

She drew herself up perceptibly. "It's my brasada, Cardigan. My house. My land. Do you think I'd let them take it that way?"

The drum of hoofs turned him in the saddle. Kamaska had remained behind at the *hacienda*, and his horse was lathered with the hard ride from there as he pushed by them on his hairy mule. He halted by Balacar and Garza, speaking in a hot, breathless way, glancing back at Cardigan. Garza nodded, said something, neck-reined his horse away. Florida caught at Cardigan's hand.

"Quick, you've got to tell me. Who are you?"

"Yes," said Balacar, and he had turned back to them through the screen of mesquite. "Who are you, Cardigan?"

"Don't you know," laughed Pinto from behind them. "He's Lieutenant Dixon's brother."

A dull flush reddened Balacar's heavy-fleshed face, and he controlled his anger badly. "We have found mustang sign. We'll be riding."

He reined his horse in beside Florida and Kamaska dropped back till he was just ahead of Cardigan, and they broke into a trot through the brush that way. Cardigan watched for them to come up with Garza, but the man did not appear. Aragonza was trailing, and kept dismounting to check the sign. They crossed a portion of brush that had been swept by the fire. There was a great stretch of blackened stubble, still glowing and snapping sullenly in places, reaching to a sandy river bed which the fire had been unable to leap. They plodded through the white sand and into thick brush beyond.

"Evidently a large cut of *mestenos* was driven this way by the fire," said Balacar.

None of them answered, and Cardigan gripped his reins more tightly with the thickening of the sullen antipathy which lay between all of them. Pinto was grinning blandly at Innocencio, and the knife-man shifted uncomfortably in his saddle, his forehead still red and lacerated where Cardigan had struck him with the table leg. Then a startled, crashing sound broke from the thickets ahead, and Aragonza shouted back at them.

"¡*Mestenos*! Head them off. They are cutting toward you. Head them off."

A mustang with great singe marks blackening his dun hide burst through mesquite with the berries caught like brown bubbles in his mane. His wild eyes rolled white as he saw them, and he turned on a hind leg like a roper, taking another direction through the brush. With a hoarse shout, Kamaska was after him. Another *mesteno* crashed into the open, and then three mares clattered in from the mesquite. Cardigan spurred his dun so that it nudged into Florida's pony before digging into its gallop.

"Don't get separated," he shouted in her ear, and then was past her.

He sensed her horse following behind him, and saw Pinto line out after Florida. Then he was into the chaparral, with the mares making a great crashing before him. Keeping his eyes open, as Florida had told him, was next to impossible. Every time a clawing mat of mesquite or a hackberry branch thrust itself out at him, his head jerked aside, and his eyes twitched with the violent instinct to shut. Yet he forced himself to keep them open, smashing hell-for-leather into the *mogote*, and found he could dodge the malignant brush with more ease than before. He ducked under a post-oak and, where he would have missed the *agrito* beyond that if he had allowed his eyes to close, and probably would have had his leg swept out of the stirrup, he spotted the thorny, crawling spread and swept his leg up to avoid it.

He neck-reined the dun violently to one side and scraped past the thick, shaggy trunk of a hackberry. Then he pulled up and turned the blowing animal, waiting for Florida. It was when his own noise had stopped that he realized there was no sound behind him. He had purposely not gone far, only riding enough to penetrate the first thicket. An insidious fear fingered him. He was just touching his dun's flanks to send it back when the sound came. It stiffened him in the saddle, and he felt the blood drain from his face, and his lips formed the word soundlessly.

"*La onza.*"

With an abrupt motion, Cardigan kicked his dun back through the mesquite and into the clearing. It was empty. He opened his mouth to call Florida, then closed it. He turned the dun, a strange, clawing sensation tightening his vitals. Then it came.

"Card, watch out! Card, watch out! Card. . . !"

There was terror riding the hoarse, cracked shouts, and then agony, as the intelligible words became a wild, shrill scream, and that scream was so imbedded within Cardigan's memory by now that he raked his dun without thought and drove it toward the sound with all the coals on. He exploded through a mass of *gran-jeno* and ducked flat on his dun to tear beneath a low stretch of *chaparro prieto* and jerked aside from a clawing arm of mesquite. The screams had stopped by now and he had smashed a straight line a hundred yards through the brush before he pulled his lathered dun up, trying to place the spot where the sound had just come from.

The brush was utterly silent, save for his dun's heavy breathing. He tried another tack through the mesquite, going slower. Finally he went back to the original clearing and started circling out from it. He lost track of the time it took him to find Pinto. He pulled through a stand of torn, prickly pear into a small opening. Pinto was lying face down. Most of his shirt was gone, and the flesh across his back was ripped away so deeply the white pattern of his bones was visible, and the ground beneath him was soaked with blood.

Cardigan got off his horse slowly, his face set in a stiff, terrible mask. It didn't matter what Pinto had been. It didn't matter that he hadn't known him long. All that mattered in that moment was the feeling of utter loss in Cardigan. The vagrant, poignant memory of a reckless laugh passed through him, and of a swaggering figure in the saddle, and of a cheerful Texas lullaby sung one night up by the Nueces when the going had gotten especially tough.

It must have been the sepulchral rustle of mesquite that caused Cardigan to turn around. Africano stood there, bare, leprous torso covered with fresh brush scratches, black chest rising and falling heavily. Cardigan drew a sharp breath, turning toward him.

"Africano. . . ."

"Careful, *señor!*" It was a sharp command, but more than that, stopping Cardigan, was the guttural warning of the dogs.

"I don't have to touch you, Africano." Cardigan pulled his gun. His lips were flat against his teeth. "I don't have to touch you to kill you."

Africano was staring at Parker. "You think . . . me?"

"What else?" Cardigan's voice was brittle and he was trembling a little now. "You've been around every time. *Nagualismo?* Go ahead. Go ahead and change back into that *onza* before I put a slug through your black brisket. I'd like to see you try."

"No, *señor*, no. I'm not *nagual*. Kamaska's loco. Just because I come from Yucatan? That was a long time ago, *señor*. I was a *niñito*, a baby. Garza is from Yucatan, too. This is my country, *señor*, my *brasada*. Do you think I'd let them take it, Balacar and the others? I've been trying to help the *señorita*. When you came, I thought it was to get Balacar. I have tried to help you, *señor*. . . ."

"By running around changing yourself into an *onza* and tearing people up?" said Cardigan bitterly.

"No, I tell you I am not *nagual*. Didn't I give you Balacar's briefcase when I found it? Didn't I tell you of George Weaver? I was trying to warn you of *la onza* that night of the fire, but I got there too late. I used to work at *Hacienda del Diablo*, but Garza ran me off when I found out what they were up to and threatened to tell the *señorita* if they didn't leave. They have tried to find me and kill me ever since. And now she knows, doesn't she . . . ?" Africano stopped abruptly, his black head raising, and then shouted. "*Señor*, behind you. . . !"

It was his own whirling motion that saved Cardigan, carrying him partially to one side. The hilt of the *belduque* tapped at his shirt as it hummed past him, driving into Africano's chest. The man made a gurgling sound and fell against Cardigan, knocking the Remington upward with its first shot. The slug shattered through the brush above Innocencio's head, where he stood across the clearing. Before Cardigan could jump away from Africano's body and throw down on his second shot, the two dogs had leaped past him, snarling savagely.

"Kamaska!" shouted Innocencio, trying to turn and run, "Kamaska," and then the ferocious animals were on him, and he went down with a pitiful shout beneath their snarling, slashing fury.

Kamaska came into the open from the other side, and Cardigan had his gun cocked, and he fired with the conversion held straight out at the level of his hip. The square, apelike Mexican grunted, and reached out with both arms, and kept on coming toward Cardigan in that heavy, shuffling stride. Cardigan fired again, without throwing his gun up. Kamaska flinched, and kept coming. The Remington bucked with Cardigan's third shot. Kamaska made a sick sound with the impact of that one, and staggered a little, and then put his foot down in another step, grunting with the pain it caused him, and came on, grunting with each step. Cardigan's lips peeled away from his teeth in a grim desperation, and he dropped the hammer on his fourth one. Kamaska made no sound with that one driving through his thick, square belly. He took another step, his hands spastically spread out in front of him. His face contorted with the effort his will was making to drive him on that last step. His foot struck the ground with a solid, thumping sound. His thick, callused fingers touched Cardigan. Then they slid down the front of Cardigan's shirt, and Kamaska's weight almost knocked Cardigan over, falling against him, and sliding to the ground.

"*Señor.* . . .

It was Africano, trying to raise himself on an elbow, the *belduque* protruding from his chest. The dogs were worrying at Innocencio's body across the clearing, growling and snarling. Cardigan squatted down to Africano, and the man waved a hand at Pinto.

"You know . . . you know what that means?"

"It means you got what was coming to you and. . . ."

"No, no, I'm not *nagual*." Africano licked lips flecked with blood. "I mean that they would kill Parker?"

"What do you mean, they?"

"They no longer think he is Lieutenant Dixon. They must have found the real Lieutenant Dixon!"

X

There was something strident about the utter silence of *Hacienda del Diablo* that caught at Cardigan. He hauled his dun to a stop just inside the fringe of brush, searching the compound for signs of life. Africano had died in the thicket there with Pinto Parker; and the dun was shaking and heaving beneath Cardigan, he had driven it so brutally to reach the spread. It came to him now with a shock that there were no mustangs in the corrals. Neck-reining the dun abruptly into the open, he spurred the flagging animal across the porch. His Remington was in his hand as he swung off the blown horse, and his heels tapped across the flagstones in a grim deliberateness. The heavy door stood ajar. Cardigan slid in with his back coming up against one wall and his gun covering the living room that ran the length of the front of the building. One man was in the room. He sat on the floor, slumped against the wall near the hooded fireplace, legs thrust out before him, head on his chest. The wall above his head was pocked with bullet holes that had dripped yellow adobe down onto his white head. Two big, stag-gripped Colts lay one on either side of him.

"Esperanza?" said Cardigan.

The old cook had trouble raising his head and focusing his eyes. "Cardigan," he croaked. "I thought you was dead. Balacar sent Innocencio and Kamaska out to kill you and Parker."

"Lieutenant Dixon?" said Cardigan.

"How did you know?" Esperanza made a vague movement with his hands, licking his lips. "Dixon came while all of you were gone into the brush. He said the two men who'd been guiding him had been killed almost a week ago by some nigger, just before he reached the Comanche Trail. I figure it must have been Africano. Africano run Dixon's string of mules off into the brush and scattered them. That's how you and Parker must have come across the one Garza found you with. By the time Dixon got the mules rounded up, he was lost in the brush. He tried to find his way alone, but he said this nigger kept trying to kill him and get the mules again. Finally Dixon killed all the mules and cached their loads of Krags and started out alone to find us. . . ." Esperanza trailed off, making that motion with his hand again. "*Agua*, Cardigan, *agua*. These holes in my *estomago* give a *hombre* a *diablo*'s own thirst."

Cardigan got a clay pitcher of water off the table, and Esperanza slopped it all over his chest drinking, finally pushing it away. "Kamaska lit out to tell Balacar the real Dixon is finally here, and they come back. They had to bring Florida in on the end of a gun. Garza claimed you and Parker had been taken care of, but Balacar sent Kamaska and Innocencio to make sure. He wanted them to bring your head back in a saddlebag. He said he wouldn't believe you were dead till he saw that. He said that's the kind of a *hombre* you are."

"Who let the mustangs out?"

"Florida. She wanted to stop Balacar from getting the guns, I guess. She's been against this from the beginning, only me and Kamaska and the others were too dumb to see that. Garza paid us extra *dinero* and promised us we'd ride high beside him as soon as they got those guns. We always thought Florida would be with them, but I guess they only wanted to use her till they got the mustangs broke. She got out somehow while Balacar and Dixon were talking and let all the horses loose, and that made them mad. They started knocking her around, and I see what they really had intended with her all along. I'm her *hombre*, Cardigan. I been on *hacienda* with her grandfather and her father and her, and they can't do that. You see what I got for my trouble. Aragonza. I never see a man pull his gun so fast. I had mine already out before he started. *Madre de Dios*." He licked his lips again, blinking his eyes almost sleepily. Then, with a perceptible effort, he focused them again, reaching up feebly to clutch at Cardigan, his voice a hoarse croak. "You've got to get them, Cardigan. You got to stop them. Once Balacar gets those guns, there'll be no stopping him. He can get mustangs again. That ain't hard. Maybe it'll take him time, but he can get them. It's the guns."

He drew a long breath.

"The whole thing hinges on them. Once they're in his hands, the brasada's going to burn from one end to the other. You think that was a good fire at *Mogotes Oros*? You wait till Balacar gets going. This whole border country won't be safe for a man like you to set foot in. They'll raze every town from here to Austin. There won't be a cattle ranch left south of the Nueces. And nobody'll be able to stop them, Cardigan, five hundred men with Krags under a soldier like Balacar in this brush. Nobody's been able to clean the brush of rustlers and killers in the last hundred years. What chance do you think they'll have with an organized army? And Florida"—his hand tugged at Cardigan's shirt with a spasmodic fear—"you got to stop them, Cardigan. Before they get those guns. She's with them and Balacar'll kill her as soon as he has the Krags for sure. The only reason he kept her alive was her influence with the *brasaderos* but, as soon as he gets those guns, he won't need her any more. From the description Dixon gave of the place he cached those Krags, I'd say Rio Frio."

"My horse is done," said Cardigan.

"There's some old brush ponies staked out behind the cookhouse. They ain't these mustangs, but they'll take you where you need to go."

Cardigan rose, took a step toward the door, then turned. Esperanza waved him on.

"Go ahead, go ahead. Ain't no use waiting to see me sack my kack." He took a gasping breath. "Make it before night comes, Cardigan. I heard *la onza* a while back. Make it before night comes or you'll have the *nagual* on you out there."

"I don't think so," said Cardigan. "I think that's already taken care of."

It was a stringy-backed, hammer-headed gelding no more than fifteen hands high, scarred from nose to tail by the brush and, once Cardigan touched its hoary flanks, the evil little beast threw itself into a mad gallop, crashing through the brasada as if it hated every thicket personally, throwing itself broadside through *mogotes* of chaparral, driving tumultuously through a bunch of mesquite with its head down and little eyes glittering belligerently, dashing across open spaces in a driving impatience to be at the brush again. Cardigan had taken some wild rides in his day, but this sat the fanciest saddle. It was a constant battle to remain on the horse, ducking flat along its cockleburred mane or throwing himself off to one side, riding its rump, its neck, its flanks, not spending five minutes of the whole time sitting straight in the saddle. Yet, with all its apparent rage at the brush, the horse took him through *mogotes* the dun could never have negotiated, bursting thickets the devil himself would have gone around, penetrating seemingly impenetrable chaparral, crashing prickly pear so solid it looked fit to stop a herd of steers. And all the time it was Florida's admonition. Keep your eyes open, keep your eyes open.

There was a post-oak that batted his head and left him sick and dizzy and reeling in the rawhide-lashed brushpopper's saddle, and mesquite that caught at his face while he was off to the side and left his flesh torn and bleeding, and *agrito* that ripped his Levi's to shreds, and nopal that jabbed his hands and arms like bayonets. He seemed lost in a mad nightmare, filled with the roaring crash of brush and the clatter of chaparral and the squashing pop of prickly pear.

Esperanza had said Rio Frio, just south of where they had hunted *mestenos* that first time, and the best Cardigan knew was to drive in a straight line with the sun on his left. Soon he was fighting the brush as bitterly as the pony, flinging a curse at each jabbing *comal*, shouting a hoarse execration at every low-reaching hackberry branch. He had gotten the feel of it now, and was going more by sense than sight, his swing to the side automatic when a post-oak loomed ahead, his jerk up instinctive to avoid the clawing arms of *comal* before his face, riding like a drunken man, swaying and cursing and shouting and panting and bleeding.

He crossed a great, blackened stretch, where the fire had burned itself out in some pear flats, and ran again into the thickets. There was no trailing for him; he knew too little of the brush for that. He struck a wet creek finally and knew it to be Rio Frio, for there was no other water within miles, and turned down the dribble, fighting through cottonwoods and hackberries festooned thick with parasite moss and the constant pop and crash of brush as he burst through it to hear any sounds; and he came upon them in a mad rush, tearing through a screening thicket of huisache that grew down into the river, and almost running down Aragonza on the other side.

"Cardigan!" shouted Aragonza, jumping backward.

The man's first surprise kept him from any action and, by the time he was ready, Cardigan had hauled his heaving pony to a stop and slid off and stood there, swaying and bleeding and panting, his legs spread out beneath him, his torso bent forward slightly. *I never see a man pull his gun so fast!* It was in Cardigan like that, what Esperanza had said, and he was waiting, with the knowledge. *I never see a man pull his gun so fast.*

"Go ahead," he said.

Aragonza went. His right arm was still in that black sling, but Cardigan had seen enough to know the man was as good with either hand and, when the Durango serape flapped against Aragonza's *charro* vest with his blinding movement, whatever had been in Cardigan's mind was swept from it as instinct and habit reared up from his unconscious in an inundating wave. He felt his whole body sweep into motion, and that was his last conscious sensation till the crash of guns jarred through him. It must have been the jolt of Cardigan's slug striking Aragonza that made the man pull his trigger, spasmodically, for Aragonza had not lifted his gun high enough to be in line. With the smoking six-shooter still pointed at the ground, Aragonza sobbed in a strangled way and fell over on his face.

The brush pony had been spooked by the gunfire, and bolted for the mesquite, but the clatter of the men bursting into the open from there caused the animal to rear up and whirl back toward Cardigan. With all his concentration on Aragonza, Cardigan's awareness of Florida had been but a dim one in those first moments, where she was standing on the far side of the clearing.

"Cardigan!" he heard her cry, and with the brush horse charging wildly at him, he threw down on the trio who erupted from the thicket behind Florida. He had to snap his shot at the first man he saw, and it was Comal Garza, coming out of the mesquite with berries dripping all over his shoulders, and that Ward-Burton hugged in against his belly as he snapped the bolt. Cardigan's gun bucked in his hand, and he had time to see Garza's face twist, and then the horse's shoulder crashed into him, spinning him around.

Desperately, Cardigan tried to keep his feet. He spun into a hackberry, hearing the horse thunder on into the brasada behind him, and then reeled off the tree and went to his hands and knees in the sand facing away from the hackberry, a foot behind his head. He flopped over onto his back with his gun in both hands. In that position, lying there flat with his feet toward them and the gun sighted down his belly through his toes, he saw *Tio* Balacar. Balacar must have been the one to fire that first shot, for he was still coming forward in a stiff-legged run, and he had already thrown his gun down for the second shot. Cardigan thumbed desperately at his own hammer, knowing his head would be blown off before he could ever fire.

He recoiled to the roar of the shot. Then he lay there, his gun still gripped in both hands, not yet cocked, realizing it hadn't been Balacar's gun which had made the sound. *Tio* staggered on forward a couple of steps, his face blank with a stunned surprise, and then a glazed opacity dulled the brilliance of his little black eyes and, when he fell forward, one of his arms dropped across Cardigan's leg.

Florida was standing above Garza, with Garza's smoking Ward-Burton still held across one hip. She was not faced toward Balacar any more. She had snapped the bolt of the gun again, and her thumb was still over the breech where she had jammed in a fresh shell. The third man who had been running out with Balacar and Garza was halted, a frustrated rage showing in the way his mouth worked as he stared at the weapon, his hand still gripped on the flap of a holster at his hip, holding it open over the butt of an Army Colt he hadn't been able to draw.

Cardigan got to his feet, stepping over Balacar, slipping the Colt from the man's holster, and it was rather a statement than a question. "Lieutenant Dixon."

"Yeah," said the man sullenly.

"I'm Marshal Edward Cardigan, United States government, and I'm taking you back for desertion, theft of government property, and fomenting activity inimical to the government of the country, and that's tantamount to treason, and they usually hang a man for that."

Florida was staring at Cardigan, wide-eyed, and her words were hardly audible. "Marshal . . . Edward . . . Cardigan . . . ?"

"You can see why I couldn't tell you." He was turned toward her, and it was spilling out now, the way he'd wanted it to come for so long, the way he'd wanted to let her know she wasn't alone. "I didn't know whether you were with them or not, Florida, for sure. I couldn't take a chance. I had a job to do, and I couldn't take a chance. So much more depended on it than just you and me. The lives of so many men who would have died if I'd failed, men like Masset and Weaver and Smithers."

"Weaver was a marshal too?"

"Yes, the first one they sent in to find out what was going on down here. Lieutenant Dixon was in the Quartermaster Corps at San Antone. Balacar reached him. It's usually money, in a case like that. Enough money. Dixon got assigned to a detail transporting those Krags from San Antone to Fort Leaton. At the Nueces, two Mexicans met the detachment and, with their help, Dixon got the guns into the brush. Two of the troopers were killed during the ruckus. Our office had word that Balacar was active somehow north of the border, and when the Krags disappeared that way, and with the reports Masset's office had been sending in about this *na-gualismo* business going on south of the Comanche Trail, the government decided it was time for them to step in down here and try and clean it up.

"After Weaver disappeared, I was assigned. Instead of coming straight in, I figured it would be better if I dallied onto someone who knew the brasada and who would be accepted in here among the class of men who ran the brush. We had tabs on the local rustlers and border-hoppers working out of San Antone and other towns near the brush. In Brownsville I finally tied in with Pinto and Navasato to run a bunch of Big Skillet beef across the border. Pinto never suspected who I was till right at the last. . . ."

He trailed off, and she looked up at him, sensing what was in his mind. "He wouldn't blame you, Cardigan. He didn't. He stuck, didn't he? Even after he began to understand how you'd used him."

"It didn't matter at first." Cardigan's voice was guttural. "He was just a two-bit rustler, and he was just someone who could get me in here. But you know Pinto. After being with him that way, riding with him, camping, fighting, drinking"—he moved his head in a helpless, frustrated way—"I can't help how I feel. It doesn't matter what he was or what he may have done. I can't help how I feel."

"He understood, Cardigan. He wouldn't have had you any other way. You're that kind. Pinto understood what kind you were and admired you for it, and whatever happened he never blamed you."

It was the rustling sound that made Cardigan realize how much of their attention had been focused on Dixon. Florida stood in front of where Garza lay, and it had hidden his movement just long enough. Both Florida and Cardigan whirled toward him, but he was already on his feet, and plunging into the brush. Florida tried to fire, but she hadn't shoved the fresh shell home hard enough, and the Ward-Burton jammed on her. Cardigan had put his Remington away, and it took him that long to draw it, and then it was Florida, shouting, "Cardigan, look out. Dixon. Cardigan. . . ."

He whirled back, the Remington out, firing after Dixon as the man leaped into the mesquite. He heard Dixon cry out in pain, and then crash on through the thicket. Cardigan plunged after him.

"Garza," called the woman. "What about Garza?"

"Dixon's the man I want," shouted Cardigan, smashing through some prickly pear. "Garza won't go far with that slug I put through his belly."

He was still shouting when the sound came. He stopped shouting, and stopped running, and stood there, with his mouth open. Bursting through the pear after him, Florida ran into Cardigan, almost knocking both of them over, and then, against him like that, she stiffened, and her fingers tightened on his arm. It rose above the brasada like the scream of a woman in mortal pain, weird, terrifying, unearthly. It was the same sound Cardigan had heard before Navasato, and Masset, and Pinto. He felt a suffocating constriction in his chest, as the cry died, and Dixon must have stopped running somewhere ahead of them, for an utter silence settled over the brush.

"No, Cardigan," whispered the woman, "no, no, no."

"Cardigan." It was Dixon's shout, shocking them, coming shrill and cracked from ahead. "Cardigan, for God's sake, Cardigan! Help me, Cardigan! For God's sake, Cardigan. . . !"

Cardigan made an impulsive movement toward the sound that carried him halfway through a lane between mesquite thickets with the woman clinging to him, and then Dixon's screams had stopped, too. Gun gripped in a white-knuckled hand, Cardigan forced himself onward. Sweat was running down the deep grooves from his nose to his lips as he passed the mesquite and forced his way through thickly entwined chaparral. There was an open spot beyond the chaparral. Dixon lay there, face down. Florida stared a moment, then turned her face to Cardigan's chest with a small sob.

"I was a fool," Cardigan muttered thickly.

"A fool?"

"I thought Africano was the *nagual.*"

Her face turned upward with a jerk, and her eyes were shining up at him in a wide fear. "You mean . . . Garza?"

XI

Night touched the brasada with its ghostly hands, and the *chaparro prieto* stood in sinister silence along Rio Frio. From somewhere far off a coyote mourned through the darkness. And nearer, through the mesquite, back in the secretive pear, the sibilant, chuckling crackle of movement through the brush mocked them.

No telling how long they had crouched there, above the torn, dead body of Lieutenant Dixon. No telling how long they had waited. It seemed an eternity to Cardigan. His hand about the Remington was aching from its tight grip, and his palm was sticky with sweat against the butt. The woman, beside him, was still having those fits of trembling, her breathing coming out in small, choked spurts. She watched him intently with the fear in her big, dark eyes, and her lips kept forming his name, as if it were the last thing she clung to.

"Cardigan . . . Cardigan . . . Cardigan."

He couldn't blame Florida. He was terrified himself. A deep, instinctive, primal fear, that rose from the first fear the first man had felt for the night, and the unknown. He licked his lips, remembering the twisted horror on Navasato's face when they had found him that way.

"Cardigan . . . Cardigan."

He took a careful breath, trying to blot from his mind the picture of Sheriff Masset's bloody, rended body.

"Cardigan."

He almost shut his eyes to keep from seeing Pinto Parker, lying there, torn, shattered, dead.

"Cardigan."

And still the sound, quietly out there, circling them, stalking them. The rustle of mesquite that might have been the wind, only there was no wind. The faint sibilance of something brushing the curly red gramma. The barely perceptible crunch of prickly pear.

And the tracks, Cardigan. Hadn't Pinto said it? *Just like cat tracks. Only they couldn't have been. Cats don't grow that big in Texas, or anywhere.*

He tried to swallow past the thickening in his throat, and almost choked. He felt his fingers digging into the flesh of Florida's arm, and tried to ease the grip. And still the sounds. A sibilant rattle. *Agrito?* A faint tapping. Mesquite berries knocked from a branch. A scraping whisper. *Nopal?*

"Cardigan, I don't think I can stand it. . . ."

"Sh"—he put his finger across her wet lips—"it won't do us any good to move. It'll just give us away."

And the tracks, Cardigan. A jaguar, perhaps. Too big. Cats don't grow that big in Texas. Or anywhere. What is it, Africano? What is *la onza?*

There it was again. Mesquite? Oh, hell! He shifted his position to ease aching muscles. How could you tell if it was mesquite? How could you tell anything? What did it matter? It was out there. That's all that mattered.

La onza is a hybrid, señor. A cross between a bull-tiger and a she-lion. There is nothing more deadly. There is nothing more terrible.

"Cardigan. . . ."

He squeezed her arm hard enough to make her wince, lifting his gun a little. It seemed to be nearer now. From the right? He turned that way slightly, cocking his head. Or the left? He began to shift back, and then stopped, the maddening frustration of it sweeping him. He bit his lips to keep from cursing, or standing up, or crying, he didn't know what. He realized he was breathing hoarsely, and tried to stifle it. Tears were running silently down the woman's face. She was biting her lips too, and blood reddened the tears as they reached her chin.

"Cardigan!"

It came all at once, the crash of brush and that terrible screaming sound that no cat could ever make and the woman shouting at him, and the bellow of his gun as he whirled and saw the huge, blurred silhouette of it, hurtling down on them. He caught Florida with a sweep of his free arm, knocking her back and aside, and jumped back himself to fire again, not throwing down this time, dropping his thumb on the hammer from where he held the gun at his hip.

He had a kaleidoscopic sense of evil little eyes gleaming green as they were caught in the moonlight and white fangs in a great, velvety snout and the blasting heat of stinking breath as the beast let out another of those unearthly screams, and then he was being thrown back by its terrible weight and impetus, all the air exploding from him in an agonized gasp. He had no conscious feeling of shouting again. With those terrible talons ripping at him, he felt the gun explode somewhere down by his hip.

He tried to get to his feet, crying out in pain as a swipe of the huge paw caught his upflung arm, tearing it away from his face. His impression of the animal was still blurred and unreal, and still going backward, he gained his feet, and managed a stumbling step on into the thicket, and jerked the Remington into line again to fire point-blank at the huge, snarling face before him. The screaming sound it made deafened him this time, drowning the report of the gun.

A great suffocation gripped him, and after that, nothing.

XII

It was a voice. Coming in from somewhere, Cardigan knew that, if he knew nothing else. It was a voice.

"It looks like my *onza* has eliminated Marshal Edward Cardigan now, too, my dear, doesn't it?"

"Your *onza*."

That was another voice, trembling, afraid, yet brave, with the kind of courage a man has who will go out to meet what he fears, or a woman.

"Then you're the *nagual*."

There was a laugh coming to Cardigan through succeeding layers of pain, now, that spread over him and spun through his brain. "My dear Florida, surely you don't believe that *nagualismo* rot. I'm no more a *nagual* than Africano was. The only rapport I have with *la onza* is that I've had the animal since it was a cub. It will do my bidding as Africano's dogs did his."

"Don't be fantastic. How can you train a beast like that? Even if it did exist."

"It does exist." The man's voice again. "And I did train it. Isn't that more logical to believe than the fact that I change myself from a man to an animal? They train ordinary cats, don't they? They train tigers to obey the whip. You'd be surprised what those Caribs can teach a jaguar. Why not an *onza*? You should see the beast, Florida. You will. It eats from my hand. Anybody else it will rend to shreds. It took time, of course, and patience. But so does a good horse."

"But why? Are you crazy? . . . a sadist?"

"No more than is a man who trains his dog to protect him. You'll have to admit it was an admirable expedient. There have been ordinary murders through this stretch of the brush for hundreds of years, but that didn't keep men from running it. You saw what happened with my *onza*. These Mexican *brasaderos* have enough Indian in them to know *nagualismo*. Even white men. Look at Masset. It kept them out of Cañada Diablo, didn't it? Every new kill by *la onza* was another brick in the wall of superstitious fear keeping the *brasaderos* out of Cañada Diablo, and we could work here in perfect safety till everything was ready."

A growing acceptance was in the woman's voice. "Did Balacar know?"

"Nobody knew," he answered her. "I kept *la onza* chained in those caves south of Rio Frio. When we first heard Parker and Cardigan were coming through with a bunch of cattle, I let it out, thinking they were just rustlers. Then, after it had killed Navasato, I found that dead mule and the Krag with his body, and thought it meant one of them was Dixon. Africano had stampeded Dixon's mules, and this one must have been caught by the *onza* about the same time it found Navasato."

Cardigan was trying to squirm from beneath the ponderous weight of the animal lying across him now. He was sobbing with the agony in him. He wrested one leg from beneath the great, white-furred belly and rolled from under a bloody paw. The man was still talking from the thicket farther on.

"When Kamaska came, telling us the real Dixon had arrived at the *hacienda*, I told Balacar to go on and I would take care of Parker and Cardigan. *Tio* must have sent Innocencio and Kamaska to make sure. He didn't know about the *onza*. If they hadn't bungled it, the *onza* would have had Cardigan there. When I realized Cardigan had escaped, I followed him with the *onza*. I reached you here just about the time he did, didn't I? And now it's just you and me. We can do the same thing *Tio* wanted. We can have an empire here. We can live like Cortina. Did you ever see his *hacienda*, Florida? Even his peons had silver-mounted saddles. Five hundred Krags and the men to use them and the brasada, Florida. Nothing can beat that combination."

"It's already beaten," she sobbed. "One man beat it. Maybe he's dead now, but he beat it. You won't last the night out with that slug Cardigan put through your belly."

"Maybe you'd like me to call the *onza*, Florida."

"The *onza*?" Fear shook her voice.

"It will eat out of my hand," said Garza.

"This one won't eat out of your hand, Garza," said Cardigan.

He must have made a shocking sight, stepping from the thicket. His shirt was torn completely from his torso, claw marks drawing their viscid, red grooves from his collarbone to his belt, his left arm hanging torn and useless by his side, dripping blood off the limp fingers, the flesh ripped in a patch from his forehead.

"Cardigan," gasped the woman, and he had time to see the desperate joy in her face before she had hidden it against his chest, and he didn't mind the pain that caused him, as his one good arm encircled her pliant waist. He looked over his shoulder at the defeat in Garza's face, and he wanted to hate the man, for Pinto, and couldn't because there wasn't that much emotion left in him.

"The guns?" he said gutturally.

"Down by the river," said Florida, her voice muffled against him. "Dixon cached them under a cutbank. We've got to get you to a doctor, Cardigan, we've got to get you to a doctor."

"You come too?"

"Yes, you know I will. You can't make it alone."

"I don't mean. . . ," he began. "Esperanza's dead by now back at your spread. All the others. Half the brush is burnt out by that fire. It will never be the same again."

She lifted her head to look at him, and understanding of what he was asking entered her eyes. What had happened was still too strong within both of them for either to put this in words so soon, yet her answer encompassed all his questions, spoken and unspoken. "You know I will," she repeated.

THE CONESTOGA PIRATE

DAN CUSHMAN was born in Osceola County, Michigan, and grew up on the Cree Indian reservation in Montana. In the early 1940s his novelette-length stories began appearing regularly in such Fiction House magazines as *North-West Romances* and *Frontier Stories*. Later in the decade his North-Western and Western stories as well as fiction set in the Far East and Africa began appearing in *Action Stories*, *Adventure*, and *Short Stories*. "The Phantom Herds of Furnace Flat" was his first appearance in *Lariat Story Magazine* (3/45). It was followed by "Stranger's Luck" (3/46), "I. O. U.—One Bullet" (5/46), "Boothill Loves a Pilgrim" (11/46), both "Longhorn Puzzle" (1/47) and "Where Smokepoles Never Rust" (3/47) under the byline Tom O'Neill, "His Last Prisoner" (5/47), "Burned with the Coyote Brand" (7/47), and "She-Wolf of the Rio Grande" (3/49).

Dan Cushman and Les Savage, Jr., were the mainstays in Fiction House magazines throughout the 1940s. The Tom O'Neill byline came about because Cushman was also the author of a series of stories about Armless O'Neil in *Jungle Stories* and *Action Stories*. Now some of his finest stories from both *North-West Romances* and *Lariat* have been assembled in VOYAGEURS OF THE MIDNIGHT SUN (Capra Press, 1995).

STAY AWAY, JOE (Viking, 1953) is an amusing novel about the mixture, and occasional collision, of Indian culture and Anglo-American culture among the Métis (French-Indians) living on a reservation in Montana. The novel became a bestseller and remains a classic to this day, greatly loved especially by Indians from many nations for its truthfulness and humor. ". . . It is a *funny* novel," William Bloodworth wrote in TWENTIETH CENTURY WESTERN AUTHORS (St. James Press, 1991), "the humor of which derives partly from the mixture of traditional and white influences on Cushman's contemporary Indian characters. Such humor may suggest a greater respect for Indians than one might find in novels that are more intentionally respectful."

Yet, while humor is also Cushman's hallmark in such later novels as THE OLD COPPER COLLAR (Ballantine, 1957) and GOODBYE, OLD DRY (Doubleday, 1959), he also produced significant historical fiction in THE SILVER MOUNTAIN (Appleton Century Crofts, 1957), concerned with the mining and politics of silver in Montana in the 1890s. This novel won a Golden Spur Award from the Western Writers of America. In 1996 it will be reprinted for the first time in an unabridged paperback edition by Leisure Books.

The character of Comanche John, a Montana road agent, was born in the pages of *Frontier Stories* in "The Conestoga Wagon" (Winter 44) where he is known as Dutch John. He is still Dutch John in "No Gold on Boot Hill" in *Action Stories* (Summer 45). Finally, in "Comanche John—Dead or Alive!" in *Frontier Stories* (Winter 46) he emerges with the moniker he carries ever after in numerous short adventures and in three of Cushman's novels, MONTANA, HERE I BE (Macmillan, 1950), THE RIPPER FROM RAWHIDE (Macmillan, 1952), and THE FASTEST GUN (Dell First Edition, 1955). John's first appearance has not previously been collected.

I

The pack-horse grazing near the campfire snorted, stood with lifted head peering into the twilight.

"Bear likely," said the grizzled man, jiggling the venison in the long-armed skillet. "Saw a trail over yonder in the cottonwoods when I fetched kindling."

But his younger companion was unconvinced. His eyes tried to pierce the gloom which hung deep in the underbrush. Then, distantly, came the clack of hoofs on rocks.

The grizzled one, hearing the sound, pushed the skillet to a cool edge of the fire, stepped away from the direct rays while his hand went to the long-barreled Navy six at his belt. And for many seconds the two listened.

The elder man was under medium stature. His hair, once dark but now silvered, fell to his collar. He was dressed from hand to foot in buckskin. His companion was far younger—in his early twenties, although his beard tended to deny his youth. He was slim, supple as a young birch, stood with the confidence of one long used to the wilderness.

"Sounds like two horses to me, Bogey," the young man said. "Some trapper, I suppose."

Nearby, a horse snorted and whinnied. An answering whinny came from the direction of the trail. The *thlot-thlot* of hoofs hesitated, and grew louder. In a moment, a lone rider, leading a pack-horse, appeared in the fringe of firelight.

He paused there, partially hidden in shadow. A black slouch hat was pulled low over his eyes. His face was covered with matted beard which was no less black or disreputable than his headgear. When his eyes fell on old Bogey, he gave a shout of pleasure.

"Well, shoot me for a Blackfoot, if it ain't old Bogey!" He leaped from his mount, strode over, extending his hand.

"Dutch John!" Bogey pumped the traveler's hand vigorously. "I heard tell you up and went to Mexico."

"No Mexico for me. I been in Californy."

"Gold huntin'?"

"Yep. Come over from Placerville this summer. Camp there got too full of law and order." Dutch John circled his neck with a grimy forefinger ending with a circular motion by his left ear indicative of a hangman's noose. He winked, shot a spurt of tobacco juice at the fire where it spluttered on a hot coal. "There was some lonely wayfarers relieved of excess weight which they carried, and a pack of folks suspected me. Of course I was innocent as a babe unborn. . . ." His matted whiskers parted to reveal a set of tobacco-stained teeth when he smiled.

"This here is Wils Fleming, my pardner," Bogey said, motioning to the tall young man. "Wils, shake hands with Dutch John."

Dutch John was medium in stature, perhaps thirty-five years old, although there was about him that peculiar ageless quality which years in the open so often give a man. Wils could tell he hailed from "civilization" because he wore gray homespun trousers and horsehide boots rather than the fringed buckskin of Indian country. His eyes were hard, calculating, and perhaps cruel; his manner of wearing his Navy pistols—slung low and far forward—testified to his expectation of trouble.

"Which way you headed?" John asked.

"The Deer Lodge Valley," answered Wils.

"Dear Lodge! No Deer Lodge for mine."

"No?"

"No sir! Me, I'm trailin' for the real diggin's . . . the Grasshopper . . . Bannack!"

"Bannack?"

Dutch John snorted. "Don't tell me you ain't heard tell of Bannack yet. It happened nigh three months ago."

Wils and Bogey registered in the negative, drew closer, listened.

"It was this-away. I was headed up to Orofino from Salt Lake, but I met a fellow named Joe Craves t'other side of Fort Hall. He and two half-breeds was headed down for provisions. He'd come from Bannack . . . said the gravel of the Grasshopper was yellow with the stuff. Greatest strike ever in the Northwest. There'll be a rush for it when the news gets to the Salmon River diggin's. But I'll be there ahead of 'em."

Bogey, listening, commenced rubbing his palm. Wils looked thoughtfully in the fire.

"Better come along," Dutch John urged.

"How about it, Wils?'

"Sure, I'm for it."

"Got provisions?" John asked hopefully.

"Little. Managed to pick up some flour at Fort Hall."

"Good. I ain't got any myself. Been livin' on jerky straight for the last two or three days. But share and share alike is my motto. . . ." John glanced first at Bogey and then at Wils while his thumb ran back and forth in the strap which held a pistol—but the implied threat in this action was not necessary. The two gladly invited him to share their meager supplies.

"Flour will be worth more'n gold dust over in Bannack before spring comes, I reckon," John said. "Joe Graves and his 'breeds won't get back with a wagon train before then, and a man can get mighty sick of deer meat in that time."

The meeting was at the mouth of Horse Creek on the Snake River, in the wild Northwest; a Northwest of two or three roads, a couple dozen beaten trails; a country dominated by the Hudson's Bay Company, the American Fur Company, and the Blackfeet.

Ten years before a half-breed named Benetsee unearthed a fragment of gold worth about ten cents from a prospect hole he had scratched out with the branch of an elkhorn at Deer Lodge. But the great strike waited on John White who, on July 26, 1862, sunk his pick into the gilded sands of the Grasshopper, at a spot which was later known throughout the world as "White Bar," a symbol of riches.

It was Bannack!

Toward this Eldorado the trio followed up the Snake, crossed the barren lava expanse to where Lost River and Birch Creek sank away in the thirsty formations. On the second morning they turned up a sage-dotted plain which separated two northerly running mountain ranges, following a trail which would lead them through the rugged Bitterroots by way of Lemhi Pass, and to Bannack.

At late morning, Wils reined in, pointed out a string of white dots several miles ahead; the dots wound serpent-like, kicked up a haze of dust which hung blue in the atmosphere. "Wagon train," he said. "Suppose they're headed for Bannack?"

By noon they overtook it. Evidently the train was on the point of leaving the trail, for it had turned eastward, and then paused for the noon meal.

In all, there were about thirty wagons. Many were pulled in tandem by six or eight horse-teams. In these arrangements, the canvas-topped "schooners" would be in front with one or more loaded supply wagons in the rear. As the trio rode by, the faces of women and children peered from the rear puckers of several schooners.

"Settlers," Bogey growled as if the word had an unpleasant flavor. "Saw a train of 'em on the south Snake two years ago. Country's gettin' right crowded."

At one wagon they noticed several men gathered watching their approach.

"Be you headed for Bannack?" Dutch John asked as soon as they were within speaking distance.

"Bannack?" asked one. They glanced at one another. Obviously the word was new to them.

"Sure . . . the Grasshopper diggin's. Biggest gold strike the North-west ever seen. Bigger'n Fraser or the Salmon."

"Did you say gold strike?" A tall, finely built man had ridden up just in time to hear the end of John's remark. He rode unusually erect. He was perhaps thirty. Unlike the bearded men who were grouped by the wagon, he was clean shaven except for carefully groomed sideburns which extended lower than the base of his ear. There was about him that which stamped him a man of the world—but for all that, it was plain the others did not look on him as their leader.

"Bet your life it's a gold strike," answered Dutch John. "At Bannack, over the Bitterroots. Up two hundred miles to the north."

"When did the strike take place?"

"July. We heard from the first man out."

"Plenty for us all, so I hear tell," Bogey put in.

There are few who can resist the lure of gold. Already the words had wrought a noticeable change on the ever-growing group at the wagon. But there was one ancient man, bearded, lean as a scare-crow; he stroked his ragged gray beard and shook his head. "We came to make homes," he said. "We're headed for them mountains yonder . . . for Paradise Valley."

Dutch John was unimpressed. "Paradise Valley? I never heard of them diggin's."

"They're not diggin's. Not gold diggin's, anyhow." The gray one fixed John with his Old-Testament eyes. "Paradise Valley is broad and grassy; there's good pure spring water and black soil. We didn't come to dig gold . . . we came to farm."

"Farm!" John aimed a spurt of tobacco juice at a wagon wheel. "Farmin's for squaws and Chinee."

"Farming is the most noble of callings! Farming is God's work!"

"A sky pilot!" John evidently considered a person of such ilk be-neath his contempt for he turned his attention in another direction. His eyes sought out a man who seemed to be their leader. "Got plenty of beans and flour for the winter?"

"More than enough. We planned to have enough to carry us until our first harvest."

"Fine." John rubbed his hands. "Share and share alike's my motto. Long as we tell you how to get to the diggin's, I reckon you folks won't object to us takin' our share of the provisions."

The leader—his name was Matthew Ebbert—did not immediately comment on this. His eyes were thoughtful. A good portion of the group appeared to be awaiting his decision, but one of the wagoners struck fist against palm with resolution.

"I'm headed for Bannack," he announced.

A woman whose face looked out from beneath the tunnel of a long sunbonnet clutched him by the arm. "Jason, I don't want to go to a mining camp," she half-whispered. "I want a home . . . our own land. . . ."

But her husband was determined. He jerked his arm away. "To hell with farmin'. This is our chance to get a stake. It's Bannack for me!"

His words seemed to stampede a good portion of his fellows. "Bannack for me, too," shouted one, and another: "Farmin' can wait, gold won't."

"What say you, Ebbert?" one asked of the leader.

Ebbert still hesitated. He glanced at the faces around him. The temper of the majority was apparent. Then he spoke reluctantly. "I say, those who want to go to Bannack, go. And those who want to go to Paradise, go."

"But that will mean splitting the train," cried the parson.

Ebbert nodded grimly.

"Who's talking about splitting the train?" The question came from a girl who had ridden up just in time to hear the parson's remark.

She sat her horse like a veteran. She wore a split buckskin skirt and beaded jacket; her hair was tucked beneath a broad sombrero.

The parson turned to her. "These fellows have brought news of a gold strike up North somewhere, and now your paw says, split the wagon train."

"No. We can't do it. We all started together . . . for Paradise Valley, and that's where we're going." She glanced around, her eyes troubled at finding her words had won so little support.

"No, Nora," Ebbert answered. "I'm afraid it's not that easy. Some of the boys want to go to the valley, but most lean toward Bannack; the wagon train will be split whether we want it or not."

"You, Boone." She now turned to the tall, shaven man who had ridden up a while before. "You stop them, can't you?"

"Sorry? Nora. Afraid I can't. Your father's right. We'll have to split. There's no other way."

She looked searchingly at Boone for a moment, then back to her father. An expression of doubt appeared in her face. "But we're going to Paradise . . . ."

"Well. . . ." the word drifted off uncertainly. Matthew Ebbert was plainly uncomfortable. He ran fingers through his whiskers, gazed off at the white clouds which flecked the deep autumn sky over Saddle Mountain.

"You don't intend to go to this . . . this . . . Bannack?"

"Yes, daughter," he answered with decision. "We're going to Bannack. Paradise will have to wait."

Hearing this, the parson snorted with disgust. Nora turned to the tall man—he was evidently more than just a friend. "Boone, how about you?" she asked.

"It will have to be Bannack," he answered, a note of softness creeping into his cold voice. "It's our chance for a fortune, Nora."

Thus rebuffed on all sides, the girl seemed to resign herself. "Then, of course I'll have to go, too." Her even tones masked the turbulent emotions which were sweeping her.

The parson had stalked off toward his wagon. But now he turned, and his spindly legs carried him back. "Then by jimmys, I'll go to Bannack, too," he announced, his high voice quavering with emotion. "I dreamed of a farm in Paradise Valley . . . a place where I could live out my last few years in peace. But I'll give that up."

"But there'll be plenty going on to the Valley, Parson. You can go along with them," Ebbert said.

"No. If Boone and Nora go to Bannack, I go, too." He sighed. "I've dreamed and dreamed of marryin' them in their own little home in Paradise Valley. But if it's to be Bannack. . . ." He tossed his hands in a gesture of resignation.

"But Parson. . . ." Nora was on the point of objecting to his sacrifice, perhaps say another minister could be found, but she paused, afraid of hurting the old man's feelings. Then, for the first time she took notice of the three whose story of Bannack gold had disrupted the unified purpose of the group.

Her glance swept over Dutch John, whose lips curled in amusement at the scene, and over Bogey who seemed taken aback by the vigor of her objections, to fasten on Wils. He sat his horse tall and impassive. Although he was the youngest of the trio, there was something in his manner which stamped him as their leader.

"Why couldn't you let us go our way in peace?" she demanded. "Why did you have to come with your story of gold? If you'd waited another day . . . yes, another hour or two, we'd never have met." Her eyes darted fire. "See what your news has done? It's split our group. Before you came, all they wanted were homes. Now they're mad with lust for gold. . . ."

Without giving him time for an answer, she swung her horse around, cracked her quirt, went galloping to the far end of the train.

But the last glimpse Wils caught was not of eyes which darted fire: it was the face of a girl whose lip trembled in disappointment.

Dutch John whistled admiringly. "Ain't she the scorpion?" he asked.

II

Fewer than a third of the party held to the original purpose. Grimly, perhaps a little regretfully, these drew their wagons from the line and headed northeastward in the direction of a low flank of the Bitterroots, around which lay their valley.

After they were gone, Matthew Ebbert strode over to where Wils, Bogey, and Dutch John had dismounted and now sat in the sagebrush eating jerky.

"Any of you men ever been to Bannack?" he asked.

Wils shook his head. "There wasn't any such place as Bannack when I came over the Lemhi Pass last fall."

"But do you know how to get there?"

"Sure. Just follow up Birch Creek here. You drop over the divide and follow the Lemhi River until you see the pass toward the east. Bannack is on the other side . . . maybe forty miles."

"How do you recognize the pass when you reach it?"

Wils shrugged. "Just have to know, that's all. Maybe I could draw out sort of a map."

"No. I'd rather have you guide us."

Wils looked questioningly at his companions.

"We haven't much money," Ebbert went on. "But we have plenty of supplies. There are many supply wagons loaded with flour, and with grains which we intended to use for seed. We'll give you an equal share."

Dutch John rubbed his hands. He knew the supplies would be worth a fortune in the new-born settlement that winter. "An equal share, hey?"

"It would be more than you'd need for an entire year . . . even if you had a family."

"Go ahead, Wils," John urged.

"All right, we'll guide you," Wils answered.

Gleeful at this, Dutch John sawed off a large chunk of jerky with his bowie knife, poked it in his cheek—with his thumb there to let it soak like a dried-out chew of tobacco. "Share and share alike is my motto. Once we get to Bannack, we'll divide the stores up equal!"

A horse kicked dirt as it was pulled to a stop. "What's that about dividing the supplies?" a man asked.

Wils looked up and recognized Boone Logan. A second later, six others came to a stop behind him. There was something about these which set them apart from the honest homeseekers who made up the bulk of the party.

Ebbert answered, "I've offered these men equal shares in the supplies provided they guide us to Bannack."

Even though he maintained a poker face, there was no doubting Boone Logan's opinion. "We can get along quite well without them," he said coldly. "If they're short on provisions, load their pack-horses with flour, beans, whatever they want. But no more of this about guides."

"Have you ever been there?" Ebbert demanded.

"Where?"

"To Bannack . . . or over Lemhi Pass?"

Logan hesitated. "No. But two of the men here have been to Fort Benton . . . Mex and Jodel."

Ebbert turned to them. "Have you ever been over Lemhi?"

"Mex" and "Jodel" exchanged glances. Then one of them spoke up—it was Jodel, a greasy-looking man with a heavy, truculent face. "No. We went east of the mountains, from Fort Laramie."

"We need someone who has traveled the pass." Ebbert's manner of saying this indicated his mind had been made up.

Boone Logan turned pale around the lips, and his hand clutched the reins until his knuckles turned white. But he said no more. After meeting the elder man's steady glance for a moment, he cracked his quirt sharply across his horse's belly, started off at a lope, his followers at his heels.

Dutch John, thoughtfully masticating his jerky, watched him go. "That fellow's right nasty," he commented.

"Boone Logan is my future son-in-law," Ebbert said with a note of disapproval of John's opinion. But John was undismayed; he picked a string of jerky from between his teeth with the point of his bowie, and then answered.

"I don't give a damn if he's your blood brother. I'll call a snake by his true name whenever I run onto him."

Ebbert turned away, his face troubled.

The wagons, Bannack bound, soon started. All afternoon they creaked up the valley of the Birch, pausing only after the sun dropped from sight beyond the Lemhis. Wils, Bogey, and Dutch John were just cleaning up after the evening meal when a girl appeared in the firelight. It was Nora Ebbert.

"I'm sorry I lost my temper this afternoon," she said simply.

Wils was a little ill at ease, not used to having women—and especially ones as beautiful as this—insert themselves in the light of his campfire. He studied her for a moment as she stood there, her eyes mysterious in night shadow, the firelight golden in her hair. "That's all right," he said with one of his best smiles.

She went on: "It wasn't your fault the wagon train split. It was the fault of those who would rather seek gold than something more worthwhile." Then she dropped the subject. "How far is it to Bannack?"

"About three days on horseback, but much longer for the wagon train. We'll be lucky to get there in ten days. You can never tell about October."

"You mean it might storm. What then?"

"Then we'll probably be on this side until spring."

"Are you through with your supper?"

"Yes."

"Will you come to our wagon? Father sent for you."

The two walked across the piece of ground which the wagons circled. It was dark now and the wagon tops shone ghostly white in the flickering light of a dozen campfires. There was talking and laughter. And someone played a banjo. It seemed strange and unreal to Wils—this center of light and sound in the midst of the vast wilderness, a wilderness which seemed to crowd in with the night. As if in recognition of his thoughts, the wilderness intruded even more closely when a coyote howled on the hillside.

"Is there just you and your father?" Wils asked.

"Yes. Mother died four years ago, in Missouri. I have a brother in California. Father and I left this spring for Paradise Valley. Boone . . . Mr. Logan . . . had been there. He told us about it."

"It's too bad we had to spoil your plans."

Nora smiled. "One never knows what is for the best. . . ."

Matthew Ebbert had questions concerning the route. They talked for half an hour. When Wils started back to camp, he was accosted by Boone Logan.

"Come in, Fleming," Boone said cordially, motioning toward his wagon.

Wils followed the big man up the stairs which were dropped down from the high wagonbox. Inside, Logan dug a live ember from the stove, held it to the wick of a tallow lamp which he blew to flame. He motioned his visitor to a chair, eased himself to the edge of the bunk.

"I'm surprised you'd want to be slowed up on your trip to Bannack, Fleming. Why don't you go on and leave us? Get there before the good placer ground is all gone. We'll find the way, provided you leave us instructions."

Wils had expected something like this. But why was the man so determined they should not go along? Surely it was not the share in the provisions—Logan himself had offered to load their pack-horses with food. Perhaps it was something more personal, but Wils dismissed the idea.

"I don't mind being held up a few days," he said. "I'd hate to see this outfit start the wrong trail through the Bitterroots. If it blizzards, which is likely, there'll be no track to follow. And there are plenty of false breaks which lead only to blank walls three thousand feet high."

"Don't be swayed too far by your charity." A sarcastic note had found its way into Logan's voice. "I've had no trouble guiding this train up till now."

Wils fastened Logan with his cool gray eyes. "Why are you so damned set on getting rid of me?" he asked in an even tone.

"Maybe it's because, as guide, I don't care to have my position undermined."

But his words did not ring true. Suspicious of Logan from the start, Wils now became convinced that there was something underhand, perhaps sinister, afoot. For some reason, a vision of Nora flashed in his mind. It was distasteful to associate her with this man—her future husband. What, he wondered, had prompted her to accept Logan's offer of marriage—but true, he was handsome, and a man of the world.

"I've accepted Ebbert's offer, and I'll stick to it," Wils said.

"Maybe this will help you alter your decision." Logan pulled a weighty buckskin bag from his jacket pocket. It jingled when he tossed it in Wils's lap. "Couple hundred there," he commented.

The action was unexpected. Wils allowed the money to lay for a moment; then the full import of it appeared to him. So Logan expected him to sell out for this poke of gold coin! He threw it to the floor at Logan's feet, stood up.

"I'll get my gold in Bannack," he said coldly.

Logan's eyes narrowed until they became slits, cutting his deeply tanned face. The veins stood out on his temples. He crouched forward, buckskin tightening around the tensed muscles at his shoulders. Wils watched the hand which hovered for a moment over the pistol butt. Then Logan relaxed a little and spoke.

"I advise you and your friends to be gone when morning comes, Fleming. And if you mention this little episode to Ebbert, or to Miss Ebbert. . . ." He did not complete the threat, at least with words, but his fingers significantly tapped his gun butt.

Wils answered, "I intend to guide this train to Bannack. As for the Ebberts, I'll tell them what I choose."

Their eyes met for a few seconds, then Wils turned, leaped down from the wagon, and hunted out the low-flickering campfire where Dutch John, become mellow in the early autumn starlight, played low and dolefully on a mouth organ while Bogey sang:

> Oh, I'm goin' to Orofino
> That's the place for me,
> I'm goin' to Fraser River
> With the washbowl on my knee.

The train started with the dawn. Soon left behind were the barren, sage-dotted lava plains. Here the country was greener and more rugged.

Boone Logan kept to himself during the morning. At noon he spoke briefly with Matthew Ebbert, and after that he and his six companions—Mex, Jodel and the rest—disappeared until nightfall. "Scouting for Blackfeet," someone said, although this was not hostile country.

The next day also passed uneventfully, but Wils did not relax his caution. He knew Logan would sooner or later attempt to carry out his threat.

On both afternoons Wils and his two companions rode ahead to choose the train's campsite. On the third afternoon Wils was ready to start, but neither Bogey nor Dutch John was to be found—they were behind somewhere catching trout for supper. So Wils set out alone.

After traveling several miles he caught sight of a rider out ahead. He urged his horse to a gallop. It was Nora Ebbert.

"Hello, Wils," she smiled. "Looking for a campsite?"

He nodded, was about to say something when a herd of deer caught Nora's eye. They grazed on a hillside a short distance from the trail.

"Look!" she exclaimed. "A white deer."

They reined in. "Looks like an albino," Wils said.

They headed up the hillside, but the deer, alarmed at their approach, started off on little stiff jumps and were soon hidden from view by a rise of ground. When the riders gained this point, the animals had found shelter in a patch of evergreen.

It had been a greater climb than Wils or Nora had imagined. They paused to rest their mounts after the steep ascent. From this vantage point could be surveyed a great, undulating expanse of hilly country. The wagon train was not yet in sight, but from that direction came a group of swiftly riding horsemen.

"Wonder who they could be?" Wils pondered as he watched their approach.

The girl shook her head. "Maybe they're strangers."

"No. They're from our outfit. They're in too big a hurry to be going far, and besides, they have no pack animals."

A troubled expression knit Nora's brow when they started down the hillside.

At the trail, Wils asked: "Who are those men of Boone Logan's?"

"Men of Boone's. . . . ?" Nora seemed upset by the question. She glanced sharply at Wils, then away.

"Yes. Jodel and that bunch. They aren't like the rest of the party."

After a moment's silence she answered: "We met them at Fort Laramie. Some of them Boone knew . . . he had been out here before, you know, along the Overland Trail to California."

"Were they planning to live at the valley?"

"I don't suppose so. Boone said we would go through Blackfoot country, so we would need them to scout for war parties."

Wils dropped the subject. For the next couple of miles the girl seemed preoccupied with some problem of her own.

The trail now led through a flat which was spongy with water. Wils examined it doubtfully. "Wagons can't get through there. Too heavily loaded." He looked for a route on higher ground. A hillside invited his inspection. As he pointed his horse up the climb, he did not notice how near the riders had approached from down the valley.

A shot cracked. The wind from a bullet fanned his cheek, flung up a shower of rock fragments where it plowed the dirt.

Wils turned his horse. More guns spat out. Bullets kicked up dirt on every side. Down the hill his horse plunged. A jutting flank of the hill gave temporary protection. He looked around for Nora; she was still in the swampy depression and hidden from the horsemen.

"What is it?" she cried.

But he had no time to explain. He lashed his horse to a run, motioned for the girl to follow. In a few seconds she was abreast of him.

The protecting flank of hill was soon left behind. Before them was a broad spread of land destitute of protection. Two wind-sculptured fingers of sandstone stood out from the rimrock eight hundred yards to the right. Toward these they spurred their horses.

The spat of gunfire from behind rose over the clatter and thud of hoofs. A bullet cuffed the ground ahead. Another, striking a rock, droned hornet-like as it glanced away.

Wils unholstered his pistol. It was a new type, throwing a slug no more than half the size of the conventional Navy Colt, but it carried like a rifle. He was tempted to risk a shot. The riders were grouped, making a good target. He fired. One of the horses faltered, drove nose downward to earth, its four feet pointed skyward for a moment, and the rest was obscured in dust.

Suddenly the shots and the pursuit stopped. Once gaining the security of the rocks, Wils and Nora looked back.

The riders had formed a group and sat looking in their direction. A hundred yards in their rear the fallen horse was a still dark spot in the crisp autumn-hued grass. And from it a man came limping.

"Too bad I got the horse," Wils muttered. He looked across at the girl. Her breast rose and fell excitedly beneath her buckskin blouse. Her hair had escaped from beneath the sombrero; windblown, it hung down her back in loose brown masses which reached the saddle cantle. Her eyes danced with excitement and anger.

"Those . . . highwaymen!"

"I doubt that they're highwaymen," Wils answered. He had an idea of their identity. "I wonder why they quit following so suddenly?"

Wils shook his head, watched the riders who picked up their unmounted comrade and started back in the direction from whence they came.

"My hair," Nora laughed. She started tucking it back beneath her sombrero. "It got loose down there. Strange thing, as soon as it did, they stopped shooting. It must be a charm."

"Yes," Wils smiled. "It may have been more of a charm than you think."

From a distance, he estimated, they would mistake her for a man. They probably thought her to be old Bogey who wore buckskin, rode a bay horse too. But Bogey's hair was cropped off at the collar. Nora's long tresses flying behind would be instantly recognized.

The two circled the rimrock until they sighted the train. It was then near sundown, so they signaled the lead team, and the wagons creaked into a circle. Soon a dozen campfires sent pillars of smoke into the chill autumn air.

III

The trout which Bogey and Dutch John had snared from the creek tasted excellent after their dreary deermeat diet. While Wils ate, he told of his experiences of the afternoon.

"It's that blasted Logan and his gang!" Bogey's voice shook with anger.

"Yep!" Dutch John, who took man's perfidy as a matter of course, was inclined to a practical view. "It would be a pretty rough job cleanin' 'em out. I reckon I'll have to treat this Logan to a pistol ball. You know what the fee-loso-pher said: 'When the head is gone. . . .' "

"That will be our last resort," said Wils.

"Last resort!" John paused in the course of taking a great bite from the boiled trout he held in his fingers. "Down in Californy, where I hail from, killin' was the first resort."

Their conversation was interrupted by the appearance of Matthew Ebbert. "Can I speak to you a minute?" he asked of Wils.

Ebbert led the way to his wagon. "Nora told me what happened," he said. "Who were those men, Wils?"

"Couldn't see their faces."

"But you have an opinion."

"Sure. I think they were those men of Logan's."

Ebbert walked for a while in worried silence. There was no doubt he too suspected them. "Boone was with the train all afternoon."

"But his men . . . Jodel and the rest?"

"We aren't sure. We mustn't condemn anyone without proof. You're likely to meet highwaymen along the trail any time." But Ebbert's attempt to palliate the circumstance was weak.

"By the way, why was Logan so set against me joining the train in the first place?"

"He's a strange man in some ways. It might be . . . well, he has a jealous disposition."

"Jealous?"

"Don't misunderstand me. I'm not doubting my daughter. But it might seem to him that Nora is paying you too many favors."

"Then you believe he was at the bottom of this thing?"

"I don't say that. I don't even believe it. He's a man of importance in Missouri. Comes from one of the best families. He was educated for the bar. He wouldn't stoop to . . . murder."

They were now at Ebbert's wagon. The stovepipe thrust through the canvas roof belched smoke, and from the doorway was wafted the odor of baking bread.

"Have a bite with us?" Ebbert asked.

Wils accepted with alacrity. Inside, Nora was just placing the loaves to cool. She smiled when he entered.

There were two others in the wagon. One was a heavy-handed teamster named Ceiver; he had belligerent black whiskers. The other was his wife, Prudence. She was also muscular and belligerent.

"Heard about the trouble you had this afternoon," Ceiver growled, "and, if you want my opinion, we made a poor choice in a man to guide us. We should have found one without so many enemies."

"Now, Tom," Ebbert temporized. "There's just a possibility we're harboring the enemies right here in our own group."

But Ceiver scorned the suggestion. "I know what you mean by that. But you have no cause to suspect them. Why would those boys start out to kill Fleming? Or Nora? No. It's some personal feud of his own."

Wils had taken this much in silence, but with mounting anger. He started to address Ceiver, when Prudence cut him off.

"Don't pay no heed to my man there. He's bull-headed as a por-key-pine in August." She turned on her husband who obviously quailed beneath her glance. "Ceiver!" she boomed. "Keep your bird-cage shut. This young man's here as a guest." Then to Wils: "Prudence Ceiver's the name. Glad to meet wi' ye."

They shook hands. Her palm was hard and big-boned like a man's.

When Wils returned to camp neither Dutch John nor Bogey was in sight. But shouting voices attracted his attention to the right, beyond a small knoll where a wagon had been pulled some distance from the circle. He imagined hearing Bogey's voice.

Gripped by an unexplainable foreboding, he started over to investigate. His walk soon quickened to a run. He made the top of the knoll, burst around the wagon. And there was old Bogey—a Bogey with blood streaming from the corners of his mouth; it had run down his chin and saturated the front of his buckskin shirt. He was on hands and knees, and standing over him was Boone Logan.

"Bogey!" Wils shouted, flinging aside the men who stood watching.

Logan turned on him. Wils pulled up, dropped his hand to his pistol, but something rammed him in the back. "Stick 'em up," a harsh voice sounded in his ear.

Wils turned his head, glimpsed the leering, greasy face of Jodel.

"Ever see a man shot through the spine?" Jodel growled with a lopsided smile which exposed a row of snaggled yellow teeth. "They just lay and kick, like a chicken with his head cut off."

Wils could do nothing but obey. He lifted his hands. Boone Logan, who had watched this, smiled coldly and turned his attention once again to the old man who was just struggling to his feet.

Bogey made an effort to put up his fists and fight back. But his guard was flecked away. Logan swung a terrific right-hand smash. It caught Bogey high on the cheek; he staggered as if hit by a sledge, would have gone down had not his assailant stepped in and seized him by the hair. Logan thrust him back on his wobbly legs, then drove another blow. It made a sickening thump when it landed— like a hammer striking a pumpkin. When Bogey went to the ground, he struck across the extending wagon tongue. He lay there as if his back were broken.

"Logan, I'll kill you for this," Wils said.

"You aren't in a very good position to talk of killing," Logan smiled.

With a brutal laugh at this, Jodel thrust the barrel of his pistol against Wils's spine with a force which, coming unexpectedly, all but knocked him from his feet.

Logan nudged Bogey with the toe of his expensive boot. "That's what happens to those who come around and make threats. Take him back to your camp." Then he turned and started toward the circle of wagons.

Wils, still covered by Jodel's revolver, gathered the old man in his arms and carried him away. At camp he found Dutch John who had returned after picketing horses. Wils told briefly what had happened. By that time, Bogey had started to come around. When Wils looked up, John was gone.

On glimpsing signs of approaching consciousness from Bogey, John had strolled leisurely in the direction of Logan's camp. The twilight was deepening, but he could still see well enough. Over there, six men had gathered around a newly kindled campfire. John approached quietly, sat on the wagon tongue watching for several seconds before anyone noticed his arrival.

"Hello, boys," he said cordially. "See you beat up on old Bogey. That's somethin' I been longin' to see done for quite some spell."

They scrutinized him doubtfully. "You mean you're glad to see him beat up?" Jodel croaked.

"That's right. We ain't travelin' together anymore." Dutch John's disreputable beard parted to expose his teeth in a lopsided smile. "Surprised, ain't you?"

"What do you want?" one asked suspiciously.

"Reckoned maybe I'd jine up with you."

They looked at one another questioningly.

"I'd be right handy," he hastened to assure them. "For instance, I might give you a few tips on pumpin' lead. You was right awkward in that little affair this afternoon. . . ."

"Hush up!" Mex, the dark one, said, looking off toward the other wagons.

From that direction someone was approaching. It proved to be Tom Ceiver, the man Wils had met in Ebbert's wagon a few minutes before. Ceiver nodded shortly to the six near the fire, looked suspiciously at Dutch John who still roosted on the wagon tongue.

"Why hush up?" John asked. He gave the impression of carelessness, but his eyes watched narrowly every move the others made. Then he explained to Ceiver. "I was just ruminatin' with the boys on what a botchy job they made of that shootin' this afternoon. Now for instance. . . ." he nodded to Jodel. "You, Jodel! Step over there away from the rest. About a step or two more. There. That's fine. Now I'll show you a little gun trick I learned in Californy."

Jodel was nervous, but John spoke soothingly. "Don't hop around so much. Stand real still, it works better that-a-way."

Then, with scarcely a perceptible movement, with a hitch of his shoulder only, it seemed, the Navy pistol flicked from its holster. A report split the twilight air. Jodel sagged. Without a word, or a movement of his hands, he pitched head foremost in the dust. The bullet had found his heart.

Such was their consternation at this act, none of the others spoke a word. They drew back instinctively.

Dutch John held the gun muzzle up, blew the smoke from the barrel. "You see, it was right easy. Nice clean job. Californy style. If any of you boys want more lessons, just say the word."

John spat distantly at the campfire. Gun in hand he stepped sidewise around the wagon. There he leaned almost double and watched the group from underneath, but none seemed to have stomach for a fight.

"That was murder! Plain out-and-out murder!" It was Ceiver's outraged voice. "He won't get away with this, I'm telling you . . . !"

"What was that shot?" Wils asked when Dutch John returned to camp.

"That? It was me givin' our friend Jodel a lesson in the fine art of pistol shootin'."

"What do you mean?"

"I just killed Jodel."

"By crackies, I was aimin' on gettin' him myself," Bogey said through swollen lips. He was propped against a bedroll, unable to move about.

"Yes, sir, nice and clean a job as I ever turned in . . . 'less maybe it was that guard I picked off the Yuba coach that time. A-course the guard was tougher because he had me dodgin' buckshot." John set to loading powder, ball, and cap in his pistol's empty chamber. He took considerable time about it, then minutely inspected each load in his other gun. One cap failed to please him, so he inserted another one. "Can't be too careful about these things," he muttered.

"I suppose all hell will break loose now," Wils said. "But I guess it doesn't make much difference. I made a promise to Logan when I was over there with a gun in my back, and it's a promise I aim to keep."

"Now don't go off half-cocked with your powder wet," John cautioned. "I'll get him when the time comes."

Wils shook his head. John fished a gold piece from his jeans pocket. "Tell you what, I'll flip you for him."

But Wils wasn't listening. His attention was drawn to the people who were running to the place where Jodel lay dead. "There's likely to be trouble," he said. "Maybe a lot more trouble than we cut out for ourselves."

"Um-m." Dutch John pocketed the gold piece. His eyes grew shifty. Evidently he had not forgotten a similar group which became "the law" over in Placerville. "That's somethin' else they have over in Californy," he muttered, "them pesky Californy collars."

John went quickly over to where his horse was staked, ran hand over hand up the picket rope until he grasped the halter. He led the animal to where his saddle lay, threw it on, pulled tight the cinch. Almost before Wils or Bogey realized what he was about, he was mounted and signaling farewell.

"I'll be seein' you in Bannack," he grinned.

"Wait! If you're goin', we're goin' too." Bogey attempted to get up. But Wils restrained him. "It's no use, Bogey. You can't travel tonight."

John snapped his quirt, and the horse started off toward the trail. "There he goes now!" someone shouted. A dozen men came running. A rifle cracked. The horse stumbled, went to his knees, sent John pitching over his head to the ground. He lay stunned for a fatal moment, attempted to regain his feet, but they had borne down on him.

"Stick 'em up, we got you covered," Ceiver shouted.

Wils ran to the scene. He elbowed his way through the men who obstructed him, tried to speak, but no one would listen.

"Here's his pal, let's string him up too." It was one of Boone Logan's five remaining henchmen.

"String 'em both up," a wagoner cried.

"Get a rope!"

A rough hand was laid on Wils's shoulder, spun him around. He jerked away. With a continuing movement, he whipped his pistol from the holster, backed away. The mob fell silent—hesitated.

"Release him!" Wils said, motioning toward Dutch John with the muzzle. But he noticed the eyes which had been on him now shifted to something in his rear. He dared not glance around. A footstep cracked the dry grass behind him.

"Drop the gun, Fleming." It was Logan's cool voice. "It wouldn't hurt my feelings to have to pull this trigger."

Wils dropped the gun, slowly raised his arms, turned. He noticed Ebbert a few steps at Logan's rear, and running to catch up came Nora and Prudence Ceiver.

"What's going on here?" Ebbert demanded.

"This man killed Jodel," one of the wagoners answered, pointing to Dutch John. "We're going to hang him."

Ebbert raised his hand in a gesture which asked for coolness and deliberation.

Tom Ceiver spoke up: "A murderer deserves to get hung. And this murder was in cold blood. I saw it." He advanced on Ebbert, his black whiskers bristling.

"I'm still running this wagon train," Ebbert said coolly. "And there'll be no lynching. If there's anyone hanged, it will be after a fair trial."

"All right, let's hang him after a fair trial," Ceiver answered.

The word "trial" seemed to make Logan coldly furious. He whirled on Ebbert, glowered down on him. "What damned women's talk is that? String these two fellows up!" Then he caught sight of Nora and said no more.

"I don't know what's in the back of your mind, Logan." Ebbert's use of the name "Logan" instead of "Boone" called attention to the rift which was growing between them. "You may think it's time to take command. But I don't. I'll do the ordering here just as long as these men here want me instead of you." He turned, faced the group. Not one pair of eyes challenged him. He nodded toward Dutch John. "Bring him to the wagon." Then to Wils: "Take your gun, but don't cause us any more trouble."

IV

A great bonfire crackled beside Ebbert's wagon. He presided from a chair which had been moved down for him. At one side ranged six wagoners who were chosen as a jury. Dutch John, apparently but little perturbed, sat in the center of things, chewing tobacco and spitting at the fire.

The trial had not yet begun, but Parson Joe had seized the opportunity to speak his mind. "See what happened when you chose gold instead of Paradise Valley? A killin' already, and now probably a hangin'. The next thing we'll be fightin' amongst ourselves . . . you mark my words. It ain't followin' the Lord, that's what it ain't. Sometimes I think it must have been the old boy with the horns hisself which sent these three fellows into our midst to lead us from the true course . . . to send us off to this Gommorrah of a city called Bannack. . . ."

"Why'd you come, Parson?" one of the wagoners asked with a laugh.

"It wasn't for the gold. I'd ten times rather have gone to the valley. I come because here was where I was needed the most."

"Court will come to order," Ebbert said. "We're here to try a man for murder."

The "trial" took about ten minutes. The jury seemed not swayed by the testimony of Logan's henchmen; what influenced them most heavily was the word of Tom Ceiver, for he was one of their own number. He damned the crime as a black one.

"It was trickery, that's what it was. He shot Jodel down without giving him a chance. If it had been a fair and square gun duel, it would be different. But this wasn't. I say, hang him."

Then Wils told his story, and Bogey recounted the beating he had received at Logan's hand. But Logan stood up and denied everything.

"I never struck this man. He got bruised up in a fight over at his own camp. Now they've thought it over and are trying to pin it on me in hopes it will win sympathy for that murderer there. A fine story!" He laughed and most of the jury laughed too. But one person who did not smile was Nora Ebbert. She looked grimly into the crackling fire, and her jaw was set.

"Well, boys, what's your decision?"

The jury did not hesitate. "Hang him," they chorused.

Parson Joe, who had anticipated the verdict, and perhaps inwardly applauded it, stepped forward as nimbly as his shaky old legs would carry him. It was a great moment in his ministerial career and he intended to make the most of it. He addressed Dutch John in sepulchral tone: "You are about to meet your Maker, and I'm willin' to give spiritual assistance and succor in your hour of need."

Dutch John grinned at the parson, aimed a spurt of tobacco juice at the fire. "Reckon it's a little late for me to be doin' much prayin', Parson."

"It's never too late to come into the fold, brother. It says right in the Good Book: the Lord is a skillion times happier over gettin' back one single lost sheep which has strayed than in keepin' all the rest of his flock. 'For the last shall be first and. . . .' "

"I ain't strayed from the fold. I ain't ever been thar," John guffawed. "Besides, Parson, I ain't a sheep, I'm a wolf."

"Is there a tree hereabouts?" someone asked.

John turned from the parson, directing his attention to the speaker. "Do you know how to tie the knot? I reckon I'll have to teach you Missouri farmers how it's done. Them Californy collars is tricky affairs."

"We'll tie it to fit your neck. We may not know much about a Californy collar, but we're right handy with Pike County cravats guaranteed to wear a lifetime."

"By the way, where is a tree?" Ceiver asked.

The question struck everyone silent. Indeed, where was a tree? Along the creek were willows, and here and there a few spindly quaking asps. These wouldn't do for a hanging. Besides, it was now dark. Stringing a man up would not be as easy as it first sounded. They pondered, spoke together in low tones. "How about it, Ebbert?" one asked.

"We'll wait till morning." Then to Ceiver: "You've taken lots of interest in this thing. I'll make it your responsibility to watch the prisoner until sunup."

They decided to keep John in Ceiver's wagon. Prudence left to stay with Nora for the night. Over a bench which sat by one wall they tossed a quilt; there Dutch John, tied hand and foot, was told he could sit or lie as pleased him. There seemed little chance for him to escape from his bonds but, to make doubly sure, two guards were posted at the door of the wagon, while Ceiver himself flopped down on the bed inside. Thus Dutch John was between them.

The bonfire slowly died to a bed of ghostly blue flicker. A cold wind, reminder of approaching winter, sprang from the north. It bent down the dry grasses, moaned complainingly around the sides of the wagon. The two guards outside pulled their jackets more closely about them, and finally they crawled inside. Ceiver snored.

At his own camp, Wils lay watching the moon climb high from the jagged horizon. Two hours passed before he crawled quietly from his bed. Bogey made a movement to follow, but Wils restrained him. "I'll get along better alone," he said.

He made a wide circle, then slowly crept toward the wagon where John was held prisoner. Up above the moon shone intermittently. He advanced only while it was hidden. Whenever its edge broke from behind the cloud, he would lie flat in the grass. Thus he advanced until a bare forty yards separated him from the wagon. The moon brightened; he watched, but there was no movement near the wagon, no sign of the guards.

A cloud sailed over. In the moment of darkness he rose on hands and knees preparatory to going closer. He would chance it all the way to the wagon this time.

But he stopped. Quickly he dropped flat again. Someone was there. He could make out a vague shape—a head and shoulders which, like a shadow, moved along the canvas wagon top.

For many minutes he lay still watching. But no sound came to his ears, and the shadow was not again visible. He began to think his eyes had played him false.

Someone shouted. There followed the thud of running feet. Off in the darkness a horse snorted. It was followed by the sound of galloping hoofs. From beside Ceiver's wagon, several guns cut loose, sending red streaks of flame toward the retreating hoofbeats.

Many voices sounded. "He got away!" were the words on many lips. The question came, "How?" but apparently none could answer.

Wils dared not wait to learn more. What if they should discover him gone from his bed? He ran swiftly back to his camp, pulled off his boots. Even while doing this, someone was approaching from out of the gloom.

Wils asked with feigned drowsiness, "What's the shooting?"

Two men drew near. One recognized him. "The tall one's here," he said.

"How about the other?"

"He's here too."

Wils began pulling on his boots. "You still haven't told me what the shooting was," he complained.

"Yes, what the thunder's going on?" Bogey put in.

"Your pardner got away. Somebody slit the canvas behind him and cut his ropes in two."

Darkness hid the surprise on Wils's face; this had been his own plan. Bogey, of course, still thought Wils had done it.

Someone else approached. "Find them?" By his voice, it was Boone Logan.

"They were here, in bed."

Logan grumbled something and turned away.

The fire was again burning brightly when Wils and Bogey reached the scene. Cursing and pacing back and forth was big Tom Ceiver. "Took my guns, the dirty thief!" Then he spied Wils. "He's the fellow that cut 'em loose. He had plenty of time to get back and play 'possum.

There followed ugly mutterings among the men. "Ought to string 'em up and not wait for morning this time," someone said.

"Hold on!" It was Matthew Ebbert. He was emerging from Ceiver's wagon. "We have no reason to believe that Fleming here had anything to do with it."

Ceiver paused, looked incredulous. "What? No reason? Why, it's as plain as light. Who else would want to cut him loose?"

"Maybe you, Ceiver."

This knocked the breath from the black-whiskered man for a moment "No time to joke," he finally answered.

"I'm not joking."

"Not joking! I never heard anything so ridiculous in my life."

"Then maybe you could explain why your bowie knife was laying on the wagon floor right where Dutch John's ropes were cut?"

In proof of this, Ebbert held the bowie out in the light of the fire. Unusual in design, it had a handle mounted with a young deer's hoof. Many recognized it instantly. Ceiver's jaw sagged. He was too astounded for the moment to deny anything.

His wife's voice cut in, "You sure been a hero tonight, Paw. Not only do you cut him loose, but you furnish him a brace of pistols."

Ignoring Prudence, Ceiver turned on Ebbert. "It's a damned lie. I never cut him loose, and you know it. You're trying to shield somebody. The last time I saw that knife it was sticking in the table top at the back of the wagon."

But few were listening to him now. They still snickered at his wife's words. Off in the shadow, Logan glowered.

Ebbert said, "We'll never settle it tonight, and we'll never catch Dutch John, either . . . not that it makes much difference. I don't imagine he'll bother us anymore. Let's roll in and get some sleep."

As Wils turned toward his camp, he noticed Nora for the first time. She stood at the door of the wagon. Her lips were drawn in a firm line. But when she caught Wils's glance, the line softened, and she smiled.

Bogey spent a poor night. His back pained where it had struck across the wagon tongue. Next morning, when he attempted to ride, his face grew white and he nearly fell to the ground. Nora, who saw him, insisted that he ride in her father's wagon. Reluctantly he accepted. "Shunted off with the women," he sighed as he lay down in Matthew Ebbert's bunk.

Wils discovered that the knife incident had not convinced the wagoners of his innocence. They were cold toward him. He kept to himself at the head end of the train.

At mid-morning they passed over a low divide from where the waters flowed north—north, but not to Bannack. This stream, the headwaters of the Lemhi, was turned away by the snow-burdened Bitterroots, divide of the continent which reared mightily to the east; it flowed westward to join the Salmon—treacherous "River of No Return"—and roar down unconquerable cañons, at last to falter and join placidly with the Snake flowing to the Pacific. Beyond the Bitterroots sprang headwaters of the Gulf-bound Missouri.

In the afternoon Nora joined him. They rode together for several miles without either mentioning the happenings of the previous night.

She asked, "How long before we reach Lemhi Pass?"

"About four days if everything goes right."

"And how long to Bannack?"

He calculated. "Two days more, barring storms."

Storms! Nora looked off at the forbidding mountains with a shudder.

Wils pointed north. "The pass is over there, around that peak . . . though you can't tell it's a pass from here."

"You mean a wagon can get through the mountains there?"

"It can if it hurries." When Wils spoke these ominous words, his eyes were on the black bank of clouds building over the northern horizon.

"Do you suppose Dutch John is beyond the pass already?"

"Perhaps." And after a pause, "I suppose you believe I cut him loose."

Nora shook her head. "No, I don't believe you did it. I thought the question was settled last night."

"You mean Ceiver actually did free him?"

"I prefer to believe that." Nora smiled. "It's handy to believe it."

Wils studied the girl's face, but it told him nothing.

She went on in a musing tone, "Some of the men are a little worried over the prospect of meeting Dutch John when they get to Bannack."

"I suppose you'll marry Boone Logan when you get there. . . ." Wils didn't realize he was saying these words until they had already passed his lips. It was as though his most intimate thoughts had found the power of speech. Nora looked at him with a startled, searching expression, then turned her eyes away. A minute passed. The clack of hoofs on stones and the soft creak of saddle leather were the only sounds that filled the void which these words seemed to have pointed out between them.

Her voice, when she answered, was scarcely audible. "Yes, we are to be married at the end of the trip."

"I gathered as much from things the parson said." Wils tried for a pleasant, perhaps casual tone, but a tremor in his voice informed against him.

Suddenly, impulsively, the girl pulled her horse to a stop, faced about. Her eyes were intense to the point of tears. "Wils! Does it make any difference to you . . . that is . . . oh, I don't know what I'm trying to say!"

She made a move as if to turn her pony towards the train, but Wils grasped the bridle. For a moment he was so near he sensed the warmth of her body—could inhale the fresh redolence of her hair. Their eyes met.

He spoke huskily. "Yes, it makes a lot of difference to me."

His arm reached out as if to grasp her about the waist, but her horse jerked, twisting the bridle free of Wils's fingers. Nora drove her heels to the animal's side, sent it galloping toward the train. Her eyes were turned away when she passed him and her lips were drawn in a thin line. The hint of a sob was catching at her throat.

The coolness which had grown between Matthew Ebbert and Boone Logan had become obvious to all. Preoccupied and serious, Ebbert would joggle along in the high wagon seat, or walk silently beside his mules, while Logan who, until now, had been his frequent companion, spent his time in confidence with first one and then another wagoner. He seemed to have plenty to talk about.

For Wils's part, he took no chance on ambush these days. Never did he ride beyond sight of the train, and after dark he took the precaution to carry his robes away to a secluded spot where Logan's men could not find him while he slept. He had no hankering for a knife between the ribs.

The evening after Wils's conversation with Nora, Matthew Ebbert hunted out his lonely campfire.

"I don't like the feel of this wind," Ebbert said by way of introduction. He wore a homespun shawl as protection against the breeze which, judging from its piercing bite, had been born on snowfields.

"It doesn't feel good," Wils answered laconically—he had faced the uncertainties of Northwestern winters long enough to expect the worst.

"What if the pass gets snowed full?"

Wils shrugged. "Then we'll have to winter at Fort Lemhi."

"And wait until spring?"

"We have plenty of provisions. If some are in a bigger hurry, they might be able to make the pass on horseback."

The lines on Ebbert's face seemed deep tonight, its bold relief accentuated by the fire which flickered alternately light and dim in the cutting wind. Wils guessed there was something in addition to the possibility of blizzard which worried him—and this supposition was strengthened by his next words.

"I'd like to talk to you, Wils . . . something important. But it's too cold here for an old man. We can go to Ceiver's wagon. Prudence and Nora are keeping Bogey company. And Ceiver . . . well, he's not there."

Wils poured water on the fire, then dug it under. It was evergreen country here and the wind might carry lingering embers to the inflammable needles. After the fire had become a steaming heap, he started with Ebbert for the wagon.

It was so dark that neither of them noticed the shadow which lurked a few rods at their rear.

They entered Ceiver's wagon and closed the flap. It was draughty cold, darker, even, than outside. Ebbert felt around for the little iron stove, but the fire had long been dead.

Wils asked, "Want me to run over to your wagon for a light?"

"No. I'd rather you wouldn't. No use advertising our being here. It would only worry them more than they are already."

Ebbert struck flint on steel. After several unsuccessful attempts a spark took hold and the tinder flared. He applied it to the wick of the tallow lamp. The interior of the wagon became visible in the smoky-yellow light—flickering light, for the flame bellied as if each flare would be its last as the wind sought out a hundred crannies for entrance.

Ebbert started in his tired voice. "Things haven't been going too well. You have probably noticed Logan's confidential talks with the men: he's been spreading it around that you released Dutch John and the two of you . . . are planning an ambush."

"So that's what he's been saying!"

"It was only tonight I learned from Ceiver what it was. Many believe him . . . even Ceiver."

"Ceiver's always been suspicious of me."

"You see the position in which it places me."

Wils pondered a moment. "Just one question. Do *you* believe it?"

"No. I've always trusted you."

"How does Logan say this ambush of mine is to be carried out?"

"He says you won't lead us to Lemhi Pass at all. Instead, you will lead us along some blind trail . . . one which allows no retreat . . . and there Dutch John and his gang will kill us all. After that, the train and supplies will be taken on to Bannack and sold for a fortune."

"Apparently I have it well planned. Well, what do you suggest?"

Ebbert shook his head. "It's not easy. I can't see Logan's purpose in spreading such a story. He admits he's never been through the country, and yet he wants to guide us. I hate to say this, Wils, but the men won't follow you much farther."

"What does Logan suggest for me, the rope?"

"Yes. And he's found support . . . with Ceiver, for instance. They say, 'If we let him go, won't he ride ahead and lead the gang back on us?' "

"Nice fellow, Logan. He has ideas. I wonder. . . ." Wils pondered the uncertain flame of the tallow lamp. In the interim the wind moaned drearily, set to flapping the loose ends of canvas, made the wagon shake with interrupted rhythm on its leather springs. Wils shook his head, evidently in dismissal of some thought he had not put in words.

Ebbert said, "It's unsafe for you here another day. Tonight there's a meeting in Donovan's wagon. In fact, it's going on now."

"Weren't you invited?"

"No. They didn't ask me because they know how I stand."

"It appears Logan is taking over the command."

"Yes."

"So I'd better leave tonight?"

"It's the only safe way."

"I'm not looking for a safe way."

"Perhaps not, but you can't guide us if you're dead."

Wils smiled. "No, only in spirit."

"I'd prefer you in the flesh. Now here's my plan . . . but first, how far is it to Lemhi Pass?"

"Maybe two days for the train."

"No, by horseback."

"Six, maybe seven hours."

"Good. I'll ride there with you tonight. We'll start now. Then I'll have time to return and guide the trail. You can go on to Bannack."

"But how about Bogey? He still can't ride."

"He'll be safe, I believe. None of the men are suspicious of him."

"Very well, I'll take you to the pass. Once there you can't get off the trail except in this direction." Wils pointed straight down. "One thing more . . . the provisions. . . ."

Ebbert paused. Some sound outside the wagon attracted his attention. Wils, too, heard it. They both listened. It was an indescribable sound, more motion, it seemed, than anything else—as if some weight had been placed at one side of the wagon, interrupting, for a second, its rhythmical shaking. For a moment only the moaning wind, the fluttering canvas, and the soft creak of the leather springs filled the void of silence.

The elder man smiled, relaxed. "Thought I heard something. Guess this business is getting me a bit jumpy. But what I was. . . ."

The sentence was never completed. Close, almost in the room, a gun crashed. Ebbert, struck, spun on the balls of his feet. His hands clutched the table edge. Then he slumped to the floor.

By reflex, Wils whipped out his gun, spun toward the opening at the front of the wagon from whence the shot had come. But the killer was gone. Wils had no opportunity to fire a shot in return.

A second later Prudence Ceiver rushed in. "What was . . . ." she started, and her eyes fell on Ebbert's still form. She pulled back in shocked horror. Then she stared at the gun in Wils's hand. He guessed the thought in her mind.

"It wasn't me. Somebody shot through the front."

Nora Ebbert followed Prudence through the door. She looked, for a moment, at her father. Then, without uttering a word, she dropped to her knees at his side. After several seconds she whispered his name.

Outside someone shouted, "It's in Ceiver's wagon." A moment later the wagon seemed full of men. They pushed to glimpse the dead man on the floor. Nora, oblivious to them, stared at his still form and kept repeating his name.

Someone forced his way through the crowd. It was Boone Logan. He lifted the girl to her feet. "Nora, you'd better go," he said softly. Then to Prudence, "Take her to the wagon." The men made way for the two women as they left. Logan turned, pointed an accusing finger at Wils. "Grab that man. He's the murderer."

"I never killed Ebbert," Wils answered evenly. "He was shot from outside . . . through that opening."

Ceiver came forward. "Let me examine your gun. If there's an empty chamber, we'll know you're the man."

Wils's mind raced over past events. He had fired one shot during the trip—the day he and Nora were pursued by the six riders. With a shock it came to him that he had never reloaded the empty chamber.

But Logan was unaware of this. He cut in, "No use of looking at his gun. He's had time to reload it."

Wils's hopes rose. Would Boone Logan unintentionally be his salvation? But no. The others were all looking expectantly at the gun. He must act, and act quickly.

He made a bluff at it: "All right, Ceiver, I'd be glad to have you examine my gun." He stepped forward as if to offer it butt first, for examination. In doing this, his step carried him opposite the slit in the canvas through which Dutch John had gained freedom, a slit now loosely sewed together. He hurled himself shoulder first at the spot. There was a rending of cloth, and within the second he was on the ground outside. He leaped to his feet, slipped away in the darkness.

Men fell over one another rushing from the wagon. Someone fired at random off in the darkness.

Swiftly but silently, Wils circled the camp. A deeper shadow ahead marked a grove of evergreens by the creek where he had moved his bed intending to spend the night safe from Logan's treachery. It was so dark he could see scarcely a yard ahead. His feet groped down a rock-strewn incline. Nearby he could hear the creek rolling over boulders. Something seized his feet; tripped him. A picket rope. Here was a piece of fortune! Hand over hand he ran down the rope until his hand reached a horse's halter. He led the animal away.

The general form of the country was now emerging as his eyes grew more accustomed to the darkness. Off there were the rough outlines of the hills, and just ahead the deep blackness of the evergreen grove near the creek. He led the horse into the grove, saddled it, quickly rolled together a robe and a piece of jerky and tied these behind the saddle. Then, mounting, he gave the horse rein to pick his way up the creek.

From the camp came a medley of excited voices. The voices were angry, but any attempt at pursuit was frustrated by the darkness.

That night he did not pause. Morning dawned gray, a subdued light filtered through low-hanging mists. The mountains were close now. Evergreen branches frequently slapped at him as he rode along. Towards noon he shot a blue grouse which roosted in the low branches of a lodgepole. He paused an hour to roast it; then rode on. By mid-afternoon he was at the gulch through which the trail climbed up towards Lemhi Pass.

Here, at last, he paused to make a decision: should he continue to Bannack, or should he keep watch on the wagon train?

▼

That morning Matthew Ebbert was laid away in a lonely grave beside the trail. Parson Joe stood by the rocky grave and preached a sermon—fervent, though with a brevity demanded by the exigencies of October. Then, leaving a pine slab hopefully reared against the timeless seasons, the train creaked north.

In the excitement, none seemed to have remembered the existence of old Bogey. After the funeral he found himself alone with Nora and Prudence.

"Don't you believe a word about Wils shootin' your paw," he said to the girl. "That boy ain't got a deed like that in his hide."

Nora didn't answer. She did not wish to believe in Wils's guilt either. But what else could she believe?

Bogey could read this thought in her eyes, so he went on, "Of course, I've got no way of provin' just who did commit the murder . . . though I got a pretty close idea. But it couldn't have been Wils."

"Why?" growled Prudence, not unsympathetically.

"Why? Because, first off, Ebbert was the best friend he had in the train. If Wils had wanted to shoot somebody, he'd have chose Logan . . . there'd be some sense in that. Second, if he'd fired that shot . . . mind I say if he had . . . why, he'd have lit out *pronto*. He had the time. He wouldn't have waited with a pistol in his hand."

All this seemed plausible, and for a moment Nora found herself believing it. But there was the fact of Wils's flight, a tacit admission of guilt, which cast doubt on anything Bogey could say.

She asked, "But why did he run away?"

The old man was silent for a moment. "It's got me stumped," he admitted.

"All he needed to do was show his revolver for examination. You said so yourself, Prudence. . . ." Nora, almost in tears, pressed her hand to the elder woman's breast.

Prudence patted her soothingly. "There, there, honey. If it's true, it's best to face it."

"It ain't true," cried Bogey.

"Hush up, you old varmint. Can't you see what you're doin' to this here pore child?"

With a sigh, Bogey lay back in the joggling wagon, gazed thoughtfully at the half-translucent canvas ceiling. Slowly an expression of determination became fixed in his eyes. Later, when Nora had moved up to the driver's seat, he asked, "You had a good look at Ebbert after he was dead, didn't you, Prudence?"

"Sure. Helped lay him out in his last bib and tucker."

"Where did the bullet hit him?"

"Right above the heart."

"Go clean through?"

"Yes."

"Come out lower than where it went in?"

"A bit lower."

"Must have been fired from somewhere up above!"

"I see what you're getting at, but it don't prove a thing. It might be that Ebbert was leaning forward when the bullet hit him. Or it might have glanced from a rib. Besides, Wils was considerably taller."

Bogey grunted, pondered for a moment. He thought: if the bullet was aimed down, and if it passed through Ebbert's body, then it was lodged somewhere in Ceiver's wagon. He asked, "By the way, did you see where the bullet lodged?"

"No!"

"Did you look?"

"A little."

"Hm-m. I'd like powerful well to find that bullet." Bogey sat up with a movement which indicated his invalid days were over, sprained back or not. "Yes sir, I have to find that bullet!"

"What can that prove?"

"Plenty. I can prove it didn't come from Wils's gun."

"But his gun ain't even here."

"Maybe not. But I'll lay gold coin against Jeff Davis greenbacks that Nora remembers it. You see, it wasn't an ordinary Navy Colt like most of the boys carry. It was a new sort of gun; used a one-hundred-fifty grain slug instead of a two-fifty. Had a longer range and a heap smaller bore; more powder and less ball. He bought it off a drummer in Salt Lake this spring."

Prudence's eyes lit up. "Say, maybe you fetched yourself an idea." She stepped to the front of the wagon and spoke to Nora through the aperture, "Did you ever notice anything special about Wils's gun?"

"Yes, it had pearl stocks, and an octagon barrel. . . ."

"But anything about the kind of a load it shot?"

"I remember thinking the bore looked like a toy pistol, it was so small. But it carried out a long way. Why?"

"Nothing, honey, nothing at all." She turned back to Bogey with ill-repressed excitement. "Get your shoes on, you old rebel. We're going to have a look for that bullet."

But they searched the wagon without finding a trace of it. After an hour, they gave up. Bogey returned to his bunk, heaved a profound sigh. "It couldn't just evaporate," he said.

Prudence shook her head in doleful agreement.

That night the train camped on a park overlooking the creek. Next evening, with good fortune, it might reach the pass.

But dawn came through a haze of sifting snowflakes. Boone Logan looked apprehensively at the mountains and cursed, then he ordered the train on. At noon the snow was soggy underfoot. It balled with earth and clung to the wagon wheels in sticky masses; it obstructed and rendered insecure the hoofs of the horses.

Logan held a conference with his henchmen; afterward he prophesied clearing weather and ordered a halt. But his five henchmen rode on— to ascertain, he said, whether it was still possible to travel the pass.

A few minutes after the train halted, the boy who drove for Parson Joe—Tod Warner—appeared at the door to Nora's wagon. He stamped wet snow from his boots, panted from exertion and excitement. "Parson Joe is mighty sick this morning," he said. "He's had the misery all night."

Nora was little perturbed. "It's his lumbago again!"

"No, ma'am. Not lumbago this time. It's in here." Tod indicated his chest.

"A cold?"

"More'n a cold. Chills and fever all night long. Reckon he drank a bucket of water. Thought sure enough he'd die, but he wouldn't let me send for help. But now he's asking for you, Miss Nora."

Nora tossed a shawl about her head and shoulders, followed Tod down the steps. The parson's wagon was a hundred yards distant beyond a clump of quaking asp. She ran most of the way.

Inside, Tod had left a good fire. The parson, with closed eyes, lay beneath a buffalo robe, trembling with ague. He opened his intense blue eyes when Nora leaned over him.

"Not too close, child," he warned in a wheezy, scarcely audible voice. "Not too close, it might be ketchin'."

"Parson, why didn't you send for me sooner?"

"Never mind, child. It don't make no never mind. Nobody can help me now. My sands has just about run out and the good Lord is makin' ready to fetch me home."

"No. You'll be all right. Tod, put a stone on the fire. We'll wrap it and put it on the parson's chest."

"No, child. No hot stone for me. Nothin' but prayer, and one other thing. . . ." He reached up and took Nora's hand. His palm was hot ; the skin was like old paper.

"What other thing, Parson?"

"It's about you. My fondest hope has been to unite Boone and you in bonds of holy wedlock. That's the chief reason I chose Bannack instead of goin' on to Paradise Valley. But now it don't look like I'll ever get to Bannack."

"Parson, don't say that!"

"It's true. By tomorrow I'll be gone. I ain't complainin'. I'm happy to go."

Tod, listening in the background, sniffled audibly.

The parson went on, "That is, I'll be glad to go providin' this thing ain't left undone. Before I die I want you and Boone to come before me, each takin' the other's hand . . . like two lovers with their whole lives and this great new country spread before 'em . . . and let me jine you forever. There won't be no preachers in Bannack where you're goin', child. And no book of God's word. The only book there will be the Devil's book of fifty-two pages; and the only god will be Mammon."

Nora's eyes cast about like a trapped animal's. Her free hand clutched convulsively at her shawl. She tried to put his mind on other things: "No, Parson, not now. You must sleep, then you'll feel better. You just have a touch of chills and fever."

"Nope, I'm a goner sure as shootin'. In my Father's house there are many mansions, and I'll soon be tradin' this here ornery old prairie schooner for one of 'em. Tod. . . ."

"Yes, Parson."

"You'd better run out and fetch Boone."

Tod ran to do the parson's bidding

Nora paled. "But we can't be married now. My dress . . . and Father buried only yesterday. . . ."

"Child, buckskin is as honorable as snow-white linen. And as for your paw . . . well, I know he'd be wantin' it this-a-way."

The parson made a move to sit up, but he dropped back to the bunk. "Pshaw, I forgot the witnesses. Who would you want? Prudence and Tom?"

"After a while . . . but you must rest now."

But the parson would have none of resting. Not even an hour's delay would he tolerate.

Boone Logan, handsome, broad of shoulder, stepped through the door followed by Tod. A few snowflakes glistened for a second on his jacket. He leaned over and took Nora's hand, squeezed it, but she avoided his eyes. On the parson he looked with studied solemnity. "How are you, Parson?" he asked.

"Poorly. I'm about to pass over the great divide, Boone, and I don't mean Lemhi, neither. So, as a last act, I'm hankerin' to jine you two young folks in the bonds of wedlock."

Logan looked at Nora. "Do you want to?" he asked.

For a moment she was silent, studying the parson's brown, dehydrated hand which lay in hers. But her eyes did not see the hand. Her eyes saw Wils Fleming—as she remembered, tall, with something of the whiplash about him; handsome with that devil-may-care way of sitting his horse in long-stirruped Indian style. But Wils was gone already to Bannack, perhaps. And Wils had killed her father. Her eyes found the parson's. In them was such a depth of pleading she could not refuse.

"You will?" Boone asked softly.

"Yes," she said.

"Fetch the witnesses," cried Parson Joe.

Nora said quickly, "No. Give me . . . just an hour."

"Fiddlesticks! Why wait? A woman can waste more time!"

Boone said magnanimously, "An hour isn't long, Parson."

"All right," the old man resigned. "One hour." He heaved a great, satisfied sigh. "My dyin' day' and the happiest day in my life. . . ."

VI

That morning, Bogey had declared his back cured—or practically so. He drove the team until the train stopped that noon and, while the scene just recounted was taking place, he was out hobbling horses. Coming back to the wagon, he was hopeful that Prudence would reward his activity with a cup of coffee. The door to the wagon was ajar, so he walked in. Prudence was speaking to Nora.

"But why today? It's foolishness. There's no need for such a hurry. Marriage can wait till you get to Bannack."

Bogey cut in, "Marriage! Who's gettin' married?"

Nora dropped her eyes.

"You figurin' on gettin' married?" he pursued.

"Yes, Bogey."

"To Boone?"

She nodded.

Prudence, now aided by Bogey's presence, spoke firmly. "But not today!"

"It will have to be today. Parson Joe's . . . going to die."

Prudence promptly exploded. "Die! He's been headed for the Great Beyond ever since I first laid eyes on him five years ago. Look at last winter. He said he was a goner then. Why, that time he even gave instructions for buildin' his coffin! He ain't that far yet."

"He's really sick. He's telling the truth."

"Well, so be it. But you needn't get married to please some old decrepit sky pilot."

"I'm sorry. It's no use arguing. I'm going to be married in an hour . . . half an hour now. I've promised."

Bogey asked, "You wouldn't keep your promise if it meant marrying the man that planned your father's murder, would you?"

"No, of course I wouldn't."

Without saying more, Bogey turned and left the wagon. He found Ceiver's wagon, now deserted. This time, somehow, he must find the bullet.

He worked systematically. First he climbed atop a low stool at the front with his head on a level with the aperture through which the bullet had been fired. He sighted at the spot where Ebbert had most likely stood. Fired at this angle, the bullet would strike the wall about eight inches above the floor. But the wall and floor were unscarred—he knew that from his search the other day. Obviously, something was wrong. Had some other object stopped the bullet's flight, an object subsequently moved?

"Let's see," he muttered. "Ebbert stood here. Turned, fell here. Wils must have been here. Then he jumped through this tear. Hello. . . ." The old family table of the Ceiver's now stood before the rent in the canvas. "He couldn't have jumped the table. It must have been put here since."

He had examined the table before, but he slid it in the only possible direction—toward the back—and again sighted from the aperture. One table leg near the wall was now in the path of fire. On hands and knees he scrutinized it.

The leg was of mossy oak, large enough to stop a bullet. But it was unmarked. He looked closely—then, in surprise, more closely still. What occupied his attention was not a bullet hole—it was a fresh crack which split apart the time-honored varnish to expose the wood's white heart.

"Funny what would cause a crack like that," he muttered. "Look's like some pressure is holdin' it apart from inside."

He shook the leg—it was loose. It twisted in his fingers. And as it turned there was exposed a gaping bullet hole. It was large, a hole made from the slug of a Navy pistol.

Working feverishly, he started to dig at the bullet with his bowie. He thought better of it; instead, twisted the leg from the table; left the table teetering there while he ran for Ebbert's wagon.

Gleefully he hammered on the door. Silence! He looked in. The wagon was deserted. "Parson's wagon," he muttered.

He ran outside. But which wagon was it? They stretched at intervals for half a mile along the edge of the park. He ran north, caught sight of a man gathering dry twigs beneath a clump of fir trees.

"Where's the parson's wagon?" he panted.

The man's mouth fell agape at sight of Bogey's standing there with the mossy table leg over his shoulder like some Brobdignagian ball-bat.

"Where's Parson Joe's, you idjut?" Bogey screamed.

"Back thar," the man pointed south.

Bogey turned, raced away. There were four wagons around the grove of quaking asp at which the man had pointed. Bogey hammered at the first one. The man who answered was small, freckled, had suspicious eyes.

"Where's Parson Joe's?" Bogey asked.

"What you want with the parson?"

Bogey gave up, ran to the next wagon, opened the flap without knocking, and glanced inside. There, with joined hands, and facing Parson Joe's bunk, stood Boone and Nora. At their right and left were Prudence and Joe Ceiver. All looked startled at Bogey and his table leg.

"Stop this foolishness," cried Bogey.

His words, and the impetuousness of his appearance, shocked them all to silence. Parson Joe let fall the shaky hand which held the Bible. With an unusual effort, he sat upright in his bunk. "This is no foolishness," he quavered. "This here is a sacred ceremony you're interruptin'."

"Maybe you won't be so durned anxious to go on with it when you hear what I got to say." Bogey pointed toward Logan with a finger which trembled with excitement. "Miss Nora, there's the man which plotted your father's murder!"

Logan spun on Bogey. He loomed over the elder man with fists clenched. But Ceiver stepped between them. "Calm down, Boone," he said. Then, to Bogey, "Get out of here! And be gone from the wagon train by five minutes. If you think you'll stop this wedding, you're wrong. You can't, because the wedding is all over."

"All over!" Bogey glanced at Nora. With an inclination of her head she indicated Ceiver was telling the truth. "Too late!" Bogey said in a hollow voice. Then he seemed to grasp his resolve. He was still not beaten. "By thunder, it's not either too late!"

He spun away from Ceiver, pistol in hand, might have fired, but Prudence grasped his wrist, forced him tight against the wall by superior weight. Bogey struggled impotently in her grasp.

She whispered, "Put that gun away, you fool. Want to spoil everything? Let me handle this."

Bogey relaxed. Freed, he reluctantly drooped back the pistol in its holster.

Prudence turned on Logan and her husband. "Get out of here," she commanded.

Logan glowered. "Get out! Me get out?"

"Yes. Both of you."

Logan hesitated, finally said, "Very well. Come, Nora."

"No. Nora stays."

"Listen, I don't know what's on your mind . . . but Nora is my wife, and she goes with me."

But Prudence stood her ground. She took Nora by the shoulders, and drew her close. "I said, get out. Haven't you any feeling in your hide for this poor girl?"

"What's goin' on here?" Parson Joe wailed, but no one heeded him.

Logan turned abruptly and clomped through the flap door. It slapped shut behind him.

"What's in your head, Prudence?"

"Never mind. You go, too."

"You don't put store in what Bogey says, do you?"

"Never mind, just git."

Tom Ceiver did as he was told.

A moment of quiet followed. Parson Joe sighed; he relaxed, supinely peaceful with hands folded across his chest, his eyes closed. A smile relaxed his lips.

Prudence said, "Let's see that table leg."

Bogey triumphantly handed it over. She examined the hole and nodded her satisfaction. "It's from a big-bore gun, right enough. How come we didn't find it the other day?"

"The leg was loose. The force of the bullet striking it must have turned it around so the bullet hole couldn't be seen."

"What does it all mean?" Nora asked.

"This is the bullet which killed your paw," Bogey explained. "But it never came from Wils's gun. Wils's gun didn't throw a slug more'n half this size."

Prudence dug out the ball with a butcher knife and dropped it in Nora's hand.

She looked at it for a moment. "No, this isn't from Wils's gun."

Bogey thought of something. "Miss Nora, you remember the day he shot at those men back on Birch creek?"

"Of course."

"How many times did he shoot?"

"Only once."

"Did he reload the empty cylinder while he was with you?"

"No."

"And he didn't reload in camp that night, either. I remember Dutch John puttin' cap and ball in his pistol, but not Wils."

Prudence demanded, "What you gettin' at?"

"Just this: Wils likely never did reload that cylinder. And if he didn't, he couldn't show his pistol to be examined. . . ."

"Glory be!" breathed Prudence.

Nora's eyes flashed. "Then it was someone else!"

Bogey responded, "Sure it was. And I don't have to guess much as to who, either. I could have spit on him not three minutes ago."

"But it couldn't have been Boone."

"Couldn't have, hey? Well, he was Johnny-on-the-spot to accuse Wils by time the shot quit echoing."

Prudence shook her head. "Boone was at that meetin' in Donovan's wagon when the shot was heard. A dozen men can prove that."

"How about his men?"

Prudence stepped to the door, thrust out her head, and bellowed, "Ceiver!"

Her husband was sitting on the steps at her feet. "What do you want?"

"Come in here. Ceiver, were all of Logan's scouts in Donovan's wagon at the time Ebbert was shot?"

"All but Mex. He was hobbling horses."

"Mex, hey? So it was him!"

"What about him? You mean he killed Ebbert?"

"That's right."

Nora sank to a chair. Her lips were drawn in a tight line. Her hands clenched until the knuckles were bloodless. Prudence thrust out her jaw and looked belligerent. Bogey fingered the pistol at his belt. An expression of doubt had even found its way to Tom Ceiver's face. But in the bunk, oblivious to the scene just enacted, Parson Joe sighed in deep contentment. He muttered, "The happiest day of my life, jining these two happy young folk in the bonds of wedlock."

VII

That afternoon Bogey pointed his horse up the trail toward the pass.

"Don't come back without Wils," Prudence had admonished.

"I'll bring him back. You watch over Nora."

"Don't worry. I'll see to it that Logan scoundrel don't take his nuptials too seriously."

It was heavy going through the wet snow. Bogey didn't press his horse, for he knew all its strength might be needed before the trip ended.

Near nightfall he sighted two riders approaching from up the trail. They proved to be Indians—a buck and his squaw. Bogey pulled his horse across the trail, held up his hand, palm forward, in signal of friendship. The Indian pulled up, returned the signal.

"How!" said Bogey.

"How!" the Indian answered. He was old, had a parchment face wrinkled by many seasons. His squaw was young—he must be a man of importance in his tribe, Bogey thought.

"How far to Lemhi Pass?" Bogey asked. The Indian shook his head. Bogey repeated the question in the dialect of the Crows, but the Indian still responded in the negative. He was probably a Shoshone, or a Bannack. Bogey thereupon motioned toward the mountains at the east, and with a zigzag gesture indicated a trail. The buck nodded and, without speaking, but with eloquent use of his fingers, pointed to the peak ahead, held up two fingers, motioned north with his thumb, spread fore and middle fingers, then gestured east with both hands. After this he proudly expended his entire fund of English: "Fort Benton, four sleeps."

These directions satisfied Bogey: he was to pass this and the next mountain, go east when the trail forked. The Indian, who supposed him headed for Fort Benton, estimated the distance at four days' travel.

Bogey dipped into his pouch for a fragment of blackstrap tobacco and three rifle balls which he proffered as a gift. In exchange, the Indian drew forth a once gaudy, but now bedraggled, fragment of calico; this he presented in return. They parted with a sign of friendship.

A DAY HAD PASSED since Wils had gained the foot of the steep ascent of Lemhi Pass. Here he must decide his course: would he do the sensible thing—continue on to Bannack; or would he wait to fight it out with Logan and his henchmen?

It was not an easy decision. He pondered at length, the while allowing his horse to pick its leisurely way up the steepening trail. They proceeded thus, without destination, for five or six miles.

A voice sounded a few yards to his rear, "Waal, if it ain't Wils!"

Dutch John was emerging from a clump of jackpine near the trail. He led his horse, was just returning a pistol to its holster.

"Dutch John! I thought you'd be in Bannack by now."

"Reckon I would be." John aimed a spurt of tobacco juice at a white quartzite boulder. "Reckon I would, only certain things held me up . . . or t'other way around." He winked, drew the back of his hand across his disreputable black whiskers. "You see, I been doin' a little minin' right here in the pass. Likely spot."

"Mining?" Wils looked doubtfully at the inhospitable cliffs, and down at the torrent which frothed over jagged boulders in the gulch.

"Yep!" To prove his assertion, John drew from his saddlebag two weighty buckskin pokes. "Gold," he said, hefting them expertly. "That Bannack must be a right rich spot. Leastwise, the pilgrims comin' out has a powerful lot more'n the ones goin' in."

Wils made no question of John's mining methods. In the North-west of 1862 it was neither polite nor healthful to question another's line of business.

"Business is good, Wils, better jine me."

"Sorry, John, it's not my line."

"Well, every man for his principles, I say. But share and share alike is my motto." In proof of this philosophy, he held out one of the bags of gold. "Take it, there's plenty where this came from."

Wils shook his head. So, with a resigned gesture, John put the gold back in the saddlebag. "You run into all kinds on a gold rush," he muttered. "Headin' for Bannack?"

Wils shook his head doubtfully. Then he told of Ebbert's murder and of his own escape.

"I don't reckon I'd worry much more about 'em," John said.

"I wouldn't except for Bogey, and those two women."

"Ah-ha!" John sagely nodded his head.

"And I believe Logan has some scheme

"May be. That fellow's a rattler, right enough."

"The train should heave in sight tomorrow. I think I'll keep an eye on it."

Wils turned back down the trail. Without question, Dutch John did likewise

Dutch John said, "Thanks for cuttin' me loose t'other night. Looked like I'd staked claim on one of them Californy collars for sure."

"Me cut you loose?" And Wils gave his version of John's escape, of his own approach to the wagon, of the dark form which appeared, and finally of the unexpected turn of affairs through the discovery of Ceiver's bowie.

John, marveling, shook his head. "I was just sittin' thar, tied good and snug', tryin' to wear one of the ropes thin on the edge of the bench. Then I heard the sound of cloth being cut right behind my back. I reckoned it was you. I dropped my hands low, and somebody cut the ropes. The knife was put in my hand, so I did the rest . . . snitched Ceiver's guns and lit out. I forgot the knife . . . lucky, too, way it worked out."

Darkness came early, and that night it snowed. All next day the two watched for the train. At dark, Wils grew worried. "This trifling snow shouldn't hold them up. Suppose they got off the trail?"

Dutch John shrugged. "Tomorrow we'll ride back and have a look-see."

That night the two slept not an hour's travel from where Bogey had camped beneath his spreading evergreen. Dawn came misty and sunless through a sky of lead gray warning of blizzard. Neither Wils nor John mentioned the weather, but both mutely recognized that the wagons which negotiated Lemhi before spring would have to hurry. They started down the trail. In the distance, a rider approached. It was Bogey.

He took scarcely time for greeting; instead he gave a rapid account of happenings since Wils's departure. "We got to get back," he concluded. "Nora needs you."

Words seemed to fail Wils for a moment. Finally he burst out, "But she's Logan's wife . . . don't you understand that?"

"Wife! Them few triflin' parson's words ain't so important. . . ."

"Yes they are, Bogey."

"Then he can annul it."

Dutch John patted a revolver, "I got the best annuller you ever saw, right here. Maybe that girl would appreciate the happy state of widda-hood."

"Yes," Wils said after a moment's consideration, "we have to go back. She . . . and Prudence are our friends. We can't abandon them."

They started down the trail, expecting the train with each mile after the first ten, but there was no sign of it. Finally they rode atop a promontory from which a vast area spread beneath their gaze—an area limited only by the purple haze of fall, by the jagged outlines of the Bitterroots, the Salmons, and more distant ranges. The valley itself was visible almost to the Birch Creek divide—but no wagon train was there.

Bogey finally asked, "Think they took the wrong trail?"

Wils answered grimly. "Maybe it's the wrong trail Logan had in mind all along."

"It's likely," John mused. "Blind trail in the mountains; Injun attack, say . . . that game's been played before. The provisions on that train would be worth as much as gold in Bannack."

Wils asked Bogey, "Was Logan there when you left?"

"He was, but his men weren't. They left to look for the pass."

Wils cursed under his breath. He looked up and to the south where a light spot in the clouds told the sun's position. It was late morning. Then he cracked his horse sharply with the quirt. "We'll have to hurry," he said through clenched teeth, "and hurry like hell."

Down the hill they went, clattering over stones, paying no heed to branches which snatched at clothing and slapped their faces. In the snow were the impressions of the hoofs of three horses—Bogey's, and the two Indians he had encountered the night before. At last, on nearing the train's campsite of the previous day, they found the wagon tracks. These had headed across the valley toward a cleft in the foothills backed by precipitous mountain walls. Without comment they turned, urged heir horses to greater speed.

From the distance came the rattle of gunfire.

*   *   *

AFTER BOGEY DEPARTED, Prudence returned to the wagon where Nora was sitting. She went to the corner where the guns were kept, and hauled out a big-bore shotgun. From the barrel she dug the wad, and poured out its charge of birdshot. Then, after adding a few grains of powder, she poured in a heavy load of buckshot, rewadded, inserted a fresh cap for good measure, and leaned the gun against the wall within reach of her rocking chair.

"Great thing in an emergency," she growled. "If the devil was on my heels and I only had one shot . . . give me buck!"

After that, she and Nora waited nervously but, when darkness fell, Logan had not returned. Prudence lit the tallow lamp, but its sad, reddish flare seemed so ineffectual against the gloom that she became reckless and dipped into her hoard of tallow candles, one of which she lighted and placed in a brass holder beneath a chimney. After that, she brewed coffee, and the two felt better.

Tom Ceiver came in, poured a cup of coffee.

"Where's Logan?" his wife asked.

"Out exploring the pass."

"Humph! Thought he knew the country so well!"

"It's not only the pass. This happens to be Blackfoot country. He and his men are out scouting a raiding party."

At the word "Blackfoot" the two women became tense. The Blackfoot nation was the scourge of the Northwest; well they knew the fate of other emigrants who had become the prey of those painted horsemen.

A little later a sharp rap came at the rear of the wagon. Unconsciously Prudence checked the position of the shotgun. She said, "Come in."

The door opened to admit Boone Logan. He didn't glance at Tom or Prudence—his gaze was for Nora. He smiled. But the girl did not lift her eyes; they narrowed and grew hard as she looked at the floor, and her mouth set in a line remindful of her father's.

"May I have coffee?" Boone asked, noticing the pot which still bubbled on the stove.

Prudence answered, "Help yourself."

Ceiver attempted to smooth the atmosphere: "Any Blackfoot signs?"

Logan maintained silence until he had drunk half his coffee, then he answered, "Yes. I don't want to scare anybody, but they're about. I have the men watching them. So we'll get warning before an attack. However, it would be well to start early tomorrow."

He finished his coffee, set down the cup. Then he stepped over and set a hand on Nora's shoulder. His eyes narrowed with a hard glitter when he noticed how she flinched beneath his touch. He appeared to hesitate for a moment, then he said, "My wagon isn't exactly the place I'd want to take a bride. But we'll have a real home . . . in Bannack."

Nora didn't answer. Logan looked at her for a few seconds, then turned his gaze on Prudence. He could not help read the suspicion on their faces. Without speaking more he left the wagon. They all breathed more easily when the flap shut behind him.

With the first gray hint of morning the wagoners were out unhobbling their horses, hitching them between traces which each morning grew more stiff with cold. Smoke billowed from some of the stovepipes but, reading a warning in the leaden sky, most of the travelers ate hurriedly of cold beans or jerky.

Nora ran down and called on the parson. Inside his wagon a lamp cut the pre-dawn gloom. The old man sat in his bunk taking nourishment. "Feel a lot better," he confided a trifle sheepishly. "Reckon I'll get a chance to convert them Bannack heathens after all."

The parson's good health irked Nora—of course she wanted to see him recover—but the fact stood out that his chills and fever hadn't been serious, yet because of them she was now Logan's wife. After a few words she returned to her wagon.

The air soon rang with the cries of teamsters, with the sing and pop of long-lash whips. The wheels creaked in the cold, and soon the dozen divisions of the train were in motion northward.

Boone Logan rode ahead, tall, erect, his ringed buckskin aflutter. A while later two riders approached from up the trail. Logan galloped ahead to meet them. The teamsters looked to their priming, for these two were Indians, and this was Blackfoot country.

But they proved to be only a peaceful old Shoshone and his squaw who sat stoically by the trail and watched as the train rolled by.

A short time later Logan turned abruptly toward the east. He motioned the lead team to follow. He led the way across the valley to a gulch which in turn pointed toward what appeared to be a cleft in the mountain wall. "It's Lemhi!" "It's the pass!" were the words which ran along the line of wagons.

It was fair going the first two miles, but as the gulch narrowed the road became only a wide deer trail which followed sidehills among evergreens. After a long, continuous climb it dropped to the floor of a grassy park, spongy with springs. A herd of twenty deer watched with jet eyes, tame as milk cows, even curiously following a few stiff jumps at a time—but no one shot, for the air bore snow flurries and the idea of haste was uppermost in all minds.

Climbing from the park toward an area of spectacular cliffs, the trail was difficult and rocky. Twice the drivers of the lead team were forced to pry slide rock from the trail which, when free, went rolling and crashing in a series of leaps only to stop at the gulch's bottom far below. Always, now, the wagon wheels clung precariously to the trail. Some of the more timorous shouted questions to Logan, but he rode ahead unheeding.

High above a golden eagle veered in small circles, effortlessly, on set pinions. Then with a flap of gathering wings he came to perch on a crag which stood spire-like away from the vertical porphyry cliff.

At last, on reaching a broad sweep of treeless mountainside, Logan signaled a halt. Almost in unison with his gesture a teamster shouted, "Indian!" and pointed toward a feather-decked figure which appeared atop a large rock two hundred yards above.

A chilling scream rent the air. Guns crashed from all around. Men toppled from several driver's seats.

Somebody raced from a wagon, started dragging away a wounded man. A gun spat out from behind a nearby rock. The man sprawled over his wounded comrade.

One frantic driver commenced lashing his horses, turned them downhill in an attempt to escape the way he had come; but the wagon faltered as it turned, it swayed, hung for a moment on two wheels, then plunged, crashing toward the abyss, the terrified horses squealing with fright, feet flying in a horrible tangle. From the wagon's rear a barrel of flour rolled, leaped high in the air, shattered with a cloud of white.

Logan ostentatiously found refuge between two rocks; fired at something. He turned, motioned to the driver of the lead team who had hidden in his wagon when the shooting commenced. "They'll get you there," he shouted. "Come here."

The man hesitated for a moment, then he leaped from the wagon. Bent double he hopped like a jackrabbit over the sliderock. But a waiting pistol, not thirty feet distant, cut him down.

The firing then ceased; the horses became calm; and the silence of the mountain fastness was again complete.

Prudence Ceiver peeped through a rent she had cut in the canvas of the wagon and spotted a glint of gunshine up the hill. She looked down the long barrel of her rifle, waited perhaps a minute. Something dark appeared around the edge of a stone. She squeezed the trigger. A man stumbled into view, pitched face down.

"One," she growled. She dumped another charge of powder down the barrel. But something closer attracted her attention, so she passed the rifle over to Nora and kept watch with the shotgun.

Boone Logan attached a white handkerchief to the barrel of his gun and waved it as if asking for a truce. A feather-decked man appeared briefly to motion, then hid again. Logan climbed down the hill. Soon he emerged from the parley and, still bearing his white flag, advanced along the train.

"They'll let us go, but we'll have to leave the horses and wagons," he announced along the line. "Get ready and follow me."

But when Prudence heard his words, she thrust out her head and bellowed, "Stay hid, you fools, or he'll get us all killed. Don't you see it's his own gang fixed up like Injuns?"

Logan spun on her as if stung by a whiplash. Fury twisted his face. He dropped the kerchief-draped barrel as if to shoot, then thought better of it and forced a smile.

"You'd better come," he shouted. "It's your only chance."

The sound of a different gun cut the air. It came from back toward the trail. One of the befeathered men sprang up, then fell. His companions—there were but three left now—leaped to find someplace safe from this unexpected attack. But one was knocked down as he sought to escape. Wounded, he crawled desperately on all fours. The head and shoulders of a black-whiskered man in a disreputable slouch hat appeared momentarily over a rock, his pistol bobbed up, cracked, and the wounded man lay still.

Prudence, watching, gasped in surprise, "Dutch John!"

Nora asked, "What's that?"

"Looks like Bogey brung back the whole crew!"

Boone Logan jumped behind the wagons, ran quickly along the line until he reached Ebbert's. He entered. "Come, Nora. We still have time to escape. We can reach my horse along this side. He'll carry us around the mountain to safety."

But the girl drew back, an expression of revulsion answering him.

He repeated, "Come!"

"I'll stay here, you . . . murderer."

"You little fool! Call me murderer? I'll tell you who attacked us . . . it was Wils Fleming and those highwaymen friends of his." He took a stride as if to seize Nora and drag her with him.

"Stay where y'are!" It was Prudence's voice which cut the air.

He drew up short, for the shotgun was trained at his heart.

She said, "There's a dozen buck in this bar'l, enough to blow you to the blackest spot in hell, I reckon."

They faced each other a second. He spoke in an icy voice. "You wouldn't dare pull that trigger."

"Don't pass the end of that table," said Prudence.

He laughed through his teeth, commenced a stride.

The gun leaped with a roar in Prudence's hands. The concussion of the charge spun him half around. He fell heavily to the floor.

For a few seconds the women stared at him, but with more relief than horror. Then their attention was drawn outside where a perfect fusillade had broken out: the last two of Logan's men had broken and run for it, and with disastrous results.

Dutch John, atop his rock, turned to Wils and swore as the last of them went down from the well-directed bullet of a wagoner. "Just my luck! Whenever I get some good wing shootin' stirred up, some-body has to horn in and spile it."

That afternoon the train managed to turn on the dangerous mountain trail and descend. Toward evening the sun broke warm and yellow through a rift in the clouds—assurance that the year's first blizzard was not in the offing after all. The camp was at the approach to Lemhi.

While Wils and his two companions were having supper at Nora's wagon, the flap raised to admit Parson Joe, hale and hearty after his attack of chills and fever.

"I come to apologize for marryin' you off to that varmint, and to congratulate you on bein' a widda."

Nora smiled. "That's all right, Parson."

"But," he went on, looking from her to Wils and back again, "mebby I'll get to perform a ceremony over in Bannack after all."

And the smiles on Wils's and Nora's lips left him in no doubt.

Over by the kettle, Dutch John sliced off a strip of venison with his keen bowie. He pondered the parson's words and looked specu-latively at the bunk where Joe Ceiver lay with a bullet-shattered arm. "Got a might good idee to finish off this pesky Ceiver fellow so Prudence and I can make it a double," he said.

But Prudence shook her head. "I don't reckon you're the marryin' kind, John. But just the same, I'm right glad I cut you loose the night they was measurin' you for that Pike County cravat."

REACH HIGH, TOPHAND!

DWIGHT BENNETT NEWTON was born in Kansas City, Missouri, and went on to complete work for a master's degree in history at the University of Missouri. From the time he first discovered Max Brand in Street & Smith's *Western Story Magazine*, he knew he wanted to be an author of Western fiction. He began contributing Western stories and novelettes to the Red Circle group of Western pulp magazines published by Newsstand in the late 1930s. During the Second World War, Newton served in the U.S. Army Engineers and fell in love with the central Oregon region while stationed there. He would later become a permanent resident of that state and Oregon frequently serves as the locale for many of his finest novels.

"Smoke-Pole Rendezvous in Abilene" with Wild Bill Hickok as one of the characters was his first story to be published in *Lariat Story Magazine* (7/46). It was followed by other notable contributions, "Born to the Brand" (9/46), "Drifters Spell Trouble" (1/47), "Saga of the Tombstone Kid" (9/47), and "Swing High, Nester!" (3/49). Captain Joseph T. Shaw encouraged his clients such as Dan Cushman and Frank Bonham to establish personal relationships with editors. Newton was a client of the August Lenniger Literary Agency and Lenniger did not believe in it. As a consequence Newton never had any direct contact with Malcolm Reiss while the latter was principal editor and general manager at Fiction House. However, Reiss knew Newton's work well enough that when he invited him to contribute a book-length manuscript for *Two Western Books* and Newton sent in a short outline, Reiss could tell Lenniger after accepting it, "Newton usually knows what he's doing."

"All the characters in the novelette are real people—even the villain," Lenniger wrote to Newton after reading the first story he submitted to the agency. What makes his fiction so special is this combination of characters who seem real and about whom a reader comes to care a great deal and Newton's fundamental humanity, his realization early on (perhaps because of his study of history) that little that happened in the West was ever simple but rather made desperately complicated through the conjunction of numerous opposed forces working at cross purposes. Yet through all of the turmoil on the frontier a basic human decency did emerge. It was this which made the American frontier experience so profoundly unique and produced a heritage of remarkable human beings of which the nation they built could be proud, always. Newton knew this and it elevates his magazine fiction to a level that demands the best of it be preserved permanently, and these are the same qualities which also characterize so many of his subsequent novels.

Among his finest novels are AMBUSH RECKONING (Ace, 1968), HELL-BENT FOR A HANGROPE (Ace, 1954), and THE LURKING GUN (Ace, 1961), now reprinted in a single triple-action mass merchandise edition by Leisure Books, LONE GUN originally published by Perma Books in 1956 as THE AVENGER but now with its title restored in a hardcover Gunsmoke edition from Chivers, and THE BIG LAND (Doubleday, 1972) which is available in a full-length audio version from Books on Tape.

"Reach High, Top Hand!" first appeared in *Lariat Story Magazine* (7/47). It has not been otherwise collected. However, Newton did expand this story to form his novel, TOP HAND (Perma Books, 1955), first published under the Dwight Bennett byline.

I

The railroad depot at Sage Flats, Wyoming, had a new station master who was no friend to Sam Wills. Unfortunately, too, because on a warm day like this the depot platform was one of the few comfortable places in town. Even when a summer sun baked the vastly rolling wastes of gray sage and sand and bunch grass, and the twin lines of the U.P. tracks were eye-punishing streaks of brightness running moltenly east and west between Green River and the far-off divide at Laramie, a breeze from low hills on the north horizon always managed somehow to breathe along this shadowed platform and make it ideal for a pleasant nap.

But today, barely an hour after stretching out on an empty baggage truck with a half-filled mail sack for a pillow, Sam was suddenly startled awake by a rough hand on his shoulder and a voice that said: "All right, move on now! The Limited is due by in ten minutes and it don't look good for the town to have bums sleepin' all over the depot!"

Sam did not argue. He pulled his battered hat down over brown locks that were already becoming tinged with gray, and with hands shoved deeply into empty pockets, shuffled away from there. The blue-clad station master watched him go, scowling in distaste.

Over on the siding, a milling of dust and noise above the loading chutes drew Sam's attention. While he dozed, a small shipment of cattle had come in from one of the ranches on the Flats and was moving into the pen prior to being prodded up the ramp and into the cars. Something from the past stirred deeply within him as he leaned his shoulders against a corner of the depot and looked and listened to that familiar scene beneath the white-hot Wyoming sky. Behind him the station man's sharp voice called out: "I said move on and I meant it! Get clear away!" But Sam Wills hardly heard.

He was already moving across packed earth and beneath blasting sunlight toward the activity in the pens.

Now he could smell the dust and the sweat. He could see the horsemen and hear their cussing as they prodded the last of the big steers through the gate. Sam sauntered over to the fence, swung up and leaned across the top rail for a look at the bald-face critters bellowing and stirring within.

They were B-in-the-Box cattle. Good beef, too, Sam Wills considered, appraising them with a cowman's eye. Another tidy penny for the box safe in old Harry Benton's office. He thought this idly enough, without any hint of rancor, although rich Harry Benton was Sam's own father-in-law and the trouble between them was of fifteen years' standing.

It got so, after so long a time as fifteen years, you could come to take a thing like that for granted. Sam never bothered anymore. That was just about his strongest characteristic—not bothering.

Now, satisfied with his look at the cattle in the pen, Sam hopped down from the fence again and, as it would happen, straight into the path of a horseman who came loping along the side of the pen. The first he knew of it was a blow from the muscled shoulder that drove him hard into the rails. He caught his balance, turned as the horseman brought his mount out of a stumble and then reined about.

The rider was old Benton's foreman, a solid, black-haired man by the name of Tedrow. He shouted at Sam: "What's the matter with you? Too drunk to keep out of a man's way?" And then he saw who it was he had run down and a look of wry amusement wrapped his dark features.

"Well, well!" he grunted. "The great cowman himself! What you doing down here, has-been . . . studyin' to get your old job back? Figurin' how you used to do things better in the old days?"

Sam, his shoulders in the faded old coat pressed back against the corral poles, looked at the man in the saddle without answering. There were things he might have said—that he had likely been rodding B-in-the-Box before Cal Tedrow even won his first spurs as a green cowhand. But this probably did not even enter Sam's head. He had long been out of the habit of talking back to anyone.

Now other punchers had appeared out of the dust and confusion of the loading pens and they were watching Sam and their boss with grins on sweaty faces. Cal Tedrow liked an audience. He took this one into the joke with a broad wink, jerked his thumb at the man on the ground. "You know, I hear the boy used to be pretty sharp in the old days. He was a top hand that reached too high and look where he landed! Say, Sam, how much washing did the missus take in last week?"

Sam shoved away from the fence. He only meant to put his back to this crew and walk away from their mocking laughter; but Cal Tedrow must have misconstrued his intentions. The foreman's face went quickly hard and he barked: "Don't try to start nothin'!" And with a quick thrust of a boot caught Sam in the chest and shoved him back and down. Then he looked at the others, and whirling his bronc went larruping off through the drifting dust.

In another moment Sam Wills was alone. He got up slowly; slapped the loose, powder-dry dust out of his worn clothing and dragged on his battered hat. There was the beginning of anger in his stolid, aging face, but it had settled into apathy again as Sam left the loading pens and chutes behind him and headed for the false-fronted buildings of Sage Flat's main street.

It was a warm day all right, one to drain the energy from a man. You almost thought you could hear the paint blistering on the houses of town; and beyond them, far off across a gray expanse of rolling sage, the low-lying hills to northward seemed to shimmer behind curtains of heated air. A ragged clump of tumbleweed came scooting along the rutted street on a hot breath of wind, and tired ponies at the hitch rails stamped fretfully as blown dust whipped and stung their sweaty hides.

Ambling up the warped plank sidewalk Sam blinked into the heat haze and thought how nice a drink would feel in his dry throat; but he didn't have any money and his credit was no good in any of the town's three saloons. Just to make sure he stopped under the meager shade of a wooden awning and felt through all his pockets.

Clean empty!

No point in approaching Myra again, either. His ears still stung from the tongue-lashing he'd received the last time he'd ventured to ask his wife for money. He shrugged philosophically and moved on along the street.

Harry Benton's own saddler was racked before the hardware store. That was sort of interesting. The store had belonged to Sam at one time, long ago right after the big trouble with Benton when he'd had to quit working cattle, and turned to other ways to make a living.

But no B-in-the-Box mount had ever gnawed the store's hitch rail the few months Sam owned the place; for Harry Benton had blackballed him, and naturally the rest of the range had danced to Harry's tune. Sam was forced to go out of business, and that had sort of been the beginning of the end. He usually didn't think much about it anymore; but right now, because of that scene with Cal Tedrow, there was a stirring of anger in Sam against B-in-the-Box and everything connected with it.

Maybe that was why he refused to step off the sidewalk as Benton came out of the store. They met head-on.

Harry Benton was an old man, but his spirit was as high as ever.

In the days when Sam Wills ramrodded for him he had been solid, and stubborn, with a shock of hair as fiery as his temper. The stubbornness remained; for the rest, Harry was bent with time and his head was white, and only the blazing eyes—though a little dimmed—were much the same.

As he saw Sam Wills now, those eyes took on a kindling of wrath and scorn that was all he ever had for this son-in-law of his. Sam stood his ground and for a moment they were halted like that—the wealthy cattle baron and the forty-year-old scarecrow, unshaven, in his broken relics of clothing.

"Well!" old Harry bit out. "You steppin' out of my road, you whelp? Or am I gonna have to kick you out of it?"

His words carried. A face or two appeared to watch with interest this encounter in the hot and empty street. It was Sam Wills's place, now, to step meekly into the dust and let the most important rancher on the Flats have the walk to himself.

He had never failed before in such a situation. Yet, somehow, the things that had happened to him today had built an unfamiliar core of resistance within the derelict. From somewhere came words of mild defiance.

"I reckon the sidewalk was built wide enough for two men at once!"

"*Men?*" Benton spat the word. "When have you counted yourself in that class? What man could fall as low as you've come . . . and dragged my daughter with you."

A sudden mask dropped over Sam's features. Without a word he shoved past Benton. Behind him he heard Harry's cry of fury. "You come back here! I ain't finished talkin'. . . ."

In the middle of a word the voice choked off. Sam stopped involuntarily, turned half around. He saw Harry's face, distorted and purple; he heard the gasp that dragged through the old man's lips. Then suddenly he was hurrying back. He got there just as the taut body slumped forward.

Sam caught him, found almost no weight in the rancher's wasted body. Harry was fighting for breath, his mouth gaping, the silvered hair streaming down into his face as the expensive hat fell and rolled on the splintered walk at their feet. He got one word out: "Heart. . . ."

In desperation Sam looked around him. Other men were coming. Sam saw the open door of the hardware store near at hand, and supporting Harry awkwardly, got him inside. The proprietor was not there. Sam sighted a packing box and dragged the sick man over, let him down upon it with his back against the side of the counter.

Head lolling, Harry croaked out: "*Bottle.* . . ." One thin hand was trying to gesture toward the pocket of his coat. Sam dug into it quickly, found Benton's medicine and the silver spoon he always carried. Sam had seen him pour out the dose and make a face over it, many times. Now with fumbling fingers he got the bottle's cap off, brimmed the bowl of the spoon. "Here you are!" he grunted, and he put the spoon to Benton's lips.

At that moment a spasm ran through the thin body. The jaw, suddenly slack, dropped open and the head sagged forward. The medicine spilled futilely, untasted, over Harry's lifeless chin and his clothing; and Sam straightened slowly, the empty spoon and bottle in his hands.

Harry Benton would never need another dose of his heart medicine, now.

The things that happened those next few minutes were a jumble and confusion to Sam. Men came hurrying in from the street with a clomp of boots and rattle of spur chains, raising an alarmed and excited babble of voices. Almost at once they had the store packed, and the concentrated smell of strong men and horse sweat was nearly unbearable. But somebody had sent for the doctor and when he came they made room for one more.

"I knew it!" the medico kept saying half to himself, as he stooped to Harry's sprawled, limp form. "I told him all along he'd go out this way. And with this heat we's been having. . . ."

It seemed a little indecent for them to crowd around the dead man that way. Sam had been quickly shoved into a corner by the front window where he stood shuffling from one foot to the other thinking someone might want to ask him some questions. Nobody seemed to. The sun came in through the plate glass window like a furnace blast and the sweat crawled down Sam's spine. He was miserable.

Finally they picked up all that was left of Benton and carried him up the street to the doctor's office, and after that the crowd in the store thinned out some. Sam moved outside, too, glad to get away from the concentrated heat of that plate glass window. He felt lost, as though there was something he should do or say; but no one had invited him to make any statement although there had been many a hard look thrown his way and he'd heard more than one remark about what a shame it was Harry Benton should die like that—from a heart attack brought on by quarreling with his no-good son-in-law.

And then Sam thought of Myra, and he quailed inwardly. Myra would have to be told, and no putting it off either. Somehow he had forgotten that part of it, until just this moment. With great misgivings, he started for home.

He met his wife within a block of the house. For someone else, with that eager interest most people have in being the first with bad news, had already been to her, and she was heading for the doctor's office. She had on a faded dress; her thin face was pale in the hard glare of the sunlight. A pang of regret for many things touched Sam when he saw her.

"You heard about it?" he asked, clumsily, and fumbled to take one of her work-roughened hands. "I'm sorry, Myra. . . ."

She barely paused in her quick stride. Her jaw set as she looked at him coldly. "Sorry? That's a new one!" she said, bitterly. "You killed my mother; and now Dad!"

"That ain't hardly fair!" Sam protested.

She jerked her hand away from him. "I don't want to talk to you! I don't want to hear your voice or see your face either. Not just now . . . it'd be too much!"

Her voice broke in a sob. She stepped past her husband and continued on her way.

Sam looked after her for a long minute and then he gave his characteristic shrug that meant, "What the hell!" He went on to the house, turning in at the littered yard of packed bare earth, stepping up to the sagging porch, shuffling across the threshold of the two-roomed, sparsely furnished shack. He felt at a loss, purposeless. He moved one of Myra's wash tubs off of a chair at the rickety kitchen table and sat down. One hand drummed idly on the table top as he stared through the window at clothes drying on the line outside. A tang of sage came on the hot, dusty air that breathed faintly across the open sill.

Presently he shoved to his feet again—restless, weighted by an undefined depression. A drink was really what he wanted; Sam went suddenly to the cupboard, shoving aside Myra's ironing board with its pile of waiting clothes, and fished down an old cracked teapot from the topmost shelf. There were a few crumpled bills stuffed inside it. Sam glanced around furtively, then quickly removed one and shoved it into a pocket. He went out again through the front door and turned along the street that led to the heart of town.

II

On the steps of the Shorthorn Bar a voice calling his name made him turn with a guilty start. Homer Lowndes was coming toward him across the dusty street, his tall and cadaverous form dressed immaculately. He loomed a head taller than Sam as he hitched his long legs up the steps to the saloon porch. He said crisply: "I saw you from my window, Sam, and I would like to have a few minutes of your time. It's a matter of some importance."

Sam scowled. He didn't much care for Lowndes, mainly because the lawyer was a deacon of the Methodist church and had been a leader in the often-voiced opinion that Sam Wills should be run out of town. Sam also had an inborn distaste for the two big buck teeth that thrust out below his upper lip on the rare occasions when Homer Lowndes allowed himself the luxury of a smile. But the lawyer was not smiling now. Something told Sam he had better not decline.

They went across to the two-story brick building that housed Homer's office; the lawyer's gaunt body preceding Sam up the dark stairway to the second floor. He used a key on the office door, thrust it open, and stood aside to usher his visitor in ahead of him. That was Homer Lowndes for you: lock everything up tight as a vault just to run across the street and back.

The bare elegance of the office furnishings oppressed Sam, made him snake off his hat and run stubby fingers nervously through uncombed hair.

Lowndes went to the bookcase whose gleaming doors housed his thick and musty lawbooks. A clink of glass on glass, a gurgle of liquid, brought Sam's head up then in a quick surprise. He stared as the lawyer brought a tumbler partly filled with amber whiskey and set it on the edge of the desk beside him.

"Might as well have your drink and get it over with," Lowndes muttered. "Then maybe you can put your mind on what I'm going to tell you!"

It was a good brand of whiskey, and Sam downed it and put back the glass with shaking fingers.

"Thanks!" he grunted, still not looking at the lawyer squarely. Lowndes waved the word aside with an airy gesture.

He folded his lean body into the chair behind the desk then, and he got down to business with characteristic abruptness. "So your father-in-law is dead!"

Sam only nodded, waiting.

"You're aware, I suppose, that Myra is Harry Benton's sole survivor . . . which means that she stands to inherit the B-in-the-Box ranch, lock, stock, and barrel. I don't doubt at all that you've had that fact in mind all these years!"

His voice was dry and caustic as he added that last but Sam was somehow too astounded to take offense at the meaning Homer put into it. He said slowly: "Why, no, I didn't know that. Harry said a long time ago that he was going to cut her off and leave everything to charity."

"Harry Benton made two wills," Lowndes went on, as though Sam had not spoken; and opening a drawer of his desk he brought out a couple of legal documents and placed them on the blotter in front of him, neatly, side by side. He speared a thin, bony finger at the first of these. "This was drawn up more than fifteen years ago . . .

before Myra left home to marry you and before his wife died. By its terms the ranch and stock were to go to the mother; or in case of her decease, to Myra. All very simple."

The long finger rose, hovered above the second document and then pounced upon it. "But this one, drawn five years afterwards, supersedes the other. There has been none later. It is Benton's last will and testament. And let me read you one paragraph from it."

He picked up the document, opened it, cleared his throat, sliding the dry upper lip back from the ugly teeth. He found the place, and intoned in a sing-song voice: "If at the date of my decease my daughter, Myra Benton Wills, has become a widow; or if, within a month of the reading of this will, she becomes a widow or seeks legal divorce from her husband, Samuel Wills, then my estate shall pass to her *in toto*. If, however, at the end of said month, she has not sued for divorce, or if the divorce be not granted, then she is to receive one hundred dollars and the rest of the estate shall pass to the benefit of such charitable institutions as is hereinafter provided in this my last will and testament."

The voice ceased. Lowndes folded the document and placed it again beside the other will, and then he lifted his eyes and looked at Sam. "You see his purpose? Even in the grave, Benton will not give over his attempt to dissolve your marriage to his daughter. This is his last move . . . this choice he offers her. Which do you think she will take? Which," he added, slowly and deliberately, "do you think she *should* take?"

Hot words that had been trembling to spill from Sam's lips melted away to nothing. There was that in the probing voice of the other that made him turn square and face the truth. And the picture he saw—the picture of himself, and of what these fifteen wasted years had meant—was one that hurt.

"You're right, Homer!" he grunted then, bitterly. "And so was Benton, fifteen years ago, when he wouldn't give his consent to Myra marrying me. I'm no good for her!"

Lowndes shrugged a little, frowned thoughtfully at the bony yellow fingers folded before him on the desk top. "Well, we might as well be fair. You're a good cowman, Sam. You had made Harry a fine foreman, but because you had the audacity to marry his daughter he kicked you out and blackballed you so that no other rancher hereabouts dared hire you."

He looked up again and there was a strange glint, almost of friendliness, in his sharp eyes. "You see, I do know quite a bit about your story, Sam, even if I am a newcomer in Sage Flats. At one time I imagine I made things rather hot for you . . . before I started inquiring around and began piecing together what I learned.

"Sam, if you could have left this region, you'd have had no trouble to make a good place somewhere else. But Mrs. Benton came down with a stroke, brought on by all the family argument, and Myra insisted on being near her mother. So you gave up cattle and opened a hardware store. It failed. You tried one thing after another; and every time Harry Benton broke you. And still Myra's mother hung on and on . . . for over five years more."

Sam sighed. "That's true enough, Homer, but it's no excuse. If I'd been any good, Harry couldn't have licked me. I just didn't have the backbone. Because Mrs. Benton did die, finally, and then it was already too late. That was my chance to break away, to try for a fresh start. Myra was willing and anxious then to go. But I just didn't want to! I was a failure, and I'd got used to it. I'd got. . . ." He glanced down at himself. "It's got down to this . . . and I stayed there!"

"I know," the lawyer agreed. "You'd become a worthless, no-good bum who'd let his wife break her back at other people's washing just to keep the pair of you alive. They tell me she was a very sweet and pretty girl when she lost her head over you fifteen years ago, Sam. Those years certainly haven't been easy on her. But now. . . ."

He picked up the document he had read, looked at it and then at Sam. The latter's mouth hardened. "Yeah, I guess I know what you mean. Well, you needn't worry, Homer," he added, bitterly. "After fifteen years of the life I've given her there's no doubt in my mind which choice she's going to make. She despises me, I know that well enough. And I promise I won't give any trouble or fight the divorce. In fact. . . ." He looked at Lowndes sharply. "I'll even make a deal. For fifty dollars I'll leave town right now and never come back, and she can claim desertion or whatever else she wants to call it. All the money she's ever going to have, it ought to be worth that much to her to be rid of me!"

The lawyer raised an eyebrow curiously. "Where will you go?"

"To hell, most likely!" Sam told him. "I been headed that way a long time now!"

The bony hands spread in a brief gesture. "I could suggest this to her. Or advance you the money myself. Yes," he went on, "it's a very intelligent solution: a bribe for you, clear title to a ranch for your wife. There's just one thing. Myra is only a woman . . . not even a young woman, anymore. How is she going to hold on to that ranch once she owns it?"

Sam shrugged. "She's got a foreman. She's got Cal Tedrow."

"Precisely!"

Their eyes locked. Each read his own thought reflected in the other's. Sam said, "Then you don't like Tedrow either?"

"I don't trust him. Harry Benton scoffed whenever I tried to warn him, but I am reasonably sure Tedrow is not above stealing cattle from his own employer. Now, if a woman should come into control of B-in-the-Box, seems to me it would be a field day for him. He'd rob her blind!"

Sam Wills frowned. "What's on your mind, then?"

"Just this: In spite of everything, I'm confident that the one person in this world still most interested in Myra's welfare . . . in seeing her established and her ranch set in working order . . . that person is a man named Sam Wills! Deny it if you like. Nevertheless, I'd like to offer an alternative suggestion to the one that you just made." He picked up the document he had read aloud, looked at it, then dropped it into a drawer and shut the drawer with his knee. "Let's just leave that where it is for the time being." He picked up the second will—the old one. "I shall file this original will and I'll announce it as Benton's final testament. Under its terms your wife can then take possession of B-in-the-Box with no provisos.

"Now, here is my proposition. Today. . . ." He looked at a calendar on the wall. "Today is the seventh. Exactly three weeks from now I am going to the ranch for another look through Benton's papers, and there . . . quite by accident . . . I shall discover the later will. You, Sam, will have until that day to set matters straight at the ranch and replace Cal Tedrow with a dependable foreman; one who you know will serve Myra faithfully after . . . after the true will has been made public."

Sam hesitated. "That don't give me much time!"

"I'm sorry. By suppressing that will for even three weeks I am stepping outside the letter of the law, a thing I've never done before in my career! There are many people hereabouts, I'm sure, that know or suspect its existence; I would not dare delay any longer in producing it!"

Sam got slowly to his feet. The lawyer did likewise. A hard gleam was in Sam's eye. He said: "Except for one thing I would tell you to take your proposition and stuff it! If you want to know what I think, I got good suspicion you've got an eye on that ranch yourself! I know lawyers and I know there's a reason for you being so damn solicitous about my wife's welfare. I wouldn't even put it past you to try and marry her yourself, Homer, once you're rid of me, if B-in-the-Box came with her!

"Well, good luck to you if you can swing it! But me, I resent being a tool for anybody. I'd tell you to go to hell . . . except I can't resist an opportunity to stand up to Cal Tedrow and tell him he's lost his job!"

Lowndes's face showed no anger; only its normal cold frostiness. "You'll go through with it then?"

"Yeah," said Sam. "But only for three weeks!" And there was a fire in him that had not been there in many a long year.

It was a breathless day with no relief from the high sun's torment when Sam Wills hired a livery stable team and wagon and drove Myra out of Sage Flats to take over her father's ranch. They didn't have much to say to one another that day. Sam, with the ribbons in his hands, looked sidelong at his wife from time to time, sensing the tumult of emotions that must be concealed behind her tired eyes and thin, stony features.

The big house, sitting on a hill with poplars tall and green about it and the barns and corrals and outbuildings behind, would be a matter of memories for her. Sam thought: She was born in that house, and she left it for me because her dad and mother wouldn't have me. And now she's coming back . . . fifteen years older, and no one there to greet her. A sudden access of pity flooded through him, and Sam wanted very much to say something to his wife—just a word or so. But communication had long ago become a difficult thing between these two. Sam merely shrugged, and halting his team under the shade trees jumped down into the grass and came around the back of the wagon, reached up and gave his wife a hand to help her down. She said, "You going to see to the team?"

He glanced at the wagon. Beyond, he could see men lounging about the door of the bunkhouse. The B-in-the-Box riders were staying close today as the new owners moved in. Sam grunted: "I'll have one of the hands run the rig back to town."

But he had taken only a few steps in their direction when Myra called him. She was at the top of the steps now, in the shade of the veranda; and he thought that her voice sounded almost a little frightened. "Maybe . . . maybe you'd better come with me, Sam."

Somehow relieved at having put off his encounter with the ranch crew, Sam came back and moved slowly up the broad steps. He took the key from Myra, unlocked the door, and shoved it open. Myra stepped inside. Sam followed.

The last time they had gone through that door together—even now he could remember the delicious terror of it, as fortified with the courage of youth and of a fact accomplished they had walked in, timidly, and shown Harry Benton the brand-new wedding ring on Myra's hand. Sam wondered if she felt this too; wondered if that was the reason she called him back and wanted him with her now.

But quickly the spell had passed, and again they were two shabby, aging people wandering through the empty house. Sam didn't try to talk, but let her take the impact of each well-remembered room in silence. She paused a long time in the doorway of the bedchamber where her mother had died. After that they went down the stairs again and into the low-ceilinged living room, and here Myra lowered herself stiffly to one of the pair of comfortable, leather-bound settees. Sam stood by the cold fireplace, staring at the cougar skin on the hardwood floor.

The sound of sobbing jerked his head up suddenly. Myra had her head bowed against her hands and he watched awkwardly, not knowing what to say as her thin shoulders jerked to her weeping. But she didn't stop, kept right on crying as he had not seen her do in many years. On an impulse then he moved to her, put a hand upon her faded hair. "Please, Myra!" he mumbled. "Ain't any good cryin'. . . ."

Suddenly she had stopped, and reaching up she seized his shabby coat sleeve and drew him toward her. "Sit down, Sam!" He obeyed, uneasily, his shapeless hat upon his knee. She was very serious, but not cross now as he had grown accustomed to finding her. "We've got to have a talk . . . about everything."

"Yes," said Sam.

"It's not easy, what I want to say. Coming here like this to my home after all these years. I feel old and lost. And yet . . . there's a chance now, Sam! A chance to make something of the little time that's left, and maybe forget what's come between."

He could say nothing, merely sit and look at her tired and patient face.

"I'll need help, Sam," this worn and graying woman beside him was saying now. "I can't go it all alone. Won't . . . won't you try, now, again? We've hurt each other, I know. I held you back when you might have gone ahead; but you. . . ."

"You don't need to say it," he muttered. "I know my shortcomings, I reckon." He stood up suddenly. "I'm no good, Myra, and it ain't likely there's much left in me worth saving. But I used to know something about a ranch . . . I'm goin' outside now," he added, gruffly, "and size up the crew."

He was glad to escape from her, and her tired, accusing eyes. Dragging on the shapeless hat, he went out through the dark front hall and upon the broad veranda, closing the big door behind him. And there were the men of B-in-the-Box, gathered in the shade of the bunkhouse, waiting motionless with their eyes upon him. Sam steeled himself to face them.

III

Under the hard glare of the sun, he went toward the silent group. Nothing had changed much around the ranch headquarters, he had time to notice, since the days when he had been foreman here at B-in-the-Box. The same buildings, except for the fine new barn. The big house itself had a new wing that had been completed only a year or so before; the extension contained Benton's office and a spare storeroom or two.

There were ten riders on the payroll. Two or three got to their feet as Sam came up but the others merely lounged and stared at him and he stood facing them, a scarecrow of a man in his battered clothing. Most of them were armed, but Sam's gun and belt had long ago gone as a trade-in for booze.

Big, dark-haired Cal Tedrow stood leaning against the side of the door, hat pushed back. Sam felt that here was the most effective place to affirm his authority. He cleared his throat, said with a firmness of tone he had not used to any man for a long spell of years: "You want to quit now, Tedrow, or wait to get fired?"

The foreman straightened, putting his feet down flat upon the earth; his dark face shot forward. He began to swear at Sam Wills in a flat, monotonous voice. The others heard him in silence, watching the faces of the two intently as though waiting to see how this would develop. "You worthless, drunken bum! You can't fire me!"

"Your pay stopped five minutes ago. You better draw it and ride!" Sam said.

"Yeah?" Tedrow spat into the dust. "We'll see about that." He came away from the door, and Sam tensed thinking the man was coming at him; Sam's liquor-softened body would make no match for Tedrow's whang-leather toughness. But the foreman did not want a battle. He went straight past Sam Wills toward the house. He pounded at the door. Sam knew then what was in the other's mind.

Myra opened the door, looked blankly at Tedrow. And then the latter was saying, in a voice that carried clearly to the men before the bunkhouse: "Ma'am, you're your own boss, but I'm telling you flatly you can't run this ranch without a damn good ramrod. I've served your dad for three years; I know this ranch and I know its problems. And now that character," he added, with a contemptuous glance at Sam, "tells me I'm through here. I won't accept that from anyone but you, direct!"

There was a silence. Sam, with all these cowhands looking on, stood there and endured Tedrow's glance; and he endured the humility of having his own wife weigh him in the balance, publicly, in front of the hired ranch crew.

But then Myra said, in a voice that sounded thin and without too much conviction: "My husband is in charge of operating the ranch. If he thinks best to do this, then it stands."

"You're making a bad mistake, Mrs. Wills!" Tedrow stated, angrily. "That man ain't capable of rodding a spread like this! He's a has-been . . . a no-good drunk! Your dad built a fine ranch. He'll tear it down in a year's time!"

"We don't need to argue," she cut him off. "If you will step into the office, I'll pay you the money you have coming."

Tedrow went dark with cold fury. "All right!" he bit out. "I will!"

She held open the door for him and he entered, moving stiffly, not removing the big hat from his head. And slowly, deliberately, six of the men before the bunkhouse came to their feet and they too moved toward the porch.

Sam caught one of them by the arm, dragged him around. "Where are you going?"

The man looked at the other five, back at Sam. "I dunno about them. Me, I'm drawing my time. I just don't care to work here no longer."

Sam stood aside, and watched the B-in-the-Box crew melt away and leave him standing there in the hot sunlight with bowed shoulders and empty hands.

The last man had been paid, and Myra returned the cash box to the office safe where old Harry Benton, distrusting banks, had always kept his money and papers. She came out into the dark hall of the new wing and found Sam waiting, not able to meet her eye directly as she faced him. The front door slammed shut behind the last of the crew. Sam muttered: "Thanks for backing me against Tedrow!"

"You're my husband," she retorted, rather sharply. "I couldn't very well have done anything else . . . it wouldn't have looked right! But. . . ." She looked at him closely, in the shadowed hall. "Are you sure it was the best move? You see what happened."

"Yeah, I see. I had my reasons, though," Sam added. "Right now I'm going to saddle up and take a look around; see how large a crew we really need to run this ranch. After that I'll go out and find them!"

Starting for the corral to find a mount, he halted in sudden surprise as he noticed three cowpunchers still lounging in the shade by the bunkhouse. He headed in their direction. "Ain't you three gone yet?" he demanded, in a sour tone.

One got to his feet—a tall, lean youth, who could make a quick move without seeming to put any effort into it. "Then are we fired too, Mr. Wills?"

Sam looked at the three of them. "No . . . not if you ain't of a mind to quit. I just thought everybody left with Tedrow."

"Hunh-uh," said the youngster. "We three don't like Tedrow."

"I see." Sam was thoughtful. "What's you fellows' names?"

"Bob Redpath." The others identified themselves as Norrell and Lang.

"Set down, Bob," said Sam. "I guess you boys see what I'm up against. I have to take over this spread . . . cold . . . and run it without any crew to speak of. I don't know anything about the shape the range or the stock are in. And . . . ," he added slowly, "it's been a long time since I thought much about such things. . . . Now, you fellows got any suggestions?"

Norrell and Lang exchanged glances. The latter said: "Shucks, neither of us been on the payroll but just a few weeks. But Red-path's ridden for B-in-the-Box nearly a year now."

"The spread's in pretty good shape, Mr. Wills," Bob Redpath spoke up. "There are a couple of things, though. . . ."

"Well?"

"We been losing some cattle," said the young man, earnestly. "Not heavy . . . just a trickle, a few head now and then. Once or twice, though, Tedrow would have us make a good-sized gather, and then we'd leave them alone for a night and next day they'd be gone. Speaking mighty plain," he added, "Tedrow and some of his pals was generally away from the bunkhouse on those nights."

Sam looked at him sharply. "Like that, huh? Did you ever say anything about this to Harry Benton?"

"Couldn't. None of the hands ever was able to talk to the boss except through Tedrow . . . that's the way Benton run this ranch. Common cowhands was too far beneath him."

Sam nodded, for surely he, more than any other, had felt the weight of old Benton's autocratic notions.

Redpath said: "And it was the same about the dam."

"What dam?"

"Well, that's the other thing I meant to tell you about. You see, B-in-the-Box has a good graze, but it ain't getting the water it needs. And there's a place I've noticed along the creek where it seems to me a dam could be thrown up pretty cheap and backfill a natural little reservoir. Then, with irrigation ditches put out from there. . . ."

Sam got to his feet quickly. "Wait a minute, Bob," he said. "Let's just saddle up and go take a look at that place. You boys," he added to Norrell and Lang, "hang around a spell, will you?"

Complete as his memory was of the whole stretch of that range, Sam could not have named a place for a dam until Redpath took him to the spot and pointed it out. "Well, I'll be juggered," Sam muttered. "It wouldn't take much to close off this narrow point and the hills behind it form a perfect cup. Yeah . . . a good idea, come to think of it. Seems like the creek's smaller than in the old days. Maybe the springs back in the hills are giving out, and in that case we'd better start thinking about impounding this water while we can."

"I'm glad you agree," said Bob Redpath, modestly. "Seemed to me I was right."

Sam looked at him thoughtfully. "There's a head on your shoulders, Bob. And from remarks you've let drop I fancy you got your share of savvy about cattle and horses, too. How would you like a try at rodding this outfit?"

The younger man turned toward him, slowly. "Me? Fill Tedrow's job?"

"I'd like you to take a whack at it. Your first chore will be to build you a crew."

"Why. . . ." Bob looked both confused and pleased. "I'd like it fine, Mr. Wills; I really would. Only. . . . Why do you want a foreman at all, if I ain't being too personal? Why don't you rod the B-in-the-Box yourself?"

Sam could feel the color rising in his face. His fingers tightened on the reins. He started to say: "I ain't gonna be around long enough." He changed that to: "I got my reasons!" And abruptly reined his bronc about and headed him back across the swells of sage and bunch grass. Bob fell in beside him. The new foreman looked puzzled.

Next morning Sam and Bob took the buckboard into Sage Flats. Before they left Myra gave Sam a list. "Here's some things I'll be needing. I think you can get most of them at Logan's and we'll put an order in to the mail order house at Kansas City for the rest."

He took the paper, glanced at the items. "Good night!" he exclaimed. "You're really going to make the place over, aren't you?"

"I laid awake most of the night, planning," she admitted, and there was a tone in her voice and a color in her thin cheeks that Sam could not remember having found there in years. "This house is a gloomy place. Dad didn't seem to care how it looked. But I'm going to put up some new drapes and liven things a little bit." Almost shyly she added: "Do . . . do you think I'm being silly?"

"Good Lord, no!" he blurted. "Seems to me you're just enjoying yourself, Myra. It's high time you was!" And then she smiled at him!

It lasted just an instant, that smile, but it was compounded of many things—of understanding, even of forgiveness. It took away the years that were piled about her eyes and her mouth, and it smoothed the harshness from her brow; so that, for the moment, this person smiling at him was a girl that he had loved fifteen long years ago.

But the moment passed quickly, and Myra was turning away from him to the iron box safe. "I'll give you the money now," she said briskly, and opening the cash box began counting out a handful of bills.

Then suddenly she faltered, made a move as though to stuff the money back into the box.

Sam blurted out: "That's all right . . . I'll tell Logan to charge it to you. Not so much danger that way of me getting sidetracked at the Shorthorn Bar!"

He saw her jaw go firm. With quick determination, she shut the lid of the box and handed the money to him. "I like best trading in cash." She hesitated. "I've given you a little extra. Why not stop in at the clothing store and buy some new duds? A rancher ought to look the part, you know, and that outfit of yours has seen its best days. . . ."

The money rode heavy in his pocket all the way to town. He had little to say to Bob Redpath.

When they nosed their team and buckboard into a hitchrack before the general store and Sam swung down to snub the reins, he happened to glance at the brick building across the way and there he saw the lean and yellow face of Homer Lowndes at the open window. Sam looked away quickly.

Bob joined him on the board sidewalk. "What's the program, Mr. Wills?"

"I dunno. I got some shopping to do first. Maybe you can nose around and see if there's riders in town looking for work. Sign on any that look good to you."

His new foreman agreed, and they parted. Sam went into the general store. Old man Logan scowled when he saw who it was.

"Another scorcher today," said Sam, as he handed over the list and the merchant scanned it though his glasses. In answer, Logan only raised his brows in a sideward glance at him, and with a sour grunt moved away.

He set out the goods perfunctorily, gave Sam back the paper and snatched the money that was handed him. He made change and turned his back without a word.

Sam gathered up his bundles and dumped them grimly into the rear of the buckboard. It positively hurt, he knew, for the good people of this town to have to deal with him in any way—to accept now as an equal the derelict they had never noticed before, unless to throw him out or sic the dogs on him.

And of course, they were right! Those who had despised Sam Wills had always secretly pitied his wife; and now his change of station was due to her and her alone. It was Myra's money, not his own, that he was spending today.

As he hooked the buckboard tailgate a sudden commotion down the street broke in on Sam's reflections. A fight had started. Two men were in the dust, slugging it out, while others came yelling and shouting to watch, the planks of the walk drumming under their feet. And then one of the combatants went down and through swirling dust Sam caught a better glimpse of the other, standing over him. It was Bob Redpath.

Sam started in that direction as fast as he could run, but liquor had broken his wind and the fight was over before he reached there. The man Bob had licked was getting up, slinking away through the crowd with a hand clamped to his jaw; and Bob turned to a bunch of men on the post office steps, fists clenched, and bareheaded, "Any more of you want the same?"

There were no takers. A few turned hastily and walked away; but another spoke up quickly; "I've changed my mind about that job, friend. If you'll take me, I'd like to sign on."

Two or three others echoed his words. Redpath nodded. "All right," he said. "Get your broncs and meet me in ten minutes."

Then as they scattered he turned away, ignoring the curious glances of the onlookers, and he came face to face with Sam Wills. "Oh . . . howdy," said Bob, grinning sheepishly.

"Been hiring riders?" said Sam. He glanced at the bruised knuckles Bob was wiping on his shirt front. Bob followed his glance, tried to laugh as he flexed the hand.

"Little argument," he said, carelessly. He would talk no more about it.

Bob and Sam headed again for the buckboard. Within a few minutes four cowpunchers with trail-stained clothing, and soogans and warbags strapped behind their high-cantled saddles, had ridden up singly and joined them. Bob introduced them to Sam, who allowed that the B-in-the-Box foreman had signed up a good bunch of men.

"I've finished my shopping," Sam said then, indicating the load of goods in the back of the wagon. "So we might as well be heading home. Unless," he suggested, idly, "you'd like a drink first?"

Bob Redpath gave him a sharp look, ducked his head quickly. "Ain't particularly thirsty," he muttered. "But I'll step inside with you."

"Oh no." Sam took the reins. "I was just thinking you might want one."

He clucked to the horses.

IV

"What were you fighting about?" Sam demanded, suddenly, when they were about halfway to the ranch.

He saw the confusion that gripped the youngster. Bob tried to tell him, "It wasn't anything. . . ." Sam cut him off.

"Maybe he said he wanted nothing to do with an outfit run by the town bum. Was that it?"

Redpath colored. "Did I . . . ?"

"No, you didn't say anything of the kind," muttered Sam. "I just guessed it. Well, that's a stigma this ranch won't have to put up with forever!"

At the B-in-the-Box Redpath showed the new hands to their quarters. Sam unloaded the buckboard. Myra was delighted by the things he had brought. "These are just right!" she exclaimed, unrolling a bolt of flowered drapery goods. "They'll make up into nice curtains and put a touch of color into this drab living room. See?"

She spread it at arm's length to show the effect. And something about her face, peering at him excitedly above the brightly colored goods, touched him deeply. "Gosh, Myra," he blurted. "You ought to get you a dress made out of something like that. It makes you look younger . . . like when you was a girl!"

"Why, Sam!" Her cheeks colored with pleasure. She dropped the goods across one arm and raised her free hand, self-consciously, to smooth her faded hair. She stopped then, expression changing. "I told you to buy yourself some clothes," she said, in her old tone of suspicion. "What did you do with the money?"

"Oh." He dug into his pocket, pulled out the bills and looked at them. "Guess I just forgot," he mumbled. He tossed the money on the table. "Bet you thought I'd get plastered with that, didn't you?" He shrugged, turned abruptly, and shuffled out of the room.

"Wait!" Myra cried. "Sam, I'm sorry, I. . . ."

But he would not come back, and her voice was cut away by the door's closing.

Time was running out, however, and the three weeks' grace Homer Lowndes had granted him were almost over. A few days before the end of that period the lawyer himself dropped by. He was the first caller Myra had received since inheriting B-in-the-Box, and his coming filled her with an obvious and almost childlike excitement.

She served him tea and cake in the old swing on the veranda, wearing a flowered dress she'd found at the store in Sage Flats shortly after Sam offered his suggestion; and the change it made in her was startling. Lowndes, recovered from his first astonishment, responded with an unctuous charm and showed his buck teeth in a yellow smile that Sam, who observed the scene from time to time around the corner of the house, found revolting.

Before he left, Lowndes found a chance to draw Sam aside. "How is everything going?" the lawyer wanted to know.

"To schedule," Sam told him. "She's got a dandy foreman now, and the ranch is in good shape."

"Cal Tedrow?"

"I hear he's still in the neighborhood with a half dozen hardcases that quit their jobs the same day I fired him. I hope he doesn't give any trouble. Otherwise, Myra should be able to get along quite well after . . . after I leave."

"Good!" Lowndes hesitated a moment. "I must say, Wills, that your wife is still a most attractive woman! I would never have dreamed what a change this inheritance could make in her."

Sam only shrugged; but after Lowndes had left he cursed and let off steam by kicking an empty can across the dusty ground. "The damned hypocrite!" he muttered. "Got his cap set for her already . . . and the ranch, too. And here my hands are tied, and he knows it!"

One result of the lawyer's visit, however, was to break the ice with the people of Sage Flats. The wives of other ranchers began dropping in to call on the woman who had formerly done their cleaning and washing. Myra received them all graciously, and what was past seemed now forgotten. Today she was owner of the district's biggest cattle ranch. And with every day that passed she appeared to grow younger, more like the girl she had once been.

After one of these visits, Sam came up the front steps to find her seated alone in the veranda swing, and she stared at him with a strange look in her eyes. "Sam!" she exclaimed.

He stopped, put a shoulder against the pillar beside the steps. "What is it?"

"Just now . . . sitting here this way . . . I was reminded of that first day, a long time ago. Do you remember?"

He nodded, slowly. "Yeah, I remember. . . ."

Coming up those same steps, tall and brown and strong in his youthfulness; and she sitting in that same swing, brown hair loose about her shoulders, eyes bright and a charming color in the fresh, soft curve of her cheek. She had spoken his name; with a touch of his hatbrim he'd started past toward the door, only to have her call him back again.

"Are you mad at me, Sam?"

He stared at her, "Mad at you, Miss Benton?"

"You never even speak to me anymore. I'm sorry if I've done something to offend you. . . ."

Consternation was in him, and he swallowed twice before he could speak. "Gosh, Miss Benton! How could you offend anyone? I been pretty busy, that's all. Your dad's waiting in the house to see me, right now."

"Oh. You better go along then." And the sun came out in her face. "I only wanted to ask you about the hurt foal."

"Why, I'll be glad to take you down to the pasture to see it, later on, if you'd like."

And that was all—just the few, half-stumbling words, and the unspoken thing that passed between them, going deeper than any words. And then the brief, sweet moment ending as Harry Benton came striding to the door looking for his foreman—and the quick suspicion that flashed into the older man's face as he found the pair of them together and read the last looks in their eyes. . . .

"YAH," said Sam, and ran his fingers through graying hair. "That was a good many days ago!"

"You coming up the steps just now reminded me," said Myra. She rose, went to her husband; and then she kissed him, swiftly, and stepped back. She laughed at the look on his face. "Do you mind so much? I just felt like doing it. . . ."

He couldn't answer. It had been a long, long time since any show of affection had passed between these two.

"I told you to buy some new clothes, Sam!" she said suddenly. "I meant it, too. I want you to go right into town and do it . . . this very afternoon! And I'll not have any excuses this time!"

A turmoil rode within Sam as he took the trail to Sage Flats under the hot sun. It was not going to be so easy to go away and give up everything. Not the ranch—losing that would mean very little to him. But Myra—Sam realized the truth. He still loved his wife, and in spite of everything he thought, there was still some tenderness left in her heart for him.

He knew a sudden wild impulse. Defy Homer Lowndes and the second will! Let him produce it—and then let Myra decide! Perhaps—but that would solve nothing. The old problem would be with them again. Myra would be left without her father's ranch, and with a weakling of a husband on her hands.

Sam was swinging down from his bronc as this truth struck him, his fingers fumbling to knot the reins about the hitch rack before the Shorthorn Bar. A moment later, without quite knowing how he got there, he was leaning on the mahogany with a boot on the rail, and his voice sounded to him like a croak as he ordered: "Whisky!"

The barkeep, knowing him from the old days, gave Sam a hard look and automatically he dug into a pants pocket, his stubby fingers finding the money Myra had given him. The clothes he needed wouldn't take all of that. He fished out a bill, slapped it down on the bar, and then his first drink in weeks was in his hand and he emptied the glass quickly, set it down gasping for breath.

Above the saloon's swinging doors, across the white-hot blast of the street, he could see the windows of Homer Lowndes's office. How long was it since he had sat in front of Homer's desk, and drunk the stingy glassful of liquor Homer offered him? It must be— Good Lord! Day after tomorrow, the three weeks would be up. Then Lowndes would produce that second will, which even now must be waiting in the drawer of his desk where Sam had seen it placed.

A sudden sweat broke out on Sam's forehead, as an idea struck him with brutal force. "You damn fool!" he muttered, softly. "Why hadn't you thought of that?"

Get to that office, perhaps at night. Pick the lock on the door some way. Find that will and destroy it—and then let the ghost of Harry Benton—and Homer Lowndes too, try to do anything about it!

The idea was so sound, so foolproof, that it turned Sam all a-tremble. He needed another drink to steady his nerves and clear his brain so he could think about it. He would have to do this very carefully, not take any chance of being caught! He motioned to the bartender, got his glass filled again. "Leave the bottle set there," he ordered as an afterthought, and lifted the amber liquid to his mouth. . . .

V

"Hey, Mr. Wills! Sam!" The hand was shaking him again. Sam tried to sit up but the pain in his head was too much. Bob Redpath's urgent voice faded out. Lying back, Sam tried to figure out where he was and what was happening. He must have passed out completely; next thing he knew Bob was back and a hand was under his head, raising him, and there was a pungent, steamy odor in his nostrils.

Bob said: "Come on, drink this, Sam! It's strong, black coffee. It'll do you good!"

The last thing in the world he wanted just then was coffee, but the thick china mug was against his lips, insistently, and he gulped it down. He gasped over it, with the bite of the hot liquid eating at the fog that filled his head. Then here came the cup, full again. "More," insisted Bob. "Drink it up!"

"No!" groaned Sam, trying to push the cup away. "No, please. . . ."

But it went burning down his throat. He shook his head, ran the back of a hand shakily across his mouth, found the scrape of beard stubble. And then his eyes came open, blearily, and the face of Bob Redpath swam slowly into focus. "Where . . . ?" Sam muttered thickly. "What . . . ?"

"You're in Sage Flats," his foreman told him. "Right at the edge of town. I saw your bronc grazing and found you here in the weeds beside the road."

Sam tried to sit up, to look around; but the effort was too much and he collapsed against Bob. He ran a furry tongue across his lips. "A drink!" he begged, brokenly. "For the love of. . . ."

"No! You've already had too much. I got a whole pot of coffee from the eat shack yonder and you're gonna drink every drop if it takes that to sober you up. Come on, now!"

There was no resisting that firm voice or the hands that forced the cup against his lips. Sam let the scalding liquid pour into him; then a spasm seized him and he rolled over face down into the ditch and was sick. He lost all the coffee, and everything else; until his stomach churned on emptiness, and a great weakness and trembling took him.

"Good enough!" said Bob grimly. "Now we'll shove some breakfast into you and you'll be good as new."

"Lemme alone!" moaned Sam, his fingers digging at the sandy soil. "I wanna die!"

The other jerked him up, clear up to his feet. "Now listen! You got to sober up and pay attention to me. There's been trouble. Cal Tedrow!"

That name served to clear Sam's head. Staggering uncertainly on swaying legs, he blinked at the other. "What's he done?" he demanded. "He hurt Myra? Damn you, what's he done?"

"He just turned bronco, is all. Him and his crew made a try last night for that hundred head we're holding for the Wagon Gap shipment. Luckily, I had some men spotted there and they busted up the raid . . . killed a couple of his riders, and scattered the rest. The sheriff's got a posse on the trail now!"

"When . . . when did you say all this was?" Sam demanded.

"Last night." He added dryly, "It's early morning now, you know."

Then, with a groan, Sam saw the pieces begin falling into place. "And I went and fell off my bronc trying to get home," he said, bitterly. "And lay here in a ditch all night . . . while this was going on!"

"I found you hadn't been in your room," said Bob. "That's how I came looking for you and caught sight of your bronc. Now, we got to get you back on your feet *pronto*, and head for home."

"Like this?" Sam looked down at himself, at his clothing foul with filth and mud. He remembered, shoved a hand frantically into his pocket. It was empty.

"Drunk it up!" he exclaimed, self-hatred twisting his wan, bearded face. "The money Myra gave me for new clothes. I can't ever face her again, Bob! I'm no good! I didn't even. . . ." He almost said: *I didn't even have the guts to do the job I planned, and rob Lowndes's office.* But he held it back.

"Now listen to me, Mr. Wills," said Bob, earnestly. "I happen to have money with me. We'll get some breakfast. Then as soon as the store opens we'll buy you those clothes . . . you can pay me back later. And we'll tell your wife something to explain where you were last night."

"No, no!" Sam mumbled, shaking his head in misery. "There's no point in it. Why waste your time, kid?"

But Bob Redpath had a stubborn quality in him, and when the two of them came to B-in-the-Box in midmorning Sam was wearing the new shirt and riding pants, and boots, and hat. Sam rode with head sagging, his spirit low.

Myra was waiting in the yard for them, consternation showing in her as she saw Sam's wan, sick face. "Is he hurt?" she demanded.

"No, Miz' Wills," Bob explained. "Your husband's pretty well worn out, is all. He was in the saddle all night trying to overtake Tedrow's crew . . . that's why he never come home."

"Help me get him into the house!" Myra exclaimed. Still weak and shaky, Sam had to let them ease him down from the saddle and then, one on each side, support him as he stumbled up the steps and into the coolness of the house. And then he was in his own room, on the bed, and the new boots were being taken from his feet. "Thanks, Bob," Myra said. The door closed and they were alone.

On a chair by his bed, Myra had a hand on his hot, dry forehead. And she was saying: "You shouldn't have tried it, Sam! You're not as young as you used to be. And you wouldn't have had a chance if you'd happened to catch up with that gang. But I'm proud of you just the same!" She added: "You look mighty nice in your new outfit, too, Sam. But now, you get some rest."

Sam twisted feverishly, overcome with shame. "No, no!" he cracked. "It ain't true . . . it ain't. . . ." He wanted to blurt out the facts.

"What is it, Sam?" said Myra.

He groaned. "Nothin'," he grunted. "I dunno what I'm saying!"

"You get some sleep!" she ordered. At the door she paused. "Can I bring you a little something to eat first? You must be starved, too."

"No! Just . . . leave me alone!"

For a long time he lay there wrestling with a problem that was too much for him. And then at last he slept, a troubled rest; and when he awoke night had come again and all was stillness in the dark of the room.

He pawed aside the blankets, dropped his stockinged feet to the floor and sat up on the edge of the bed. His head ached sharply; he waited a moment for it to clear.

He had slept all day. And tomorrow was the deadline Homer Lowndes had set for him! Well, he knew now what he had to do; and he knew that, somewhere, he had found the strength to accomplish it. He was ravenously hungry, but there was no time to think of food. He got up, padded across the room, and found the lamp on the dresser. He located a match, lighted it.

A clock beside the lamp said ten thirty; he would have to be in town by midnight for that was when the westbound stopped at the depot and took on water at the tower.

A sick-looking face, clouded with day-old beard stubble, peered back at Sam from the mirror above the dresser. He looked down at himself, at the new clothes. And then, in a corner of the room, he spotted the bundle of mud-caked rags that someone must have found tied to the cantle of his saddle, and brought in while he slept and left here.

Moving hastily, Sam undressed and got into the clammy wreckage of his old clothing. The new garments he rolled up and tied in a bundle, and then as an afterthought he dug out a paper and pencil from a drawer of the dresser and leaned to scribble a hasty note:

Bob:

I can't pay you for these but maybe you can sell them and get part of your money back. You shouldn't have bought them. You shouldn't have wasted your time or your lies trying to save me.

The rods is the only place for me and that's where I'm headed. I'm taking one of the horses but I'll leave it at the stable back of the railroad depot. So long, Bob. When Lowndes comes out tomorrow you'll find out why I'm doing this—for my wife's sake! I'm afraid she might not have made the right choice—that she thinks I'm worth keeping. You and I though, we know different. We know the truth about me!

I leave the ranch in your hands. They're good ones.

Sam Wills

He folded this, tucked it into a pocket of the shirt where Bob would surely find it. Then, with the bundle under his arm, he tiptoed out.

Bob Redpath slept in the bunkhouse with the rest of the hands. Sam knew that most, if not all, of the half dozen B-in-the-Box riders would be gone from the ranch tonight—some guarding the cattle that Tedrow had almost got away with, others riding with the sheriff's posse if it, indeed, was still in the field. Sam stole out of the house without waking his wife, and then across the dark ranch yard. The bunkhouse door was open. He set the bundle of clothes where Bob couldn't fail to see it; and then he made for the corral.

A number of horses were in the pen. He would find saddle and bridle and blanket in the tack room of the big barn, next to it. Sam swung open the barn door, moved into the big room redolent with the odors of hay and grain and animals. The tack room was up front. Sam walked into it—and straight into a gun barrel that rammed hard against his belly. Tedrow's voice said: "We was beginning to think maybe you weren't headed this way after all, Sam!"

He sucked in breath, sharply. "Tedrow!" he muttered. "What are you doing here?"

"It's as good a place as any, ain't it, with the law out in the hills looking for us?"

"You're through in this country!" said Sam. "Don't you know that?"

He heard the fury behind the other's reply: "Yeah . . . thanks to you, you worthless bum! But me, I don't care to leave empty-handed . . . not when there's a safe full of cash that I might just as well tap, first. That's why we doubled back and stopped off here."

"Are you talking about . . . ?"

"Shut up!" the ex-foreman growled. He added: "Search the guy, Nick, and see he ain't got a gun on him."

Rough hands seized Sam, felt for a weapon. "Nothin', Cal."

"All right," said Tedrow. "Start walking, mister. And no noise!"

Halfway through the big building they hauled up suddenly. One of the men whispered: "Somebody coming!"

"In here . . . quick!" Sam was pushed bodily into a stall, and the others crowded in after him. A man's figure blocked out the opening of the barn's doorway, then Bob Redpath called softly: "Sam! Mr. Wills!"

The gun in his ribs, and the harsh breathing of Tedrow against his ear, held Sam taut and silent. The man at the door said: "Are you still here, Sam? I woke up and I found the note you left. You're making an awful mistake, Sam! Believe me, you are!"

The silence rang out; no sound except the scurrying of a rat somewhere in the hay. Suddenly Bob came running by them, and into the tack room. He came out again and they could tell he was lugging a heavy saddle with him. And then he had left the barn and the one called Nick said, tightly: "Maybe we shoulda stopped him, Cal. Maybe he guessed something!"

"No he didn't!" Sam said, hastily. "He just decided I had already left and he's saddling a bronc to ride to Sage Flats and try and head me off."

Cal Tedrow said: "All right. We'll just wait here a few minutes."

And presently a horse left the corral and the sound of its hoof-beats drummed away to silence; and then Sam knew that except for himself and Myra, and maybe the old crippled cook, the ranch was now deserted. "Okay," grunted Tedrow. "Let's go!"

They moved across the darkness of the yard—Tedrow, and Sam, and two of Harry Benton's renegade hands. When they reached the new wing of the house, Tedrow said: "We'll try this side door. If it's locked, we can force a window."

But the door was open and they trooped through it silently. Tedrow closed and locked the hall door and said softly: "Light a lamp, somebody. We'll just make ourselves at home."

Nick got the wick burning. He was a big-boned, towheaded waddy; the third man Sam recognized as a skinny hand who was generally known as "Rooster." Sam faced Tedrow now in the lamplight, and he knew he made a shabby, unimpressive appearance. But he said, stoutly: "You can't get away with it!"

"Cut out the nonsense!" growled the ex-foreman, and he shoved Sam around toward the iron box safe in the corner of the room. "Get over there and open that tin can for us, real quick!"

Sam shook his head. "But I . . . I don't know the combination to that safe!"

"You don't!"

Rooster snorted. "He's lyin'."

"No . . . no, maybe not." Tedrow looked very sour. "Come to think of it, if that wife of his has got any brains in her skull, she wouldn't tell this boozehound how to get to her money."

"Then what'll we do?" demanded Nick.

"Fetch the woman in here," answered Tedrow. "We can make her tell us the combination."

Sam choked out: "No. . . ." But no one paid him any attention. Suddenly Rooster was saying:

"Boss, I think I can open this crackerbox by touch. Just be quiet a minute and lemme hear the tumblers fall. . . ."

He was on his knees in front of the safe, a look of pained concentration on his bony features, working the dial with deft, lean fingers. The other two were watching him, waiting, all their attention on Rooster's effort.

Sam was thinking of Harry Benton's will—how it said that Myra would have to be a widow to inherit B-in-the-Box. He was thinking just then that there was more than one way to make a widow out of a woman. And the thought made him suddenly reckless, suddenly indifferent to whatever might happen to himself.

Nick was standing next to him, eyes trained on Rooster and the safe, and the gun butt in Nick's holster was thrust, invitingly, almost into Sam's fingers. Very calmly, Sam pulled it out and before Nick could do more than give a startled squawk the barrel of his own weapon was laid across the side of his head and he dropped cold, striking a corner of the rolltop desk. The safe had swung open and Rooster was reaching for the metal cash box as Nick's fall interrupted him. He whirled, startled, and the box dropped to the carpet followed by a snow of papers. Rooster was digging for his own revolver. Sam squeezed the trigger. The concussion of the shot was terrific in that closed space. Sam had not fired a gun in years, but he had a feeling that his bullet had gone home even before he saw Rooster sag against the safe.

And then Tedrow hit him with a heavy fist that took Sam across the side of the face. Sam went down. His fingers opened, letting the gun drop. But in agony he held on to consciousness and would not go clear under. He was rolling as he hit the floor, and he just missed the toe of the boot that Tedrow aimed at Sam's face. He caught that boot in his hands, instead, and with what little strength he had in him Sam gave Tedrow's leg a jerk.

It was just enough to throw him off balance, to swing him around clutching at the desk for support. His hand struck the kerosene lamp, sent it crashing over in a spray of broken glass and burning oil. And then he too hit the floor and Sam threw himself at him.

Somewhere in the house he heard Myra screaming, calling his

name. He could not think about that. Tedrow was more than he could handle—a tough frame of bone and sinew, and hands that could beat and batter the other man's soft body. Sam endured that punishment, tried to hold Tedrow and drive home a blow that could have some effect on him. His fists bounced off the man like rubber, harmlessly. Tedrow had lost his gun, but he wouldn't need it. Grappling there on the floor of the office, Sam could see him faintly—black hair streaming into a sweating face, eyes glistening.

But how *could* he see . . . ? Sam knew, then. The lamp! It had smashed, and burning oil had ignited dry timbers. Flames were running halfway up the ceiling, in that corner. They had caught the drapes Myra hung at the window, and found here new fuel. The whole wing would go, the entire house. . . .

Desperation gave Sam new strength to battle the darkness that Tedrow's blows were putting inside him. He felt the man's cheek splat beneath one knuckle-bruising blow; that had been a good one. He broke loose, rolled; felt the edge of the heavy desk cutting into his shoulder. Tedrow, coming to his knees, dived forward.

At the last second Sam twisted, let the man go past him against the desk. Tedrow dropped with a groan. At once Sam was on him, pounding Cal's head against the desk—again and again, until the man was still.

Staggering, he came to his feet in a nightmare of leaping flames and dancing shadows. Beyond the door of the office Myra was calling his name. "Stay back!" he cried through the thin partition, his voice a croak. "Get help . . . water! Before this fire spreads!"

On the floor were the huddled shapes of three men. He couldn't leave them here. Sam grabbed a chair and smashed the window. Air rushing in fanned the flames to new fury, and the curtains swayed, dripping fire. Sam got a grip under Tedrow's armpits and dragged him to the opening. Somehow he shoved him through the opening. There were two others left.

Firebrands were dropping around him and he was staggering, coughing on wood smoke, when the last man was saved. After that he went to hands and knees, groping; found the cash box where Rooster had dropped it. There were papers, too—deeds, letters, old tally books. He couldn't save them all. But he got an armful of them, and the box, and then he stumbled to the window and he went through it head first, out of that room choked with smoke and flame. He dived through the shattered window as though into cool water; but it was hard earth that received him.

VI

He was in his own bed again. The biting smell of wood smoke was everywhere. His face and his hands felt stiff and hot with burning fire; he stared dumbly at white bandages, not quite registering yet what had happened, or how he came to be here.

Myra said: "I taped up the blisters with tea leaves. That ought to take the burn out of them." Sam saw her, then, kneeling beside him. It was daylight.

"Did . . . did you get the fire put out?" he demanded anxiously.

"Yes . . . the cook and I; and some of the boys were close enough to see the reflection in the sky and they rode in fast. We lost the new wing, but the rest of the house will be all right with some patching."

Sam said, quickly: "You got the money?"

"Oh, yes! And Cal Tedrow and the other two . . . they've already been taken in to jail. Oh, Sam!" Tears were in her eyes and her voice. "I'm proud of you. The world will know, now, that I haven't been mistaken in you all these years!"

"Now, wait," he exclaimed, miserably. "Night before last. . . ."

"Forget night before last!" she retorted, smiling. "Did you think I'd never seen you with a hangover before? But you can't explain away what happened in the office. Why, I wouldn't trade you, Sam, for any man I've ever known!"

What he might have said to that was broken off by a voice sounding in the doorway. "Am I interrupting something?" It was Homer Lowndes, his yellow features broken in a smug smile of pleasure; and then Sam remembered what day this was.

"Well, well!" said the lawyer, and the look he laid on Sam was a sardonic one. "Looks like our little man has turned into a hero overnight. Yes, sir, the whole damn range is talking about you."

"Skip the humor!" growled Sam, and he braced himself. "Just hurry up and tell us what you come out here for this morning."

The face dropped its smiling mask. "All right, I'll do that. From what I was told by my predecessor in the law office at Sage Flats, there's reason to believe that Harry Benton must have left another will . . . later than the one I filed three weeks ago. I've been worried about it. So I came here today to make a final search and see if I couldn't find it among his papers."

"Another will?" repeated Myra, blankly.

"You heard him," Sam muttered. "Well, go ahead and look, damn you!"

"Oh, I already have," said Homer, blandly. "You know, that was a bad fire you had last night. If such a will ever did exist, it must have got burnt to ashes. I couldn't find a trace!"

Dumbly, Sam Wills heard him; and it took a long moment for the meaning of what the lawyer had said to strike home. But then he caught the wink Homer gave him, and he thought: Good Lord! The old devil's got a heart after all!

Lowndes was saying: "Even if Harry did intend a different way of disposing of his estate, seems to me this was still the best way it could have worked out. I reckon the ranch is in good enough hands." He smiled at both of them. "Good day, Sam. Good day, Mrs. Wills. I won't be bothering you anymore."

Sam lay back on the pillow and his wife's hand was on his shoulder. Sam did not say anything. He was too full of wonder and happiness for speech.

FURNACE FLAT

(CECIL FRANCIS) FRANK BONHAM was born in Los Angeles, California. He attended Glendale Junior College and was able to enroll as a junior at U.C.L.A., but his further education was cut short when he suffered a debilitating asthma attack while he walked through the Chemistry Building on campus. So, during that winter at twenty years of age, he went to a cabin his parents owned at Big Bear Lake to recuperate and started writing short stories. Out of 107 stories he wrote over the next two years, he managed to sell seven.

Bonham answered an advertisement in a Glendale newspaper for a "secretary-collaborator" and by this means came to meet Ed Earl Repp. Repp was in his late thirties and had established himself as a screenwriter for low-grade "B" Western films. Seeing the success of Harry F. Olmsted who had an entire stable of writers ghosting stories for him for the Western pulp magazines, Repp decided to do the same thing. Frank Bonham and Tom W. Blackburn would be the foremost names among later Western writers who underwent an apprenticeship with Repp, where they wrote the stories, Repp submitted them, and they were published under Repp's name with an even division of the income between the two. Bonham felt he had to do it because by this means he was able to earn $125 a week, but he remained resentful about the apprenticeship for the rest of his life. He later described his position with Repp as that of "a slave" and felt "I went into indentured service with this man." Bonham's parting from Repp was fraught with bad feeling. Even as late as a year before his death, Bonham wrote with some bitterness about the episode in an article titled "Tarzana Nights" now reprinted in THE BEST WESTERN STORIES OF FRANK BONHAM (Ohio University Press, 1989).

By 1941 his fiction under his own name was headlining Street & Smith's *Western Story Magazine* and by the end of the decade his Western novels were being serialized in *The Saturday Evening Post*. "I have tried to avoid," Bonham once confessed, "the conventional cowboy story, but I think it was probably a mistake. That is like trying to avoid crime in writing a mystery book. I just happened to be more interested in stagecoaching, mining, railroading. . . ." Yet, notwithstanding, it is precisely the interesting—and by comparison with the majority of Western novels—exotic backgrounds of Bonham's novels which give them an added dimension. The historical aspects of his Western fiction early drew accolades from reviewers so that on one occasion the *Long Beach Press Telegram* predicted that "when the time comes to find an author who can best fill the gap in Western fiction left by Ernest Haycox, it may be that Frank Bonham will serve well."

Frank Bonham's memorable short novels in *Lariat Story Magazine* were "She-Boss of the Devil's Graze" (5/43) and "The Canyon of Maverick Brands" (1/44). All of his novels are uniformly fine, but the very best include LOST STAGE VALLEY (Simon & Schuster, 1948), BOLD PASSAGE (Simon & Schuster, 1950), SNAKETRACK (Simon & Schuster, 1952), NIGHT RAID (Ballantine, 1954), and THE EYE OF THE HUNTER (Evans, 1989). Mike Tilden at Popular Publications told Bonham's agent, Captain Joseph T. Shaw, the same man who had once edited *Black Mask Magazine*, that he would gladly buy any story Frank Bonham wrote. "Furnace Flat" first appeared under the title "Gun-Dog of Furnace Flat" in *New Western* (12/48) and has never otherwise been reprinted.

I

"LONG HARD LIFE OF GRADY RYAN"

It was dusk when Ryan came down from the mines. He drew his pay, the last he would ever receive from Furnace Flat Borax Company, and hurried to the Miners' Bar. All day he had been thinking that the old boraxer called Mysterious Smith would become suspicious at the last minute and pull out without him. But when he stepped into the saloon, still in his dusty work clothes, miner's cap on the side of his head and pipe in his teeth, he saw Smith at the table in back near the mechanical piano.

Ryan bought a beer and carried it over. A big, black-jowled man of thirty-two, he looked rough and sober. He sat down and sprinkled salt in the beer.

Mysterious Smith kept his eyes on Ryan's face. Smith looked no different from a score of other wanderers of Death Valley and the Panamint, a bearded apostle of the pick and shovel. He was dark as mahogany and had a chest like a wine-barrel. "Well?" he said.

Grady Ryan nodded. "Did it. Turned my singlejack for the last time. Drew my pay. Thirty-six dollars for us to sink in chuck. Still taking off tonight?"

"The burros are loaded, all but the grub. Got any girls you'll be mooning over, better say good-bye to them and get it out of your system. Maybe you ain't coming back so soon."

"No girls," said Ryan. "I only mine the ore that pays."

Smith said: "You don't look like you'd been mining anything too rich. If we don't hit it this time, you better marry a rich widow."

He had a realistic, tart sort of humor which had a sting. Ryan perceived that he had dug down through his tough hide to the thing that had been disturbing him more and more the last few years. The fact that at thirty-two he was precisely where he had been at twenty, still knocking around the desert turning over rocks, hunting the lodestone that kept them coming back all their lives.

You did it so long, and then you couldn't quit. You did a hitch in the mines for an outfit, spent six months living on beans and saleratus biscuits in a box cañon, sinking test shafts and tunnels, and stumbled back disillusioned and sick of it. But after a few months you were ready to go again, your guts knotted up with eagerness, your eyes raving over a story about a strike at Skidoo or Mahogany Flat. This expedition with Mysterious Smith was merely the latest, certainly not the last, of a long series of failures entitled "The Life of Grady Ryan."

It was between shifts. They had the saloon almost to themselves. "Look," Ryan said suddenly. "Just how much chance have we really got to sink our picks into something?"

"Purty good, purty good." It was the least mysterious thing Mysterious Smith had said yet. It was spoken with a glint in eyes bleached like old denim.

Ryan put a question that was like the probing tap of a geologist's hammer. "Then I don't see why the hell you're letting me in on it, if you think there's something in the bag."

"Feller's all got different talents," said Smith, getting mysterious again.

The saloon door opened and a gang of borax muckers came in, men Ryan had worked with off and on for a couple of years. Among them were Tom Lund, his drift boss, and Pat Hoagland. Hoagland was mine superintendent, a sturdy, affable, double-dealing roughneck who knew more about mining than a company president ever would. Hoagland had instituted the practice of charging miners for the candles and carbide they used. A man had better keep his own time card, Ryan knew, or he would come out owing the company.

Hoagland came over and laid a hand on his shoulder. He wore a canvas-brown mustache and let his long hair curl above his collar. "Good luck, Grady," he said. "Maybe it's the right thing you're doing . . . though I doubt it."

"Smith and I," Ryan said, "are going to find the Lost Gunsight. Next time you see me I'll be buying cigars, instead of candles."

Hoagland's laugh resembled the grunt of a wild boar. He glanced at Smith. "I'll bet you know where all the gold in Death Valley is, come to that."

Smith said, "All that glitters is not gold."

Hoagland looked pained. He started for the bar, but turned back to Grady. "Kane would like to talk to you before you go. He'll be in his office for an hour tonight, if you've got time."

"Hell, I haven't even got a dress suit. I can't go up there looking like a mucker."

"Kane," said Hoagland, "was a mucker before he was a million-aire." He went over and found his special bottle waiting for him.

Grady winked at the prospector. "And he's going to be a mucker again, or I don't know a sick mine when I see it. Suppose you buy the groceries," he said. "I'll go up to the boarding house for my stuff. See you at Maggie Conway's for supper."

Smith grunted. " 'Tain't safe."

Ryan chuckled. "Who's Maggie Conway? Just another Cousin Jack's daughter. The girl I'm looking for has her picture on the double-eagle."

But he thought of Margaret Conway as he walked up the steep, straight road between the lava-stone buildings. If she were just an-other Cousin Jack's daughter, it was because he had kept her that way in his mind. She had the warmth and ingenuousness of her Cornish womenfolk, with a little bit of their quickness in her speech and a lot of their good humor.

Ryan had become so practiced at self-deception that he was not sure whether it was because of her that he hungered so for a real strike, or simply for himself. But he did know that it shamed him to be in debt to her for meals and, the few times he had asked leave to call on her, that he could not even afford a turn-out to take her riding. And that gnawed at him.

It was early January, the air thin and sharp as chilled wine. Night cold was invading the ugly mining town in the parched hills east of Death Valley. Above Furnace Flat's sheet-metal hives, the hills were stark and colorful, birthmarked with patches of strawberry, stained with green-stone, rotted with slanting ledges of rim rock like outcrops of rusting iron.

It was a capricious country, ready to dump gold in your lap or burn you to cracklings beside a spring it had whimsically sucked dry. Or ready simply to wear you down from vainglorious manhood into premature senescence.

Kane's office was in a big two-story headquarters building against a hillside. The boom and clatter of the mill was a discreet distance away, but the dust of it was like talcum powder all over the building and its windows. Ryan arrived in the office of Borax Kane.

He had seen Kane frequently, but had never spoken to him. The president of Furnace Flats Borax Company was a broad-shouldered man of fifty, several inches under six feet. He sat at a rough pine desk with a clutter of papers and three brimming ashtrays. He was smok-ing cigarettes, which seemed to Ryan a rather effeminate gesture.

He failed to acknowledge the mucker for a few moments; then he said without looking up: "Take a chair."

He went on signing papers while Ryan stood there with fury mounting in him, staring down at the red, veinous face with its turgid eyes and slack whiskey-mouth. Finally Kane sat back. He looked surprised at the scowl in the other's eyes—it had the effect of bringing him to his feet with an affectation of pleasure. "Sorry to make you wait, Mister. Pretty busy this time of year."

"So am I," Ryan told him.

Kane fumbled a box of cigars, almost spilled them and held them out to Ryan. Ryan took three. He kept his slow, gray-eyed gaze on the man, wondering what the hell was wrong with him. He was like a speaker who had forgotten his lines. Kane kept dodging the cigarette smoke, blinking, moving his head as though he hated the stuff but couldn't remove the cigarette from his lips. Ryan bit the end off one of the cigars.

"Why the hell don't you throw that thing away and have a cigar?"

Kane grunted, "Nothing I'd like better. The doctor took me off cigars last year. Kidneys. Damned nuisance." His flabby, rutted face annoyed the miner, somehow. "Ryan," he said, "Hoagland tells me you're quitting us. Why?"

"If I could eat the candles I have to buy," Grady said, "I might see the sense in staying."

"You can't eat desert holly, either," Borax Kane smiled. "You must feel fairly sure of yourself to give up a good job. We've let off twenty percent of our workers, you know."

Ryan said: "Yep." He saw through Kane like polished glass now.

Kane dropped the cigarette on the floor and stepped carefully on it. The racket of the mill was a muffled booming in the room. "What are you and Smith looking for?"

"I think he's got a popcorn mine staked out."

Kane sat down, two displeased lines between his eyes. "Why are you taking this attitude?" he demanded. "I asked Hoagland to send you up so I could wish you well, and. . . . Well, I'm interested in all our employees. Hoagland's mentioned you several times as being one of his best men. Frankly, I have a feeling that a man as determined and as thorough as you are may have some luck. I think I can make it a little easier for you on this trip. Whatever you're looking for." He handed Ryan a check. It was for two hundred dollars.

Ryan looked at both sides of it. "I was reading in a Mojave paper where the stockholders were climbing all over you because they didn't get any dividends last year. Sure you can spare this?"

There was color under Kane's heavy jowls. The essential nature of the man surfaced in his eyes. "It isn't that the borax is running any less high-grade," he retorted. "I had my own reasons for building up the surplus fund. Which naturally wouldn't be clear to stockholders."

Ryan flapped the check. "This buys you how much of what we find?"

"I thought of a forty percent interest. Fifty would be customary, but since there are two of you. . . ."

Ryan let the check flutter to the floor. "Maybe you ought to go prospecting, too. I don't have to get my news about the mines from the newspapers, you know. I'm one of the boys that digs the stuff you sell. It ain't running so sweet these days. Unless you hit a new ledge, I'd say your stockholders were going to be auctioning off some equipment in a couple of years."

Kane snapped: "Forget the whole thing! Men have been licked before you because they were under-capitalized! You could hit a mountain of solid gold and still lose your shirt because it costs too much for you to get it out. But once you leave here, you won't come back to anything as good as I'm prepared to offer."

"I don't know where the idea got started that Smith and I own a mine," Ryan shrugged, "but I hope it's true. If we do, we'll damn well not sell it to a scrounging rock merchant."

He went out. Below him, lights gleamed in the early darkness. I've done it now! he thought. Whatever he did, he would never be able to return to Furnace Flat. Yet it was pleasant to reflect that Borax Kane was in a more uncomfortable spot than any of his workers.

All they had was a wife and a few kids to ride them for not making any more money. Kane had a few thousand stockholders to apologize to each time he skipped a dividend.

II

"HALO OF THE TOMMYKNOCKERS"

It was eight o'clock when he left the company rooming house with his belongings. A remembered feeling as of a hairspring jiggling inside him began. A man his age ought to be rid of illusions of big strikes. But there was always the chance. . . .

Just this one last trip! One more pull at the bottle, bartender, before you cork it. But suddenly the bottle was empty, the visions old, the drinker disillusioned of his drink, but betrothed to it forever.

Ryan started down the hill with his old rattan suitcase on his shoulder. It was amusing, the way even Kane credited Mysterious Smith with having a hidden claim. Rot! Smith wouldn't be letting other men in on it if he had. Put a beard on a man, fill his mouth with secret gibberish, and they whispered of buried treasure and divining rods.

Smith was not at the cafe. Grady had kept a single dollar of his pay; he could eat sparingly on this. Margaret Conway placed steel knife, fork, and spoon before him with efficient, slender fingers. She gave him what seemed a special smile; it puzzled him.

A light-limbed blond girl, she wore her hair up, a pencil thrust into it. She wore a starched blue-and-white blouse that made her look like an illustration for a James Whitcomb Riley poem. Her skirt was long and dark, snug about the hips and full below; she seemed to Ryan something entirely too fragile and feminine for this country.

He had mulligan, pie, and coffee. All through the meal, as she passed near him going to and from the kitchen, he kept wanting to say something to her, something significant but not too significant.

Well, Mysterious Smith and I are going out prospecting together. I'll be coming back rich and full of ideas in a couple of months.

No good. He'd be coming back broke and hungry. But one of these days he would see a ring on her hand when she set out the silver, and soon after that she would be merely another miner's wife, just a woman to tip his hat to on the street.

Ryan ended by saying nothing. He laid the dollar on the counter, took his hat from a nail, and walked out. He had the feeling that he was walking out of her life and, though he knew he had never really been in it, it took some of the shine off the trip.

Suddenly he heard the door open again as he moved away. He turned. She stood in the doorway, hands on hips, slim with the light behind her, the dream a man saw on lonely trails.

"Grady," she said, "they tell me you're leaving. Is that the only good-bye you've got for me . . . a silver dollar?"

He went back. "Chloriders come, and chloriders go, but Ryan goes more than anybody," he grinned. "I'll be back one day, do another hitch for Kane, and take off again."

"You aren't a man to stay with a thing, are you?"

"I've stayed with the valley fourteen winters and one summer."

Maggie Conway tucked the pencil in her hair. It made him think of a schoolteacher, a young and pretty schoolteacher, but one trying to get a point across.

"Staying with the valley is just a way of not staying with anything," she said. "You're a young and stout one, Grady Ryan, but you won't always be. Why don't you stay with Furnace Flat?"

"I'll be stout longer following a jackass than I will be digging widow-makers."

"I was watching to see you make drift boss, superintendent, and then go after old Kane's job. You don't have to stay in the mine, you know."

"Those things make good reading, Maggie. But I've yet to see it happen. For me, the caper is to hunt the lodestone. Aaron Winters found it, One-Eye Thompson and some others. Maybe it's in the cards for me. If it is. . . ." His tongue ran down. Thin ice crackled under him. "Well, the first thing I'll do," he smiled, "is to pay my grub bill at Maggie Conway's."

She made an impatient gesture. For a long time the violet-gray eyes speculated on him with something of the same look she had given him in the restaurant. "There's something . . . Grady!" she said suddenly. "You're going to strike it this time! It's on you. The look is on you. That's what I saw when I was putting out your silver!"

Ryan laughed. "So the Cousin Jane broke her needle last night, and now she looks everywhere for omens! Have the Tommyknockers hung a halo over my ear?"

"It wouldn't hurt some people I know to keep right with the little people." She continued to stare at him in a kind of awe.

"No," he told her. "It isn't the little people . . . it's the big people who make our luck. Men like Kane and the Mojave bankers. What can the Tommyknockers do for a chlorider who has to sneak out of town to beat an eleven-dollar restaurant bill?"

Suddenly the inhibitions lost their grip on him. Banter and bitterness both fled from him. He was reaching out to hold her waist between his hands, pulling her close to him and saying roughly:

"Maggie, I'm nearly out of brags, but here's my last: I'm going to lick this God-forsaken valley! I'm going to find something so rich the bankers will climb over each other to invest in me. When I do . . . though it may take twenty years . . . I'm coming back to Furnace Flat. That was the big thing you saw on me, my wanting you. Nothing else. But it's enough to make me shine like a gilt Indian."

She pulled him out of the light of the cafe window. Her lips laughed up at him. "You don't even stay with a brag all the way, do you?"

Ryan's arm crushed her body against him, his fingers dug into the golden tangle of her hair, his mouth pressing hers hard. When he let her go, he felt wrung out, burned down to the core, exalted and yet sorry.

"And now I'm wanting to ask you to wait," he said bitterly. "I'm full to the ears of promises. But all I'm saying is: I'm coming back. Rich or poor I'm coming back. I hope you're still here, but I'm not asking you to be."

"I'll be here," she whispered. "I'll be here till April, and we're going out on the parlor car of the Tonopah and Tidewater in style. Because you're on your way!"

Ryan clung hard to his convictions. "I'm a burned-out chlorider at thirty-two. I believe an assay when I run it myself. I believe in a gold-piece after I've bitten it. You don't go off glory-holing with a cañon rat like Mysterious Smith if you're any more than a cañon rat yourself. We're putting our stake on the double zero, but the odds haven't changed any."

Margaret put her finger on his lips. "You are going to hit it," she said slowly. "That's as sure as the sun's coming up tomorrow! Name it after them, will you? 'The Tommyknocker Mine!' They'd like it."

Ryan kissed her again. "I'll build a home for aged Tommyknockers, if I hit it. And one for you. On top of Nob Hill, in San Francisco. That's no cheap brag."

THEY TRAVELED THAT NIGHT until sunup, making dry camp in a region of twisting, painted mole-burrows. After a few hours' rest they went on. Mysterious Smith was a taciturn traveler. A grunt was a full speech.

It seemed to Ryan that he knew where he was going, but it was a back-and-switching route he took to get there. He had thought he knew the valley, but Smith led him into cañons he had never seen, under an eroded rim of green rocks he did not know at all, and on the fourth evening he threw off on a high ridge between two cañons. The cañons were narrow slots of burnt ochre, gouged with caves. The ridge was like a dinosaur's backbone, hairless and bony, supporting a few desert holly.

Ryan scratched his head. "Seems like we've passed a dozen camp sites better than this."

Smith snapped: "Seems like it suits me."

Grady shrugged and started breaking up pieces of greasewood with which he had festooned his gear during the last hour. Smith stopped him. "Not yit." He led him down to one of the caves they had passed on the switchbacking climb from one of the cañons. He walked into it and sat down.

In Ryan's mind, a dark suspicion lurched up. The old man was crazy. Camp above and then come down to roost in a cave! But he carried it off casually, stooping to enter the cave and sitting down cross-legged.

"Damnedest spot I was ever in," he confessed. "I keep hoping you've already got a ledge spotted, but I know dang well you haven't, or you wouldn't be letting anybody else come along."

Smith slipped out his upper plate, removed a shred of chewed wood-fiber from between two teeth, and slipped the pink horseshoe back into his mouth. " 'Tis so, I reckon. For both of us. First time I ever went prospecting with anybody. You'll do, though. Talk too much, but you'll do."

Ryan cleared his throat. "I keep wondering why you asked me to come along."

Smith peered down the cañon. "I've got some rocks staked out, all right. Nothing much. Fellers got to get their sights down. They look for borax like they'd look for a field of cut diamonds. It don't come that way anymore. But this sorta suited me, and I riz a couple of monuments. Took a little sack of ore samples to town with me.

Damned if I didn't misput them. Knew right where they were, but when I come back to camp from town they were gone. I got the idea somebody else liked them."

Ryan's mind shot with the clarity of a carbide beam to the session in Borax Kane's office. It was all plain, now. Mysterious Smith was a long way from being crazy. But somebody else was crazy to think he could be gotten around.

"That was two months ago. I've been kinda watching you. I like you, Ryan. You don't kid yourself nor try to kid the next man. You know the desert can't be licked, but you like it for what it is. So when I knew I had to have a pardner, I began thinking about you. I ain't so tarnal old, not what you call downright decrepit, but I ain't fit for a real battle.

"We're going to have a battle before we get our test shafts sunk, and another one keeping the rocks for ourselves. And I'd like a younglin' to help me make it. Is it worth half a borax mine . . . I ain't guessing what kind . . . to risk having your behind shot off?"

Up the twisting little cañon drifted the scuff of mule shoes. Grady smiled. "They didn't lose much time, did they . . . ? Sure, it's worth it! You cover me. I'll go down and talk to them. When'd you spot them?"

"Yesterday. We're a long way from the borax, you understand, but I wanted them to catch up to us where we could handle 'em. Wonder if Kane had the guts to come hisself?"

III

"BORAX BONANZA!"

First came the burros, a pair of strong, mouse-gray animals carrying light packs. Pat Hoagland came after them, peering upward along the ridge. The mine boss was dusty and flushed; he wore a winter army shirt and geologist's breeches terminating in lace boots.

Close behind him strode another man, younger than Hoagland and taller, hatless, his hair blond and his skin dark. This man was familiar to Ryan, too. He was one of the geologists, a man named Fisher, with the distrust of the comparatively uneducated for the over-educated, Ryan had never cottoned to him. He was one of the whiz boys who would spend five minutes in a drift, announce that shoring would be necessary, and get out before the hanging wall fell.

Fisher said suddenly, stopping to thrust at the ground with a stick: "Look here!"

Hoagland went back. Fisher was examining a clutch of fresh burro sign. "Can't be an hour old!"

"We'd better throw off here. We don't want to run into them tonight. They've run the legs off us," he said, "but we're closing in!"

Ryan walked from behind a pitted lava buttress. "You're doing better than that," he told Hoagland. "You're there."

Both men turned with a quick rustling of gravel under their feet. They looked so tense, so guilty, that Ryan began to chuckle. "You fellows look like you were about to break into somebody's bank."

"We have as much right . . . ." Fisher began hotly; but Hoagland cut in angrily. "Sure we're following you. That's our privilege, isn't it?"

Ryan shrugged. He carried no gun, and suspected that Hoagland might be filling with a false confidence because of the Colt at his hip. "If you want to play it all the way out," he declared.

"Play it out? We'll play it any way we want. We're curious to know why you sneaked out of town in the middle of the night. I say we'll find out." He was an odd combination of saloon roughneck and professional man. About all the gloss engineering school had put on him was to teach him how to frame a threat in parlor language.

Fisher came in impulsively. "What's the matter with you valley men? You came out here with a little homemade geology and a pick, starve for six months digging in a spot a trained geologist could tell you was barren, and then refuse the help of someone like Borax Kane who wants to set you up!"

Ryan could taste temper on his tongue like salt. "Kane," he said, "has been setting me up for quite a spell. I could almost eat on his set-up. If you want to take your burros back with you, start now."

Hoagland shook his head, a grin tucked in the corners of his mouth. "Don't mind us. We'll just trail along. We're not claim-jumpers. But the law only allows you so many feet anyway. We'll take the leavings."

"Right. But not until we know what's leavings and what isn't. If we strike anything, we'll run some honest-to-God tests before we decide what's for us and what's for the rest of you."

Hoagland looked back at Fisher with a grin, then started past Ryan. Grady brought a fist from his hip in a short, decisive uppercut. Hoagland tried to sway out of line; the blow landed on the edge of his jaw, sent him reeling against the cañon wall and sliding down at the base of it. He was coming up immediately, getting to his knees before he thought of the Colt.

Fisher was ahead of him, there. He carried a small .32 revolver in a hip pocket. He had it halfway out of his pocket when the cañon shook under the dynamiting roar of a rifle a hundred feet above. A slug howled off the pocked lava wall. Fisher stood paralyzed.

Ryan said: "Take it out, but throw it where it won't tempt you. Same for you, Hoagland. And then come up fighting, if you've the guts for using your fists anymore."

Both men rid themselves of their weapons. Hoagland looked steady enough when he got on his feet. He started slowly toward Ryan, but Grady suddenly launched a drive that smashed him back against the cañon wall. They went down together, Hoagland's hands groping at Ryan's throat.

Ryan threw him off but, as they scrambled up, Hoagland began slinging long punches from his shoulders. He was a strong and zealous opponent, surprisingly solid, an executive whose impatient energy carried him into every activity his mind entered. The miner suddenly found himself on the defensive.

A fist smashed his mouth. Another crashed against his ear and filled his head with a dark roaring. Hoagland's face seemed to balloon and devour him, hard and eager, betraying a sort of surprised pleasure, as if the man were thinking: This mucker isn't so tough! Why don't I do more of this?

Ryan stood up to him, but Hoagland was on the march, taking a stride after each swing; and not many of the thrashing blows missed.

Suddenly Ryan found himself looking at the gritty earth from an all-fours position. He rose to his knees, started swaying at the rugged, unmarked face of the mine boss. He lumbered up thickly. Pat Hoagland stepped forward with his left foot and drove his right hand into Grady's face.

He was on his back. He was licked. He was tasting blood and thinking that he was glad it was over. Yet that small and ill-natured monitor which dwells in some men's minds was frantically trying to whip him up, like a testy mule-whacker. *I'd rather die than be licked by a college man!* he thought.

Through a blanket-thickness he heard Fisher exclaim enthusiastically: "My God, Mr. Hoagland!"

Up there on the cliff, Mysterious Smith must be indulging in some profane thinking. He had mistaken a cut-proud capon for a fighting cock.

Grady Ryan took a shuddering breath and propped himself up with a hand outstretched behind him. He was a bloody, dirt-smeared relic of the overly ambitious fighter who had swung at Hoagland a few minutes ago. He drew one foot up, rolled over onto all fours, and stood up. Pat Hoagland shook his head.

"You've had enough, you damned fool!" But as the miner started for him, he fired a long blow at Grady's head. It rocked the dark, battered head but did not slow him. He came on, shoulders hunched, face tipped down, eyes glaring up at Hoagland. Again the mine boss stabbed, but Grady knocked this one aside and abruptly seized him by the shirt and swung a haymaker. It landed on the side of Hoagland's head.

He reeled aside, pivoted and lurched back, an intemperate fury on him. He closed with Grady and pumped one to his belly. Grady took it and snapped his head down, striking Hoagland on the nose. Hoagland blurted something and tried to back away. Ryan had a hand behind his neck and held him while he slugged at this jaw. It jolted him. Another punch cut the hard skin under his eye.

Ryan saw him foggily. The blow to the belly had robbed him of the strength he needed to finish it. A cold greenness flowed through him, but he continued to stand there. He saw Pat Hoagland coming forward, gathering everything into a single blow that started slowly and gained momentum.

Ryan tipped his head. The punch tore his ear. Grady brought his fist up like a miner ramming a stull home under a timber, not with an explosion of speed, but with a dogged force that kept moving. It took Hoagland under the chin and stood him up stiff as a hung hide.

When he sank down, he sank all the way. He sat heavily on the gravel, slowly fell over on his side and lay twistedly with his cheek against the earth.

Mysterious Smith had come down from the rocks. He was there to give Ryan a drink from a pint bottle and to strike him once on the shoulder. Then he left Grady to sit on a rock with a gun on Fisher while he brought back the burros. He cut the lashings and dumped all their gear on the ground. Throwing out a few cans of beans, he set fire to the oiled tarps and burned everything but the beans and the burros.

When Pat Hoagland came around, Smith told him: "There's easier ways of mining than this. Easier places to travel than where we're goin', too. So long, boys."

The secret map in the head of Mysterious Smith led them both down more barren washes, across rocky hogbacks, winding in and out along the gaudy bluffs of the Funeral Mountains. On a clear, crisp morning, as Ryan threw a hitch over his packsaddle, he glanced up and saw Smith regarding him.

"Got any secret vices a future pardner ought to know about?" Smith asked.

"One. My guts growl when I'm hungry."

Smith walked up and down, a perplexed, barrel-chested old chlo-rider. "I'm seventy-four years old, and I got'n two dollars to my name. But I'm going to die in the damnedest mansion *this* valley ever seen! I'd kill the man that tried to do me out a dollar of this fortune. I've lost two others when my pardner's ree-lations set the lawyers on me. It ain't a-goin' to happen to me again. *Look!*" he yelled suddenly.

He ran up the slope. They were camped at the bottom of a wide wash from which rusty ridges ran up in rimrock steps. Smith was tugging at a clump of creosote brush. He pulled it away and revealed a hole not much larger than a coyote hole. "Git yer lamp!" he screeched. "Show you sumpthin', pardner!"

A kind of excitement he had thought buried with his youth fountained up in Grady Ryan. Lamp fizzing, he crawled through the adit after Smith. Just inside, the tunnel flared to regulation dimensions, about six feet wide and seven feet high. Mysterious Smith had said borax did not come high grade anymore. But the drift had been cut through a vein of borax as pure as diamond. In the shrill carbide light, a galaxy of stubby borax crystals gleamed all about them. It was the purest borax Grady Ryan had ever seen. It was bonanza borax.

IV
"PAY THROUGH THE NOSE!"

The drift was already nearly a hundred feet deep. They brought the burros inside after enlarging the adit, screened it again as best they could, and made the drift their camp. They spent two weeks probing around the cañon for new outcrops. They never found another like the first, but a narrower ledge of the same clear mineral was opened down along the dry wash.

"You name this'n," Smith invited. "I called the first the Bellyache Number One, because I had the gripes the day I struck that chimney."

Ryan thought of a blonde girl who looked like a picture in a poetry book and who surely had the vision of the Cornishmen. "What about the Tommyknocker?"

"Suit yourself." Smith packed his burro, and again checked the monuments about the Bellyache. Ryan was ready to travel. "Sure you ain't got any kin?" Smith asked suspiciously.

"I've got an aunt somewhere. Haven't seen her in years."

Ryan did not look at him when he spoke. As he heard Smith's pipe strike the ground, he looked about. Blood choked the prospector's features. His eyes were small blue marbles in a stricken face. He backed off a pace.

"So you ain't got any kinfolk . . . but you've got an aunt!"

"I told you I haven't seen her since. . . ."

"You'll see her soon enough after she hears you're rich! It's off!" he yelled. "It's all off!"

"It's too late to call it off," Ryan snapped. "I grubstaked you. I took a licking for you. We're pardners, now, like it or not."

Smith made a sobby sound and leaped on him. He was heavy and compact; they fell and rolled. Ryan pinned him flat and sat on his chest.

"Now, you old catamount! You'll not have any kin-trouble with me, but you'll have every other kind if you try to deal me the split-card!"

Smith squeezed his eyes shut. After a moment Ryan got off him. Smith got up, panting.

"You get your cut; don't squall so. But I keep the Bellyache. You got no more share in it than I have in yours. That pays you off. I'll have no part of you. Kinfolk-lousy!"

"It's going to take two separate outfits to work them if we split up. Two freight outfits to reach the T. & T., too."

Smith's salmon-pink plates showed in a laugh. "Freight outfits! And you call yourself a valley man. Ryan, you're only four miles from Furnace Flat!"

Yelling with idiot glee, he drove his burro up the cañon.

Ryan hurried after him. Four miles. A mine was valued in this country in direct ratio to its nearness to a railroad. He savored it. The T. & T. would build a spur. It was the warp and woof of luck. The Tommyknockers were in this one for sure.

GRADY RYAN spent a month at grips with a misconception. He was green enough at good fortune to think that certain benefits were automatic: Good clothes, a rig to take your girl out in, pale-green cigars. As it worked out, he spent a month in the direst poverty.

He could sell the mine for ten thousand cash, but he couldn't borrow a dime on it. He must sink new drifts before anyone would risk money on him. He took Margaret Conway for a walk one night.

"I haven't forgotten that house on Nob Hill, Maggie. But that and the fine clothes will have to wait. Could you carry me another month on that grub bill?"

"All your life," she laughed. "The gilt is still on you."

Miners settled like locusts upon the Cinnabar Flat area. Every un-filed claim was taken overnight. Most of them were middling chimneys of mixed tuff and borax. Grady had his eye on them. He would buy them at a dime a dozen after he made his peace with the banks.

He borrowed two hundred dollars from Tom Lund, his old drift boss, and hired Tom and a few other boys away from Borax Kane. They achieved enough footage in the first month to start Ryan and a sack of samples across the valley to Mojave to try to dig up cash to go on.

The bank did not want his paper. They turned him over to a fat Swiss in a back room, who extracted a deed and the first install-ment of twelve percent on twenty thousand dollars before Grady ever saw the money.

Twenty thousand would barely buy some second-hand machinery

and get him started. In the meantime, the Swiss would drink his beer and think fondly on the mine he expected to own.

It was warm when he returned: Cinnabar Flat was two thousand feet below Furnace Flat; summer would strike like a bronze gong. A Tonapah & Tidewater spur was already building to the mines. Smith was pulling out tons of borax and even Kane had some gopher holes producing.

Ryan was just in time for an auction of mine machinery at the Blue Gravel diggings. He rented a turn-out and joined the caravan streaming over the hills one morning. Maggie rode with him, starched and cool in blue and white. She opened her handbag to take out a sheaf of yellow backs.

"There's why I could carry you," she said. "There's more money in filling miner's stomachs than in digging ore. Fifteen hundred dollars, Grady! How much Tommyknocker stock will that buy me?"

Ryan shook his head. A gang of worries chased about his mind. "Stick to filling their stomachs. If I go under, it'll be alone."

She sat back indignantly. "You'd turn me down for my share, after I called the turn for you?"

"Your share," said Ryan, "is half of everything I make. But God knows how I'll squeeze out the money I already owe, with the mines shut down for five months this summer and the interest still snowballing."

The Blue Gravel mine was on a hillside sage-tufted like a candlewick spread. In a junkyard of rusting equipment, a flat spring-wagon had been parked as an auctioneer's platform. Grady saw Borax Kane with the auctioneer.

The day was savagely hot. The auctioneer, a corpulent big man wearing a black suit and stock and too dignified to remove his coat, looked as though he were strangling. He took a drink from Kane's pint. His lips were flaccid and his face purple as he pressed a handkerchief repeatedly to the glistening crown of his head.

Yonder was Mysterious Smith, with his superintendent. He looked no different, a man too old and withdrawn to change—suspicious, close, and wistful.

Brannigan, the auctioneer, climbed the wagon and pounded on a box with a wrench. He went through the wherefores and put a selection of office furniture on the block. Ryan took it from a disinterested rival for two hundred. Other small lots went cheaply. Then the heavy equipment went up. It would go as a single lot if a bidder could be found.

"The entire operating equipment of the United Metals Corporation," Brannigan panted. The heat had his face blooming; his eyes were choked in moist red flesh. "Equipment used and unused, as she stands . . . strap-iron railway supplies, timbering and head-frames. Gentlemen, what am I bid?"

Down to a dollar, Ryan knew what he could afford to bid. Twelve thousand would leave his blood white as milk. "Eight thousand," he said.

Smith said: "Nine."

Brannigan tapped the box. "Do I hear ten?"

On a long chance, Ryan made a jump bid: "Eleven!"

Smith turned slowly and stared at him. The small blue eyes were steady and venomous. He turned back, cleared his throat—and said nothing. Joy surged up in Ryan; another thousand to get it down to Cinnabar Flat. He was set!

Suddenly Margaret was whispering: "I'm not just going to watch this game, Grady Ryan. I'm going to be in it. Either you sell me stock, or I loan it to Smith!"

"I told you why I can't take your money. If you want to wreck me, this is as good a way as any."

"I don't want to wreck you. But I practically helped find that mine. And I want to take any risk there is along the way, and not have people saying Maggie Conway married the Tommyknocker mines, not Grady Ryan. Do I get my stock?"

Brannigan struck the box. "Eleven thousand once!"

Ryan was a man who led more easily than he pushed. He was also a man with old-fashioned ideas about widows and orphans. He thought of how far that fifteen hundred would take her if she ever really needed it.

He called to Brannigan: "Get on with it!"

The auctioneer pounded the box a second time. Maggie's chin went up. She ran over to Mysterious Smith and put an arm about his shoulders. She whispered to him. Smith's head did not turn, but suddenly he called out: "Twelve!"

Ryan stood like a man on a rock. "Thirteen," he said.

Maggie stared her fury at him. Ryan felt relief softening his joints; he let out his breath. Smith was boxed for fair.

"Thirteen thousand once. Thirteen thousand twice!"

Someone was moving through the crowd. Borax Kane reached Smith's side and began to talk in a confidential, smiling way to him. Ryan bawled: "Pound it out!"

"Just a moment!" Kane said. "Smith, I'd like to. . . ."

"*Pound it out!*" Ryan roared. He started for the wagon.

Brannigan raised the wrench. Then his face acquired a foolish slack-mouth look. He reached blindly before him; someone was there to catch him just as he collapsed.

In the shade of the wagon, a canteen dumped over his head and his coat and stock pulled off, he began to come around. Outlanders did damn fool things in the valley. All this time, Ryan had to listen to the bland chicanery of Borax Kane while they waited for Brannigan to come to.

"I'll back you up to three thousand, Smith. You've got a real mine down there."

"Going to keep it for myself, too," said Smith doggedly.

"What good is a mine without any machinery?"

Maggie counseled vociferously, but Smith's sandbagged features admitted he had to have machinery; he was licked without it. At last he agreed. As they hoisted Brannigan to the wagon again, sodden and mauve-featured, Mysterious Smith cracked:

"Fifteen thousand! Now, by . . . !" He wheeled and gave Grady Ryan a triumphant stare.

"Fifteen-five," Ryan said. I can raise the money to operate from the Swiss. Might as well go down in a cloud of smoke.

Smith did not react. He was beyond it. He had a shirt-tail partner, no machinery, and owed money he probably could not pay. Brannigan hammered the deal down. Grady went forward to pay up. He stopped by Kane. Kane's big, drink-pocked face was pleased. A red smile wreathed his face.

"Good luck with that machinery, Ryan. You don't need to feel sorry for Smith, because there is all the machinery he needs right at Furnace Flat . . . for a consideration!"

V

"THE SIGN OF DEATH"

Kane and Hoagland moved their men and their methods to Cinnabar Flat like a couple of cavalry generals taking a town. Overnight, Mysterious Smith became merely an old chlorider who visited his mines like a man bringing flowers to a sick friend. He collected a few dollars a week for food and beer.

Grady went ahead doggedly. He had Tom Lund steal a gang of hardrockers from Kane. Short of cash, he sold them on a deal by which he retained half their pay for a year, paying six percent. He and Kane sweated each other's games. Knowing each other's finances, knowing neither could weather a summer on interest without production.

On a hot evening in late May, Grady walked down the street of Furnace Flat to the cafe. It was after the dinner hour. The cafe was closed, but through the window he could see Maggie with her fat Irish cook packing heavy restaurant china in newspapers as carefully as though it were bone.

Margaret let him in with prim coolness. Ryan had got over his pique, but women had the faculty of nursing a grudge as they might a child. She tried to serve him pie and coffee without recognizing him, but Grady caught her hands and pulled her down to him. He gave her a peck on the cheek.

"As a millionaire customer," he said, "I'm entitled to service."

"You'll get the same service they all get."

Ryan watched the women place china ceremoniously in a crate. It came to him that packing china was an odd occupation for this time of night. Margaret flipped up an arch glance when he asked about it.

"I don't know about miners, but restaurant people have enough sense to get out of the valley in summer. I'm leaving on the first of June. We were going out in April, before . . . remember? When are you going to let your men pull out?"

Sooner or later, someone had to ask it. Ryan had kept hoping it would be Borax Kane who made the decision, so that Kane would be the black dog of Furnace Flat, the first man to condemn his men to the valley heat.

"Haven't decided," he said.

Margaret crossed the floor and looked into his eyes. "You're not shutting down at all!" she declared.

Ryan stirred uncomfortably. "I didn't say that. . . ."

"But I can read it on you! Grady, it will hit a hundred and twenty-five down there!"

"Not in the mines. If I can get them underground, they won't be any hotter below than they would be in winter. At worst, I'll operate the night shift alone."

Afterward, Grady remembered the way she had looked at him. "Get out of it, Grady," she said slowly. "Get out of it while you can. They've taken off their blessing. I can see it on you!"

"If they've had their blessing on me so far, I may do better after they take it off," Ryan said. He got up to leave. Someone else entered the restaurant. It was Tom Lund.

"I tried to catch you before you left," Lund said. He was a strapping redhead with a face like something carved artlessly from rock, his cheekbones jutting, mouth wide and jaws square. He carried his worries in his eyes, hazel under bleached, thorny brows. He had a miner's hands and thick, strong wrists. Lund was a man without artifices. Where another might have broken his news carefully, Lund blurted:

"Hoagland's driven into one of our ledges. He's been high-grading our rock for two weeks!"

Ryan strode past Lund. Margaret ran after him to get between him and the door.

"Don't go down there, Grady! Talk to Kane . . . but don't go down. I tell you they've taken off the blessing!"

Grady moved her aside. "The trouble is underground. The ironing out of it will be too. And the only blessing I'll need is these two fists."

*   *   *

"I COULDN'T get the notion of rock like that coming out of the coyote hole it did," Lund told him. They were on a hand car coasting down to the mines, the air rushing past them, hot and dry. "It was pure colemanite, but the drift it came out of was the old Slab Bacon claim . . . not worth the powder to blow it up. But I had it from one of their men today that Fisher's drove a shoo-fly into our own main ledge."

"What have you done about it?"

"Jawed with Hoagland and that fool Fisher. They claim there ain't any such cut . . . but they're not welcoming visitors."

"They'll welcome me." Ryan took a sullen joy in the development.

Flares lighted the night operations in the broken rimrock cañon. Borax rattled and roared down the hurries into T. & T. ore-cars. A dull hammer-stroke marked the bursting of dynamite in a deep mine. Ryan picked up an armload of dan at one of his own mines, some fuse and caps, and started up the hill. Tom Lund carried a six-foot drill and sledge. They had donned lamps and caps.

At the foot of the Slab Bacon chute, ore cars on a precarious hillside trestle were receiving clattering loads of borax. The dust was heavy and stifling. They climbed the slope through a rubbish of spilled rock, broken timbers, and boxes. A short line of tiny mule-cars was backed out to the grizzly, where workmen in dust-chalked clothing, their faces pallid in a greasy dusk of oil flares, were tending them.

Grady halted, set down his load of dynamite, and lighted his lamp. "Sure about this?" he asked Lund.

Lund's lamp spat into life. "This guy had all the directions and footage. It checks out that they're only using this as a portal." Abruptly he said: "Here they come!"

Grady saw the pair coming down from a shed. They were Pat Hoagland and Borax Kane's blond whiz-boy, Fisher. Hoagland carried an oil lantern, setting it down when they had reached the others. The mine boss rocked on his feet with his hands on his hips.

There was still a fat wad of cartilage above his right eye, where Ryan had hit him that day. It gave his face a slightly lopsided look and, knowing Hoagland's compulsion to exert his will on others, rather than to have it exerted on him, Ryan knew that he must be conscious of that scar whenever he talked to any man.

"You boys going to do a little mining?"

"A little unmining," Ryan told him. "That's good-looking rock out there. I looked this hole over when it was sold. I wouldn't have guessed it would give anything but cotton-ball."

Fisher's face was clamped in an expression of nervous determination. "You can't always 'guess' what's in a mine by the kind of surface rock it shows."

"That's right. If there's ore in there, I've learned something about mining. I'd like to see just how you opened up this seam."

Hoagland rubbed his hands together, still pleased, still poised like a boulder on a cliff. "We have a mine tour about once every six months for the stockholders. Why don't you sit on your hands until then? We'll show you how to make a borax mine pay."

"You'll show me how to make somebody else's mine pay, you mean."

Hoagland's eyes picked up the harsh gleam of the lamps. "That's too subtle for me."

Grady was aware that the white carbide light was dulling Hoagland's vision. "Too subtle?" he said. "Try this."

He had picked up the sledge as the others came down the tracks. He held it by the head with one hand and swung the handle in a short arc to the side of the miner's head. Hoagland stumbled forward. He was not out, but he was not quite capable of co-ordinating thoughts and actions. He fell and lay on the tracks with a thick-tongued moan.

Fisher was coming in with a strangled curse. As he passed Lund, the redhead slammed one into the side of the head. Fisher staggered and went to his knees.

They picked up their tools and walked quickly into the tunnel. They followed on down the tracks. The timbering stretched away from them in a geometrical diminuendo of angles. The trace of borax seam on the wall began to fade. It died in a cavern where every ounce of worthwhile rock had been chipped away. Off to the left, a new drift opened up. The polished strap-iron rails caught the carbide lights as they followed them. There was no sign of borax anywhere but along the tracks, where it had spilled from laden cars.

The tunnel was heavily timbered; seams and faults made the whole section dangerous. The tunnel ran in defiance of geological formations—in defiance of mining law, too, boring through the mountain toward Tommyknocker Number 3.

Suddenly they were in borax again. The clink of a sledge became audible. Past a turn they saw in the distance a miner holding a six-foot drill while another man swung a double-jack. These men turned suddenly.

Ryan jerked his thumb. "Out."

The men got out. They knew they had been in Tommyknocker rock for two weeks. This was no concern of theirs, but they knew it was Ryan's.

Ryan walked after them until he had left the borax deposit behind, reaching the area rotten with faults. It took little work with the drill to open a hole he could load with a charge of dynamite sufficient almost to lift off the top of the hill. Then they walked another hundred feet and opened a second seam.

Grady measured fuse. "Go on," he told Lund. "I can take it from here."

"Hell with that! I'll run down and light that first fuse. You start this one when you hear me coming."

A toothed edge seemed to be at Ryan's nerves. He had never felt mine-fear before. "I said get out!"

Tom Lund hesitated. Then he shrugged and started off.

Ryan touched the first fuse with his lamp and sprinted. He lighted the second, and legged it so hard that he bumped solidly into the man coming the other way before he saw him. He fell and rolled, lost his lamp and had a glimpse of a lean, wild-eyed man rising out of the dust ten feet beyond him. Fisher had gotten past Tom Lund.

A coal oil lantern burned on its side near him, chimney shattered. Fisher's hand snatched up a rock, his arm drew back, and he hurled it at Ryan's head before Ryan had time to duck.

VI

"SNOW"

In the darkness he ran on. Ryan pressed his hand against his ear. The rock had gouged it as it whirled by. For one moment he hovered in a humming darkness; then, his head clearing, he came up on his knees and shouted:

"*Fisher!*"

Fisher was out of sight around the bend. His footfalls ran brokenly down the drift. Ryan's act was not humanitarian. They would call it manslaughter if the engineer died in an unauthorized blast.

Fisher lurched along a hundred feet ahead of him as Ryan followed. Fisher reached the first fuse, yanked it from the charge, and stood uncertainly. Ryan could feel the clammy fright that had suddenly come home to the man: Was that another fuse burning down there?

Fisher started back, hesitated, and looked once more at the sparkling hole in the blackness. Even he knew what a blast could do to this kind of formation. He pulled his fears into one last impulse and his long stork-legs carried him toward the dynamite.

Ryan hurled the rock. It caught Fisher on the leg. He sprawled. Ryan got him by the back of the neck and rushed him back down the drift. Fisher was not fighting Ryan, but stumbling helplessly. They were at the turn where they had collided when the vast, paralyzing explosion of gases shook the mine.

Ryan was down on hands and knees in the blackness, hearing nothing but a roar of giant waters, feeling the thud of rocks against his body. He let himself slump onto the foot wall. It was too big to fear. He was a tiny black speck of life against a sky, not worth reaching for, but death was impartial.

Then there was a crumpling roar ahead of him, and afterward it seemed as though a cork had been twisted into a bottle. Sound ceased. You couldn't call that pattering of small stones up and down the drift genuine sound, not in this place of massive concussion.

He heard his lamp fizzing like a beer bottle getting ready to let loose. His hand encountered the warm metal and he flicked the flint wheel. Fisher sat against the side wall with blood streaming down his face. Ryan had forgotten him. Terror was microscopic in its effect, excluding everything but selfish thoughts.

Fisher leaped to his feet. Ryan's eyes went with old training to the hanging-wall. He saw the great slab of gneiss suspended over their heads, sinking gently toward them.

He came to his feet and started Fisher along the tunnel. Shortly he heard the brief, crumpling sound of the rock falling. They kept walking until they saw the mass of stone clogging the shattered tunnel, its jagged shoulder veiled in gray rock-dust. Fisher pivoted suddenly and swung a blow wildly at Ryan's jaw. It hit Ryan on the side of the head and jarred him.

"Crazy bull-headed boraxer! Dynamite us both to hell, will you? Die like drowned-out gophers!"

Ryan swerved into the geologist. He turned the man's jaw with a short, chopping punch. It hurled Fisher back against a stull and dropped him in a loose, gangling huddle. He began to sob.

Grady went back to work. There was not a foot of the drift he would care to spend five minutes in. He examined the slide. They were sealed in.

He told Fisher gruffly: "This isn't a coal mine. Nobody's going to die of black damp or poison gas. After we get used to it, we'll start moving rocks around."

By Ryan's watch, it was twenty hours later when they paused in a spell of careful work on the slide to listen. Fisher had been docile ever since the fight. Now he started tearing rocks aside with a wild yell.

"They're coming!"

Half the town of Furnace Flat was waiting to see them stagger out of the Slab Bacon. Tom Lund was the first man to seize Grady, tears in his Irish-blue eyes.

"The damn fool was laying for me! Hit me with a rock and I never come around for an hour."

Borax Kane was there to receive his geologist like a lost son. But Fisher's eyes, striking Ryan's for an instant, were ashamed. This man, they said, has seen the core of me—the sawdust where there should be courage. And this shame, Grady knew, could turn a man like him into an enemy more dangerous than two-fisted Pat Hoagland.

Margaret got through the crowd to him. Ryan held her, filled with an aching relief. "You will defy every omen under the sun!" she told him. "Do you believe me, now?"

Ryan hesitated, moved through gratitude to admit he had been wrong about everything; but a man's convictions were hard to shake. "I believe that college geologists should stay where they belong . . . in offices."

Margaret regarded him steadily. "I've bought two tickets to Tonopah. It was a deal I made with them; if they brought you out, I'd get you away from Cinnabar Flat for the summer."

Ryan shook his head. "You give the little people credit for knowing everything. Will they tell me how to keep the mines if I close them?"

"Perhaps if you'd go, they would. I'm using my ticket on the first of June. You can use yours when you feel like it. But you won't find Maggie Conway waiting long in Tonopah."

Maggie ran off to the railroad. There was a sharpness in the heart of Grady Ryan, but he was still standing there when she took a seat on the little car with its row of benches. He and Tom Lund drifted over to a flat-car and sat on the edge of it while it filled. Lund seemed waiting for him to say something. At last he asked Grady: "What'll I tell the boys?"

"Tell 'em I'm alive, if you think they'd be interested."

"No, I mean. . . . Well, there's enough Cousin Jacks among them to keep the old superstitions alive. This looks bad to them. The owner of a mine nearly dying underground. What shall I tell them?"

"Tell them," Ryan said, "that we're going to work all summer. Extra pay. They'll bunk at Furnace Flat. I don't see why it should be so different from any other time of year."

Lund was silent a while. "Kind of forgot what summer's like, ain't you?"

"I know better than most. But we're going to try it, anyhow."

Though Grady Ryan did not know it, that was the night before summer. By ten o'clock the following day, every miner and mucker in Cinnabar Flat knew it would be a day to remember. The thermometer just inside the big Tommyknocker Number One registered one hundred and thirteen. It was one hundred and seventeen by noon.

A wind roused off the desert, rushing up the cañon with its kiln-like breath to carry gray clouds of dust into the mines. At two it was a hundred and twenty, and Grady had the good sense to dismiss all outside workers.

The heat continued to roast Cinnabar Flat all week. Suddenly it was apparent that it would not let up until winter. Five months of skull-cracking heat ahead! Ryan went on summer schedule, put out water barrels and raised wages.

Kane posted a notice on his bulletin board.

Owing to unfair competition by the Ryan mines, we are forced to continue mining operations beyond our regular closing date.

And also, Grady speculated, owing to some unpaid notes and failing mines. The rich Bellyache ledge was not living up to expectations. Ryan's Number One, after a slow start, was expanding and becoming purer. Despite the heat, he was almost optimistic by the night Lund came shamefacedly with a miner's delegation to the small sheet-metal office building.

"I tried to talk these stiffs out of it," he explained, "but they will say their piece. They say they're quittin'. They want the wages you've held back."

Ryan had been working with a desk which had come apart. Furniture had to be made in the valley, without glue, to endure the heat. He stood in the doorway, shirtless, sweating, a dark, blunt-chinned man with temper in his face.

"What's the matter?" he demanded. "Tired of waiting for that spree?"

"Tired of the heat!" a miner shot back.

"What heat? It averages sixty in the mines. That's cool enough for anybody."

"It don't average sixty after you come out at seven A.M.! Better'n a hundred, and you can have my share of sleeping in a sheetmetal shack, even at Furnace Flat."

"Where do you think I sleep? You can bunk in one of the mines, if you want."

Someone laughed. "Work, sleep, and eat underground! We ain't gophers, Ryan."

Lund put in an apologetic complaint. "The watermen don't keep the barrels full, either, Grady. They're always dryin' out and fallin' apart. And the chuck at Maggie's is gettin' worse. Meat spoils so fast she's serving nothing but salt-cured bullhide."

"All right," Ryan said. "If you're bound to quit, you'll quit. But I can't pay your back wages. The agreement was that I kept them for a year. In a year, you'll get the money with interest."

There was a muttering of displeasure. "That was the promise," Lund reminded them. "Take it or leave it. But if you quit, you'll probably wander off to the gold mines or God knows where and lose out on it. Take a hitch in your belts and stay."

In the end, they decided to stay. Lund remained after they left. "There's something else," he said. "Did you specify seasoned lumber when you bought your timbering?"

Something in Ryan slowed up and held its breath. "I picked it out myself."

"Maybe you'd better let me pick it out next time," Lund growled. "There's a lot of sags showing up. Some places the stulls and timbers are beginning to separate. The boys are grousin' about snow in every damn' drift we're working."

"I'll look 'em over," Ryan promised.

He said it casually enough, but it had the impact of a rock between the eyes. Snow! Catastrophe dust—the gentle sift of earth that preceded a cave-in. It meant faulty or inadequate timbering; and to replace timbering would mean the finish.

He spent the better part of one night examining the stulls and timbers of the main drifts. Lund was right. Almost imperceptibly, the overheads were bowing. In other spots, the stulls had developed bad cracks.

Ryan closeted himself with his books and did some figuring. New timbering at six thousand. Labor at about half that. Lost time. . . .

He was scared. He wanted to tell everyone to keep his voice down, to walk softly, not to drop anything heavy. It was not immediately serious. But if the settling process continued, it would soon be serious enough to close the Tommyknocker mines for good.

He had a heretical thought, one at variance with his nature; that no matter how much he made, it could never make up to him for the things he had lost. Maggie. Mysterious Smith. Some cherished illusions. Happiness and the struggle for money were incompatible.

When they touched, one was quick to tarnish. In this case, both had tarnished.

VII

"GIANTS IN THE EARTH"

On the first of June, Maggie Conway closed her cafe and moved over to Tonopah. For Ryan, the edge was off everything. He ate at a third-rate beanery and thought of Maggie's cherry pie. He rode home from work through amber dawns and dreamed of her hair.

The stark beauty of the winter season had burned out in dust and heat. Sand and salt-storms raging down in the furnace called Death Valley invaded the cañons, fouling machinery with grit. At night, the ninety-degree heat was bearable. But by day, Cinnabar Flat was a ghost camp.

Yet the ore coming out of Ryan's mines was clear as rock candy. Mill checks began to flutter back to him. Some of the pressure eased off. He'd lick them with this summer-club of his! He could meet his first interest payment handily, get the Swiss to set the installment on the principal over till fall, and catch up then.

He was thinking this the night Borax Kane came to call. Beyond him in the flare-lit darkness, Grady made out the barrel-shaped form of Mysterious Smith. Grady let them in. In the lamplight, Kane's face was a harsh pattern of impatience and anger bottled up until they soured. He wore a neckband shirt without the boiled collar, and his pants were dusty and creaseless.

Smith, the patriarch of all prospectors, carried a large volume which Ryan discovered was a Bible. There was something withdrawn about his eyes. Ryan thought: the old son's going to make a speech!

Kane shot a glance at the heat-curled wall calendar. "June sixteen! Hell of a time to be in the valley. How much longer are we going to pussyfoot around this way?"

"I'm not pussyfooting. I'm mining borax with both hands."

"And losing money every day."

"A *good* mine will always pay itself off."

Kane let the mark slide off. Mysterious Smith stood by the door, gazing down the dim cañon.

"Look here," Kane suddenly blurted. "We're a couple of strong mules, you and I, but we're pulling in the wrong directions. Now, Smith and I . . . ." he glanced with some uncertainty at the boraxer, "we've been talking about a merger."

Smith said: "Two wrongs do not make a right."

Kane looked disgusted. Grady laughed. "Nor two bad mines a good. What's the matter, Mysterious . . . Bellyache mine go bad?"

Smith shook his head slowly. "It's not that. It's the hatred and strife that are wrong."

"They didn't used to disagree with you."

Kane's temper suddenly ripped out at the seams. He strode to Grady's reeling desk and began to pound on it. "I've had enough of backing and filling over this. I've got you in a corner, Ryan, and you'll come out of it on my terms. We're going to merge, whether you like it or not, and the terms will be a lot more to your interest if you co-operate."

Grady said stonily: "So *you've* got *me* in a corner, now!"

Borax Kane was taking a paper from an envelope. He unfolded it and let the miner have a brief glimpse of it before he replaced it. Grady felt a cold finger trace his spine. "That looked like my signature!"

"It should! That piece of paper was signed in Mojave. It was for a loan made by a man named Zeelendorf. It cost me a cut of the Bellyache mines, but the point is. . . ."

Ryan could read the page entire. "The point is, I owe you instead of the Swiss, now."

"You may find me a less co-operative creditor," Kane remarked. "I see that you've got an installment of interest and principal due next week. I'll want it all in cash, unless we work out something else before then."

All at once he went stumbling backward out the door. The ledger Ryan had flung struck him in the chest. He rolled down the slope a short distance and got up shouting obscenities. Ryan heard him stumbling away in the darkness. He slumped into a chair, breathing hard, glaring at Smith. Smith shook his head.

"You shouldn't have did that, boy."

"I didn't have a gun. It was all I could grab."

"You didn't used to be so buttish. Use' to be slow-goin' and smilin'. Money's changed you."

"Not money. Lack of money, Mysterious."

Smith deposited the twenty-pound Bible on a table and opened it to a place marked with a bartender's suds knife. "I think I got this all figgered out. It's all right here in the Book," he read.

" 'Vanity of vanities, saith the Preacher, Behold all is vanity.' "

As he read, Ryan perceived that he had found the irrefutable apology for failure: the Lord wanted it that way. He said wearily, "That's okay. That's good stuff, Smith. But . . . damn it!" he said wryly. "Don't you wish we could've cut the mustard? You and I should never have busted up. We'd have stood this valley on its ear. We'd have had buckets of money by now. Remember that house you were going to build?"

Smith's eyes filled. He closed the Book slowly, stood looking down at it and declared plaintively: "Now you've went and took that away from me. What's the matter with you, man? You're bitter to the core."

"Just about," Ryan sighed. "And if I don't find. . . ." Suddenly he sat up straight.

Smith's face, too, acquired a curious look. He appeared to listen. "You hear somethin'?"

Ryan did. He had heard the sound several times in his life. Californians were bound to: a distant, shaking rumble. Then the shack began to rock. It was like being in a box-car taking a turn, giving itself a shake and then straightening out. It went on for a full half-minute, dust sifting down to them, the hanging lamp swinging, sheet-metal siding chattering. It was over, then. It might be the last, or it might be the beginning or end; it was an earthquake.

Smith grunted. "Glad I ain't in a mine tonight. But we're purty well timbered. Not like when I was a young feller. Your legs for stulls and shoulders for timbers! Better come up with me and have a shot of holy water, Grady."

Ryan got the words through the dust in his mouth. "No, I think I'll stick around a while yet. See you in town, Smith."

As the old man went out, Ryan thought: You missed a bet, old-timer! The Lord has just spoken, and you didn't even hear his voice! It was practically supernatural. One minute he was saying the Bible was all right, if you believed that sort of thing. The next. . . .

Catastrophe! Rigidly he kept his mind from plunging into conjecture. Falling rocks, broken timbers, crushed bodies of miners—these things were swirling in the darkness just beyond the shores of consciousness.

Smith's Bible lay on the desk. He turned it. The stuff the prospector had found so comforting was, he decided, downright level-headed. This preaching had come out of a wise head.

He looked up, his eyes softening. Maggie, girl, I wish I'd turned an ear to you. You had something to tell me, if I'd been able to hear you. If I'd closed up, I wouldn't have had those boys in the mines tonight.

He read on for a half-hour. And by this device Grady Ryan killed the half-hour before they came for him.

Tom Lund came alone, blundering up the path like a blind man. He stopped in the doorway, gripping both jambs, dirty, sweating, and scared. "Cave-in in Number One! Haven't checked all the rest. Did you feel it?"

Grady got his cap and lamp and went with him. Up and down the cañon, men were scampering like ants. Inside the main Tommy-knocker drift, they squeezed along between the walls and a line of orecars carrying out tons of cleared rock. Shattered timbers thrust up from the flotsam. Grady worked through a gang of muckers. Jury timbering had been thrown up. Slabs of rock the size of an ore-car had fallen. They were being laboriously dragged back to where they could be handled. Ryan took his place with the men.

It was three in the morning when they cleared a snake-hole. Shouts came to them from beyond, and presently a face showed in the aperture as a miner crawled through. Four men came out. They told of two more trapped under the rocks.

At five, they recovered the bodies. A pearly daylight suffused the hot morning sky when they reached the grass. Ryan watched them carry the tarpaulin-draped bodies down to the railroad. He had an impulse to explain that it wasn't his fault; that an earthquake could catch anybody napping.

Yet he knew the best defense he could make was to keep his mouth shut and try to salvage enough out of the wreckage of the Ryan mines to help out the widows.

It was all cut and dried, the whole heartbreaking business closed. The fight that had begun one night over a table in a saloon was ended. There was nothing to do now but purge the soul with whiskey in that same saloon. Something holy about whiskey, too. Holy water, saloon variety. Beyond this point cares dared not tread.

He rode up to Furnace Flat with a carload of weary muckers. In the saloon, they left him alone, a hulking, haunt-eyed man frowning into a whiskey glass, as if words of wisdom might be written there. Certainly he had found them nowhere else.

Presently Pat Hoagland, Fisher, and some of the Furnace Flat men came in. Hoagland wore a look of sanctimonious gravity. But inside he must have been ready to erupt with glee.

Grady drank for an hour. He sat listening to the senseless hammering dissonance of the mechanical piano, taking his liquor with beer chasers. It was like pouring whiskey down a drain. It muddled without touching his grief. He kept seeing the broken forms of two miners who, but for him, would have been alive now. And yet he would have taken a miner's oath that those timbers would hold.

Hoagland stopped by to lay a hand on his shoulder and say: "Sorry, old man." He jumped as Grady started up, but Grady let himself sullenly back into the chair and merely watched as the Kane crowd departed.

It was not long after this that red-headed Tom Lund barged into the saloon. Lund carried a short length of shattered twelve-by-twelve. His cap was off; he was filthy with rock dust, but there was a kind of shine to him. He walked across the floor straight to where Ryan sat swaying on his chair.

VIII
"BLACK DOG OF CINNABAR FLAT"

Lund put the timber down on the table so heavily the legs creaked. He scrubbed dirt away from the wood with a muddy handkerchief. "Look there! What do you call that?"

Ryan looked at the timber, with its splintered end and deep saw-marks, without comprehending. "I call that a busted timber," he told Lund, thickly.

Lund said: "I call it shenanigans!" The broken nail of his forefinger indicated four deep, blade-thick ruts across the wood. It was at the fourth that the tough grain of wood had broken. "I found a dozen of these doctored jobs in Number One alone. Don't know how many in the other mines."

"Saws slip," Ryan said obtusely.

"Four on one timber? Four inches deep? The hell they do!"

Ryan frowned. He discerned suddenly that it had been one of the cuts which caused the timber to break. Slowly he pushed his chair back. He stared at Lund. "Who set this thing up?"

Lund's tawny eyes pinched. "That's what I've been trying to find out! I knew it was a gang of company busters I hired away from

Hoagland. Thought they came along kind of easy. You won't find any of them on the payroll now. They've quit, a man at a time, not even squawking about leaving half their wages. Why not? I'd reckon they were drawing pay up the line. I've talked to some boys who swear those busters practically locked them out of the mine while they done the timbering!"

The whiskey finally caught fire. It warmed, fountained up darkly inside Ryan, turned loose something that had been a long time bound. He started across the room, lurched against a table and tipped it over. He had to grope his way. Lund grabbed an arm and steered him to the bar.

"Get Mr. Ryan some coffee! Grady, I'm going to make a speech. Soak up about a gallon of coffee while I talk."

Ryan never knew what Lund said, but he was conscious of loud voices in the saloon and men swarming about him, and someone yelling in a high, old-man's voice:

"Bring that stick along! We're going to nail Kane and Hoagland up for everybody in Furnace Flat to see."

He turned and saw Mysterious Smith near him. Smith came over and gripped his arm. "Forty years in the valley, and I never seen a thing like this before. Won't again, neither."

"Tell you a better stunt," Lund declared. "Re-timbering is going to wreck the Tommyknocker. Kane knew that when he sent his hunkies in to high-grade us. I'll work for beans until we get them all tore out and replaced. Anybody going to help me?"

It seemed that nearly everyone was. But Ryan himself cooled the idea.

"That's great. But what are we going to use for timbers?"

Lund laughed. "Excuse the boss, boys. He's drunk. Kane's got a whole timber-camp down there. All the twelve-by-twelves we'll need and, if we run short, we'll take them out of his mines. Why don't we start now, before it gets too hot?"

Ryan, beginning to sober, was carried out with them.

Hell was a great place to be from. You could not evaluate the things you had until you'd spent a few weeks there. This was his conviction as they rattled along on the flat-car. The heat seemed wonderful, the gaunt walls of calico stone beautiful. But the finest thing of all was to have been the black dog of Cinnabar Flat, and to be accepted again by the sort of men you understood and respected.

At six o'clock, the heat already pouring down into the cañon, the mines were deserted. Fine, thought Ryan. No one to object when they took the timbers. But he'd be having a talk with Kane and Hoagland one day. A moment later, scanning the sheet-metal building which was the local Furnace Flat office, he saw that the mines were not entirely deserted. Someone stood at a window, watching the work train coast in.

He waved the donkeyman on when the train began to slow. "We'll pick up granny-bars before we go on up," he called.

Lund was not deceived. "Sure granny-bars will do the job?"

"I've got a couple of hollow crowbars with .45 caliber ammunition in the office," Ryan told him.

While the workmen swarmed up the slope to the tool crib, he and Tom secured guns from the office and started up the tracks to the Bellyache. Mysterious Smith had, mysteriously, disappeared. There were just the two of them walking up the tracks to the main hoppers, climbing along the hurry-chute toward the gleaming corrugated shed leaning on stilts against the flank of the mountain. Two men without much shelter.

The heat rose up sulphurously from the cañon as if from a river of molten iron. It must be hell in the shack, Ryan thought. The men in there must have good reason to stay inside.

They were within a hundred feet. A rough mule-trail led from the chutes to the office. When they had gone a short distance along it, someone shouted. Hoagland stood in the doorway with a rifle.

"Leave the guns if you're coming in!"

Ryan stopped, his eyes taking inventory of the closest boulders. "The guns," he said, "are the reasons we're coming in."

He took two strides more when Hoagland snapped the gun up. A bullet slashed through a gray holly at the side of the trail. Grady dived for a rock. He heard Lund digging in behind him.

Lining the Colt out across the rock, he sent a slug crashing into the wall. It opened a small perforation in the metal, and perhaps in someone inside. With the echoes still pouring down the cañon, he sprinted another twenty feet up the trail. Kane's ill-tempered voice reached him.

"I'll kill you both quicker than I would a chuckawalla if you try to break in here! But I'm willing to dicker."

"So am I. Here's my second offer." The bullet passed through the wall.

"So help us God, Ryan!" shouted Hoagland. "We mean business. If you're coming here with any notion that we were responsible for your cave-in, leave it behind. We can adjust this."

"One way," said Ryan.

Lund's gun crashed, the report striking Ryan heavily as he crouched ahead of him. He heard Hoagland yell again: "Let the damned fools have it!"

At the adit of a mine above them, a gun roared. Grit exploded at Grady's side. He began to crawl, but Hoagland took a snapshot that struck in front of him and forced him to flatten against the ground. He wriggled around into a shallow depression, hearing Lund grunt and swear as he, too, sought shelter from both points. Another shot screamed down at him. It passed so close that the sound on the gravel was like a cap-crack.

Hoagland or Kane fired once more from the building. Lund cried out, gripping his forearm the way a man did with more than a scratch. In a moment he picked up his Colt and fired wildly at the shack, but dropped the gun immediately and tried to stanch the blood gouting from his arm.

Ryan turned back. He could lie here and be picked over like carrion, or he could make a run for it. He took shells from his pocket and re-loaded the gun. He pulled his legs up under him, and braced himself.

Someone called to him. It was the pink-gummed voice of Mysterious Smith. "I figger to fire a stick o' dan over thataway directly, Ryan. I'd lay still if I was you."

Ryan froze. From the sound, he figured Smith must be below the shed, somewhere between it and the railroad. For an instant Hoagland was exposed at a window.

Up in the mine, Fisher began wildly pumping shots down the slope. But Smith appeared to be well hidden. A moment later something tan and cylindrical arched from the rocks, struck the tin roof, and rolled off, to lie close beside the shack.

Fisher was screaming: "It's a trick! Stay inside!"

But the men inside would not gamble. They lurched into the brassy sunlight, Hoagland firing as he came. He ran up the slope toward the mine, Kane sprinting for a rock and flopping beside it. Grady took cool aim at his former boss's running figure. He pressed the trigger and felt the good, solid buck of the gun. Hoagland broke stride and went down hard.

Mysterious Smith took Kane from the back. Ethics, when dealing with men whose ethics were those of a sand rattler, seemed foolish. Kane bleated like a sheep.

Fisher, not a man to stick by a partner any more than a principle, came out of the mine with his hands up.

A moment later there was a concussive blast close against the side of the shack. One wall was crushed inward as dust rose about the building. Smith, it seemed, had not been bluffing. . . .

Grady Ryan left Furnace Flat on the narrow-gage for Tonopah that night, after seeing Tom Lund taken care of in the company infirmary. He and Smith had had a brief talk about the possibility of a merger. In a new burst of religion, Smith wanted to call the outfit the Golden Rule mines.

"Credit where credit's due," Ryan argued. "You name yours whatever you want. I'll keep on calling mine the Tommyknocker."

He thought Maggie would like that. It was a lot of foolishness, of course. But if you had to believe in superstitions, the little people were good ones to stick with.

COLT-CURE FOR
WOOLLY FEVER

JONATHAN HURFF GLIDDEN was born in Kewanee, Illinois, and was graduated from the University of Illinois with a degree in English literature. He came first to write Western fiction because of prompting from his brother, Frederick Dilley Glidden, who wrote Western fiction under the pseudonym Luke Short. In his career as a Western writer, he published sixteen Western novels and over 120 Western novelettes and short stories for the magazine market. From the beginning, he was a dedicated craftsman who revised and polished his fiction until it shone as a fine gem. His Peter Dawson novels are noted for their adept plotting, interesting and well-developed characters, their authentically researched historical backgrounds, and his stylistic flair. His first novel, THE CRIMSON HORSE-SHOE, won the Dodd, Mead Prize as the best Western of the year 1941 and ran serially in Street & Smith's *Western Story Magazine* prior to book publication.

During the Second World War, Glidden served with the U.S. Strategic and Tactical Air Force in the United Kingdom. Later in 1950 he served for a time as Assistant to Chief of Station in Germany. After the war, his novels were frequently serialized in *The Saturday Evening Post*. Peter Dawson titles such as HIGH COUNTRY (Dodd, Mead, 1947), GUNSMOKE GRAZE (Dodd, Mead, 1942), and DEAD MAN PASS (Dodd, Mead, 1954) have all recently been reprinted by Chivers Press in hardcover Gunsmoke editions. ROYAL GORGE (Dodd, Mead, 1948) is also generally conceded to be among his masterpieces, although Peter Dawson was an extremely consistent writer and virtually all his fiction has retained its classic stature among readers of all generations. His short story "Long Gone" in *Zane Grey's Western Magazine* (3/50) was adapted for the screen as FACE OF A FUGITIVE (Columbia, 1959) starring Fred MacMurray and James Coburn.

One of Jon Glidden's finest techniques was his ability after the fashion of Charles Dickens and Leo Tolstoy to tell his stories via a series of dramatic vignettes which focus on a wide assortment of different characters, all tending to develop their own lives, situations, and predicaments, while at the same time propelling the general plot of the story toward a suspenseful conclusion. He was no less gifted as a master of the short story and DARK RIDERS OF DOOM is the title of the first collection of his short novels and stories.

Elmer Kelton, himself a respected author of Western fiction, once observed that he had read all of Luke Short's stories and novels and that never once did one of the protagonists so much as crack a smile. Jon's model had always been Ernest Haycox among Western authors and he began in the serials and stories he wrote after the war to experiment with character and narrative technique in a fashion his brother never did. "Colt-Cure for Woolly Fever" is a humorous story, abandoning the reliance on serious circumstances, grim conflicts, and sober protagonists which had come to characterize so much of the Western fiction being written at the time, and thus setting the stage for the return of stories which stressed comedic elements, a quality that had become increasingly scarce in Western fiction written during the Depression and the war. This story first appeared in *Big-Book Western* (2/49) and has not otherwise been collected.

I

"BIG BILL"

They watched the stranger on the palomino coming down the pass trail, Jesusita leaning languorously in the *cantina* doorway in one of those typically provocative attitudes that was Big Bill's reason for staying on here the last four days. Now, annoyed by the way she studied this oncoming rider so fixedly, he tongued his tobacco from one cheek to the other and spat expertly between his boots cocked on the *portal* wall. As the resulting puff of dust jumped from the roadway beyond, he observed sourly: "Never did see a runt forkin' that good a horse but what it was stole."

Jesusita shrugged one shoulder, her dark eyes smoldering as they rocked around to him, then away again. He had decided from the first that this look betrayed her passion for him, though his several attempts at acting on that assumption had resulted only in the left side of his face being slapped hard.

So now, misinterpreting her glance as he usually did, he told her, "Say the word, *Muchacha*, and that palomino's yours."

"Hah! The gringo talk beeg!" she said derisively, expansively, the firm yet gentle lines of her upper body standing out sharply with her quick intake of breath. "I no want the *caballo*, no notheeng from you!" And as she turned in through the doors and left him, Big Bill chuckled so hard that his paunch bobbed, and he swore for the two hundred and thirty-seventh time that she would be his.

Everisto, her cousin, had been whittling at a knot on the step log, his ever drowsy glance on the rider who was coming into sight again from behind the spruce. And now as he pried away a chip he said, "Thees runt, you call heem. He wear the two beeg guns and he's not so leetle. The horse, she's too beeg to make heem look beeg."

Bill scowled, eyeing the rider intently. "He's a runt," was his considered opinion.

Shortly he and Everisto went indoors, both acting on the same impulse yet neither aware of its furtive quality. At such a remote place as this it was safest to show no curiosity over strangers. The *cantina*, with its offering of food and lodging, had thrived first because of Jesusita's beauty and secondly because she, Everisto, and Papa who spent most of his hours asleep by the stove, all pretended to see nothing and know even less than nothing about the comings and goings along this trail.

For the trail led from sheep country in the broad valley below to a vast cattle range the other side of the pass and, with the feeling strong between the two factions, the running of such an establishment called for a certain finesse.

So when the stranger got down from his palomino and stepped in through the swing doors some minutes later, Jesusita was behind the bar rinsing lamp chimneys in hot soapy water. Big Bill was bellied to the counter opposite her sipping a glass of tequila. Everisto was doing something with a deck of cards at the room's only table and Papa's unshaven chin was resting exactly where it usually did, on the front of his none too clean flannel shirt. His snoring only heightened the room's midday somnolence and struck a note in harmony with the buzzing of the flies at the windows.

"Afternoon, folks," said the stranger pleasantly.

"*Buenos tardes, Señor,*" murmured Jesusita.

Her demure greeting was so at odds with that bolt-of-lightning quality Bill had so constantly sampled from her that Bill now pushed his paunch two inches from the bar and turned to eye the stranger. What he saw rocked him back on his run-over heels.

The man was, as Everisto had said, not small. Big Bill still topped his even six feet by a good four inches, but that wasn't what Bill noticed. Nor did he particularly note the stranger's blondness, or the lean, handsome face.

There was something else to displease his belligerent eye. The stranger's outfit was expensive. A nicely pressed black coat hung open over a fiery red shirt. The boots below clean waist-overalls, also pressed, were fancy-stitched and polished till they shone. The pale gray hat was new, expensive, and didn't show any dust.

Despite all this it was three other items that had jolted Bill. Two were a matching pair of horn-handled Colts riding low along the stranger's flat thighs, the holsters thonged. The third was the ivory handle of a knife showing above the top of the polished right boot.

Big Bill took a certain pride in the armament he carried, and on his ability to use same. He'd done some carving on the cedar handle of his Navy Colt in the way of uniform notches representing certain luckless individuals who had had various and sundry fallings-out with him.

A long time ago he'd worn a matching weapon, but an empty pocket and a smooth-tongued Mexican over in 'Cruces had whittled him down to being a one-gun man; he'd never bothered to replace the missing weapon. He always carried a big clasp knife in a pocket of his Levi's, one that would snap open, and on several occasions he had wielded it in what he invariably called self-defense—though his favorite close-in weapon was the neck end of a broken bottle.

He was big. He could use knife, gun, or bottle expertly. He'd never run across the man he couldn't lick. Nor had he ever missed an opportunity for showing himself the better man when meeting any individual who had the look of thinking himself able to take care of trouble.

So now, after his deliberate inspection of the fancied-up stranger, Big Bill even more deliberately scowled and, disdaining any reply to the other's greeting, turned back to his glass.

"The handle's Matt, folks," the stranger said affably then. "Who'll wet their whistle with me? Make it whiskey, Señorita."

Everisto at once came over to the counter, grinning and nodding as he took the bottle the stranger passed him and filled his glass. "*Gracias, Señor, gracias,*" he said.

The stranger offered Big Bill the bottle then and Bill said with a surly snarl, "I pass."

"Every man to his own taste," Matt drawled.

If he hadn't turned his back on Big Bill just then, the thing might have been settled sooner. All Bill could think of to do was to glower at Jesusita, which only made the smile she was giving the stranger more radiant.

This Matt took up his glass now, drawling, "To all beautiful women," and drank the toast with his pale blue laughing eyes taking in Jesusita's dark loveliness.

Afterward he tossed a silver dollar to the counter and Jesusita made change, a half dollar and two dimes. Whereupon the stranger stared down at the coins, saying, "You didn't take out enough, Miss."

She made a pretty play of hands and shoulders in telling him, "Fifteen cents the dreenk, Señor."

"Cheap," he said.

Big Bill had suddenly had enough of this folderol. He pounded the bar loudly.

"Sheep?" he roared. "What about sheep?" and wheeled with the clumsiness of a grizzly to throw what tequila remained in his glass squarely into the stranger's eyes.

If he hadn't thought to draw his .44 at the same time, he wouldn't have lived to add his bit to the lurid history of Chiricahua County. For, though nearly blinded, Matt's right hand dropped to his Colt so fast the eye could scarcely follow.

The hammer click of Bill's weapon was all that stopped the stranger's draw. Smiling broadly then, the tequila dripping from his chin, Matt lifted his empty hand carefully and laid it palm down on the bar. And Jesusita picked that moment to burst into a torrent of Spanish, which dealt plainly with the obscurity of Big Bill's ancestry.

Presently, when he had blinked his eyes clear of the fiery liquid, Matt politely raised a hand and motioned Jesusita to silence. Then he looked up at Bill, who held the Colt still lined at the middle button on his shirt. "Just what did I say to upset you, friend?"

"Sheep! What the hell else?" Bill roared, Jesusita's tongue-lashing having blunted the sharp edge of his temper not at all. "The only sheepman I drink alongside is a dead one!"

"Now you've got me wrong," Matt drawled smoothly. "Fact is, I can't stand the stink of sheep. So tell the señorita you're sorry. Then you can put that hog-leg away and fill your glass again. It's my treat."

"Sorry for what?" Bill's roar hadn't diminished. "Turn yourself around and keep them hands where they are!"

For a fraction of a second he caught the wintry look in the stranger's eyes and should have been warned by it. But the chip he'd put on his shoulder was too big to let fall now and, reaching out roughly and grabbing this Matt by the arm, he pushed him around. Then, ramming the muzzle of his Colt in at the man's spine—he had a second warning there, for the muscles along that back were like oak—he relieved him of his pair of matched .45s.

Using his own weapon to push the stranger away from him, he bellowed, "Next time you figure to drink alongside a cattleman, bring your big brother with you, runt!" And with that he headed for the doors, satisfied that when Jesusita had time to consider the last few moments she would see him for what he was—a brave and strong man.

He carried Matt's two guns by their trigger guards hanging from his big left index finger, and as he came up on the doors he reached out with his other hand to push them aside.

That hand was touching the wood when he felt what he thought was a fly touch his ear. A wing of brightly reflected sunlight flashed past his eye. There came a thrumming sound and the door stirred slightly away from his hand.

A split second later he saw the ivory-handled knife that had grazed his ear quivering in the door panel. And behind him he caught the sound of something thudding solidly against the bar.

"Now hold on," came Matt's mild drawl.

The color drained from Big Bill's face. He stood there rigid, his back still to the room. He was remembering the shotgun Jesusita always kept under the bar, which would account for the sound he had just heard, and he was imagining its front bead centering the small of his back. So he stood rooted as he was, staring at the knife and blinking away a sudden flow of perspiration from his forehead that trickled down into his eyes and off the end of his bulbous nose.

"You forgot to tell the *señorita* you're sorry, friend," Matt told him.

Big Bill thought to drop the three guns then and they clumped solidly to the hard-packed earth floor as he tried to speak, but couldn't. He swallowed to rid his throat of its cottony dryness and then, strictly because he was as afraid as he'd ever been, he said meekly, haltingly:

"I . . . I reckon I done wrong, *Muchacha.*"

"Now that's a real nice sentiment," Matt North told him. "You can trot along if you feel like it." And Big Bill shouldered out through the doors and was gone.

"Ornery cuss, eh?" Matt said, setting the bottle back on the bar. He had been holding it ready in case his swift knife throw hadn't completely awed the big man, and it was its accidental banging against the counter that had made Big Bill think of the shotgun.

"Beel, she's the beeg peeg!"

Jesusita sighed with relief at the relaxing of the tension. And now her eyes flashed with loathing. "He come here three, four day ago. He say to me, '*Muchacha*, you and me go to see priest an' get married, no? You leave thees place w'ere the mens she's always trying to kees you and make the love. W'at about eet, Jesusita?'

"An' I tell heem no man make the love to me for I heet and bite if she do. So Beeg Beel he laugh and peench me on the arm. I heet heem. Then he peench me other places and I heet heem some more. But still she theenk thees is the way I make the love to heem, so he 'ang 'round. I take hees monee and let heem make the beeg eyes. W'at I care?"

Matt was only vaguely aware of what she had been saying, so entranced was he by the play of her eyes and graceful, quick motions of her hands. He knew he was staring at her calf-eyed, but didn't care. And now he let out a gusty breath, saying, "'Sita, you're the prettiest thing I ever laid eyes on!"

She liked that. Everisto, watching, could hardly believe his eyes, for he knew she had been telling the truth about not tolerating the advances of men customers. Yet here she was, smiling in confusion, obviously liking this stranger's words.

"Tha's wot Beel say, 'You beauteeful, *Muchacha*,' " Jesusita put in hastily now. "So w'en he say eet I heet heem. Like thees."

And before Matt could dodge she leaned over the counter and

slapped him across the face so hard his head rocked to the side. But then instantly there was a look of contrition in her eyes and she was crying, "Oh, *Señor*, I no mean that!" Just as quickly as she'd moved a moment ago she now leaned closer to him and, patting his cheek, murmured, "*Pobrecito*! For a meenute I theenk you Beel. I too sorry, *Señor* Matt!"

"Didn't hurt a bit, *Señorita*." Matt was rubbing his cheek. "Not a bit."

"Matt," she sighed, elbows on the counter, her face close to his and her eyes ever so soft. "That's one nice 'andle. Matt. Veree nice."

She had such a gone look right then that Matt gulped and reached for the bottle. He poured himself a drink and downed it at one swallow, for he was a slow hand with the opposite sex and this girl with the flashing eyes was sweeping him off his feet. He wanted to touch her, maybe even try a kiss. Instead he blurted out:

"Couldn't we . . . that is, couldn't you and me go down to town some night and kick up our heels at a dance, 'Sita?"

She drew away, wide-eyed in alarm. "No, no! Papa he take the belt and wheep." Unashamedly her hand went to her backside. "You come see me 'ere, Matt. We seet on the *portal* one night teel Papa asleep, no?"

"Sure," Matt gulped. "Sure thing."

"But not in the town," Jesusita said, wrinkling her nose. "The town she steenk of cheep. Once it was *differente*. W'en I the leetle girl everyone they 'appy. Papa, 'e was the *vaquero* then. He rope the beeg steer and tweest 'is tail an' he wear the wot you call bool-'ide pants. But then the cheep mans come in and weeth the gons they fight and drive the cattlemans out. So now Papa 'e 'ave the seekness of the 'eart and he seet there all day dreaming of w'en 'e was the wan fine *vaquero* and ron the cattle."

Matt's look had turned grave and now he glanced at Papa in the chair by the stove and nodded, drawling, "I've heard about your ruckus here. No one's tried to push these sheep-lovers out of the valley since then?"

"They always talking." She lifted her shoulders eloquently. "But no one, he do notheeng. Beel, he say he go down to rob the bank because he hate the cheep man. But all she do ees talk beeg. Beeg Weend, I call heem. He got the beeg talk from the beeg belly."

Matt's glance went to the doors. "So Bill would like to bust open the bank, eh?"

"He like to fine. But he no have w'at you call the gotts."

"Guts."

"Tha's w'at I say, Matt. The gotts."

Matt's glance was still on the doors and now he drawled absent-mindedly, "Maybe Bill and I could get along." He moved on over from the bar then and picked up the guns, holstering his own pair and ramming Bill's through the belt of his Levi's.

He was standing there looking out over the doors when Jesusita cried quickly in alarm, "You no go out there, Matt! Beel, he keel you. He the wan toff *hombre*! He got the rifle on 'is 'orse."

Matt's lean face broke into a smile. "So I see. He's got the rifle right enough. But not his horse. He's gettin' onto Whitey."

"W'itey?"

"My palomino."

His smile still holding, he turned and came back to the bar. He picked up the bottle and laid two silver dollars on the counter, telling her, "This Bill and I are going to make some medicine, 'Sita."

Then, as he went to the doors again, she cried, "Matt, stay weeth me!" But he only shook his head and stepped out onto the *portal*.

At that moment Big Bill, astride the palomino, was turning out from the *cantina*'s tie-rail. He saw Matt and, his look turning ugly, leveled the .30-30 Winchester he had been holding with stock cradled against his thigh.

"Back in there, runt!" he called hoarsely, trying to quiet the palomino's head-tossing and nervous side-stepping.

Matt's smile only widened and for several seconds he watched the muzzle of Bill's rifle bob up and down to the nervous pitching of the animal. Then abruptly he whistled.

At that sound the palomino suddenly reared high on hind legs. And Bill, dropping the carbine and reaching for the horn a split-second too late, slid heavily down over the animal's rump and hit the ground with a pained grunt. The palomino at once quieted and walked on past the rail and in under the *portal* to rub his nose fondly along Matt's arm.

There was a point beyond which Matt didn't want to humiliate the big man, so he wasn't smiling now as he drawled, "Whitey's a handful, Bill. Should've warned you. That's a trick I taught him."

Big Bill's face was dark with an apoplectic look and his furious glance went to the carbine. But it was too far beyond his reach to give him a chance against even an average draw. So he picked his hat out of the road, beat the dust from it, clamped it on his head and heaved his vast hulk erect. Matt sauntered on out and, drawing Bill's .44, held it out to him butt foremost. At the same time he hefted the bottle in his other hand, saying, "Let's you and me pick a spot of shade and wash the dust out of our windpipes. I got something to talk over with you."

Bill's angry glance became uncertain now. With a down-lipped sneer he took his gun and stood glowering down on the smaller man, as though undecided as to what to do next. But something in Matt's eyes made him finally holster the weapon. Then, grudgingly, he accepted the bottle as Matt uncorked it and offered it.

They each took a long pull at the bottle and then Matt led the way to the shady side of the *cantina*. There he sat with his back to the wall, putting the bottle between them as Bill joined him. And Bill was still studying him suspiciously as he said:

"The girl in there says you got a notion to bust open the bank down below, Bill. Now you and me got something in common."

"What?" Bill growled

"Hatin' sheep," Matt told him. "And wantin' to lay hands on some easy sheep money."

Bill's frown faded before a slow surprise. "Well, I . . . that is, you might say I got my eye on that there bank," he admitted haltingly.

"Think the two of us together could pull the thing off?"

Bill blinked, obviously caught unawares. And as he hesitated Matt drawled, " 'Course, if you think it's too risky. . . ."

"Who the hell said I thought that?"

Bill had swallowed his tobacco when he sat so suddenly there in the road, and now he took a plug of the weed from a shirt pocket, needing time to think. He bit off a generous hunk, then handed it to Matt. And after Matt had taken his bite, they silently passed the bottle between them again. Finally Bill said:

"Ain't nothin' to be afraid of. Except maybe for that tin safe bein' so full of money two men couldn't haul it all away."

"We could make two trips," Matt said blandly, making Bill blink again and wonder just what this stranger's nerves were made of.

"Here's the way she looks to me," Bill went on, groping his way through his slow thoughts and trying to remember how the bank had looked on his trip down to Pleasantville day before yesterday in Jesusita's buckboard.

"They've ordered a new safe shipped in. But she ain't here yet, which has caught 'em with their galluses down. They've got the back wall of the bank knocked out with a hole big enough to drive a team through. So they can get the new safe in when she comes. The thing's boarded over now and that sheep-lovin' sheriff, Clyde Case, takes turns with his deputy day and night watchin' to see no one comes along with a hammer and breaks in. Must be close to thirty or forty thousand in the old safe."

"How much of a job will it be to open the thing?"

Big Bill laughed so hard his paunch shook. He made another pass at the bottle before he answered, "I got a knife in my pocket'll do the job slick as a whistle."

"Then let's do it tonight."

Matt's words made Bill sit straighter. "Tonight?" he echoed. "I . . . well, y'see, I was thinkin' me and Jesusita might go for a walk up toward the pass tonight."

"Now that's a shame," Matt said innocently. "Here I thought you might help."

Things were moving too fast for Bill. "Hadn't we ought to go down there and look the thing over first? You, I mean."

Matt nodded. "Just what I was thinkin'. Give me the rest of the afternoon and I'll meet you wherever you say. Let the girl wait, Bill."

The big man sighed, for the way Matt talked made the thing sound easy. Then he remembered something and, scowling at Matt, said, "You looked pretty sweet on her in there."

Matt's wide grin held a guilty look. "Sure. I always give 'em a try, Bill. But if she's yours, I'll lay off."

"She damn' well is!" Bill flared. "You and me got to get that straight if we're sidin' each other."

"That's easy," Matt said. He held out his hand. "So long as we're partners we don't mix our women. Okay?"

Bill nodded. He was smiling for the first time as he wrapped his big fist around Matt's and shook it.

II

"SHEEP TOWN"

The men and women in Pleasantville who observed Matt's arrival were unanimous in their reactions. Most of the men wished they could own the horse and most of the women would have given anything to own the man, so by the time he turned in at the livery corral to leave the palomino, more than a few of the folks were already curious about him.

He went straight to the hotel, his bedroll slung over his shoulder, and there were half a dozen townsmen in the lobby to overhear him tell the clerk as he signed the book, "The best room you got, friend. With a bath."

"Mister, there ain't a foot o' plumbin' on the premises."

Matt's brows lifted in polite surprise. "No? Well, maybe I'll build a hotel of my own with some. This is sure a wore-out-lookin' settlement, friend. Give me the best you got."

Once he and the clerk had climbed the stairs from the lobby the several men who had overheard these remarks hastened to discuss them, quickly forgetting their anger over the slighting way he had spoken of the town. One of the group went to the desk for a look at the register and shortly rejoined the others to say, "Calls himself North, Matthew V. North."

They made several conjectures on the stranger's identity, most of which were based on his asking for a bath and his look of affluence, and by the time Matt came down the stairs again they were very respectful in the way they answered his casual nod.

Matt's next stop along the street was at a shack with a shingle hanging over its door bearing the legend, LAND FOR SALE. RANCH AND TOWN PROPERTIES. He was in there a good twenty minutes and as soon as he left, crossing over to the bank, Mayor Williams and two other men who had been in the hotel lobby went into the shack to ask what had gone on.

"Plenty," they were told. "North took out options on every outfit we got for sale, includin' Ives's place. And on those eight lots down the street where we give up buildin' the new opera house."

"God in heaven!" the mayor breathed. "Who is he?"

"Calls himself North, Matthew. . . ."

"We know that! But where's he from?"

"He didn't say and I didn't ask. One thing, though. He ain't so taken with the idea of runnin' sheep."

The mayor and his companions looked at each other as their informant shortly continued, "I told him if he was settlin' here it'd be sheep or nothin'. He just looked at me sort of queer, like I needed a haircut maybe or a shave. Said he'd think it over, that he wanted to invest around a hundred thousand in good grass and town lots and. . . ."

"A hundred thousand?" one of the others whispered. Then, finding his voice, he said quickly, "Let's get on over and see Caleb. He may know more about North."

But two minutes later Caleb West, president of the bank, couldn't add much to what they already knew of the stranger—except that he'd refused to bank any money until the present safe was replaced by an adequate vault.

"Vault?" the mayor said. "You didn't order no vault, Caleb."

"Who said I did?" Caleb countered in irritation. "But I can order one in place of the new safe, can't I? Fact is, I already got a man ridin' across to Junction to send a telegram about it."

While they were speculating further on the importance of this Matthew North's arrival, and on what his money would do for the town, Sheriff Clyde Case joined them and was presently inserting a new note into their conversation as he observed: "You boys better let me take a look at my dodgers before you get so steamed up over this bird."

"Clyde, for the love of the good Lord, why spoil our fun?" Banker West asked. "You'd suspect your grandmother of bein' a squaw woman if she hadn't lived long enough to let you have a good look at her."

He, like the rest, had little patience with the sheriff for the reason that Case had twelve years ago kept plenty far out of the way of flying lead during the war with the cattlemen.

"You go look through your dodgers, Clyde," the mayor said. "But danged if we'll let you insult this gentleman and scare him off."

So Case, grumbling about their ingratitude when he was only looking after their best interests, left the bank and went to his office and stubbornly set about going through his disorderly collection of reward notices.

He was halfway through the stack when Matt came in off the walk, saying pleasantly, "Afternoon, Sheriff. Have a cigar?"

Clyde had a guilty, surprised look as he got out of his chair and took the cigar. "Thanks, Mr. North," he said respectfully. "I been hearin' about you. Have my chair."

But Matt was noticing the dodgers and now taking his own cigar from his mouth and nodding down to the desk, said, "That's a funny thing. I dropped in here for this very reason, Sheriff. To look through your wanted notices."

Clyde Case's weasel-eyed glance turned impassive. He ran a thumb along his tobacco-yellowed brown mustache, put the cigar in his mouth and started chewing it as he asked off-handedly, "Lookin' for one in particular?"

"Sure am." Matt watched the lawman's jaws working at the cigar. He regretted having given Case the smoke now, for he had just spent one of his last few dollars on eight fine cigars and he could already see that this one was wasted.

So as he sighed his disappointment he told Case, "On the way over here I ran onto a jasper that had a mean pair of ears. Big as a house, a front on him like a barrel. A nose too big for his face and they called him Bill."

"Big Bill!" Case nearly choked on the cigar. He got red in the face and his voice was trembling when he went on, "That yellow-livered coyote! Mean as a grizzly and twice as dangerous. Tell me where I can find him and I'll blow a hole through his back. His back, mind you! He's wanted on any one of ten counts that'll hang him."

"Now hold on," Matt said mildly. "Don't get so aforesaid. For all I know this Big Bill may be three hundred miles from here by now. On the other hand, he was headed this way."

"The hell you say!" Case stepped quickly to the door, stuck his head out and bawled, "Avery! Get across here!"

"What's up?" Matt asked.

"Avery's my deputy," Case told him, his look worried as he chewed the cigar furiously. "Mr. North, you got much ready cash on you?"

Matt frowned. "Would a couple thousand be what you call ready?"

The sheriff's eyes bugged open. "Ready and then some! Well, you hide that there money *pronto*! If Big Bill breezes through here and finds there's a well-heeled stranger in town, he'll take every damn' nickel you got."

"No one takes my nickels," Matt drawled.

"You pay attention to what I'm tellin' you!" said the lawman excitedly. He gave a start as the door opened. But when he saw who it was, a tow-headed youth who was working at his teeth with a splinter of wood, he said officiously, "Avery, go to the hardware and get every shotgun Blaine's got in the place. Hand 'em out to the best shots. Beginnin' at dark, we're goin' to have twenty armed men prowlin' this street."

"How come?" Avery wanted to know.

"How come! Big Bill's been seen close to here and for all we know he. . . ."

The sheriff's words broke off, for he was speaking at an empty door. Avery had already left, on the run.

"Why get so het up?" Matt asked. "If the law gets this spooky over one lone wolf, maybe I ought to look for some other place to settle."

"Mr. North, you got us wrong," Clyde hastened to assure him. And for the next several minutes he did his best to convince Matt that Pleasantville was exactly what the name would indicate, a pleasant place to live, safe as the inside of a church at meeting time, the best climate in the world, the best of everything.

"Take grass, for instance," he ended by saying. "I hear you're of a mind to buy some land. Well, sir, there ain't an animal ever lived was so sick that a week on this grass wouldn't cure him. It's plumb past believin', but we never lose a head of anything in this valley except for butcherin' or some pet critter now and then dyin' of old age. Ever see anything to beat the looks of them sheep you passed on the way in?"

"I kind of hoped to run cattle, Sheriff."

Case stiffened, started to look angry, decided for private reasons not to. He shook his head. "Nope, sheep's all we run here. The time was, ten or twelve years ago, when they ran cattle. Them damn' critters near ruined the valley. You know how cattle are, pullin' the grass up by the roots and. . . ."

"I always thought it was the other way around."

"No sir! You take my word for it, neighbor, it's cattle and not sheep that ruin the range. So," the lawman went on, deciding he had proven his point, "a few of us up and decide we'll save what's left. For a week or two it was Nip and Tuck, the lead flyin' so thick you didn't dare set foot outdoors by day. Then finally we drove Matt Rivers and his gang. . . ."

"Did you say 'Matt Rivers'?"

The sheriff nodded. "Matt Rivers. He was leader of them cattlemen. Set up a lot like you, come to think of it. Your build, them big shoulders and all. And pale hair like yours."

"That's funny," Matt drawled. "Matt's my first name, too. We got a parcel of Rivers in one branch of our family and for a minute here I was thinkin' this man you mention might be some kin. But I reckon not."

"Probably not or you'd have heard of him before now. We chased him and his bunch over the pass and later we heard he had died from a chunk of lead through his middle. They tell me you've taken out an option to buy Ives's place, among others. That's the old Rivers layout, the old Anvil brand."

"Y' don't say!"

"Yep. And a right nice layout it is, too. Ives, he wants to sell on account of bein' ready to retire. He's made a big killin' up there on that Anvil grass with all the water and meadow he's got and he'll sell for the right price. Thirty thousand, they say."

Matt nodded. "That's the price quoted to me."

The sheriff had become quite affable and now slapped Matt on the back, saying, "Well, sir, you couldn't find a better place at a better price. Take it before Ives changes his mind. And try sheep, Mr. North. You can't go wrong on a wool crop."

"I'll think it over." Matt lifted a hand, drawled, "See you later, Sheriff," and left.

He hadn't gone twenty steps when a portly individual standing at the walk's edge below the jail stopped him. "Mr. North, let me introduce myself. I'm Mayor Williams." He took Matt's hand and pumped it hard, adding affably, "Some of the boys are hoisting one across in the Nugget, since it's the shank of the day. We'd admire to have you join us."

"Now that's real white of you," Matt said and, the mayor linking an arm in his, let himself be led across the street to a saloon.

III

"DOUBLE-CROSS"

During the hour he spent in very pleasant company in the Nugget, he several times put a hand in his near-empty pocket, announcing that the next round of drinks was his. But each time his offer brought a storm of protest, for several others had joined the gathering and new money was anything but scarce.

Several of these last joiners were carrying shotguns—the ones the sheriff had ordered handed out at the hardware store—and as they took their drinks they passed the guns across the bar to the apron for safekeeping, so that by the real shank of the evening, supper time, the back-bar looked like a gun-case with its array of new and shiny weapons.

When the subject of eating presented itself, Matt was invited to dine with several of the town's most eminent citizens. He accepted graciously. The meal was larded with much boisterous whiskey-livened talk and consumed an hour and a half. Toward the end of it Matt was beginning to feel uneasy and kept glancing at the clock over the counter.

Finally, when it appeared that the evening had only begun, he rose from his chair and announced, "Gents, I thank you for one fine mess of food. But there's work to be done. If this curly wolf Big Bill is really due to shoot up the town tonight, let's get set for him."

"Why, I'd almost forgot Big Bill," the mayor said. He wasn't too steady on his feet as he rose to stand alongside Matt, who noticed him licking his lips and wondered at the reason until the mayor said loudly to the others, "Boys, the nights are gettin' right chill. What say we get ourselves a bottle or two to help us last till mornin'?"

There was a general agreement. Someone reminded the assemblage that they had left their guns at the Nugget, so they straggled out and across the street, a man on either side of the newcomer and both calling him "Matt" now instead of "Mr. North."

When they were finally gathered in front of the Nugget, armed with their shotguns and a quart bottle for every other man, the mayor spoke for all of them in asking, "Where do you want us, Matt?"

This matter took some thought and for a moment Matt didn't answer. Then finally he drawled, "I don't know the town, boys. Let the sheriff decide."

"Where the hell is Clyde?" someone asked.

"Out behind the bank watchin' the alley, ain't he?"

"Someone go get him."

"Tell you what," Matt inserted, knowing it was well past the hour he had set for meeting Big Bill. "I'd like to wander on out the street and look it over, get the lay of the land. While you're gettin' the sheriff, I'll roam about by myself a minute or two."

Mayor Williams wanted to come with him but Matt took him aside and said quietly, "Better stay with the bunch. They're likkered up and need watchin'. Keep your eye on them. I'll be right back."

Williams was swaying a little and had to stand spraddle-legged to keep his balance. He, like the others, had had a lot to drink. Now he was licking his lips again, wanting more as he said, "Y' know, Matt, I think Clyde thought this Big Bill business up as a joke on us. Whyn't we all just go in there, set ourselves down and enjoy a few more drinks and some cigars? Maybe a game of draw?"

"It wasn't Clyde thought it up, it was me."

"So it was, so it was," Williams grumbled. "Well, you get on and I'll keep an eye on this bunch."

Matt went on before the mayor could change his mind. Half a minute's walk brought him abreast the big livery corral. The street was dark here and after a look both ways along the walks he climbed the gate and hurried on toward the back of the big enclosure, the shadowy shapes of several horses drifting out of his way in the darkness ahead. He found that his steps were slightly uncertain and wished now he hadn't taken so many drinks.

He was coming up on the spidery black silhouette of the windmill beyond the back rails when he remembered the big log watering trough. A sigh of relief escaped him as he took off his hat and coat and, laying them aside, dipped his head into the cold water brimming in the trough. Then, for some strange reason, he got to thinking of 'Sita and just stood there for a minute or two.

He was scrubbing his face again presently, feeling his senses steadying under the chill bite of the water, when a sound made him wheel around. Instinctively, in one smooth flow of motion, he palmed the Colt from his right thigh, softly asking, "Who is it?"

"Me," answered a deep-toned voice—Big Bill's. "Where you been all this time?"

"Layin' the way for an easy job," Matt answered. He dropped the Colt back into its scabbard, pulling out the tails of his shirt and using them to dry his head. Then, without giving Bill a chance to complain further, he said, "Now here's what we do." And he went on to explain exactly what was to happen.

He ended half a minute's steady talk by saying, "So it'll be a cinch. Remember, there'll be a loose board. When I light my cigar, you go in that way. Be quiet while you're inside and wait in there till I come after you. Where the hell's all the gunny-sacks?"

"Tied to my hull."

"Then we're all set, Bill. Give me fifteen minutes."

But something was bothering Big Bill, for he made no move to walk away. And shortly he said in a voice that grated, "One man double-crossed me once. I drop by the cemetery at Socorro every now and then to take flowers off his grave. His family leaves 'em."

"That's not the way you'd want your grave treated, Bill."

"You mind this, now," Bill growled, in no mood for nonsense. "I get my half . . . no matter what."

"And see that I get mine," Matt said. "After all, I'm leaving the business of the split to you."

Without another word, Bill turned and walked away in the darkness.

IV

"NO DAMN' DINERO!"

Mayor Williams and four men were set to watch the lower end of the street while another group stationed themselves along the stretch of awninged walk above the hardware store. "Me, I'll go give the sheriff a hand," Matt offered. No one questioned his statement. It was as easy as that. So he went on down to the bank.

Taking the narrow passageway alongside the bank, he was careful to be loudly whistling a tune, trusting Clyde Case's steadiness not at all.

"Who the hell's makin' so much noise?" came the sheriff's sharp query as Matt stepped out of the back end of the passageway.

"Me, Sheriff. How do things look?"

"Oh, you, Mr. North." Case came up out of the shadows. "They don't look so good if you ask me."

"Why not?"

"We need more men back here."

"You and me can handle our end," Matt drawled.

That seemed to quiet the lawman's jumpy nerves somewhat and for a minute or two they talked in low voices, Matt telling Case how the townsmen had distributed themselves along the street. Then, presently, Matt asked, "How easy would it be for a man to break into the bank?"

"How easy is it for a kid to fight his way into a sack of candy?"

Matt whistled softly. "Y' don't say. Let's take a look."

Case led the way on along the bank's back wall and after several steps they came up on a portion of the wall that showed a lighter shadow. "If that ain't a pretty sight!" the lawman said disgustedly.

It wasn't very strong, Matt could see, even in this poor light. A rectangular hole about as tall as he was and twice as wide had been boarded up. He stepped in close to it, swung a boot back and kicked hard at one of the wide boards, drawling, "Flimsy, eh?"

"Don't!" Case snapped worriedly. "Hell, you'll kick the whole thing loose."

He was more right than he imagined. For Matt had seen the base of that one board swing out, the nails pulled free under his kick. Here was the first thing of the several he had mentioned to Big Bill already accomplished. Now for the second, he told himself as he said, "Let's take a look up at the other end."

He and Case walked on to the far end of the wall. And now he took a cigar, his last, from the pocket of his coat. "What's up in there?" he asked, nodding up a passageway even narrower than the one he had traveled from the street.

"Nothin'." Case stepped into the passageway, adding, "Nothin' but a rain barrel in here you got to watch out for. Right here."

"Glad to know about it." Matt wiped a match alight along the seat of his pants and as it flared held it out openly and unshielded by his hands to light his cigar.

"Put that damn' thing out!" the sheriff breathed softly, excitedly. "You want your face shot in?"

Matt shook the match out, saying apologetically, "Didn't think, I reckon. You really do expect this Big Bill, Sheriff?"

"You're damn' right I do!"

"Then you lead right on. Show me how to get to the street from here. I'll watch this side from the . . . from the front."

Matt's last three words had been spoken more loudly than the rest. For a moment ago a sound had shuttled along the alley and, standing as he was now, he saw a shadow moving across toward the bank's rear wall from a shed across the way.

He breathed a vast sigh of relief—Case was in the passageway, unable to see. Now he quickly turned and made plenty of noise in stumbling after the lawman up the length of the narrow corridor. Big Bill was on his way into the bank. He could only hope that Bill would follow the rest of his instructions to the letter.

Case stopped at the head of the passageway, saying in a low voice, "Now, if I was you, I'd stand right here. You can see both ways along the street and, if there's any trouble out back, I'll holler."

"Better make it good and loud."

"I will." The lawman stepped out onto the walk.

Matt watched him saunter along the front of the bank and try the doors. Then he went on.

By that time Matt already had one boot off and was pulling at the other. Then Case stepped out of sight into the passageway along the bank's far wall. Laying his boots aside and drawing one of his Colts, Matt turned and cat-footed fast back along his corridor to the alley. When he turned into the alley, it was to hug the shadows close to the wall.

He ran the last few steps across to the foot of that far passageway, making no noise, and as a last precaution took off his hat and dropped it, coming to a crouch at the wall end. His head low to the ground, he looked around the corner.

He heard Case stumbling toward him close by. But it was so black down that narrow alleyway that he couldn't see so much as a shadow. There was barely time for him to come erect and lift the .45 before Clyde Case stepped out into the open.

Once he had his target, Matt swung his blow expertly. The barrel of the Colt caught the sheriff above the ear, denting in the side of his hat. Case sighed softly. His knees buckled. And it was no trick at all for Matt to catch him as he fell, unconscious.

Matt laid the lawman down gently, wheeling immediately to walk over to the boarded-up section of the wall. He holstered the Colt as he pulled aside the loose board and whispered, "Okay, Bill! Everything's set."

He had barely spoken before the big man edged sideways through the narrow opening that barely let him squeeze through. Bill carried a bulging gunny sack in each hand and one of these he quickly held out to Matt, saying brusquely, "Here, take it."

Matt took the sack and hefted it, asking, "How'd it go?"

Bill chuckled in a deep, excited voice. "Nothin' to it. Didn't even have to use the knife. Brother, we made a haul! Now how do I get out of here?"

"Just the way you came, Bill."

Matt was still speaking when Bill made a sudden move, his ham-like fist awkwardly pulling the Navy Colt from holster. As he leveled the weapon at Matt and backed away a step, he snarled, "Reach for the back of your neck, runt!"

Matt was careful to keep his hands well away from his sides as he dropped the sack and lifted them. And as he locked his hands behind his neck, Bill said hoarsely, "I told you no one had ever double-crossed me!"

"No one's tryin' to double-cross you, Bill."

"Damn' right they ain't!" Bill said. He started backing away into the shadows. "You just stay set till I'm gone, runt! If you move a finger, I let daylight through you!"

Matt wasn't particularly alarmed. But he stayed as he was for better than a minute after Bill had edged out of sight into the blackness. At the end of that interval he thought he heard the slow hoof-falls of a horse going away across the rocky hillside above the alley.

Yet he wasn't sure Bill had gone until he softly called, "You still there?"

There was no answer and, letting out a gusty breath, he brought his hands down. He picked up the sack and reached into it. A slow smile came to his face as he brought out a handful of paper. Even in this faint light he could see that it was scrap paper.

When he had emptied the sack, he found that it contained nothing but more scrap paper, a bundle of blotters, several unused tablets and two empty ink bottles. Something struck him as being very funny then and he laughed softly as he stuffed the worthless junk back into the sack.

He took one parting look at Sheriff Case before he moved back up to his own passageway. When he brushed against the rain barrel, he lifted the lid, dropped the sack into it, replaced the lid and went on.

He pulled on his boots again, went to the street head of the passageway, and sat down. He was a man of patience and made himself comfortable as he settled there to wait.

Some ten minutes later a man with a shotgun cradled in the bend of his arm came sauntering along the far walk. By the time he was abreast, Matt had rolled up a smoke. And he took some pains to see that the match flared openly as he lit it.

As though that had been a prearranged signal, the man over there left the walk and angled toward him. Halfway across, he called softly, "That you, Clyde?"

"Nope," Matt answered. "Clyde's out back."

It was one of the men who had gone with Mayor Williams. "Nothin' doin' so far as I can see," he told Matt as he joined him. "Think I'll go chew the fat with Clyde for a while."

"This is a lot of hogwash." Matt yawned. "No one's goin' to bust into this place. Wish I could get some sleep."

"Me, too. Let's see if I can talk Clyde into lettin' us call it off." And the man walked away, taking the far passageway toward the bank's rear.

It came sooner than Matt had expected, in less than a minute, in fact. Suddenly a shout echoed up out of the alley. It was high-pitched, almost a scream. Matt grinned and, just to see what would happen, drew one of his Colts. He pointed it roofward along the passageway and thumbed three fast, deafening shots, bellowing, "Stop! Stop!"

Hardly had the sound of his shots died out before someone yelled stridently far up the street. A shotgun's boom rode over the town as Matt ran back toward the alley. He had nearly reached it when the man back there shouted, "Don't shoot! It's me. Red."

And Matt, turning into the alley, called breathlessly, "Did you get him?"

"Who?"

"How would I know who?" Matt said acidly. "Who was it you yelled at? I saw him cross right here goin' down the alley."

"I didn't yell at no one. It's Clyde."

"So it was Clyde?" Matt asked, hearing others running toward them along the alley now.

"Hell, no, it wasn't Clyde! It was, I mean! He's here. Out cold!" And now at the sound of quick-pounding boots coming along the alley the speaker lifted his voice again, bawling, "Damn it, don't none of you shoot!"

Shortly one of the men who gathered about the sheriff lit a lantern and, as confused talk began, at least two men claimed to have seen a rider heading out of the alley. But they had seen this supposed rider going in opposite directions and Matt added to the confusion by giving his version of having shot at someone afoot.

Suddenly a man at the back fringe of the crowd bawled out, "God A'mighty, here's a loose board!"

"Where?"

"Where the hell you think? Here!"

The others forgot their unconscious sheriff then and crowded around the man who was reaching out to pull the loose board in the wall aside. As he did so several groans escaped the others. Someone breathed in an awed whisper, "The safe!" and pushed the first man out of the way to squeeze in through the opening. The rest, hit by a sudden panic, started shoving and crowding forward, trying to be the first to follow the leader.

The man with the lantern was the last one in and, as the wavering light thinned the corners of the big room, he was the only one who found the voice to speak. "Cleaned!"

Big Bill had made a mess of things. Papers were strewn every which way in front of the safe's open door. Several empty metal boxes, their lids twisted off, lay in the litter. A rack of trays from the safe sat in a lopsided stack on the floor of the nearest teller's cage.

When no one spoke over quite an interval, Matt said, "We're wastin' time, gents. Let's throw our hulls on some nags and take a look around."

But the man nearest him slowly shook his head. "Wouldn't be no use, Mister," he said. "Whoever did it was smart enough to head for the pass off north of here."

"Then let's get up there and head him off."

"Hunh-uh! That's cattle country beyond. No sheepman's used that pass for the last ten years and ever come back."

Once again a weighty silence settled over the eerily lit room. These men were speechless, dumbfounded, staring fixedly at the open safe. And shortly one of them breathed in a hushed voice, "Not one damn' dollar left! We're stone broke! You and me and all the rest! Even Caleb West!"

Only then did the full impact of their predicament seem to strike home to them. They looked at each other stupidly, disbelievingly.

And it was in this moment that Matt quietly told them, "Don't get in such a lather, boys. When we find out how much is missin', maybe I can help."

V

"JUDAS BABY"

Only one thing had gone amiss in all of Matt's calculations. The next morning after breakfast he ambled on along the street past the crowd gathered in front of the bank as far as the livery corral.

The palomino was gone.

Well, he thought, I reckon Whitey and the money are both at the same place. He really didn't feel very bad about it, nor was he very surprised.

Along about nine o'clock as he sat on the hotel veranda, a man came over from the bank and stopped below him on the walk, saying respectfully, "Caleb West and the directors would like to see you across there, Mr. North."

Matt said, "Sure," and came down off the veranda to walk back over with the man. The crowd in front of the bank, such a big one that it spilled off the walk into the street, opened silently before him and his companion, and on his way to the doors he heard a woman say in a loud whisper, "That's him! They say he's our only hope."

Inside, on the way to Caleb West's private office, Matt saw that no attempt had been made at cleaning up the litter alongside the safe.

There were eight men in the banker's office, which was clouded with cigar smoke. The four sitting at the long table at the room's center rose respectfully at Matt's entry and it was West himself who offered his chair, saying, "Here, sit at the head, Matt."

But Matt shook his head. "Always did think better on my feet, thanks." He pulled his coat open, thrust hands in pockets and went to stand with his back to the window, asking abruptly, "What's on your minds?"

Caleb West cleared his throat. With a nervous glance at the others he began, "Well, Matt . . . Mr. North, that is . . . we're sort of . . . well, I guess you'd say. . . ."

"I guess your bank is about busted," Matt cut in. "Is that what you're tryin' to say, Caleb?"

The banker nodded glumly.

"And you want to know if I'm goin' to help you?" Matt asked.

"Well, we kinda hoped you'd. . . ."

"Let's not beat about the bush," Matt interrupted again, rather sharply this time. "You've had some bad luck. If you close your doors, this range dries up and blows away. You need ready cash to stay in business. Correct?"

"You said a mouthful," Mayor Williams put in quietly.

"How much did you lose?"

"Eighty-seven thousand four hundred two dollars and sixty-nine cents," the banker stated.

Matt's soft whistle was absolutely genuine. "Now that's a wad of money, even for me," he drawled, frowning. He had never been particularly quick at figures and now, after a few seconds, asked, "How much would it take to keep you on your feet?"

Caleb West shrugged worriedly. "That's a matter of question, Matt."

Let's see, Matt was thinking, Ives is asking thirty for the layout. Thirty from eighty-seven odd is . . . is around fifty some. And he asked, "Could you limp along on fifty thousand?"

The gladness that replaced the worry on Caleb's face was really touching. "We could, Matt, we could. And every man, woman and child in the valley would thank you from the bottoms of their hearts."

Matt was impressed but tried not to show it. In fact he was frowning as he drawled, "I can swing that much without too much trouble." There was an excited mutter of voices at the table and now Mayor Williams and the others sat straighter, looking less like a pack of whipped dogs.

"But," Matt went on, "there's one big hitch. Maybe you remember me sayin' a couple times yesterday that I don't take to sheep."

They looked at each other nervously and with some alarm and Mayor Williams said, "Matt, it's somethin' you can get used to."

Matt shook his head. "Not me." And he let those words lie by themselves over the following silence.

Shortly a man at the table's far end asked meekly, "Then it's no go?"

"If you stick to sheep," Matt told him. "Look, gents," he continued with a seemingly vast patience, "I just happened to stop here because this valley looked good. And because I was lookin' around for a few hundred or so sections of land to throw some beef onto."

"A few hundred?" Williams breathed in awe. "But there ain't that much for sale around here."

"There will be if I pull out and wait maybe a year," Matt reminded him. "Let this bank go broke and in a year I can buy land here at thirty cents on the dollar."

"You wouldn't do that, Matt!" Caleb West said in a small voice.

"I damn' well would if it's either that or live around the stink of sheep."

When he had finished speaking, they looked at each other skeptically. And it was finally Williams who had the nerve to speak up: "That's puttin' it to us straight, boys. I, for one, could live just as long if Jenny never cooked another of those mutton shoulder roasts." He shuddered convincingly. "And the air around here could be a bit sweeter."

"Cattle will pay a man almost as good as sheep," Caleb conceded.

Then one of the others banged his fist on the table, saying tartly, "I'm switchin' over! I was raised to hate sheep and here I been messin' with a wool crop the past ten years." He sighed audibly, feelingly. "It'll be a relief to ship them stinkin' critters and settle down to some clean honest ranchin'."

There was more talk, a lot more, but by the time the courthouse clock was striking ten Matt was astride a livery horse and leaving the town behind him. Everything was settled. For a long-term loan of fifty thousand dollars, the directors guaranteed him that any outfit doing business with the bank would either change over to beef or be denied any financial help whatsoever. There were hardly any brands in the valley that could get along without bank money at some time or another.

So he was whistling as he rode along. He was on his way, so he told them, over the pass to the railroad to have the money sent in by express. He had assumed a distant air when they became curious as to his background. Thinking back on that he could smile now.

And just for the fun of it, he went through his pockets to see exactly what he was worth. The total came to four dollars and sixteen cents and in this moment he reflected somewhat bleakly that he would have to stay away from poker layouts, one having rid him of a year's savings two nights before he started over the pass to meet Jesusita.

'Sita!

He'd had too much on his mind to spare her many thoughts but now she became the core about which much of his thinking revolved. He was still trying to picture the brightness of her eyes, her slenderness and grace, and wondering how much room there was in her heart for such a man as he when he brought the *cantina* in sight two hours later.

He was swinging from the saddle at the rail by the *portal* when the doors swung open to frame a vision of radiant loveliness for him. Her black wavy hair shone like ebony and fell loosely about her shoulders. Those gently rounded shoulders were half revealed by a white embroidered blouse of some filmy material that barely clung to them. About her small waist ran a belt of broad silver conchas and below that a long black silk skirt nearly swept the dust as she ran out, white petticoats showing, to cry:

"Matt. Oh my poor Matt! I all the time theenk you keeled!"

He couldn't help but put his arms about her as she threw herself against him. And then, unashamedly, she took his face in her hands and pulled it down to smother it with kisses. She kissed his cheeks, chin, eyes and then his mouth.

Finally, to get a breath, she drew away and her flashing dark eyes laughed up at him. Then all at once her look turned grave, alarmed. "Matt, you hide queek! Beeg Beel, he's around some-wheres. He tell me he keel you, pool your arms off and heet you in the face weeth them. All in the fight over me.

"So last night I cry and thees morning I still cry and Beel he say I am his now because he won me from you. I heet him again but he only laugh. And then I find he gives Papa the monee, lots of *dinero*. So Papa he tell me we go across to the town weeth the railroad and be married. And now Beel somew'ere out back heetch-ing the team for the treep. Oh, Matt, now you save me from Beel!"

"That I'll do," Matt drawled.

He took her by the shoulders, the excitement strong in him as he said, "But first, we got to get something settled, *Muchacha*. Down in the valley there's a ranch. It's got a big house of 'dobe shaped like the letter H. There's cottonwoods and willows all 'round and a crick runnin' right past the porch. And off behind there are hills covered with pines and down below there's a meadow with a big ponderosa standin' square in the middle of it all by itself and. . . ."

"The Anvil, the Reevers place," Jesusita put in, nodding quickly. "Papa he work there for old Matt Reevers before the sheepmans she come. He was the wan fine *vaquero*. And Papa he steel tell how he teach the leetle Reevers to ride, the leetle boy."

Matt's look became a wondering one and he asked, "Papa couldn't be Miguel, could he?"

"Miguel, sure. He's Papa. Why? You know heem?"

"No. I . . . that is, someone down below mentioned him to me." Then, to cover his confusion, he shook her gently by the shoulders, saying, " 'Sita, I've just bought the. . . ."

His words broke off a fraction of a second as he noticed the *canti-na's* swing doors slowly inching apart. He waited to be sure that they didn't open any further before going on in a louder voice, "I've just bought the Anvil. How would Papa and your brother like to come there to live? Papa could look after the horse string all on his own. Your brother would maybe run the kitchen for the crew. How does that sound?"

"Everisto, he my cosin."

There was a warmth and a tenderness in her eyes as she looked up at him, softly asking, "And me, Matt?"

Matt shrugged, finding it hard to speak. "That's up to you, 'Sita. I'm nothin' but a top hand that's been pretty fiddle-footed and never saved a nickel. Maybe I'd make you a poor husband."

"Oh, Matt!"

Again she threw her arms around him and kissed his face and now Matt noticed the doors come open violently. Inside, in the deep shadow, he saw a high shape and his frame went rigid.

But then the doors swung slowly shut once more and he breathed a sigh of relief and gave his attention to the immediate problem.

Jesusita was saying excitedly, "We go now, thees afternoon! I shot thees place, lock it and leave it forever. Wait, I tell Papa and Everisto." And she whirled and ran to the door.

From out back came the soft squeal of door hinges. And Matt, putting his own meaning to the sound, said loudly although he was talking to himself, "Big Bill's wanted on about ten counts. He'll hang if he ever shows his face in this country again."

He went silent a moment and now heard the slow, measured hoof-thuds of a horse he assumed was walking toward him along the *cantina*'s far wall. And as he moved in toward the 'dobe wall that enclosed the *portal*, he went on speaking in that same loud voice, "There's a big reward out on him if you get him and. . . ."

The palomino, Big Bill in the saddle, suddenly lunged into the open from around the building's far front corner. The Navy Colt was in Bill's hand. It swung down and into line with Matt as Matt forgot his dignity and dove sprawling behind the wall.

A sudden deafening explosion marked the instant 'dobe plaster sprayed from the top of the wall. And over the fast drumming of the palomino's hoofs rose Big Bill's strident shout:

"Come on out and fight, runt!"

Matt's impulse was to reach for one of his .45s. Instead, he smiled. Then, taking off his hat, he crawled to the wall's edge and looked on out to the road.

The palomino was running fast, already out of sure range for a Colt. Yet Bill, facing about in the saddle, threw two more shots at the wall and Matt had to duck back again to keep from getting bullet-splashed dirt in his eyes.

Several seconds later Matt came erect and stepped out into the open. The palomino's swift-reaching run was something to delight the eye and for a moment he watched in admiration.

But Big Bill was headed toward the pass as fast as he could ride and this realization suddenly sobered Matt. He breathed, "The poor fool never learns."

Then, putting fingers between his lips, he gave a piercing whistle, so loud that the echo of it racketed back from the near piney slope.

He was watching the palomino's stride break as Jesusita ran out through the doors crying, "Matt! Who is the shots?"

"Watch!" was all Matt said. She looked up the trail in time to see the horse slide to a sudden stop, then rear sharply, viciously. But this time Big Bill wasn't unseated as he had been here in front of the *cantina* yesterday. He dug in his spurs, grabbed the horn, and commenced sawing at the reins.

Matt's look turned worried. He lifted his hand again, whistled once more.

This had its immediate effect. The palomino came down on all four feet. Then suddenly his forelegs buckled, his head went down and it was all Big Bill could do to take his boot from the stirrup and jump for his life as the horse threatened to roll onto him.

Matt would have lost a horse then if the palomino hadn't been fast getting onto his feet again and going away. For Bill, lying there in the dust, had to roll over to pull his Colt.

Bill's first shot struck between the horse's flying hooves. His second was wild because Matt had quickly drawn one of the .45s and thrown a shot at him. A geyser of dust spurted up two feet out from Bill's head. Then, as Matt fired again, the big man hauled himself to his feet and started running in panic.

Never had Big Bill made such tracks. He went out the trail almost as fast as the palomino was running in along it. And, just for the fun of it, Matt deliberately took another shot and still another.

"Keel heem!" Jesusita cried, her eyes flashing hate at the big man. "Keel heem dead, Matt!"

Possibly, had his next shot been lucky, Matt could have winged Big Bill. But he was telling himself, "He's scared, really scared, and he'll never be back. So he threw the bullet a pace or two ahead of Bill and to one side. And now he burst out laughing as Bill dodged aside, stumbled, rolled in the dust and picked himself up again.

Jesusita was laughing, too, as Bill rounded a far bend and disappeared behind the pines. "Beel, he have the sore feet tonight," she said, turning to Matt.

But he wasn't looking her way. The palomino, chest heaving, was standing beside him now and with one hand he was stroking the animal's neck while the other fumbled at the thongs of the nearest pouch on the saddle's cantle.

He got the pouch open finally and looked inside. And Jesusita, not understanding his relieved smile just then, asked, "What ees it, Matt?"

"Nothin'," he drawled, tying the pouch's thong once more. "Nothin' at all. Just something I loaned Bill last night. For a minute there I thought he forgot to give it back."

He faced her again, grinning broadly.

"Now let's get a move on, 'Sita. I'd like to have a look at that layout before dark."

STAGE TO DEATH

WAYNE D(ANIEL) OVERHOLSER won three Golden Spur awards from the Western Writers of America and has a long list of fine Western titles to his credit. He was born in Pomeroy, Washington, and attended the University of Montana, University of Oregon, and the University of Southern California before becoming a public school teacher and principal in various Oregon communities. He began writing for Western pulp magazines in 1936 and within a couple of years was a regular contributor to Street & Smith's *Western Story Magazine*, Popular Publications' *Fifteen Western Tales*, and Fiction House's *Action Stories* and *Frontier Stories*.

BUCKAROO'S CODE (Macmillan, 1948) was Overholser's first Western novel and remains one of his best. In the 1950s and 1960s, having retired from academic work to concentrate on writing, he would publish as many as four books a year under his own name or a pseudonym, most prominently the Joseph Wayne byline. THE BITTER NIGHT (Macmillan, 1961), THE LONE DEPUTY (Macmillan, 1957), and THE VIOLENT LAND (Macmillan, 1954) are among the finest of the early Wayne D. Overholser titles, although virtually all of his titles for Macmillan are outstanding in one way or another. He was asked by William MacLeod Raine, one of the most respected of Western authors, to complete his last novel when for reasons of worsening health Raine was unable to finish HIGH GRASS VALLEY (Houghton Mifflin, 1955). Indeed, Overholser often proved to be a capable collaborator with other Western writers, COLORADO GOLD (Ballantine, 1958) with Giff Cheshire published under his Lee Leighton byline and Cheshire's Chad Merriman byline and SHOWDOWN AT STONY CREEK (Dell, 1957) with Lewis B. Patten published under the Joseph Wayne name perhaps being the finest of them.

An Overholser Western novel, no matter under what name they have been published, is based on a solid knowledge of the history and customs of the 19th-century West, particularly when set in his two favorite Western states, Oregon and Colorado. Some of his novels are first person narratives, a technique that tends to bring an added dimension of vividness to the frontier experiences of his narrators and frequently, as in CAST A LONG SHADOW (Macmillan, 1955), the female characters one encounters are among the most memorable. Overholser wrote his numerous novels with a consistent skill and an uncommon sensitivity to the depths of human character. Almost invariably, his stories weave a spell of their own with their scenes and images of social and economic forces often in conflict and

407

the diverse ways of life and personalities that made the American Western frontier so unique a time and place in human history.

Many of his Macmillan titles are being reprinted in mass merchandise paperback editions by Leisure Books, several titles have appeared in hardcover reprint editions from Chivers in Gunsmoke, and several of his short stories are available in paperback audio from Durkin Hayes. His two contributions to *Lariat Story Magazine* were "The Educated Lobo" (5/44) and the story which follows, "Stage to Death" (11/44). It has not been previously collected.

I

It had rained hard for two days, hard enough to turn the Suntex County roads into greasy gumbo and bring the creeks and rivers boiling over their banks. It had stopped now, but the May sky was still as gray as a goose wing, and bore promise of another downpour.

Bill Mason, stage guard on the Opal City to Tamarack run, stood against the bar in the Last Chance Saloon, and stared thoughtfully through the fly-specked window at the leaden sky. In a few minutes the stage would pull out for Tamarack. Maybe it would get through and maybe it wouldn't, for it had to cross Sundown and Piute Rivers, and both were mud-yellow, roaring torrents.

"Hello, Billy Bock," a man said softly.

Icy fingers knotted Bill's stomach muscles. He hadn't been called Billy Bock since he'd been a wild young hellion back in the Colorado mining camps. Here in Oregon nobody knew who he was. Nobody knew what he'd been. Nobody knew about the bank job in Silver Creek where he'd had his first and last taste of the owlhoot, and found it not to his liking. He was Bill Mason, stage guard, with a three-year perfect record to his credit.

Slowly Bill's eyes turned to the man who had come up behind him. He was a stranger clad in a yellow slicker, a leggy man almost as tall as Bill with a saber-like nose and a pair of eyes as hard and sharp as chipped obsidian. A tough hand, Bill saw, with the stamp of the owlhoot upon him.

"You got me wrong, feller," Bill made himself say. "My handle's Mason. Bill Mason."

"Sure, I know." The man's voice was so low that his words barely reached Bill's ears. "You're Bill Mason now, all right. It wouldn't do to be Billy Bock out here. Some folks wouldn't like it if they found out the gent they looked up to on account of his guts and fast guns had committed a robbery back in Silver Creek, Colorado."

The icy fingers took another tie on the knot in Bill's stomach. He'd never seen the man before, but the man knew. There was no use arguing. Bill had drifted for years after the Silver Creek episode, trying to get away from his past and forget it. He thought he'd done that here in Opal City. Now suddenly he realized these three years had been a fool's paradise. For a moment he stared unseeingly at the amber liquid in the glass before him, a long moment while the past caught up with him and held him in its long and cruel tentacles.

"You seem to know quite a bit, feller," Bill said then.

"Yeah, quite a bit," the man murmured. "I ain't got nothing against you, Billy Bock. Neither's the Domino Kid."

Bill's eyes stabbed at the man. "I don't know the Domino Kid. What's he got to do with it?"

"Plenty. You'd know the Kid all right if you seen him without his mask, but we'll let that go. What I'm getting at is whether you're gonna be smart so we can make a deal, or if you're gonna be fool enough to make me tell them certain folks about the Silver Creek job."

"What's the deal?"

"In a few minutes you'll be heading out with Mack Travers. Your box is gonna be heavy, heavy enough to make good picking for the Kid. Now the Kid don't want no trouble. Of course if there is trouble, I reckon he can handle it, and the way the weather is, he could get clear before the sheriff caught his trail. Still and all, the Kid don't like shooting. If you'd just hand the box down, and forget your guns, I'll ride on, and nobody's gonna know about Silver Creek."

Bill looked down at the glass again. "Mebbe them certain folks wouldn't believe your yarn."

"And again they might. Travers is no friend of yours. Neither is Eli Krone in Tamarack. Even Sam Benton might do a little quizzing around if he knew what I know."

All that was true enough. Both Travers and Krone, the Tamarack agent, were new men, and they'd plainly showed their dislike for Bill. Why, he didn't know, but he did know he valued Sam Benton's friendship and trust. Benton was the super, and he'd given Bill his job. Then there was Laura Benton, Sam's girl. Six months ago she'd returned to Opal City from Portland where she'd been going to school. From the moment Bill had seen her standing beside Sam's desk, he'd known exactly what the future would be for him without Laura. Balancing that knowledge had been the bitter realization that a man with his past could never tell her how he felt.

"Well?" the man asked. "What's it going to be?"

Bill gulped his drink, and slid the glass back across the bar. "How'd you know so much about the set-up here?"

"That's none of your business. I'm asking one question and I want the answer."

Bill drew paper and tobacco from his pocket. His fingers trembled a little as he spilled the tobacco into the brown paper. There was only one answer he could make, and he knew the price he'd pay in making it. Sam Benton had trusted him. Benton hadn't asked him for his pedigree. There was only one way to return a trust like that.

"The answer is that you can go to hell," Bill said evenly as he shaped up his smoke.

The man grinned wolfishly. "I ain't surprised. It's sure funny how righteous a gent gets when he thinks he's got a good thing. You're a fool, Billy Bock. You rode with Stony Krass once. That put a brand on you you'll always wear. After you think about it a spell mebbe you'll get over being a fool. I ain't telling Benton now what I know. I'm giving you a chance. The Domino Kid is taking the box between here and Tamarack. If you go for your guns, Benton will hear the dirt. Think it over."

The man stepped around Bill, and strode out of the saloon. A moment later he rode by on a big roan gelding, headed west for Tamarack.

Bill laid a coin on the bar.

"Better have another drink," the apron said as he came up. "It'll be a hard trip to Tamarack today."

"That it will," Bill agreed. "No, one's enough."

"I hear the Piute and Sundown are running chuck full. If them bridges go out, you'll be stuck on the peninsula. Looks to me like Sam's a fool to send you out."

Bill shrugged. "The mail has to go through. I reckon the bridges will be there long enough for us to get over 'em."

The stage was standing in front of the office when Bill reached it. Mack Travers scowled. "I didn't look for you to show up. I figgered mebbe you was too yaller to make the trip today."

Bill's fists knotted. "Mack, one of these days you're gonna waggle that long tongue of yours too much. I don't like sitting beside you no more than you do me, but there ain't no sense in acting like a mangy hound with a sore tail even if you are one."

Travers's beefy face reddened with anger. He started to say something, and didn't, for Sam Benton appeared in the doorway behind Bill. He called, "Bill, come in here a minute."

Bill felt the icy fingers working his stomach muscles again. Maybe the sharp-nosed stranger had told him already.

Benton was pacing the length of the office when Bill went in. He was a white-haired, steady-eyed oldster who had done just about everything for Wells Fargo in the years he'd been with them. He stopped pacing now, and looked at Bill worriedly.

"It's gonna be a hell of a trip," Benton said bluntly. "The road's slick and the bridges may go out any time. What's more, you've got a heavy box. You'll have the mine payroll, and a sack of gold for the Tamarack bank. To make it worse, you've got four passengers, one of 'em Laura."

"Laura?" Bill stared at the super in amazement. "What are you letting her go for?"

"I don't tell Laura what she can or can't do," Benton snapped. "She's twenty-one, and she knows how things are as well as I do. Besides, she's told folks she's going, and there'd be a row if I tried to keep her from it." He looked at Bill narrowly. "I was thinking mebbe you wouldn't want to go today."

Bill couldn't tell, as he met Benton's gaze, whether the sharp-nosed man had stopped and told Benton or not. He asked quietly, "Are you telling me I'm fired, Sam?"

"No," Benton answered. "You've got the best record of any guard I've got. I just thought maybe you wouldn't want to go today."

"I heard a yarn about the Domino Kid being between here and Tamarack," Bill said, and saw the super's face whiten.

"That heller?" Benton rumbled. "I don't believe it. The last thing I heard he was clear over on Snake River."

"Just a rumor," Bill said mildly. "A gent in the Last Chance was telling me about it. If you ain't firing me, I'm going. I figger I'd do as well handling the Kid as anybody. But there's one thing Sam. I'm not riding with Travers after this trip."

Sam Benton nodded somberly. "He's an ornery cuss all right, and he ain't too smart about some things, but he's a steady enough driver. He'll get the stage through if anybody can."

Laura Benton came in then from the street. She looked prettier than ever, Bill thought, in her plum-colored taffeta dress and the bright blue bonnet that matched her eyes. Again that chill spasm hit his stomach, for the past was rushing up once more, dispelling the bright promise that her presence always held for him, a promise that could never be borne out.

"You shouldn't be going today," Bill said roughly. "It's a dangerous trip. There's nothing in Tamarack that warrants taking the risk."

"That's what a man would say." Laura's full, red lips smiled at him, but there was that in her eyes telling Bill he could say nothing to change her mind. "With Mack Travers driving, and you riding shotgun, I'm taking no risk. My best friend is getting married in Tamarack tomorrow, Bill. I wouldn't miss it for anything."

"You see?" Sam spread his hands helplessly. "She'll go. Hell or high water wouldn't stop her."

Bill said nothing more. He helped Travers carry the heavy box to the stage and slide it under the seat. Laura stepped inside. Bill climbed to the seat beside Travers, and they rolled down the muddy street to the hotel. Three passengers got in there. One was Joe Higgins, a bleary-eyed whiskey drummer, the second a sheepman from Tamarack named Hank Fletcher. The third Bill didn't know. He was a slim, dapper man in a black broadcloth suit. He wore two guns on his lean hips, and there was a sort of feline toughness about him that Bill noted.

Later, when the town was behind them, and they were wheeling through the sticky gumbo, Bill asked, "Who's the dude?"

"Dunno." Travers spat over the wheel. "Stranger in town." He looked at Bill and grinned sourly. "You worried, Mason? Think mebbe we got the Domino Kid with us?"

"Mebbe." Bill looked at the driver narrowly. "How come you think he's in these parts?"

Travers shrugged his thick shoulders. "You never know where that hellion's gonna be. I'd heard he was around. That's why I figgered you wouldn't be going today. I reckon he's one *hombre* you wouldn't care to swap lead with."

Bill kept a tight rein on his temper. That was Travers clean through. He'd go out of his way to make a man mad for no reason.

For an hour they rode in silence under a lowering sky. Carefully Bill went over in his mind the route between Opal City and Tamarack, picking out the spots where the Domino Kid might set his trap. It wouldn't be on the flat between Opal City and the Sundown Cañon, nor would it likely be between the Piute west rim and Tamarack. There were two sharp grades down to the rivers, and two hard climbs above them. The chances were the Kid would strike near the top of one of the climbs.

No one seemed to know anything about the Domino Kid except that he wore a black and white checked mask—that he was deadly with six-guns. There was no description of his looks because no one had ever seen his face when he was holding up a stage, but he'd just about match the dude in the coach in size. He usually worked with two men. Bill had never heard of him operating in Oregon, but the outlaw had found it too hot in Montana and Wyoming where he had been working. There was a good chance the Domino Kid had moved west.

Bill thought again about Stony Krass, the outlaw with whom he had ridden when they'd held up the Silver Creek bank. Bill had heard he'd been shot a year or so after that, but someone in Krass's crowd must have spotted Bill Mason as the Billy Bock of the Colorado mining camps. Otherwise the sharp-nosed stranger would never have known who he was.

They started down the steep grade to Sundown River, slithering perilously close to the edge as they swung around the curves. Bill held his shotgun between his legs, eyes on the road below, but it was from habit more than any thought the Domino Kid would be here. He was thinking about the stranger, about Laura Benton, and he wondered bitterly why life had brought them together after it was too late.

Then they'd reached the bottom, and swung south along the river bank. A quarter of a mile upstream was the bridge, the muddy, yellow torrent sweeping fiercely under it. A mass of logs and debris was jammed against the pier, and it seemed to Bill that the bridge was about ready to go.

"It don't look good, Travers," he said. "You'd better let the passengers out before you. . . ."

"You're yaller," Travers snarled. "Yaller like that damned soup. Hang on. I'll get you over. Or mebbe you want to get down."

"Go ahead," Bill said through tight lips. "We'll all get wet together." It seemed to him, as it had more than once before, that the driver was trying to prod him into making some locoed move. He didn't understand why, but he kept a tight rein on his temper. There would come a time for settlement with Travers.

The stage swung west, rumbling on across the swaying bridge, and reached the west side. Travers leered at Bill.

"I reckon you'd had us sitting all night waiting for the water to go down. There ain't no room for a yaller-bellied jigger in this business."

Bill's fists clenched. "Travers, I'm a mite tired of hearing that kind of gab. When we get to Tamarack, I'm gonna shove it down your throat."

"Yeah, sure," Travers mocked. "You'll play. . . ."

A timber-splintering crash came from behind them as the river triumphed, and swept the span downstream. Travers whipped a glance behind them, and what he saw brought a strained look into his beefy face.

"Sure," Bill jeered, "you've had us all taking a cold bath, and heading downstream for the Columbia."

For once Travers was silent. The road tilted sharply now, bringing the horses to a slow, slogging pace. This was where Bill had guessed the Domino Kid would be. Bill gripped his shotgun, eyes hard on the narrow road above, nerves taut as his gaze searched every boulder and break in the steep walls ahead.

Slowly they crawled up the gash of a road as gray clouds dropped lower. Then they were on top and leveling out across the summit. The road swung south again. They were across the divide, and starting down the grade to the Piute. It twisted a thousand feet below them, running as yellow and fiercely as the Sundown. The bridge across it was much like the one that had gone out behind them. Bill wondered what Travers would do when he reached it.

The coach swayed ponderously down the grade, sliding close to the edge and back again as the straining driver gripped the brake handle and called to the horses. A grim look came to Bill Mason's lean face as he considered the possibility of the bridge below them being out. They'd be marooned here on the peninsula between the rivers, for days perhaps, without food and without water. Bill thought of the Domino Kid, and he thought of Laura Benton in the coach, and he swore softly.

Then they were down, and rolling upstream alongside the river. The bridge was still in place. There was no log jam against it, but muddy water was running over the plank floor. Fifty yards or more above the bridge was a homesteader's deserted shack and barn. Travers didn't make the turn toward the bridge, but tooled the coach off the road, and across the meadow to the barn. Bill looked at Travers sharply, but the driver kept his eyes straight ahead, his mouth a hard line across his red face.

When the horses stopped beside the barn, Hank Fletcher poked his head out, and yelled, "Hey, you mule-headed numbskull, what are you doing here?"

Travers climbed down. "Mebbe you want to take a swim, Fletcher, but I don't. We're staying here tonight."

"What the hell," the sheep rancher bawled. "I've got to be in Tamarack tonight."

"Walking's good," Travers said laconically. "We just missed getting our feet wet when we crossed the Sundown. I can't tell what shape this bridge is in, but I ain't taking no chances. We'll stay here tonight. It ain't cold, and it ain't raining. You'll be all right. Come morning, if the water's down, we'll go on."

Fletcher started to curse again. Bill had come up behind Travers, his shotgun in his hand. He said, "Shut up, sheep herder, or I'll pull you out of there, and throw you into the Piute."

The sheepman subsided. Bill wheeled, and went into the barn. The roof of the house had fallen in, but the barn was in fair shape. If it rained during the night, they might get wet, but it was better than sleeping in the mud. He left the barn, and walked to the bridge. For a time he stood looking at it, wondering why Travers had decided not to cross it. It didn't add up right. But Bill figured he'd know the answer before daylight.

II

Travers was unhitching the horses when Bill came up. "You open your mug about me being scared of crossing the Piute, and I'll pull it out of your head, Mason," the driver snarled.

"I wouldn't think of it, Mack. I don't need to say anything."

"It was just the smart thing to do," Travers muttered. "No use taking chances."

"Sure, and we'll be handy for the Domino Kid if he is holing up around here."

"That's your job," he said sullenly.

"Yeah," Bill agreed. "That's my job. I aim to make it tough for the Kid, and anybody that's aiding him."

"Keep an eye on that gun-packing dude," Travers muttered, and turned back to his horses.

The passengers were huddled in the barn. Laura looked at Bill, and challenged him with a smile. "I guess you're still thinking I shouldn't have come."

"When's the wedding?" Bill asked.

"Tomorrow afternoon," Laura answered.

"Mebbe you'll make it yet."

Bill explored the barn. Stalls ran along one-half of the north side. The other half was a large, rectangular pen. The floor of the south end was covered with musty straw. He went back to the passengers. "I'll see if we can rustle an axe. We can chance a fire here in the pen. It'll be mighty cold by morning if we don't have one."

The dude's brows lifted. "I'd rather be cold than have our hotel burn up," he said sourly.

"It won't burn," Bill said, and left the barn.

Bill searched the shack. In a lean-to behind it, he found a rusty axe. He split some dry wood he found in the lean-to, and carried it to the barn.

Joe Higgins, the whiskey drummer, had opened his bag, and was sampling a bottle. Bill dropped the wood, jerked the bottle from Higgins's mouth, and tossed it into the straw. Higgins spluttered an oath, and swung his right fist at Bill.

"Behave," Bill snapped, and caught the drummer's fist but Higgins was in no mood to behave. He slashed his left fist into Bill's face, tried to twist free, and failed. It wasn't a hard blow, but it was enough to snap the last shred of Bill's temper. He jerked the drummer toward him, stooped, and in a continuation of the same lightning movement he raised his shoulder into the man's middle, and pinwheeled the drummer through the air behind him. Higgins smashed into the wall, bounced off, and hit the earth floor in a wind-driving fall.

Travers had been standing in the runway at the end of the barn watching Bill. Now he let out a bellow of rage, his red face contorted by a swift rush of fury.

"You can't throw my passengers around," Travers roared, and started toward Bill. "Shuck off your gun belts, and we'll see who's running this outfit."

"Suits me," Bill rasped. He unbuckled his gun belts and handed them to Laura. "Come on, Mack. You've been wanting this for a long time."

Travers came in a rush, big fists flying. Bill was lighter than Travers, but faster. He pivoted lightly to one side, clipped Travers hard on the side of the head, and sent him spinning into the wall. Travers smashed against the boards, spun away, and came rushing. This time Bill met him with an impact that jarred the building. Bill's fists beat viciously into the driver's thick muscled stomach, battered his head back with short, trip-hammer punches, and drove him into a corner. Travers plunged to one side and backed away.

Bill kept after Travers, never letting him get set for a solid counter punch. Travers was bleeding from mouth and nose, and his eyes were beginning to close. He drove a few blows home, but Bill kept him enough off-balance so that his fists did little more than sting Bill's face. They made a complete circle, Bill stalking as a cougar might stalk his prey.

"Come on and fight," Bill taunted. "You've been calling the wrong man yellow, Travers."

Travers held his ground then, great fists sweeping at Bill's face. One of them landed, the first effective blow the driver had smashed home. Fireworks exploded before Bill's eyes. He took a battering fist on his shoulder, blocked another with his arms and, when his vision had cleared, he drove in hard. Travers didn't back up in time. Bill rocked the driver's head with a pile-driving right, and he heard Laura cry out. Once more Bill's fist cracked against Travers's jaw. The driver started to go down, great arms sagging. As he fell, Bill hit him with all his one hundred and eighty pounds of hard muscle behind the blow. Travers fell soddenly into the ancient litter of the stable floor, and lay still.

Bill sleeved sweat from his forehead. As he took the gun belts from Laura, he saw that she was staring steadily at Travers's still body. Then she raised her eyes to Bill's. "Did you have to do that?"

Bill laughed harshly. "What did you want me to do?" He buckled on the belts, and began to build a fire in the center of the pen. The gunslung dude came up to him.

"Queer business," he said. "What's behind it?"

Bill straightened up. The whiskey drummer, Higgins, was on his feet now, and Fletcher was eyeing him curiously.

"I'm not just sure," Bill said. "I've got it pretty straight that the Domino Kid is around here expecting to grab that express box. I haven't figured out why Travers didn't cross the bridge. Mebbe he knows more than I do, but it don't look to me like the bridge over the Piute is half as dangerous to travel as the one we crossed."

"We beat that one by seconds," the dude said thoughtfully, "but I didn't think it looked quite right when he turned off here."

"I'm guessing the Kid was somewhere on the road beyond the Piute," Bill went on. "Mebbe just below the rim. It's steep right there, and we'd have been moving slow. I figger we're as well off here as we could have been if the Kid had tackled us below the rim. That's why you ain't taking on a skinful of your forty-rod, Higgins. Before the night's over, we may need all the guns we've got." Travers had come around now, his hate-filled eyes on Bill. "From here on in I'm running things. You hear that, Travers?" The driver nodded sullenly, and made no move to get up. "You, Higgins?" The whiskey drummer bobbed his head. "All right. Some of you will get some sleep. Laura, we can fix you a bed over there in the straw. The rest of us will stay here. If we ain't lucky, we'll be stopping lead by morning."

For a time none of them said anything. They stood looking at Bill until the gun-packing dude said, "I've heard of the Domino Kid. If he is around, we'll be lucky if we don't all stop some lead."

Travers got up and lurched out of the barn. Bill nodded at Higgins and Fletcher. "Go over to the lean-to, and get some wood," he ordered. When they were gone, Bill said, "It's gonna be tough sledding here tonight. I'm not sure of Travers. If he's thrown in with the Kid, he may get the drop on us."

There was a bleak smile on the dude's face. "Could be you're suspicious of me, too. I hope you'll believe me. I'm Brad Buckley. I'd heard the Tamarack Bar was for sale. I'm going over to see about it." He lowered his voice. "I'm packing a nice chunk of dinero. I might just as well stop some of the Kid's lead if I lose it."

"You look like you might be some help when the shooting starts," Bill said. "Higgins won't, and Fletcher's the kind that's likely to start things at the wrong time." He looked at Laura, and slowly shook his head. "Lady, I'm sure sorry you're here."

"I'm not." There was no fear in her blue eyes when she looked up at Bill. "I wouldn't miss this for the world."

Bill groaned. "I suppose you think it'll be as much fun as a wedding."

"Certainly, and a lot more exciting."

Bill threw up his hands. "All right. Just stick around. You'll have your excitement. Buckley, when I'm not here, I want you to stay here with Laura. She might be as profitable for the Kid as the express box."

III

It was dusk when Bill left the barn and walked to the coach. A few minutes later he came back with the express box, and dropped it outside the pen in the straw. Fletcher and Higgins were standing beside Buckley at the fire. Neither Laura nor Travers was in sight.

"Where's Laura?" Bill demanded.

Buckley looked around in surprise. "I dunno. Thought she was in here."

Bill swore. "Where's Travers?"

"He hasn't been here since he got up after his licking," Buckley answered.

Bill wheeled out of the barn. It had begun to rain again, not heavily, but enough to make a person wet, and Laura was out in it. He circled the barn, searched the house, and finally found her standing beside the bridge.

"What are you doing here?"

"Getting rained on," she said flippantly. "If you don't get me to that wedding, Bill Mason, I'll never speak to you again."

"All I want is to get you out of here alive," Bill snapped. "After this you stay in the barn. Did you see Travers?"

"Bill," she grabbed his arm, the flippancy gone from her voice now, "Travers is over there on the other side of the river. Why would he be there?"

"My guess is he's expecting to find the Domino Kid. Come on. You're getting back to the barn. When the blow-off comes, you get down behind a manger and stay there."

"Yes," Laura said meekly, and walked back to the barn, her arm through Bill's.

For one short moment Bill dreamed a dream that had been with him from the time he'd first seen Laura. Then, like all dreams, it was gone, for the past had rushed up again. Silver Creek. Stony Krass. The sharp-nosed stranger. Billy Bock the bank robber.

"What are you thinking, Bill?" Laura asked.

Bill looked down at her, and he thought bitterly he could never tell her what he had really been thinking. He said, "I was thinking about how to keep you out of the Domino Kid's hands. He may get the idea your dad would dig deep into his pocket to get you back with your hide all in one piece."

For a long time they sat around the fire while darkness came and the rain pounded against the roof. "What do you figure about Travers?" Buckley asked suddenly.

"If he comes in, don't take any chances." Bill took off his slicker. "In the dark and that rain, the Domino Kid and an army could sneak up on us. One of us has got to stay outside. Who wants the first crack at it?"

Hank Fletcher pulled at the ends of his scraggly mustache. "Reckon it might as well be me."

"Fire a shot if you need any help," Bill said, "and keep fairly close to the barn. Come in every half hour or so."

"Sure," Fletcher said. He slipped into the slicker, and went out.

Bill picked up Higgins's coat. "Come on, Laura. You're going to bed." He laid the coat on the straw on the other side of the row of mangers but, when he came back, Laura hadn't stirred.

"I'm not sleepy," she said defiantly.

"All right," Bill said. "Get in the way if you want to."

They sat around the fire, talking little. Higgins kept licking his lips, and looking at his bag. Buckley stared somberly into the fire. Bill moved to the door occasionally, and looked out into the rainy night, Laura's eyes following him where she sat across the fire from Buckley. Once she got up and moved to him.

"Did you see Fletcher?" she asked.

"No." Bill answered. "I'm going out and look." He stepped out of the barn. Five minutes he was back. He hesitated a moment, eyes on Laura. "You might as well know. Fletcher's out there by the coach, dead. He's been knifed."

For the first time real fear came into Laura Benton's blue eyes. She clutched Bill's arm. "The Domino Kid?" she asked.

Bill nodded somberly. "I'd never heard he was a knifer. Gunslingers don't usually have any need for knives." He'd been holding a hand behind his back. Now he brought it around him, and showed Laura the bloody, long-bladed knife he held. The handle showed a black and white checked design. "That was in Fletcher's chest. Reckon it's the Domino Kid's all right."

Buckley was standing across the fire from Bill, staring at Bill's face rather than the knife. Joe Higgins was still crouched by the fire, whiskey-bleared eyes wide with fear, the smell of liquor about him.

"Damn you, Higgins," Bill roared. "You've been into your bag again. How can you do any straight shooting if you're gonna fill your hide with your rotten whiskey?"

Higgins licked his lips. "I just had a snort," he whined. "I ain't got a gun anyway."

"Buckley's got two," Bill snapped. "When they rush us, you'll need. . . ."

Buckley had stepped away from the fire, and for the moment Bill's eyes had not been on him. In that moment his hand darted down, and plucked a gun. Laura cried out.

"Take it easy." Buckley was grinning broadly, his eyes on Bill. "The Domino Kid plays it a little different this time, *hombre*. He rides along nice and comfortable in the stage, holes up with you when Travers gets scared of the bridge, and now he rakes in the pot. I've heard how fast you are with your guns, Mason. I figured this would be the easiest way since you didn't want to play smart, and tell Poke you'd sit tight."

Bill could curse himself for a fool. The Domino Kid had played him for a sucker. He'd been suspicious of the dude at first, and then he'd believed his story about going to Tamarack to buy the saloon.

Laura's fingers tightened on Bill's arm. "You're the Domino Kid?" she asked. "You couldn't have knifed Fletcher."

Buckley laughed softly. "I'm the Domino Kid all right, and I knew this was the time to hit the stage. Your smart gun guard there gave me another idea. I'll take you along. It might just be your dad thinks enough of you to pay. No, I didn't knife Fletcher. I've got a couple of good men out there." He whistled. A moment later Travers and the sharp-nosed man came in. "You got the horses, Poke?"

The sharp-nosed man nodded. "Mine and yours, and one for Travers."

"Good." Buckley nodded, his eyes not leaving Bill's face. "Harness up the horses, Travers. We're taking the stage. I figure somebody'll be out tomorrow finding out why the stage didn't get in, and they might be suspicious if they see it. Did you gents go through the mail bags?"

"Nothing there," Travers said. "We was at it when Fletcher showed up. That's why we had to beef him."

"Get at the horses, Travers," Buckley ordered. "Poke, the box is over there. Put it on the stage."

Bill tensed. He'd been waiting for a break, and it hadn't come. Buckley had expected him to make a try for his guns. Even a killer like the Domino Kid wanted an excuse to kill a man.

Buckley couldn't turn down the temptation to do some bragging. "I've never failed on a job," he said. "The reason I've never failed is because I don't tackle one that hasn't been thoroughly planned. After Travers caught on here, he kept me informed. Then when he recognized Eli Krone, he brought him in, and we were set. I reckon we might even pull another job or two before Sam gets wise. That's what was wrong with Stony Krass, Billy Bock. He just rode blind, and started shooting. Men like that don't last long. You've got to work at this same as anything else."

Poke had carried the box back to the coach. Travers led the horses outside, and Poke came back in.

"All set, Kid," Poke said.

But Buckley was enjoying himself too much to go yet. He drew a black and white checked hood from his pocket, and tossed it at Bill's feet. "That's my brand, gun guard. I'll leave it here with your carcass so the sheriff'll know who pulled the job. I always believe in advertising. It's easier when you keep folks scared." He nodded at Laura. "You get in the stage. Your friend Mason here will be kind of messed up when I get done. I'm right sorry about this, Mason. From all I hear, you've been a good guard, but good guards make my business tough."

"Hold on," Bill said. The only thing he could do was to play for time, and hope that something would break. "Was this all planned with Travers?"

"Sure," Buckley said, his tone faintly mocking. "We didn't plan on the Sundown bridge going out like it did, but it made it reasonable when Travers pulled in here. That was a chunk of luck for us."

"From what I've heard of the Domino Kid," Bill said, "he was the kind of gent who'd give a man a chance with his gun. You act like you're gonna smoke me down cold."

"I let you keep your guns thinking the tough Bill Mason might make a play," Buckley sneered, his cat-bright eyes never wavering from Bill's face, "but hell, you haven't even tried, so I'll have to do it this way."

"How come you knew about the Silver Creek job," Bill asked, "and Stony Krass?"

"That was Eli Krone." Buckley laughed softly. "This is a hell of a way for a gun guard to die, but it'll have to do."

Buckley thumbed back the hammer of his gun. "Poke, get this gal out of here. She don't seem to be able to go by herself."

IV

Then the whole thing broke, and in a way Bill hadn't expected. Nobody had been watching Joe Higgins. The whiskey drummer was still hunkered by the fire, but it had finally dawned on his liquor-fogged brain that if Bill died, he'd die, too. He'd crept toward Buckley, and the outlaw didn't see him until he'd wrapped his arms around Buckley's legs. Poke apparently hadn't seen the whiskey-drummer moving, either, for he'd been moving toward Laura.

Bill wheeled away from the fire, grabbing a gun as he moved. Buckley fired point blank at Higgins. Poke, too, clawed for his gun, but he was far too slow. Bill pitched his first shot at Poke, and whirled toward Buckley just as the outlaw kicked himself free from Higgins's relaxed grip. Buckley swept his gun up toward Bill, but he'd lost a valuable second, a second long enough for Bill to line his gun on Buckley and squeeze the trigger. Buckley lurched with the impact of the slug, fired wildly once, and sprawled headlong toward the fire.

Poke was dead. Bill saw that, and he saw that his second bullet had ended the career of the Domino Kid, but Mack Travers was outside on the stage seat. Bill raced for the barn door. Travers already had the coach moving. He saw Bill come out, and curled his blacksnake over the horses' heads, the report of it mingling with the roar of Bill's gun. Bill fired again, and missed. Then the big coach was rumbling toward the bridge. Bill raced after it, but there was no catching up with it now.

Bill stopped, gun held high, but he held his fire. The gold was in the stagecoach, but the chances were good Mack Travers would never find it.

Besides, he'd likely go on to Tamarack and meet Eli Krone. Bill pictured the Tamarack agent's bearded face, tried to place him, and failed. He had no proof now against the agent except what the Domino Kid had said, but if Travers went on to Tamarack, Bill Mason would get the proof he needed.

When Bill got back to the barn, he found Laura bending over Bill Higgins. The whiskey drummer's shirt was soaked with blood, but he was alive. Laura had torn a piece off her underskirt, and bound the wound. Bill examined it, Higgins watching him worriedly.

"You're hit bad enough so that you can't ride a horse," Bill said, "but looks to me like you'll make it all right if you lie still. Laura and me will head for Tamarack. We'll send a doc back. There's enough wood here for you to keep the fire going till morning. The sky's clearing up. I reckon the rain's over, and tomorrow will be warmer." Bill stood up, and looked down at the wounded man. "Joe, you did a mighty brave thing. We'd both be dead by now if you hadn't taken a hand."

Higgins's white-lipped mouth shaped into a small grin. He whispered, "I knew that, Bill. The heller figured I was so no-account he didn't have to watch me. All he bothered to do was to keep his eyes on you. Say, throw the carcasses out, will you, Bill? They make plumb unpleasant company."

Bill dragged the bodies out of the barn, and threw Higgins's coat over him. Then he said, "We'll get you to Tamarack in time for that wedding, Laura. Let's ride. I don't know what these horses are like, but we'll find out."

Laura faced Bill, and for the first time since he'd known her, she seemed at a loss for something to say. "Bill, I . . . I, well, I guess you were right," she said contritely. "I had no business coming today."

"It's a little late now to think about that." Bill grinned at her. "Let's travel."

Bill could have caught the stage before it reached Tamarack, but he wanted to catch Eli Krone red-handed. His career as a gun guard was over. It was a fact he must face now, just as he had faced the fact that he could never tell Laura Benton how he felt about her. She knew now who he was, what he had been. As she rode beside him through the rain, across the bridge and on up the long grade to the west rim, she said nothing about it, but she'd heard the Domino Kid, and the outlaw had said enough.

There was just one more thing Bill Mason could do for Sam Benton before he left the country. That was to prove to him the part Eli Krone had in the Domino Kid's sinister scheme. It was seldom Benton made a mistake in a man, and he hated to admit it when he did. He'd have to be shown hard, solid proof. So Bill and Laura stayed behind the stage after it reached the flat between the rim and Tamarack. The moon broke through the clouds.

When they were within a mile of Tamarack, Bill said, "I'm going on ahead, Laura. You follow along behind like we've been doing so you'll know if Travers stops or pulls off. If he does, you circle, and hightail it into town and find me. I'll be somewhere around the office."

"What are you going to do, Bill?'

"I aim to get the deadwood on Eli Krone," Bill said. "I'll get ahead of Travers, and be in Tamarack when he drives up. Chances are Krone will be in his office, waiting to make the split with Travers and the Domino Kid. You follow him in, but don't let him see you. Your dad keeps a room in the hotel. You go on to it."

Bill left her then. He made a wide circle around Travers, keeping a low ridge between him and the coach. It was nearly dawn when Bill rode into Tamarack, and the moon was again smothered behind thick clouds. There was a light in the express office window. Aside from that the town appeared lifeless.

Bill rode to the rear of the office, and left his horse behind it. He crouched in the alley beside the building, aware of voices from its interior. He couldn't make out what was being said, but one of the men was Sam Benton. The other was Eli Krone. With hard riding Benton could have reached Tamarack from Opal City by going south and crossing the upper bridges. Likely he had heard the lower bridge across the Sundown had gone out, and he had come on to see if the stage had reached Tamarack.

Then Bill heard the rumble of the coach. Krone and Benton must have heard it, too, for they came out and stood on the porch. The coach appeared out of the darkness. Krone said harshly, "You see, Sam. Mason ain't there. I'm betting Mack saved the gold for you." Even before the coach stopped rolling, Krone shouted, "What the hell happened, Mack?"

Travers pulled his horses to a stop. "Plenty. The Domino Kid was laying for us at the Piute Bridge. Mason was in with him, but I got both of 'em."

"Is Laura all right," Benton asked.

"I reckon," Travers answered as he threw down the box. "The passengers are all in that barn above the bridge. I had to get on as fast as I could. They had a slick trap fixed up, but I got 'em."

Travers was on the ground now. He and Krone picked up the box, and carried it inside. Cold rage poured through Bill Mason then. Sam Benton was cursing Travers for leaving his daughter behind. The thing didn't make sense, and in a minute Sam would see it. Travers couldn't afford to wait long. He knew Bill was behind them. They'd kill Sam Benton, and open the express box.

Softly Bill stepped around the corner, and crossed the porch. He passed a window just as Eli Krone was slashing down at Benton's head with a gun barrel. He'd waited too long, Bill thought desperately as he palmed a gun, went into the room.

Travers had the box open, his back to the door, and was cursing bitterly. "Rocks, Eli. Look! That damned Mason ran a sandy on us."

Then Krone saw Bill in the doorway, a bearded, bald-headed man, utter amazement mirrored in his pale eyes. Instantly his gun came up, and spat its tongue of orange flame at Bill. Lead splintered the door jamb. That was the last shot Eli Krone fired, for Bill Mason's gun was bucking in his palm. He'd squeezed his trigger a split second before the agent had. Krone spilled forward over a chair, and onto the floor.

Mack Travers had spun away from the table, and around, plucking gun as he turned. For this short interval it seemed to Bill Mason that time was flowing strongly against him. Travers had the first shot, and he didn't miss. There was the numbing impact of a slug ripping into Bill's left shoulder. He lurched with the slap of it, fired, and missed, and Travers, hurrying his second shot, missed, too.

Bill steadied, then. Time was on his side now. It was enough. This time he didn't miss. Once, twice, Bill's hammer dropped in a cold and merciless rhythm. Travers fell. In a sort of dogged determination Travers fought to his knees, hand groping blindly for his gun. He found it, raised it from the floor, but there was not the strength in his great body to prong back the hammer. He fell forward on his face, dead.

Outside there was the hoof pound of Laura's horse. Lights flamed to life along Tamarack's Main Street as gunfire broke into men's sleep, and brought them scurrying out of their rooms. A moment later Doc Bevins was in the office, hair rumpled, his black bag in his hand. An hour after that the crowd was gone, and a buckboard had been sent to Piute Bridge for Joe Higgins. Sam Benton had nothing more than a headache, but Bill Mason's bullet-ripped shoulder would be a long time mending.

Benton sat at the table in the office facing Bill, Laura beside him. She didn't smile when Bill said, "It's morning, Laura. You'd better go get some sleep if you're going to look pretty for the wedding."

"That's not the wedding that counts," Laura said.

Bill looked at her, and for a moment he was stunned by the implication of her words.

Sam Benton chuckled softly. "It's quite a girl I've got, Bill. She's like a good horse. Needs a tight rein, but she'll go a long ways with the right man."

The right man! Bill stood up. "I guess I'm done in these parts," he said hoarsely. "I'll be riding on to some place they don't know I used to be called Billy Bock."

"You'll be riding nowhere," Benton snapped. "Don't be a fool. Sit down. I've suspicioned about you for a long time, but it makes no never mind to me. A man's past is his past. It's the present and the future I'm thinking about."

Bill sat down, his face showing his surprise. "You knew?"

"Well, I had an idea. I got a letter quite a spell ago from Tamarack signed 'Friend' by some jayhoo who didn't have guts enough to put his own handle down. I reckon it must of been Krone. The letter said you'd been with Stony Krass when the Silver Creek bank had been held up. I wrote to Silver Creek, and the sheriff wrote back they didn't have no count against any Billy Bock. Stony Krass was dead, and the money had been recovered. They didn't know who all was in the outfit, but the case was closed as far as they were concerned."

"If you knew. . . ."

Benton held up his hand. "Of course I didn't really know. I figgered somebody was trying to get rid of my best gun guard. Hell, man, you'd had plenty of chance to sell me out, and you hadn't. Yesterday that sharp-nosed stranger who was in Opal City came in, and gave me another yarn about you being an owlhooter. That was why I thought mebbe you wouldn't want to make this run. I figgered that if you really had anything to be afraid of, you'd want to drift, but you didn't. Now that I've got the yarn about what happened at the bridge, I'll go so far as to promise you a job as long you want it."

"This Krone," Bill said thoughtfully. "The Domino Kid said he knew me, but I can't place him."

"He was giving me a big talk before the stage showed up about how he's lived in Silver Creek, and he saw you holding the horses for Stony Krass's bunch when they knocked the bank over. I've heard him say he used to have a head of black hair. Now that he's bald-headed and raised a beard, I reckon he's changed."

Bill remembered then, a new man named York Logan who'd joined the outfit shortly before the Silver Creek holdup. Logan, without the hair and with the heavy beard, must and could have been Eli Krone.

"It was a slick trick all around," Benton went on, "just like one of the Domino Kid's jobs, only it backfired on him when that Poke *hombre* couldn't work you. I reckon Travers and Krone wouldn't have found the gold for a long time after you put it into one of Laura's bags."

"Only Laura won't have the clothes she figgered on wearing to the wedding," Bill said.

"It doesn't matter," Laura murmured. "I told you that wasn't the wedding that mattered."

She was coming toward Bill, her eyes on him, trying to tell him, just as her father had said, that the past is past, and the future is the only part of life that counts. Bill smiled a little then, and put his good right arm around her. It was the future he could see now, running its clear and promising trail ahead of him through the years, a trail that held a promise of reality for the dreams he'd dreamed. It looked to Bill, the way Laura was raising her face to his, that she was seeing the same long trail.

STAGECOACH PASS

GIFF(ORD) CHESHIRE was born on a homestead in Cheshire, Oregon. The county was named for his grandfather who had crossed the plains in 1852 by wagon from Tennessee and the homestead was the same one his grandfather had claimed upon his arrival. Cheshire's early life was colored by the atmosphere of the Old West which in the first decade of the century had not yet been modified by the automobile. He attended public schools in Junction City and, following high school, enlisted in the U.S. Marine Corps and saw duty in Central America. In 1929 he came to the Portland area in Oregon and from 1929 to 1943 worked for the U.S. Corps of Engineers. By 1944, after moving to Beaverton, Oregon, he found he could make a living writing Western and North-Western short fiction for the magazine market and presently stories under the byline Giff Cheshire began appearing in *10 Story Western*, *New Western*—for which editor Mike Tilden suggested he create a series character: Tunin' Tedro, a piano tuner and gun artist, was the result—and *Star Western*. In 1944 his gross income from magazine stories was $1,046.20. In 1945 Cheshire became a client of the August Lenniger Literary Agency and his net income for that year from stories his agent sold was $5,011.20, a considerable improvement.

"White-Water Hi-Jack" in *North-West Romances* (Spring, 46) was his first appearance in a Fiction House magazine. It was followed by "River Man" in *Action Stories* (Fall, 46) and "Rattlers Make Poor Neighbors" in *Lariat Story Magazine* (1/47). His short story, "Strangers in the Evening," in *Zane Grey's Western Magazine* (10/49) won a Zane Grey Story Award in 1949 and was reprinted in the paperback collection, ZANE GREY WESTERN AWARD STORIES (Dell, 1951). *Zane Grey's Western Magazine* attracted writers like Les Savage, Jr., and Thomas Thompson because it paid them 4¢ a word whereas Fiction House never went above 2¢ in its entire history except for Walt Coburn in the 1920s and early 1930s. However, for the majority of writers contributing to *Zane Grey's Western Magazine*, and Cheshire was among them, the rate remained 2¢ a word.

Cheshire's first book-length Western was BLOOD ON THE SUN (Fawcett, 1952) published under the byline Chad Merriman. Fawcett Gold Medal paid him an advance of $2,000 for this paperback original, just what he was paid as an advance for his first hardcover Western novel, STARLIGHT BASIN (Random House, 1954), published under his own name. The Chad Merriman novels, first at Fawcett and later at Ballantine, are among his best work, and BLOOD ON THE SUN has just been reprinted in a hardcover edition by Chivers Press in the Gunsmoke series. While in his off-moments Cheshire did write a series of potboilers under the pseudonym Ford Pendleton for Graphic Books in the early 1950s, in general his Western fiction is informed by a wider historical panorama of the frontier than just cattle ranching and frequently the settings for his later novels are in his native Oregon. THUNDER ON THE MOUNTAIN (Doubleday, 1960) focuses on Chief Joseph and the Nez Percé war, and WENATCHEE BEND (Doubleday, 1966) and A MIGHTY BIG RIVER (Ballantine, 1967) are among his best-known titles. To this select group, though, should also be added such equally fine novels as EDGE OF THE DESERT (Doubleday, 1958) and STRONGHOLD (Doubleday, 1963). It was because he was so steeped in technical knowledge of mining on the frontier that Wayne D. Overholser asked him to collaborate on COLORADO GOLD (Ballantine, 1958).

"Stage Coach Pass" was completed on August 17, 1949. It appeared in *Blue Book* (1/50), a magazine then owned by McCall Corporation which also owned *Red Book*. This is the first time it has been anthologized.

The rider brought his horse along the drifted edge of the stage road, halting as he came abreast the Concord's high box. Stolid and preoccupied in the pelting snow-laden wind, the driver had given him only half an eye until then. He swore in surprise and pulled down the three spans of straining horses. The big Sacramento-Roseburg stage settled to a clogged stop on the unbroken road.

"Dave," he said, "what are you doing down here in this weather?"

There was nothing above the mountain notch but a depth of black sky filled with the snow. Powdery mists moved along the high timbered walls of the cañon, torn and driven by the wind. Now and then the depressed evergreens spilled their burden in an abrupt, silent crash.

The rider was young. His cheeks were blue and stiffened as he stared up at the man on the box.

"Sam, you've got to get home. It's Ellen. She fell down the stairs, and had her baby. She wants you, and the doc says you ought to be there. It's bad."

The driver swore again—softly, because of the two women within the stage. He was a blocky figure, bundled, his big Jehu's hat flattened about ears and cheeks and held there by a knitted scarf.

"Dave, I'll be lucky to get this rig across the Umpquas before it bogs down." Sam Inset shrugged his head upward at the threatening sky. "It's only starting."

Dave Judd nodded. He was Ellen's younger brother, and concern for her had flogged him the seventy miles from Looking Glass Valley. He kept staring up at his brother-in-law, his chilled face held in a grim set.

"This horse'll get you there before the road chokes up. If he plays out, you can swap for another. Ellen had a hard tumble, and it hurt her bad. She wants you, Sam . . . she needs you. I can put your stage through. You gotta go."

"Yeah, I ought to. I sure wish I could."

The man above was disturbed, and worry flooded his level gray eyes. Sam Inset was the best man on this swing line of the Overland. If the three adult passengers had felt concerned about the brewing storm, the knowledge that he was on the box would have comforted them. He simply inspired confidence when you looked at him. And seeing him, nobody would doubt his love for the girl he had married a year before, who had gone back to the valley to visit her folks before the expected child tied her down. Dave could always feel Sam's kindly concern just by being near him.

The coach door swung open. A fat female face, ringed with curls and under a poke-bonnet, was thrust out above ample shoulders and bosom. The woman stared at Dave, then lifted a querulous voice:

"Driver, what're we waiting for? We ain't got time for roadside gassing." The woman frowned as she listened for Sam's reply, which did not come. With a look of grim satisfaction she banged the door shut again.

Dave looked up at Sam, desperation swelling in him. He was dog-tired, for he had been in the saddle since the small hours of the morning, bucking the freezing wind—remembering a young mother's frightened calls for her husband, her frantic fear that the threatened blizzard would pin Sam down short of the Roseburg terminal. Dave was twenty, and his sister was two years younger.

He understood the struggle putting its signs on Sam's rugged face. His responsibility was to his passengers, no matter what. The high climb to Stagecoach Pass, the steep decline, Cow Creek Cañon, Cañon Creek Cañon—all lay ahead. Unconsciously Dave spread a thick-gloved palm and watched three fat snowflakes land upon it. Sam would never get the stage clear through. He'd be lucky to reach the next station at Six Bit Ranch.

Sam Inset twisted the lines about the brake pedal and swung down. He stared at Dave an instant, then walked back to the stagecoach door. Dave dismounted and walked over there, hoping he could say something to help explain this thing to the passengers. The heavy woman who had objected to the stop sat beside an equally fat boy. On the forward seat was an old man who looked sick and half asleep, and who even now was paying no attention. Beside him sat a girl, as pretty as Ellen, and about her age.

Sam looked at them thoughtfully. "Just heard my wife's bad off . . . a six months' baby. If the snow gets much deeper, there's a chance we won't get past the next station. This here's Dave Judd, her brother. A mighty good driver. If you're willing, he'll get you as far as I could. And I'll try to get home."

The fat woman listened with rounding eyes and opening mouth. "Risk our lives to a kid that don't look dry behind the ears? Driver, are you out of your head?"

Sam shrugged, and his voice was like a sigh. "All right, ma'am. Just thought I'd ask."

The girl had listened with interest, and she said quickly: "Oh, please go." She stared at the fat woman a long moment, less critically than thoughtfully. "Who could want you to do otherwise?"

The woman opened her mouth and closed it without speaking. Then she shrugged in reluctant consent.

Sam looked at the old man, who still had not roused from his stupor. The girl said: "I'll speak for my father. He'd say for you to go."

"Thanks." Sam looked gratefully at both women and swung around.

He took Dave ahead to get out of earshot of the coach. "You'll be lucky to get to Six Bit Ranch, kid. But you got to do it. I have no right to do this, even for Ellen. But I got to do it, too. Don't care if they fire me. It's my passengers. I'm responsible for them. *You got to do as good as I would . . . or better.*"

Dave nodded.

"I'll get 'em through, Sam . . . I swear I will. You go on. I'll get 'em through in spite of everything."

Sam stared at him again, then turned toward the horse. The wind was filling the cañon now with an ever-insistent whine. Sam swung up and was gone, simply dissolving into the curtain ahead. Dave climbed to the box, his thoughts momentarily upon his brother-in-law. Six Bit Ranch was only six or seven miles ahead, though beyond the high mountain pass. Sam had seventy miles to go, and he'd keep going as long as he could, or stop and freeze where he was halted.

It was colder on the box, but Dave was used to that, riding against it as he had been doing for many hours. He unwrapped the lines, laced them through his fingers, and started the stage. Fatigue racked him, and he realized he was hungry, for he had eaten nothing since the night before. But he had a job ahead. He understood that. Though he had grown up around horses and knew their ways, he had never handled anything like three spans hooked to a big stagecoach—with passengers depending on him, and with the blizzard he had raced since leaving home still pitted against him. "*You got to do as good as I would, or better,*" Sam had said: and Dave fully understood the size of that order.

He tried to relax but couldn't, and he gave the horses and road ahead a steady stare. The California-Oregon road climbed on into the Umpquas. The spans were hock-deep in the snow, which kept up an unremitting fall. The animals were sharp-shod and kept their pace, though it was cautious and plodding. An hour passed, and then another; and from landmarks he could recognize through the thick and gloomy downfall, he knew they were nearing the mountain divide.

He felt better when they topped the rise, followed the ridge for a time, then started down. The weight would be off the horses; they could travel faster, and the snow was not yet threateningly deep. He had a wish to share his rising spirits with the girl in the stage. He had liked the way she had encouraged Sam to go. But the fat woman with the oversized young one—Dave scowled.

He heard the growling rumble long before he saw anything. The cold flooding his body deepened, and he was suddenly on his numbed feet staring down the long grade. There were high mountain rises above them again. But he could see only a short stretch of the road and the vanishing tracks of Sam's hurried horse. The big Concord was rolling easily now, slackening the traces.

Then he saw it—an enormous débris of snow studded with young evergreens. It lay deeply across the road, baleful, beyond the soft curtain of falling snow. It angled hard against the bald mountainside, which was scooped along the stretch whence it had come. The slide ran on below, disappearing into the cañon. But it had found a base down there and come to rest—piled high as his head across the road.

He pulled down the horses two lengths from the place, physical illness holding him motionless for a long moment. Then he fought down the stupor, shook off the fear. Securing the lines, he swung to the ground and walked forward. He hadn't needed to. It was real and not a figment of his overwrought imagination, which he had actually hoped for a moment that it was.

You got to do as good as I would, or better. . . . Dave held to those words, fighting down the panic in him. The air was colder at this height, with a cutting drive. The snowfall was heavier, the carpet on the ground much deeper. The next stage station was probably only four or five miles ahead now, but it might as well be a thousand.

"What are we stopped for, driver?"

Dave hauled around to see that the fat woman had again opened the door and thrust out her head. The question had probably come on its own impetus, for she had recognized the obstruction, and horror had painted itself grotesquely on her heavy face. He walked back, but the woman had banged the door shut as if she too had hoped she could make it all unreal that way.

He was thinking furiously. He knew he would find shovel, axe, and other tools in the boot. But it would take unending hours to

clear a way through that snowbank large enough to drive the outfit through.

The door opened again, and the girl got out. Beyond her, as she
descended, Dave saw the fear-stupefied face of the fat woman. The
little boy had been leavened by her emotion and was whimpering.
The girl shut the door and walked to Dave.

"We . . . we won't be able to get to the station, will we?" There
was worry in her voice, but it was controlled, as were the features
of her striking face.

For some reason Dave felt the impulse to confide all to her, knowing she would understand and might even be as helpful as she had
been before.

"Unless we try to walk," he said. "That'd be risky. We'd have to
climb up the mountain and around the slide, and it'd be deeper up
there. We'd still have four-five miles to follow the road. Your dad
. . . he looked kind of sick."

"He is," the girl said. "He's worn out. We were nineteen days on
the Overland to Sacramento . . . three days more here. I . . . I'm
afraid he couldn't stand an ordeal like trying to walk out."

Dave nodded, for he had sensed that at the start. He might help
the fat woman and her boy wallow through, but this girl would
never leave her father. He tried to make light of it and said: "I sure
appreciated your coaxing Sam to go, Miss."

She smiled slightly. "It was you, mostly. You looked so desperate.
I hope he makes it and your sister will be all right." She was
thoughtful a moment. "You came from the north. Do you know
where Looking Glass Valley is?"

"Why, yes. I live there."

"Do you know the Gills?"

"I sure do. They're our next neighbors."

"Well!" the girl said. "Edith Gill's my sister. We're going out to
live with them. I'm Amy McDowell."

"Well, now," Dave said, and for some reason he felt better. "Then
you'll be next neighbors, too."

Amy McDowell let a slight worry show. "If we get there. We'll
freeze to death if we have to stay here too long, won't we?"

"Not if I can help it," Dave said, turning quickly to hide his face.

He swung into action, his mind settled, a plan roughly shaped.
He opened the boot, removed some of the luggage, and took out
shovel and axe. He hoped to discover a piece of tarp, and relief filled
him when he did. Then he drove the stagecoach as close to the
slide as the triple spans would permit. It was when he started to
unhook the horses that the fat woman finally created the crisis
he expected.

This time she descended heavily from the coach and stumped
toward him.

"You aim to dig in and try and wait it out?"

"I aim to keep you warm as I can while I try to dig through."

The sunken eyes rounded, outrage climbing above the fear. "You couldn't dig through that drift in a month of Sundays. Why can't you notch a trail we could follow across the top on foot?"

"There's no telling what that slide's resting on, down in the cañon, ma'am. It could move again any minute."

"Better risk that than freezing to death."

Dave turned toward her. "The old gentleman's sick, ma'am. He couldn't make it."

The woman sucked in her lower lip and nibbled on it. She kept looking at Dave. "In a case like this it's your duty to save those as can be saved, ain't it? Me and the boy could walk it." She smiled, with a fawning touch to it. "With your help, that is."

"Ma'am, that'd still be a gamble. The best chance for everybody is right here."

Anger came then, and the puffed jaw shoved out. "Then help us across the slide, and me and the boy'll go on by ourselves."

"I can't let you, ma'am." Dave stiffened, and stared straight into her eyes. "You'd lose your head before you'd gone a mile. You just ain't got the stuff it'd take to get you through by yourself. And I won't desert anybody, no matter what."

The woman swung heavily, paused in long thought, then climbed back into the Concord.

Dave unhitched the horses and moved them around behind the stagecoach. Working the front wheels and straining with all his strength, he got the big vehicle as close as he could to the slide, angling it on the road until it stood across the wind. Then he bunched the animals on the upwind side so that, with mountainside, slide and stagecoach, they formed a crude and windy box.

He took the tarpaulin and climbed to the deck of the Concord. Its panels were thin, and he draped the canvas on the windward side, the air current slatting it hard against the body. He secured the upper edge, then swung to the ground.

The axe was sharp, for drivers on this swing line often had downfall to clear from the road. He took it, with the shovel, and climbed gingerly onto the slide. The pelting snow with its vapors formed a curtain so thick he could not trace its course far down into the cañon. But the slide seemed stabilized, and he trusted himself to it and began to dig out one of the small evergreen saplings it had carried down.

In half an hour he had a fire started in the windbreak, with four saplings crosshatched upon it. The needles flared up, the brisking blaze throwing its heat onto the near side of the Concord. If he could keep this side hot enough, it would help warm them inside.

When the fire was going good, he got the foot-warmer out of the

Concord. It was a large, oval tube that, in cold weather, was refilled with heated sand at each station. He placed the warmer beside the fire, close enough to heat quickly. The rough enclosure blunted the force of the freezing wind, and the mountain updraft carried the smoke away. He removed his gloves and warmed his hands as if he were washing them in the heat.

A childish voice rose in a wail: "Ma, I'm hungry."

Dave frowned, waiting for the fat woman's answer, but she kept quiet. He put the warmer back inside. Then he took the axe and began to work his patient way up the mountainside. Time after time he wallowed down again, dragging heavy limbs from the low-skirted evergreens. He built the fire a little bigger, and when he put his hand on the outside panels of the Concord he found them hot.

He opened the door and asked, "Warm enough?"

Amy McDowell smiled at him. "Why, we're quite comfortable."

The little boy scowled at Dave. "I'm hungry."

"If you want to chew on a snowball," Dave said, "I'll bring you one." He shut the door roughly.

He kept bringing in fuel until dusk began to thicken the obscurity of the storm. The signaled night lent a deep melancholy to the high mountain scene. Dave began to grow aware of a persistent dizziness within himself. He was exhausted, chilled too deeply to be warmed by his moments at the fire, and he needed food. From time to time he would take snow into his mouth and let it melt. Despite the numbness of his face, hands and feet, a fever seemed starting in him. But his hardest work lay ahead.

When he was assured of fuel enough to last through the hours of night, he took the shovel. Ever since they had halted, he had no intention of trying to clear the road. But a ramp might be notched to the top of the slide, tramped and packed as he worked at it. And then it could extend across what he now knew to be a distance of two hundred feet. Then down again. A man might accomplish that—if he could hold out.

He swung into the rhythm of shoveling, and kept at it until the torturing cold drove him down to the fire. Soon it was full dark, the steadily continuing snowfall detectable only in the firelight and the soft impact on his face. He got his ramp built, and by that time it was tramped enough to give a possible footing to the horses. He began to extend the notch across the slide.

The boy started to wail, steadily, his complaint raveling into the low moan of the wind. As Dave descended the ramp, he felt himself sway for a moment. He opened the coach door with a rough jerk, but at that moment Amy McDowell spoke up.

"Ma'am, he gets his feeling from you. If you'd try to feel hopeful. . . ."

"He's hungry," the fat woman snapped, "and so am I. He's scared, and so am I. If we ever get out of this, I'll see that driver's fired."

"Ma'am," Amy McDowell said, and her voice was sharp, "the regular driver could no more have prevented the snowslide than this one. He could have done no more toward taking care of us. For your boy's sake, you ought to keep up your courage."

"He deserted us!" the woman screeched. "To die in the blizzard while he saved his own skin!"

"Lady . . . ," Dave began—then closed the door sharply before he said too much. But a numbing new fear had climbed into him. She was going to make trouble, even if he succeeded in bringing them through. It would cost Sam his job. Disgracing him. *You've got to do as good as I would, or better. . . .*

Daylight found him on the far side and digging a careful descent. All night he had tramped back and forth to refreshen the fire, halting to warm himself only when he was too numb to go on. In some dimmed part of his mind he understood that he was wretchedly sick. It was a fact he didn't dare to face. And in all the long night there had been only one bright spot, when Amy McDowell emerged and insisted on relieving him at the shovel. He had refused, but the offer had strengthened him.

The downfall seemed a little less in the dawn, but maybe that was only the effect of the growing light. But Dave knew a good four inches had been added to the blanket already on the road. The horses might pull it, but there would be slow, hard going all the way down the mountain. There might be other drifts, as bad or worse than this, before they reached the little Cow Creek valley.

But the big, untested thing was still at this site. He couldn't see the bottom of the slide even yet. Was it stable enough to hold the weight and jar of the heavy vehicle and horses, even if they could cross without bogging hopelessly? It needed only to start moving again to sweep the whole outfit into the murky depths of the cañon.

He didn't dare pause to think about it. Returning to the stage, he began to lead the chilled horses forward and to hook up. Inevitably, the Concord door burst open.

"Driver!" the fat woman called shrilly. "You ain't going to drive us over that?"

"No ma'am," Dave said. "You're going to walk while I drive over light."

"What if it sweeps you down? How'd we get on?"

"Ma'am, you can worry about that. If it sweeps me down, I'll have my own hands full, and I won't be around to see the rumpus you'll raise when I get you through."

When he had hitched up, he helped the passengers out. The old man was still dull-eyed, sunken within himself, obviously played out. But if he had made a complaint yet, Dave hadn't heard it. Amy

McDowell gave him a brief smile, and he saw that the hope in her eyes, which had never died, was bright now. She had trusted him. The fat woman stalked to the fire with her son, and appropriated the space on the warmest, downwind side.

"Luck!" whispered Amy McDowell as she passed close to Dave.

He didn't mount the box. Holding the reins, he stood on the upper side of the stage by the front wheel. The vehicle had been so close that by the time he was hitched the leaders stood upon the slide, the swing span on the ramp, and the wheelers at the bottom. He spoke gently, casually, to the animals. Numbed, they were eager for motion. They tightened the trace chains, and lifted the Concord out of its small drift.

They sank to their knees but kept their footing. The stagecoach plowed deep, but slowly moved to the top of the ramp. The drag lightened there, and the outfit crept out onto the slide, barely contained by the notch Dave had dug with so much labor. His heart was slamming; he held his breath, and the old dizziness haunted him every step across. Yet nothing moved but stage, horses, and himself. He let the outfit roll down the far ramp; then in spite of himself he buckled and fell into the untramped snow on that side.

He was up instantly and looked back to see the fat woman tramping energetically across the slide, dragging her boy. Dave went back to help old man McDowell up the climb and across the top, Amy supporting her father on the other side.

Dave couldn't hold himself in, and he said: "Ma'am, you've had a real worry with your sick dad, and you never peeped."

She smiled across at him. "Don't call me ma'am, Dave. Not if we're going to be next neighbors. Will we get down now?"

"I can't tell you a thing beyond the stretch I can see, which ain't much," Dave said. Then he added, "Amy."

He got his passengers inside, gathered his tools from careful habit, and put them in the boot. He felt better when he mounted to the box, and knew it was because of the girl he had found in the storm. But he was sick, though he still couldn't admit it fully. He started the spans on their wallowing way through the heavy snow, hardly daring to watch ahead for fear of what he might see.

It gave him only an edgy relief when he realized that distance was slipping behind. Then, when the road came abruptly onto the valley floor, exultation beyond repressing swept up in him, and he let out a yell. The flats presented even deeper drifts, but a half hour later he saw the muggy outlines of the stage station.

A man came onto the long-roofed porch, waving his arms in excitement. Dave brought the stage to a halt there, and for a moment thought he was going to pitch from the box. He managed to swing down, hearing the station-keeper jabber: "Never been so glad to see anybody. Inset said to watch for you. Nearly rid out to meet you, but the missus said I'd only freeze afore I got there."

Dave knew he had to hold on a few seconds longer. The station-man might remember, but the others wouldn't know. He supported himself limply on the front wheel, gasping: "Feet . . . hands . . . frost-bitten, I reckon . . . mustn't go in where it's warm . . . mustn't . . . rub snow . . . ." Then he slumped and fell into the soft carpet under his feet.

He wasn't surprised to learn he had slept the clock around. He found himself alone in the bedroom of this settler's cabin that doubled as a stage way-station. His first thoughts were not of his passengers, who were safe now, but of Sam Inset. A wish that was close to a prayer filled his being. Sam must have got through. It had to be that way. And Ellen—she and her new baby had to be all right.

He saw his clothes over a chair, and they had been dried carefully. He stared at his hands and worked his fingers. He slid a hand under the covers and felt of his feet. They were tender but unbandaged. He had come through all right. Then he realized how enormously hungry he was. He got his clothes on, but the boots were too much. He padded down the stairway in his stocking feet, his whole body sore and aching.

The stairs came into the cabin's big livingroom at one side of the huge fireplace. There was a crackling fire, and the room's warmth wrapped about him. He saw Amy and the fat woman and little boy seated about the room, and looking at him with varied expressions. The old man, he supposed, was resting up in bed somewhere, too.

The fat woman was scowling at him, but Amy smiled and said: "You look fine, Dave. Did you notice it's stopped snowing? Hasn't since yesterday afternoon."

"That's fine," Dave said. "Then we'll get on . . . if I can get boots on my feet. But first somebody's got to scare me up something to eat."

"You can ride as a passenger from here on, and without any boots if need be," Amy said. "The company sent a man out from Roseburg to help you. Your brother-in-law asked them to, after he'd seen your sister. So there's word: she's better. Having him there did that for her, I know."

Dave closed his eyes for a moment, then opened them. There was still the fat woman and the complaint she was going to make against Sam. The company knew of the defection by now, but if a passenger raised hob, they could not treat it lightly. Then the station-woman came in, and he went out to the lean-to kitchen to eat.

The relief driver and station-keeper came in together from the barn. The company man had made a long, hard ride from the division point after the snow stopped the day before. Just because it was good to hear, Dave made him restate the fact that he had seen Sam, that Sam had said Ellen and the premature baby were better. Then he followed the other men into the big main room.

The company man looked at the women and said: "Well, we can roll again whenever you're ready, and nobody the worse for wear."

"Nobody the worse . . . !" the fat woman gasped.

Amy's voice cut her off. She had drawn the little boy to her and lifted him onto her lap. She smiled up at the company man. "You should have seen this brave little fellow. He was just awfully hungry, but after I told him how brave he was, there wasn't a whimper out of him."

The company man glanced skeptically at the boy. "He looks like a jim-dandy."

The boy stared back, then began to grin. "Gee whiz, it was fun!" he announced.

Amy sent a friendly look toward the fat woman, who was still scowling a trifle. "His mother's lucky to have him, and I'll bet she's proud. Think what the neighbors will say about the frightful experience we all shared together."

The fat woman began to smile.

They were almost ready to leave when Dave got a chance to speak to Amy alone. He gulped: "That was sure fine, and it surprised even her the way you turned her feelings right side out. I sure appreciate it, and so'll Sam."

Amy dismissed it. "We're going to be next neighbors. That means people who live close to each other. We're going to, aren't we?"

Dave pulled in a long breath. "I sure hope so," he said.

PAYROLL OF THE DEAD

(CHARLES) STEVE FRAZEE was born in Salida, Colorado, and during the decade 1926-1936 he worked in heavy construction and mining in his native state. He also managed to pay his way through Western State College in Gunnison, Colorado, from which in 1937 he was graduated with a Bachelor's degree in journalism. That same year he also married. He began making major contributions to the Western pulp magazines with stories set in the American West as well as a number of North-Western tales published in *Adventure* in the late 1940s. Few can match his Western novels which are notable for their evocative, lyrical descriptions of the open range and the awesome power of natural forces and their effects on human efforts. CRY, COYOTE (Macmillan, 1955) is memorable for its strong female protagonists who actually influence most of the major events and bring about the resolution of the central conflict in this story of wheat growers and expansionist cattlemen. It has recently been reprinted in a hardcover edition by Chivers Press in the Gunsmoke series. HIGH CAGE (Macmillan, 1957) concerns five miners and a woman snowbound at an isolated gold mine on top of Bulmer Peak in which the twin themes of the lust for gold and the struggle against the savagery of both the elements and human nature interplay with increasing, almost tormented, intensity. BRAGG'S FANCY WOMAN (Ballantine, 1966) concerns a free-spirited woman who is able to tame a family of thieves. RENDEZVOUS (Macmillan, 1958) ranks as one of the finest mountain man books.

Not surprisingly, many of Frazee's stories have become the basis for motion pictures. "Death Rides This Trail" in *Western Story* (10/52) was filmed as WILD HERITAGE (Universal, 1958); "The Devil's Grubstake" in *Fifteen Western Tales* (5/54), which the author had originally titled "The Singing Sands," was filmed as GOLD OF THE SEVEN SAINTS (Warner Bros., 1961); and "Many Rivers to Cross" in *Argosy* (3/53) was brought to the screen as MANY RIVERS TO CROSS (M-G-M, 1955). When Frazee came to expand the story he had wanted to call "The Singing Sands" into a novel, he proposed this title again to the book publisher, but the book publisher altered it prior to publication to DESERT GUNS (Dell First Edition, 1957) and, of course, the producers of the motion picture version rejected the author's preferred title even though it was on the original Warner Bros. contract. For its appearance in paperback audio from Durkin Hayes, the title has at last been restored to what the author wanted and the story is now finally titled "The Singing Sands."

According to Bill Pronzini in the second edition of TWENTIETH CENTURY

WESTERN WRITERS (St. James Press, 1991), a Steve Frazee story is possessed of "flawless characterization, particularly when it involves the clash
of human passions; believable dialogue; and the ability to create and sustain damp-palmed suspense." "Knife in the Back" first appeared in *Complete Western Book Magazine* (3/57) and it was first anthologized by Scott
Meredith in BAR 6 ROUNDUP OF BEST WESTERN STORIES (Dutton,
1957). For the latter appearance, Meredith, who was Frazee's agent at the
time, restored the author's original title for this story, "Payroll of the Dead,"
and that same courtesy has been extended to the author for its appearance here.

I

"COME OUT AND FIGHT"

When Jim Bennington knew for sure that the second Sioux was
staying with him on the left bank of the river, he paddled his soggy
boat closer to the heavy current on his right, despite his being a
poor swimmer. The Yellowstone was running tawny from rains deep
in the mountains. The surface of it was making a seething sound
and Bennington could feel the tremendous power of the river shuddering through his boat.

The crude craft was made of singed buffalo hides lashed to a
framework of wild cherry wood. Bennington had started to pattern
it along canoe lines and more by accident than design the boat had
wound up tapered at both ends like the splinter of an angry cougar's eye. It rode low in the water but it rode well—when it was not
six inches awash inside, as it was now from leakage of the pitch-
daubed seams.

Three miles upstream Bennington had thought to stop and remelt
his supply of pitch for a fresh caulking job. He was swinging toward
shore when the over-eager Sioux, painted black and red for the
glory trail, rose in the willows and fired an arrow so close to Bennington's head that the feathered end whisked his neck in passing.

The Sioux had nocked a second arrow and the string was almost
at his ear when Bennington caught him belly-deep with a rifle shot.
The Indian's glory trail ended as he crumpled forward from the
bank into the river. The boat spun with the current and was floating
backward when a second warrior came leaping through the rust-
brown willows. Bennington drove the Indian flat with two shots,
but he knew that the rocking and pitching of the boat had made
him miss.

The second warrior's rifle shot ripped the apron of elk skin
around the cockpit of the boat. By then the current was spinning
Bennington. He had to drop his rifle between his knees and grab

the paddle as the boat crashed sidewise into the curling wildness of fast water.

When he got straightened out, Bennington looked back and saw the Sioux dragging his companion up the bank. Great store these Lakotas set by the bodies of their dead. Bennington hoped that the survivor had his bellyful for one day; it depended on his mettle as an individual. But no such luck, for the Indian then got on a gray horse and started following downriver.

All the way from Sarsi country, bad cess to it, small groups of Sioux had kept Bennington jumping. For some reason the high plains were unduly astir. Bennington had hoped to save both work and trouble by sticking to the river.

Now he had a fair share of both. The mettle of the Sioux was tough; he kept coming. And the boat was getting so heavy that Bennington knew he would have to go ashore soon or sink. Leaping water swept him through a cut between bare hills. He saw the gray horse falling behind as it had to climb and then work its way across deep gullies.

Riding almost in the middle of the river, Bennington scanned the east bank for a good landing place. He did not like the looks of the wild water he would have to cross, but the thing to do was to put the river between him and the persistent Indian.

He started to turn across the stream. A sudden rush of water came up around his thighs, above the lashed crosspieces of the seat. A seam had popped and there was no time to make it over to the right bank. With a landman's distrust of water he had held himself ready to unload at any time; his cartridge bag and other items he could not afford to lose were around his neck on rawhide thongs and his Remington was between his knees.

The kayak still held together. He decided to make the west bank if he could, the near side, where a gravel bar of the color that gave the river its name came out like a long tongue. There was a wide streak of bad water between him and the slow swirling pool against the bar but that did not worry him as much as the position of the Sioux.

The bow of the boat came around stubbornly as he dug his paddle deep and leaned on it. He was taking water fast and it gave him a moment of panic. The bow came around. He began to paddle with all his might. Once across that churning leap of white water, he could jump out and drag the boat ashore.

He saw the rock too late. The boat went into it sidewise and began to tip upstream. Bennington grabbed his rifle and kicked free an instant before the terrible weight of the Yellowstone filled the boat, snapped the cherry wood longerons and the lashed frames, and wrapped the boat like a wet hide around the rock.

Bennington went under when he struck the water. The current

twisted him in a helpless sprawl. He hit himself in the chest with the butt plate of the rifle as he flailed his arms in a wild swimming motion. He came up. His legs struck a submerged rock and the tawny waters knocked him under again.

Still clinging hard to the rifle, he dog-paddled with both hands. It was partly the swing of the current and partly his own efforts that carried him out of the heavy surge of water into the quiet rim of the pool beside the gravel bar.

His feet struck bottom. He took two stumbling steps toward shore, gasping from the cold and the shock. The pool was cutting a hard, chill line just at the V of his buckskin shirt.

The Sioux stepped to the edge of the gravel with his gun half raised. Bennington recognized it as an old English trade musket. The Sioux's round, hard eyes were both wide open as the rifle came against his shoulder. They did not change, but his lips went tight, and the start of that was the warning Bennington acted on.

He ducked deep into the water. He could not hear. He had no way at all to judge the success of his timing, and so he had to come up almost instantly, either to meet the smash of the ball into his face, or to know that he had a little longer to live.

The warrior was just lowering the musket. A bloom of smoke was drifting away from the muzzle. Bennington brought his own rifle clear of the water. He allowed bare time for the water to run from the barrel before he pulled the trigger.

The hammer snapped and that was all.

He tried again. The second water-ruined cartridge was a brother to the first.

The Sioux, Uncpapa he was, dark and happy now, tossed his rifle aside and put an arrow to his bow. He made a motion of drawing it. He grinned when he saw how Bennington tensed himself to duck. Underwater Bennington had shifted his rifle to his left hand. His knife was in his right.

He said, "Come out and fight me here." If he could get closer, he would throw the knife. He stepped ahead and felt the gravel bottom sloping sharply inshore. One more step and he would be floundering over his head.

The Uncpapa answered with grim humor. "I am not a beaver, White Rain, who loves the Crows."

Bennington thought, he knows who I am and he knows that I was camping with Stunned Elk's horse stealers. Neither of the thoughts was helpful. The small party of raiding Crows with whom he had camped a few days while building the boat had thought him crazy. They had sat in the shade shaking their heads as he lashed the framework of the boat together.

Two days before it was finished they had gone down the Yellowstone on their ponies. Their opinion of Bennington must be right. No doubt they were alive and dry and healthy; he was up to his neck, fifteen feet out in the water, facing a war-smeared Sioux who didn't give a damn about counting coup on a live white man.

Bennington again invited the warrior to join him. It was only talk and they both knew it. The Uncpapa's stone-solid eyes glinted as Bennington edged downstream and almost went under when he struck another sloped-off place. Bennington lurched as he regained his balance. He was trapped. The Sioux was well aware of it or Bennington would have been dead before this.

Strong and seething the river ran at Bennington's back. He could feel it holding his buckskins tight against his body. He could twist sidewise and dive for the heavy current, let his rifle go, and try to swim out of arrow range. It was only a flashing thought; he was not that kind of swimmer. Before he was across the white water that had wrecked his boat, the Sioux would have him stuck up with arrows like one of the floating buffalo carcasses that Ree boys used for target practice on the Missouri.

Without raising his bow to full position the warrior sliced an arrow close to Bennington. He grinned with broad humor as the white man ducked. It never paid to curse a mortal foe in combat. You taunted him, insulted him, but you did not curse him. Bennington could not help it; he was too scared. He cursed the Sioux in English.

He brought his knife up toward his chest. It would not be an easy throw because the water would impede his arm during the final quick jerk and cast.

"White Rain who loves the Crows." The Sioux chugged another arrow close to Bennington and then at once laid another shaft on the twisted string. The first two had been flint-headed. This third was a steel point, well serrated, faintly shining with bear fat.

The Indian had enough of sport. It never lasted too long with any of them. The arrow lay flat across the bow while the warrior told Bennington that he, a white man, had killed High Wound upstream. Now White Rain, who loved Crows, was going where all the soldiers had gone.

Bennington threw the knife. He made the cast half blinded by the explosion of water from the sudden surfacing of his arm. It might have been a good throw but the Sioux leaped aside with smooth, instinctive coordination of mind and coppery muscle.

He was done with humor now. He raised the bow and his lips began to tighten. Bennington saw the scars of the Sun Dance on his broad chest muscles as the bow ends bent back.

Bennington drove sidewise into the current. He went under and felt the sudden rip of the wild, cold power against him. He came up in spite of himself. He heard the rifle shot as the current shot him downstream. He tried to look back but the white waves slapped across his face, blinding him, strangling him when he gasped for air.

In spite of his efforts to dog-paddle across the current, the river dragged him with it. He shot another desperate look across his shoulder and this time, before the leaping water whacked the vision from his eyes, he saw a white man striding from the willows with a smoking rifle. The Sioux was down.

He heard another shot as he paddled high, like a swimming hog, splashing toward the tip of the gravel bar.

II

"SOME JOB"

Otis Dameyer made a fine figure of a man as he stood on the bank watching Bennington diving to recover his rifle. Dameyer was all the way from St. Louis on some kind of Army business that he had hinted at before he shut up, as if he did not trust Bennington.

Up from his third dive, Bennington rested, as well as a man could rest neck-deep in water with the cold soaked all the way into his marrow bones. Dameyer looked like an officer, all right, Bennington judged.

He was big-framed and lean, with a cavalryman's flat-muscled legs. His eyes were a bold, staring blue. His hair was dark bronze. It appeared that he had trimmed lately with scissors the curling tightness of his short beard. He had a wide mouth with full lips, the kind that can go in an instant from ready humor to cruelty.

"You might have dropped it out in the current, Bennington," Dameyer said. "Try farther out."

He talked like an officer too, Bennington thought. Nobody was going to recover a rifle out in that current, but it was not there; it must be closer inshore, somewhere in the deep pool just beyond the strip of high bottom.

Three dives later Bennington found it. He come up sputtering and cold-weary and splashed toward shore. Dameyer was dragging the dead Sioux toward the water.

"Leave him there!" Bennington reached the shore and staggered up. The sun instantly made him feel ten degrees warmer.

"Why?" Dameyer asked.

"It won't hide anything to dump him in the river. The Uncpapas will know we got him anyway." Give any dead Indian a right to be borne away and scaffolded by his friends. Pushing the water from his shaggy black hair, Bennington watched Dameyer's face and knew instinctively that the man would not understand.

"How do you know he's an Uncpapa?"

That would be hard to explain to Dameyer too, so Bennington said, "I know," and let it go at that.

Bennington looked at the Sioux. That second shot had come from Dameyer's pistol, a wasted shot; and then Dameyer had started to throw the warrior into the river.

In the willows the big gray horse came forward to meet Bennington. The saddle was Sioux and so were the nose hitch and war rope. The brand on the hip was a big U S. Bennington removed the saddle. Along the back and barrel of the horse the marks of a McClellan saddle were still worn into the hair. He raised the mount's feet one by one. They were still well shod.

"One of our horses, of course," Dameyer said. "I shouldn't be a bit surprised if they got him when they butchered the paymaster's guard a few weeks ago near Bismarck. You heard about that?"

"No." Bennington put the saddle back on the horse.

"How long have you been out?"

"Over a year."

"I see." Dameyer smiled. "Then you wouldn't hear much about Army news, of course."

"Not a word." A poor year, unless you figured experience worth something. Bennington had been close enough to the Pacific to trade for a pack of sea otter skins that would have put St. Louis buyers on edge. The Blackfeet had the furs now.

He led the horse from the willows. Out in the white water the rock was clean again. His rag of a boat had torn loose and floated away. Whoever had told him he was a boatsman?

"Over a year, eh?" Dameyer said pleasantly. He lit a cigar. It was so out of place that Bennington stared at it resentfully. "You've really lost track of civilization."

"I'll catch up when I hit Fort Lincoln."

"Former Army man?"

"Yes."

"Confederate cavalry, no doubt?"

Bennington looked at the teeth of the gray. Six years old, he guessed. "So my accent still sticks a little, huh?"

"Quite a little. Louisiana or Mississippi?"

"I was a private in the Iron Brigade, the 2nd Wisconsin." The First Brigade of the First Division of the First Corps. Why was it every damned fool he met had to assume he had been in the Southern army just because he was a Southerner?

"No offense, Bennington." Dameyer was persistent. "You still act cavalry to me. After the war?"

"I was in the Seventh, yes."

"Fine regiment." Dameyer was relishing his cigar. "They were camped on the Heart River when I came out. I stopped with them

overnight. I knew Colonel Benteen during the war." He found another cigar and gave it to Bennington. It was not manners; it was
more like a bribe.

After the weird Indian mixtures Bennington had been smoking,
the cigar tasted good. The gray horse pleased him; it was transpor-
tation that would not go sidewise the instant he quit steering it.

"How did you like it?" Dameyer asked.

"Like what?"

"Service with the Seventh."

How indeed? Bennington had ridden since he was five. That part
of it was fine, but that was very little of his service. Most of it was
boredom, waiting, regulations that galled after the easy discipline
and hard fighting unity of the Iron Brigade. For being drunk one
night below New Fort Hays Bennington had been put in the guard-
house pit, on orders of Colonel Custer.

Bennington remembered the pit, a hole in the ground, banked
over with poles and dirt. He had spent five days there. That was
part of service with the Seventh Cavalry too.

He answered Dameyer's question. "It was all right, if you like
the cavalry."

"It so happens that I do." Dameyer studied Bennington from bold,
blue eyes. "It's about mess time. Let's eat and talk something over."

Bennington was cleaning and drying his rifle when Dameyer
brought two horses from the willows downstream. The way the
pack-horse was laden, it looked as if Dameyer intended to go all
the way to the Columbia without shooting game. Twenty feet from
the dead Sioux the two men cooked and ate.

"I'll stand obliged for some hardtack and bacon," Bennington
said, "enough to take me down to Lincoln on the gray."

"You're not taking the gray. It's government property. You're not
going down to Fort Lincoln anyway, Bennington." Dameyer was
rock-tough one instant, and the next moment he smiled as if apolo-
gizing for his harshness. "I think you'll change your mind when
you hear what I have to say."

The Army never changed wherever you encountered it. Bennington watched Dameyer recover his cigar from a log where he had
placed it while eating. The end was chewed into a long, twisted
mess. Dameyer cut it off with a hunting knife and relit the stogie.

"There was about twenty-five thousand dollars in the payroll wagon
old Sitting Bull got a few weeks ago. At least it was some of Bull's warriors, we're sure. They may have thrown the money away by now. Again,
maybe not. My job is to find out and to recover any part of it that's left."

"Some job," Bennington said.

Dameyer watched him coldly. "The Army thinks it's worth a try.
The Sioux have no use for money, probably don't know the meaning
of it. They killed the paymaster's guard and looted the wagon in

hopes of finding arms, perhaps. At any rate, we know they carried off the money."

"Near Bismarck?"

Dameyer nodded. "It's scattered on the prairie from there to the head of the Missouri."

Bennington looked out at the river. He was anxious to be on his way.

"I'm ordered to go right to Sitting Bull himself to see what can be done," Dameyer said.

"That was an easy order for somebody to give. Do you know where he is?"

"We heard the White Rain Mountains," Dameyer said. "I'll be frank with you. I had an Army scout with me until I told him what the orders were. He turned around and rode back." There was shrewd opaqueness in the round blue eyes. "It wasn't all chance that brought me here in time to save your hide, Bennington. I've been watching you for two days."

It sounded like a lie to Bennington. "How so?"

"Two days ago I met the Sioux you were camped with when you were building your boat. Old Stunned Elk could talk a little English and I can work by hands fairly well. He told me you'd be coming down the Yellowstone anytime, if you lived to make it." Dameyer smiled. "You barely did."

If you were any good, you did not keep reminding a man that you had saved his life. Possibly Dameyer did not know any better. He certainly was ignorant in other things, almost unbelievably so. Stunned Elk's bunch were Crows. Dameyer had called them Sioux.

The Army had chosen a green apple for an impossible task. Bennington looked Dameyer over carefully, as if he had not seen him right the first time. The man had a tough, sure cast to him, without doubt. That he had come this far alone proved that he was determined to carry out his orders, even if he did not know a Crow from a Sioux.

Army stubbornness was fine, but it also could get you killed in a hurry.

Bennington said, "Did you reload that rifle after you shot?"

Surprised at the sudden veering, Dameyer stared at Bennington, and then he colored slightly. "I didn't, for a fact." Then he defended himself. "I still had the Colt."

"Sure." Bennington picked up the war rope of the gray. "Sitting Bull may be in the White Rain Mountains, or on the Rosebud, or clear up on the Marias." He shook his head. "How about the hardtack and bacon, Lieutenant?" Dameyer was no lieutenant and Bennington was sure of it.

"*Captain* Dameyer," the man said gently, automatically. He watched Bennington's hand on the war rope.

He had not been a captain very long or he would not be so conscious of the rank, Bennington thought. Just how far was he going with that bluff about not letting Bennington have the gray?

"That's government property, mister. I'll need that horse." Dameyer did not reach toward his pistol. His voice did not rise. "The supplies I can spare you, but not the gray." He was cold-blooded and well poised; he was not bluffing.

Bennington could make a fight of it and take the horse. It would be a bad fight too. He might have to hurt Dameyer. He kept looking at the officer and knew it would be worse than that: he would have to kill Dameyer to get the gray. After all, the man was going in and Bennington was going out. It did not make sense to fight a fellow white man, and an Army captain in the bargain, over a government horse.

Bennington thought it over. When he was sure that he was not backing down, he dropped the war rope.

Dameyer showed no expression of triumph. "You've been out a year. Why not another week or two?"

"It's a crazy job. You're wasting time, Dameyer."

"Couldn't you find Sitting Bull's Oglalas?"

Uncpapas, damn it. "Sure, I could find Sitting Bull." Be taken to him, rather. You never *found* a particular Indian in this forbidding country.

"Well then?" Dameyer said.

It was all very simple to him. He was an Army officer acting on orders. Orders were all right when someone with sense gave them. Dameyer would go blundering on and get himself killed.

"I know you can do it," Dameyer said. "Stunned Elk told me that you were one of the best . . . ."

"Yeah, sure, me and Charley Reynolds and Yellowstone Kelly. No thanks, Dameyer."

"That's odd. Lonesome Charley Reynolds was the scout who turned back on me."

"He was smart."

Dameyer shrugged. "Take the gray, Bennington. I'll get along." He walked over to his pack-horse.

The order-dedicated, Indian-ignorant idiot was going through with it. Maybe he was a fool but you had to hand it to him for having guts and determination.

And he had not tried to prod Bennington with any hints about being paid as a scout. Bennington looked at the captain's rifle leaning against a log, still unloaded. Wasn't that something? Yet, except for that rifle, Bennington would be lying dead somewhere along the gravel bar, with his legs in the water, with a round area gleaming on his skull.

III
"FOOL'S MISSION"

Dameyer was digging into his pack.

"Never mind," Bennington said. He got on the gray and started upriver. He had always been somewhat of a fool himself.

Captain Dameyer came along behind him without a word. Dameyer showed no triumph. He acted as if he had known from the first that Bennington would go along with him. With brass and confidence like that the man would be a brigadier before his hair was gray.

The Sioux that Bennington had pumped through the stomach was not dead. He lay where his companion had dragged him, and his horse, a mean-looking blue pony, was still close to him.

"Well, by Judas!" Dameyer said, when he saw the Sioux's eyelids flicker over the gray haze that was beginning to deaden the dark brown of his eyes. He drew his pistol.

"Put that away." Bennington got down and knelt beside the dying Sioux. The glazing eyes cleared for an instant as hatred swept the cloud away. "Sitting Bull. Where is he?" Bennington asked in Sioux.

The Indian's eyelids flickered. He got his hand on his knife and there was still a little strength in him as he struggled to keep Bennington from taking it out of his hand. When his wrist failed, the Sioux tried to bend his head down to bite Bennington's wrist.

"No use, Dameyer." Bennington stood up.

Dameyer still had his pistol in his hand. He shot the Indian in the chest and the warrior gave a small, conclusive jerk.

Bennington swung around angrily. "You're alone the next time you don't listen to me."

"He could have crawled away and got well. Look what happened when they shot Rain-in-the-Face and bayoneted him and left him for dead . . . ."

"You'll listen to me from now on, or I'll take that pony and you can go it alone."

Dameyer began to reload his pistol. "You're the scout. I'll listen."

Bennington led the pony close to the Sioux. As a gesture of respect to the warrior he wished to kill it, but he did not like the idea of another unnecessary shot. He tied the pony to the willows. Other Sioux would be here before long; the land was swarming with them.

Until dusk Bennington set a fast pace. They were between the Rosebud and the mouth of the Big Horn River. Just before dark they crossed the Yellowstone, went over two long ranges of dry hills, and camped at Red Springs. Bennington was uneasy then: they had not seen an Indian all afternoon, or any fresh sign.

Dameyer wanted a fire. Bennington said no, and there was no fire. In the dark, making a long tour around the camp, he almost stepped on a rattlesnake that sent its dry, deadly warning as Bennington leaped sidewise in the deep grass. The incident shook him all out of proportion to its importance.

Dameyer was in his blankets when Bennington went back to camp. Dameyer was not worrying about anything. He yawned and said, "All quiet, huh?"

"Quiet enough for us to lose our horses. I'll stand the first four hours to midnight."

"Fair enough."

"Where did Lonesome Charley turn back?"

"About twenty miles out of Lincoln. Why?"

"Was he all right? He wasn't sick, was he?"

"No," Dameyer said. "He told me it was a fool's mission."

It was too. "Who assigned him to you?"

"Colonel Custer, of course." Dameyer yawned again.

Charley Reynolds was not the kind to turn back for anything less than extraordinary reasons; but maybe he had thought Captain Dameyer was reason enough. No Army scout was forced to take idiotic orders like a soldier. Still, it worried Bennington.

It did not worry Dameyer at all. He went to sleep in five minutes, snoring like a fat hound. Bennington kept thumping him with the toe of his moccasin, making him turn over. Between going out to the horses and trotting back to keep Dameyer's snores from being heard by every restless Sioux in Montana Territory, Bennington spent a bad four hours.

He did not trust Dameyer after the first watch was over. For a while Bennington lay unsleeping in his blankets. But Dameyer stayed alert. He went out to the horses. He moved around without too much noise. Bennington went to sleep. Four hours a night was about all either of them would get from now on.

At four in the morning Dameyer was ready to go on. Whatever else he lacked, he had toughness and an eagerness to do his job.

They quartered away from the rising sun, riding the long, rolling hills. It was a big and lonely land they crossed and it seemed to be uninhabited. Bennington had seen it that way at times, but he had never accepted a clump of trees, a thicket, the willows beside a stream, or any other cover, at face value.

"Who said Sitting Bull was in the White Rains?"

"Scouts. Bloody Knife and some of the others Custer seems to trust so much."

It did not matter. The White Rains were as good a place as any to head for. They would find Sitting Bull when they ran into Sioux who were disposed to, or who could be persuaded to, take white men to him. Some of it depended on the fact not being known that the two of them had killed High Wound and the other Uncpapa.

In the afternoon they were fifteen miles from the Yellowstone, going southwest toward Tullock Forks. Bennington held it unlikely that they would reach the Little Big Horn without running headlong into Sioux.

He kept wondering about the marks of wood cutting he had seen late yesterday afternoon. While they were still on the west bank of the river, he had looked across the swift water and had seen where trees had been chopped on the east bank, even cottonwoods that burned poorly in steamboat fireboxes. Dameyer had been ducking branches and hustling the pack-horse along. Bennington doubted that he had observed the marks across the river.

"How long were you at Fort Lincoln?" Bennington asked.

"Several days."

"Did any steamers go up the Missouri?"

"I heard that the *Far West* left from Fort Buford sometime last month on Army business."

"To the Yellowstone?"

"Up the Yellowstone, they said."

The *Far West* was nearly two hundred feet long. It could be handled on the Yellowstone, Bennington guessed, but it would be a mean and dangerous task. He asked, "Where was it headed?"

"I haven't the least idea," Dameyer said. "I'm only a dumb captain."

"What outfit?"

"The Sixth Engineers."

Engineers! Bennington said it under his breath like a curse. They could corduroy a road through a swamp or maybe get some sort of boat bridge across a river, but what did they know about Indians?

If Captain Dameyer observed Bennington's disgusted reaction, he gave no sign of it. Dameyer rode along in obvious enjoyment of the country, relaxed and easy, smoking a cigar. He acted as if the sight of a hundred Indians rocketing down suddenly from the next bare ridge would not even give him a start.

I'll find out about that pose before this is over, Bennington thought.

He found out soon.

There were about twenty-five in the bunch. Dameyer and Bennington came upon them unexpectedly, if you could call a quarter of a mile a distance "coming upon." It was close enough. There were men, women, and children in the bunch. Immediately there was a furious stirring of movement.

The women and kids went at a run up a ridge. Bennington saw a child fall from a travois. An old squaw with her gray hair streaming dropped off a calico pony and scooped up the child, running with him.

Bennington saw a headdress blossom suddenly on one of the warriors milling between him and the fleeing squaws. Two of the bucks cut off at a high lope to gain the top of a knobby hill. The others seemed to be racing aimlessly, kicking dust in all directions.

It was a heap of activity for the size of the alarm: two white men sitting their horses quietly on a ridge. Bennington made the peace signal. He said, "Just sit, Dameyer. They're coming."

"Good!"

Bennington shot the captain a quick glance. The man was not scared. Maybe he didn't have sense enough to be scared. Bennington watched the signals of the two warriors who had gained the knobby hill to see what kind of support lay behind the white men. They sent the truth down to the others. The others let out long, quavering cries and came on in a rush.

"What kind of Sioux?" Dameyer asked. He might have been asking for information to put in a report, for all the emotion he showed.

"Don't know," Bennington answered. He swallowed slowly. He and Dameyer had excited the band far too much for normal circumstances. He saw the feathers in the tails of the ponies as the Indians came charging.

"Sit quiet," he said. "Don't get excited."

Dameyer's voice held an amused tone, "Take some of that medicine yourself, White Rain."

The Indians split their charge, winging out on both sides of the motionless white men. In the center, the chief with the headdress shouted, "Hi-yi-yi!" in a drawn-out, trembling call that carried far across the hot, dry hills.

"Musical bugger," Dameyer said, and Bennington wished he would keep his mouth shut.

Bennington looked from side to side. The flankers were obeying; they were watching their chief. For the moment at least everything depended on the man with the headdress.

The chief slowed his pony from its flashing run. He shifted his rifle and raised his arm, and then he dropped down to a walk and came up the hill toward the white men.

They were Cheyennes, Bennington saw then. The chief was Blue Buffalo. Three years before Bennington had seen him in the camp of the Oglalas, with whom the Cheyennes were strong brothers. Bennington dropped his hand and made the signs, and said, "I am glad to see Blue Buffalo once more."

IV
"BAD MOMENT"

For just an instant his use of the chief's name raised little sparks of surprise in the Cheyenne's eyes. The warriors crowded in, dark with suspicion and hatred. Magnificent physical specimens, they were, the tallest and the most clean cut of all plains tribes.

One of them reached out to snatch Dameyer's rifle. Without moving the weapon, Dameyer shook his head, smiling. His eyes were like round rocks and there was no fear in him. The warrior wheeled his pony back. His companions laughed. The warrior raised a Springfield carbine.

He said harshly, "We have seen too much blood. Blue Buffalo says it."

The warrior lowered the carbine and rode to the outer edge of the group. Across the hills the squaws had stopped and were looking back, with the dust of their flight settling around them.

"We are in peace," Bennington said. "We would speak with Tatanka. We have heard he is in the White Rain Mountains."

Blue Buffalo was willing to parley, but he did not get down to go through the usual ceremonies. Urgency was in him. It might be, too, Bennington thought, that guilt was riding him. At least he was not at ease. His eyes moved with a sharp kind of worry as he followed Bennington's casual glances at certain equipment of the warriors: five or six Springfield carbines, shot boxes of Army issue, a sergeant's chevrons on a patch of torn blue cloth tied in the tail of one of the ponies.

"Tatanka is gone," the chief said.

"Where has he gone?"

Blue Buffalo pointed. "Down the Rosebud, beyond the Yellowstone. Far away."

Another warrior slammed his pony in close to Dameyer. He held a knife close to the captain's face. With that and the dark stare of glittering eyes he tried to strike terror into Dameyer.

Dameyer grinned pleasantly. "Put that away, bucko, or I'll drop your guts in your lap with it."

The warrior did not understand the words but he understood the fearlessness of the captain. Blue Buffalo grunted angrily and waved the buck aside. Blue Buffalo said to Bennington, "You are scouts for Man Without Hip?"

For General Terry. Bennington shook his head.

"For White Whiskers?"

General Gibbon. Bennington shook his head. "Alone we seek Tatanka to speak with him."

Once more Blue Buffalo pointed north and east toward the Rose-bud. He started to turn away.

One of the Cheyennes said angrily, pointing at Bennington, "He rides the horse of Stab Bear!"

"Before that it was the horse of the Great White Father." Bennington said, "and now it is his again." He gave the Cheyenne a hard stare. It was a bad moment. There were no rules to judge Indian behavior. The Cheyennes could catch fire and rub him and Dameyer out in moments. Bennington slid his hand back and rested his thumb on the hammer of his rifle.

Blue Buffalo put his pony around again. Fury glittered in his look as he watched Bennington, and then the heat began to die. He became sullen, discouraged, almost afraid. He waved for his warriors to follow him.

They did not have to obey him. They put their savage hatred against Dameyer and Bennington. A small, quick move, a tiny crack of fear in the white men and the thing would have exploded. Lacking either, one of the warriors could have boiled over anyway.

Dameyer threw contempt like words from his odd blue eyes. Bennington sat quietly with his hand on the rifle, with his face grave and steady, with all his fear jammed down where it did not show.

"There has been too much blood," Blue Buffalo said.

The Cheyennes listened to their chief. As they rode away one of them smashed in close to the white men and lashed the pack-horse so that it jumped and tried to break loose. The warrior who had turned back from grabbing Dameyer's rifle swerved his pony and struck the captain across the shoulder with a string of scalps.

Dameyer smiled faintly. "The next Sioux I shoot in the guts won't get a mercy shot."

It was not worth saying that the band was Cheyenne, not Sioux. For a man who knew little about Indians, Dameyer had stood up to their bullying tactics like a veteran. Maybe it was not so important to know one tribe from another. Maybe the Army knew its business, after all, when it sent Dameyer.

But Bennington was not obliged to like him; a man without fear was inhuman.

"What did they say about Sitting Bull?" the captain asked.

"We're going the wrong way."

"Maybe they lied."

"Maybe they did." Bennington turned the gray and started across the hills toward the Rosebud.

Dameyer followed him. "They'd been in a scrap against our cavalry, did you notice?"

Bennington grunted. How could he have missed noticing? Three Springfield carbines, odds and ends of cavalry equipment; but there had not been an Army horse in the bunch. Blue Buffalo was headed toward one of the reservations. Before he reached there, the carbines and other Army gear would be well concealed.

Blue Buffalo had been ill at ease. There had been guilt in that repeated talk about too much blood already. Whatever kind of skirmish the Cheyennes had been in, they had won, or else they would have been in a much uglier mood.

"Did the Sioux burn that payroll wagon?" Bennington asked Dameyer suddenly.

"No. Why?"

"I'll bet they burned it. There went your money, Dameyer. We're risking our hair over nothing."

"They took the money, be sure of that. All we have to do is find out how much of it they hung on to." Dameyer squinted at the distance ahead. "How far to the Yellowstone?"

"We ain't even to the Rosebud yet." For some reason despite Dameyer's actually being a pleasant man, Bennington wanted to quarrel with him. He could not name the quality of character that irritated him. It wasn't entirely Dameyer's bold, almost insolent, disregard of danger, nor his flashes of arrogance, but that was part of it.

It must be, Bennington decided, a deep coldness in Dameyer that was difficult to describe and not always easily apparent.

Bennington remembered something that had flashed in and out of his mind while they were waiting for the Cheyennes to come up. "Where'd you get my name . . . White Rain?" He used the Sioux words.

"From Stunned Elk's bunch."

"Tell me something about Stunned Elk's braids, Dameyer."

"One of them was turning gray. The other was still mostly black." Dameyer chuckled. "It gave him a lopsided look."

That was Stunned Elk, sure enough, but the Crows had their own name for Bennington. *Cha,* Wolf Hair. "You didn't get my name from Stunned Elk, Dameyer."

Dameyer gave the impression of shrugging. "Where are we likely to run into Sioux again?"

"Anywhere," Bennington answered curtly. The Uncpapa Dameyer had killed by the river had called Bennington by name, at least twice, but Dameyer was not supposed to understand Sioux.

Bennington tested that supposition. "You heard Stab Bear use my name, Dameyer."

"Stab Bear?"

"The Uncpapa you killed."

"Stab Bear, White Rain." Dameyer chuckled. He found two cigars and tossed one across to Bennington. "Sure, I heard him. I understand enough Lakota to catch a few words now and then. It's like letting people think you're stone deaf. You hear a lot that you wouldn't catch otherwise."

"If you were that near, you sure shaved things close before you shot him."

"Didn't I?" Dameyer met Bennington's angry stare with good humor. "It was a funny sight, you'll have to allow. You up to your ears in the water, the Sioux slicing arrows at you . . . I got him in time. What more do you want?"

They struck the Rosebud the next morning. Bennington had gone up it in June the year before when the delicate odor of wild roses filled the whole valley. Now there was the biting smell of hot dust raised by the horses. Suddenly Bennington asked, "What month is this?"

"July." Dameyer calculated. "The thirteenth. July 13, 1876." He smiled to himself.

Of Indian sign there was plenty. All along the way the grass had been grazed down by ponies. There were campsites where lodge poles still stood. The staked circles and the fire pits were weeks old, but the enormity of the campsites, strung for miles along the river, made Bennington uneasy.

Thousands of Sioux had ridden here this summer. The unshod hoofs of their ponies had pounded a trail hundreds of yards wide beside the stream. There were marks of shod horses too, widely dispersed among the more blurry outlines of the plains ponies. Cavalry even under the most careless of lieutenants on scout did not spread out like that.

Bennington rode with a tingling down his spine. He was not positive about the picture he was reading here, but it seemed to have an ugly look. When they stopped to re t the horses at noon, he found an Army canteen under a bullberry bush.

"Some careless recruit will pay for that, " Dameyer said.

"I'd say he already had."

As usual, Dameyer switched his position when there was no point in carrying on pretense. "The Indians have run off a batch of Army horses, for certain, wouldn't you say?"

Bennington looked out at the marks of plains cavalry that had passed in numbers greater than the strength of some corps he had seen during the war. He was tired of jostling words with Captain Dameyer of the Sixth Engineers, who said the obvious or lied beyond comprehension.

They made twenty-five miles that day and were still about twenty-five miles from the Yellowstone when they camped.

Again Bennington took the first watch, sitting in a clump of bushes far enough from the Rosebud so that the sound of it neither lulled him not dulled his ears. Tonight Dameyer slept silently. Even the horses were unusually quiet.

It seemed to Bennington that the host which had passed up and down the valley was all around him now in the ghostly starlight, not threatening but riding by in endless strength, going to some appointed place.

The pale-set stars and a sensing of time slipping through the barrier of midnight told Bennington when to rouse Dameyer, who came from his blankets instantly alert.

Dameyer pulled on his boots. The breech of his Springfield made light metallic sounds as he put in a fresh cartridge. Then for a moment he was stock still. "It's strangely quiet, isn't it?" His voice was a murmur.

"The Indians are long gone from here." Bennington believed it, but still he felt the presence, the ownership, the flowing splendor, and the dark savageness of a people whose mark would be forever on the land.

"Tomorrow we'll find them," Dameyer said.

"We're weeks behind this migration." Suddenly Bennington had a hope and a wish that Captain Dameyer would give up when they reached the Yellowstone again.

"Weeks then," Dameyer said. "We'll find them." He rose and made a tall, broad shape against the night. He walked confidently into the hushed darkness to take his post.

V

"BIG WORDS"

In the morning Dameyer was eager to move on. Bennington had never seen a man so anxious to find Sioux. Bennington himself had lived among them when circumstance forced him to do so, but he had never considered them blood brothers, or even been entirely at ease in their camps.

Captain Dameyer was fairly busting to get right in the middle of the most bitter of all the Sioux, the bands from all the seven councils, the fiercely independent dissidents who would have no peace on white men's terms, who followed the harsh counsel of Tatanka, Sitting Bull.

All the way down the Rosebud Bennington looked moodily at the fat U-marks of steel-foot horses sprinkled among the tramplings of thousands of ponies. It was no small scout detail the Sioux had rubbed out to get those horses. Of course it was possible that each horse did not represent a dead cavalryman: the Indians might have stampeded the mounts of several companies engaged in a skirmish.

He asked, "Did soldiers go up the river from Buford with the *Far West?*"

"I think so," Dameyer said. "A few companies of cavalry pacing along on the bank, some of the Sixth Infantry on the boat itself. Why?"

It was always *why* with Captain Dameyer. Bennington did not answer. He kept searching out the marks of shod horses in the wide trail.

"That's not our business," Dameyer said. "Forget everything but the orders."

Now it was "our" business and "our" orders as Dameyer assumed that Bennington was solidly stuck with the detail. That was not the case at all; Dameyer just might lose a second scout when they came to the Yellowstone.

Out in the chopped swath where the Indians had ridden Bennington stopped to look down on torn strips of faded blue cloth. Squaws had used them as diapers for their infants. The sun pressed hot upon his back. The land was big and empty.

Those pieces of cavalry blue, used like an insult, cast here in the dust, seemed to express the shocking hatred of the Sioux for white soldiers.

Dameyer said, "How far to the Yellowstone now?"

"We'll get there soon enough."

They came upon a dead horse, a cavalry mount with the McClellan still on it. Bennington got down and walked around it. The horse had been shot in the head at close range. He stepped close and lifted the canteen on the saddle. It was empty. The horse had bloated and popped and now the flesh was sagging away and the yellow teeth of the animal made a long snarl.

Dameyer gave it a glance and said, "Let's get on." A mile farther on he pointed to the left. "Let's cut across to the islands. We can make an easier ford there, rather than following the Rosebud all the way down."

That was so but how did Dameyer know it? He had given the impression of being lost ever since Bennington met him. "The Sioux stayed with the Rosebud," Bennington said.

"Bully for them. Let's cut off toward the islands. We'll find the Sioux if we just keep riding in their general direction." Now he was the martinet condescending to explain his order.

He was right but Bennington still wanted to be stubborn. His dislike of the man had grown to where it overshadowed his puzzling about Dameyer's character.

"Is there any particular advantage in staying right in the middle of this Indian pike?" Dameyer asked.

Bennington led the way off to the west, toward the islands in the Yellowstone. They came to the river and Bennington stopped to cool the horses before making the crossing. He said, "We've gone in a circle, almost. How'd you know these islands were here in the bend?"

Dameyer broke off a handful of willow tops and tried to rub the dust from his high Wellington boots. "Good Lord, man, I rode past the islands on the way to find you. Besides, I've got a map."

"I might let you depend on that map from here on."

Dameyer smiled. "Another boating expedition, eh?"

"No, I'll ride."

"Do so if you wish." Dameyer squinted across the river. "What's the best route for me to take after I cross?"

He could be bluffing but it did not seem so. With a singleness of purpose that was at once admirable and enraging, the captain was going on with his assignment. Money taken from a paymaster's wagon. Dust scattered on the wind.

Bennington felt like cursing but he knew he was going to stick. At the first, if he had known how much of a liar Dameyer was, he would not have gone with him. Clever liars were generally also clever cowards, but Dameyer was a combination that utterly stumped Bennington.

"We reach Sitting Bull, say. All you're obliged to do is get some report of what happened to the money, is that it?"

There was a hard challenge in Dameyer's stare. "Are you suggesting something else?"

"You don't expect to recover any of the money, do you?"

"I do, if they've got any of it. Every note goes back to the government. Were you hinting at something else?"

Bennington had not been hinting at anything else. He had been trying to estimate the length of their stay in Sitting Bull's camp, in case they ever got there. For his part he wished to visit the Sioux as briefly as possible.

Dameyer had taken a different meaning from the question. Just how genuine was his outrage? Bennington said, "You'll see that I get paid as a scout?"

"I'll try. That's all I can promise."

No amount of money was worth the risk that lay ahead. If Dameyer had made at any time glib promises about Bennington's being rewarded for his services, Bennington would have distrusted him; but now the officer's blunt honesty in the face of his own need of help settled Bennington's mind.

Sun glint from the water bounced in Dameyer's crisp bronze whiskers as he mounted. Bennington studied out the first island. It was covered with a dense growth of willows and the upstream end of it was strewn with debris from floods. Most of the heavy water was on the far side, for the stream between here and the island was shallow enough to show bottom.

The river was less than belly deep on the horse as Bennington approached the island. He was turning to see how Dameyer was coming with the pack-horse when he saw a small movement in the willows.

There was one Sioux, crouched low. He rose as Bennington turned his rifle to bear on him. Then there were a dozen Indians who rose suddenly to full height from the willows. Bennington saw the rifles, the war arrows steady on the bows, the grim, dark faces.

Even devoid of paint they were the most murderous-looking band of Oglala Bad Faces Bennington had ever encountered.

Their coppery skins were gleaming wet from the swim to the island. The white men had stumbled into the trap with no resistance, so that for a moment the Sioux were at a loss. It would not last long, their lack of design.

Fear rocked up and down in Bennington, but his face was grave as he rested his rifle across his thighs and said, "We seek Tatanka Watanka." Most of the fierce dark eyes were on Dameyer. The Indians were hoping he would try to fight or run. Without turning Bennington said, "Don't try anything, Captain."

Dameyer's answer was as cool as the river. "I guess we found them, didn't we?" He came splashing on and several warriors waded out to meet him. They cut the tow rope of the pack-horse. They punched at the pack, testing for loot, as they brought Dameyer ashore.

A brawny warrior grinned at Dameyer. He said, "Friend," and reached his hand up, and like a fool the captain reached down to meet the gesture. The next instant the Sioux jerked him from the saddle. They pounded him brutally while they were taking his weapons. They kicked him to his feet at last and turned to Bennington, closing in around him.

"We are in peace. We are not scouts. We have come from the White Father to speak to Tatanka," Bennington said.

"Tatanka does not speak to mice."

"Tatanka sets the hoofs of his pony on mice."

"And on white man soldiers."

"Tatanka does not know the White Father."

"He will speak to us. The White Father has sent us. We are only two. We are here," Bennington said. That they were still alive was because it had pleased the Oglalas to let them walk straight into a trap. The Sioux were not given to making captives of grown white men. Bennington and Dameyer would die here or they would go to Sitting Bull's camp as visitors.

Still on his horse, Bennington knew that he held a small advantage. When they dragged him from it the gates of savagery would swing wide open and he and Dameyer would die quite simply. He glanced down at Dameyer. The captain's face was bloody. The roughing he had taken had roused a horrible temper in him and now with attention centered on Bennington, Dameyer was sizing up the chances more from the standpoint of anger in him than from logic.

"I will not argue with children," Bennington said. "We have come to see the Water Pourer, whose medicine is powerful. He has dreamed already of our coming. He will be displeased if his dream is violated by careless children."

One of the warriors growled, "Hear the big words of this white man, this mouse, whose heart squeaked with terror when he saw us."

"Let the white scouts swim to the next island while we shoot our arrows at them."

That suggestion fell sensibly among the Oglalas; there was little sport in clubbing to death two enemies who had offered no fight. Several warriors grunted approval of the idea.

"White Rain has said his words." Bennington gave the warriors a contemptuous look, and then he raised his eyes to look above their heads, as if they were miserable objects who did not concern him; but from the edge of his eye he watched Dameyer.

Dameyer was not as hurt as he had pretended. Dameyer was reaching under his shirt. The idiot had some kind of small handgun there. He was pulling it free when Bennington swung his rifle. The barrel cracked down on Dameyer's head and the captain buckled at the knees.

The sudden move startled the Sioux. The warriors close to Dameyer fell back. Bennington dropped from his horse quickly and took the wicked little handgun away from Dameyer. A big Oglala stepped in to crush the captain's head with a war axe. Bennington shoved him back with an open hand.

"My friend is a child too," he said. Bennington tossed the handgun down. "We have come to see Tatanka!" he shouted. "We have had enough of your foolish acts!" He glared around him savagely, letting anger hide his fear.

The Sioux went into council. Two of them had recognized the gray horse. They were in favor of killing the white men without further delay. Older warriors ruled against them. After all, White Rain had spoken of a dream. Tatanka had many dreams. Perhaps White Rain had spoken with a split tongue, but it was not safe to disregard dreams.

Better to let Tatanka Watanka decide if the white men were liars.

Dameyer lurched to his feet. All the heat was out of him and the shrewd determination was in his face again. "I almost ruined it, didn't I? Are they taking us to old Bull?"

"We'll see." You could not figure the captain out. He was the strangest mixture of fire and ice Bennington had ever known. At least his head for once had been put to a good use.

The Bad Faces took the white men's weapons. Two of the younger warriors started to loot the pack and were stopped by Clouds Floating, a scarred Oglala who seemed to have the most rank. It was he who told Bennington, "We go to Tatanka."

"What did he say about Sitting Bull?" Dameyer asked quickly.

"They're taking us to his camp."

"We did it!" Dameyer's confidence was back with a surge.

VI

"SITTING BULL"

Three warriors took the horses across swift water to the next island. Dameyer was a miserable swimmer also. Bennington saw him plunge in without a trace of fear but a moment later the captain was in trouble. Two young Sioux rocking along in the current beside Dameyer laughed at his spluttering and his frantic efforts to stay afloat. They let him almost drown before they grabbed his hair and towed him ashore.

Dameyer choked and gasped but when he was able he looked at the two warriors and grinned.

In the cottonwoods on the west bank five young boys were watching the ponies. Angry because he had missed the fun, one of them jabbed Bennington in the rump with a knife choked down at the point between thumb and forefinger.

Bennington knocked him heels-up in the air and turned away before the youth landed. The Oglalas laughed.

Dameyer said, "I see there *is* a proper time to lose one's temper, after all."

Bennington glanced at a bugle hanging on the saddle of a young Indian's pony. There were two blood bay horses in the bunch, shod horses with government brands.

"You know what, Bennington, I'm going to pay you directly one hundred dollars from the payroll money. That's a whole month's pay for a scout."

Bennington gave the captain a narrow, disliking look.

For three days they rode northward with the Sioux. They crossed the Missouri and continued on into country that Bennington did not know. When they crossed the trail of a Crow war party, five of the warriors and three of the young boys went after their ancient enemies.

Late on the fourth day Bennington saw the Sioux camp ahead. It was the largest he had ever seen. Clouds Floating let out a shout and went zig-zagging ahead on his pony. The rest of the escort, stolid with their importance, took Bennington and Dameyer on at a steady pace, ignoring the shouted questions of young men watching the pony herd.

Bennington held to a solemn expression as he made a quick estimate of the number of big cavalry horses in the herd. There were at least two hundred. He gave Dameyer a bitter look, but the captain's eyes were on the camp.

The excitement Clouds Floating had raised by his approach, the signal that he had found white men, was dying away as the Sioux escort took Bennington and Dameyer past lodges of the Minneconjou, Brule, and Sans Arc. On ahead, set apart from all the others, Bennington saw a yellow council tent.

A group of chiefs stopped the escort and asked questions. Bennington recognized Gall, in whose camp he had once spent a month. Black thoughts were setting behind Gall's face as he looked at Bennington, who gave the signs that he was glad to see the chief again.

Gall turned away. Behind him banks of stone-faced warriors stood silent, their faces bad. And it was that way as the escort took the white men on through the camp, a bad quietness and a hatred showing starkly in all the Sioux. The chiefs now walked ahead of the cavalcade and the crowd closed in behind.

They passed lodges of the Cheyenne. Bennington saw Little Chief, the tall, thin-lipped orator, who folded his arms and stood impassively, giving Bennington no recognition whatsoever. When they came to the Uncpapa lodges a squaw and an old gray-haired woman pushed forward. They put their hands on their mouths as they stared at the horse Bennington was riding, and then they both broke into a loud wailing, sawing the air with their arms and rocking their bodies forward.

The keening lament of the women of Stab Bear, dead beside the Yellowstone, broke with a rawing effect on Bennington's nerves.

Captain Dameyer swung his head from side to side and watched the camp with high contempt. It was the right thing to do, but he was not acting, and therein lay another dark bundle of worry for Bennington: the Sioux understood acting and could admire it, but a genuine contempt of them was a deadly mistake.

Two hundred cavalry horses were in their pony herd at this moment because someone had shown contempt of a great, free people.

They came to the red and black lodge of Sitting Bull. Tatanka stood before it with Rain-in-the-Face, whose eyes were glowing with cruel, sharp intelligence. Rain-in-the-Face was standing by aid of a stick crutch and Bennington saw the queer hanging of his foot, as if the toes only could touch the ground.

Bennington said, "The White Father has sent a soldier and White Rain to speak to Tatanka Watanka." He gave the marks of respect to Sitting Bull.

The down-drooping lips of the Sioux's greatest medicine man tightened. The deep lines running from the corners of his bold nose grew stronger. His cloudy eyes looked at the white men as if they were pieces of spoiled meat. Sitting Bull had grown gray listening to the broken words of white men.

He turned his back and went into his lodge. Hobbling on his crutch, Rain-in-the-Face followed him. A feral rumbling came from the Sioux.

"That was the old boy himself!" Dameyer said excitedly. "Tell him to come back out here. Tell him . . . ."

"Shut up," Bennington growled. He watched Gall and Bad Hip and Little Wound go into an impromptu conference. Clouds Floating stood aside, glowering, angry, as if he had been reprimanded for bringing the white men into camp. Sitting Bull had turned his back upon them, and now their position was worse than precarious.

Dameyer did not observe this at all; he started to complain again about Sitting Bull. He stopped when warriors grabbed the bridles of the horses and led them away. Bennington took a deep breath. Gall had saved their hides, Pizi, the irreconcilable, the white man hater, the true, hard man of the Sioux.

Inside a lodge guarded by the *akecita*, the Indian police, Bennington stood between the door flap and the fire pit and fought down a desire to kill Dameyer with his bare hands. From what he had learned from Clouds Floating, from what he had seen in the camp, the cavalry horses, the great number of wounded Sioux, Bennington had pieced together a grim and ugly picture.

Dameyer sat down on a pile of buffalo robes. He started to pull off his boots. "Give me a hand here, will you?" When Bennington did not move, Dameyer lay back on the robes and sighed with utter relaxation. "You wouldn't believe it, but I'm a little tired. When will we have the council with old Bull?"

"We never will," Bennington said. His voice was calm. "You start telling the truth or I'm going to kill you."

Dameyer started to smile and then gave proper assessment to what he had heard, and his face grew sober. "I think you've guessed the truth, Bennington. You came along of your own free will, so don't act like a Puritan now."

"You'd better talk, Dameyer!"

The captain bunched a robe under his head to gain more comfort. "The cavalry had a couple of scraps with the Sioux. Crook got his nose bloodied. Custer lost half his command, about three hundred men, over the Little Big Horn. He got killed himself, by the way."

"I said I wanted the truth!"

"You're getting it. You damned fool, do you think any man is immortal? Custer lost five companies of the Seventh, right down to the last man. Reno and Benteen took a bad mauling but the infantry came up the river in time to save them."

The casualness of Dameyer's words made Bennington say, "You're no officer. You never were."

"That's right," Dameyer said agreeably. "I'm a man looking out for himself, the same as you. There was no paymaster's wagon robbed near Bismarck. You guessed that before we started to cross the Yellowstone the second time."

I didn't, Bennington thought.

"But don't fret yourself," Dameyer went on, "there's money here for us. All we have to do is talk Sitting Bull out of it, and that can be done."

"What money?"

"The Seventh was paid about a month before the fight. They never had a chance to spend a cent. Most of that money is right here in this camp, Bennington. Figure the privates at thirteen dollars, about three hundred of them, average the officers' pay at . . . ."

Bennington turned away with a sickness in him. He stumbled to the door of the lodge and looked out directly at a Fox warrior standing guard twenty feet away. Beyond the Sioux a group of curious children were watching the tent. One of them had a rag on a willow stick.

It was the lower bar of a swallow-tailed pennant, a blue bar with the handles of crossed sabers standing against it in white. Bennington had seen it many times, George Custer's personal pennant. . . .

Dameyer was still talking and his words drained Bennington's strength like a knife plunged into his back: " . . . even if half of it was thrown away or lost, we still can figure on several thousand dollars. It's nobody's money, Bennington. The Indians have no use for it. I've got an idea of what to tell them about it, but you'll have to make the spiel of course."

The warrior waved the children away. They trotted off, shouting, and the blue bar waved and flapped on the stick.

Bennington grasped the sides of the opening, gathering the hide in a grip that made his knuckles stand white. He looked over his shoulder at Dameyer. "You filthy, miserable bastard."

Dameyer began to search under his shirt. "Right at the start I saw that you were soft inside, Bennington."

Bennington walked as far as the fire pit before the sounds of the village around him brought him control.

VII

"BARGAIN"

"That's right," Dameyer said. He relaxed again and his fingers began to tug at the thing he'd been probing for under his shirt. "We're stuck. We've got to work together. What we think of each other has nothing to do with the problem." His smile was engaging. From under his shirt he pulled two cigars wrapped in oiled silk.

"These are the last, Bennington." Dameyer tossed one across the lodge. It struck Bennington's shirt and fell into the fire pit.

"Here's what you tell them, Bennington: those green pieces of paper they took have the names and identification of the soldiers they killed. They chopped the dead to pieces . . . you know how Sioux perform. Tell old Bull that the White Father"—Dameyer's mouth curled with dry amusement—"has to know who his dead soldiers are, so that he can do them honor. The only way he can tell is to have the pieces of green paper."

Dameyer lit his cigar. He lay back on the robes again with his hands behind his head. "It ought to work, don't you think? The Sioux honor their dead enemies, and we're not asking for anything that's useful to them."

With all his anger drained away and only a sense of helpless wonder left, Bennington stared down at Dameyer. Who spawned such men? What kind of blankness was inside them?

"It might work," Bennington said tonelessly.

"Good! Then we're agreed. A third of the money goes to you. That beats a hundred dollars, doesn't it?"

"Yes, it does." Bennington walked over to the door flap again.

"When do you suppose they'll have a council? Tonight?"

"Likely." No matter what kind of slime had been forced on him, Bennington wanted to stay alive. He would use his wits and lie with a grave expression, assuming that the Sioux chiefs granted him the right to speak before them.

He looked through the doorway, past the *akecita* guards, on to the free hills beyond the stream where the camp was set. On the Little Big Horn . . . Custer wiped out? It was not possible. There had been fighting, yes, and the cavalry had been hurt, but. . . .

A tall Cheyenne came by with a hunting party that was blood-smeared. The Cheyenne stopped to ask one of the guards what was going on. Bennington kept staring at the horse the tall Cut Arm rode and, when the hunting party went on, Bennington stepped out to follow the horse with his eyes. A Fox warrior forced him back inside with a lance.

Bennington had seen enough. The sorrel was one of Custer's favorite horses, white-stockinged all the way around, a blazed forehead. Its name was Vic.

Bennington looked at Dameyer. With the cigar gone dead in his teeth Dameyer was sleeping peacefully. Snoring.

Somewhere in the valley of the Greasy Grass near the bright blue loops of the river, was it? Bennington knew the country well. He and Dameyer had been almost there when they turned back to the Rosebud after meeting the Cheyennes.

In the evening an old squaw whose hands were mutilated from mourning her dead brought food to the lodge and went away without ever looking directly into the eyes of the white men.

Dameyer roused, refreshed and confident. He retrieved the cigar that had fallen from his mouth while he slept. He picked the other cigar from the fire pit and put it inside his shirt. "Well, they're not trying to starve us, eh Bennington?" He ate with his fingers and sucked the juices from them afterward and once more asked when the council would be.

Darkness came and there was a council. Bennington heard the crier going about the camp, an old man with a deep voice. "Two white soldiers who fought against us on the Greasy Grass have come into the camp to speak to Tatanka, who will not hear their words. The chiefs will council. High Wound and Stab Bear, of the great Uncpapas, have been killed by these two white men."

The crier went away. A silence came upon the camp. Bennington heard but faintly the distant counciling of the chiefs. Quite likely Sitting Bull was not with them, or else he listened in silence, for he was no longer a warrior. His power came from dreams, from the slyness of a great intelligence; but in the end life or death for Bennington and Dameyer would be largely Sitting Bull's decision.

After two hours the council ended. No one came for the white men. Dameyer said angrily, "Tell these guards we want to talk to Sitting Bull."

"You tell them." Bennington pulled off his moccasins and went to bed.

He had never slept completely relaxed in an Indian camp. He knew when the guard changed, and later he was aware of the man who came toward the lodge and held a low-voiced conversation with the *akecita*. The flap scraped back and the man came into the darkness of the lodge. He spoke Bennington's Sioux name.

"I here." Bennington threw off the robes.

"Why are you here?" the man asked.

The darkness gave gravity to the lie Bennington told about the payroll of dead soldiers on the Greasy Grass. At first it was all a lie and then it became mixed with truths which fell simply from

Bennington's lips. He told the visitor that the quarrel of the White Father with the Sioux was one thing, and that the honoring of dead on both sides was another thing.

"The White Father did not send us to say that there will be no more fighting, or ask the Sioux not to fight again. We are not chiefs. We are only men. With the pieces of paper we will know the dead. We will honor them. This is all we ask of the Sioux, who honor their warriors who die bravely."

There was a long silence from the man who stood before Bennington. Meager starlight came through the smoke hole of the lodge but it was not enough to reveal more than the gloomy outlines of the Sioux. Doubt rode the Indian's silence.

"These pieces of paper are traded among white men as ponies are traded among my people," the visitor said.

The man was making sure that Bennington did not mistake him for a simpleton.

"It is so," Bennington said. "The pieces of green paper are used among white men to buy what they wish from each other, but if the paper is returned to us, it will be used only to honor the soldiers who were killed."

Again the long silence ran before the dark figure spoke. "Five suns ago a dream was told in this camp. In the dream four white men were seen riding to the camp. They came to say that the White Father wishes peace, that the soldiers even now hunting for the Sioux will be sent away. You have not said this. You are only two. Where are the other two?"

This time it was Bennington who was long silent, with his mind racing over the implications of the statement and the questions. When the visitor first spoke, he had been reasonably sure of his identity, and now he was certain. Bennington asked a bargaining question of his own. "Will White Rain be heard by council?"

The visitor grunted in the affirmative.

Bennington took his time. His next words would trap him hopelessly if he had guessed wrong, or they would save both him and Dameyer. He said, "The dream was good. There were four white men sent. One turned back from fear. The other grew so sick with boils upon his back that he could not ride. Two are here. The others were chiefs and the White Father had told them to speak to the Sioux, to say that the soldiers would be sent away, to say that peace would be.

"I am not a chief and my friend is not a chief. We were to ask only for the pieces of paper to honor our dead, but I know what the others were to say and so I will say it to the council. The dream was good."

After a moment Sitting Bull turned swiftly and ducked through the lodge opening and was gone.

"What was that about?" Dameyer asked quickly.

A bargain? Yes, surely it must be a bargain. Tatanka was no chief. He was not even a warrior. There were Sioux who said he had no heart for fighting. It was known that he never went into battle. And yet he was the strong man of the Sioux and ruled a large number of them through a mixture of intelligence and medicine.

Dameyer said, "Who was that? What did he say?"

"I thought you understood some Sioux."

"Not the way you two grunted it. Who was it? Did you ask him about the money?"

"It was Pte. He said he would see about the money."

"Pte?" Dameyer asked. "Sitting Bull is the man we want."

"Pte is sacred to the Sioux." Buffalo were not only sacred but very useful to the Sioux. Bennington got back into his blankets. It was not luck that he had struck upon an Indian dream as an argument when Clouds Floating and his bunch had taken him and Bennington. Indians lived by visions.

Sitting Bull was full of dreams based on logic, or one might say that where the dream ended and logic began, a fine line lay almost indiscernible. After the great victory of the Sioux over the Seventh, was it not natural that white men would come to the Indians to talk? Sitting Bull had seen that this would be so, and if he had presented it as a result of a vision, rather than the work of a shrewd mind, that was his business.

Let him stand secure as a man of true visions. After all, he had missed but slightly the number of emissaries presumably sent by the White Father. Bennington was willing, even quite anxious, to establish the lie that Tatanka had not missed the number at all.

In fact, Bennington's life depended on it.

"Did this Pte say we would get the money?" Dameyer asked.

"He said the council would hear us."

VIII

"DEATH ALL AROUND"

They were taken in mid-morning to the meeting of chiefs outside the yellow lodge. The Sioux war leaders had already passed through their ceremonies. No pipe was offered the white men, no gestures of respect. They came as beggars to be heard.

Bennington had a long bad moment when he looked at the hostile faces, Rain-in-the-Face, Kicking Bear, Pizi, the great, straight man of the Sioux, Crazy Horse, Bear Rib, Bad Hip, Little Chief of the Cheyennes, and many others.

Sitting Bull was there, dressed in a black and white calico shirt, his strong legs wrapped in leggings of black cloth, his cloudy eyes showing nothing, his gray hair running down to frame his broad face into narrowness.

The Sioux gave Little Chief the honor of speaking all the wrongs long held against the white man by the Sioux and Cheyennes. The list was long, his voice was good, and when he made a killing point, the ranks of Sioux standing in hard quietness behind the council growled their approval like a chant. After a long time Little Chief wanted to know why two white men had come here.

In the strong daylight with the unwavering eyes of a fierce people upon him, Bennington found the lie hard to tell, but he told it with all the power and imagery he could muster.

The council listened. They were not impressed by the White Father's need of small scraps of green paper to tell the names of his dead soldiers on the Greasy Grass.

Bennington knew that he had to do much better. He spoke of the dream. "When we left the fort on the river, we said among ourselves that our coming was known. Tatanka Watanka sees that which others do not see, and so we were sure that he would know of our coming. There were four of us. One grew sick and fear overcame the other. Two of us are here.

"The other two were to speak of peace. I do not know everything they were to say and so I will not make up words, but I do know that they were to speak to Tatanka and the chiefs about peace."

Bennington saw belief come to the faces of the Sioux. It was simple for them to believe what they had heard already from Sitting Bull. Behind the chiefs the listening warriors shifted their eyes to the medicine man, paying respect.

Sitting Bull showed nothing. His eyes were drawn down tightly. His thin upper lip jutted slightly over the lower. He sat with his arms crossed and he gave the impression that he had heard nothing.

There was no more for Bennington to say. He looked above the Sioux, beyond the pony herd, out to the tawny hills. He was sweating. He waited.

Kicking Bear said, "We will consider the words of the white man." He looked to Sitting Bull, who held his withdrawn pose, not hearing.

Gall motioned to the picked warriors of the *akecita*.

They escorted Bennington and Dameyer back to the lodge.

Dameyer was in a raging worry. "Sitting Bull never opened his mouth! What happened? Do we get the money?"

Bennington sat down on his robes. "We'll see."

"You're cool enough about it. Did you purposely foul up everything? I wish to hell I'd brought somebody I could trust!"

"What really happened to Charley Reynolds, Dameyer?"

"He was killed on the Little Big Horn. You didn't swallow *all* the lies I told you, did you?"

"I'm afraid so." Bennington rose and strode to the lodge door. Once more he found himself gripping the teepee hides so hard that his wrists and forearms began to ache.

The guards went away before noon.

A short time later the procession started. No warrior or even a toothless old man joined in it. Squaws and children walked past the lodge, throwing money through the doorway. There were handfuls of notes crumpled like the sprouting leaves of rhubarb. Some of the money had been smeared with filth. An ancient squaw with a face like a frost-wrinkled apple stopped in the opening, spat upon a bill, and let it flutter to the dust.

The fire of a wolf pup burned in the eyes of a young boy who swung back his arm and hurled a piece of colored cloth wrapped around a rock. It struck against the back wall of the lodge, a cavalry guidon, crumpled and dirty. Bennington picked it up, looking at the bloodstains on the circle of gilt stars.

A Cheyenne girl who could have been no more than three threw down a toy pony made of buckskin, with a ten dollar bill tied on it as a saddle blanket.

Dameyer's eyes were alive and darting as the money began to litter the lodge floor. He snatched up a wallet with worn gold initials on it and a ragged bullet hole through it. There was money inside, a thick sheaf of notes stuck together with dried blood. Dameyer took the notes and dropped the wallet into the fire pit.

A hag with live coals for eyes thrust her withered face inside and started to hurl a scalp with a five dollar bill tied in the hair. Dameyer snatched it from her hands before she had a chance to throw it.

The long line ended. Indian boys brought the white men's horses before the lodge, with all their possessions on them. Dameyer was on his hands and knees scrabbling around the lodge. "Gather it up! Let's count it."

The amount was a little more than two thousand dollars. Dameyer cursed. "They held out on us, that's what they did! Go tell Sitting Bull we won't leave until . . . ."

"We're leaving," Bennington said quietly, "while we have the chance. They haven't got any more money. They told me they threw most of it away right at the battlefield."

"Over three weeks ago!" Dameyer said savagely. "We'll go there just the same."

"Sure."

Dameyer was stuffing the money into the big pocket inside his shirt. A map and an Army tinder kit took up too much room. He threw them into the firepit. "I'll give you your share when you get me back to one of the forts, Bennington."

It was another week before they found the battlefield. Between tufts of reddish-brown grass the soil was white and ashy on the hills above the blue loops of the Little Big Horn. The wolves and birds had been here, and the wind and rain, so that the fluffy earth heaped in haste upon the bodies of the dead was mostly gone now.

Bennington got down and led his horse through the litter of rotting equipment scattered widely on the hills. Here and there were small heaps of McClellans and rifles with broken stocks, all partially burned; and the bottoms of cavalry boots with the tops cut off, already starting to curl in the sun; and horses sinking into the earth; and empty cartridge shells spilled in the grass.

He did not count but he knew that he had seen almost a hundred bodies that had been covered with sagebrush only as a burial gesture. There were soldiers here that he had known, but there was no way of knowing them now.

Higher up the hill Dameyer was searching furiously for money. Bennington went up to him and on beyond him to where the basket from a *travois* was staked down over a grave, the only real grave that Bennington had seen.

This would be the burial place of Custer, the Yellow Hair.

"Keep looking, don't stand around!" Dameyer shouted. He plunged away toward a pair of pants hanging on a bush.

Across the basket of the *travois* Bennington looked down at the Sioux campsite on the other side of the river. It ran for miles. Someone had burned the lodge poles. Grass was already rising in the charred marks. "There were too many of us," Clouds Floating had said.

Bennington led his horse down the hill to Dameyer.

"The Sioux lied," Dameyer said. He was hot and sweating. "I haven't seen a single bill. You can't tell me that the other soldiers picked them all up. They weren't here long enough even to bury their dead. I tell you the Sioux lied, and you . . . ."

Dameyer was looking into the muzzle of Bennington's pistol. With his free hand Bennington was pulling the cavalry guidon from under his shirt.

"What's the idea?" Dameyer asked.

"I've been wanting to kill you for a long time."

"You fool! I'll give you your third of the money."

What made a man like Dameyer? What was left out of his insides, or so badly twisted that he was incomplete? Musing, staring, with the pistol in his hand, Bennington shook his head.

"Half the money then!" Dameyer shouted.

With a slow motion Bennington tossed the guidon to Dameyer.

"Pile it on that." He watched the notes tumbling from inside Dameyer's shirt. He watched the man counting. "Put it *all* down there."

Dameyer was like a cornered wolf, but he saw the curious listlessness in Bennington's eyes. He obeyed.

The money lay on the stained guidon and on the ashy soil around it. Bennington tossed down his tinder kit.

"You're crazy!" Dameyer shouted. "No, I won't!"

"Burn it."

"You're crazy!"

"Burn it."

"That's senseless, Bennington!" Dameyer flung his arm in a wide gesture. "It won't help them. It won't help anybody." Crouched on his knees he stared up at Bennington. "You've gone Indian. You're starting to believe that story you told the Sioux about honoring . . . ."

Bennington cocked the pistol.

Death was all around Dameyer and death was looking at him. His hands trembled as he ignited the tinder. The guidon turned brown, then black. A small, red-edged hole appeared in it. The hole spread but there was no flame until the money caught fire. It burned with an orange flame, with little smoke, charring away slowly.

Dameyer stared down in anguish. His heart was truly on the ground, where the wisps of smoke were dying away. "Why did you do that, Bennington?"

With the pistol Bennington motioned for Dameyer to walk away from him. The man started. He swung around and cried, "To think that I saved your life!"

"I just saved yours. Get out of my sight, Dameyer."

Bennington rode away from the mutilation and horror. From a hill above the high bluffs on the river he looked back and saw Dameyer going toward the Indian campsite. He would look there for money. He would look forever for money.

When Dameyer was completely out of sight, Bennington began to feel free and clean once more. He turned the tired gray horse toward the Rosebud.

THE CLOWN

VERNE ATHANAS was born in Cleft, Idaho. His father was a construction foreman and so his growing years were spent constantly on the move, wherever the present job happened to be. Schooling was sporadic although he did attend classes long enough in such places as an Oregon logging location designated simply as Camp 2 to learn how to read and write. In 1936 he married Alice Spencer and they came to reside in Ashland, Oregon. Writing was a career that came to him from necessity rather than by design. At eleven Athanas was stricken by rheumatic fever that later led to the chronic heart disease which plagued his adult life. He began writing Western fiction for the magazine markets in the late 1940s. If there is a predominant theme in his fiction, it is the specter of relentless determination required of a person in winning through on the American frontier in a life-struggle with the land and the hostile human environment. In his brief writing career, which spanned only fourteen years, he wrote only three novels but in them he sought to expand the conventions of the traditional Western story and in ROGUE VALLEY (Simon & Schuster, 1953) produced his masterpiece. In THE PROUD ONES (Simon & Schuster, 1952), about a lawman and his limping deputy, he created a story which not only inspired a motion picture but also the long running "Gunsmoke" series on radio and then television. MAVERICK (Dell First Edition, 1956) was his final novel, a cattle drive story which had appeared originally as a serial in *The Country Gentleman* (9/51-12/51). Many of his finest short stories are now being collected into single-author volumes. In his concern for psychological themes in his Western novels and stories he was clearly in the tradition of Les Savage, Jr., and T. T. Flynn and in his care for accuracy in historical detail he emulated the work of another Oregon author, Ernest Haycox.

Verne Athanas came on the scene too late to have his fiction published in *Lariat Story Magazine*, although he did make notable appearances in other Fiction House magazines, such as *Action Stories*, *Indian Stories*, and *Frontier Stories*. "The Clown" was Verne's original title for this story but it was changed to "Boy with a Gun" when it was published in *The Saturday Evening Post* (6/24/61). It was first anthologized as "The Clown" in SEARCH FOR THE HIDDEN PLACES (McKay, 1963) edited by E. D. Mygatt. The version which follows is based on the author's own typescript.

His name was Mike, and he was having a whale of a time in the hunting camp, even with the chore-boy work. As soon as this bunch of sports filled their licenses on buck deer, he and Uncle Lutey were going to hunt on their own. There were slick pine needles underfoot and the wondrous clean scent of morning in the high mountains, and he was just fifteen and, had he not felt the weight of his past three years, he would likely have yelled like an Indian and run for the sheer joy of it, like any twelve-year-old. But he didn't; and, when he came to the last turn in the trail, he saw the bear pawing through the scant remnants of yesterday's garbage.

Actually it was a pretty silly looking bear. For one thing it looked as if it had just got up and hadn't combed its hair yet. Its head was small, and its neck long, and some genetic accident had lightened the fur about its eyes, so that it had a high-browed, astonished look, and another lightened patch about its mouth gave it a clownish grin, a wide comic grin made all the more preposterous by the intent and dedicated way it turned and sniffed and daintily nibbled at small bits of garbage.

The boy moved back carefully, feeling a trembling excitement, and a branch caught on his sleeve and made a horrible racket. He froze, but the bear paid no heed. He retreated until he was out of the bear's sight, and then he turned and sprinted for the camp.

He cried in a desperate tone just above a whisper, "Uncle Lutey! Uncle Lutey, there's a bear up at the garbage pit! I saw him! He's up there right now!"

Lutey swung his axe and the split halves of the block fell apart on the woodpile.

"Big 'un?" he asked calmly. He was stocky, Uncle Lutey, solid and compact as an oak stump. His pate was shiny bald, under his battered old hat, and he had ruddy apple cheeks and faint blond eyebrows and an expression generally amiable.

The boy cried in incredulous dismay, "Uncle Lutey, aren't you. . . . He'll get away!"

Lutey said quietly, "So?"

"Why, why—he's a *bear!* He's up there eating our garbage!"

"Well," said Lutey dryly, "I see you managed to save what you took out today."

The boy hastily put down the garbage pail he was still carrying, feeling the hot red of embarrassment flood his face. He wheeled away and went to his tent and got out his .22 rifle. Uncle Lutey met him at the tent flaps.

"All right," said Uncle Lutey. "Mebbe I shouldn't have funned you, but you know better than to go takin' on like some of them city sports, Mike, boy." He waited and the boy looked hotly into his eyes, and saw the uncle he loved and respected above most men, and he looked down and said, "Well, heck, I just. . . . He is a wild bear, ain't he, Uncle Lutey?"

"That's the only kind we got, boy. Now you put that popgun away, an' we'll go on up an' have a look at him if he's still there."

"Well, shouldn't I take the gun, just in case?"

Lutey grinned at him. "All you'd do is irritate him with it. An' it ain't no real smart trick to get yourself caught lookin' an irritated bear right in the eyeballs. Now come on."

The bear was still there. Uncle Lutey knelt behind a big manzanita bush and watched, his .30-30 across his thigh, scarcely any bluing left to the metal, the battered stock almost entirely innocent of its original varnish.

The bear nosed in the garbage, to the dull clanking of flattened cans, took a final lick at something, lifted its clownish head and looked around vaguely. The boy, in jerking anguish, whispered, "He's getting away, Uncle Lutey. He's getting away!"

The bear went at a ridiculous rolling gait across the clearing and then was gone. The boy stared in complete disbelief. "You let him get away," he said.

Said Uncle Lutey, "Now look. This is a huntin' camp. The sports come up here an' pay good money for a chance at good huntin'. You ain't improvin' it with any extra shootin'. Second, we don't need no bear. And third, you leave that bear alone, you hear me?"

"Yes sir," he said in an offended voice.

Uncle Lutey looked at him and grinned, reached out and roughed his hair in a gesture half chiding, half affectionate.

"Bloodthirsty pup," he said. "Go on down to the grove an' pick off some of them magpies. They'll fly twenty miles to pick at a sore on a sick old cow."

He was still offended, but he couldn't stay mad under Uncle Lutey's amused scrutiny for long, and finally he grinned sheepishly and followed his uncle back to the camp.

Uncle Lutey was his dad's half brother, and a lot older. His real name was Luther, but nobody ever called him that. Uncle Lutey wasn't like any of the rest of the family. He'd been in the Forest Service and in the Army and a ranch hand and a Government hunter, and he took a little logging contract once and went broke and got disgusted and went out in the hills and lived for two years off coyote bounties. Finally, he said, he decided to give civilization one more chance and, the next they'd heard, he was working for an outfitter who had set up a string of hunting camps in the back country. Mike wouldn't have traded his invitation to come deer hunting this fall for a hatful of diamonds. Until the bear.

Somehow he couldn't get that bear out of his mind. He was walking through the woods, and it was stalking him. He turned, and it was upon him, a gaping redness of jaw and whiteness of teeth, and the little .22 was jammed—it would not fire, and the terrible jaws tore at his belly and back and thigh, while he struck at it with futile, slow-motion blows of his fists.

When he caught himself musing, he knew it was silly; but he went with great caution to the pit, and felt a sense of relief, and then, a resentment, as of having been cheated somehow, when there was no bear, no sign of it. After supper that night, he asked very casually, "Did you ever kill a bear, Uncle Lutey?"

"Couple," said Uncle Lutey.

"What did you do with 'em?" asked one of the sports.

"Et 'em."

"Don't know whether I'd be much enthused about bear meat," said the sport.

"Ain't bad if you're hungry," said Uncle Lutey.

"What kind of gun did you use?" This was the other sport, the one with the .270 rifle with the carved stock and special barrel.

"Old .30-30," said Lutey.

"Not much gun for a bear, is it?"

" 'Tis if you hit 'em right."

"Well, hell, so's a .22 if you stick it right in their ear."

Mike said, "I killed a beef steer with a .22 once." He hadn't, but his father's farmer friend had, before butchering, last fall.

The big sport, the one named Wally, said, "How many points did it have, kid?"

The other one, the gun crank, said, "Well, that's not what I said. A tame cow in a pen, that's not the same as hunting."

Mike felt himself flushing wrathfully. It seemed it always came out like this. He'd ask Uncle Lutey, and the rest of them had taken the whole thing over, and they didn't even bother to call him by his name. He was just the kid. He was as big as the little one, the gun crank, but that didn't make any difference. He got up and stalked out to the little tent he and Uncle Lutey slept in. It was early still, but he opened his sleeping bag with a quick, zipping noise and went to bed.

He dreamed about the bear that night. Next morning, on his way up with the garbage bucket, he took the .22. He heard the clunk of a tin can against a rock before he made the last turn. He put the pail down, and he moved, crouching, around the screen of brush, and then he could see over the massive shoulder of the great gray boulder—half buried yonder—to the rocky, sand-floored area which was the garbage pit.

The clown was again nosing through the camp's leavings, with its wide-eyed astonished look, its comic unchanging grin, still rumpled and frowzy-looking.

He didn't actually will any of it. It just seemed that the little rifle came up all on its own. His thumb slid the safety catch through its short arc from **Safe** to **Fire**. The front sight snuggled into the notch of the rear sight; all these things did themselves, without his thinking, without his effort; but he did not stop them, he did not hesitate.

A small detached part of him touched fleetingly on Uncle Lutey, then pushed him aside. What came after that was very like the unconscious, uncontrolled violence of the first man dropping off a limb onto the back of his prey, a sharp rock in his hand. As primitive as that, it was.

The shot snapped peevishly. The lank clownish bear flinched, snaked its head around and clacked its jaws at its own shoulder. Incredibly, it turned back and began snuffling at the garbage. He fired again.

The bear jerked half around this time, snapping at the air, looking accusingly about, high, low and around, as if for the stinging insect which had bitten it.

He got a trifle panicky then. He'd seen a .22-short drop a fat hog in its tracks, seen a long-rifle dump a steer. He pulled the sights into line on the scant sloping forehead and squeezed off. He saw the red furrow plowed, saw the spatter of hair and blood, heard the diminishing whine of the ricochet. The bear ducked its head, pawed at the streak, and a rather ludicrous whining sound came from it. He whacked another shot into the muscle of the neck, and the bear wheeled and began its incredible fast run, and he got in three more into the back and rump as it ran in its torment.

The firing pin fell on the empty chamber; then, half sick with fear and excitement, he yanked out the magazine tube and dug into his pocket for more cartridges, and he heard Uncle Lutey crying in a distant, enraged voice, "Oh, you tarnation idjut! You damned bloodthirsty whelp!"

Then Uncle Lutey came running, hurdling a bleached windfallen snag, ducking his bald pate to bull his way through a stand of manzanita. He plowed to a halt, threw up the short battered .30-30 and loosed the bellowing shot on the swing, levered, still swinging, shot again, swore loudly, violently and took a short frustrated run aside with the little gun held poised; then he lowered the weapon and turned. Under his wispy blond eyebrows, his eyes were very cold and pale and gray-blue. The little crabapple knots in his cheeks stood round and ruddy. He said thinly, "You had to do it, didn't you?"

He reached out and took the sleek .22 in his right hand. He held it by the small of the stock and walked to where the great gray stone stood out of the earth. Deliberately, almost dispassionately, he raised it, brought it down. He lifted and struck methodically, violently, and blued bits of metal were battered and bent and twisted. Screws tore from their metal embrace in agonized shrieks almost drowned under the splitting of wood. When he was finished, the .22 was irreparably ruined. He turned, and the nostrils of his small button nose were flared with the force of his breathing.

"Had to do it, didn't you?" he cried again. "Oh, damn it, boy!"

Mike stood, uncertainly, half sickened in reaction, frightened half to death. So he looked at Uncle Lutey, afraid but not retreating, wishing he could, but knowing he couldn't, and Uncle Lutey's eyes were harder to meet than the shattering eye of the sun itself.

Then, little by little, the fire went out of Uncle Lutey; the screwed-down violence within him seemed to lessen, and then, in a sudden shocking gesture, he tossed the .30-30 at Mike and threw an arm out violently. "There's a blood trail. Get on it!"

He got on it. He went uncertainly across the clearing, and the bear's scuffed prints were plain enough. Just inside the yonder shelter of brush the earth was scuffed and torn, as if the bear had fallen and then scrambled up, and here there was blood, a great sprayed gout of blood, and there a splash, and beyond. . . .

He wasn't quite sure where he lost the track. Somewhere between the thickets' far edge and the slanting spine of the stony ridge he came to a stop and looked about, with a sinking sensation of loss, of disorientation. No stone had been disturbed, at least to his eye. No blood showed. Nothing. He stood alone on the steep slope scabrous with volcanic rock and ash, small grasses and shrub clinging with bitter tenacity to all the small crevices and fissures. If the bear had been this way, they did not care or show, not by so much as a bruised or juiceless leaf or bent dry stalk.

He heard the sound and wheeled on it, and Uncle Lutey came through the thinning edge of the fir thicket and trudged up to him, looking tired and grim and unfriendly.

"Lost him?"

"I guess so."

"Circle. Like I showed you on deer tracks. He won't be hidin' his trail, sick as he is."

He circled. A hundred feet above he found a splash, darkening red, a small rock turned, its underbelly paler and unweathered, compared to the rest around it.

"Here," he said, and Uncle Lutey came and nodded, and they went on.

They topped the ridge, and Uncle Lutey stared gloomily downslope. "Figgered," he said. He led off down the long far slope. The trail pitched sharply down and into a fern-shouldered creek bank. In the soft shoulder ferns were uprooted, two long slide marks showed on the bank. Hurrying water had washed all else away. Uncle Lutey plunged in, ignoring the rush of water that went over the tops of his ten-inch laced boots. Mike thought maybe the bear had gone through like that, lunging and driving, the water rushing and soaking its rumpled furry hide.

Mike plunged in—as Uncle Lutey had done, as probably the bear had done—and his ankle turned under, and a small hot knife drove itself clear to the bone, and he went in a headlong sousing splash. The water rammed itself into his mouth and halfway down his throat and snatched at him and rolled him and simultaneously struck him head to heels with a searing cold shock.

His lashing hand bruised itself on slick bottom stone; he bucked up with his rump, trying to get his feet under him and his head up out of this chill strangler which was trying to kill him; he came up and cleared the water from his throat in a choking bawl and fell down again as his leg buckled under him; he lunged forward again, gasping with shock. He crawled his way up the ferny bank and sat, streaming water, gasping and choking. Somehow he still held the .30-30, and he laid it aside and reached almost fearfully for the ankle that had buckled under him. Uncle Lutey came and knelt by him.

"Lemme have a look at it, lad," he said

Mike unlaced the ankle-high shoe and slid it off. He made a grunting sound through his clenched teeth. He almost went up like a rocket when Uncle Lutey gently moved the foot.

"Probably a sprain," decided Uncle Lutey, "which means some-thin's tore instead of broke."

He rocked back on his heels and looked at Mike, and Mike read it as a compound of pity and contempt. "You won't walk much further on that," said Uncle Lutey, "sprain *or* break."

It was a thought warm and comforting. He didn't have to go on. He couldn't go on. He didn't have to see the clown bear again. He didn't have to go on and on with this cold black ball swinging and sagging in the pit of his stomach. "The hell I don't," he said. He didn't mean to say it. He didn't want to say it. But he said it.

Uncle Lutey looked at him. "Don't be a damn fool," he said. "You'll do good to make it back to camp."

He didn't look at Uncle Lutey. He tried to remember. There was something in the first-aid book. Triangular bandage. He didn't have a triangular bandage. There was the bandanna in his hip pocket. Folded cornerwise and then again and again until it looked more like a red cravat than anything else. The middle under the arch and the ends around the back of the heel and crossed at the instep and under the sides of the arch bight, and boy, it hurt, trying to get the ends yanked far enough through to tie over the instep. It was clumsy, but it locked the ankle pretty solid. He pulled on the wet shoe and that hurt, too, and it wouldn't lace more than a few holes over the wet sock and the wet bandage.

He tried getting up. His lips peeled back from his teeth, and he held back the cry only with great effort, seeing the thin grin on Uncle Lutey's face. Then he realized that Uncle Lutey was only matching his own pained grimace, feeling the pain as he was feeling it, and it shamed and angered him. He loosed his grip on his uncle's arm and let his weight come solidly on the ankle, and in his mind he roared silently and profanely at the sword of pain which slashed at him. He took a hobbling step, and another.

He swung on Uncle Lutey, grinning the grin that was almost pure pain, and he said through his teeth, "O.K., I can make it now."

Lutey said quietly, "Look, now, you could cripple yourself for good that way."

He said through the hurting grin, "My foot, ain't it?"

Lutey looked at him, a good long look. Then he said, "All right. Lemme cut you a stick an' get some of the water off of the gun."

Lutey wiped down the .30-30 as best he could, dried off the cartridges, and shoved them back into the magazine. He cut Mike a staff, heavy as a shovel handle and some four feet long. Mike leaned on it and reached out for the carbine.

Lutey said dryly, "Don't try to be too damn big a hero, boy. I got a good hunch where that bear's headin'. Save your strength. You'll need it." He swung away then, carrying the gun, and Mike hobbled after him. It hurt. It hurt like everything. But it felt better than turning back.

The sun was straight overhead. His shadow was no blacker than the black burned earth underfoot. The burn was hell-cooled a little. It had burned a year ago, or two—not much more. For the earth still shrank from the flame which had roared here; and only here and there were stubborn brush clumps pushing up from the crowns burned over and buried under ash and charcoal. What had been a great forest thicket was jackstrawed poles now, heat-hardened giants' lances of wood insulated in black char, heaped and tangled and interlaced down a long dry cañon.

The clown bear's track led straight into it. Into it and through it, squeezed between charred boles scarcely a foot apart, diving into a laced tangle; a maze that smeared a man with its coated smut, a powdered lampblack that found its own grease in a man's sweat and there mixed and clung.

Mike swallowed black cotton in his throat, and it didn't swallow worth a hoot. All the inner recesses of his nostrils were burning, and he breathed through his open mouth in gasping inhalations. He swung up a leg to cross still another charred pole and bumped the bandaged ankle in the half-laced shoe, and it didn't hurt at all, except that he went over the pole in a slow-motion fall, a silly, aimless fall, with the black spears wheeling against the blue sky and the hard black powder-coated earth coming up and smacking him alongside the face, and *Hoo, boy, that was a jolt, and maybe I just ought to lie here a minute and get my bearings,* and Uncle Lutey, leaning down, looking concerned.

"Mike," said Uncle Lutey from somewhere way, way off. "You all right, boy?"

He pushed himself up, feeling foolish. "I'm all right."

Lutey said, still from far away, "Better rest a bit, boy. Why don't you set down while I take a little jog ahead an' see if that little spring's plumb dried out?"

There was a ringing in his ears that faded in and out, came nigh and went distant. "I'll make it," he said.

He hobbled, hurting. He and the bear. He and Lutey, ducking and lunging and working through the down stuff ahead like a beagle through a briar patch. But there wasn't any end to this dismal blackened hell of a tangle.

He knew. The bear knew. There wasn't any end. There wasn't anything but the steady wrenching pain of one hurting step after another, one and another, and another and another, on and on into the endless tangle, because the bear had to go here—something made the bear go here—and he had to follow, and he'd forgotten why, now, but he had to follow, because that was the way it was.

He could smell wetness. It was impossible, but he could.

"Well, that's it, what's left of it," said Uncle Lutey. "Was a nice little spring, 'fore the fire." Now there was only a swale of damp earth, pocked with animal tracks and littered with their droppings.

"He wallered there," said Uncle Lutey, pointing, and the bear's tracks went over and through the others, and there was a trough in the muddy middle of this circle of wet earth, small ridges pushed up so recently that they slid and crumbled at the edges as they watched. Uncle Lutey stooped, put a hand on the wet earth, and then knelt and began digging with his hands and a slab-ended stub of a limb.

Mike sat down—almost fell down, really. He thought vaguely maybe he ought to help, but he simply sat, the seat of his jeans growing warmly damp. Uncle Lutey stopped digging and water seeped slow as death into the bottom of the hole he'd dug. Black water. Lutey scooped it out with his cupped hands, threw it aside and waited again, and again water seeped in, a trifle cleaner now, and he scooped up a double handful and splashed it on his face, sluicing soot and small dirty rivers. He snorted prodigiously and wiped the wet back of his hand across his mouth. Water came back into the hole, antagonizingly slow.

Finally he said, "O.K., have a drink."

"Go ahead," Mike croaked. "You first." But Uncle Lutey knelt, waiting, and Mike went down onto his belly and thrust his head down into the hole and sucked up water. It tasted like wet burned wood and smelled like swamp and he'd never had a better drink in his life. He hoisted himself up.

Uncle Lutey drank. He looked across at Mike, then said, "No sense lyin' to you, boy. I didn't think he'd make it this far. The last couple hours, I didn't think you'd make it. Now we got anyway another mile of this, an' then the creek we crossed way up yonder and this draw come together. But it ain't no creek no more. It's swamp. Mean swamp. There's places you could lose a herd of cattle, much less a bear tryin' to find himself a place to hide out an' heal up."

Mike doubled his good leg under him. He gripped the staff with both hands and the end of it sank into the damp earth as his weight came on it, and he pried himself up and onto his feet.

"He ain't goin' to heal up," he said.

"No," said Uncle Lutey reluctantly.

"All right then," said Mike. He stooped and got the .30-30. He straightened, feeling a little dizzy and at the same time stronger for the short rest and the drink of water. He turned and hobbled past the last track in the soft damp earth, ducked under a chest-high windfall, not waiting for Uncle Lutey, not looking back.

Almost imperceptibly the cañon walls fell away on either side. He plodded on. Uncle Lutey came alongside and tried to take the gun from him, and he shrugged him off almost without knowing he did it. The tangle of charred poles gave way to brush and scrub, and then suddenly he was in a rank thicket of fir and aspen and then aspen and willow, and now there was no horizon, nothing but the lush and crowding growth, and once he stepped down into a place as solid as any to the eye and went halfway to his knee in a pocket of muck.

The trail was a scarcely visible furrow in the rank grass. It skirted an island of cattails and went straight into a wall of willows. Mike dropped the staff, held the .30-30 in his right hand, hauled himself through the stubborn slick-barked tangle with the other. The ankle didn't hurt any more. It was merely a dully aching club end, swung none too dependably from his knee. Usually when he put his weight on it, it held and, when it didn't, he caught himself on the willows.

He came on the bear without warning. It lay, hind legs back and forelegs out, flat on its belly, head down on forepaws but not asleep, for the eyes followed him, and slow, dragging breaths moved the shaggy sides, and soft bubbling sounds came and went.

Mike moved as a sleepwalker might, in a wondering numbness, limping toward the bear, and the little eyes followed him, but with detachment, with a vast indifference.

Lutey cried an alarm, "Now, dammit, boy, be careful!" but Mike kept on until he stood no more than ten feet from the bear, and the bear raised its clownish head and looked at him, and its mouth fell open in a vacuous idiotic grin, where Lutey's last bullet had struck and broken its jaw. The grinning mouth drooled its slow red drip, and suddenly the bear went all misty and blurry, and a great twisting knot came in Mike's belly. He couldn't look into the eyes watching him so disinterestedly and dispassionately from under the high clownish brows.

He moved aside, and the head turned slowly to follow him, though the bear did not move otherwise, and from somewhere far away Uncle Lutey cried again, "Mike!" The bear looked back in Uncle Lutey's direction and took those terribly disinterested eyes away, and Mike thrust the muzzle almost against the side of the clownish head with its ridiculous uncombed look and pulled the trigger.

The recoiling rifle almost tore itself from his hands. The bear's head jolted to the impact and then fell to its forepaws. A slow, sighing breath came from it, and the shoulders sank, and the hind legs made one long, slow sleepy stretching motion, and then there was nothing—no motion, no sound, nothing.

Mike fell to his knees. Something crowded up in his throat. Something harsh choking and bitter. "I'm sorry," he said, almost without knowing he'd said it. "I'm sorry."

He reached out a hand and touched the coarse, unkempt hair, felt a small low-set ear bend under his touch, felt the warmth of life still under the unkemptness, and suddenly he was crying as he hadn't cried since he was ten years old, crying desperately and full-heartedly and without any reservations at all, with his hand clutching desperately in the long shaggy fur of the dead clownish bear.

AFTER WHAT SEEMED A LONG TIME, Lutey said from somewhere behind him, "Look, its a couple miles over to the other camp. I'm goin' to borrow a couple horses. You stay put till I get back, now."

He didn't trust his voice. He just bobbed his head without looking around, and it must have been all right, because Uncle Lutey went away without saying any more. He wiped his eyes and scrubbed at his nose with a sleeve and felt himself completely emptied out and used up. He was asleep, with his head against the bear's shaggy shoulder, when Uncle Lutey came back and shook him.

Uncle Lutey said gruffly, not looking at him, "Well, guess we can skin him out, save the hide, anyway. Doubt anybody'd eat the meat, gun shot an' fevered the way it is."

Mike looked up in protest. "I don't want the hide," he said. "I don't want anything." He swallowed. "Uncle Lutey?"

"Yuh, boy."

"Is it a law . . . like with a deer . . . that you got to . . . to take it, save the meat and like that?"

"Well, no, not really. He's a varmit, the law says. I never held with killing somethin' an' just leavin' it lay, but why?"

"Well, I . . . ,"—he looked away from Uncle Lutey, feeling like a fool, but going on with it,—"I'd kind of like to bury him. Like . . . you know . . . ?"

He waited a moment, afraid to look at Lutey, afraid of what he'd see on his face. Finally his uncle said, "Figgered you might, boy. Fetched one of them foldin' Army shovels from the other camp."

He looked up at Uncle Lutey then, and Lutey looked back; and Lutey said, "Had it in my mind a time or two to rub it in a little, Mike. Ask you how you liked it, hot an' dirty an' hurtin' an' beat out. But I didn't have to do that, because it wasn't me teachin' you no lesson. You know it, an' you done your own teachin'. You do wrong, an' it costs you . . . one way or another. How much of it you remember an' how much you learn by it, that's up to you. Now, come on. I'll help you."

Mike sat, looking his uncle full in the face. "Thanks," he said. "Thanks, Uncle Lutey."

"Why," said Lutey, "you're welcome."

And, somehow, the old and trite response satisfied them both.

THE SILENT OUTCAST

LAURAN PAINE, who under his own name and various pseudonyms has written over 900 books, was born in Duluth, Minnesota, a descendant of the Revolutionary War patriot and author, Thomas Paine. His family moved to California when he was at an early age and his apprenticeship as a Western writer came about through the years he spent in the livestock trade, rodeos, and even motion pictures where he served as an extra because of his expert horsemanship in several films starring movie cowboy, Johnny Mack Brown. In the late 1930s, Paine trapped wild horses in northern Arizona and even, for a time, worked as a professional farrier. Paine came to know the Old West through the eyes of many who had been born in the previous century and he learned that Western life had been very different from the way it was portrayed on the screen. "I knew men who had killed other men," he later recalled. "But they were the exceptions. Prior to and during the Depression, people were just too busy eking out an existence to indulge in Saturday-night brawls." He served in the U. S. Navy in the Second World War and began writing for Western pulp magazines following his discharge. It is interesting to note that all of his earliest novels (written under his own name and the pseudonym Mark Carrel) were published in the British market and he soon had as strong a following in that country as in the United States.

Paine's Western fiction is characterized by strong plots, authenticity, an apparently effortless ability to construct situation and character, and a preference for building his stories upon a solid foundation of historical fact. ADOBE EMPIRE (Hamilton, 1955), one of his best novels, is a fictionalized account of the last twenty years in the life of trader William Bent and, in an off-trail way, has a melancholy, bittersweet texture that is not easily forgotten. It was first published in the United States in 1993 by Chivers North America. MOON PRAIRIE (Hamilton, 1950), first published in the United States in 1994 by Thorndike Press, is a memorable story set during the mountain man period of the frontier. In later novels such as THE HOMESTEADERS (Walker, 1986) or THE OPEN RANGE MEN (Walker, 1990), Paine showed that the special magic and power of his stories and characters had only matured along with his basic themes of changing times, changing attitudes, learning from experience, respecting nature, and the yearning for a simpler, more moderate way of life.

Double-Action Western was first published by Winford Publications, Inc., beginning with the issue dated September, 1934. Abner J. Sundell was the editor. The magazine proved sufficiently successful that the next year Winford launched *Real Western* and in 1937 *Famous Western*. In early 1940 Winford Publications put all of its double-action magazine group on hiatus. They were eventually acquired by Columbia Publications, Inc. Robert W. Lowndes became editor for the Western magazines, *Real Western*, *Famous Western*, and *Double-Action Western*. Lauran Paine began writing extensively for the double-action group in the early 1950s and Lowndes proved to be a mentor for him. "The Silent Outcast" first appeared in *Double-Action Western* (1/54) and has not been previously collected.

I

The saga of Caleb Doorn was well known across the wide, savage frontier. In lonely trapper's camps, in the buffalo chip evening fires of cattle drovers, hide hunters, explorers, soldiers, scouts, even Indian teepees, his story was told, along with the legends of his feats. Still, there were very few of these hardy, courageous souls who had ever seen him, or who would associate the lean, gray-eyed man lounging against a rough log pole before Elmore's Emporium, in Willow Creek, with the savage, daring fighting man who had been court-martialed at Santa Fé and drummed off the post for insubordination. Caleb Doorn was more than a legend; he was almost a myth. To the whites he was a dread, yet fascinating man, lethal with a Kiowa-Apache scalping knife, a long, cumbersome dragoon pistol, or with his fists and booted feet. He had refused to advance against a bristling Comanche village with his unprotected troop of cavalry and had been dismissed from the Army. He wasn't a coward, the whites agreed; he just wouldn't take orders.

By the Indians he was grudgingly admired; he was their kind of a fighting man. He fought and thought independently, as a man should, not as a machine, to be ordered here and there regardless of circumstances. They had reason to know him well, for Caleb Doorn's bridle and knife sheath were decorated with little wisps of black, coarse hair. Indian hair.

Among the slightly grinning fraternity of frontiersmen who challenged the Indians, the whites, the soldiers and even Nature herself, Caleb Doorn was openly agreed with and liked. This reckless, loose brotherhood of marked men was scornful of regimentation, authority, or rule by anything except their own force. They laughed derisively at the soldiers, smiled grimly at the Indians, and out-maneuvered both in an era of lawlessness and violence that kept the far country open only to the daring and able.

Willow Creek was a small trading settlement nestled along a busy little creek fed from the run-off snow waters of the Bitteroot Mountains. It consisted of six log buildings that housed a saloon, a church, Elmore's Emporium, a massive, well-stocked old trading post, and the several houses that sheltered the permanent residents.

In the spring of the year, the little creek at the edge of Willow Creek blossomed out with wild flowers and emigrant wagons, their dusty, worn sailcloth coverings off-white and stained as the bone-weary, gaunt travelers rested before taking up the trackless battle over the mountains and through the Indian country. Caleb Doorn, fringed buckskin pants and long hunting-shirt mildly greasy and stained, leaned indolently against the massive log that helped support the rough board overhang before Elmore's store and watched apathetically as a small band of dirty, creaking wagons pulled frowsily up to the creek. His right hand hung unconsciously beside the sky blue, beaded scalping-knife with its forked, stag handle. At the bottom of the gaudy sheath hung a small circular twig from which dangled three miserly tufts of black, rank hair. On the opposite hip, suspended from the sweat-stained, wide, dark belt that encircled his waist hung a long-barreled cavalry pistol of Colt's manufacture. The bead-encrusted moccasins finished off the lean-hipped, broad-shouldered figure and the deep-set, calm, and thoughtful gray eyes seemed to be lethargic; but they didn't miss a thing as the ragged travelers down at the creek went about setting up camp.

Caleb Doorn, on first sight, appeared deceptively docile and lazy, but a closer study showed small things that had been unnoticed at first. There was the impassiveness of the eyes; the slight prominence of the rounded jaw and chin; the thin, slightly hawkish nose and the quick, gracefully casual movements of the muscular body. All the things one had heard then began to suddenly take creditable shape, for there was a hard-to-define capability about the man that was at once a warning and a promise that, once aroused, Caleb Doorn would be very dangerous.

The emigrants down at the creek were nothing out of the ordinary. There were scrawny women, gaunt, hollow-cheeked men, and fragile, solemn-faced youngsters. The wagons were battered and scarred and the livestock was thin and dry-eyed with fatigue. Automatically the travelers set up their camp and built small, fragrant fires; spirits arose gradually and nasal voices sang out to one another. The sounds drifted up to the solid section of Willow Creek, and the Emporium's proprietor—short, hard-eyed, capable and, dogmatic Si Elmore—came out onto the plank walk built under the overhang of his store and looked callously down at the emigrant camp.

Speaking to no one in particular, he grunted aloud, "More of 'em. Means the pass is open again. Reckon the Oregon and Californy travelers'll be commencin' to come again. That means spring is here." He turned abruptly and saw Doorn watching the camp too. "Caleb, 'pears to me that Californy oughta be filled up by now."

Doorn tossed a casual, disinterested look at Elmore, grunted audibly, and returned to his speculative watching of the emigrants. His thoughts were somber and shrewd. The nation had recently gone through one of the worst civil wars in history and never had a country been better equipped to turn its face westward than was America. Eighty percent—perhaps more—of the emigrants had borne guns through the bloody conflict; and now, trained and inured to hardship, they were setting out to conquer and open up their newest possession, the American West. It wasn't like the Crusades, he thought, where the warriors rode forth full of pride and piety, to be butchered by a savage and fanatical foe who knew all about contemporary fighting. These people were as hard and as ruthless, at the core, as the land and the savages they were pitting themselves against. He straightened up and walked silently away, balanced on the balls of his feet like a mountain man. Elmore watched him head toward the camp along the river with a thoughtful gaze. He shook his head slightly and went back into the store.

"California?" Doorn watched the man as he spoke.

The sun-tanned, hawk-faced emigrant looked closely at Doorn before nodding his head. He guessed the frontiersman to be a squawman, one of those white men who forsook their own kind and went Indian. As yet he was new on the frontier, and beads and buckskin meant only one thing to him: Injuns.

"I reckon. At least we're headin' that way."

Doorn nodded slowly. "You're the first party through so far this year. You goin' to wait for another train before goin' on?"

The man snorted derisively. "Hell, no. What fer?"

"Indians."

"Ain't seen any yet that'd scare me, and we've come a long ways."

Doorn's eyes were sardonic. It was an old story to him; the plains and forests were full of unknown graves and scattered bones. Scorn, contempt, and over-confidence had accounted for more butchery on the trail than ignorance. He let his eyes wander from the thick, black, low-heeled boots of the emigrant up past his shapeless, dirty woolen britches tucked into the boots. He saw the scarred old cartridge belt, the battered pistol, a butternut shirt of homespun, faded cloth, and the bewhiskered, lined face of a young man whose life had left harshness and hardship etched deep into every pore. The eyes were good, Doorn decided. Young and brazenly courageous, but good steady eyes.

"You the leader of this train?"

"Yep. Name's Josh Harris." The man looked inquiringly at Doorn. "You a . . . a . . . a native?"

Doorn didn't smile, although he felt like it. The emigrant's fumbling over the insulting term, "squawman," wasn't new to him. He nodded and shrugged a little when he answered. "I reckon you could call me that."

His pensive eyes went beyond the younger man to the vast, rolling, endless landscape of primeval wilderness ringed with majestic, purplish mountains in the hazy distance. "At least I been out here a long time. Long enough to know you'll never get to California with only three, four wagons."

The emigrant smiled slyly. "We got somethin' that'll guarantee our passage among the heathens." Doorn eyed the man carefully and said nothing. Finally the younger man turned and beckoned to Doorn. "Come with me fer a second. I'll show you our passport to Californy."

Together they walked through the motley, ragged camp, with its swirling little gusts of wood smoke, to a wagon, older than the rest, patched and warped. The emigrant jumped lightly to the high poop from the wheel hub and Caleb followed him. Inside the wagon, among the soiled, pathetic possessions of the young man's family, Doorn saw something that made him catch his breath. Sitting defiantly, arms bound tightly behind her back, large, obsidian eyes blazing scorn and contempt, sat an Indian girl. Doorn looked up quickly to the emigrant who was smiling broadly, wolfishly. The man nodded indifferently toward the girl.

"That there's our passport. Won't no Injuns jump us if they know we'll crack her skull when they do."

Anger leaped into Caleb's face, anger and contempt mixed with a little frustration. For a long moment he didn't speak. The Indian girl was tall and shapely with jet black hair, full, firm lips, and a thin bridged nose below expressive, haughty eyes. Her clothing was chalky white, beaded buckskin with long, graceful fringes that waved sinuously when she moved. The emigrant was startled when he looked at her. For the first time since her capture, she was smiling slightly, her eyes on Caleb Doorn.

"Where'd you get her?"

"Caught her bathin' in a little creek about twenty miles back." Harris wagged his head slowly and looked balefully at the captive. "Damned heathen. Fought like a cougar. Like to laid out three men afore we got ropes on her."

"You'd better release her."

"Not by a damned sight."

"You're new on the frontier. Her people will attack you for kidnapping her. If you kill her when they attack, they'll kill every man, woman, and child in your party."

Harris shook his head grimly. "They won't attack us while we have her for a hostage."

Doorn sighed in exasperation. "Harris, you're a fool. Indians don't value life like we do. First, they'll attack you for stealing her; second, they'll fight like demons if you harm her. Alive or dead, you signed your own death warrant when you tied her up."

The emigrant shook his head doggedly, stubbornly. It wasn't in his make-up to concede a point in an argument. "She stays here, our prisoner."

Doorn turned abruptly toward the handsome Indian girl and knelt beside her. His tongue wrapped itself readily around the guttural, moist dialect of her people, the dreaded Blackfeet. "Who are you?"

"Singing In The Clouds."

"Who is your father?"

"Two Shoots, hereditary chieftain of the Siksika."

"How is it that you are here?"

The girl's black eyes swung venomously toward Josh Harris, who was listening to the unfamiliar Algonquin tongue with uneasiness on his frowning features. "He and four other white men caught me in a creek, taking my bath. They roped me, tied me, and made me their prisoner. The Blackfeet are not at war with the whites, but my family will avenge me." The words were spat out and there was no mistaking the anger behind them.

Josh Harris shuffled his feet uncomfortably and looked away. Doorn continued squatting in silence for a long time.

Singing In The Clouds turned her handsome face to him, studied his thoughtful features for a moment, and spoke again. "I know you. You are Many Coups, the white man, Caleb Doorn. Called by the Sioux, Silent Outcast." Doorn nodded soberly and remained silent. "You have argued with this outlander. You asked him to release me."

Doorn's head came up. "Do you speak English?"

"Well enough to understand what was said."

"Do these white emigrants know that?"

"No, Many Coups, they do not. I have pretended not to speak their tongue. It is better that way. They say what they wish in front of me. To them I am a dirty heathen." Again the eyes flashed and Doorn felt an inner thrill at the scorn and rampant fury in their passionate depths. "It is good that I know what they plan. If they are attacked, I am to be offered as a peace-token or killed."

A sardonic smile showed her even, pearly white teeth. "Whether I live or die, these fools will learn a deadly lesson, will they not?"

Doorn ignored the question. "Singing In The Clouds, if I can get them to set you free, will you repay me by telling your people to let them go across the great hills without trouble?"

"Will you be with them?"

"No. I am waiting at Willow Creek for a white soldier and his troops. I am to guide them south to the land of the Mexicans where there will soon be a war."

"Then I will not try to protect these travelers."

Doorn looked into the uncompromising eyes and saw no mercy.

For a long, electric moment, their eyes remained locked. Doorn knew better than to let his gaze falter before an Indian, for the plains people evaluated a man by his courage alone, and a weak, unsteady eye was, to them, a sure sign of cowardice and treachery. Singing In The Clouds suddenly averted her gaze and a soft, dark blush swept over her. She had heard many stories of this celebrated, morose outcast and in her heart she recognized that here was a man she could live beside. The thought caused a wave of confusion within her firm, large breast, and she looked away in half fright, half surprise.

Caleb's voice was low when next he spoke. "Then I must go with them. Singing In The Clouds, they are fools, but they shouldn't be killed because of their ignorance. They will not wait for another train. They will go on alone. Let them go, Singing In The Clouds. They are not going to stop in the land of the Blackfeet. Let them go far beyond your home, to the land that meets the great sea."

Without looking up, she answered stubbornly in a warm voice. "Only if you go with them."

"Then I will go with them. Is it that the brave Blackfeet want me out of their country too?"

"No, Silent Outcast," in using the Sioux name instead of the Blackfeet name, Singing In The Clouds was acknowledging belief in all the firelight legends she had heard of this strange man. "No; the Blackfeet respect you. But unless you go with these fools, the Blackfeet will not respect them, and their bones will . . . ."

"I go with them, then." Doorn arose abruptly, looked for a long moment into the black eyes of the girl, drew his heavy-handled scalping knife, leaned forward, and slashed the ropes that held her in a quick, fluid movement. Josh Harris leaped forward with a deep growl as the girl flexed her aching arms. Doorn turned on him, his knife held menacingly.

"Don't make it any worse, Harris. This girl goes free."

"Who the hell d'ya think you are, comin' in here and cuttin' our prisoner loose. She . . . ."

Doorn's knife slid noiselessly into its beaded sheath as he interrupted the angry emigrant. "I'm still leaving you a hostage, Harris. I'll go with you myself." The emigrant looked uncertainly from the girl to Doorn.

"What can you do for us? That there Injun girl would be a better trade, in a pinch, than you'd be."

Doorn smiled softly, his eyes watching Harris like a hawk. "Go on up to the Willow Creek store and ask Elmore about me. I reckon he'll figure you got the best of the trade. I'll get you through the Blackfeet if anybody can."

Josh Harris wasn't a quick-tempered man, and the complications that had suddenly engulfed his plan of using the Indian girl for a hostage made him wonder if, after all, the strange white man wasn't right. Without a word he swung around, clambered out of the wagon and, taking long, purposeful steps, headed toward the Willow Creek general store.

II

Doorn helped the girl to the ground, scowled at the startled emigrants, and hustled her toward the village before any of the watching wagoners could collect their wits sufficiently to question him. Once behind Elmore's massive log building, Doorn yanked free the tied reins of a saddleless little sorrel mare, boosted the girl up, and pointed back the way the wagons had come.

"Don't stay on the trail, and don't stop until you get back to the Siksika. Go."

Singing In The Clouds looked down at his bronzed, lean face for a quiet moment, then nodded her head gently. "I owe you something, Silent Outcast."

Caleb managed a crooked little smile. "You owe me nothing. Would any sane man . . . Indian or white . . . try to keep a hawk in a cage, or an oriole hidden, or a beautiful woman a slave?" He shook his head emphatically, answering his own questions in Algonquin. "No. Only a fool would try. Don't blame them for their ignorance, Singing In The Clouds. Pity them for the great store of knowledge they don't possess. Go."

The girl nodded again, took a fleeting, hungry look at his face again, whirled the sorrel mare and loped off. Caleb Doorn stood slouching in the shade of a massive old cottonwood watching the lithe, supple body sway rhythmically with the jerky stride of the little mare, lost in thought. That was the finest specimen of an Indian maiden he had ever seen. The fragrant, caressing touch of a vagrant spring zephyr blew over him and the rich luxury of the wild land rode headily on its breath. Doorn sighed and scratched his ribs lustily.

Evidently Elmore had given Doorn a good send-off. At any rate Josh Harris, deeply impressed, met him when he returned to the emigrants' camp along the creek. "If you'll tell me where your horse is, I'll send a boy for it."

Doorn shook his head. "I don't have one anymore."

"You mean you give it to that girl?"

Doorn shrugged. "Wasn't much account anyway. It was a Cheyenne pony I got when I was ridin' in a Sioux raiding party." He let his eyes roam over the emigrants, who had heard who he was and were surreptitiously studying him. "Maybe I can buy one from you folks."

Harris motioned toward an iron stew pot suspended from a bowed twig. "Come on, let's eat. I haven't had my mornin' meal yet. Hell, I got six, seven good horses. You can have your pick. Be glad to have someone else worry about one of 'em for a while. Anyway, I got all I can do keepin' things runnin' 'thout worryin' about extra horses."

Harris's wife, a youngish woman looking washed-out with a thin-lipped mouth and hard, tired eyes, nodded respectfully at Caleb and handed both men a wooden bowl full of a watery, aromatic stew.

They sat and ate. Caleb hadn't known he was hungry until he ate. "How long you goin' to stay at Willow Creek?"

"Leavin' right after we eat. Only stopped to get three wheels re-tired anyway. Figger to get across them mountains afore it sets in hot. They say the land on the other side is a reg'lar desert and hotter'n hell 'thout water."

Doorn nodded. "That's right. But this early in the year there ought to be plenty of water for a while yet." He ate slowly, his eyes roaming over the gaunt people, taciturn and tired, and the listless oxen and horses. "You oughta have a week or so to rest up the stock, though, from the looks of things."

Harris frowned into his stew bowl. "I know it, but we can't rest this side of them hills." His face brightened. "We'll lay over a week or two when we get onto the desert. That'll give the critters a chance to pick up. The folks, too."

Doorn watched a bony mare suckling a knobby-kneed little colt who was frantically hunting for milk that wasn't there. "It's bad to start over the hills with weak stock. There's a lot of bones up there. Not just animals, either, that've been caused by failing critters."

Harris's scowl was coming back. Doorn saw the stubborn set of his jaw and decided to say no more. "Well, we got no choice, Doorn, so I reckon we'll have to try it. Through?" Doorn nodded and handed the empty bowl to Harris's wife, who quickly sluiced it out and packed it away.

Three men approached Harris and he nodded to them, pointing a blunt forefinger at Caleb. "Mr. Doorn's goin' to guide us over the passes through them mountains yonder?" The three men looked gravely at Caleb, who stood up and nodded to them. One of the men, a wizened little man of indeterminate years and mousey hair, spat lustily into the dust before he spoke. "Reckon we got a chance, just three wagons?"

Doorn shrugged and Harris jumped into the breach. "Sure. What's to stop us?"

One of the other men, a big-handed farmer fresh from the Union

Army, named Jack Bedford, grinned sourly. "You always bein' in a hurry has made us right good time, Josh, but I allow the stock's in pretty hard shape to go a-scalin' them hills up ahead."

Harris's eyes clouded and that peculiar set that Doorn had noticed to his jaw came out. "Jack, we got a goal. We gotta get across them deserts afore summer sets in, you fellers know all that." He shrugged slightly, resignedly. "Sure, the critters'll suffer, but they'll get their rest pretty soon. Now let's git hitched."

He turned to the unspoken member of the trio, a dark, thick-shouldered man who chewed tobacco with the rhythmic monotony of a cow chewing her cud. "Seth, fetch up that chunky bay horse of mine, will you? Doorn, here, will need it to ride ahead and scout out the trails."

The three men nodded and walked away. Harris watched them go for a speculative moment, his frown slight but unmistakable. "Always a-worryin', them fellers are."

Storekeeper Elmore, dry washing his pudgy hands on a flour sack apron, stood beside a tall, graceful Delaware Indian and watched the creaking, lurching wagons start the torturous, gradual climb into the balsam-scented mountains ahead. He wagged his head disapprovingly."Now just how in hell's that there sol'jer, Gin'l Kearney, gonna find his way into the Mexican country down south?"

The Delaware, without taking his eyes off of the tall, buckskin-clad figure ahead of the lazy dust stirred up by the ponderous wagons, spoke softly. "I take sol'jers. Caleb Doorn tell me, he no back three, five days, I take 'em."

Elmore was a little appeased but his garrulous features were still on the distant horseman who rode erect, his long rifle balanced across his lap, at the head of the small caravan. "Well, that's better, but I'll be damned if I can figger out Doorn. What're three half-rotten old wagons and a scrubby crew of half-starved clod-hoppers to him? Hell, don't he know this time of the year the Injuns are all moving through the mountains, headin' fer their summer huntin' grounds?"

The Delaware looked distastefully at Elmore and nodded his head as he turned away. "Caleb Doorn know that, too. He no take pioneers over passes otherwise. He no live in log store. He know things." The Indian was moving away when Elmore turned his indignant eyes on him.

The first day, the little caravan rumbled and groaned over eleven miles of fairly good trail. They could have ground out another mile or two but Caleb, conscious of the heaving, bony sides of livestock, held them down.

The worst was yet to come. Their night camp was in a little clearing where the charred, scattered remains of old campfires were all around them. The emigrants' spirits were higher than they had been in days. Jack Bedford brought a small, thick oaken cask to Harris's cooking fire after everyone had eaten, and the carefully hoarded liquor trickled agreeably down the throats of the men. Massive, slow-thinking and good-natured Seth Overholt smacked his lips and spat out his cud of tobacco before he drank. Harris took two large swallows and Caleb mixed his whiskey into his tin cup of hot tea.

The older, dried up little man, an ex-Texas Confederate cavalryman, held his scraggly beard up with one hand as the fiery liquid burned its way down past his gullet. He set the jug down and turned to Doorn. "You figured keeping that there Injun girl was bad medicine, Josh tells us."

Caleb nodded emphatically. "Stealing her was bad enough. You haven't heard the last of it yet, unless the Blackfeet have changed a helluva lot this past year."

The little man ran a dirty hand over the stubble along the sharp edge of his lower jaw. "Might be right at that. I recollect, once, back in Texas, an Injun name of Big Tree, gettin' all riled up over something sort of like that. Finally got hung, but he sure lifted a lot of hair afore he was caught up with." He spread his hands palms up in a deprecatory way. " 'Course them was Comanches."

Doorn smiled slightly. "Comanches are tough, but don't think Northern Cheyennes, Sioux, and Blackfeet aren't just as bad. Fact is, I'd rather fight almost anybody except a riled-up Blackfoot, and that goes for the short, heavy Apaches that live out on the desert you got to cross before you get to California."

The second day put nine more miles between the emigrant train and Willow Creek. The train camped late in the afternoon on a promontory overlooking the pine and fir dotted off-side of the mountains. Doorn had used the easiest, most-traveled passes, and the weak horses and oxen were holding out better than he had expected. The sun was riding above the horizon when the women built their small cooking fires and the men turned the hobbled horses loose to graze overnight on the knee-high, tough buffalo grass that grew among the trees.

Doorn and the four emigrants were sitting in the cool shade of a mammoth old pine tree, resting and content, when Caleb's sunken, brooding eyes, level and indifferent, caught a movement among the trees on the far side of the wagon clearing. He said nothing to the others and watched for a repetition as desultory, relaxed talk among the pioneers went unheeded around him. Again there was a slight, shadowy wisp of movement.

Doorn was certain now. Calmly, almost casually, he broke in on the conversation of the men. "Don't do anything conspicuous, like grabbing a gun or a knife. Just sit as you are."

He looked at Jack Bedford, who was puffing peaceably on a black and stubby little pipe stoked with kinnikinnik tobacco. "Keep right on puffing, Jack." The men were suddenly tense, although they made no overt moves. "In those pines across the clearing I saw some movement. Maybe it's only some varmint."

The old Texan, squint-eyed and sober, grunted dryly. "And then again, it might be a whole passel of redskins, too." He wagged his old head shrewdly. "Danged sly, them redskins. Seen 'em slip up like that many a time back in Texas."

Josh Harris tried to act unconcerned, but Doorn saw the bunching muscles along toward the back of his stubborn jaw. He recognized the sign; Harris was going to be dogmatically stubborn. Caleb decided on a bold front.

He looked directly toward where he had seen the movements and called out, "If our cousins will come out, we will smoke a pipe and eat meat."

The emigrant women looked up, startled and frightened, at Doorn's shout in Algonquin. Fearfully they followed his gaze toward the distant trees. For a long, silent moment there was no answer, then suddenly seven tall, gruesomely-painted Indians stepped into plain view. The emigrants gasped, and one of the women couldn't smother the small shriek that arose wildly in her throat.

Doorn didn't bat an eye, but his heart sank within him; the strangers were Sioux warriors, not Blackfeet. They stood fully exposed, their rifles lying casually across the crooks of their arms, scalps dangling from their belts and their bodies painted, as well as their faces, to indicate a raiding party. Doorn appraised the muscular, stringy bodies and read the painted symbols of the Sioux fighting societies.

He arose and held up his hand, palm outward, the age-old sign of peace, indicating that an open palm held no weapons and plotted no treachery. The Sioux remained motionless. Doorn affected not to notice the slight and walked gracefully forward while the seated emigrants watched, fascinated, their fingers lying close to their pistols and Jack Bedford's pipe emitting a series of gusty little blobs of smoke under the impetus of his badly shaken nerves.

III

One of the Sioux, a head taller and ten years younger than Caleb, took two firm steps forward and stopped. The white man faced him and their eyes locked. There was a grudging respect in the crossed glances. Both recognized in the other a strong man.

The Sioux spoke, in English, which mildly surprised Doorn. "You not many. Very foolish."

Doorn nodded solemnly. "These emigrants are going far beyond the big desert. I only guide them through the Blackfoot country, over the mountains."

The beady black eyes never flickered. "You, Silent Outcast. I see you twice, now." He shook his head in a tight little back-and-forth movement. "No good. Emigrants give us horses and flour."

Caleb's hand was resting casually on the hilt of his heavy knife and the Sioux let his dark eyes lower meaningfully as the white frontiersman spoke. "We travel in peace. The emigrants' horses are poor and weak; the Sioux don't want them."

"We take 'em and scalps, too, if you no give 'em." He nodded toward the hand on the knife-hilt. "No good. I can take knife from you."

Doorn's face was a frozen mask and his eyes were hooded beneath the drooping lids that sheltered the bright, deadly orbs beneath. "Try it." His voice was very soft and the other Indians, sensing friction, watched in anticipation.

For a silent moment the tall Sioux looked with confident irony at the smaller white man, then he shrugged and handed his rifle to one of his companions with several guttural words. The other Sioux formed a small, loose circle.

Doorn read the sign easily. There was going to be a fight. He spoke coldly, without taking his eyes from the warrior. "The emigrants will shoot."

Scorn dripped from the Indian's words. "Let them. They will never live to tell of it."

Doorn raised his voice a little, still watching the big savage. "Harris, I'm going to fight this Injun. Don't shoot until the fight is over. If I lose, you must kill the women first."

The emigrants arose lazily and stood near their wagons where they could see the combatants, leaning on their long rifles. The women and children had miraculously disappeared inside the great rolling hulks that had been their homes for many months.

Harris, lips flat against his teeth, threw his words toward Jack Bedford and the Texan. "Them Injuns are probably only an advance war party. If Doorn loses, we're in fer it."

Bedford and the older man didn't answer; their eyes were glued on the circling fighters, but the thick-shouldered, tobacco-chewing emigrant with the thick thatch of black, curly hair, was half smiling. He was a good rough-and-tumble fighter himself, and the prospect of being killed later was secondary to the tableau now unfolding a few hundred feet away. He shrugged and spoke softly. "Never heard of Injuns comin' right out inter the open and wantin' ter fight, man-to-man, before."

The Texan squinted sagely. "I figger that they're afraid to commence a shootin' attack 'cause they're a war party in their enemies' territory. If the Blackfeet didn't hear the shootin', some whites might, so I sort of allow they want to count a coup on us 'thout no noise."

He nodded approvingly. "It'd be quite a war honor if they could slip inter Blackfoot country and collect some white scalps . . . right under the noses of the Blackfeet and whites, alike." The others only half-heard him as they watched Caleb and the tall Sioux warrior.

Caleb Doorn was appraising the big Sioux. His adversary was confident of his ability to beat the white man. He moved with a half-smile on his face and his large, black eyes were probing, reading and measuring his man without the grimness that usually marked an Indian fighter. Doorn turned slowly, standing in the same place, as the Sioux circled him. If he could keep the man moving, he had one slight advantage. The Sioux would have to carry the fight to him. Doorn's massive knife was lying edgewise in his fist while the Sioux's knife, a Green River dagger with a nicked, razor-sharp edge, was held a little forward from the side, like the shiny, sullen tongue of a deadly snake.

The Indian, seeing no immediate opening, began to weary of the by-play. His face had an annoyed, angry flush on it and the half-smile had turned down at the lips, into a sneer. He was crouching from the waist up, his sinewy legs bent a little at the knees. Doorn knew he would spring in soon, and balanced on his toes. The sun was sinking a little lower all the time but its head was still a life-giving elixir. The Sioux began an unintelligible dirge, deep in his throat. Doorn suspected it of being a victory song, being sung softly in anticipation, but the words were unfamiliar to him.

When the Indian closed, it was no surprise to Caleb; but he hadn't expected the wary strategy that went with the lunge. The warrior had shot forward like a lightning streak and dropped almost to his knees as he went. Doorn saw, too late, that the Sioux was coming in under his guard. Desperately he tried to lower his knife to meet the attack, but only by dodging wildly backwards and sideways did he avoid receiving the glittering Green River knife in his groin, where it had been calculated to enter his body, ripping upwards, to disembowel him. Even so, the Sioux knife struck hard against his brass belt-buckle, the force of the blow, since he was back-pedaling when it struck, knocked him off-balance and he went over backwards. The watching Sioux warriors leaned forward eagerly and gave approving cries of encouragement when their tall champion, twisting in his momentum, threw his own body across the white man's prone form.

Caleb squinted hard against the blinding flash of the sunlight and grabbed desperately for the Sioux's knife arm. The man was a squirming, convulsing bundle of steel-like muscles that rippled and writhed as he tried to turn his body enough to straddle the frontiersman. Doorn felt the closeness of the blow as the Sioux aimed a violent thrust at his head. He had rolled frantically away fast enough so that the knife missed his throat by inches and struck, jarringly, into the soft, spongy earth. Before the Sioux could withdraw his blade, Caleb had grabbed the bronzed wrist in an iron grip and fought to bring up his own knife, in part restricted by the rigid body of his enemy.

The smell of the warrior's sweat-drenched body was like death in Caleb's nose, and the straining of his own body made him dizzy. As his knife came up, the Sioux tried to grab Caleb's hand. He missed, spun crazily, and lunged with a dawning desperation for the blade again. Doorn, still beneath the massive form, yanked back his arm, felt the keen blade slice across the Sioux's palm and heaved with all his strength, throwing the other violently sideways, even as the Indian roared in pain and killing fury as his hot, spurting blood ran gushingly from the torn hand.

Doorn rolled wildly sideways, released the Indian's knife-hand and spun lightly to his feet. He reached up quickly and wiped away the blinding rivulet of sweat that was running into his eyes. The Sioux, mad with anger, reckless and wild, roared an oath and rushed forward, head down and knife-arm extended. Caleb was panting and weak from the exertion, but he kept a cool mind.

As the big man came in, Doorn stepped wide to one side and swung his own knife like a club. His aim was faulty, though, and instead of cutting deep into the Sioux's skull only a tiny jar told him that he had struck at all. The Sioux watchers groaned and the charging Indian, past Caleb, straightened up, dazed, and held an exploratory hand to the side of his head. His left ear was gone, sliced off as neatly and cleanly as though a surgeon had done it.

Bleeding profusely now, hacked and gory, his blood mixing with the awesome, running symbols daubed in black and red and yellow over his shiny, dusky body, the Sioux came in without caution, slashing with the blindness of a doomed man. Caleb tried to dodge away and felt the sullen, burning sensation of a deep cut along his left side, just over the ribs. He jumped backward, so as not to be overwhelmed again by the maddened attack, dropped to one knee and braced against the rush that brought his enemy in close. Then Caleb's knife, slippery with blood, flashed unerringly inward and upwards.

For an awful, deadly quiet moment, the big warrior looked down at Doorn, his knife poised and ready. His face was so close that Caleb could see the little fantail of wrinkles around his squinted eyes. He shuddered, dropped his knife, and his knees buckled as he fell in a writhing heap to the pine-scented earth; a gush of hot, bubbly breath, laden with foam-flecked blood, cascaded from his nose and mouth. Caleb stood poised and ready over his dying adversary, looking at the dumbfounded Sioux warriors. The Indians were glassy-eyed as they watched the disemboweled warrior twitching and gasping on the blood-soaked ground. Slowly they looked up. Doorn, ashen-faced and thin-lipped, was waiting. His fringed hunting shirt was a spectacle of splattered gore, and his wounded side was dripping warm blood that mixed on the earth with the congealing little pools of the dying man's blood.

Without a word, three of the remaining warriors went forward and lifted their fallen comrade and carried him stoically out of the little glen. The other Sioux fighting men were staring bitterly at the white man. They eventually turned and followed their companions into the gloom of the shadowy forest. Caleb turned and walked wearily back to the emigrants, expecting to feel the tearing agony of a rifle ball in his back any second, but almost too tired and spent to care.

Night spread its somber blanket of darkness over the fearful little emigrant camp. Caleb had explained to the settlers that Indians, in general, would not fight at night, believing that a warrior killed in the dark would never find his way into the Hereafter, through the darkness. However, aching in every joint, he joined the others in a hidden cordon, scattered among the bushes and trees outside the wagon encampment site, where each of the four men kept a wide-eyed, sleepless vigil, lest the Sioux should return for vengeance.

Dawn was an interminable surcease that seemed forever in coming. The emigrants, half afraid to move, slipped back to the wagons with the first glow of pink off in the east. Their women and children, white-faced and shaking, were set to barricading the wagons. There was a fresh, saintly fragrance in the air when the first rifle shot came spanking down the wind to them. Doorn, sore and stiff, his wounded side a searing, fire-like burden with every breath, told the others in curt, clipped sentences, that yesterday had been a picnic. Today—this morning, in fact—was the deciding moment for them all. He minced no words when he told them that only a miracle would see them ever leave the mountains alive, and he had never seen a miracle in his life.

Grimly the men set the women to loading rifles while they peered cautiously from under the great sailcloth shrouds where they were secured to the high, gracefully curving wagon boxes. No movement met their slitted eyes. No birds sang; no crickets croaked in their hidden, grassy world. Doorn shook his head. "They're out there all right. Stand ready, boys. They've got to do this in a hurry and they know it. The noise of those rifle shots will carry a long way."

He had scarcely stopped speaking when a furious fusillade

sprang up, not three hundred feet from the wagons. Splinters flew as the balls riddled the wooden sides. Jack Bedford thrust his rifle quickly out of a wagon, sighted, and fired. He swore and reached for another rifle. Caleb saw two flitting shapes, and methodically threw two rapid shots from his Colt at them. An Indian screamed exultantly and the emigrants shuddered. The old Texan fired, swore, exchanged rifles and fired again. This time there was a harsh smile on his face. An attacking Sioux toppled grotesquely out of the crotch of a tree and hit the ground with a sodden, dull thud.

IV

They were coming in now, throwing caution to the winds, anxious to finish it off and disappear with their trophies, and to exact every last drop of revenge. Caleb saw them charging through the trees, four hate-maddened, powerful, painted savages, running recklessly in zig-zag lines that made accurate rifle fire impossible. Caleb shouted to the others and threw himself flat, cocking his long barreled six-gun.

Josh Harris swore furiously. "A firebrand!"

Caleb hadn't seen it. One of the Sioux tossed a big pitch firebrand in a large, drooping arc. It fell squarely on the sagging top of the wagon they were all crouching in, and the dry, half rotten old sailcloth caught like tinder. He felt the sting of molten pitch and cloth as the fire raged overhead and leaped to his feet. "Run for it. Try to get to the next wagon, up ahead." He swung to Harris. "Get the women and kids out of here. We'll try to cover them. Hurry!"

It was useless and Caleb knew it. The besiegers were in the trees on the far side of the clearing now, as they had planned to be, crouching, their rifles steady and waiting for the first emigrant to make a break from the fiery arc of the burning wagon. Caleb's heart sank and he muttered a rusty, half-forgotten prayer as the old Texan's wife, a thin, sparse woman, white-faced and resolute, leaped awkwardly from the wagon. Three half-crazed youngsters followed the old woman. She ran with desperate agility toward the wagon ahead, keeping her own body between the Indians and the children. The horror-stricken emigrants were firing frantically into the trees where they knew the savages were hiding—firing without a target, but with the hope that their volley might spoil the Sioux' aim.

The thunderous roar of guns was deafening and the acrid, eye-stinging fumes from the spent ammunition made a sulphurous odor that encompassed the emigrant camp and its grassy little clearing. The old woman was shoving the children into the wagon when Caleb saw her sag. His throat was tight. She jerked spasmodically twice more, as leaden balls ripped and plowed into her flesh; she sagged, tried to force herself upright, then collapsed.

A wild, terrifying shriek split the air and made Doorn jump involuntarily. He swung around just in time to see the old Texan, a bowie knife in one hand and his old cap and ball pistol in the other, leap out of the wagon. Instead of running toward the other wagon, he screamed wild, blasphemous curses in a shrill, ragged voice and charged across the little meadow toward the woods where the hidden Sioux were watching. The others in the wagon dared not fire as long as the old man was running forward in their line of fire. A breathtaking moment of suspense overhung the battle ground. It lasted a short few seconds, then a Sioux rifle, hidden and muted by the dense foliage, coughed its deadly message. The old Texan missed his footing, stumbled, recovered his balance and charged on, his pistol spitting fire and smoke. Again a Sioux rifle roared and this time the little old man fell limply, his feet beating a tiny tattoo out in the tall grass, the rest of his body lying hidden in the thick underbrush.

The little tragedy was over and the rifles began their furious cannonade again. Josh Harris and Jack Bedford ran with the rest of the emigrant women and children for the next wagon as the fire ate lividly into what remained of the other one. Caleb and the tobacco-chewing, thick-shouldered emigrant, dodged and streaked after the others. Caleb threw himself into the wagon as a bullet struck inches behind him. He turned quickly and grabbed the sweaty shirt of the other man and yanked with all his might. The emigrant was almost into the enclosure of pitted, scarred wood when a strange, horrified look spread over his face and, with an unexpected impetus, he lunged far over Caleb's crouching form and fell among the débris. Caleb helped him into a crouching position before he noticed the thin trickle of blood running down the man's trousers.

"Hard hit?"

His jaws working wildly on the mangled cud of tobacco, the man looked up at Caleb in disbelief. "Look," he said incredulously, pointing to his posterior. "Shot plumb through the rear end."

Caleb felt no humor right then. The Sioux ball had penetrated the man's buttocks from side to side. It wasn't for a long time afterwards that the humor of the incredulous emigrant and his half-embarrassed, half-painful grimace of pain struck his funny bone. "Set still and take it easy, if you can."

The man's eyes crinkled a little through the grime of his lined, powder-grimed face. "I can take it easy, I reckon. But, by gawd, it'll be a danged long time afore I do any sittin'."

The Sioux firing had ceased and Caleb guessed the reason. They were circling around, getting ready to throw another firebrand. He cautioned the others and the silence was even worse than the bedlam of the attack. Suddenly a wild, deep-throated scream broke across the cool mountain meadow. A crazy patchwork of erratic rifle fire blossomed out behind the wagons. It swelled and roared into a deafening crescendo. The emigrants turned white faces to one another.

Doorn felt dread and shattered hope in his bowels. "Must be the rest of their war party."

Josh Harris, his face working like a man demented, jumped to his feet. "If we gotta die, let's do it standin' up, not hidin' in here like a passel of mice."

Caleb, being next to him, heard every word; but the others couldn't make out what he was screaming over the crashing, roaring medley of gunfire that sent bullets all around them with an abandon that was overwhelming. He saw the madness in Harris's eyes and lashed out with his fist. Harris collapsed in a heap among the broken furniture and sweaty bodies of his comrades.

As suddenly as it started, the gunfire stopped. A pall of awful silence hung over the crouched, bleary-eyed emigrants as they huddled low in the old Conestoga. Caleb risked a hazardous peek and his eyes widened. Systematically scalping fallen Indians were other Indians! A dawning realization swept over him. He took a better look, recognized the clothing and the painted symbols of the Blackfeet, and hurried out of the wagon, followed by stunned, dizzy and completely exhausted emigrants.

While Caleb Doorn, a wraith in fringed, smoke-tanned buckskin, blood spattered and grim, stood watching the Blackfeet among the pathetic little clutch of dazed emigrants, the Indians arose from their grisly chore and stood in silent wariness. Caleb let his gaze roam from the scorched, churned-up clearing with its rank odor and bullet-scarred trees to the fringes of the forest all around the wagons. There were Indians everywhere. If they came for war, resistance would be useless and brief.

He licked his chapped lips and turned his blood-shot eyes to Josh Harris. "They're Blackfeet."

"War party?"

"I reckon. They're painted and armed for war, but I see women among them too, which isn't customary."

"Sure's a helluva lot of 'em."

Doorn nodded wearily. "Biggest war party I ever saw. They must've been slippin' up on us when they ran into what was left of those Sioux. That'd account for all that shootin' back among the trees." He nodded thoughtfully. "They sure made quick work of 'em."

Harris, his jaw slack and tired, nodded glumly. "Yeah, well, what do we do now?"

Doorn shrugged. "I'll go council with 'em." He drew himself erect with an effort.

Josh Harris laid a restraining hand on his sleeve, hard and rank with caked blood. "No fightin'. If they're gonna fight, then by gawd, we'll all fight this time. You aren't in no shape . . . ."

Doorn shrugged off the hand. "Let's wait and see."

He walked slowly across the bruised and broken grass toward the largest gathering of Blackfeet, who were standing looking down at the dead Texan. They watched him come up with impassive faces. Caleb raised his arm and held his hand, palm outward, toward them. One of the Blackfeet, an old man with a deeply-lined, scarred face and badly-healed broken nose, returned the salute while the others remained stolidly motionless.

Caleb's throat was dry and his voice sounded oddly harsh in his own ears when he spoke. "It is well my brothers came when they did."

The older man grunted wryly, a flicker of a bitter smile on his face. "It is better yet that Silent Outcast made the emigrants release my daughter, Singing In The Clouds."

Doorn grunted. "You are Two Shoots?"

"Yes. And I know you: Silent Outcast."

There was a moment of awkward silence, then Doorn motioned to a scalped, gory-skulled Sioux lying in the brush nearby. "Sioux raiding party?"

Two Shoots was not to be put aside. He ignored Doorn's remark, his frosty old eyes unblinkingly on Caleb. "Singing In The Clouds said you gave her your horse?"

Doorn flushed uncomfortably; he didn't want to discuss the girl nor her enforced release from the emigrants. It was thin ice with the hot-tempered, vengeful-minded Blackfeet. He made a wry face. "It would have been a long walk back to the Siksika."

His tart tone amused Two Shoots, although his face remained saturninely half smiling. "I will give you many horses for that favor."

Caleb's face burned a quick red. "Dammit. I don't want your horses. Keep 'em. The emigrants are fools. They thought by keeping Singing In The Clouds that no Indians would attack them."

"Did they think she could save them from the Sioux?"

"I told you they are fools. One Western Indian looks like another to them."

Two Shoots let his mud-colored eyes glide over Doorn's shoulder to rest balefully on the little crowd of rigid, silent emigrants huddled near their wagons. He jutted his chin toward them and spoke without taking his brooding stare from them. "They travel westward, on the great trail?"

"Yes. To the land that meets the sea."

"It is well. Such fools would not live long in the land of the Blackfeet." He turned back to Doorn. "We were following your trail. I wanted to give you horses and frighten these fools for my daughter."

He turned to a lean, stalwart man behind him. "Take your fighting men and guide these white fools beyond our land. Take them out onto the big desert and leave them there." His battle-scarred face swung back to Caleb and his eyes were intense and watchful. "You, Silent Outcast, will return to the Siksika with me."

Doorn frowned. "Why?"

Two Shoots held out his hand, palm upwards and open. "Because Singing In The Clouds wishes it."

Doorn looked into the fierce eyes for a long, thoughtful moment and the vision of a tall, graceful olive-skinned, black-eyed beauty floated across his inner vision. It was an apparition of pure loveliness that had a warm, generous smile hovering over the full, red lips. A fantasy that was designed to take the hollow loneliness out of a wilderness man's solitary, brooding life. Slowly his hand came up and lay for a fleeting, warm second over the open palm of Two Shoots. "You will see that the emigrants are taken safely onto their trail?"

"Yes."

"I come with you to the Siksika, to Singing In The Clouds."

Two Shoots's battered features spread into a toothy, strong smile and he nodded his head wisely. "Had I returned without you, I might have become an emigrant, too. It is well."

Caleb smiled for the first time in a long while and the two men walked into the forest, toward the painted, pastoral horse herd, side by side.

GUN THIS MAN DOWN

LEWIS B(YFORD) PATTEN wrote more than ninety Western novels in thirty years and three of them won Golden Spur Awards from the Western Writers of America and the author himself the Golden Saddleman Award. Indeed, this points up the most remarkable aspect of his work, his remarkable consistency and craftsmanship. He was born in Denver, Colorado, and served in the U.S. Navy 1933-1937. He was educated at the University of Denver during the war years and became an auditor for the Colorado Department of Revenue during the 1940s.

It was first with "Too Good With a Gun" in *Zane Grey's Western Magazine* (4/50) that Patten began contributing significantly to Western pulp magazines, fiction that was from the beginning fresh and unique and revealed a lifelong concern with the sociological and psychological affects of group psychology on the frontier. He became a professional writer exclusively upon publication of his first novel, MASSACRE AT WHITE RIVER (Ace, 1952). The dominant theme in much of his fiction has to do with the notion of justice and, its opposite, injustice. In his first novel the focus is on the exploitation of the Ute Indians but, as Patten matured as a writer, he explored this theme in poignant detail in small towns throughout the early West. Crimes, such as rape or lynching, were often at the center of his stories. MAN OUTGUNNED (Doubleday, 1976) opens at a Fourth of July picnic in a small town being interrupted by an invading gang of robbers. THE ANGRY TOWN OF PAWNEE BLUFFS (Doubleday, 1974) finds a small town victimized by its own lynch-mob mentality set off by an attack on two girls. LYNCHING AT BROKEN BUTTE (Doubleday, 1974) goes beyond Walter Van Tilburg Clark's THE OX-BOW INCIDENT (Random House, 1940) and shows how the guilt that pervades a small town after two innocent men are lynched breeds more violence. A DEATH IN INDIAN WELLS (Doubleday, 1970) finds a wounded Cheyenne displayed in a cage; when the half-breed son of the local sheriff takes the body back to the Cheyennes for burial, more violence erupts.

Once the values embodied in these small towns are examined closely, they are found to be wanting. Conformity is always easier than taking a stand. Yet, in Patten's view of the American West, there is usually a man or a woman who refuses to conform. Among other fine titles, always a difficult choice, must surely be included A KILLING AT KIOWA (Signet, 1972), RIDE A CROOKED TRAIL (Signet, 1976), THE LAW IN COTTONWOOD (Doubleday, 1978) recently reprinted both in a hardcover edition by Chivers Press in the Gunsmoke series and in the ongoing Patten double-action mass merchandise series from Leisure Books, and DEATH RIDES A BLACK HORSE (Doubleday, 1978).

"Gun This Man Down" was first published in *Dime Western* (3/54). This marks the first time it has been collected.

I

"HOMECOMING"

Matt Hurst stepped down off the train onto the wooden platform and eyed the town with eyes as bleak as the leaden sky. Snow drove along the ground before the biting January wind, forming tiny dunes as variable as a woman's moods.

He stood for a long moment while his mind digested the unpleasantness of his memories, then he picked up his carpetbag with his left hand, tossed his sacked saddle over his right shoulder, and strode down the slight rise of ground between railroad station and town.

A man's eyes, resting on his home after five years, ought to show something besides this cold unfriendliness. Else why would a man come home? There were a lot of reasons, he reflected, among them a deep need to understand the things that had happened, and a possibility of exacting vengeance.

A few scattered horses lined the town's hitchrails, rumps to the wind, tails whipping between their legs. A lone woman hurried along the street clutching her skirts to keep the wind from lifting them. Smoke rose briefly from half a hundred tin chimneys before the wind snatched it away. And on the far side of town, a school bell clanged for the noon hour.

Hurst looked at the town and cursed.

The hotel, a yellow framed structure with a balcony across the front at the second story level, seemed to recoil from each new blast of wind, wind that came howling off the rolling sagebrush country to the north of town. Matt shouldered open the door, came into the lobby in a swirling cloud of snow, and dropped his bag and saddle beside the door.

Nothing changes, he thought as he looked around at the game heads hung from the smoky walls, at the worn red lobby carpet, littered as always with cigar ashes and cigarette butts. Nothing changed, not even the sour-faced, bespectacled room clerk, Rudy Littlefield.

Matt stepped across the lobby to the desk and flipped open the register. He signed Matt Hurst and looked up at Rudy, a mocking, challenging smile on his lips.

He wasn't a tall man, nor was he overly broad. Unprepossessing because his heavy sheepskin covered and concealed the long, smooth muscles of his shoulders, the deep power of his chest. Un-prepossessing until you let your glance dwell on his cold gray eyes, on his mouth so thin and hard and bitter.

Littlefield breathed, "Matt Hurst! I thought you looked familiar. You've growed since I seen you last."

His eyes took on a gleeful excitement. Matt said dryly, "Give me a room and the key to it. Then you can run out and tell the town I'm back."

Rudy eyed the low-slung Colt revolver that peeped from beneath Matt's hip-length sheepskin. He said, "What you goin' to do Matt?"

"Do? What should I do?"

Rudy flushed and stammered. "Well you know . . . I mean, you come back to do something about Dan and Will and Frankie, didn't you?"

Matt said, "A room and a key, Rudy."

Let them worry. Let them stew and wonder why he was back. Let them wonder because he was wondering himself. He hated the town and the people in it. He hated the slot they'd shoved him in ever since he was old enough to remember things.

Dell Tillman had always said, "You don't tame a wolf whelp by treating him good. He's what he is, and sooner or later he'll turn on you."

That was what Matt Hurst was—a wolf whelp. A wolf pup that had run away to keep from being smeared with the same brush that had tarred his father and his brothers. He knew now that he should have stuck.

If he had, maybe things would be different. Maybe Dan and Will and Frankie would still be alive.

Or maybe he should have stayed away. What could possibly be accomplished by returning? One man cannot obtain vengeance against an entire community. And even if he could, would not the very act of obtaining it hurt him more than it hurt the ones against whom he acted?

The carpeting on the steps was a little more frayed than Matt remembered, the hallways a little more dingy. Cooking odors from the hotel kitchen lifted up the stairwell and invariably announced what was being served at the next meal. Today it appeared to be sauerkraut. Matt felt the sudden pangs of hunger.

So immersed was he in his thoughts that he did not notice the girl until he was face to face with her. She stepped to one side to pass, and Matt, stepping aside himself, unwittingly moved the same way and found himself still facing her.

Quickly, embarrassedly, he stepped back, and the girl did the same. She laughed, a pleasant, musical laugh, and said, "You stand still. I'll move aside."

Matt flushed, feeling like a fool. "All right," he growled. The girl kept her glance on him with a close interest that further flustered him. And he began to notice her for the first time.

Her hair was like honey in color, having a light yellow sheen on top, deeper, darker highlights beneath. Her skin was smooth and white, her lips full and soft. Her dress seemed unnecessarily tight at waist and bodice, plainly outlining her rather startling figure.

She asked, "You're new in town, aren't you?"

He nodded and she said, "I'm Lily Kibben."

"Matt Hurst." The way he said it, the name was a curse. Lily's eyes widened, and her smile faded.

She murmured, "I see," and stepped quickly past.

He turned and watched her back as she descended the stairs, smiling wryly at her reaction to his name. The wolf whelp is home. That was what all the town would be saying. The wolf whelp is home and there's going to be trouble.

All right, damn it! Trouble hadn't been all that was on his mind when he started back. But if they wanted trouble, then let them have it.

He found his room and opened the door. He strode to the window and looked down into the gloomy street. He saw Rudy Littlefield come out of the Bullshead saloon across the street and hurry back toward the hotel. He saw Alfred Polk and Dell Tillman come through the heavy winter doors and follow Rudy. Matt moved close to the glass and stared insolently down at them. Rudy glanced up as he approached the hotel, saw Matt and dropped his glance hastily. Tillman followed the direction of Rudy's glance with his own and scowled when he saw Matt in the window.

Matt grinned. He shucked out of the sheepskin and eased the .45 out of its holster. He spun the cylinder and checked the loads. When he replaced it, he seated it lightly. Maybe they figured on exterminating the Hurst clan once and for all, and he didn't intend to be caught unawares.

He waited in the small room's center, not afraid, but feeling the same tight emptiness in his stomach that fear could engender. He was lonely, really, and angry at himself for being so. And he resented the fact that his homecoming stirred no welcome in a single one of the town's inhabitants. Why? He had never done anything to deserve this. But he was Dan Hurst's son, and because he was, they hated and distrusted him.

He heard Tillman's heavy, arrogant tread on the stairs, heard Dell's tread alone. But he knew the sheriff was with Dell and remembered the light way Polk had of walking.

It was Tillman who rapped on the door, loudly, imperatively. Matt Hurst felt his anger rising.

He said shortly, "Come in." And the door banged open. Tillman stepped in first, scowling.

He was a big man, big of body, always appearing larger because of the power he wielded and of which he was so aware. He wore a neatly-trimmed beard, and his eyes above it always looked at a man as though he were one of nature's unpleasant mistakes. He looked at Matt that way now. "Why the hell did you come back?"

Matt stared at him coolly for a moment, trying hard to hold his temper. He said at last, "Damn you, you're in my room. You aren't here because I asked you either, so keep a civil tongue in your head. I came back because I took a notion to, and maybe because I heard a thing or two."

Alf Polk stepped from behind Tillman, graying, aging, but still with that indefinable quality of confidence and efficiency exuding from him. He said calmly, "Dell, quiet down a mite. Let me talk to Matt."

Dell glared at the sheriff. Alf muttered, "Matt, Dan and your brothers were killed by a posse acting on my orders. They were caught over in Trout Creek Pass with a herd of DT stock."

"How'd they die?" He thought Dell Tillman's eyes flickered as he asked. And Alf Polk looked at the floor a moment before he answered. Finally he said with a sigh, "I guess you'll find out anyway. Dan and Frankie were shot. Will was hanged."

Matt felt a surge of passion. "That was on your orders too, I suppose."

"No." Alf seemed a little tired suddenly. "No, you know better than that, Matt. I wouldn't order such a thing."

All at once Matt knew that if they didn't get out, and quickly, he wasn't going to be responsible. A lifetime of hatred and resentment seemed to boil abruptly to the surface. He said, his voice even and low-pitched, "Get out of here! Both of you! Get out while you can!"

Tillman opened his mouth to bluster, but Alf caught him by the elbow and pushed him around toward the door. His softly breathed words were barely audible to Matt, "Don't be a fool, Dell. Do what he says."

When Tillman was gone, the sheriff turned in the doorway. "Why'd you come back, Matt? You've never done anything that's outside the law. You were doing all right over in Utah." His voice was calm and soothing, a little cautious too.

Matt flared, "If you don't know, I couldn't tell you. They were all I had. When I got word they had all been killed, I wanted to know how they died. I guess I knew why. But I had to know how."

"Now you know. What you figure on doin' about it?"

Matt's voice was savage, taunting, "Suppose you figure that one out, Sheriff."

Alf Polk shrugged. "Suit yourself, Matt. But be mighty careful. You know how folks react to the name Hurst around here. I'll let you alone until you step out of line. When you do, I'm coming after you."

Matt sneered, "Or send a posse out under your orders . . . with Dell at its head."

Alf looked at him steadily for a long moment. At last he said, "All right. Rub it in. Maybe I deserve it at that," and backed slowly from the room.

Matt Hurst sat down on the edge of the bed and buried his face in his hands. He was shaking with suppressed rage.

Well, he could do the obvious, the thing everybody expected him to do. He could kill Dell Tillman. Then run—and keep on running.

He could carry it farther than that. He could find the names of the men who had comprised that posse, and exact vengeance against each one of them. He shook his head. He'd never get that job done. Because Alf would pick him up long before he finished. He could call it a bad job and get out of town.

Or he could go out to the home place and take up where Dan and his brothers had left off.

For some reason, this course appealed to him most. Let Tillman stew a while.

He got up and spilled some of the cold water from the white china pitcher into the graniteware pan. He washed his face and dampened his black, curly hair. He dried off on the thin hotel towel and ran a comb through his hair. Then he headed downstairs toward the hotel dining room.

He caught himself thinking of that girl—Lily Kibben—and wondering who she was. She must have come to town after he had left.

Morose, lonely, and very much on the defensive, he came into the dining room and halted in the doorway to eye the thin crowd. Over in the corner sat Dell Tillman and the sheriff, Alf Polk. Both of them watched him warily. Nearer to the door sat Lily Kibben, alone. She held her glance on him longer than necessary and, while it was strictly neutral, Matt thought he detected a hesitant invitation in it too.

On impulse he headed for her table and paused there, looking down, frowning at his own unexpected temerity. He said, "Mind if I join you?" And cursed himself inwardly for laying himself wide open for refusal.

For an instant he thought she would refuse, for into her expression came a definite aloofness. Then she smiled, "Of course not. Sit down."

He released a slow sigh, pulled out a chair and sat. He found himself grinning at her and said, "I shouldn't have done that."

"Why?"

"Because it would have tickled Tillman to see you refuse."

"But I didn't refuse."

"You were thinking about it though." This girl was the first one he had encountered here in Granada who looked at him as though he were a person and who seemed able to forget that his name was Hurst.

"Yes. I guess I was. But not for the reason you think. I might have refused any strange man." Her expression was calm and thoughtful, her lips relaxed and pleasant. But her eyes held the faintest shadow of bitterness.

She looked directly at him and said honestly, "Perhaps we're the same kind. You see, I am not particularly well liked in Granada either."

"Why?" He almost snapped the question.

Her face flushed faintly and she looked away. "I'm not married. I own this hotel, which is a thing no lady should own, and worse, I run it myself. They place me just a little above the dancehall girls." She smiled ruefully. "So you see, I can understand your feelings."

Susan Davenport, who had been the hotel's waitress as long as Matt could remember, came up behind her and looked at Matt. "What are you goin' to have, Matt?" Her stance was hostile, her eyes cold.

Matt said, "Sauerkraut's on the menu, isn't it?"

"All right." She went away, her back stiff and straight, with uncompromising disapproval.

Matt grinned for the second time at Lily. "I'm going to have to get used to that."

She looked at him seriously. "Why did you come back? What can you possibly hope to gain?"

He shrugged. "I don't know. I'll be damned if I do."

He noticed her staring at something over his shoulder, and turned his head. Another girl had come into the dining room, and was striding toward Tillman's table. Lily whispered, "You should remember her. That's Elaine Tillman."

Matt stared, thinking, *Five years makes a lot of difference.* As indeed it did. When Matt had left, Elaine had been a lanky kid in pigtails. There was nothing lanky about her now. Nothing lanky and nothing childish. She pulled out a chair at Tillman's table and sat down. Tillman spoke to her and she turned her head to stare at Matt.

Matt could recall a time when he had been friendly with Elaine, even could remember having a crush on her. But her cool glance revealed nothing of that, for it held only the hostility he was growing so used to.

Yet for some reason, Elaine's hostility angered him inordinately. He stared back at her, deliberately insolent until she flushed and looked away. Tillman half rose from his chair, growling something angry, but Alf Polk pulled him down again.

And Matt Hurst laughed aloud, mockingly, bitterly.

Lily finished her coffee and stood up, suddenly cool. "I guess I was mistaken about you."

"Why?"

"I thought you might be above that, but it appears that I was wrong." She walked across the room and entered the kitchen.

Susan Davenport brought his dinner, looking oddly relieved. She was an old maid, fiftyish probably and as skinny as an old cow in the spring. She said, "You stay away from Lily, Matt Hurst."

Matt grunted, "She's twenty-one, isn't she?"

Susan slammed his water glass down so hard that water slopped on the table. "You stay away from her. Hear?"

Matt said, "Maybe. Maybe not." He looked across at Tillman, at the sheriff, at Elaine Tillman. He looked up at Susan and thought, *Keep baiting me, all of you. Keep at it. Maybe if you do you can make me blow up. Then you'll have an excuse to do what you've been wanting to do.*

Susan paled under the concentrated virulence of his glance. She backed away, turned, and fled to the kitchen.

Matt ate hurriedly, hungrily. When he was finished, he tossed a dollar onto the table and got to his feet.

He wanted a drink. He wanted a fight. He wanted something that would work this enraged helplessness out of him. But he thought, *You'd better get out of town before you do something crazy.*

He stalked out through the lobby and onto the boardwalk before the hotel. The wind whipped his clothes, penetrating with a cold chill. Snow stung his exposed flesh, as he narrowed his eyes against it. "Tomorrow," he muttered. "Tomorrow I'll ride out home."

Abruptly he crossed the street toward the Bullshead. He banged through the doors and stalked to the bar.

Tillman must have paid his crew today, he thought. There were a full half dozen of them here, drinking at the bar with big, blond Olaf Skjerik, the foreman.

Olaf swung to face Matt, his hand hovering close to his gun. He said harshly, "What the hell did you come back for? You got any ideas of squarin' up for Dan and his thievin' litter? If you have, go right ahead. I'm ready."

He stood cool and still, his back to the bar. Matt felt his own hand tense, felt the fingers form a claw a scant two inches above his gun grips. He looked at Olaf, at the five DT punchers he'd have to fight too. He won the battle with himself and said mildly, "With five men backing you, I guess you are ready, Olaf. It takes consider-able courage for six men to brace one, doesn't it?"

Arms swinging at his side, he walked over to the bar. He laid a silver dollar down, having first carefully fished it out of his vest pocket. Not looking at Olaf, he took the bottle from the bartender and poured his glass full. He tossed it down and another after it.

Liquor always made him reckless, and he knew this was no time for recklessness. Yet he couldn't seem to control the compulsions that drove him.

Olaf and the DT crew watched him and conversed in low tones. Matt had just finished the fourth drink when Dell Tillman banged in, bringing a gust of icy wind and a cloud of swirling snow with him.

He stood at the door with the collar of his mackinaw turned up about his ears and said harshly, "Olaf, I want to talk to you."

"Sure, boss. Sure." Olaf crossed the room. Matt turned his back. Tingles of uneasiness ran the length as he listened to the low, indistinguishable murmur of their voices. It took no particular astuteness to guess that they were discussing him.

Abruptly he whirled and walked toward the door. Some perverse obstinacy prevented him from sidling around Tillman's bulky figure, and he jostled the DT owner deliberately.

Tillman showed remarkable restraint, moving aside with only a muttered curse. But Olaf's hand snaked after his gun, coming away only at Tillman's curt, "Olaf! No!"

Matt felt a growing tension within himself. He knew the smart thing would be to get out of town before touchy tempers exploded into violence.

And he might have done this. But standing on the walk before the Bullshead was Elaine Tillman, waiting in shivering silence for her father to reappear.

Matt scowled at her. She said, "Matt, why did you have to come back? Couldn't you let well enough alone?" Even with her cheeks red from the cold, she was beautiful. Her eyes were large, deep brown in color. Her hair was jet black, lying in windblown tendrils about her face where it had escaped from the level shawl tied under her small chin.

Matt growled, "You defend shooting Dan and Frankie down? You defend hanging Will?"

"They were rustling Matt. They were caught with the goods."

"There are courts in Granada County. So far as I know, the penalty for rustling isn't death. It's two years in the state pen."

She shrugged helplessly. "So Dad and Olaf were wrong. Are you going to right that wrong with more killing?"

It was Matt's turn to shrug. He was watching a strange, glowing fire in her eyes. He was watching her mouth turn soft and slack with the thoughts filling her lovely head.

She stepped close to him, and looked up with provocation that may have been entirely unintentional. "Matt, I'm thinking of you."

His mouth twisted. "Sure. Sure you are. I could tell that back in the hotel dining room."

"You're bitter Matt. Too bitter. You can't spend your life collecting for every wrong that's ever done you."

She swayed against him. And Matt did what any man would do. His arms went around her with the latent hunger of a man who has known few women, who is suddenly offered something by a woman's eyes.

And perversely, she regretted the offering instantly as his hands touched her. She struggled.

The saloon door banged open behind Matt. He felt the tug at his belt as his gun was lifted from its holster. And he felt the savage, terrible force of a knee in the small of his back.

He released Elaine and tried to turn. Men were piling out of the Bullshead, but it was Dell who held him. It was Dell who held him with knee at his back and powerful hands on his shoulders while Olaf smashed a giant, hard fist into his unprotected face.

Numb with shock, Matt nevertheless exploded into furious action. He twisted against Dell's grip and the knee slid away. His fist crashed into Dell's face with a chunking noise that left Dell's nose a flattened, bloody mess. Dell turned him loose.

Matt's own straining against the suddenly releasing grip threw him away, threw him across the walk and into the street.

Olaf and his five came lunging after him like a pack of wolves at a fresh kill. And Matt, crouched there in the street, fought desperately and hopelessly for his life.

As Matt came to his feet from that first fall in the street, three simultaneous blows thudded into his body. And all of the hatred he felt for this town and its people came boiling to the surface of his brain. His face twisted, savage, utterly naked in its unmasked passions.

Hatred blazed from his slitted eyes. The wind beat against him, whipped his clothing against his body. He lunged, and an outstretched foot tripped him up. Before he could rise, a kick landed in his ribs, another on the side of his head. Two of the men piled down atop of him and held him pinned to the frozen ground while they beat at him with their fists.

Dimly he heard Tillman's hoarsely shouted order, "Let him up! You can hurt him more that way!"

The two that held him down rolled aside. As Matt stumbled to his knees, he drove himself forward, elbowing one of them in the groin. Matt kicked him viciously as he stepped away.

And they were on him again. Elbows, knees, fists banged into him. A man behind him kicked him in the ankle, and it gave way temporarily. Matt lunged against another of the men, clutching at him for support. And drove his head upward against the man's chin.

It snapped the man's mouth shut and he almost bit his tongue in two. Matt felt the ankle supporting his weight again and shoved the man away from him. He threw a looping left as he did so and felt a wild satisfaction at the solid way it landed.

He heard Tillman's shouting, "Get him! Get him!" and he thought he heard Elaine's sharp cry.

A hard shoulder drove upward against his jaw, snapping his head back with an audible crack. The landscape and the men closing in whirled before his vision for an instant.

He saw Elaine, wide-eyed with a sort of fascinated horror. There was something primitive in her parted lips, in her hastened breathing, in the hot lights that played in her eyes. But there was no pity in her.

Olaf Skjerik slammed against him then and drove him back against a building wall. Matt twisted, slamming both fists down against the back of Olaf's bowed neck. The man fell like a stunned steer.

He had cut the odds to three to one, and there was solid satisfaction in that. One whom he had downed lay rolling in the frozen street, groaning with pain. Another sat on the edge of the walk, head down, spitting blood between his knees and gagging. Olaf lay utterly still. Matt stepped away from him, nimbly avoiding a rush by two of those remaining. But the third drew his gun and brought it slashing at Matt in a wide, wild swing. The barrel tip grazed his forehead and a flood of gushing blood blinded him. He swiped at his eyes with the back of a numbed hand.

A fist smashed his lip against his teeth. Another rocked his head and blurred his reason. And the gun barrel got him a second time, driving him down into a bottomless pit of darkness.

But not stealing all consciousness or all feeling. Helpless, motionless, he lay on his back in the street while they kicked and beat at him with frustrated and senseless rage.

Until Alf Polk came running across from the hotel, shouting, "Get away from him! All of you!"

It was blessed relief when the hard, raining kicks stopped landing. It was blessed relief to sink away into that bottomless pit where there was no pain but where everlasting hostility hovered in the air like a curse.

II

"BRAND HIM RENEGADE!"

He was no longer in the street, when his consciousness came back. There was warmth around him, softness under him. His hand moved and felt the rough warmth of a woolen blanket. He opened his eyes and stared upward at the cracked ceiling of his room in the hotel.

He lifted the hand and felt his throbbing face, touching the bandages there. He groaned. Then he saw Alf Polk.

Polk said softly, "Coming out of it, Matt?"

Matt rolled onto his side and groaned again in protest at the pain that shot through his bruised and battered body. It was an effort, but he brought an elbow under him and raised his head and upper body.

His vision cleared and he had the oddest impression of Polk. He thought there was actual pain in the man's face, haunted shame in his eyes. But then it was gone and the sheriff was smiling wryly.

Polk said, "Boy, will you believe me now? Will you go on back to Utah and forget this town?"

Matt shook his head. He flung the blankets back and sat on the edge of the bed, his bare feet resting on the rough board floor. He dropped his head into his hands to ease its throbbing.

In that position he said sourly, "No," and looked up. "What kind of a man are you, Alf? What hold has Tillman got over you? You let him shoot down Dan and Frankie. Maybe that couldn't be helped. But hanging Will was plain murder and there are laws against murder in every territory in the West. You're sworn to uphold the law. Why the hell don't you do it?"

Polk was silent and his eyes avoided Matt's. Matt said, "Suppose I was to swear out an assault warrant against Tillman and his crew? Would you serve it?"

Alf got up and walked to the window. He stared down into the street for a long while before he answered. At last he grunted, "Sure, kid. I'd serve it. But don't be a fool. Tillman would have his bunch out in a couple of hours. And you'd only make a laughing-stock of yourself."

"Suppose I'd swear out a murder warrant? Would you serve that?"

"I'd have to. But how long do you think you'd last if I did? You'd be the only complaining witness. How long do you think Tillman would let you live?"

"But if he didn't get me?"

Alf sighed. "Tillman would be tried. There'd be no witnesses to appear against him. The men who were along with that posse would deny it. And Matt, hard as it is to accept, there's a lot of sympathy in any cattle country for a man who catches his own rustlers."

Matt gave him a long, level stare. "Get out of here, Alf. Get out."

Polk walked to the door. His face showed no resentment, but only ill-concealed regret. "All right, kid. I'll go. But I hoped I could talk some sense into you. I hoped you'd see the way the cards are stacked. What are you going to do now?"

"I'm going home. I'll go back out to the old place and live. I'm going to gather up what cattle still carry the Rocking H brand, and pick up where old Dan left off."

"Rustling?"

Matt looked at him pityingly. "Why did I leave this country, Alf?"

"All right. You left because you wouldn't go along with Dan's rustling. But can you ever convince Tillman that you aren't sore enough to misbrand every one of his calves you find? Can you ever convince the people around here that you aren't just like Dan?"

"Tillman will never catch me red-handed. He can't if I let his stock alone."

Alf looked at him a moment more. He said, "You're a fool, Matt. You just haven't growed up yet." He shrugged as he turned away. "Go ahead, Matt. Play out your hand even when you know the deck is stacked. Only don't come crying to me after you've lost your chips." He closed the door behind him.

Matt tried to control the rage that flooded his face with blood. His head pounded. He got up, crossed the room, and peered at himself in the cracked mirror. A bandage was wound around his forehead; another covered a torn ear. Otherwise his cuts had been covered with patches of court plaster.

He was aware of stiffness around his middle, and feeling, discovered a thick tight bandage around his ribs. He wondered how many of them were broken and suddenly understood the sharp pains he'd had whenever he breathed deeply.

He sat back down on the bed, fished makings out of his sheepskin that lay on the floor by the bed and rolled himself a smoke. He touched a match to its end and inhaled deeply.

All right, he thought, *face it. The world is full of injustice and you've come smack dab up against it. What are you going to do, beat your brains out trying to fight it? Or are you going to act grown up for a change? Act grown up and take the world the way it is instead of trying to change it?*

A man can talk sense to himself but it doesn't always help. Matt's mind was made up as he rose and began to put on his clothes. Gray light filtering into the room told him that dusk was very near.

A knocking at the door startled him, and he looked anxiously for his gun. He found it on the oaken commode and picked it up. It struck him then that the knocking had not sounded like a man's knock would.

Grinning a little sheepishly he laid the gun back down and called, "Come in."

The door opened and Lily Kibben stepped into the room. Immediately her face clouded with concern. "You shouldn't be up. You have broken ribs and a concussion." She smiled faintly, "Also you have multiple lacerations, as the doctor put it."

Matt grinned at her. "In everyday language, a sore head."

"Yes." She looked at him with frank interest, a frown of puzzlement on her brow. "Why did you come back? Surely you must have known it would be like this."

"I guess I did. Let's just say I'm mule-headed. Stubborn."

"What are you going to do now?"

"Go out to the home place. Work."

"And try to prove that your father and brothers weren't guilty?"

He shook his head. "No. They were guilty all right. They'd been rustling Tillman's stock for years. I knew it and everybody else knew it too. I left in the first place because I wouldn't go along with it."

"What do you hope to prove, then?"

He said soberly, "Look. If they'd let me alone today, maybe I'd have turned around and left. It wasn't right that Dan and Frankie were shot, and it certainly wasn't right that Will was hanged. But a man can accept some things, even if they aren't right. Cattle thieves have been hanged before in cattle country.

"But they couldn't let me alone. As soon as they started pushing, I knew I couldn't leave. Do you see that?"

She said quietly, "Maybe I do see." She studied him for a moment, then said, "I was watching you across the street when the fight started. I saw you try to kiss Elaine Tillman."

Matt flushed; he started to speak and stopped, wondering why it seemed so important that he explain that.

Lily murmured, "Why did you do that? Are you in love with her?"

He shook his head positively.

"Was it worth what it cost?"

Matt felt his anger stir. He said, "If you were watching, then you know she brought it on. As soon as I touched her, she changed her mind."

Lily crossed the room and stood facing him. She asked again, "Why did you do it?" She watched him, her eyes searching beneath the surface expression of his face.

He frowned. "I don't like to admit this. I thought it was only because she was a woman asking to be kissed, and because I was a man hungry for a woman's kiss. But there was more to it than that. I wanted to show her . . . and show the town . . . that Hurst was as good a name as Tillman."

Lily smiled. She lifted her face and said, "I think I'd like it if you kissed me."

Matt's arms went out and pulled her against him. Her body was warm and soft. Her lips were loose with expectancy, her eyes bright. Matt kissed her.

At first there was only laxness in the girl, limp surrender. He tightened his arms about her, bore down brutally against her lips.

Suddenly her arms went up around his neck. Her body pressed

hungrily against him. Her lips moved beneath his. And when she drew away, she was breathing hard. She murmured almost soundlessly, "I think if I were Elaine I would regret my struggles."

Matt grinned shakily. "Thanks." He kept his eyes steadily on her, feeling the rise within himself of a hunger that dwarfed any he had ever experienced before.

Lily lowered her glance and backed away. "You must be starved. I'll send you up some food." She turned and walked swiftly through the door.

Matt sat down and pulled on his boots. Oddly, for the first time since his return, he felt proud of himself. He felt as though he were nine feet tall, as though Tillman and the sheriff were his acorn.

He heard the harsh clicking steps of Susan Davenport in the hall, and looked up as she came in with a steaming tray.

She set it down on the table. "Hmpff. Room service now, is it? What did you do to that girl?"

Matt grinned at her mockingly. "She's twenty-one, isn't she?"

"Some ways. Others, she ain't. You hurt her, Matt Hurst, and I'll. . . ."

"You'll what?"

She faced him defiantly, "I'll kill you myself."

Matt said, "I won't hurt her. Not if I can help it."

Susan flounced out of the room. Matt pulled up a chair and began to eat. He could hear the wind howling outside and he thought of the twenty miles out to Rocking H with dismal dislike. But he knew that if he didn't go out tonight he'd never go.

So he finished his dinner quickly, gulped the scalding coffee, and slipped into his sheepskin. Then he tramped downstairs and picking up his saddle and carpetbag went out into the biting wind.

He gasped as the full fury of the sub-zero blast struck him. And winced at the subsequent pain in his ribs. Bending forward against the force of it, he slogged up the street to the north until he came to the stable.

Behind him the town seemed almost deserted. Here and there an oil lamp flickered wanly in some window, but the streets were empty, and the horses of Tillman's crew were no longer racked before the Bullshead.

Inside the stable, he dumped his saddle and bag beside the door and went into the tiny tackroom that served also as an office for old Si VanNess. Si sat with his feet against the pot-bellied stove, and he looked up inquiringly as Matt came in, not recognizing him at first. "Not figgerin' to ride in this, are you, stranger?"

Matt nodded. He fished a bandanna from his pocket, took off his hat and tied the bandanna over his ears. Si recognized him and slammed his feet down onto the floor. "Matt Hurst!"

"Yeah. Matt Hurst."

"Goin' home?" There was a thinly veiled hostility in Si's voice.

Matt nodded. "I want a horse."

"Dunno. Dunno about that."

"You'd better find out fast. I'll rent him or buy him, but I want a horse."

"Reckon you better buy."

Matt shrugged resignedly. "All right. But no Hurst ever stole a horse and you damn well know it."

"No offense, Matt. No offense."

But the wizened old man didn't back down on his demand that Matt buy the horse. He shuffled into the cold, gloomy rear of the stable and returned shortly leading a big blue roan gelding. Matt carried a lantern out and set it on the floor while he went over the horse. He would not put it past Si to palm off a string-halted or smooth-mouthed horse on him. The horse was sound, however, and young, so he paid the seventy dollars Si demanded without comment.

Town fell behind, and Matt headed directly north along the road. After the first five miles, his feet were numb. He got off and walked a while.

Snow fell thicker now, and began to pile up on the ground.

A sense of hopelessness and depression increased in Matt's consciousness. *Why am I doing this?* he asked himself. It was now obvious that vengeance for the death of his father and brothers was out of the question. It was also obvious that years would be consumed in living down the bad name Hursts had always had hereabouts.

Yet hard as it was, Matt knew it was a thing he had to do if he wanted to live at peace with his own conscience.

Midnight passed. Matt walked enough to keep the circulation up in his legs and feet. He almost missed the turn that led to the Hurst ranch, but he realized it and retraced his steps. After a few moments, dismounting to walk, he saw the dim hoofprints of horses in the road before him, almost drifted over by driving snow.

Instantly he swung into the saddle, spurred to a reckless gallop. What were they up to now?

He knew, really, even before he saw the glow in the sky. He knew and rode recklessly, his face twisted into a savage, bitter pattern. They had burned him out!

As he rode up before the smoldering ruins, he was shouting at the top of his lungs—shouting curses, blasphemies—shouting threats, and almost sobbing, with hurt and cold and awful frustration.

Chilled and shaking, he piled off the horse and warmed himself in the charred and glowing embers of the house. He looked around at the firelit yard. They had burned the barn as well as the house.

But the corral stood intact. And dug into a bluff a hundred yards from the house was the spud cellar, something they couldn't burn.

This was the place Matt Hurst remembered from the time he began remembering. It was where he had been born. The buildings stood in the center of a 160-acre homestead claim. And surrounding that, was Rocking H range.

Slumped and somber, he stood and stared at what was left. He was beaten. Even Matt could see that now, and admit it because he had to. It was ride back to town, sell his horse, and get on the train for Utah. A man could stand only so much and Matt had stood it.

Something twitched at his hat, snatched it from his head. The report came instantly, a deep booming report like that of a rifle. Matt hit the ground before its roar had quite died away, lying silent and still.

So he was not even to have his chance to run? Well to hell with them! He'd not run and he'd not quit. He'd stay, and if death were his due for that, then it couldn't be helped. He'd take a few of them with him.

He made his breathing shallow and waited. After a few moments he heard a soft shuffling in the snow. It came nearer—and then a rifle muzzle dug savagely into his back. He heard a man's hoarse breathing.

Matt suddenly threw himself backward against the rifle muzzle with all the violence he could muster, rolling as he did. He came up grasping the icy gun muzzle in one hand. He pulled and the rifle bearer tumbled toward him with a sharp cry. Matt raised his knees and they caught the man in the stomach.

But with the breath that drove so savagely from him the man brought the words, "Matt! Don't!"

Matt sat up, peering down at the man's shaggy face. "Kip! What the hell are you doing here?"

"Waitin' fer you to come home." Kip struggled to his feet.

"Where were you? I didn't see anyone."

"Sure not. I was in the spud cellar." Kip's voice was cracked and reedy. "Come on. I got a fire goin' in there and it's a sight warmer than it is out here. I got coffee and whiskey too."

Matt followed him silently across the yard. A lamp was burning in the spud cellar, lighting its moldy walls and dirt floor. There was a moldy, damp smell in the air, but Kip had raked out the disintegrating sacks of rotting potatoes and the floor was as clean as it would ever be.

Kip had made a bunk out of one of the barn doors by laying it on the floor and spreading his blankets over it.

He poured out a cup of coffee, laced it stiffly with whiskey, and handed it to Matt. "You look like you could use this."

Matt asked after the first scalding sip, "Did you see them do this, Kip?"

"I did. Skjerik ramrodded this dirty job. He had three men with him."

"Tillman along?"

Kip shook his head.

"When did they do it?"

"Just after dark." The old man peered at Matt. "What hit you? A freight train?"

Matt made a twisted grin. "Same freight train that burned this place, Kip. Only it was Skjerik and six men."

"What you goin' to do about it?"

Matt shrugged. "I don't know. This is rough on me, but it wasn't for me that I came back. I came back to see if Dan and Frankie and Will got a fair shake. They didn't, but they knew the chances they ran taking Tillman's stock. They got what they knew they would if he caught them."

"You mean to say you don't know?"

"Know what?"

"That they'd quit rustling Tillman's stock. They quit when you pulled out. Dan hadn't changed a brand for damned nigh four years. He wrote a couple hundred letters to different parts of the country tryin' to find you and get you to come back. I guess he realized you was right."

Matt stared at him, his mouth hanging open. "Kip, you're crazy. Why else would Tillman go after them?"

"He needed Hurst grass. About a year ago he bought the Holt place that borders you on the west. After that, this place cut him plumb in two. He tried to buy it from Dan half a dozen times, only Dan figured maybe you'd want it some day."

A crazy, tight, nervous fury was growing in Matt. He said, "But Alf said. . . ."

"Alf," Kip snorted. "He's been courtin' that daughter of Tillman's. He'd perjure himself to St. Peter to get her."

"He's twenty years older than her." Matt was incredulous.

"Sure. Them kind want even harder than a young buck. They want so hard nothin' else matters to 'em."

"But how the hell did Tillman get away with it? There's other people in the country. Surely someone knew . . . ?"

"They knew Dan and your brothers were suspected of rustlin'. Dan didn't go around tellin' folks he'd quit. Hursts have had a bad name in these parts for so long, it'd take a sight more than Dan's words to whitewash it anyhow."

Matt whistled. "Kip, how can you be sure?"

"Boy, I was with 'em. 'Twas a blizzard, something like the one tonight. We were movin' a bunch of Rockin' H stuff in to be fed for the winter. They jumped us in that patch of timber over by Oak Springs. We made a run fer it, scatterin' like Dan said. I was lookin' back and seen Olaf and Tillman ridin' together. 'Bout then a low tree limb got me on the side of the head and dumped me out of the saddle. When I come to, I started huntin' around fer Dan and the boys. I found 'em. I found 'em all right. Dan and Frankie shot. Will hanged."

"What'd you do?"

Kip looked at the floor. He cleared his throat. His voice was low and shamed. "Nothin', boy. Nothin'. I knew the thing was so big nobody'd dare let a witness to it live. I knew it was useless to go to Alf Polk. So I just kept my mouth shut. I knew you'd hear about it and come hot-footin' it home. And I figgered I'd be a sight more use to you alive than dead."

"How's it happen they didn't look for you? Didn't they know you were working for the Rocking H?"

"That's just it. I wasn't. Nobody even knew I was in the country. I'd been in Colorado ridin' for an outfit down there durin' the summer. When they laid me off, I drifted in here to see if maybe Dan wouldn't hire me durin' the winter."

Matt realized that his fists were clenched so hard that the nails were biting into his palms. He spat his words out like bullets, "They won't get away with it. They won't get away with it."

III

"RIDE, VENGEANCE, RIDE!"

Matt lay awake most of the night, staring upward into the utter blackness of the cellar. Outside, the wind howled and whined and deposited a six-inch layer of snow on the ground. In the morning, Matt was no nearer a solution than he'd been before.

Essentially, Dan's innocence and that of his brothers made no difference at all in the solution to the problem. He was still face-to-face with the whole county's enmity; he was still confronted with the sheriff's dishonesty and dereliction of duty.

But he remembered the look of shame in Alf Polk's eyes and his words, "All right. Rub it in. Maybe I deserve it at that."

He made up his mind and rolled out of his blankets. As he did, Kip stirred and sat up sleepily. Matt built a fire in the cast-iron stove Kip had apparently salvaged from the ranch junk heap. Kip got a quarter of venison where he had hung it outside and cut off a half a dozen steaks. He mixed up some biscuits and slid them into the oven.

"Matt, you look like mebbe you've made up your mind."

Matt nodded. "I'm going to take a whirl at Alf Polk. He wasn't along on that raid when Dan and the boys were killed. Maybe he don't know it was a put up job."

"What if you're wrong?"

"I won't be any worse off than I am right now. They're doin' their damndest to get me anyway."

Kip's seamed, aged face showed his disapproval. But he only grunted. He crossed the room, got his rifle, and began to clean it. He said, "I'll get ready, son. They'll be after me quick as Alf can get in touch with Tillman."

Matt said, "Kip, it's our only chance. Some of the men who were along on that deal are bound to've read the brands on that bunch of stuff. They'll know they weren't DT stock but our own. Get 'em in a jail cell, and I'll lay you ten to one they'll talk."

Kip shrugged. "Wish I had your confidence. Well, hell, I'm old anyhow. I got to go sometime, and I'd rather go with a bullet in me than lay in a bed and die slow."

Matt grinned as he mopped gravy from his plate with a broken biscuit. "Worrying is what gave you all that gray hair."

He got up and shrugged into his sheepskin. Outside, the world was dazzling with bright sunlight on fresh snow. The sky was as blue as Lily Kibben's eyes. He got his horse from the corral where he had put him last night late and saddled up, wishing the animal had had some hay last night, or at least some grain. But the hay-stack had caught from the barn, and even yet was smoldering, sending a column of blue smoke into the sky like a signal. All the grain had been in the barn. He made a mental note to have a load of hay and grain sent out today from town.

Kip looked up at him after he had mounted. He said, "Let's see. It'll take you till ten or eleven to get to town. It'll take Alf till two to ride out to Tillman's. So I reckon we can expect company along about three or four. You be back by then?"

"Sure."

"Bring me back boxes of forty-four-fortys. Better bring a couple of boxes of forty-fives for yourself. We'll likely need 'em."

Matt snorted and rode away.

Riding, he considered Kip's doubt, weighing it against his own confidence. All depended, he was aware, upon Alf Polk's honesty. If he were mistaken in giving Alf credit for honesty, then Kip was right. They'd fight to the death right in the spud cellar.

But if Alf were honest, he'd take a posse out to DT for Tillman, Olaf Skjerik, and the men who had ridden on that murderous errand.

The air warmed rapidly under the bright sun as Matt rode. Under-foot the snow turned soft, and it was melting away from the high spots which were all but scoured clean.

Matt's mind was filled with memories of his father and two brothers and with regrets that none of Dan's many letters had found him. He would have liked to have made his peace with them before they died. He would have liked to unsay some of the harsh things he had said on the day he left.

He was touched by the fact that Dan and his brothers had given up their raids on DT stock because of his leaving. And he was more than ever determined to see that their murderers came to justice.

Engrossed by his thoughts, he did not see the rider who pulled out of a side road and stopped to wait for him until he was almost upon her.

It was Elaine Tillman. Her smile was bright as if a trifle uncertain.

He stared at her, unsmiling.

She faltered, "Matt, I'm so awfully sorry about yesterday. But I don't think I could have stopped them."

"You didn't even try. And you know damned well you were asking me to kiss you."

"Matt you're wrong. I can see how you might have got that idea, but. . . ."

Matt laughed harshly. Elaine flushed. She said defiantly, "All right. I was asking for it. But as soon as you touched me, I remembered Dad and Olaf inside the saloon. I knew they might come out at any minute. I was afraid of what they'd do if they found me in your arms. So I struggled, hoping to get loose before they came out. You mustn't blame them too much, Matt. Your father and brother stole a lot of Dad's cattle. They naturally hate the name Hurst."

Matt's expression didn't change. His eyes were bullet-cold. "Did you know they burned me out last night? House, barn, haystacks. I spent the night in the spud cellar."

Elaine showed surprise that could not have been feigned. "Matt, it couldn't have been them. Dad wouldn't do such a thing."

Again Matt laughed. "They were seen. And I'll tell you something else. Dan and Frankie and Will were driving a herd of Rocking H stuff when they were killed. It was deliberate, cold-blooded murder. They hadn't stolen a DT critter for four years . . . not since I pulled out of the country. And Dell Tillman knew it."

Elaine's eyes blazed. "Matt Hurst, you're a liar."

He shook his head. "I've got proof of it."

"Proof. Proof. What proof could you have?"

He smiled coldly. "An eyewitness."

"Who?"

"Same one that saw them burn the buildings at Rocking H last night. Kip Reynolds."

She pulled up her horse and stared at him. She must have read truth and sincerity in his eyes, for she suddenly slumped in the saddle and the fight went out of her.

"What are you going to do?"

"I'm going to see Tillman and Skjerik dangling at the end of a rope. I'm going to see every man that was with them that night rotting in the state pen. I'm going to see Alf Polk driven out of the country, disgraced because he permitted it to go unpunished. And I'm going to see the name of Hurst respected and that of Tillman dirtied the way my own name has been dirtied."

"Is that all you want, Matt?"

"Not altogether. I want the buildings at Rocking H paid for."

Suddenly Elaine slipped out of the saddle. She walked up to the side of Matt's horse and stood looking up at him. Tears of humiliation stood out in her eyes. She fumbled in the pocket of her wolfskin coat, but Matt paid little attention to that. He thought she was searching for a handkerchief.

She said, "Matt, please. I've had no hand in all these things. Must I suffer too?" Her hand came out of her pocket and she caught at Matt's cinch as the horse sidestepped nervously away.

She was pleading, "Matt, you used to like me. And I liked you, Matt, only I was afraid of Dad."

Matt felt a moment's doubt. Then his mind pictured Will, swinging in the icy breeze because Tillman was greedy, pictured Dan and Frankie, still on the ground while snow drifted over their unfeeling faces—because Tillman was greedy.

She said quickly, "Matt, is it all dead, your feeling for me? Because if it isn't, we can still be happy." She made a shaky smile, and in her eyes was promise, invitation. "Get down, Matt. Please."

Matt's eyes searched her face. Odd, the resemblance it bore to her father's even while it was entirely different. Odd, that resemblance—the same arrogance, carefully masked, the same unbending ruthlessness. Dell would do anything to attain his ends, and Matt knew suddenly that Elaine would too.

He wanted to laugh, to mock her offer. But his innate sense of chivalry would not permit it. He said gently, "It's too late, Elaine. Too many things have happened. I couldn't let Dell get away with those three murders even if I wanted to."

Now, her carefully masked arrogance and ruthlessness showed in her face. Her expression contorted with balked, frustrated fury.

Matt's horse suddenly shied away from the girl. Matt felt his saddle turn and felt himself dumped onto the snowy ground. Elaine stood ten feet away, looking at him, a cryptic smile on her face, a small pocket knife in her hand.

Matt struggled to his feet, more surprised than angered. "What the hell did you do that for?"

She laughed softly, mockingly, and her eyes held a gleam of triumph. "You're beaten, Matt Hurst. Do you know what I'm going to do?"

He shook his head, thoroughly puzzled.

She put the knife in her pocket, and her hand came out holding a derringer, which she pointed steadily at him. "I'm going to tear my clothes and scratch my face. I'm going to ride into town and say that you attacked me." Her free hand went to her face and her nails raked deliberate gashes across her cheek. Matt tensed, started toward her, but a freezing of her glance, a tightening of her hand around the grip of the gun halted him.

She said, "Matt, don't do it, or I'll kill you."

"You wouldn't get away with it." But he knew he was wrong. She would get away with it. The word of a Tillman was better than that of a Hurst any day. He stopped, holding his hands rigidly at his sides while he watched the mounting hysteria in Elaine.

She caught the neck of her coat and ripped it open, and the buttons popped off onto the snowy ground. She caught at her bodice and ripped it downward, exposing to his startled eyes a smoothly rounded, swelling white breast.

Again Matt tensed, wanting desperately to halt this. There was something indecent about it that shocked him. Yet what could he do? Even if he escaped being shot by that steady gun in her hand, what would have been accomplished? He could not restrain her indefinitely. He could not hold her here all day.

He whispered, "Elaine, stop it. This is crazy."

"Is it? I don't think so. I think it's the only way I can beat you Matt."

Her hand went upward to her hair, deliberately began pulling the hairpins and dropping them. Her hair streamed in a cascade about her shoulders.

And Matt knew an empty, defeated feeling. She was right. He was helpless to stop her and he was beaten. He'd had Tillman right where he wanted him; he'd been able to foresee justice done for the murder of his father and brothers. Now, all hope of that was gone.

The townspeople would believe Elaine. Nothing would suit them better than to believe that this final degradation was possible for a Hurst.

Still holding the tiny gun on him, Elaine walked over and mounted her horse. She rode away, unspeaking but smiling triumphantly.

With violent trembling fingers, Matt got out his pocket knife and walked over to where his saddle lay. He began to mend his cinch.

His emotions ran the gamut, in the next few moments, from utter despair to towering rage. He cut holes in each end of the cut cinch latigo, then cut off one end of his leather saddle strings, and with this laced the two ends together.

He caught his horse and slammed the saddle up with unnecessary viciousness. The horse shied and looked at him with reproachful eyes. Matt leaped into the saddle, but he did not dig in his spurs. Instead, he looked toward town, looked back toward Rocking H, and then looked in the direction of Tillman's DT.

An idea began to blossom in his head, giving hope to his reluctance to run.

When he did finally sink his spurs, his horse was headed for Tillman's place. He was through running. If he ran now, he knew what the end would be. They'd hunt him down on Elaine Tillman's testimony until they found him. And they'd find him if it took ten years. When they did, there could be no end but the hangman's noose. Not even a trial to precede it. For only this way could the men of the frontier keep their women safe from the riffraff that prowled its lonely reaches.

Matt's horse pounded away the few short miles that lay between the place that Elaine had left him and the Tillman ranch. A little before eight he topped a rise and looked down into its yard. He knew the next few minutes would draw heavily on his dwindling patience. So he steeled himself to wait.

Apparently breakfast had been over for some time. Yet the crew was still in the bunkhouse, receiving instructions on the day's tasks. Matt saw Tillman come out onto the long veranda of the house, pause and light a cigar.

Hatred poured through Matt like a poison. His hands trembled and his face went white. It took all of his self-control to keep his hand off the grips of his gun, even though he knew this was an impossible range for a revolver.

Tillman puffed luxuriously for a few moments, then strolled ponderously toward the bunkhouse. He met Olaf at the door, and the crew spilled out around the two as they stood talking.

There was a brief commotion in the corral as each roped out a horse for the day. Then the crew mounted, split, and in two bunches rode at a slow trot away from the ranch. Leaving Tillman and Skjerik in the bunkhouse doorway.

The sound of their talk carried clearly in the crisp air if the words did not. Matt began to curse softly, virulently under his breath.

"Separate, damn you. Separate. I can't jump you both and I've got to have Tillman."

As though in immediate recognition of his command, Olaf slouched away toward the corral. And moments later rode out on the trail of one of the crews.

Matt did not move. Tillman watched Olaf until he was out of sight. Then he turned and made his way toward the house.

Matt wasted no time at all now. At a run, he caught his horse and swung himself to the saddle. He urged the horse into a swift, relatively silent running walk and headed off the rise toward the ranchyard, hoping that Tillman would not pause at the window and look out.

He reached the yard without incident. Still it was touchy, for one of the crew might return after something forgotten in the morning's haste.

He tied his horse to the porch rail and, walking soundlessly, mounted the steps. Since the morning was fairly warm, Tillman had left the door ajar. Matt took an instant to draw his gun and thumb back the hammer and then he stepped into the house.

The huge front room was empty. Matt tried to recall from the couple of times he had been in this house where the office was exactly. He decided it was off the oak-paneled dining room.

He saw that he had been right an instant before he stepped into the office doorway, the gun steady in his hand.

Dell Tillman looked up with surprised annoyance that changed in a miraculously short instant to pure undistilled rage. He said, "Get out of here."

Matt's lips curled unpleasantly. "Not until you come with me."

"Are you crazy? Have you gone plumb nuts?" His hand yanked open one of the desk drawers before him and dived inside.

But Matt was quicker. With two swift strides he reached the desk and, leaning over it, slashed savagely at Tillman's face. The gun barrel caught Tillman's nose, broke the cartilage in it and shoved it to one side, bleeding internally and purpling outside.

Tillman forgot the gun in the drawer. He clapped a hand to his nose, and tears of pain stood out in his eyes and rolled across his cheeks. But he uttered no sound.

His eyes were blazing coals as they stared their defiance at Matt.

Matt said evenly, "You're coming with me."

Matt's gun barrel slashed again. This time it caught Tillman on the side of his jaw. The sound of bone breaking was plain in the room. And this time, a howl of pain, almost a sob, came from Tillman's tight-held lips.

His other hand went up and shoved his sagging jaw back into place. Pain whitened his face and brought beads of sweat out on his broad forehead.

Matt said evenly, hiding the sickness that seared his soul, "Get on your feet and come with me. Or do you want another taste of this?"

Tillman cringed. He got up and came around the desk, still holding his shattered jaw carefully in one hand. He said weakly, "Let me tie this up. Man, I've got to have a doctor."

"Later," Matt laughed sourly. "I want it to hurt you till we get where we're going. I want it to hurt you bad. Maybe if it hurts you enough, you'll want to talk. Maybe you'll want to tell me everything you know without making me hit you again."

He herded Tillman ahead of him out the door. Tillman winced as the cold air touched the exposed roots of his broken teeth. Matt crossed the yard and, watching Tillman out of the corner of his eyes, roped a horse out of the corral. He pulled a saddle from the top rail and cinched it down on the horse's back. He walked across the yard, mounted, and returned.

"Get up," he said curtly. "And don't forget. There's nothing but death in this for me if I get caught. If we run into someone, I'm going to kill you first. With a shot right in the belly where it'll hurt before it kills you."

Tillman mounted painfully. And Matt headed out at a trot.

A trot is the most painful gait imaginable for a man in pain anyway. With Tillman's broken and sagging jaw, it was torture. Whenever Tillman would pale and sway in the saddle, Matt would slow to a walk. And when Tillman would apparently recover, he'd again urge the horses into that bone-jolting trot.

Twice, Tillman tried to speak, but Matt only said brutally, "Shut up!"

Just before noon, they reached the dug-out spud cellar on Rocking H. Kip came out of the cellar door and stood, rifle in hand, watching. Matt said harshly to Tillman, "Get down!"

Tillman slid off his horse, nearly collapsing as his feet touched the ground. Matt dropped his horse's reins. He shoved Tillman ahead of him to the dug-out door.

Kip's eyes widened, "What'd you do to him?"

"It's a long story that I'll tell you later. Something came up that made me change my plans this morning. Go look in my bag. You'll find a paper and pencil. Bring it out. I want to write down what Tillman's got to say."

Tillman showed no resistance, indicated no will to refuse.

Kip came back with a pad and pencil and Matt sat down with his back to the door. On the top of the sheet he wrote, STATEMENT, and the date, JANUARY 27, 1887.

He looked up at Tillman. "Make it easy on yourself. What happened the day you jumped Dan and my two brothers."

Tillman hesitated. Matt said, "Kip, hit him in the jaw with your fist."

Kip started toward Tillman. But Tillman said, "No. I'll tell you."

"Go ahead." Matt poised the pencil and began to write swiftly as Tillman talked.

"I rode in that morning and told Alf that Dan was moving a herd of DT stock. Alf deputized me and Olaf, and we took Sam Willis, Joe Furness, and Utah Dunning."

"Five of you then."

Tillman nodded. "We caught them over by Oak Springs."

"Did they have any DT stock?"

Tillman shook his head after a wary glance at Kip. "Only Rocking H stuff. We jumped them and shot two of them down. We caught Will and strung him up."

"Did your crew get a look at the cattle?"

Tillman shook his head. "It was snowing. Nobody was payin' any attention to the cattle, and they scattered anyhow. But Joe Furness's horse was shot out from under him and while he was lying there a little bunch of the cattle went past him. He asked Olaf about it later. Olaf told him he'd kill him if he opened his mouth about it."

Matt began to grin. He looked up at Kip. "We've got two eyewitnesses then."

Tillman looked surprised. Matt said, "There was a fourth man along with them that day. Kip here. He'd just drifted in from Colorado and Dan agreed to give him his keep for his winter's work."

He got up and handed the pad to Tillman. "Sign it."

Tillman did. Matt folded up the paper and handed it to Kip. "Keep this. When the sheriff arrives, pay no mind to what he's got to say about me. But make him read this."

Kip grinned. "All right."

But Matt did not return the grin. He said soberly, "You haven't heard the worst of it yet. I'm supposed to have attacked Elaine Tillman. If I can talk my way out of that one, I'll be better than I think I am."

Tillman's face grew slowly purple. Matt said, "Do you know what your daughter did? She cut my cinch this morning so I couldn't beat her to town. She clawed her own face and half tore her clothes off. Then she took out for town."

Tillman lunged at him. "Liar!"

Kip tripped the man. But his eyes were cold as he looked at Matt. "I hope he's wrong, Matt. I got no use for a man that'll force a woman."

Matt grinned sourly. "Even you huh, Kip?" He mounted and rode away fuming.

Halfway to town, Matt topped a low rise of ground over which the road ran and saw the sheriff's posse sweeping toward him. He was about to leave the road and seek concealment when the sheriff led his men off the road, taking the more direct route across country toward Rocking H.

Matt, mostly concealed by the rise, sat looking ruefully after them. A man wouldn't have a chance with a bunch like that. He wouldn't even get back to town. They'd hunt around until they found a cottonwood limb strong enough to hold him and then they'd hang him.

Shrugging, he lifted the blue roan to a mile-eating, rolling lope, and stayed with the gait steadily all the way to the outskirts of Granada. There, he left the horse in an abandoned, sagging building and proceeded on foot.

He walked openly down the street toward the center of town, nervous and very much alert, ready at an instant's notice to snake his gun from its holster and start blasting away. He didn't intend to be taken alive, to be hanged for a crime of which he was wholly innocent.

The very unexpectedness of his presence here must have carried him through, for he reached the alley behind the hotel without incident, save for a searching stare given him by an oldster who came out of the Chinese restaurant next door to dump a pan of dishwater.

He went on past the hotel, waiting until this oldster should go back inside the restaurant. When he did, Matt whirled and ran back to the rear door of the hotel. He entered, closed the door behind him, and stood back to the wall, waiting for his eyes to become accustomed to this dimness after the sun-glare on new snow outside.

He stood in a storeroom, piled high with canned goods, barrels of sugar, molasses, and crackers.

There were two doors leading out. One, Matt surmised, led to the kitchen, and he guessed that the one which showed the most wear was probably the kitchen door. He crossed the room and opened the other one.

Cautiously he peered through. He was looking into a long hallway, which ended in the lobby thirty feet away.

He slipped through the door and closed it behind him. He advanced along the hallway until he could look into the lobby. Now, he realized, he needed some luck. Somehow, he had to find Lily Kibben without being seen himself.

The lobby was deserted, save for the clerk poring over a ledger at the desk. It was mid-afternoon, and Matt knew the dining room would also be deserted. The chances were good that Lily was in her room on the second floor.

He made the stairway without being seen and crept silently upward. He reached the top and paused, trying to remember the direction Lily had been coming from when he'd met her that first day.

He had a vague memory of her coming from around to the left of the stairway—and there were only two rooms there.

He knocked softly on the first one, numbered 203. He got no answer, so he moved on to the second, 205. He heard steps inside the room, and grew tense as he waited.

When Lily opened the door, he released a long sigh of relief.

Her face, when she saw him, seemed to smooth out into cautious neutrality. "What are you doing here? Don't you know how dangerous it . . . ?"

"I know." He shoved past her and closed the door. "First of all, do you believe I attacked Elaine?" he asked levelly.

"Did you?"

"No. I didn't."

"Then who did?" Her eyes withheld judgment.

"Nobody." He crossed the room and sat down tiredly on the bed. He looked around him. Lily's room was a feminine room, from frilly lace curtains at the window to the satin spread on which he sat. A feminine room that had a light fragrance of woman and woman's perfume.

"I don't understand."

"I met her on the road this morning. I told her I had proof that my father and brothers had been driving their own stock the day they were jumped by Tillman. I told her I was going to the sheriff with the proof."

"What was the proof?"

"An eyewitness Tillman didn't know existed. An old-timer that's been around Rocking H off and on for years. He told me Dan hadn't mis-branded a steer since I left four years ago. He told me Tillman wanted Rocking H and that was why he rigged up that rustling scheme."

"Then what happened?"

"When Elaine became convinced that I was telling the truth, she started to plead with me." Matt felt a flush stealing into his face. He said, "She came over to my horse and grabbed hold of the cinch. First thing I knew, I was on the ground, and my saddle was too. She'd cut the latigo. She pulled a gun on me, said she'd shoot if I tried to stop her. She clawed her face, ripped her clothes and took down her hair. She told me I'd best get out of the country because she was going into Granada and tell that I'd attacked her."

For the first time, Lily's expression showed belief. "What did you do?"

"What could I do? I could have made a try for her gun, and maybe I'd have got it. But that wouldn't have helped. I couldn't hold her there forever. I figured I was cooked. But I wasn't going to let her stunt get Tillman out of paying for killing Dan and my brothers. So I rode over to DT and kidnapped him. I beat him up some with my gun barrel. I took him over to Rocking H and made him confess in front of Kip Reynolds."

"Matt, Matt, what are you going to do now? They'll lynch you if they can catch you."

"I know it." He got up and faced her, standing close. "I just wanted you to know the truth from me. I didn't want you thinking that what Elaine said was true."

If he had needed a reward for the risks he had taken coming here, he got it now. He found it in the shining brightness of Lily's eyes. "Thank you, Matt."

He turned toward the door. Lily asked, "What are you going to do?"

He shrugged. "Run, I guess. I don't see how I can save myself. But at least, Tillman and Olaf Skjerik will pay for what they did. I only wish there wasn't so damned much snow on the ground. I won't have much chance. . . ."

Lily interrupted excitedly, "Matt, wait. Did you struggle at all with Elaine this morning?"

"I never touched her."

"Matt, are you sure? It's important. Are you sure you never touched her?"

He nodded, puzzled. Flushed, excited, Lily began to talk. As she did, a flicker of hope began to glow in Matt's eyes. Ten minutes later, he slipped swiftly down the stairs, back to the alley by the same route he had followed coming in.

There was no difference in the way he walked when he came to the street. Before, he had come with his head averted, with his hat pulled low over his eyes. Now, he strolled along boldly, looking each man he met straight in the eyes.

The third one recognized him. Matt saw the man's face pale, saw his mouth drop open. He went on past, and felt the man's eyes boring into his back. He waited another instant and then he stole a quick look behind him. The man was running frantically along the street toward the center of town.

When he was out of effective pistol range, the man began to yell, "It's Hurst! Matt Hurst! He's right here in town, bold as brass. The damned skunk!"

Matt smiled faintly. He continued to walk unhurriedly. A rifle boomed out behind him and the bullet tore splinters from the frame building wall beside him.

Feigning surprise, Matt looked around. He could see them coming, a ragged line of them, like skirmishers in an Indian battle. As they came, order began to emerge from their confusion. Matt heard the authoritative voice of Judge Fisher, saw his tall, spare figure in the vanguard of the approaching mob.

Matt broke into a hard run.

He went around a corner, running as hard as he could. In seconds, a few of that mob would be mounted. They'd run down a man afoot in no time.

He reached his horse. He heard the howl of the mob plainly and knew they were drawing close, too close. He heard the pound of hoofbeats.

He mounted and spurred his horse savagely out the door and into the open, ducking low to avoid the door-frame. And went out of town at a hard run with his mounted pursuers only a short hundred feet behind.

For the first two miles, Matt rode as hard as he could, and barely managed to stay out of range of their booming guns. But at last, they apparently decided to wait for the remainder of the mob to catch up, and so slowed to a walk. They had seen the plain trail he made in the snow and had known he could not get away. Matt put about a mile between himself and his pursuers, and then slowed his horse as well. The animal was breathing hard, was sweating heavily. And he was tired. Hardly in condition to serve a man who had to escape.

At a walk, then, Matt left the road and pointed the horse toward Rocking H. But as he rose, he began to doubt the wisdom of Lily's suggestion. He began to doubt, and loosened the bandanna around his throat instinctively as he thought of the rope they would put around his neck.

Clouds had drifted across the sun, black, lowering clouds that forecast another storm. Matt tipped up his face and tried to estimate how long it would hold off before it struck. Four or five hours, he hoped. Four or five hours.

Always behind him were the angry ones, the ones who wanted his blood. A couple of miles short of Rocking H another group pounded up to join the first. Immediately they all surged forward at a hard run.

Matt shrugged and touched the roan with his spurs. Rested a little, the animal answered with a burst of speed. And at last, Matt rode in sight of the Rocking H.

The yard was jammed with the horses of the sheriff's posse. There was a cluster of men before the dug-out cellar. Matt saw Tillman sitting dejectedly on a box. A white bandage around his jaw, tied up on top of his head, made him stand out plainly.

Matt galloped into the yard yelling, "Here I am Sheriff! Come and get me." And pounded out away from it before they recovered from their surprise enough to reach for their guns.

Immediately after leaving, Matt slowed the roan a little. He knew they'd be milling around in the yard for a while before they got organized. Grimly he realized that when they did, there would be over fifty of them on his trail.

He reached the place where the lane to DT joined the road well ahead of them. He dismounted, concealed his horse in a dry wash, and with his rifle poked up out of that same wash, settled himself to wait.

IV

"LAST ROUNDUP"

Lily had barely reached the street when she heard the cry lifted, "There he goes! Get him, damn it, get him!"

Immediately, almost, from the doors along the street, men ran out, carrying rifles, revolvers, pitchforks. They formed a ragged line across the width of the street, grim-faced men who advanced toward the edge of town with purposeful determination.

There was something cold about them all that struck terror to Lily's heart. They would be merciless when they caught Matt. For in the minds of all he was convicted, guilty. The word of a woman, particularly a woman such as Elaine Tillman, could not be doubted.

Judge Fisher took charge, shouting crisp, concise orders. He sent half a dozen men to the livery stable after horses. He instructed those others who had horses saddled to get them immediately and try to head Matt off.

And less than two minutes later, six horsemen swept out of town, a short forty yards behind the fleeing Matt Hurst.

Lily felt a cold touch of fear in her spine. She knew abruptly that if her plan failed, then Matt Hurst's blood would be on her hands.

She was thinking, too, that the sheriff was in love with Elaine, thinking that he would not be inclined to believe Matt's story that Elaine had deliberately lied about his attacking her. She was aware as well that Matt, knowing his own innocence, would rely too much on his ability to convince others of it.

Yet she knew the men of this country. And she knew that not one of them would consent to a hanging if a woman were present.

She broke abruptly away from the hotel veranda and, lifting her skirts, ran swiftly as she could toward the stable. Si VanNess firmly and stubbornly refused to catch and saddle her horse until all of the men waiting were mounted and gone. Lily was forced to wait helplessly, fuming.

At last her horse was ready and, although she was wearing a full-length skirt, Lily mounted astride. She was not much of a rider, and her horse was old and patient. Lily had no spurs, but a small quirt which she had never used hung from her saddle-horn. She took it down and belabored the old horse's rump until he lifted resentfully into a half-hearted trot.

The miles dropped behind with agonizing slowness. Tears of helpless frustration welled up into Lily's blue eyes and ran across her cheeks unheeded. "Oh God," she prayed. "Let me get there in time. Let me get there in time."

She thought of the short time she had known Matt Hurst, and of how much he had come to mean to her. She knew that in Matt was a great capacity for living, for laughing, and loving.

She wondered if his feelings toward her were the same as hers toward him. Perhaps he had only felt a normal man's hunger for a woman, and perhaps that explained his taking her in his arms, his kissing her.

The thought depressed her, and again she began to quirt her horse. She had to beat them to Matt. She had to.

She almost passed the turnoff that went into Tillman's place, but reined in abruptly and whirled around as a call came to her from a dry wash off from the road.

"Lily! Turn that horse around and get back into town. They'll be here any minute."

Lily started to protest, but hardly had she uttered a half dozen words when she heard the confused, distant shout of the posse.

She heard Matt's urgent shout. "Distract them for just a minute. Stop them here at the forks. Then you get back into town."

She had no time to answer that, for they were upon her, pulling their plunging horses to a sliding halt. Lily raised her hand.

The sheriff scowled at her and growled irritably, "What are you doing away out here, Miss Kibben? Don't you know Matt Hurst is somewheres around?" He turned to his posse. "Samuels, ride into town with her. See she gets there safe."

For an instant there was silence. It was broken by Matt's cold, clipped voice from the draw, "Don't a damned one of you stir a hair. I've got a rifle here and I'll use it, make no mistake about that."

Someone in the group stirred, and the rifle barked. Matt said sharply, "Think I'm fooling? The next bullet will kill someone."

The sheriff growled, "Careful boys. Do what he says. Any man that would. . . ."

Matt snarled, "Shut up."

Judge Fisher asked, "What's the idea, Hurst? What do you want?"

"I want you to look at something. You and the sheriff. The rest of you stay put."

Fisher shrugged wearily. "I suppose you want us to believe you never touched Miss Tillman."

"Exactly that. Lily, take the sheriff and the judge and circle around to Tillman's lane. Pick up Elaine's tracks in the snow and follow them here to the main road."

"What'll that prove?"

Matt said, "It will prove that I was never closer than ten feet to Elaine except at the time she cut my cinch latigo. You'll find her hairpins and buttons from her coat lying there at the fork and not a damned track but hers anywhere around." Matt permitted himself a faint, sour grin. "I'm a slick article, Judge, but not slick enough to attack a woman without my tracks mixin' with hers. Go on, take a look."

Judge Fisher reined his horse over and crossed to the Tillman lane. With his eyes on the ground, with the sheriff and Lily following him, he traced Elaine's tracks to the main road, careful not to cross or foul any of them with his own.

When he looked up, he said, "Elaine Tillman lied. Tracks say Matt's telling the truth."

There was a sudden, swelling murmur from the packed group of men. The judge yelled, "All right. Any of you that want to, come over here and look for yourselves. Careful, though, I don't want these tracks messed up."

A man in the crowd said plaintively, "Now why in hell would a woman do a thing like that?"

And the sheriff replied, his voice faint and weak, "I reckon she done it to save Dell."

Lily felt tears of relief welling up in her eyes. Still holding the rifle cautiously, Matt climbed up out of the wash. He looked directly at the sheriff and said harshly, "You've got Dell Tillman. You've got his confession and two witnesses to back it up. What are you going to do about it?"

The sheriff said, "I'll bring Tillman in," but Lily knew he was lying. There was a shiftiness about the sheriff's eyes that betrayed him. Lily looked at the man and felt a reluctant pity. Alf Polk was in a squeeze, all right. He was desperately in love with Elaine. He had probably talked to Elaine before leaving town, and Lily guessed she had put the same price on herself for Alf that she had for Matt, that price being Dell's freedom.

It was a price Alf was prepared to pay. The shiftiness of his eyes told Lily that. The sheriff turned toward the posse. "Go on back to town. I won't need any help bringing in Tillman."

That was apparently the final tip-off to Matt, if one had been needed. He walked over to the wash and got his horse. He rode back and looked at Lily with warmth in his eyes. "Go with them. I'll see you later."

"What are you going to do?"

"I've got to see Kip. And Lily?"

"What, Matt?"

"I owe you more than I can ever pay. I owe you my life."

She was wordless, but her eyes told him many things. Her eyes promised him the world if he came back to her. And her eyes told him that she knew what he intended to do, but her lips were silent.

Her smile was tight, perhaps a little sad, for she knew he was going into worse danger now than any before.

Matt wheeled his horse and rode away at a gallop. He turned at the crest and looked back. Lily had not moved. She was watching him, and she lifted a hand in farewell, as he rode down the slope and dropped from sight.

Riding out, he had pointed his horse toward Rocking H. But as soon as he dropped out of sight, he veered away from that course and took a direct one toward Tillman's DT. Three miles lay between the turnoff and Tillman's ranch. Matt covered them in less than twenty minutes.

He rode in openly, and his eyes were quick to spot the horses, sweated and unsaddled, which had been turned into the corral to cool.

Matt rode up to the bunkhouse and quickly swung down from his horse. He called, "Olaf!"

Olaf Skjerik came to the door hulking, blond, cold as ice and scowling.

Matt said, "Call out your crew."

"Get the hell out of here, before somethin' happens to you. I still remember that clout you gave me on the neck."

"You'll get more than that before I'm through."

Olaf started toward him, and the crew came pouring out of the bunkhouse behind Olaf.

Matt said sharply, "Hold it!"

There was that in his stance, and in his expression, that stopped Olaf as though he had walked into a wall. He looked disturbed for a moment, then gathered himself for a rush.

Matt said evenly, "The jig's up, Olaf. Tillman's confessed to the sheriff that you and he murdered Dan and my brothers. He's confessed that they weren't moving DT stock but their own. Somebody saw what happened that day. Kip Reynolds was along."

He grinned at Olaf's open-mouthed amazement, fully aware that when the big foreman recovered from it he'd be as dangerous as a grizzly bear.

Matt went on, "Joe Furness got a look at some of the brands that day. And you told Joe you'd kill him if he told, didn't you? Well you won't be killing anyone, Olaf. Because you'll be in jail. And when you are, Joe will tell what he knows."

Behind Olaf he noticed Joe Furness slipping furtively away, and let him go because this suited his purpose.

He said, "The other two will probably be let off pretty easy. They thought what they were doing was on the level, if not quite legal. But you knew better."

Olaf's mouth snapped shut, and his eyes glittered. His huge body seemed to go tense and still. Matt said swiftly, "The rest of you stay out of this and you'll be all right. Olaf's figuring on making a play. He knows he's hooked. Stay out of it, hear?"

Matt knew his own skill with a gun. He knew himself to be fairly fast. He knew as well that Olaf Skjerik, for all his bulk, was supposed to have a lightning draw. It was probably what Tillman had hired him for.

Behind Olaf, Tillman's crew scrambled aside, leaving open space behind the foreman. To right and left they scattered, and Matt knew that unless they stayed neutral, he was finished.

But he faced this as he had faced everything else since he had alighted from the train at Granada—with fatalistic concern. Whatever the outcome of this battle, he had won. He clung to that belief. He had won vengeance for Dan and Frankie and Will, and he had cleared the Hurst name.

But remembering Lily Kibben, he knew he did not want to die.

Olaf fell into a half-crouch, his hand but an inch from the butt of his gun.

Matt glued his eyes to the foreman's, and waited. The waiting grew long and intolerable and at last he said hoarsely, "Scared, Olaf? You've got guts enough to hang an innocent man, but have you got guts enough to face one who can shoot back?"

Olaf's face twitched. And Matt heard the slightest of movements behind him and off to one side, toward the house.

He felt cold sweat break over his body. He dared not turn his head for even a lightning glance. Then he heard Tillman's choked, painful laugh. Saw Olaf's cruel expression of triumph.

Matt said, never taking his eyes from Olaf's face, "How did you get away from Rocking H, Dell? Didn't Alf leave a guard over you?"

Tillman chuckled, though the sound was filled with pain. Tillman said thickly, "Only Kip. He got careless and I slugged him."

There was a momentary silence. Matt's hands were sweating and he knew the palms would be slick as he grabbed for his gun. But he dared not try to wipe them on the sides of his pants. He dared not move those hands. For when he did, bullets would come at him.

Tillman growled, "Take him, Olaf!"

Olaf's hand sped for his gun. It cleared leather, the hammer coming back.

As though from far away, Matt heard a scream—a woman's scream. But there was no time for thought of anything but this. No time to look up, no time to be surprised or even to think.

A man's movements became automatic under the prod of mortal danger. Matt realized that his gun was in his hand without quite remembering how it got there. On the heels of the click of Olaf's gunhammer came that of Matt's. And quickly following that, Tillman's, unseen off there to Matt's side.

Matt's gun bucked against his palm, and Olaf's shot came like an echo. Matt felt a savage blow in his thigh. It was as if a horse had kicked it out from under him. He drove backward, falling, and at that precise instant, Tillman's gun spoke, the bullet cutting air where Matt had stood but a split second before.

Rolling, forgetting Olaf for the moment, Matt brought his gun from beneath his body and snapped a swift shot at Tillman's crouching form.

Tillman never got off a second shot. He dropped his gun and clawed at his throat an instant before he collapsed.

Matt heard the woman's screaming plainer now. He forced himself up to a sitting position and looked at Olaf.

The foreman stood solidly on his feet, his gun smoking in his hand. But he didn't fire again. He stood that way for what seemed an eternity, and at last began to sway like a giant pine in a gale.

A red spot on his shirt front began to spread. Matt struggled up to his knees, sick and dizzy with the pain in his thigh. He felt the softness of Lily as she crouched beside him, unmindful of the danger that yet lurked in Olaf Skjerik's gun.

Matt started to push her away, stopped as he saw Olaf collapse onto the hard-packed snow. He turned a little, realizing that her arms were around him, that her tear-dampened face was pressed very close against his own.

He kept saying over and over, "Lily, I told you to go to town. I told you to go to town."

He tasted her lips, salty with tears but unbelievably sweet for all of that. When she could speak, she murmured shakily, "Matt, I belong with you. I belong with you."

He murmured, "Yes," but it took her second kiss to convince him that he was not delirious, that he wasn't dreaming this. The pain of the flesh wound in his thigh disappeared and he felt as though he were ten feet tall.

THE STREETS OF LAREDO

HENRY WILSON ALLEN wrote under both the Clay Fisher and Will Henry bylines and was a five-time winner of the Golden Spur Award from the Western Writers of America. Under both bylines he is well known for the historical aspects of his Western fiction. He was born in Kansas City, Missouri. His early work was in short subject departments with various Hollywood studios and he was working at M-G-M when his first Western novel, NO SURVIVORS (Random House, 1950), was published. While numerous Western authors before Allen provided sympathetic and intelligent portraits of Indian characters, Allen from the start set out to characterize Indians in such a way as to make their viewpoints an integral part of his stories. RED BLIZZARD (Simon & Schuster, 1951) was his first Western novel under the Clay Fisher byline and remains one of his best. Some of Allen's images of Indians are of the romantic variety, to be sure, but his theme often is the failure of the American frontier experience and the romance is used to treat his tragic themes with sympathy and humanity. On the whole, the Will Henry novels tend to be based more deeply in actual historical events, whereas in the Clay Fisher titles he was more intent on a story filled with action that moves rapidly. However, this dichotomy can be misleading, since MacKENNA'S GOLD (Random House, 1963), a Will Henry Western about gold seekers, reads much as one of the finest Clay Fisher titles, THE TALL MEN (Houghton Mifflin, 1954). Both of these novels also served as the basis for memorable Western motion pictures. Allen was always experimental and THE DAY FORT LARKING FELL (Chilton, 1968) is an excellent example of a comedic Western, a tradition as old as Mark Twain and Bret Harte. His novels, I, TOM HORN (Lippincott, 1975) and FROM WHERE THE SUN NOW STANDS (Random House, 1960) in particular, remain imperishable classics of Western fiction.

"I am but a solitary horseman of the plains, born a century too late and far away," Allen once wrote about himself. He felt out of joint with his time and what alone may ultimately unify his work is the vividness of his imagination, the tremendous emotion with which he invested his characters and fashioned his Western stories. At his best, he could weave an almost incomparable spell that can involve a reader deeply in his narratives, informed always by his profound empathy with so many of the casualties of the historical process.

WESTERN ROUNDUP (Macmillan, 1961) was a collection of short stories by members of the Western Writers of America. Nelson Nye was the editor of the book, but he worked closely with Edith Nalle, then Western fiction editor at Macmillan who ably assisted Wayne D. Overholser, Steve Frazee, Noel B. Loomis, and Nye himself in producing their finest and most consistent work. "The Streets of Laredo" is a story Hank Allen wrote especially for inclusion in that anthology so it did not have a prior magazine appearance.

Call him McComas. Drifter, cowboy, cardsharp, killer. A man already on the road back from nowhere. Texas of the time was full of him and his kind. And sick with the fullness.

McComas had never been in Laredo. But his shadows, many of them, had been there before him. He knew what to expect from the townsfolk when they saw him coming on, black and weedy and beard-grown, against the late afternoon sun. They would not want him in their town, and McComas could not blame them. Yet he was tired, very tired, and had come a long, tense way that day.

He steeled himself to take their looks and to turn them away as best he might. What he wanted was a clean bed, a tub bath, a hotel meal and a short night's sleep. No women, no cards, no whisky. Just six hours with the shades drawn and no one knocking at the door. Then, God willing, he would be up in the blackness before the dawn. Up and long gone and safe over the border in Nueva Leon, Old Mexico, when that Encinal sheriff showed up to begin asking questions of the law in Laredo. The very last thing he wanted in Texas was trouble. But that was the very last thing he had ever wanted in any place, and the very first he had always gotten. In Laredo it started as it always started, everywhere, with a woman.

Still, this time it was different. This time it was like no trouble which had ever come to him before. Somehow, he knew it. He sensed it before his trim gelding, Coaly, set hoof in the streets of Laredo.

Those border towns were all laid out alike. Flat as a dropped flapjack. One wide street down the middle, running from sagebrush on one end to the river on the other. Some frame shacks and adobes flung around in the mesquite and catclaw, out where the decent people did not have to look at them. Then, the false fronts lining the main street. And, feeding off that, half a dozen dirt allies lying in two lines on either side like pigs suckling a sow asleep in the sun. After these, there were only the church, school, and cemetery. It was the latter place, clinging on the dryhill flanks of town, where the land was even too poor for the Mexican shacks, that McComas and Coaly were presently coming to.

It lay to their left, and there was a burying party moving out from town, as they moved in. McComas had to pull Coaly off the road to let the procession pass. For some reason he felt strange, and hung there to watch the little party. It was then he saw the girl.

She was young and slim, with a black Spanish *rebozo* covering her head. As the buggy in which she was riding with the frock-coated parson drew abreast of McComas, she turned and stared directly at him. But the late sun was in his eyes and he could not see her features. Then, they were gone on, leaving McComas with a peculiar, unpleasant feeling. He shook as to a chill. Then, steadied himself. It was no mystery that the sight had unsettled him. It was a funeral, and he had never liked funerals.

They always made him wonder though.

Who was it in the coffin? Was it a man or woman? Had they died peaceful or violent? What had they done wrong, or right? Would he, or she, be missed by friends, mourned by family, made over in the local newspaper, maybe even mentioned in the San Antonio and Austin City papers?

No, he decided. Not this one. There were no family and friends here. That girl riding in the preacher's rig wasn't anybody's sister. She just didn't have the look. And the two roughly dressed Mexican laborers sitting on the coffin in the wagon ahead of the buggy were certainly not kith or kin of the deceased. Neither was the seedy driver. As for the square-built man on the sorrel mare heading up the procession, he did not need the pewter star pinned on his vest to tag him for McComas. The latter could tell a deputy sheriff as far as he could see one, late sun in the eyes, or not.

The deputy could tell McComas too. And he gave him a hard looking over as he rode by. They exchanged the usual nods, careful and correct, and the deputy rode on, as any wise deputy would.

Directly, he led the buggy and the wagon into the weed-grown gate of the cemetery, and creaking up the rise to a plot on the crown of the hill. There, the drivers halted their horses, let down their cargoes. Still, McComas watched from below.

The two Mexicans strained with the coffin. It was a long coffin, and heavy. A man, McComas thought. A young man, and standing tall. One who had been taken quick, with no warning, and not long ago. No, this was no honored citizen they were putting under. Honored citizens do not come to boothill in the late afternoon with the town deputy riding shotgun over the ceremony. Nor with only a lantern-jawed, poorbones preacher and a leggy young girl in a black Mexican shawl for mourners. Not by considerable.

McComas might even know the man in that coffin. If he did not, he could describe him perilously close. All he had to do was find the nearest mirror and look into it.

Again, he shivered. And again controlled himself.

He was only tired and worn down. It was only the way he felt about funerals. He always felt dark in his mind when he saw a body going by. And who didn't, if they would be honest enough to admit it? Nobody likes to look at a coffin, even empty. When there is somebody in it and being hauled dead-march slow with the wagon sounding creaky and the people not talking and the cemetery gates waiting rusty and half-sagged just down the road, a man does not need to be on the dodge and nearly drunk from want of sleep to take a chill and to turn away and ride on feeling sad and afraid inside.

In town, McComas followed his usual line. He took a room at the best hotel, knowing that the first place the local law will look for a man is in the second and third-rate fleatraps where the average fugitive will hole up. Laredo was a chancey place. A funnel through which poured the scum of bad ones down into Old Mexico. If a man did not care to be skimmed off with the others of that outlaw dross, he had to play it differently than they did. He didn't skulk. He rode in bold as brass and bought the best. Like McComas and Coaly and the Border Star Hotel.

But, once safely in his room, McComas could not rest. He only paced the floor and peeked continually past the drawn shade down into the sun haze of the main street.

It was perhaps half an hour after signing the register that he gave it up and went downstairs for just one drink. Twenty minutes more and he was elbows-down on the bar of the Ben Hur Saloon with the girl.

Well, she was not a girl, really. Not any longer.

Young, yes. And nicely shaped. But how long did a girl stay a girl at the Laredo prices? She was like McComas. Short on the calendar count, long on the lines at mouth and eye corners. If he had been there and back, she had made the trip ahead of him.

Pretty? Not actually. Yet that face would haunt a man. McComas knew the kind. He had seen them in every town. Sometimes going by in the young dusk on the arm of an overdressed swell—through a dusty train window at the depot—passing, perfume-close, in the darkened hall of a cheap hotel. Not pretty. No, not ever pretty. But always exciting, sensuous, female and available; yours for the night, if you could beat the other fellow to them.

Billie Blossom was that kind.

Her real name? McComas did not care. She accepted McComas; he did not argue Billie Blossom.

She came swinging up to him at the bar, out of the nowhere of blue cigar smoke which hid the poker tables and the dance floor and the doleful piano player with his two-fingered, tinkly, sad chorus of "Jeannie with the Light Brown Hair." She held his eyes a long slow moment, then smiled, "Hello, cowboy, you want to buy me a drink before you swim the river?" And he stared back at her an equal long slow moment, and said, "Lady, for a smile like that I might even get an honest job and go to work."

That was the start of it.

They got a bottle and glasses from the barman, moved off through the smoke, McComas following her. She had her own table, a good one, in the rear corner with no windows and facing the street doors. They sat down, McComas pouring. She put her fingers on his hand when he had gotten her glass no more than damp. And, again, there was that smile shaking him to his boottops.

"A short drink for a long road, cowboy," she said.

He glanced at her with quick suspicion, but she had meant nothing by it.

"Yes," he nodded, "I reckon that's right," and poured his own drink to match hers. "Here's to us," he said, lifting the glass. "Been everywhere but hell, and not wanting to rush that."

She smiled and they drank the whisky, neither of them reacting to its raw bite. They sat there, then, McComas looking at her.

She was an ash blonde with smoky gray eyes. She had high cheekbones, a wide mouth, wore entirely too much paint and powder. But always there was that half curve of a smile to soften everything. Everything except the cough. McComas knew that hollow sound. The girl had consumption, and badly. He could see where the sickness had cut the flesh from her, leaving its pale hollows where the lush curves had been. Yet, despite the pallor and the wasted form, she seemed lovely to McComas.

He did not think to touch her, nor to invite her to go upstairs, and she thanked him with her eyes. They were like a young boy and girl; he not seeing her, she not seeing him, but each seeing what used to be, or might have been, or, luck willing, still might be.

McComas would not have believed that it could happen. Not to him. But it did. To him and Billie Blossom in the Ben Hur Saloon in Laredo, Texas. They had the bottle and they had the sheltered corner and they were both weary of dodging and turning away and of not being able to look straight back at honest men and women nor to close their eyes and sleep nights when they lay down and tried to do so. No-name McComas and faded Billie Blossom. Outlawed killer, dance-hall trollop. In love at first sight and trying desperately hard to find the words to tell each other so. Two hunted people locking tired eyes and trembling hands over a bareboard table and two unwashed whisky tumblers in a flyblown *cantina* at sundown of a hell's hot summer day, two miles and ten minutes easy lope from freedom and safety and a second beckoning chance in Old Mexico, across the shallow Rio Grande.

Fools they were, and lost sheep.

But, oh! that stolen hour at sunset in that smoke-filled, evil-smelling room. What things they said, what vows they made, what wild sweet promises they swore!

It was not the whisky. After the first, small drink, the second went untasted. McComas and Billie Blossom talked on, not heeding the noise and coarseness about them, forgetting who they were, and where. Others, telling of their loves, might remember scented dark parlors. Or a gilding of moonlight on flowered verandas. Or the fragrance of new-mown hay by the riverside. Or the fireflies in the loamy stardust of the summer lane. For McComas and Billie Blossom it was the rank odor of charcoal whisky, the choke of stogie cigars, the reek of bathless men and perspiring, sacheted women.

McComas did not begrudge the lack. He had Billie's blue eyes for his starry lane, her smile for his summer night. He needed no dark parlors, no willow-shaded streams. He and Billie had each other. And they had their plans.

The piano played on. It was the same tune about Jeannie and her light brown hair. McComas feared for a moment that he might show a tear, or a tremble in his voice. The song was that beautiful, and that close, to what he and Billie were feeling, that neither could speak, but only sit with their hands clasped across that old beer-stained table in the Ben Hur Saloon making their silence count more than any words. Then, McComas found his voice. As he talked, Billie nodded, yes, to everything he said, the tears glistening beneath the long black lashes which swept so low and thickly curled across her slanted cheekbones. She was crying because of her happiness, McComas knew, and his words rushed on, deeply, recklessly excited.

He did not remember all that he told her, only the salient, pressing features of it: that they would meet beyond the river when darkness fell; that they would go down into Nueva Leon, to a place McComas knew, where the grass grew long and the water ran sweet and a man could raise the finest cattle in all Mexico; that there they would find their journeys' end, rearing a family of honest, God-fearing children to give the ranch over to when McComas was too aged and saddlebent to run it himself, and when he and Billie Blossom had earned their wicker chairs and quiet hours in the cool shadows of the ranchhouse *galeria*, "somewhere down there in Nueva Leon."

It went like that, so swift and tumbling and stirring to the imagination, that McComas began to wonder if it were not all a dream. If he would not awaken on that uneasy bed upstairs in the Border Star Hotel. Awaken with the sound of the sheriff's step in the hallway outside. And his voice calling low and urgent through the door, "Open up, McComas; it's me, and I've come for you at last."

But it was no dream.

Billie proved that to McComas when she led him from the table and pulled him in under the shadows of the stairwell and gave him the longest, hardest kiss he had ever been given in his life. And when she whispered to him, "Hurry and get the horses, McComas; I will pack and meet you in the alley out back."

McComas pushed across the crowded room, the happiest he had been in his lifetime memory. But he did not allow the new feeling to narrow the sweep of his restless eyes. Nor slow his crouching, wolf-like step. Nor let his right hand stray too far from the worn wooden grip of his .44. He still knew his name was McComas, and that he was worth $500, alive or dead, to the Encinal sheriff and his La Salle County posse. It was the price of staying alive in his profession, this unthinking wariness, this perpetual attitude of *qui vive*. Especially in a strange town at sundown. With the hanging tree waiting in the next county north. And a long life and new love beckoning from across the river, from two miles south, from ten minutes away.

He went out of the batwing saloon doors, glidingly, silently, as he always went out of strange doors, anywhere.

He saw Anson Starett a half instant before the latter saw him. He could have killed him then, and he ought to have. But men like McComas did not dry-gulch men like Anson Starett. Not even when they wear the pewter star and come up on your heels hungry and hard-eyed and far too swiftly for your mind to realize and to grasp and to believe that they have cut you off at last. You do not let them live because they are gallant and tough and full of cold nerve. You do it for a far simpler reason. And a deadlier one. You do it for blind, stupid pride. You do it because you will not have it said that McComas needed the edge on any man. And while you do not, ever, willingly, give that edge away, neither do you use it to blindside a brave man like Sheriff Anson Starett of Encinal.

What you do, instead, is to keep just enough of the edge to be safe. And to give just enough of it away to be legally and morally absolved of murder. It was a fine line, but very clear to McComas. It wasn't being noble. Just practical. Every man is his own jury when he wears a gun for money. No man wants to judge himself a coward. All that has been gone through when he put on the gun to begin with. Perhaps, it was even what made him put on the gun to begin with. What did it matter now? Little, oh, very, very little. Almost nothing at all.

"*Over here, Anse*," said McComas quietly, and the guns went off.

McComas was late. Only a little, but he was late. He knew and damned himself, even as he spun to the drive of Starett's bullet, back against the front wall of the Ben Hur, then sliding down it to the boardwalk at its base.

But he had gotten Starett. He knew that. The Encinal sheriff was still standing, swaying out there in the street, but McComas had gotten him. And, he told himself, he would get him again—now—just to make sure.

It took all his will to force himself up from the rough boards beneath him. He saw the great pool of blood, where he had fallen, but it did not frighten him. Blood and the terrible shock of gunshot wounds were a part of his trade. Somehow, it was different this time, though. This time he felt extremely light and queer in the head. It was a feeling he had never had before. It was as though he were watching himself. As though he were standing to one side saying, "Come on, McComas, get up; get up and put the rest of your shots into him before he falls; drive them into him while he is still anchored by the shock of that first hit . . . ."

But McComas knew that he had him. He knew, as he steadied himself and emptied the .44 into Starett, that he had him and that everything was still all right. But he would have to hurry. He could not stay there to wait for Starett to go down. He had to get out of there while there was yet time. Before the scared sheep in the saloon got their nerve back and came pouring out into the street. Before the sound of the gunfire brought the local law running up the street to help out the sheriff from Encinal.

He thought of Billie Blossom. . . . The good Lord knew he did. But she couldn't do anything for him now. It was too late for Billie Blossom and gunfighter McComas. They had waited and talked too long. . . . Now he must get out. . . . He must not let the girl see him hurt and bleeding. . . . She must not know. . . . He had to get to his horse at the hitching rail. . . . Had to find Coaly and swing up on him and give him his sleek black head and let him go away up the main street and out of Laredo. . . . Yes, he must find Coaly at the rail . . . find him and get up on him and run! run! run! for the river . . . just he and Coaly, all alone and through the gathering dusk. . . .

He could not find Coaly, then. When he turned to the hitching rail in front of the Ben Hur, his trim black racer was not there. He was not where he had left him, all saddled and loose-tied and ready to run. McComas was feeling light and queer again. Yet he knew he was not feeling that queer. Somebody had moved his horse. Somebody had untied him and taken him, while McComas was on the boardwalk from Starett's bullet. Somebody had stolen Coaly and McComas was trapped. Trapped and very badly hurt. And left all alone to fight or die in the streets of Laredo.

It was then that he heard the whisper. Then, that he whirled, white-faced, and saw her standing at the corner of the saloon, in the alley leading to the back. Standing there with a black Mexican *rebozo* drawn tightly over her ash blond hair, shadowing and hiding her hollow cheeks and great gray eyes. McComas could not dis-

tinctly see her face. Not under the twilight masking of that dark
shawl. But he knew it was she. And he went running and stumbling
toward her, her soft voice beckoning as though from some distant
hill, yet clear as the still air of sundown—"*Here, McComas, here!
Come to my arms, come to my heart, come with me . . . .*"

He lunged on. Stumbled once. Went down. Staggered back up
and made it to her side before the first of the murmuring crowd
surged out of the Ben Hur to halt and stare at the great stain of
blood spreading from the front wall of the saloon. The moment
her white, cool hands touched him, took hold of him and held
him up, he felt the strength flow into him again. The strength
flow in and the queer cold feeling disappear from his belly and
the cottony mist dissolve from before his straining eyes. Now he
was all right.

He remembered clearly, as she helped him along the side of the
cantina, looking down at his shirtfront and seeing the pump of the
blood jumping, with each pulse, from the big hole torn midway
between breastbone and navel. He remembered thinking clearly,
"Dear Lord, he got me dead center! How could it have missed the
heart?" Yet, he remembered, even as he heard his thought-voice
ask the question, that these crazy things did happen with gun
wounds. A shot could miss a vital by half a hair's width, and do no
more harm than a fleshy scrape. There was only the shock and the
weakness of the first smash, and no real danger at all unless the
bleeding did not stop. And McComas knew that it would stop. It
was already slowing. All he had to worry about was staying with
Billie Blossom until she could get him to a horse. Then he would
be able to make it away. He could ride. He had ridden with worse
holes through him. He would make it. He would get across the river
and he and Billie would still meet on the far side.

She had a horse waiting for him. He ought to have known she
would, a girl like that, old to the ways of Texas strays and their
traffic through the border towns. He should even have known that
it would be his own horse, saddled and rested and ready to run
through the night and for the river.

Yes, she had slipped out of the Ben Hur before the others. She
had seen how it was with McComas and Anson Starett. And she
had untied Coaly and led him down the alley, to the back, where
McComas could swing up on him, now, and sweep away to the
river and over it to the life that waited beyond. To the life that
he and Billie Blossom had planned and that Anson Starett had
thought he could stop with one bullet from his swift gun. Ah,
no! Anson Starett! Not today. Not this day. Not with one bullet.
Not McComas.

There was no kiss at Coaly's side, and no time for one.

But McComas was all right again. Feeling strong as a yearling bull. Smiling, even laughing, as he leaned down from the saddle to take her pale hand and promise her that he would be waiting beyond the river.

Yet, strangely, when he said it, she was not made happy.

She shook her head quickly, looking white and frightened and talking hurriedly and low, as she pressed his hand and held it to her wasted cheek. And the tears which washed down over McComas's hand were not warm, they were cold as the lifeless clay, and McComas heard her speak with a sudden chill which went through him like an icy knife.

"No, McComas, no! Not the river! Not while there is yet daylight. You cannot cross the river until the night is down. Go back, McComas. Go back the other way. The way that you came in this afternoon, McComas. Do you remember? Back toward the cemetery on the hill. You will be safe there, McComas. No one will think to look for you there. Do you hear me, McComas? Wait there for me. High on the hill, where you saw the open grave. You can watch the Laredo road from there. You can see the river. You can see the sheriff and his posse ride out. You can see when they are gone and when it is safe for you to ride out. Then we can go, McComas. I will meet you there, on the hill, by that new grave. We will go over the river together, when it is dark and quiet and all is at peace and we know no fear. Do you understand, McComas? Oh, dear God, do you hear and understand what I am telling you, my love . . . ?"

McComas laughed again, trying to reassure her, and to reassure himself. Of course, he understood her, he said. And she was thinking smart. A sight smarter than McComas had been thinking since Starett's bullet had smashed him into that front wall and down onto the boardwalk. He got her calmed and quieted, he thought, before turning away. He was absolutely sure of it. And when he left her, turning in the saddle to look back as Coaly took him out and away from the filthy hovels of Laredo into the clean sweet smell of the mesquite and catclaw chaparral, he could still see her smiling and waving to him, slender and graceful as a willow wand moving against the long purple shadows of the sunset.

It was only a few minutes to the cemetery. McComas cut back into the main road and followed along it, unafraid. He was only a mile beyond the town but in some way he knew he would not be seen. And he was not. Two cowboys came along, loping toward Laredo, and did not give him a second glance. They did not even nod or touch their hat brims going by, and McComas smiled and told himself that it always paid to wear dark clothes and ride a black horse in his hard business—especially just at sundown in a strange town.

The rusted gates of the cemetery loomed ahead.

Just short of them, McComas decided he would take cover for a moment. There was no use abusing good luck.

Down the hill, from the new grave on the rise, were coming some familiar figures. They were the long-jawed preacher and square-built deputy sheriff he had passed earlier, on his way into Laredo. They might remember him, where two passing cowboys had shown no interest.

Up on the rise, itself, beyond the deputy and the parson's lurching buggy, McComas could see the two Mexican gravediggers putting in the last shovelsful of flinty earth to fill the fresh hole where they had lowered the long black coffin from the flatbed wagon. And he could see, up there, standing alone and slightly apart, the weeping figure of the young girl in the black *rebozo.*

McComas thought that was a kind, loyal thing for her to do. To stay to say good-bye to her lover. To wait until the preacher and the deputy and the gravediggers and the wagon driver had gone away, so that she might be alone with him. Just herself and God and the dead boy up there on that lonely, rocky rise.

Then, McComas shivered. It was the same shiver he had experienced on this same road, in this same place, earlier that afternoon. Angered, he forced himself to be calm. It was crazy to think that he knew this girl. That he had seen her before. He knew it was crazy. And, yet. . . .

The deputy and the preacher were drawing near. McComas pulled Coaly deeper into the roadside brush, beyond the sagging gates. The deputy kneed his mount into a trot. He appeared nervous. Behind him, the preacher whipped up his bony plug. The rattle of the buggy wheels on the hard ruts of the road clattered past McComas, and were gone. The latter turned his eyes once more toward the hilltop and the head-bowed girl.

He did not want to disturb her in her grief, but she was standing by the very grave where Billie Blossom had told him to meet her. And it was growing dark and Billie had wanted him to be up there so that he could see her coming from town to be with him.

He left Coaly tied in the brush and went up the hill on foot. He went quietly and carefully, so as not to bother the girl, not to violate her faithful sorrow. Fortunately, he was able to succeed. There was another grave nearby. It had a rough boulder for a headstone, and a small square of sunbleached pickets around it. McComas got up to this plot without being seen by the girl. He hid behind its rugged marker and tottering fence, watching to be sure the slender mourner had not marked his ascent.

Satisfied that she had not, he was about to turn and search the Laredo road for Billie Blossom, when he was again taken with the strange, unsettling chill of recognition for the girl in the black *re-*

bozo. This time, the chill froze his glance. He could not remove his eyes from her. And, as he stared at her, she reached into a traveling bag which sat upon the ground beside her. The bag was packed, as though for a hurried journey, its contents disordered and piled in without consideration. From among them, as McComas continued to watch, fascinated, the girl drew out a heavy Colt .41 caliber derringer. Before McComas could move, or even cry out, she raised the weapon to her temple.

He leaped up, then, and ran toward her. But he was too late. The derringer discharged once, the blast of its orange flame searing the *rebozo.* McComas knew, from the delayed, hesitating straightness with which she stood before she fell, that it had been a death-shot. When he got to her, she had slumped across the newly mounded grave, her white arms reaching out from beneath the shroud of the *rebozo* in a futile effort to reach and embrace the plain pine headboard of the grave. McComas gave the headboard but a swift side glance. It was a weathered, knotty, poor piece of wood, whipsawed in careless haste. The barn paint used to dab the deceased's name upon it had not even set dry yet. McComas did not give it a second look.

He was down on the ground beside the fallen girl, holding her gently to his breast so that he might not harm her should life, by any glad chance, be in her still.

But it was not.

McComas felt that in the limp, soft way that she lay in his arms. Then, even in the moment of touching her, the chill was in him again. He *did* know this girl. He knew her well. And more. He knew for whom she mourned; and he knew whose name was on that headboard.

It was then he shifted her slim form and slowly pulled the black *rebozo* away from the wasted oval face. The gray eyes were closed, thick lashes downswept. The ash blond hair lay in a soft wave over the bruised hole in the pale temple. It was she, Billie Blossom. The girl from the streets of Laredo.

McComas came to his feet. He did not want to look at that weathered headboard. But he had to.

There was only a single word upon it. No first name. No birth date. No line of love or sad farewell.

Just the one word:

McComas

He went down the hill, stumbling in his haste. He took Coaly out of the brush and swung up on him and sent him outward through the night and toward the river. It was a quiet night, with an infinite field of gleaming stars and a sweet warm rush of prairie wind to still his nameless fears. He had never known Coaly to fly with such a fleet, sure gait. Yet, swiftly as he went, and clearly as the starlight revealed the silvered current of the river ahead, they did not draw up to the crossing. He frowned and spoke to Coaly, and the black whickered softly in reply and sprang forward silently and with coursing, endless speed through the summer night.

That was the way that McComas remembered it.

The blackness and the silence and the stars and the rush of the warm, sweetly scented wind over the darkened prairie.

He forgot if they ever came to the river.

SELECTED FURTHER READING

The two principal reference sources for authors of Western and Frontier fiction are the second edition of TWENTIETH CENTURY WESTERN WRITERS (St. James Press, 1991) edited by Geoff Sadler and the ENCYCLOPEDIA OF FRONTIER AND WESTERN FICTION (McGraw-Hill, 1983) edited by Jon Tuska and Vicki Piekarski. The former is limited only to authors who wrote in the twentieth century and has no illustrations and generally short and not always accurate entries whereas the latter includes authors from the previous century as well as from the twentieth century. The second edition of the ENCYCLOPEDIA OF FRONTIER AND WESTERN FICTION is currently in preparation and should appear in 1998. Most of the authors included in this second edition are examined in depth in terms of their works and their bibliographies and filmographies (where they exist) are complete, some also having short fiction bibliographies as well. Where little is known of the biography of an author whose work is nonetheless significant, mini-entries in a special section have been included discussing their work. There are also numerous articles including one of considerable length on "Pulp and Slick Western Fiction" and another on "Artists and Illustrators." Illustrations include book jacket covers, pulp magazine covers, stills from motion picture versions, and author portraits.

In the recommendations which follow, titles of novels are to be found under the principal name of an author followed by works under pseudonyms where these apply. Citations are to first editions. Many of these titles have been reprinted or will be reprinted and it is suggested that the interested reader consult the most recent edition of BOOKS IN PRINT. This is a list of personal recommendations. If an author has been omitted, it is simply because for whatever reason I could not cite a novel about which I did not have some reservations, or because space simply did not permit me to cite every author who has written a Western story. Those authors whose stories appear in this collection, of course, have works recommended in the headnotes to their stories. There is no ranking here. These are all good Western stories. It is wrong to ask or expect more, although a particular book might well come to mean more to us as a reader.

Edward Abbey: THE BRAVE COWBOY (Dodd, Mead, 1956); THE MONKEY WRENCH GANG (Lippincott, 1975).

Andy Adams: THE LOG OF A COWBOY (Houghton Mifflin, 1903).

Clifton Adams: TRAGG'S CHOICE (Doubleday, 1969); THE LAST DAYS OF WOLF GARNETT (Doubleday, 1970);
   as **Clay Randall**: SIX-GUN BOSS (Random House, 1952).

Ann Ahlswede: DAY OF THE HUNTER (Ballantine, 1960); HUNT-ING WOLF (Ballantine, 1960); THE SAVAGE LAND (Ballantine, 1962).

Marvin H. Albert: THE LAW AND JAKE WADE (Fawcett Gold Medal, 1957); APACHE RISING (Fawcett Gold Medal, 1957).

George C. Appell: TROUBLE AT TULLY'S RUN (Macmillan, 1958).

Elliott Arnold: BLOOD BROTHER (Duell, Sloan, 1947).

Mary Austin: WESTERN TRAILS: A COLLECTION OF SHORT STORIES (University of Nevada Press, 1987) edited by Melody Graulich.

Todhunter Ballard: INCIDENT AT SUN MOUNTAIN (Houghton Mifflin, 1952); THE CALIFORNIAN (Doubleday, 1971).

Jane Barry: A TIME IN THE SUN (Doubleday, 1962).

Rex Beach: THE SPOILERS (Harper, 1906); THE SILVER HORDE (Harper, 1909).

Frederic Bean: TOM SPOON (Walker, 1990).

P.A. Bechko: GUNMAN'S JUSTICE (Doubleday, 1974).

James Warner Bellah: REVEILLE (Fawcett Gold Medal, 1962) [short stories].

Don Berry: TRASK (Viking, 1960).

Jack M. Bickham: THE WAR ON CHARITY ROSS (Doubleday, 1967); A BOAT NAMED DEATH (Doubleday, 1975).

Archie Binns: THE LAND IS BRIGHT (Scribners, 1939).

Curtis Bishop: BY WAY OF WYOMING (Macmillan, 1946).

Allan R. Bosworth: WHEREVER THE GRASS GROWS (Doubleday, 1941).

B. M. Bower: CHIP OF THE FLYING U (Dillingham, 1906); THE SWALLOWFORK BULLS (Little, Brown, 1929); THE WHOOP-UP TRAIL (Little, Brown, 1932).

Terrill R. Bowers: RIO GRANDE DEATH RIDE (Avalon, 1980).

W. R. Bragg: SAGEBRUSH LAWMAN (Phoenix Press, 1951).

Matt Braun: BLACK FOX (Fawcett Gold Medal, 1972).

Gwen Bristow: JUBILEE TRAIL (Thomas Y. Crowell, 1950).

Sam Brown: THE LONG SEASON (Walker, 1987).

Edgar Rice Burroughs: THE WAR CHIEF (McClurg, 1927).

Frank Calkins: THE LONG RIDER'S WINTER (Doubleday, 1983).

Benjamin Capps: SAM CHANCE (Duell, Sloan, 1965); A WOMAN OF THE PEOPLE (Duell, Sloan, 1966).

Robert Ormond Case: WHITE VICTORY (Doubleday, Doran, 1943).

Willa Cather: O PIONEERS! (Houghton Mifflin, 1913); MY ÁNTONIA (Houghton, Mifflin, 1919); DEATH COMES FOR THE ARCHBISHOP (Knopf, 1927); OBSCURE DESTINIES (Knopf, 1932) [short novels].

Tim Champlin: SUMMER OF THE SIOUX (Ballantine, 1982); COLT LIGHTNING (Ballantine, 1989).

Walter Van Tilburg Clark: THE OX-BOW INCIDENT (Random House, 1940); THE WATCHFUL GODS AND OTHER STORIES (Random House, 1950) [short stories].

Don Coldsmith: TRAIL OF THE SPANISH BIT (Doubleday, 1980).

Eli Colter: THE OUTCAST OF LAZY S (Alfred H. King, 1933).

Will Levington Comfort: APACHE (Dutton, 1931).

Merle Constiner: THE FOURTH GUNMAN (Ace, 1958).

John Byrne Cooke: THE SNOWBLIND MOON (Simon & Schuster, 1984).

Dane Coolidge: HORSE-KETCHUM OF DEATH VALLEY (Dutton, 1930); THE FIGHTING DANITES (Dutton, 1934).

Edwin Corle: FIG TREE JOHN (Liveright, 1935).

Jack Cummings: DEAD MAN'S MEDAL (Walker, 1984).

John Cunningham: WARHORSE (Macmillan, 1956).

Peggy Simson Curry: SO FAR FROM SPRING (Viking, 1956).

Don Davis (pseud. Davis Dresser): THE HANGMEN OF SLEEPY VALLEY (Morrow, 1940).

H. L. Davis: HONEY IN THE HORN (Harper, 1935); WINDS OF MORNING (Morrow, 1952).

Ivan Doig: THE McCASKILL FAMILY TRILOGY: ENGLISH CREEK (Atheneum, 1984); DANCING AT THE RASCAL FAIR (Atheneum, 1987); RIDE WITH ME, MARIAH MONTANA (Atheneum, 1990).

Harry Sinclair Drago: SMOKE OF THE .45 (Macaulay, 1923); as **Will Ermine**: PLUNDERED RANGE (Morrow, 1936); as **Bliss Lomax**: PARDNERS OF THE BADLANDS (Doubleday, Doran, 1942).

Hal Dunning: OUTLAW SHERIFF (Chelsea House, 1928).

Robert Easton: THE HAPPY MAN (Viking, 1943).

Gretel Ehrlich: HEART MOUNTAIN (Viking, 1988).

Allan Vaughan Elston: TREASURE COACH FROM DEADWOOD (Lippincott, 1962).

Louise Erdrich: LOVE MEDICINE (Holt, 1984).

Leslie Ernenwein: REBEL YELL (Dutton, 1947).

Loren D. Estleman: ACES AND EIGHTS (Doubleday, 1981).

Max Evans: THE HI LO COUNTRY (Macmillan, 1961); ROUNDERS

THREE (Doubleday, 1990) [containing THE ROUNDERS (Macmillan, 1960) and two other short novels].

Hal G. Evarts, Sr.: TUMBLEWEEDS (Little, Brown, 1923).

Cliff Farrell: WEST WITH THE MISSOURI (Random House, 1955).

Harvey Fergusson: THE CONQUEST OF DON PEDRO (Morrow, 1954).

Vardis Fisher: CITY OF ILLUSION (Harper, 1941).

L. L. Foreman: THE RENEGADE (Dutton, 1942).

Bennett Foster: WINTER QUARTERS (Doubleday, Doran, 1942).

Kenneth Fowler: JACKAL'S GOLD (Doubleday, 1980).

Norman A. Fox: ROPE THE WIND (Dodd, Mead, 1958); THE HARD PURSUED (Dodd, Mead, 1960).

Brian Garfield: VALLEY OF THE SHADOW (Doubleday, 1970).

Janice Holt Giles: THE PLUM THICKET (Houghton Mifflin, 1954); JOHNNY OSAGE (Houghton Mifflin, 1960).

Arthur Henry Gooden: GUNS ON THE HIGH MESA (Houghton Mifflin, 1943).

Ed Gorman: GUILD (Evans, 1987).

Jackson Gregory: THE SILVER STAR (Dodd, Mead, 1931); SUDDEN BILL DORN (Dodd, Mead, 1937).

Fred Grove: NO BUGLES, NO GLORY (Ballantine, 1959).

Frank Gruber: FORT STARVATION (Rinehart, 1953).

Bill Gulick: WHITE MEN, RED MEN, AND MOUNTAIN MEN (Houghton Mifflin, 1955) [short novel and short stories]; THEY CAME TO A VALLEY (Doubleday, 1966).

A. B. Guthrie, Jr.: THE BIG SKY (Sloane, 1947); THE WAY WEST (Sloane, 1949).

E. E. Halleran: OUTLAW TRAIL (Macrae Smith, 1949).

Donald Hamilton: SMOKE VALLEY (Dell, 1954).

C. William Harrison: BARBED WIRE KINGDOM (Jason, 1955).

Bret Harte: STORIES OF THE EARLY WEST (Platt & Munk, 1964) with a Foreword by Walter Van Tilburg Clark.

C(ynthia) H. Haseloff: MARAUDER (Bantam, 1982).

Charles N. Heckelmann: TRUMPETS IN THE DAWN (Doubleday, 1958).

James B. Hendryx: THE STAMPEDERS (Doubleday, 1951).

O. Henry (pseud. William Sydney Porter): HEARTS OF THE WEST (McClure, 1907) [short stories].

William Heuman: GUNHAND FROM TEXAS (Avon, 1954).

Tony Hillerman: SKINWALKERS (Harper, 1987).

Francis W. Hilton: THE LONG ROPE (Kinsey, 1935).

Douglas Hirt: DEVIL'S WIND (Doubleday, 1989).

Lee Hoffman: THE VALDEZ HORSES (Doubleday, 1967).

Ray Hogan: CONGER'S WOMAN (Doubleday, 1973); THE VENGEANCE OF FORTUNA WEST (Doubleday, 1983); THE WHIPSAW TRAIL (Doubleday, 1990).

Paul Horgan: A DISTANT TRUMPET (Farrar, Straus, 1960).

Robert J. Horton: (writing as James Roberts): WHISPERING CAÑON (Chelsea House, 1925).

Emerson Hough: THE COVERED WAGON (Appleton, 1923).

John Jakes: THE BEST WESTERN STORIES OF JOHN JAKES (Ohio University Press, 1991) edited by Bill Pronzini and Martin H. Greenberg.

Will James: SMOKY THE COWHORSE (Scribners, 1926).

Dorothy M. Johnson: INDIAN COUNTRY (Ballantine, 1953) [short stories]; THE HANGING TREE (Ballantine, 1957) [short novel and short stories].

Douglas C. Jones: Any (*and* Every) Novel This Author Has Written!

MacKinlay Kantor: WARWHOOP: TWO SHORT NOVELS OF THE FRONTIER (Random House, 1952).

Elmer Kelton: BUFFALO WAGONS (Ballantine, 1957); THE TIME IT NEVER RAINED (Doubleday, 1973); THE WOLF AND THE BUFFALO (Doubleday, 1980);

    as **Lee McElory**: THE EYES OF THE HAWK (Doubleday, 1981)

Philip Ketchum: TEXAN ON THE PROD (Popular Library, 1952).

Will C. Knott: KILLER'S CANYON (Doubleday, 1977).

Louis L'Amour: HONDO (Fawcett, 1953) [novelization of screenplay by James Edward Grant originally adapted from L'Amour's "The Gift of Cochise"]; WAR PARTY (Bantam, 1975) [short stories from the late 1940s and 1950s]; THE TRAIL TO CRAZY MAN (Bantam, 1986) [short novels from the 1940s and one from 1951]; THE RIDER OF THE RUBY HILLS (Bantam, 1986) [short novels from the 1940s and one from 1950].

Tom Lea: THE WONDERFUL COUNTRY (Little, Brown, 1952).

Elmore Leonard: ESCAPE FROM FIVE SHADOWS (Houghton Mifflin, 1956); LAST STAND AT SABRE RIVER (Dell, 1959).

Dee Linford: MAN WITHOUT A STAR (Morrow, 1952).

Caroline Lockhart: ME—SMITH (Lippincott, 1911).

Jack London: THE SON OF THE WOLF: TALES OF THE FAR NORTH (Houghton Mifflin, 1900); THE CALL OF THE WILD (Macmillan, 1903); WHITE FANG (Macmillan, 1906).

Noel M. Loomis: RIM OF THE CAPROCK (Macmillan, 1952); THE TWILIGHTERS (Macmillan, 1955); SHORT CUT TO RED RIVER (Macmillan, 1958).

Milton Lott: THE LAST HUNT (Houghton Mifflin, 1954).

Giles A. Lutz: STAGECOACH TO HELL (Doubleday, 1975).

Robert MacLeod: THE APPALOOSA (Fawcett Gold Medal, 1966); APACHE TEARS (Pocket Books, 1974).

Frederick Manfred: CONQUERING HORSE (McDowell Obolensky, 1959).

E. B. Mann: THE VALLEY OF WANTED MEN (Morrow, 1932).

Chuck Martin: GUNSMOKE BONANZA (Arcadia House, 1953).

John Joseph Mathews: SUNDOWN (Longmans, 1934).

Gary McCarthy: SODBUSTER (Doubleday, 1988); BLOOD BROTHERS (Doubleday, 1989).

Larry McMurtry: LONESOME DOVE (Simon & Schuster, 1985).

D'Arcy McNickle: WIND FROM AN ENEMY SKY (Harper, 1978).

N. Scott Momaday: HOUSE MADE OF DAWN (Harper, 1968).

Wright Morris: CEREMONY IN LONE TREE (Atheneum, 1960).

Honoré Willsie Morrow: THE HEART OF THE DESERT (Stokes, 1913); THE EXILE OF THE LARIAT (Stokes, 1923).

Clarence E. Mulford: CORSON OF THE J.C. (Doubleday, Page, 1927); TRAIL DUST (Doubleday, Doran, 1934).

John G. Neihardt: INDIAN TALES AND OTHERS (Macmillan, 1925) [short stories]; THE END OF THE DREAM & OTHER STORIES (University of Nebraska, 1991) [short stories].

Nelson C. Nye: NOT GRASS ALONE (Macmillan, 1961); MULE MAN (Doubleday, 1988);

as **Clem Colt**: QUICK TRIGGER COUNTRY (Dodd, Mead, 1955).

George W. Ogden: THE GHOST ROAD (Dodd, Mead, 1936).

Frank O'Rourke: THUNDER ON THE BUCKHORN (Random House, 1949); THE LAST CHANCE (Dell, 1956); A MULE FOR THE MARQUESA (Morrow, 1964).

Stephen Overholser: A HANGING IN STILLWATER (Doubleday, 1974); FIELD OF DEATH (Doubleday, 1977).

F. M. Parker: SKINNER (Doubleday, 1981).

Gary Paulsen: MURPHY (Walker, 1987).

Charles Portis: TRUE GRIT (Simon & Schuster, 1968).

John Prescott: ORDEAL (Random House, 1958).

Geo. W. Proctor: WALKS WITHOUT A SOUL (Doubleday, 1990).

Bill Pronzini: STARVATION CAMP (Doubleday, 1984).

William MacLeod Raine: THE SHERIFF'S SON (Houghton Mifflin, 1918); IRONHEART (Houghton Mifflin, 1923); THE DESERT'S PRICE (Doubleday, Page, 1924); THE TRAIL OF DANGER (Houghton Mifflin, 1934).

John Reese: JESUS ON HORSEBACK (Doubleday, 1970).

Frederic Remington: THE COLLECTED WRITINGS OF FREDERIC REMINGTON (Doubleday, 1979) edited by Peggy and Harold Samuels.

Eugene Manlove Rhodes: "*Pasó por Aquí*" [short novel] in ONCE IN THE SADDLE (Houghton Mifflin, 1927); THE TRUSTY KNAVES (Houghton Mifflin, 1933).

Roe Richmond: MOJAVE GUNS (Arcadia House, 1952).

Conrad Richter: EARLY AMERICANA AND OTHER STORIES (Knopf, 1936); THE SEA OF GRASS (Knopf, 1937); THE LADY (Knopf, 1957).

Frank C. Robertson: FIGHTING JACK WARBONNET (Dutton, 1939).